Praise for Ann Cleeves

RAVEN BLACK

'*Raven Black* breaks the conventional mould of British crime-writing, while retaining the traditional virtues of strong narrative and careful plotting'
Independent

'Beautifully constructed . . . a lively and surprising addition to a genre that once seemed moribund'
Times Literary Supplement

'*Raven Black* shows what a fine writer Cleeves is . . . an accomplished and thoughtful book'
Sunday Telegraph

'Ann's characterization is worthy of the best writers in the field . . . Rarely has a sense of place been so evocatively conveyed in a crime novel'
Daily Express

WHITE NIGHTS

'*White Nights* is a pleasure to read. Interesting characters, great setting, intriguing plot, and nothing to turn the sensitive stomach! And the bonus when we finish it is that we know we've got two more to look forward to'
Reginald Hill

'In true Agatha Christie style, Cleeves once again pulls the wool over our eyes with cunning and conviction'
Col

HIDDEN DEPTHS

THE SLEEPING AND THE DEAD
&
HIDDEN DEPTHS

Ann Cleeves worked as a probation officer, bird observatory cook and auxiliary coastguard before she started writing. She is a member of 'Murder Squad', working with other northern writers to promote crime fiction. In 2006 Ann was awarded the Duncan Lawrie Dagger for Best Crime Novel, for *Raven Black*. Ann lives in North Tyneside.

The novels in Ann Cleeves' Vera Stanhope series, *The Crow Trap*, *Telling Tales* and *Hidden Depths*, are available now and are forthcoming major ITV productions.

Visit the author's website at
www.anncleeves.com

Ann Cleeves

THE SLEEPING AND THE DEAD
&
HIDDEN DEPTHS

PAN BOOKS

The Sleeping and the Dead first published 2001 by Macmillan
First published by Pan Books 2002
Hidden Depths first published 2007 by Macmillan
First published by Pan Books 2007

This omnibus first published 2011 by Pan Books
an imprint of Pan Macmillan, a division of Macmillan Publishers Limited
Pan Macmillan, 20 New Wharf Road, London N1 9RR
Basingstoke and Oxford
Associated companies throughout the world
www.panmacmillan.com

ISBN 978-0-330-54541-9

1 3 5 7 9 8 6 4 2

A CIP catalogue record for this book is available from
the British Library.

Typeset by Intype Libra Ltd
Printed in the UK by CPI Mackays, Chatham ME5 8TD

THE SLEEPING AND THE DEAD

Prologue

She had the lake to herself. She wasn't given to fancies, but on a morning like this she knew the water was what she was born for. The water, then her and the canoe. Like they were one creature, one of the strange animals out of the myths they'd had to read when they were at school. But she wasn't half horse. She was half boat.

The spray deck was fastened so tightly round her waist that every movement she made with her upper body was reflected in the canoe, and if she capsized her legs would stay quite dry. Not that there was any chance of that today. The sun was already burning off the last of the mist and the lake was flat. There were mirror images of mountains all the way up the valley. The blades of her paddle sliced sharply through the water, pushing her back towards the shore.

The water level must have dropped again because the row of staithes, which had only recently appeared running out from the beach, seemed more prominent. She turned the canoe towards them, partly out of curiosity, partly to put off the moment of her return to the school. The figure floated just under the surface, moving gently. From a distance she'd thought it a piece of polythene. She tilted the paddle so one blade was submerged and pushed against the pressure of the water to stop the canoe. Still interested. Not scared. Waiting for the silt to clear. Then she found she was shaking and held on to the wooden post with her free hand to steady herself. It was as if she'd stumbled into a bad horror movie. The corpse swaying below her was white, like a wax, witchcraft effigy.

PART ONE

Chapter One

Peter Porteous walked to work. It was still a novelty.
He liked it all, the overgrown hedges, birdsong, cow
muck not dog muck on the road. Having made the
decision to walk, he walked every day. Whatever
the weather. Even in this heat. He was a man of
routine. On the edge of the town he went into the
newsagent's by the bridge to buy the *Independent*. He
checked the time on the church clock. In the office he
would drink a mug of decaffeinated coffee and begin
to sift through the overnight reports before meeting
his team at the ten o'clock briefing. And at the briefing
he knew there would be nothing to cause anxiety.
Cranford was a small town. The team covered a huge
geographical area, but there was seldom the sense of
being swamped by uncontrollable events which he had
experienced in his previous post. That was why he
had transferred to Cranford and that was why he would
enjoy it. He knew colleagues who functioned better
under pressure but he hated panic and chaos. Stress
scared him. He had designed his working life to
avoid it.

He was waiting for the kettle to boil for his coffee
when the telephone rang.

'Porteous.' He continued to make neat, pithy notes in the margin of the report on his desk.

'We've got a body, sir.'

He took a breath. 'Where?'

'In the lake. Only visible now because the water's so low. It was found by an instructor at the Adventure Centre.'

'Natural causes then?'

'Unlikely, sir.'

'Why?'

'It was tied to an anchor. Weighed down.'

'So.' The kettle clicked off. Still holding the phone he poured water on to coffee granules. 'Murder.'

There was a brief silence. Perhaps the sergeant was expecting a rush of orders. Instructions and queries fired one after another. None came. Instead Porteous asked calmly, 'Any identification?'

'Can't even tell the sex. It looks as if it's been there some time.'

'No rush then. They haven't done anything daft like trying to lift it from the water?'

'I'm not sure.'

'Tell them to leave everything as it is. Are you clear? Exactly. I want the pathologist there. I seem to remember that water has a preservative effect. Once the corpse is lifted from the lake it'll start to decompose very quickly. Make sure they understand.'

'Right, sir.'

'Get hold of Eddie Stout. Tell him I'll meet him there. And Sergeant?'

'Yes, sir.'

'I'll need a car.'

Before leaving his office Peter Porteous drank his coffee and finished reading the report on his desk.

The town had its back turned to the lake, was separated from it by a small hill and a forestry plantation. There were no views. Many of the older residents could remember the valley before it was flooded to create a vast reservoir and still disapproved. They had quite enough water. In the hills it never stopped raining. Let the city dwellers fend for themselves.

The road to the lake was signposted Cranwell Village and showed a No Through Road symbol. Beneath it was a brown tourist sign which said Cranford Water Adventure Centre. Cranwell Village was a scattering of houses on either side of the single-track road. There was a church and a pub and a country-house hotel where, the month before, Porteous had briefly attended a colleague's engagement party. Then there was a bend in the road and a sudden, startling expanse of water, this morning dazzling in the sunlight. The lake had a circumference of thirty miles. The valley twisted, so although Porteous could see across the water to the opposite bank, each end of the reservoir was invisible. The lane ended in a car park, with a grassed area to one side and a couple of picnic tables. There was a noticeboard with a map showing a series of walks and nature trails. A gravel track followed the lake a little further north to the Adventure Centre, a wooden building of Scandinavian design, surrounded by trees. Porteous parked by the noticeboard and studied it before walking up the track.

Detective Sergeant Stout had arrived before him.

His car was parked in one of the residents' marked spaces next to the building. He wore, as he always did, a suit and a tie, and looked out of place in the clearing, surrounded by trees, with pine needles underfoot. An officious garden gnome. Next to him stood a fit, middle-aged man in shorts, a black T-shirt with the Adventure Centre logo on the front in scarlet, and the rubber sandals used by climbers. Porteous always treated Stout carefully. The older man had been expected to get the promotion which had brought Porteous to the team. He was well liked but too close to retirement now to move further.

'Thank you for getting here so quickly, Eddie.' As soon as the words were spoken he thought they sounded sychophantic, insincere. Stout only nodded. 'Perhaps you could introduce us.'

Stout nodded again. He was a small, squat man with the knack of speaking without appearing to move his mouth. He would have made a brilliant ventriloquist, though Porteous had never passed on the compliment. 'This is Daniel Duncan. He's director of the Adventure Centre. One of his instructors found the body.'

Porteous held out his hand. Duncan took it reluctantly.

'Perhaps I could talk to him,' Porteous said.

'Her,' Duncan said. 'Helen Blake. She's a bit upset.'

'We should give her a few minutes then. Is there anything we can see from the shore?'

From where they were standing the view of the lake was obscured by trees. Duncan led them along a path to the back of the building, to a dinghy park, where there were half a dozen Mirror dinghies and a rack of canoes. A concrete slipway sloped gently into the water. He walked very quickly, bouncing away from them on the balls of his feet, as if he hoped the matter could be dealt with immediately.

'This is the last thing we need,' he said crossly. 'We've only been going three years and this is the first season we've shown any profit.'

'But the building must have been here longer than that.' It looked weathered. Lichen was growing on the roof.

'It's nearly ten years old. It used to be run by the council but in the last round of cuts they had to sell it off. I took it over then.'

'What was here before that?'

Duncan shrugged. 'I wouldn't know.'

'It was a caravan site,' Stout volunteered. 'A sort of holiday centre. I think the people who owned it went bust. The wooden building wasn't here then, though, and the trees have grown a lot. There was the reception and a bar nearer the lane. Brick and concrete. An ugly place. I remember it being demolished.'

Porteous leaned against the stone wall which separated the dinghy park from the shore. There was the smell of baked mud. A slight breeze moved the water but seemed not to reach him.

'Where did Ms Blake find the body?'

Duncan pointed to a rotting wooden staithe which jutted out from the water about thirty yards from the wall.

'This is the driest summer since the reservoir was built. The water's never been so low. Those posts haven't been exposed since I've been here. Not until a couple of weeks ago. I think they formed part of a jetty or a pier when the lake was first flooded. The body's near that far post.'

'So it was probably weighted and thrown from the jetty? Before it collapsed?'

Duncan shrugged again as if he wanted to disassociate himself from the enquiry.

Porteous gave up on him and turned to Stout. 'I don't suppose you remember when the jetty fell into disuse. That might help us date the body.'

'I don't think it fell down. I think the council knocked it down when the Adventure Centre was built. They didn't want the kids drowning themselves.'

Porteous pursed his lips in a soundless whistle. 'So we're talking a ten-year-old body. At least. When was the reservoir completed?'

'1968. The year Bet and I moved here.'

'So, a twenty-odd-year window of opportunity, if we accept the body's been in for ten years. It'll be a nightmare just sorting through the missing-person records.' He didn't talk as if it would be a nightmare. His voice was suddenly more cheerful. 'I don't suppose anyone obvious comes to mind? As a candidate for the victim.' He'd learned already that Eddie was famous for his memory and his local knowledge. According to the desk sergeant he went to bed reading the 'Hatches, Matches and Dispatches' column of the local paper.

'Give us a break, sir. We've no age or sex. I'm not a miracle worker.'

'That's not what I was told.'

Duncan had wandered away from them and was pulling one of the dinghies on to a trolley. Porteous joined him but didn't offer to help.

'How deep is the water there?'

'The bank's steep at this point so usually it's very deep. The post must have snapped off sometime because the jetty would have been higher than that. It's silty there too. This year? You'd probably be able to walk out in thigh waders.'

'Thanks. We'll see how the forensic team want to play it.'

He found it hard to imagine Carver, the pathologist, in thigh waders. He was a dapper man given to flamboyant ties and waistcoats. His hair was a deep oily black, which could only have come out of a bottle. Even in the Teletubby paper suit he put on to enter a crime scene he gave the impression of neatness and vanity.

'Will you wait here for Mr Carver, Eddie? I'll see if Ms Blake's up to a few questions. Mr Duncan, if you wouldn't mind . . .'

Duncan seemed at first not to have heard. He finished coiling a piece of rope, straightened, then reluctantly set off towards the Centre. Porteous followed.

'Where do you get your customers from?'

'That's hardly relevant to your enquiries, is it? If the body's as old as you think.' He stopped in his track so suddenly that Porteous almost walked into him. 'Sorry, that was rude. Everything I own is sunk into this place. I'm worried. In the summer holidays most of our clients are kids whose parents think it would be good for them to do more than sit in front of the computer screen all day. At the moment the whole place has been taken over by one school party. We're starting to attract more adult groups too – companies looking for a quick fix in corporate bonding.' He opened double doors into a wood-panelled lobby with a couple of chairs, a payphone and a drinks machine.

'Helen's through there, in the common-room. I'll be in the office if you need me.'

Helen Blake was a large-boned redhead in her early twenties. Her face was still drained of colour, so the scattering of freckles on her nose and cheekbones looked livid and raw. She was alone.

'What have you done with all the students?' He hoped the joky tone would reassure her but she looked up, startled, and some of the coffee she was holding spilled on to her jeans.

'They've got pony-trekking this morning.'

'Would you normally be with them?'

'No. I only do water sports.' She gave a laugh which rattled at the back of her throat. 'I did try riding once. I got a blister on my bum and the beast bit me.'

'How long have you been working here?' He wanted her more relaxed before he started on the difficult questions.

'This is my first season. I did sports science at university. Canoeing's my passion. I compete. I'm hoping for an Olympic trial.' She set the coffee mug on a low table. Her hand had stopped shaking.

'Do you like it here?'

'Yeah it's OK. Dan Duncan could do with being a bit more laid back, but as he always says, he's got a lot resting on this place.'

'Did you have a group with you on the water this morning?'

'No, thank God. I practise on my own before breakfast every day. One of the perks of the job.'

'Could you take me through exactly what happened?'

'I was on my way in.' The words came in breathless pants. 'I never take the students close to the old jetty. It would be tempting fate. They'd get stuck or hit one of the underwater planks and capsize. I suppose I was curious. There seems to be less water in the lake every day and I wanted to see what else might emerge. I didn't expect a body. It seemed to be floating not far from the surface. Very white. Hardly human. Not human at all.' She shivered and pulled her knees up to her chest and wrapped her arms around them.

'Could you see the anchor?'

'Not then. It was covered in silt. I put my blade in to steady the canoe and the movement of the water cleared it long enough for me to see the shape. I came in then. I couldn't look any more. Dan called the police. Two men rowed out in one of our dinghies. Perhaps they didn't believe me. Perhaps they thought I was imagining it. I wish I had been.'

'They had to check,' he said gently.

'What will happen now?'

'We're waiting for the forensic team.'

'I won't have to see it again, will I?'

'Of course not.'

'What I can't bear,' she said, 'is the thought of him out there all this time and none of us realizing. It's as if nobody missed him. As if nobody cared.'

If it was a he, Porteous thought. As she spoke he saw beyond her, through a long window, to the scene outside. Carver's Range Rover was pulling into the drive. The pathologist parked it neatly beside the Centre's minibus and climbed out. From the back seat he pulled out a pair of rubber waders. They were spotless and shiny, as black as his hair. Porteous hid a small grin behind his hand.

'What time will the children be back?' He didn't want an audience of sniggering, pointing teenagers.

'Not until late this afternoon. They've taken a picnic.' She followed his gaze. 'You'll be busy. Don't worry about me. I'm OK.'

Later he, Stout and Carver sat in the Range Rover to compare notes. Carver had with him a silver thermos flask of coffee which he passed around, wiping the cup each time with a paper handkerchief, like a priest at communion.

'Really,' he said in the prissy voice which made some of Porteous's colleagues want to thump him. 'It's most interesting. I've read about it of course, but this is the first time I've seen it.'

'Seen what?' Porteous had come across Carver when he was working in the city and was prepared to be patient with him. The man was a good pathologist and he could usually be persuaded to commit himself. Porteous would put up with a lot for that.

'Adipocere. That's what it's called. It's caused by saponification. Literally the making of soap. The effect of water on the body fat. One of the first pathologists to describe it said it's as if the corpse is encased in mutton suet. Remarkably apt as I'm sure you'll agree. Sometimes the adipocere preserves the internal organs. I won't be able to tell you that, of course, until the post-mortem. I'll do that as soon as I can. This afternoon if it can be arranged. I wouldn't be surprised if some of my colleagues didn't want to be present.' He took a fastidious sip of his coffee. 'Really, I can hardly wait.'

Chapter Two

Porteous lived in a barn as big as a church, which had
been converted into three flats. He had the top floor
to himself. Exposed rafters stretched to a sloping roof.
There were two long windows, a view over farmland.
Occasionally, if the light was right, he could see the
glint of the lake in the distance, like a child's imagined
glimpse of the sea. One wall was exposed stone, the
others plastered and whitewashed. On these he hung
the paintings he collected. He always went to the fine-
art students' finals exhibition at the university in the
city. Usually he saw something he liked.

It was early evening. Porteous didn't believe in
unnecessary overtime. It messed up his budgets, and
tasks which could normally be fitted into the working
day expanded, became more complicated, to fit the
time allowed. Tonight, despite the body in the lake, he
sent his team home at the usual time. There was
nothing they could do until they had identification.
Besides, he wanted them calm and reasonable in the
morning. He hated the frantic, febrile atmosphere
which sometimes enveloped a murder case. Rational
judgement was lost. It was as if there was something
heroic about the obsession with one victim, one perpetrator, about the lack of sleep, the passion stoked by

alcohol. He had, however, brought work home with him. He had carried six large box files up the open stairs. They contained the flimsy copies of missing-person reports between 1968 and 1985. The last five of the years which were of interest to him, 1986–1990, had been computerized, and he would check those in the morning.

He had attended Carver's post-mortem. As the pathologist had suggested, there was quite an audience. The little man had played up to them, preening himself, throwing out scientific jokes and puns which meant little to Porteous but raised a titter amongst his colleagues.

Porteous had taken notes in impeccable shorthand, following Carver's commentary exactly. The pathologist had performed like a music-hall magician, and there was likely to be as much information in the suggestion, the conjecture, the surprise discovery as in the completed official report. Porteous set his notes on the painted table which stood under one of the windows and went to the tiny kitchen to make a pot of tea. He liked Earl Grey, weak with a slice of lemon. He poured a dribble, was satisfied that it was ready and filled the cup. Then he returned to his notes and translated them in his head.

Carver had confirmed that the body had been in the water for at least ten years. The victim was a young male, aged between sixteen and twenty-five. He was five feet ten inches tall and, despite the adipocere, which usually occurred only when the victim had considerable body fat, he was of slender build. Carver had been excited by that fact, had thought it might warrant a note in a scientific journal. Enough of the organs, protected by the hard white layer of adipocere, remained for Carver to give a cause of death. The young man had been stabbed. By a knife with a short but unusually wide blade. A dagger of some sort. He had been stabbed in the back. A sharp upward movement into the heart. Either the perpetrator had known what he was doing or he had been very lucky. At this Carver had looked at his friends and grinned.

'Very exotic, gentlemen, very theatrical, as I'm sure you'll agree, for our small town in the hills.'

The body had been tied to the anchor by a piece of nylon rope, which had been looped around the waist. The young man had been clothed, though most of the garments had rotted and only tatters remained. The scraps had been retained and the forensic team was examining them. He had been wearing boots made of a soft leather or suede. Around his wrist was a plaited leather bracelet, which looked home-made. Perhaps from a bootlace.

At this Porteous stopped for a moment and took a sip of tea. He had been a child in the seventies. His only brother had been ten years older, and Porteous pictured him preparing to go out for the night. He saw him quite clearly, standing in front of the mirror in his parents' room, the only long mirror in the house. He was wearing wide trousers, desert boots, a fringed suede jacket. Around his neck was a leather thong threaded with wooden beads. The victim's bracelet suggested to Porteous the fashion of the seventies. The end of flower power. Not punk or the new romantics. He made a note and continued.

There had been some dental work. Carver announced this as if they should be grateful to him.

Which Porteous certainly was. After all this time it held the best chance of positive identification. There had not been extensive work on the teeth – one extraction and two small fillings – but a record of the mouth, perhaps even an X-ray would have been taken. There was no guarantee that the dentist was still in business or that the records had been kept but at least it provided an avenue of investigation. Porteous thought it would give his team something to do the following day. He liked to keep them busy.

He leant back in his chair and emptied the pot into his wide blue cup – part of the tea service which had been a present to himself when he moved into the barn. He stretched with satisfaction. This was why he had joined the police. Not to save the world. Not to race around the countryside in fast cars or strut the city streets in a uniform. But to bring order, to solve problems, to understand.

He set the post-mortem notes to one side and pulled the first box file towards him, savouring a moment of anticipation before opening it. This was what he loved, this precise and meticulous sorting of facts. He had never understood why his colleagues thought such work tedious.

Each report was a minor human tragedy, baldly told, given a dignity because the facts were unembellished. He sorted them first into gender and age, rejecting the menopausal women with depression, the elderly wanderers from care homes, the occasional heart-breaking ten-year-old who had gone to a friend's house to play and never returned. Still he was left with a mountain of paper. The majority of missing-person reports was for young males. They'd left home after problems at school, a row with parents, or in search of a more exciting life. He knew that many would have returned or got in touch. The relatives, simply relieved that the panic was over, would never have thought to inform the police.

He became engrossed in the task and couldn't let it go. He had planned just to sort through the paperwork but began phoning the contact numbers for relatives. Inevitably some had moved or died, but Cranford was the sort of town where people knew one another. Other phone numbers were given, alternative names suggested. The people wanted to talk. Porteous listened patiently to tales of lads who'd been scallies as youngsters but who'd gone on to do well for themselves, who'd taken university degrees, settled down, had families. The worst calls were when boys were still missing and no contact had ever been made. Porteous heard the flurry of hope in elderly voices.

'Does this mean there's some news?'

'No, no,' he said gently. 'Just checking old files.'

Some had heard about the discovery of the body in the lake on local radio and put two and two together.

'But that can't be our Alan,' one said. 'He could swim like a fish.'

He stopped when the light faded and it was too dark to read the scrawled names and numbers on the copy paper. He had reached 1980. If nothing came of the names he had set to one side he would check the files for 1980–1990, but he thought he had gone far enough. He had a picture of the victim in his head. A boy who was a teenager in the early seventies just after the lake had been flooded; who wore desert boots and a leather bootlace bracelet; who had been stabbed in the back.

He stood up and pressed the light switch. The room was lit by spots fixed to the ceiling beams. They shone through the rafters, throwing shadows on to the stripped wooden floor. He was hungry. He loved to cook; the process of peeling and chopping relaxed him. But today he wanted something quick and simple. He filled a stainless-steel pan with water for spaghetti and sweated garlic and red chilli in olive oil then covered the lot with freshly sliced Parmesan. He ate as if he hadn't seen food for days, shovelling it in with a spoon and a fork. He was sitting at the table where he'd been working and he looked out through the uncovered window at the lights which were all that remained of the roads and the farmhouses. Later he poured himself a glass of wine.

He liked to go to bed early but tonight found it impossible to let the investigation go. He thought he was as bad as the macho colleagues who bragged of their nights without sleep in pursuit of their prey. Still with his glass in his hand he read through his shortlist of candidates again, hoping to pick up on some minute detail which would point him to the man he was looking for.

He judged them, just as a betting man would pick a horse from a racing paper, using a mixture of fact, experience and superstition. There were three. After those he had picked a dozen or so more to follow up if nothing came of the first group. He set the three sheets before him in alphabetical order and read them again.

The first was Alan Brownscombe, the boy who

could swim like a fish. His parents still lived in Cranford. They came originally from the West Country and had planned on moving back there when they retired, but even after retirement they had stayed where they were – 'otherwise how would Alan know where to find us?'

Porteous had spoken to the mother. She had worked as a dinner lady in Cranwell Village First School. The father had worked for British Gas and taken a redundancy package when the company was privatized. Mrs Brownscombe could remember exactly what happened when Alan disappeared. She had the story pat, word for word, like a favourite bedtime tale repeated over and over to a child. He was the eldest of three, a bright boy, and he'd gone to Leeds University to read electrical engineering. He'd never been away from home before. Perhaps he was homesick. Perhaps the course was more demanding than he'd expected. At any rate when she managed to get through to him on the phone she sensed he was unhappy. It was Easter when he went missing. He was nineteen. It was 1978, a bit outside Porteous's preferred time-scale but not by much. Alan had come home for the holidays and managed to get a job on the caravan site by the lake, cleaning the vans before the start of the season, doing small repairs. One day he set off for work and never arrived. He didn't take anything with him other than the packet of cheese-and-pickle sandwiches she'd made up for his lunch. So far as they knew he had no money. He didn't return to university and they never saw him again.

'You say he was unhappy,' Porteous had said. The woman's West Country accent was preserved intact. If they could tell her what happened to her son, even if he were dead, she'd feel she could move home. He'd wanted to help her. 'Could he have been clinically depressed?'

'I don't know,' she'd said. 'It wasn't something you thought of then. Not with a nineteen-year-old lad. And he was home with us. We'd not have sent him back if he didn't want to go, whatever sort of noises his father was making.'

The height and the build fitted the body in the lake. She gave Porteous the name of Alan's dentist without asking why he wanted to know.

Michael Grey was reported missing only after his foster parents had died and the executors of their wills had tried to trace him. They'd left him the small house where they'd been living. He'd have been twenty-two at the time, but when a firm of solicitors tried to track him down they discovered that no one had seen him since he was eighteen. That would have been in 1972. It was a peculiar case but Porteous tried not to read too much into it. Social Services seemed not to feel too much responsibility for kids in care once they were sixteen. They drifted in a twilight world of hard-to-let flats, hostels and mates' floors. And if the next of kin had been named as one of the executors presumably there wouldn't have been much incentive to trace the boy. Perhaps they would have received the profit from the house in his absence. The description was vague. Porteous had the feeling that the person reporting Michael as missing had never seen him. Nothing ruled him out from being the dead boy in the lake, but there was nothing to suggest it. There was nothing as useful as a photograph.

Carl Jackson had lived twenty miles from Cranford with his parents, who farmed sheep on the other side of the lake. He beamed gappily from a school snap attached to the file. He was sixteen and had learning difficulties and was described by the constable who'd taken the first missing-person report as 'mentally retarded'. Because of his vulnerable status there'd been a big search for him, involving not only the police and mountain-rescue team but also members of the public. He attended Cranford Adult Training Centre and was collected every morning from the end of the farm track by a bus which picked up all the trainees from rural areas. His parents were elderly, considered by the staff at the centre as overprotective. Usually one of them waited with him for the bus and was there to meet him in the evening. In an attempt to encourage Carl's independence it was suggested that he could make the half-mile walk down the track alone. What could go wrong? The track led only to the farmhouse. It would be impossible for him to get lost. But one day, the third that this experiment in independent living was tried, he failed to arrive home. His parents waited less than half an hour before going out to look for him. Two hours later they alerted the police. It was as if he had disappeared into thin air.

Porteous had phoned the contact number without much hope of success. The Jacksons had been in their fifties when Carl had disappeared in 1969. He was answered by a machine. 'You're through to Balk Farm Computing. No one is available to take your call . . .' The farmhouse had been sold to yuppies, the land dispersed. It was happening to hill farms all over the

24

north of England. It had happened to the farm where he was living.

He looked again at the photo. Carl was dressed in a check shirt, corduroy trousers and a hand-knitted V-neck pullover. Old man's clothes. It was hard to imagine him wearing a hippy leather bracelet.

The long case clock in the corner chimed the half-hour. Half-past midnight. Porteous rinsed out his glass, stoppered the bottle and put it in the fridge. In bed he took ten minutes to go through the breathing exercise which usually helped him to relax, but he slept fitfully, haunted by the grainy photographs of Carl Jackson and Alan Brownscombe, by the fat white body in the mortuary and by Carver's grin.

Chapter Three

They sat in Porteous's office, which was so small that their knees almost touched, making an effort to get on.

Eddie Stout had seen Porteous cart off the boxes of files the night before and wondered what was going on. Was the man some sort of control freak? That wasn't his job. Didn't he trust the rest of the team? But Eddie was a Christian, a lay minister on the Methodist circuit, out every Sunday preaching to a handful of old ladies in the windswept chapels in the hills, so he had to forgive Porteous for being promoted over him and he had to make allowances. It was a strain for him, Porteous could see that. The silence between them was awkward.

Porteous liked Stout. Perhaps it would have been easier if the man had been less hospitable and generous. Why was Stout trying so hard? When Porteous had first arrived Stout had invited him to dinner at his home – an overture of friendship which had been impossible for Porteous to refuse. It had been an unexpectedly pleasant evening but Porteous felt he had disappointed Stout because he had given too little of himself away. He had taken flowers and chocolates as gifts instead of wine. Methodists didn't drink, did they?

But it seemed that nowadays they did, and after several glasses of home-brewed beer Stout had become mellow, almost Dickensian, sitting in a fat armchair, puffing his pipe, surrounded by evidence of his family. Porteous had drunk little and maintained his guard.

Stout's wife, Bet, was plump and motherly. There were two grown-up children, settled down with babies of their own, and photographs of them were on the mantelpiece and the window-sills. Then there was Ruthie, the baby, ten years younger than the others, a wild adolescent with cropped hair, who had eaten with them, entertaining them with stories about school. Afterwards she had disappeared off to a party with her boyfriend, but not without giving her father a big hug first.

'You've no family?' Bet had asked, as if it were a loss in his life, something to be pitied, to be compensated for with comforting casseroles and sticky puddings.

He had shaken his head. 'Never married.'

He had seen them looking at each other and had read their thoughts. At first they had considered that he might be one of them – a Christian. Perhaps of the happy clappy born-again variety, saving himself for the right girl. That might have explained his reluctance to go to the pub after work, to join in the swearing, the banter about women. But he hadn't used the right phrases, as recognizable as a Masonic handshake. He hadn't made himself known.

So then they had wondered if he might be gay. That too was something he was used to. It was a way for colleagues to explain his apparent celibacy, his love of art and theatre. He had heard the sniggers and the jokes, though he never responded to them. Eddie and Bet hadn't sniggered – they were too kind and too tolerant for that. But they had felt cheated because he hadn't been more open with them and they were curious. Later he was sure they would ask Ruthie what she thought. Porteous wondered what the answer would be.

Now, in his office, so close to Eddie that he could smell the tobacco, he had a sudden urge to explain. It would have been like talking to a priest or a shrink: 'Ten years ago I had a nervous breakdown. Stress. Now I avoid it. You know, prevention better than cure. And I take the medication. I like my life ordered, predictable. That's why I live alone. So I can control what goes on. It runs in the family, actually, psychiatric disorder. My dad was a nutter. He jumped off a bridge in front of the Birmingham Intercity. It's like diabetes. Genetic.'

But it wasn't like diabetes. Diabetes would have been no big deal; his promotion wouldn't have been a cause for self-congratulation on the part of his superiors. 'This shows that we take equal opportunities seriously, Peter. You're a trailblazer. But we suggest that you don't make a song and dance about it. You need authority, the confidence, you know, of your troops. Your past illness is no business of anyone else, is it?'

He was aware suddenly of Stout watching him, waiting for him to speak. God, he thought, it won't take him long to work out that I'm a headache if I sit here with my mouth open, staring into space. He pulled the three files out of his briefcase, lay them on the desk.

'Do you remember any of these, Eddie?'

Stout read them quickly, flicking his eyes occasionally back to his boss's face.

'Carl Jackson. I remember that one. I was up on the hill with everyone else searching, even when I'd come off shift. It was March but the weather was foul. Low mist. Rain. I thought I'd been mad to move away from the coast.'

'Could it be our chap in the lake?'

'I don't know why I didn't think of it before.' He seemed angry with himself.

'So it could be him?'

'Carl was murdered, if that's what you mean. There's no way he just wandered away from the track and got lost.'

'But it doesn't say anything here about a murder investigation.'

'There wasn't one. Everyone was content to put it down as an accident. According to the press, if anyone was to blame it was the social worker who suggested that he should be allowed to walk home on his own. But I talked to her in the day centre and I was impressed. She said Carl was deaf. No one had picked up how profound that disability was, and she thought he was more capable than his parents allowed him to be. In the few months since she'd known him he'd begun to read quite fluently. She thought he might catch up enough to move on to the technical college, perhaps hold down a real job. But his parents were horrified by those plans. They wanted nothing to do with them.'

'Hard, I suppose, to stop being protective after all those years.'

'There was more to it than that. They were a

strange family.' It was Stout's turn to stare into space, to drag back the memories, image by image.

'You think one of the parents was responsible for his death?'

'Not directly. The wife, Sarah, had a younger brother. I can't believe I can't remember the name. He caused me enough sleepless nights at the time. He didn't live at the farm but he'd never married and he spent a lot of time there. He was assistant manager in a hardware shop in town. It's been closed for years but it was a big place then, dealt in agricultural supplies and machinery too. In his spare time he got involved in community work.' He turned his head so he wasn't looking directly at Porteous. 'Quite a saint if you listened to Sarah. He was a scout leader in Cranford for years and ran the youth club in our church until I persuaded the committee it wasn't such a good idea.'

'Child abuse?'

'Nothing proved. Never charged.' Stout paused. 'It was before all the child-safety legislation, don't forget. Before Childline. Some people even treated it as a bit of a joke. If a pervy old man liked to touch young lads' behinds when they were horsing around, so what? At least it kept the kids off the streets. And no one else wanted the responsibility of organizing the group.'

'What put you on to him?'

'Rumours. Some of the things the kids said. The fact that he was such a loner. He never liked working with other adults. If he had an assistant it was an older lad who'd gone through the group. I had just enough to persuade my church to drop him. Tactfully of course, with a letter of thanks and a ten-quid book token. But not enough to take it further.'

'Until Carl Jackson disappeared.'

'Even then it wasn't a central line of investigation. I was a young DC. New to the district. No connections. I passed on the rumours and some enquiries were made but it seemed that the bloke had an alibi for the time Carl disappeared.' Porteous waited for Stout to continue but he was frowning, preoccupied. 'I've just remembered his name. It was Reeves. Alec Reeves.'

'You don't think much of the alibi?'

'It was half-day closing at the shop so his boss couldn't vouch for him. Reeves claimed he was at home taking one of his lads through his paces for the Queen's Scout badge.'

'And the boy bore it out?'

'Too scared or too involved not to. So far as I know no other checks were made on where they both were that afternoon.'

'Would you be able to dig out the name of the witness?'

'Aye. I made sure I kept all my notes on that one. I knew it would come back to haunt me.'

'Do you know what happened to Carl's parents? I tried to phone the farm last night. The number's the same but it seems to be some sort of office now. Computers.'

'Alf, the father, died. We didn't think he was involved in any way with Carl's disappearance. He was a grafter but not the sharpest tool in the box. Last time I heard, Sarah was in one of those old folks' council bungalows near the river. I presume she's still alive. She's one of those women you imagine would go on for ever. She'll be a good age now.'

'And Reeves?'

'Funnily enough he left the town soon after the investigation was wrapped up.' His voice, which was heavy with sarcasm, turned to a quiet desperation. 'To work as a care assistant in a children's home. I should have told someone. Said something. But he hadn't been charged and he had a lot of powerful friends. I really didn't think anyone would take any notice.'

'Do you remember where he went?'

'I don't think I ever knew. Look, I can't tell you if that body in the lake was Carl's, but if it was, I can tell you who killed him and I'm glad I'll be there to see him go down.'

'There's nothing we can do until we've checked the dental records. That's happening this morning.'

'I'd like to talk to Sarah. Now. While we've got an element of surprise.'

Porteous had never seen Eddie Stout like this. He was usually the one in the team to caution detachment: 'We don't get paid to act as judges,' he'd say. 'That's for God and the chaps with the hairy wigs.'

'She'll surely have heard about the body in the lake.'

'But no details. Not that we're calling it murder.'

Porteous wanted to say no. If he didn't feel he owed Eddie, he'd have refused immediately.

Eddie sensed the hesitation. 'If it is Carl it would give us a head start. Let me see what she's got to say for herself. You're right. Of course she'll have heard about the body in the lake. She might give something away. And I want to find out what happened to Alec Reeves. If he's still working with children I want to know about it. Things are different these days.'

God, thought Porteous, suddenly feeling very tired, I haven't been that passionate about anything in years.

He sensed that Stout wouldn't let it go and couldn't face a confrontation. He shrugged.

'Why not?' he said. 'But I'm coming with you.'

Stout drove. There was no air-conditioning in the car and even with the windows down Porteous felt sticky, slightly light-headed in the heat. The bungalows were grouped around a square of grass which was brown through lack of water. Two old men in white hats stood chatting and broke off their conversation when Stout knocked on the door.

Porteous had worked out that Sarah Jackson must be at least eighty, but she opened the door to them herself, and she recognized Stout immediately.

'Oh, it's you.' She had an underbite and a way of thrusting her jaw forwards to emphasize it. She was skinny and short and the mannerism gave her the air of an aggressive child. A cotton floral dress added to the impression. 'You might as well come in.'

She led them into a small room packed with shabby furniture which must have come from the farm.

'I heard you sold up after Alf died,' Stout said.

'I could hardly work the place on my own.'

'Good timing, just before the bottom fell out of hill farming. You were lucky.'

She glared at him. 'You make your own luck in this world.'

Porteous had the impression that this was a continuation of the sparring which had gone on twenty years before. He sat on a fireside chair that had been covered in pink stretch nylon, and watched.

'I hear there's a computer business in the old house now,' Stout said. He was still standing, looking out of the window.

'Is that what it was about?' She hardly seemed interested. 'I suppose there would be plenty of space.'

'You don't miss the place?' Stout persisted.

'It was never the same after Carl went.'

'No,' Porteous interrupted. He could feel Stout's anger across the room. 'It can't have been.'

She sniffed, slightly mollified, and perched on the edge of an overstuffed chesterfield.

'What do you want?'

'You'll have heard we found a body in Cranford Water?'

'That's nothing to do with me.'

'Why are you so certain it's not Carl in the lake?'

'Because he just wandered off. It was the sort of thing he did. I told the social workers he couldn't take in what you said to him. And it wasn't because he couldn't hear. Even with his deaf aid he had his head in the clouds. And he couldn't have walked that far without anyone seeing him. Where did you find the body? Near the Adventure Centre. That's the opposite side of the lake from the farm. A twenty-mile walk. At least. You lot were out searching before he could have made it. And, before you ask, he couldn't swim. Or row a boat.'

She spoke with confidence. It was a well-rehearsed speech.

'Someone could always have driven him in a car,' Stout said softly.

'Which someone are we talking about now?'

'Alec had a car, didn't he? A Morris 1100. Navy blue. It was his pride and joy as I remember.'

'I wondered how long it would be before you got round to Alec.' She was contemptuous, turning her back on Stout and directing the rest of the conversation at Porteous. 'My little brother was hounded out of the town by your man, just when I needed his support the most. It was rumours at first. Gossip. Snide, like a lassie. Don't trust Alec Reeves with your children. Then he went to his boss and accused Alec of taking our Carl. As if he would. He was good to the boy, more patient than me or Alf could ever be. He took him for treats, things we never had the time or the money to give him. The pictures on Saturday afternoons, picnics in the hills . . .'

She wiped the corner of her eye with an embroidered handkerchief. Porteous, who was looking closely, could see no tears.

'Please don't distress yourself,' he said. 'We thought you'd rather we came ourselves to tell you what was happening. My people are checking the dental records now – we know that Carl saw a dentist while he was at the day centre. The records are still available. You shouldn't have long to wait. We'll have a positive identification by this afternoon.'

Sarah Jackson was so angry that she seemed not to care. 'That's all very well,' she cried. 'But you shouldn't have brought that man here. It wasn't tactful. It wasn't right.'

She stood up as if she expected them to leave but Porteous stayed where he was.

'What happened to Alec when he left Cranford, Mrs Jackson?'

'He did well for himself. Better than if he'd stayed here.'

'Oh?'

'He got a job in a home for kiddies. They sent him

away to college.' She was as proud as if she'd been talking about her own son.

'Is he still there?'

'He retired. I thought he might come home then. We'd been so close, him and me. Our parents died when he was still at school. I brought him up. But he couldn't face it after what happened before. All those lies. He bought a bungalow in the Pennines not far from the school. I visit when I can. I'll go again when it's not so hot.'

'Whereabouts in the Pennines?'

'What's it to you? I'll not have him harassed.' She walked towards the door and threw it open. 'I'm an old woman. I need my peace. I've nothing more to say to you.'

They walked out into the glare of the sunshine. 'I'll be in touch this afternoon,' Porteous said, 'when we've heard back from the dentist.' But she had already shut the door on them.

They were in the station, walking up the stairs towards Porteous's office, when they heard footsteps running up behind them. It was Claire Wright, a young DC, flushed, excited, out of breath so she could hardly speak.

'We've got a match.' She bent double, gasping.

'You look as if you've just won the Great North Run.' Porteous forced himself to stay calm, to keep his voice light.

'Who?' demanded Stout. When she did not reply immediately he added, almost in a whisper, 'Is it Carl Jackson?'

By then she had caught her breath. 'Nah, nothing like. It's the lad called Michael Grey.'

'Ah.' Porteous continued up the stairs, unlocked his door and flicked the kettle on. He waited for Stout to follow.

Chapter Four

Stout stood in the doorway of Porteous's office.

'You don't seem surprised.'

'Not too surprised, no,' Porteous said. 'You were right about Sarah Jackson. She does know what happened to her son. But when we talked about the body in the lake she wasn't bothered, hardly interested. She knew it wasn't him.'

He made a mug of tea for Eddie, strong, as he knew he liked it, and waved it at him to invite him in. 'We'll have to save Carl for another day.' The words sounded unbelievably trite. 'I'm sorry, Eddie, I mean it. Now we have to concentrate on Michael Grey, find out everything there is to know about him.'

Porteous could tell the man's mind and heart weren't really in it. He was still thinking about the deaf boy everyone had labelled as dumb. When this investigation was over he'd give Eddie his head for a few weeks, let him dig around for a bit. Even if nothing came of it he deserved that much.

Soon it became clear they would find out very little about Michael Grey. Not immediately at least. At first Porteous had thought it would be easy. A piece of piss, he said to himself, though not to Eddie who disapproved of such language. Michael Grey had been fostered to a couple called Brice. Fostering meant Social Services and that meant records as long as your arm – reports for the court, case conferences, personal records kept to cover the back of whichever poor social worker had been in charge of him. There would be details of the natural family at least and of any contact between them and the boy. Michael hadn't been adopted, so he would still have been officially in care when he disappeared. Some attempt would have been made to trace him.

He sent Eddie to talk to the solicitor who'd triggered the first missing-person report after the foster parents' death. 'Find out who benefited from the will in the absence of the boy. Did anyone? Is the cash still being held in trust for him? What happens to it now?'

Stout slunk away like a sulky teenager. As soon as he had gone Porteous made an appointment with the senior social worker on duty at the town hall. The man was prepared to see him at once. The town hall was in the same street and of the same design as the police station – redbrick Victorian Gothic – though it had a depressing concrete and glass extension at the back, where the Social Services department was housed. A small middle-aged man named Jones met Porteous at reception and led him upstairs. They left behind them the screams of an elderly woman, demanding to see her social worker, and the increasingly irate reply of the receptionist who said she would have to wait.

They sat in a cubby-hole looking out on a busy open-plan office where one of the phones always seemed to be ringing. Jones was tidy, with a few wisps of hair combed over a balding pate. He was apologetic. 'After you phoned I checked our records. I like to think we're efficient in that department. But we've no details of a couple called Brice being registered as foster parents. Nothing at all. No application form, no record of training.'

'Would you still have the file after all this time?'

'Oh yes. We go back thirty years. Longer. Child protection, you see. It's important to know who's been looking after our children.'

'Could the Brices have been working for someone else? A charity, perhaps? Another authority?'

'That's what I thought!' He seemed impressed that Porteous had been thinking along the same lines. 'But I've phoned around and I can't find anyone else in the field who's heard of them. I'm not saying it's impossible that they were registered with another agency, but – if it doesn't sound too big-headed – my contacts are second to none. I'd certainly say it's unlikely.'

'You'll have a record, though, of Michael Grey?'

'No.' The man closed his mouth firmly, allowing no question. He sat back in his chair and clasped his hands round his small paunch. He seemed to be delighted by the mystery, and by Porteous's discomfort.

'But I gave you his date of birth. We found it in the dental records.' Porteous could tell he was sounding desperate. That'll teach me, he thought. A piece of piss.

'It doesn't help, I'm afraid. I've phoned the court. They keep their own records. No care or supervision order was placed on anyone called Michael Grey in the seventies anywhere in the county.' He paused, savouring the moment. 'Social Services were never involved with him either.'

40

'But they must have been.'

'Not necessarily.' Jones leaned forward, but didn't elaborate.

'I don't understand.'

'How old was he?' The tone was patronizing. An infant teacher talking to a particularly thick six-year-old. Just what I deserve, Porteous thought.

'When we think he went missing? Eighteen.'

'There you are then.' Jones leaned back in the chair once more and smirked. 'Over sixteen and we wouldn't get involved. He could have been younger than that when he started living with the foster parents, if it was an informal arrangement.'

'Perhaps you would explain.' Porteous had never minded eating humble pie. It was surprising how people liked you to grovel. The social worker was loving it.

'Let's take a hypothetical situation. Something we come across all the time. Say there's a single mum with a teenage lad. He starts to run a bit wild. Perhaps it's nothing that would get him in trouble with the police, but he's staying out late, skipping school. She begins to feel she's losing control. Now, it could be that the boy has a good relationship with her parents and they offer to have him to live with them for a while. To take the heat off her until things calm down. That would be fostering of a sort, wouldn't it? Nothing official. No need for Social Services to be involved even if the lad were under sixteen. In fact that's usually the last thing a family under stress wants. A nosy cow from the Welfare knocking on the door.'

Porteous smiled.

'So you're saying these Brices were probably relatives?'

'They might have been. Or friends. They might even have been doing it for money. All I can tell you is I don't think they were official.'

'Where do you suggest I go from here?'

'Have you got the name of the school?'

'Cranford Grammar.' That too had been in the dental records.

'Try there then. If it was an informal fostering they'd still have wanted the names of the natural parent. It's possible that he moved away from home after he started the school. Most problems of that sort start in adolescence. You might even find a couple of teachers who remember him. My kids go there and some of the staff must be close to retirement.'

He led Porteous down the concrete stairs. In the waiting-room the old lady had begun to sob.

Cranford Grammar had since become Cranford High, and when Porteous phoned the school from his office he was told that it was the last day of the summer term. The secretary sounded on the verge of hysteria. In the background he heard the high-pitched yelps of children, an impatient teacher calling for mislaid reports, a yell for silence.

'It really isn't a good time.'

Then he explained that he was running a murder inquiry and suddenly her attitude changed. Porteous had noticed it before. It wasn't a desire to be a good citizen and help the police. Murder had the same effect as the mention of celebrity, of a pop idol or football

star. She was excited. Later she would boast to her
friends that she had been involved.

He told her again what he wanted.

'I can only think of one member of staff who would
have been around then,' she said. 'Mr Westcott. He's
head of history. I know he has a free period first thing
after lunch but that's probably not the best time to talk
to him.'

'Why not?' he asked politely.

'Oh well. I suppose it'll be all right. I'll tell him
you're calling. And I'll check our records. If you come
to the office first I'll have everything ready for you.'

The electric bell sounding the end of lunch was ringing
as he got out of his car. By the time he got to the school
office the children were contained in their classrooms.
No pretence was being made to teach them. He heard
whoops of laughter, the blare of rock music. The secretary moved away from her computer screen when
she saw him and held towards him a manila envelope.
He could tell from the weight that there were only a
couple of sheets of paper inside.

'It's not much I'm afraid. After all this time . . .'

He knew that she would have done all she could
to help. There was no point in pushing for more. He
followed her directions to the staff-room. Jack Westcott
was plump and round and when Porteous pushed open
the door to the cluttered room, he was asleep.
Despite the heat he wore a tweed jacket with a loud
check and there were beads of sweat on his forehead.
Porteous leaned over him to tap him on the shoulder
and smelled whisky fumes. That explained the

secretary's feeling that the first period after lunch might not be a good time to speak to him. Jack Westcott had been celebrating the end of term in the pub. He opened rheumy eyes and with an unembarrassed jolt he sat up.

'You must be the policeman chappie.'

Porteous admitted that he was.

'Help yourself to coffee.' He nodded unsteadily towards a filter machine in the corner. 'I have mine black. Two sugars if the bastards have left any.'

He pressed on the arms of his chair as if to hoist himself out of it, but the effort was too much for him. The three remaining teachers in the room picked up their bags and wandered out. Porteous carried back the polystyrene cups of coffee and sat beside him.

'I'm here about a boy called Michael Grey. Your secretary said you might remember him. We think he could have been a bit of a troublemaker.'

'No, no no.' The words were thundered so loud that Porteous was startled. Jack Westcott set the cup on the table and shook his head as if to clear an alcoholic fug. 'He was a good chap, Michael. One of the best.'

'So you do remember him?' Porteous felt a wonderful relief. He had begun to think that Michael Grey didn't exist at all, that he was some figment of Carver's imagination.

'Of course I do. I remember all the kids. Hundreds of them. That's what teaching's all about. Not attainment targets. Not literacy hours. Not . . .' He looked about him, saw that the bulk of his audience had disappeared and lapsed in to silence.

'Tell me about him.'

'I didn't teach the boy. History wasn't one of his

subjects. Shame. He'd have been an asset to the sixth-form group. Articulate, you know.'

'So you didn't know him well?' Porteous felt the image of Michael Grey fade from his grasp. A ghostly apparition disappearing through a wall before it has even taken shape.

'I didn't say that. He was in my tutor group for nearly two years so I probably knew him better than his subject teachers.' Westcott sat back in his chair like an elderly Billy Bunter and shut his eyes. He continued to speak, unaware of Porteous taking notes. 'Michael joined us at the beginning of the lower sixth, a year older than most of them. I can't remember where he came from. Some private place, I think. I know there was a problem getting the paperwork from them. It hadn't even arrived by the time he left. I was never told why he resat the lower sixth and I didn't ask. Not my business. Some illness perhaps or emotional problem. It happens at that age. They're very intense. That's why they're such a joy to teach. I'm an old man, can't get up to much now. So I live through them. Voraciously but second hand. Much the safest way . . .'

He paused for a moment. Porteous worried that he might have fallen asleep again, but the words continued in a low-pitched growl.

'He was an exceptional boy. There was something about him. Charm, I suppose you'd call it. He had a way of winning people over.'

'Did he talk about his home life?'

'He was living with the Brices.' He lapsed again into silence. Porteous resisted the temptation to prompt him. 'Good people, the Brices. I didn't really know them myself. Met them occasionally. Parents' dos. The school play. But that's what everyone said. Of course they were religious.' He snorted, as if religion was to be disapproved of, then began to snore. He was more drunk than Porteous had first realized.

'Did he have friends?'

'What? Oh, bucketsful. I could give you a list. There was a girlfriend. What was her name? Shy little thing.'

'Did he talk about his family? I mean his real family.'

'No, but parents are an embarrassment at that age, whatever they're like. It doesn't mean anything. None of the kids talk about them.'

'Is there anything else you can tell me about him?'

'He was an actor. Brilliant. I remember his Macbeth. The best production the school ever did.' He lurched suddenly to his feet and began to quote hammily: 'Is this a dagger which I see before me?'

He flung out one arm and collapsed back into the chair. Then he fell into a deep sleep and Porteous found it impossible to rouse him.

Because it was the end of term the students must have been released early; as Porteous got to his car it was surrounded by a tide of screaming and dishevelled children. He was grateful to reach the peace of the police station. It was only when Porteous was back in his office that he opened the envelope given to him by the secretary.

There was one sheet of paper and a faded photograph. The paper was a reference, handwritten by Jack Westcott, for use in the universities selection process. It described Michael Grey in the same glowing terms he had used to Porteous. The boy's predicted A-level grades were good. It seemed that he would have had no difficulty in securing a university place. The photograph was in fact a cutting from the local paper and included a review of the production of *Macbeth*. A grainy figure stood centre stage. He was dressed in a costume obviously put together by the home-economics department. In his hand he brandished a wide-bladed knife.

Chapter Five

Porteous felt suddenly restless. He re-read Westcott's reference for Michael and set it aside. Sometimes it happened. He'd happily sit for days going over a mechanical task, then all at once feel that he was caged. He needed to pace up and down, to be somewhere, anywhere different. He'd discussed the problem with his doctor, who'd agreed that it could be a side-effect of the medication he was taking. But didn't everyone feel like that once in a while? Didn't everyone feel the need to break free?

He wandered down the stairs to the car park and was hovering there, trying to think of a legitimate journey he could make, when Eddie Stout returned from his meeting with the solicitor who'd handled the Brices' affairs.

'Any joy?' He thought he sounded businesslike. Not like someone trying to dream up an excuse not to go inside.

'I don't know. More complications.'

'We'll talk about it over a cup of tea, shall we?' Porteous said. 'Not here. Not the canteen. Let's go somewhere else.' To his own ears he sounded hysterical, but Stout seemed not to notice, even to be pleased by the suggestion.

'There's quite a nice place along by our church . . '

The walk calmed Porteous, made him slightly less jumpy. He felt his pulse slow. The café was attached to the church and was obviously run by its members. It was called the Mustard Seed. Besides tea and cakes it sold religious books and sentimental greetings cards. Again Porteous wondered if Stout saw him as a subject ripe for conversion. The building was new, airy, but as they went in Porteous had a fleeting smell of damp books and old ladies' perfume.

Perhaps Stout sensed his discomfort. He said defensively, 'It's run by volunteers. All the profit goes to our charities. I like to support it. Anyway it's a quiet place to talk.'

They were fussed over by two grey-haired grandmothers. There were frilly tablecloths and silk flowers, but the women made him Earl Grey to his exact specification and the shortbread was excellent. The church had been built as part of a new housing development, along with shops and a community centre. They looked out on to a street. A funeral service was taking place in the church next door. One of the undertaker's men was standing by the hearse, smoking a cigarette. The women were interested in what was happening and kept coming out into the room to peer through the window. At a nod from Stout they retreated behind their counter and soon became engrossed in their memories of the dead man. Porteous resisted an impulse to fidget. He wanted to arrange the sugar cubes into towers, to straighten the birthday cards on a nearby stand.

'I've finally met someone who knew Michael Grey,' he said. 'The social worker wasn't much use. He

49

decided the fostering arrangement with the Brices must have been informal, set up between them and the parents. He'd have no record of that. But he put me in touch with the school. There's a teacher called Jack Westcott, head of history. He remembered Michael quite well.'

'I'd take what Westcott said with a pinch of salt,' Stout said tartly. 'He'll have been in the Percy Arms all lunchtime.'

'Is that a regular event? I thought it was just because it was the last day of term.'

'Regular enough. He's retiring now, so the school hasn't made an issue of it. He never taught Ruth but I kept an eye on what was going on.'

I bet they love you at the school, Porteous thought. He said, 'There's written confirmation, anyway. A reference from Westcott to help Michael get a place at university.'

Stout didn't reply.

'I'm surprised you didn't know the Brices,' Porteous went on. Thinking, You know everything about every other bugger in the place.

'For some reason we never bumped into each other. I've been asking around though. Stephen Brice was an ordained priest with the Church of England. He worked in Africa before coming back to be rector here. After he retired he still did a lot of writing and teaching. People I've spoken to can't remember the lad, but they say it would be just like the Brices to take someone in. They liked young people. Set up a youth group. Run, coincidentally, by Alec Reeves.'

'Was it now?'

'Unfortunately he'd already left the area before

Michael went to live with them.' Stout shrugged. 'Like you said, I'll have to let that go.'

'What did you get out of the solicitor?'

'Everything he had to give. The Brices died just over a year after Michael disappeared. There was a car crash on the A1. Stephen died immediately. Sylvia was taken to hospital but passed away a couple of days later in intensive care. The wills were drawn up by the couple without the help of a solicitor. He said that if he'd been involved he would have worded things a bit differently, but the intention of the couple was quite clear and he has no doubt the wills are legal documents. They were found with the rest of the Brices' papers after their deaths. He was one of the executors and determined to carry out their wishes as best he could.'

Stout pulled a notebook from his pocket. 'Each of the wills was identical. The estate was to be left first to the other partner. In the event of the survivor dying it should go to "our foster son, our gift from God, known as Michael Grey, so he can lead an independent life". That was it, quoted word for word.'

'No legacies to charity or to the church?'

'No. According to the solicitor, they gave regularly in covenants while they were alive, but there was nothing in the will.'

'Doesn't that seem odd to you?'

'I don't think so. It wasn't a huge estate. Only a small terraced house and a couple of thousand in savings. Perhaps they wanted to give as much as possible to Michael.'

'Their gift from God.' Porteous tried to keep the sneer from his voice. 'They obviously thought he was still alive at the time of their deaths or they'd have changed the wills. And they must have believed the solicitor could trace him without too much difficulty. Didn't they think it odd when Michael didn't get in touch for months?'

'The solicitor said he'd never had any other clients like them. They were unworldly, as trusting as children. They didn't worry about things they couldn't change.'

That's what I try to do, Porteous thought. But I never manage it. 'What do you make of the "known as" in the phrase "known as Michael Grey"?'

'I supposed it meant the Brices considered him their son, even though he used a name different from theirs.'

'Not that Michael Grey was an assumed name?'

Stout looked up sharply from his tea. 'That would complicate matters.'

'Wouldn't it just.' But, thought Porteous, if that's the way it is I can't change it, so there's no point worrying.

They sat for a moment in silence. The coffin was carried from the church and replaced in the hearse, which drove slowly away. The congregation had spilled out on to the street and elderly men in shiny black suits stood chatting in the sunshine. One of the ladies behind the counter plucked up courage to call over to them. 'Can we get you anything else, Mr Stout?'

'Some more tea, Mavis, would be lovely.'

Still there were no other customers. After the tea had been presented Porteous said, 'What steps did the solicitor take to trace Michael Grey?'

'Much the same as we've done today. He contacted the school. He thought it most likely that Michael had gone on to further education and that the school would have the name of the college or university even if it couldn't give him his home address. At that time he thought it would be quite straightforward to find him.'

'But it wasn't.'

'Apparently Michael left quite suddenly without taking A levels.'

'The Brices must have thought they knew where he was or surely they would have got in touch with us.'

'I don't know. Unless they talked to a friend about it, we'll never find out. The solicitor did report him as a missing person when he couldn't get an address from the school. His main objective was to prove that he'd done everything possible to find Michael. Apparently that's a legal requirement. He advertised for information in the local Cranford paper, the *Newcastle Chronicle* and the London *Evening Standard*. It's standard procedure.'

'No response?'

'Not even from cranks.'

'What did the solicitor do then?'

'He didn't feel there was anything else he could do. He'd fulfilled all his legal obligations.'

'What happened to the money?'

'It went to Sylvia Brice's next of kin. Because she survived her husband by a couple of days *her* relative was the beneficiary, not his. It was actually a nephew, a commodity broker in the city. He hardly needed the cash. According to the solicitor all the family have done well for themselves. Perhaps that's why the Brices decided to leave the estate to Michael.'

'I'm glad they never knew,' Porteous said, 'that he couldn't be traced.'

'There is one complication.'

'Only one?'

'The solicitor's very keen for us to fix a date of death.'

'Aren't we all!'

Stout ignored the sarcasm and ploughed on. 'You see, if Michael's death predated the Brices' then the arrangement by which the nephew inherited was fair and legal. But suppose Michael was still alive when the Brices had the car crash. Suppose he'd just gone to earth somewhere and he was killed and dumped in the lake later. Then that would affect the inheritance.'

'In what way?'

'The cash should have gone to *his* next of kin, not the Brices.'

Porteous found that he could concentrate again on the detail. The dreadful restlessness seemed to have left him. 'I don't think that's likely, do you? He wasn't the sort of lad I imagined at first. I don't see him disappearing for months, moving from one squat to another, spending time inside. He was bright. He had a lot to lose. I think he was killed soon after he was missed at school.'

Outside, the congregation had dispersed. The grandmothers were banging pots in the kitchen to show they wanted to lock up.

Stout stood up. 'What now?'

'Back to the station to organize a press conference. It's time we went public. The school gave me a photo, a cutting from the local rag, but it could be anyone. Let's see if the paper still has the original. I know it happened nearly thirty years ago, but people round here have good memories. There'll be friends still living in the town. And enemies. Come on, Eddie. Let's make you a star.'

In fact Porteous took the press conference early the following evening. There was all the media interest he could have wished for. The body had been discovered because of the drought and the drought was a big story, so the national press was there. He had wanted to hold the conference in the high-school hall. The only certainty he had in the case was that Michael Grey had been a pupil at Cranford Grammar. He thought it might jog a few memories. But the head teacher wasn't keen. He seemed to think that even after all those years murder would be bad for the school's image. He used as an excuse the fact that the hall had already been hired out for an event in the evening. Nothing Porteous said could make him change his mind.

Instead they used the community centre next to Stout's church. It still smelled of the lunch that had been provided for the pensioners' club which had met earlier in the day – steamed fish and cabbage. Porteous sat on the stage behind a trestle table hidden by a white cloth. His answers to the press emphasized his ignorance. He didn't have an exact date of death. He hadn't traced the boy's relatives. That was why he needed their help. All he had was a body that looked like a lump of lard – this he phrased more delicately – and an old photo of a white-haired boy with a knife.

There was one moment of excitement. In the second row sat a big woman who worked for the town's free paper. When the photo was passed round Porteous could have sworn that she recognized the face. But when he looked for her later she had rushed away.

PART TWO

Chapter Six

It was hot again. The local news was all about the weather. A magistrate had been prosecuted for using a sprinkler at midnight. Tankers were driving the region's water south. The lake at Cranford was so low that flooded buildings were starting to emerge from the sludge and a body, trapped under a pier for years, had been found by a canoeist.

Hannah switched off the radio and parked her car. There was a new officer on the gate so she had to show her pass. The photograph was two years old and she saw him look at it then back at her, squinting, unsure at first that it was the same person. He pushed it back under the glass screen and Hannah stared at it too. It didn't look like her. The woman in the photograph was younger. She was smiling. Not relaxed exactly – Hannah had never been that – there was a tension around the mouth. But content, complacent even. It was taken while she was still part of a family. Before Rosie hated her. Before Jonathan left with a twenty-five-year-old PE teacher, to set up home all over again.

She had to wait for a moment in the gate room for two officers to come in through the outer door. The inner door wouldn't open until the outer was locked. Then she stood back to let them go ahead to collect their keys. She was in no hurry, early as usual. Punctuality had been a curse since childhood. She threw her tag into the chute and waited for the new man to find her keys. Ahead of her the officers were talking very loudly. She recognized them but they were too engrossed in conversation to acknowledge her. She gathered there'd been some trouble on the wing the night before. Nothing serious. She thought it had probably been caused by the heat. Those huts must be insufferable in this weather. The men walked off before she could hear any more, the heels of their highly polished shoes reflecting the sunlight. They were still talking. Every other word, she knew, would be a blasphemy.

Hannah followed them from the gatehouse and thought that generally, in the prison, the officers were less polite than the inmates. *They* were usually courteous, grovelling even, like the child in a class who is always bullied. Especially if they wanted something – to use the library on an unscheduled day, for example, or to be let off a fine for a lost or damaged book. 'Please, miss, it's not my fault. Honest,miss.'

Of course, they weren't all like that. Neither were the officers all boors. Today she was feeling particularly jaundiced, because the photograph had reminded her of a time of certainty, and because she'd had a row with Rosie last night. Rosie. Named by her parents Rosalind, she'd changed her name with her personality in adolescence. She was Hannah's only child. The night before, Rosie had come in drunk again with a gang of friends. It was midnight. Hannah's room was over the kitchen and she'd heard the freezer door open and the banging of a cooker shelf, and she knew that when she got up in the morning there'd be plates everywhere and half-eaten pizza ground into the carpet. And probably a body snoring on the sofa in the dining-room and two more in the spare bed. So she'd gone down and made a fuss. Rosie had stared at her in apparent horror and amazement, actually enjoying every minute of the drama.

'Get a life, Mum,' she'd said. 'Make some friends and get a life.'

Then she'd stormed off to spend the night in someone else's spare room.

Jonathan had never minded the late nights, the loud music, strange kids in the house. At first Hannah had been surprised by his tolerance. Then she'd been jealous of his ability to get on with Rosie's friends.

'We've all been young,' he'd say. 'Even you, Hannah.'

He'd take them to the pub at the end of the street, buying them drinks even before they were eighteen, talking music, reminiscing about bands he'd seen and festivals he'd attended. That side of his life had been new to Hannah. Perhaps he hadn't wanted to admit to a vaguely hippy past until the sixties became fashionable again. Perhaps he'd made it all up to impress the stunning sixth-form women who sat around the beaten copper tables in the Grey Horse, downing their pints of Stella as if they were glasses of lemonade. Perhaps, stirred by their admiration, that was when he recognized there were other possibilities in his life and he turned his attention to the lycra-clad Eve.

Not Eve the temptress, he had said earnestly when he explained that he was leaving. She was shy. She hadn't wanted it to happen. She'd be the last person ever to want to break up a family. They'd both fought it.

When Hannah failed to respond he had gone on more petulantly, 'At least we waited until Rosie finished her A levels before making it public.' As if that had deserved a prize. As if it hadn't been more about embarrassment, because Jonathan and Eve both taught in Rosie's school. As deputy head, Jonathan was Eve's boss.

Before leaving the gatehouse Hannah clipped the keys on to her belt and tucked them into the leather pouch which was designed to keep them hidden from view. The pouch was hardly an attractive garment but she always wore it. It was a rule and she'd never had any problems with rules. Perhaps that was why she'd settled without too much difficulty into the routine of the prison. There was a comforting hierarchy: governors of different grades, prisoners with different privileges, a system and a structure. Rosie's life seemed to have no order and that was why Hannah was alarmed for her. She had personal knowledge of how unsettling disorder could be.

The prison was category C, medium security, taking men who had been dispersed from local jails and lifers nearing the end of their sentences. It had once been an RAF base. There was still an enormous hangar which housed the workshops. The lads slept in billets where once conscripts spat on boots and folded blankets. Hannah had slipped into the way of calling them lads, though some of them were older than her. That showed, she thought, that she had become institutionalized into prison life.

The library was in a hut of its own, attached at the

back by a brick corridor to the education department. The site of the prison was vast. Now, at the beginning of July, it was a pleasant if sticky walk from the gate. There were flowers everywhere. Huge circular beds had been planted in formation as in a municipal park. The grass was closely cropped. The prison regularly won prizes for its gardens. In the winter it was a different matter. Then she came to work dressed for an expedition to the Arctic. The wind blew straight from Scandinavia. Horizontal rain and sleet seemed to last for days. Men who'd grown up in cities further south spoke of their sentence as if they'd been sent to a Siberian work camp. They called it the Gulag. The nearest railway was twenty miles away.

Hannah's orderly, Marty, was waiting outside for her, leaning against the door where the week before she had stuck a poster saying: NO SHORTS PLEASE. Since the beginning of the heatwave the men had started to dress as if for the beach. The exposed flesh and muscular thighs had seemed inappropriate for a library and, with the Governor's authority, she'd put a stop to it. As Hannah approached she realized the phone was ringing inside. Marty must have heard it, but he hadn't called or waved to hurry her along. By the time she'd unlocked the door it had stopped. Automatically she wondered if it had been her daughter. Anxiety about Rosie stayed with her constantly, eating away at her. She knew it was a silly habit, like checking the gas was switched off before leaving the house and always being early, but she couldn't help it. Knowing the history of the habit didn't help at all.

'You can't be on her back all the time,' Jonathan would say. 'Relax. What's wrong with you? Hormones, I suppose.' And if Rosie was there too they would snigger together. After all, what was more amusing than a middle-aged, menopausal woman scared to death that her reckless daughter would get into trouble? Because Rosie was reckless in an overreachingly confident way that left Hannah breathless.

Of course, she hadn't come in that morning before Hannah left for work and Hannah didn't know which friend she'd imposed on for a bed for the night. When she'd heard the phone it had occurred to her briefly that Rosie had called to apologize, but she dismissed the thought as ridiculous. Some chance. She picked up her bag, let Marty through ahead of her and locked the door behind them.

Marty was new to the job, different from any other orderlies she'd been given. It was a cushy number and the other men she'd worked with were eager to please, desperate to make themselves indispensable so she wouldn't find it easy to sack them before the end of their stint. They were only allowed six months in the job. It was a security concern. Supervisors and prisoners shouldn't have the chance to get too close. Marty was self-contained, efficient. He didn't tell her about his family or try to impress by talking about the books he'd read. He didn't say anything much unless it was about the library. Hannah thought he was probably in his thirties but he had one of those pale-skinned, freckled faces which always look boyish. She watched him lift a pile of newspapers on to a table and begin to sort them.

'Why don't you put the kettle on, Marty?'

He looked up, surprised, then nodded. Usually they had a cup of tea just before opening for the first session and today business didn't start until the period of lunchtime association at eleven thirty. But it wouldn't have occurred to him to comment.

For the first time she wondered what crime he had committed. Her friends – because she did have friends, despite Rosie's jibe – always asked about that.

'But what are they in for, Hannah?' they'd say with the disapproving curiosity of a *Telegraph* reader sneaking a look at the *Sun*. 'Who do you have to mix with in there? Rapists? Muggers of little old ladies?'

They were surprised when Hannah said she didn't know. She was never sure that they quite believed her. It was etiquette, this lack of interest. She wouldn't have enquired of the borrowers in the community library where she'd previously worked if they'd ever been prosecuted for speeding or tax evasion. Besides, it was irrelevant. It didn't matter. The prison was separate from the outside world. So long as the men fitted into the system and caused no bother, nobody much cared what had happened to bring them there. Except perhaps Arthur, her colleague. It seemed to matter to him very much.

Looking at Marty filling the kettle at the small sink in her office, she thought suddenly: it must have been an offence of violence. It was a revelation and she wondered why she hadn't realized it before. He was angry. Continually angry. He controlled it well and kept it hidden but now that it was obvious to Hannah she thought it explained a lot about him. That was why he kept himself to himself. It was the only way he could keep his anger in check.

She phoned home. There was no reply. Of course. Rosie would still be in a bed in a strange house, sleeping off the excesses of the night before. Not that she'd wake with a hangover. The young never seemed to have hangovers. Then, with the same sense of startling revelation she'd had when looking at Marty, it occurred to her that Rosie might not be on her own in bed. They never discussed her relationships with men. If ever Hannah broached the subject, talking elliptically perhaps about safe sex, she'd roll her eyes towards the ceiling and say, 'Oh Mum. Please!'

Hannah thought there was a boy. Joseph. He phoned and when Rosie was out she took messages. If she was in they talked for hours and she'd hear Rosie laughing. But when he came to the house it was always as part of a crowd and often he had his arm round another girl. If Rosie was hurt by that she didn't show it. Hannah hoped Rosie did have a love. She wanted something magic and gut-wrenching for her daughter. Don't wait, she wanted to tell her. Do it now. Soon you'll have responsibilities. You'll be too old. Trust me. I know what I'm talking about.

While Marty squatted by the tray on the floor, squeezing tea bags in the tasteful National Trust mugs she'd brought from home, Hannah started opening her mail. There wasn't much. A memo from her boss in the Central Library about budgets. An agenda for the prison librarians' summer school. A plain white envelope with a handwritten address which she recognized immediately. Something similar came every year. Before she could open it the phone rang again. It was Rosie, bristling with righteous indignation.

'Well,' she said, 'I hope you're ready to apologize.'

It caught Hannah on the hop. She didn't know whether to snap back a sarcastic answer or make an attempt to be conciliatory. She knew why that was. She was afraid Rosie would up sticks and move in with Jonathan and Eve if she upset her too much. Rosie had never mentioned it, hadn't used it as a threat, but Hannah was always aware of the possibility. In the end she wasn't given a chance to respond.

'Look,' Rosie said. 'I'm sorry. It must be a difficult time at the minute.'

Hannah could have fainted with shock. 'And for you. Waiting for your results . . .'

'Oh, sod the A levels.' She paused. 'I'm working this afternoon but I'll be home by six. You can take me to the Grey Horse. Buy me a pint.'

Hannah bit back a lecture. She was always telling Rosie she drank too much. 'OK,' she said. 'Why not? That would be great.'

When she replaced the phone Marty was standing looking at her, a mug in each hand.

'Trouble?' he asked, in an offhand sort of way to show that he wasn't prying.

'No. Not really. You know what kids are like.'

'I know what I was like when I was a kid.'

'Trouble?'

'All the time.' They smiled. He went back to sorting newspapers.

Dave the prison officer attached to the library came in, jangling his keys, demanding tea. Hannah opened her letter. Inside there was a printed invitation and a handwritten note. She read the note first. The handwriting was scrawled but familiar. She recognized it from way back. It had been dashed off in a hurry and there was a stain which could have been coffee on the back.

> *Hannah*
> *Hope this reaches you in time.*
> *You can always stay with me.*
> *Do try and make it this year.*

She didn't need to look at the signature. It was from Sally. At school Sally had been her best friend. She hadn't seen her for years but they kept in touch, spoke occasionally, sent Christmas cards. The card was an invitation to a school reunion. Cranford Grammar. Sally tried the same tactic every time something similar was arranged. Recently the invitations were always sent to the prison. Perhaps she thought it was Jonathan who prevented Hannah's attending.

Hannah threw the card on to the desk where she sat to stamp the books, then picked it up again to look at the date of the party. It was only a couple of days away, one of her late shifts. She thought it was typical of Sally to allow her so little time to come to a decision and arrange her affairs. For the first time she was tempted to go to the reunion, to see Sally and her other friends again. It was only pride which had kept her away. She propped the card between her mug and a box of library cards.

Hannah was never sure how the argument started. Perhaps she'd done something to provoke it, but she didn't think so. Rosie's phone call had made her more mellow. Later she remembered the conversation she'd heard on her way in about a disturbance on the wing. Apparently there'd been rumours of an early lock-up because of a Prison Officers' Association meeting and the whole place was still tense. There'd been no sense of that though when she'd let the men in.

In the first group there was a lad she didn't recognize as one of her regulars. He was young, squat, muscular. A tattoo of a snake twisted from his wrist to his shoulder. His hair was cropped so short that pink skin showed through the stubble. He mooched around the shelves for a bit, but Hannah didn't have the impression that he was looking seriously for anything. She noticed that Marty was keeping an eye on him too. She wondered if he was new, though he hadn't been at the last reception talk she'd given.

She came out from behind the desk. Dave was in her office with the door shut. She'd heard that he was moonlighting in one of the clubs in town. Certainly he liked to catch up on his sleep in the mornings. She approached the lad with the tattoo, thinking she could be making up a ticket while he was choosing. 'Can I help you with anything?'

He turned to face her squarely. He was slightly shorter than she was.

'Not doing you any harm, am I?'

'Of course not. I'll leave you to it.' She was thinking she'd had enough of oversensitive adolescents. Perhaps something of the weariness showed in her face, but she wasn't aware of it.

Suddenly he banged his hand on the edge of a metal shelf then lifted it towards her, a gesture of warning. She could see the red mark from the shelf on his palm.

'Don't look at me like that.'

'I'm sorry. Like what?' Out of the corner of her eye

Hannah saw Marty standing behind the man, his knees slightly bent, watching. She willed him to keep out of it.

'Like I was a piece of shite. Like I was something on the bottom of your shoe.'

'I think you'd better leave,' she said, much as she'd said to the drunken kids lounging around her kitchen the night before. 'Come back when you know how to behave properly in a library.'

'Don't worry I'm going.' He pushed out and sent one of the shelves flying. On the top was a plant – one of her attempts to cheer up the room. The pot shattered. The books were covered in dry compost. 'Do you think I want to stay here and look at an ugly cow like you?' He spoke quietly, with intense contempt, looked around the room and swaggered out.

It was the sort of incident that happened every day in the prison. There was no physical violence against her. No threat of it even. She'd handled worse in her time there. Much worse. But Hannah went to pieces. She started to shake and then to cry.

Dave the library officer emerged from her office, yawning, wanting to know what the noise was about. He was embarrassed, desperate to play the incident down so he'd not get into trouble. Hannah got rid of the other prisoners then sent him away.

Marty pulled the shelf upright and replaced the books, shaking out the compost, checking the spines so they were in order. Then he put on the kettle and made more tea.

'You need a break,' he said. 'A holiday.'

'I don't know.'

'We have to stay in this place. You can escape whenever you like.'

'Perhaps.' She sipped the tea. He'd used powdered milk and the liquid was very hot. It burnt her mouth. 'My husband left me three weeks ago. I'm not sure where I'd go on my own.'

She thought she shouldn't have spoken to a prisoner like that. They'd been taught not to give personal details away.

'What about a trip to the hills? You could look up your old friends.'

She was shocked. He must have read the card when he collected her mug. She wasn't surprised that he'd read the invitation but that he'd commented on it. It wasn't like him.

'Sorry,' he said, blushing slightly as if he'd read her thoughts. 'None of my business.'

'No.' The temptation returned to run away. 'No. It's an idea.'

Arthur Lee was sitting in his office in the education block. His door was open. He saw Hannah walking down the corridor and waved her in.

'Aren't you busy?' She had walked that way hoping to talk to him, but had to pretend she didn't want to intrude.

'Nah, it's good to see a friendly face.'

Arthur was a Home Office imposition on the education department and they'd never liked him. He was too clever and reported straight to the Governor. A psychologist by training, he ran courses in anger management, victim awareness and special sessions for sex offenders. That was another reason for his unpopularity. Since Jonathan had left, Hannah had taken to

dropping in on him more often, using him, she sometimes thought, as a personal therapist. He was in his
early fifties, the age her father had been when he
died. She'd have liked a father like Arthur, plump,
comfortable, understanding. He'd been born in Liverpool and had never lost the accent. John Peel, she
thought, without the beard.

'I hear you've had a bit of bother.'

She should have known it would be impossible to
keep the incident in the library quiet. She shrugged,
explained what had happened. 'Some lad kicking off.
Marty thinks I should take a break.'

'Marty?'

'My orderly. Fox. D Wing. You haven't had him on
one of your courses?'

She was thinking anger management. Arthur shook
his head. Perhaps he wouldn't have told her anyway.

'Sounds like good advice.'

'There's a school reunion. In Cranford. Up in the
hills where I grew up. But I'm not sure . . .'

'I'll come with you if you like.'

Hannah was surprised. She knew he was on his
own but they'd never met outside the prison. She
hadn't thought of him at all as the sort of person she'd
take to a party and needed time to get used to the idea.

'It's too far to come back the same night. I thought
I'd stay with my pal Sally. Make a weekend of it.'

'That's fine then.' His tone was easy but she felt
she'd been unkind. She didn't want to offend him.

'I'm taking my daughter out for a drink tonight.
Why don't you join us later?'

'Yeah,' he said. He seemed pleased but he never
gave much away.

Hannah wondered what Rosie would make of him. At least, she thought, it would prove to Rosie that she did have a life outside the family. She did have friends of her own.

On her way home Hannah called in to her boss at the Central Library and told her she wanted to take a week's holiday. It was short notice but something had come up. Marge, her boss, was so sympathetic that Hannah knew she'd heard about Jonathan and Eve. 'Have as long as you like, pet.'

They lived in a small town. By now it would be common knowledge.

Chapter Seven

Her mother always made her feel so sodding guilty. Rosie replaced the receiver, glad the conversation was over. The house was quiet. Mel was still asleep and Mrs and Mr Gillespie had left hours before to go to work. Mel was Rosie's best mate and had been since coming to the school three years before. She had spiky red hair and green eyes and she played the bass guitar. Rosie was starving but she could hardly pour herself a bowl of cornflakes in someone else's house. Besides, she needed to go home to change or she'd be late for work. Mel, whose parents were seriously rich and seriously generous, hadn't felt the need for employment between A levels and college. Rosie didn't mind working. It was a distraction.

Outside it was hot already, though here on the coast there was usually a breeze. Just as well because she had on what she'd been wearing in the club the night before – a lacy black dress and tarty sandals. The shoes were OK for dancing but they knackered her ankles if she tried to walk any distance. She took them off to go barefoot and as she stepped in and out of the shadow thrown by the trees she felt the changes of temperature on the soles of her feet.

The houses round here were big Edwardian semis

set back from the road. In one of these houses Joe lived. She took care not to turn her head as she sauntered past.

Her home was more ordinary. A tidy semi on a tidy estate. Her parents had bought it from new when she was five. It would have been her mother's choice. They must have realized by then that there'd be no other children. This boring three-bedroomed box would be big enough.

Inside she switched off the alarm and went straight to the kitchen. She put on the kettle, stuck a couple of pieces of bread in the toaster, took orange juice from the fridge and drank it straight from the carton. Inside her head she heard her mother telling her off about that. How pathetic could you get? She was eighteen, an adult, and there was her mother, nagging away at her, a worm inside her head: 'For goodness' sake, Rosalind, can't you get a glass?'

In her bedroom, when she switched on the light the bulb fizzled and died so she had to open the curtains. She saw the place in daylight for the first time in months. There was an unpleasant, musty smell, which she'd tried for too long to ignore. She pushed a window open. In the garden next door a neighbour was pegging baby clothes on to the line. Rosie waved to her. Before the job in the pub she used to babysit quite often. The woman waved back. Rosie saw pity on her face, imagined her gossiping to the rest of the street. 'Poor kid. Her dad's left. And they seemed such a happy family.' When the woman bent to lift more laundry from the basket Rosie stuck up two fingers at her back. She turned over the pile of clothes on her floor like a peasant turning hay with a fork. For the pub she had to wear a uniform – black trousers, white shirt, stupid little green apron and green bow-tie. The tie and the apron were still in the bag from her last shift. There was a white shirt in the pile but the collar and the cuffs were filthy and there were spatters of red wine down the chest. Her father had left clothes when he'd decamped the month before and her mother had been too civilized to throw them out. She'd moved them instead into the spare-room wardrobe. As if he might return one day as a lodger. There, on a hanger, was a single white shirt.

There was no sign of the trousers and the hassle was starting to bug her. Her mother had recently dreamed up a rule about Rosie doing her own washing and since then things had been chaotic on the clothes front. She'll not have stuck to it, Rosie thought. It'll be like all the other threats and ultimatums. She'll not have been able to stand the thought of her daughter going out in mucky pants. And sure enough her trousers were washed and dry with a load of towels in the tumble in the utility room. In the spirit of concili-ation which had led her to phone her mother she folded the towels and loaded the washing machine with part of the muck heap from the bedroom floor. She rolled the trousers into a tight ball and shook them out. She never understood why anyone bothered with ironing.

She looked at her watch. She could have done with a shower but there was no time, so she cleaned off last night's slap, put on more and she was ready. She only realized how dirty her feet were when she pushed them into her flat work shoes. No one would see. The pub was a big, white place close to the sea front. It was called the Promenade, known as the Prom. She'd got the job because she had the nerve to ask. Like all her friends she'd been drinking there since she was sixteen and she'd thought working in the place would be a dream. In fact when it was full of kids in the evenings, being behind the bar was a bit of a drag, not the buzz she'd expected. She had to watch her mates drinking, having a good time and usually she was too busy to exchange more than a couple of words. Sometimes she saw more than she wanted to, heard more too. It was as if the uniform made you invisible.

The first inkling she'd got about her father had been in the pub. Two lads, who she'd known fine well were in Year 11 and shouldn't have been in the place anyway, were playing darts. She'd been emptying ashtrays. It was a Friday night, somebody's birthday. The Prom was packed. They'd had to yell.

'They say he's going to get the sack.'

'You don't get the sack for screwing someone you work with.'

'You do if you screw them on the staff-room floor. My dad's a governor. He should know.'

'You can't blame him though, can you? I mean, have you seen her on the trampoline?'

'But what does she see in him?' The boy put his fingers in his mouth and pretended to throw up.

She'd almost gone up to them to find out who they were talking about, curious, eager to share the gossip. Then they'd seen her and something about the look that had passed between them had warned her, made her pretend not to have heard. Episodes, which had meant nothing to her at the time, slid into sharp focus. Miss Petrie volunteering to do the choreography for the play her father was directing. Miss Petrie on the school trip to Stratford, though what interest could a brainless PE teacher have in Shakespeare? Every time she thought of the two of them together she lost control of her body. Her breath came too fast and she almost fainted.

She didn't mind the pub during the day. There was a different kind of customer then. Grown-ups. Old men sitting for ages reading a paper, office workers wanting lunch, tourists.

When she got there Frank was outside watering the hanging baskets. He looked at his watch and grinned. She always turned up with only a second to spare. Frank was the manager, fat and forty, divorced. He'd been the one to give her the job. She'd chatted him up when he'd had a few drinks and allowed them a lock-in, then she'd turned up next morning for an interview he couldn't remember having arranged. She thought he'd given her a job out of embarrassment. It was only after learning about her dad and Miss Petrie (she couldn't bring herself to call her Eve) that she wondered if he might fancy her. He'd never tried anything on but she always made sure to keep her distance.

It was only twelve o'clock and the pub was nearly empty. Two old ladies with wispy hair and floaty dresses sat by the window in the dust-speckled sunlight, sipping brandy and lemonade. When Rosie went over to collect their empty glasses they continued to sit, engrossed in conversation, making no move to leave or to order more drinks. They were lost in memory. They had come to the coast when they were girls on charabanc trips from town. Back behind the bar, Rosie heard them giggle suddenly over a shared memory. It was a slightly awkward giggle. A boy was involved. Rosie thought, Is that how Mel and I will be when we're old? We'll sit in the Prom getting pissed on brandy and reminiscence, laughing about Joe. If Mel lives long enough to get old, that is.

Then, almost as if the thought had conjured him out of thin air, there Joe was, standing at the door, skinny as one of the pipecleaner men her granda used to make. She had to make an effort to compose herself, to breathe slowly and regularly. Joe saw her and smiled, showing a mouth of gappy teeth. He looked crumpled, as if he'd slept in his clothes – baggy cotton trousers and a T-shirt so tight that she could see the frame of his ribs. What could anyone in their right mind see in him? He had bigger feet than anyone else in the world. Black hair tied back in a loose ponytail. He loped to the bar.

'Mel said you'd be working.'

'You've seen Mel this morning?' She was surprised. She thought Mel would be dead to the world.

'Spoken to her on the phone.'

'Everything OK?'

He frowned without answering. She poured him a pint. Mel was usually the subject of their conversations. She demanded their attention. She had an eating disorder – anorexia, Rosie thought. Rosie didn't know the details, didn't like to ask. She suspected Joe knew more than she did.

Joe fidgeted in his pocket for money. 'Has she said anything to you?'

'What about?'

'She's really stressed out about something.'

'Isn't she always?' Rosie regretted that immediately. It sounded petty. But what was Mel about? She was bright and gorgeous and her parents doted on her. And so did Joe. So why all the shit?

Joe took the pint, stared into it. 'Have you started doing food yet? Any chance of a burger?'

Although he was so thin, there was nothing wrong with Joe's attitude to food. She shouted his order through to the kitchen. Frank came in with the watering can still in his hand, letting it drip on the carpet. He nodded to Joe, winked at Rosie. She knew she was blushing but Joe seemed too preoccupied to notice.

'We're going away,' he said. 'Mel and me.'

'I thought you were skint.' Joe worked all night shifts at the big supermarket on the ring road, but he never had any money. He spent it on drink, junk food, music, stupid presents for them all. His parents were both doctors and could have bailed him out but they said he had to learn to budget before going to university. They took university for granted; Rosie wasn't so sure. Joe hadn't done much work before the exams. He'd been too busy obsessing over Mel.

Joe shrugged. 'Mel says she needs to get away. It's like she's really spooked by something. She won't let go. But she won't talk about it either. Haven't you noticed?'

No, Rosie thought. I've had my own problems lately. If you hadn't realized.

Joe was continuing. 'Her mum and dad say they'll pay. We're only going for a week. They think she could do with a holiday. It would do her good. A friend of theirs has a villa in Portugal.'

'Very nice.' This time Rosie managed to keep her

voice noncommittal. She was thinking, It's not Mel who wants to go away. It's their idea. They've just had enough of her illness. They're fed up with seeing her like that. They want the problem to disappear for a while.

They'd sent Mel away before and Rosie couldn't blame them.

'I'm not sure I can handle it,' Joe was saying. 'It's the responsibility. What if something happens while we're away?' He paused. 'They want her to think about going into hospital but she's dead against it. They want me to persuade her.'

'She doesn't seem too bad to me,' Rosie said. 'No worse than usual.'

A punter came up to the bar. A salesman, she thought. Suit and a briefcase. He was sweating. It was very hot out now. From where she stood she could see the glare on the water as far as the horizon. Families walked past in shorts and skimpy tops and they seemed to turn pink as she watched them. Making the most of the summer. She expected the man to order a meal and a bottle of lager, but instead he barked, 'Scotch. A large one.' His voice was desperate. She watched him take it to a table in the shade, knew he'd be back in five minutes for another.

Joe slid back along the bar so he was facing her again.

'You don't have to go,' she said reasonably. 'Explain how you feel.'

'I can't let her down.'

They teased him sometimes because he'd been a choirboy as a kid. He said he'd been dragged along to church by his parents but she thought some of it had rubbed off. He had too many principles.

'When do you leave?'

'A couple of days.'

'Mel didn't say anything to me.' Rosie convinced herself that was why she was so angry. She felt herself close to tears. They were supposed to be best friends.

'She wanted to keep it a secret. I don't know why.'

Because she likes secrets, Rosie thought. She likes keeping things to herself. She's a hoarder. Perhaps that's what the stuff with food is about.

'What was all that with your mum last night?' he asked with a complete change of tone. He pulled a prim, schoolmistress face. This was the Joe the others knew, the gossip and the clown.

Rosie was cross. Hannah was an easy target. 'She's had a bad time. All the talk. You know what it must be like, finding out that your husband's a rat after twenty years. And she has it rough at work. It's not a bunch of laughs in the prison.'

'No,' he said quickly, seeing that he had offended her. 'It won't be. I didn't mean . . .'

The businessman came back to the bar. He held out his glass to her. She saw that his hand was shaking.

'Your mum's all right,' Joe said. 'We were being stupid.'

Rosie served the customer and let it go.

His burger came. He ate it quickly, holding it in his hand and tearing away at it as if he were ravenous. He stood still when he'd finished and she thought he was going to say something else about Mel. Perhaps he wanted to enlist Rosie's support in finding out what lay behind the paranoia. But he just nodded.

'See you in a week then. If I don't catch up with you before we go.'

And he was gone.

That evening at a different pub, Rosie's local, it was still warm enough to sit outside. She'd eaten the veggie lasagne her mother had cooked for dinner, had a shower and changed into a sleeveless frock. The beer garden was at the back, away from the road, though there was still a far-off hum of traffic. A row of conifers separated the pub from playing fields. There were tubs on the terrace and shrubs under the trees, a faint exotic smell of flowers and pine.

'Melanie and Joseph are going away,' Rosie said, using the full names as if it were a formal announcement. As in 'I, Melanie, take you, Joseph'. That wouldn't surprise her either. Joe was besotted enough to do it and he'd always been into crazy gestures. Melanie's parents would be delighted. Melanie would have a full-time minder and they could go back to the real business of making money.

'Isn't Melanie's name Gillespie?' her mother asked.

Rosie hardly heard. She was imagining Mel's dress, the church, the flowers. Her as chief bridesmaid. 'Yeah,' she said. 'Melanie Gillespie.'

'And her dad's the businessman?'

'That's right.'

When she'd first asked Melanie what her father did she'd said he ran a chip shop. Computer chips, it turned out. He'd set up a huge plant on the site of a derelict factory, was a major local hero because of all the jobs it provided.

'He was on the television again tonight,' Hannah said.

Mel's dad was always on the television.

'They're going to the Algarve,' Rosie said. 'Mel and Joe.'

'Will you be at a bit of a loose end then?'

'I have got other friends!'

For a while she had been watching a small, plump man hovering just out of her mother's line of vision. She thought he had been listening in, waiting for them to finish their conversation. Now he was approaching and Hannah stood up to greet him. Rosie thought, She planned this all along. She knew I'd not come if she warned me.

'This is Arthur,' Hannah said.

Rosie could tell her mother was nervous and decided to be gracious. 'Hi.'

'Arthur works with me at the prison. He's a psychologist.'

Rosie nodded. What could you say?

'Rosie was just telling me that two of her friends are going on holiday.' Hannah shot her the look Rosie remembered from Sunday-afternoon tea at her grandma and granda's house. A pleading look which said, Please behave, please don't show me up.

Rosie said nothing. Arthur smiled. It would be easy, Rosie thought, to be taken in by that smile.

Hannah continued, 'I was just going to tell her about my trip.'

'What trip?'

'There's a school reunion. I thought I should go . . .'

'Great. Can I come?' It was a malicious offer. She didn't want her mother to go off with this little round man with the beguiling smile. She wanted to pay Hannah back for treating her like a six-year-old.

'Do you really want to?'

Hannah looked so pathetically grateful that Rosie couldn't say she didn't mean it. Anyway, what was wrong with running away for a couple of days?

'Why not?'

Arthur smiled again as if this was what he'd been planning all along and he went to the bar for drinks.

Chapter Eight

Although Hannah had avoided Sally since she'd left the town to go to university, she had kept in touch with her friend's news. Sally had gone up in the world since they'd first become mates in Cranford. At school she'd lived with her parents on a small council estate, a couple of streets which ran down the hill to the west of the town. Her father had been a barber. Her mother had worked in the chemist's in the high street. There'd been a younger sister, a pretty child called Joanne. Hannah's dad had worked in the only bank in the town and they'd owned their own home, but the families' lives had been very similar. There'd been an emphasis on good manners and tidiness. Of course, after Hannah's father had died things were never the same again. Then she'd loved spending time with Sal's family. Everything in their little house had seemed safe and respectable.

Sally didn't go to university. She'd had no academic ambition though she'd been bright enough. Instead she'd got a job as office junior on the local paper. She was still there in a more glorified form, writing features and running the women's page. She'd sent Hannah a cutting when she first got the post as features editor. There had been a photograph at the top of the page and she'd put on a lot of weight. Hannah thought she made the job sound grander than it was. The paper had turned into one of those free weeklies which are seventy per cent adverts. She did write back to congratulate Sally about the promotion. She hadn't wanted to appear mean spirited.

When she was nineteen Sally married Chris, a lad they'd knocked about with. A baby arrived soon after. Chris worked for a printer and on summer evenings ran a disco in the caravan site near the lake. There was one more baby then Hannah heard that they'd separated. Much later she saw a piece in a Newcastle paper saying Chris had been sentenced to twelve months' imprisonment for selling drugs. She wondered if he would turn up at the prison, but if he had she'd never met him. Not so far as she knew. Would she have recognized him after all this time?

When Sally wrote to say that she was getting married for a second time to a local businessman, Hannah had imagined a shopkeeper or someone running a small unit on the business park near the river. A barber even, like her dad. But it turned out that Sally's new husband was an hotelier. Hannah might have gone to the wedding – in fact had been building herself up to it – but in the end she was never invited. Sally said it was a very small affair because she and Roger were busy preparing for the holiday season. The hotel was close to the lake and attracted tourists.

On the drive to Cranford Rosie fell asleep before they'd left their estate and didn't wake until they'd nearly arrived. She sat with her head tipped back, snoring slightly through an open mouth. Hannah didn't mind. It was a reminder of what she'd looked like as a small child.

She had only been back to Cranford once, for her mother's funeral, and that was in her third year of university. Because she was so far away – she had been at university in Exeter – the funeral had been organized by Hannah's aunt. Hannah had stayed with her for one night then returned to the West Country, glad of the excuse of exams.

Jonathan couldn't understand her refusal to return to the place of her birth. In the beginning at least, he had been interested in going. 'For Christ's sake, H, it's only fifty miles away. We could be there and back in an afternoon. Show me the scenes of your wild youth.' He'd thought he was being funny. Hannah had made no attempt to explain her reluctance.

They came upon the town almost before she realized, and then she saw with a start that it had hardly changed at all. It felt as she remembered it: stately, quiet, seductive; a place which was hard to leave, very different from Millhaven, the town on the coast which was now her home. That was rakish and full of people passing through – students, hotel workers, yuppies using it as a staging post. And affluent businessmen like Richard Gillespie who lived there to show they had a certain style and personality. Though no doubt he would be moving on too.

The hotel was in a village called Cranwell, very close to the lake. She must have passed through it on her way to the caravan site but she had no recollection. It was pretty enough. There was one main street with stone cottages, a small first school backing on to open fields, a large church. The hotel was down a track next to the church and was called The Old Rectory. It was a big, grey Victorian house with steep gables, an immaculate garden and a view of the graveyard. Hannah had been imagining something seedy, with draughty corridors and stained baths, and was pleasantly surprised. It had an air of class and of money. Rosie had stirred as they pulled on to the drive and now stretched, yawned and scrabbled under the seat for her shoes. Hannah wished she didn't look quite so grubby or dishevelled. She wanted Sally to admire her daughter.

There were other cars in a courtyard at the side of the house. All of them were newer and larger than Hannah's Polo – Jonathan of course had taken the Rover when he left. Rosie got out of the car and Hannah saw that the seam of her skirt had split at the back. She began to feel nervous, as if they had no right to be there. There was complete silence, of the sort that you find in small Spanish towns at siesta time. It was even hotter here than on the coast and Hannah was reminded of the dense, bright heat of a Mediterranean afternoon. Although the house was close to the main village street there was no sound of traffic or conversation. They walked through an arch and round the house to the main entrance. The front lawn was set for croquet. Two mallets lay with balls on the grass. Beyond a green wire-mesh fence was a tennis court, freshly marked. No one was about.

Rosie whistled and said, 'Not bad.' She pulled the hair back from her face, twisted it and fastened it with a comb. She looked immediately tidier. 'I can't see a pool,' she said regretfully. 'Still, in a normal summer, when would you use it? Really, it's not bad at all.'

The front door was open and led to a large wood-panelled hall with a stone fireplace. There was no reception desk, no bell to ring to attract attention. They stood for a moment. It seemed very dark after the glare outside, and wonderfully cool. Three doors led into the hall but all were shut.

'Well,' Rosie demanded. 'Are we going to stand here like lemons?' There were times when Hannah wondered that she had created such an assertive young woman. Rosie raised her voice. 'Hello,' she shouted. 'Anybody home?'

'Ssh . . .' Hannah felt awkward, as if she'd wandered into a private home and sworn at the hosts. She would have stood there all day.

Rosie began to shuffle impatiently. There was a woodblock floor. She'd learned tap dancing as a child and began to tap her heels and toes to some rhythm in her head. It was an irritating habit and came upon her whenever there was space to move. She'd never been able to stand still. In the distance a door opened and shut and they heard footsteps. Rosie continued to hop and shimmy and click her fingers. Hannah motioned at her to stop. The middle door into the hall opened and a man appeared. Beyond him she saw a corridor, a sunny window. She didn't at first take him to be Sally's husband. He was older than she would have expected, at least fifty-five, but it was more than that. He wasn't the sort of man she thought Sally would be married to. He wore an open-necked shirt, brown trousers with a neatly pressed crease and, despite the heat, a cardigan with pockets. His hair was thin and grey, too long at the back. Perhaps after Chris Sally had had enough of wild men. Rosie slid to a halt.

The man blinked in a way which Hannah found oddly familiar, smiled a thin, long smile and held out his hand.

'You must be Sally's friends.' His voice was light, clipped, a little spinsterish, and again she felt she should recognize it. 'Not a good day for a drive, I'm afraid. Poor you. This weather doesn't show any sign of breaking. I suppose we shouldn't complain. By the time you've had a chance to freshen up Sally will be home. She was sorry not to be here when you arrived, but today's a busy one for the paper. She's looking forward to the reunion.'

He picked up Hannah's holdall and directed them towards a curving staircase. Rosie went first and he stared as she walked ahead of him at the long brown legs appearing through the slit in her skirt. Hannah wanted to hit him, but knew Rosie would probably take the attention for granted. Across the graveyard the church clock struck five. The noise seemed to shock him out of a trance and he turned to Hannah, muttering something about the age of the tower. Their room was at the back of the house. It was large and high ceilinged with a full-length window looking over a rose garden and across more lawn. Beyond that, dazzling in the sunlight, was the lake.

Roger seemed to have regained his composure. He gave them an arch little smile as if he were enjoying some private joke and left them alone.

'Hey,' Rosie said. 'This is a bit of all right.'

Hannah dragged her attention from the lake and looked at the room. Solid Victorian furniture was lightened by pale yellow bedspreads and curtains. Rosie dropped the sophisticated pose she put on for her friends and became a child again. She bounced on the bed and danced around the room opening drawers and doors. 'No mini-bar but two sorts of biscuits on the tea tray and very nice smellies for the bath. And Sky.' She began to strip for the shower with a sort of mock striptease, not caring that the curtains were still open. Remembering Roger, Hannah closed them.

They had made themselves tea and were watching the early-evening news when Sally came in. Hannah thought she *had* put on weight, especially on the hips and the bust, but that she'd have known her anywhere. She was stylishly dressed in a thrown together, ramshackle way, in a cream linen skirt which came down to her ankles and a long cream top, crumpled at the back where she'd been sitting. There wasn't any awkwardness. She pulled Hannah towards her so she bounced against the pneumatic bosoms. Then she sat on the bed and started talking.

'God, what a gorgeous daughter. You're so lucky, H. I only had boys and they were monsters. They left home long ago, thank the Lord, and they only appear when they want something. Roger puts up with it, the sweetie. God knows why.' She paused. 'You know, it's so good to see you. I'd given up thinking I'd ever get you here.' She grinned wickedly. 'You didn't recognize Roger, did you? He didn't think you did.'

Hannah was embarrassed. She dredged back in her memory for the circumstances when she'd heard the pedantic voice. She had a fleeting image of school, of sitting with a crowd of others on the edge of the stage in the hall, then it was gone.

She mumbled, 'Something about him was familiar,' knowing how pathetic she sounded.

'Probably best forgotten,' Sally said. 'That's what I thought until I met him again. I came to do a feature on him when he bought this place. You won't believe it but he swept me off my feet. Perhaps this will jog your memory.' She stood up, put her hands behind her back and in a surprisingly accurate imitation of her husband's voice said, 'If that homework's not handed in tomorrow, Miss Marshall, I'll be down on you like a ton of bricks.'

It was the final phrase that released the memory. It was the threat for every occasion. Hannah started to giggle, quickly put her hand over her mouth to cover it.

'You married Spooky Spence?' It was impossible to keep the astonishment from her voice. She wanted to ask Sally how on earth she came to do anything so ridiculous.

'Exactly,' Sally said, enjoying Hannah's surprise. 'Spooky Spence.'

He had taught them Latin for O level. At the time Hannah had thought of him as middle-aged, verging on the elderly, but he could hardly have been more than thirty. Now that she had fixed him in her memory she thought his appearance had hardly changed over the years. She remembered those lessons as restful occasions. A quiet sunny classroom. Mr Spence's voice a drone in the background as they plodded through Virgil and Caesar's *Civil Wars*. And he had been involved in the school play. That was what the flash of memory had been about.

'But you couldn't stand him,' Hannah said.

Sally had never liked drama and had hated the Latin lessons. She'd never got to grips with the grammar. Spence had been quietly but menacingly sarcastic.

She grinned. 'He couldn't stand me either. He hated teaching. I mean, he didn't mind fiddling round with the theatre club but standing in front of a class all day was a nightmare. Food's always been his real passion. You wouldn't recognize him in the kitchen. When his mum died she left him a house and a bit of money. It gave him enough to set up this place. It's been an exciting project for us both.'

Rosie had been watching the conversation with interest. Perhaps she was wondering what it would be like to get involved with a teacher much older than her. A bit close to home.

'Why did you call him spooky?' It wasn't a tactful contribution, but again Sally didn't take offence.

'It was his way of appearing beside you without warning. Apparently out of thin air. When you least needed it. Like when you'd just lit a fag behind the changing rooms. Or you were planning to mitch off early before his lesson.' She grinned again at Rosie. 'Not that your mother ever did anything like that. Hannah Meek was the biggest swat in the school.'

Hannah didn't say that she remembered things rather differently. They'd called Roger spooky because of the way he looked at them. At the hems of their skirts which were still very short at the time, at the shirts bursting at the buttons over newly formed chests. There were stories that he'd been caught staring through the gym window at third-form gymnasts, at the girls in their knickers and airtex vests doing straddle jumps on the box and cartwheels on the beam.

*

Sally didn't go with them to the school for the reunion. She said she'd meet them there. She had to nip back to town. It was work. The editor was away and there was a press conference she needed to cover. Again Hannah felt she was making her work sound grander than it was.

Still, she was pleased to go in on her own, with only Rosie to keep her company. Sally would have rushed round introducing her to everyone, and she wanted a moment of anonymity. She wanted to stand just inside the door and look for Michael. She had dreamt that he would be there. If she was honest with herself, that was what the trip had been all about from the start. Michael was what had kept her away from the town for all those years and now it was Michael who had brought her back. When Roger dropped them off at the school – it seemed that he was too busy to attend the party – the futility of the venture hit her. She was embarrassed that she had allowed her fantasy to develop this far.

Michael Grey had come to the school when Hannah was in the lower sixth. He was a year older than the rest of them but for some reason had been placed in their year. She remembered having been given a number of reasons for that – he had been living abroad, had been ill, there had been a family problem. Still she didn't know which, if any, of them had been true. Certainly he hadn't been asked to retake the year because he was thick. He was quick and conscientious and the teachers loved him. He was doing art, English and biology, but art was his thing. He noticed the way things and people looked. She remembered the big, battered portfolio he used to cart around, the way he always had a smear of paint on his face.

So she collected her name badge, stood just inside the door and looked around. He wasn't in the room. She saw that immediately. Even after nearly thirty years she would have recognized him. She didn't think that was self-delusion. She would have stood there longer, but Rosie gave her a shove in the back.

'Go on then,' she said. 'Do the business.'

It turned out to be easier than Hannah had expected. Sally still hadn't arrived but Hannah was greeted by people who knew her, who were pleasant enough to say that she'd hardly changed. The name badges were in sufficiently large print to allow the possibility that this was a kind fiction, that they remembered the face only after reading her name, but soon she felt less nervous.

This hall was newly built when she was at school. Previously the dining hall had been used for everything. For the first time the students had somewhere for assembly and drama that didn't smell of school dinners. She recalled her first speech day there. Some sixth-form boys always ran a book on the length of the headmaster's lecture. Parents were invited and when Hannah won a prize for English her mother had turned up. Her husband had just died and people were still talking about it so it was a brave thing for her to do, but she was the only woman to be wearing a hat and Hannah wished that she'd stayed away.

The new hall was where school plays were performed. In Hannah's final year, Michael was Macbeth. He looked like a Viking warrior with his long white hair and papier-mâché armour. Jenny Graves was Lady

Macbeth. People said she was very good, but Hannah had been prompting and too busy following every line to notice individual performances. What she did remember was the knife, because she'd helped with props too. She didn't know where Mr Westcott had found it, but it was seriously sharp. One of the first years was messing around and cut herself. Hannah thought that nowadays, when everyone was so conscious of health and safety, it wouldn't be allowed.

Once she'd persuaded herself that of course it would have been impossible for Michael to be there, Hannah even started to enjoy herself. At first the music was far too loud for sensible conversation but someone persuaded the disc jockey to turn it down. She could catch up on news of people who had once been close friends. No one mentioned her father. She supposed, even in a town as small as this, that had been forgotten long ago.

She was talking to Paul Lord when Sally arrived. Hannah saw her from the corner of her eye, but continued the conversation. In school Paul had been something of a figure of fun – a spotty scientist, too conventional for his age, more conventional even than her. He had become rather handsome. Certainly he was married. He mentioned a wife and child. It seemed he had his own business and was doing rather well.

'What happened to that blond lad you used to knock around with?' he said suddenly. 'Did he go away to art school in the end, or did he settle for university?'

Hannah said calmly that she had no idea. Then Sally interrupted them quite rudely, taking Hannah's arm and dragging her away. Something had excited her. She could hardly contain herself. But she kept her face serious.

'There's something you have to know.'

'What is it?'

She turned everything into a drama. Hannah was expecting a piece of local gossip. Someone had run away with someone else's wife. She should know not to mention it in front of the people involved.

'The body in the lake,' Sally said.

Hannah must have looked at her stupidly. It wasn't at all what she was expecting.

'You had heard that they'd found a body in the lake?'

Hannah remembered a snatch of a radio report. 'Yes. It came to light because the water level's so low.'

'That was what the press conference was about. The police have got a positive ID at last. Dental records or something. It's too horrible to think about.' She shivered theatrically. 'It's Michael Grey. He'd been down there for nearly thirty years.'

She was whispering. Perhaps she wanted to add to the theatre of the occasion. Perhaps she didn't want to spoil the party. Hannah felt the room spin around her.

'Pull yourself together,' Sally said sharply. 'You'll have to speak to the police. We all will, but you're most likely to have something useful to say.' She looked at Hannah, waiting for a sensible response before adding impatiently, 'Michael Grey was murdered.'

Hannah remained silent. She could hardly say that the news had come as something of a relief.

Chapter Nine

So far, Rosie thought, she'd been very good, very much the mummy's girl, putting on a clean frock, tying back her hair in a French plait, saying what a brilliant time she'd been having.

The school was pretty much what she'd expected, comprehensive now, but still to Rosie's eyes, rather grand. Her high school on the coast was a seventies glass and concrete slum. The window frames had warped and the roof leaked. This was a stone building, approached by a drive through trees. There was a couple of new blocks, a scattering of mobile classrooms, but still it was hard to imagine kids dealing dope in the toilets or sniffing glue behind the bike sheds. More Mallory Towers than Grange Hill. Rosie wasn't sure about being there. 'Look,' she had said. 'I'd just be in the way.' Hannah had given her a look so geeky that Rosie could have strangled her but not deserted her.

They had been early of course. Her mother was always early. It drove Rosie crazy. There had been people in the hall, but they were still setting out food and glasses. Rosie had taken her mother's arm. She was shaking.

'Why don't you give me a guided tour of the place before we go in?'

They had walked together round the outside of the building, peering in through windows. Hannah had pointed out the domestic-science block, the room where Roger had taught Latin, the sixth-form common-room. Rosie had listened. She had felt supportive and grown up. She had even wondered if she should bring up the subject of Eve and Jonathan – they had never really discussed it – but she hadn't wanted to spoil things and had left Hannah to her memories.

When they returned the party had begun. The hall doubled as a theatre and it was blacked out by heavy curtains and lit by coloured spots. Outside the sun was still shining. On the stage sat a DJ playing seventies music. The lines on his face were so deep that they seemed chiselled. It was hard to tell whether his head was bald or shaved. But he still seemed younger than the people standing awkwardly in the hall, juggling paper plates and plastic glasses. He put on a David Bowie. 'Life on Mars'. It had always been one of Rosie's favourites and she was itching to dance. If Joe had been there she'd have dragged him on to the floor to get things moving.

There'd been a bit of a queue at the door, where a fat woman stood behind a table doling out laminated name badges. She was short sighted and had to squint like a mole over the table to find the one she was looking for. Hannah had found her own. Hannah Meek. How bloody appropriate, Rosie had thought. The fat woman had stared at them, as if the name or her mother's face should trigger a memory, but the effort had seemed too much for her because she just shook her head, smiled vaguely and let them walk on into the hall.

At first everything was as tedious and civilized as Rosie had expected it to be. She was introduced to old friends of her mother's. She smiled a lot, was polite and dutiful. When she laughed she felt as if she were making too much noise. The people she met seemed frozen in middle age. It was impossible to imagine them being yelled at by a teacher in this hall, or sitting at small tables to take exams. They talked about their children, the iniquities of student fees and student loans, their homes and their foreign holidays. All the time the rhythm of the music nipped at her ankles and made her want to sway away from them back into the middle of the floor.

This is *your* music, she wanted to say. Doesn't it take you back to how you were?

And sometimes she saw a woman or a man with dreamy eyes, who would look at her with a start, as if they were staring at themselves or a girl they fancied. But it didn't last, and when someone did start the dancing it was a peculiar shuffle as if they all had arthritic knees or a broom handle strapped to their spines.

Then she looked up at the stage and saw the DJ, who must have been at least as old as her mother and the others in the room, but who didn't seem it. He seemed to be laughing at them too. She moved through the dancers and hoisted herself on to the stage so her legs dangled over the edge. He didn't look at her.

'A bit young for this, aren't you?'

'I came with my mum.'

'Who was she, then?' Now he did turn to eye her up. 'I might know her.'

'Did you come to this school too?' For some reason

it seemed unlikely. He looked too different from the smartly dressed men and women. She thought he must be a refugee from the city.

'No, not bright enough. I was at the secondary modern. But I used to hang around with some of them.'

'Hannah Meek,' she said. 'That was what my mother was called then.'

'Yes,' he said. 'I can see.'

'Can you?' She had seen the occasional photo of her mother as a young woman and saw no resemblance. Her mother was so reined in. Her features were small and sharp.

'She was skinnier of course.'

She felt her face colour. Most people were skinnier than her. Hannah said she was over sensitive. 'Carry on like that and you'll end up like Melanie Gillespie.' As if she wouldn't have adored to be the same weight as Mel.

'But you're bonnier,' the DJ said after some consideration. Rosie could have kissed him.

'Can you recognize her?' she said, falling into the joky, flirty voice she used with the older punters at the Prom. She didn't have to shout. Someone had moaned about the music being too loud and he'd turned it down. He scanned the room but so briefly that she thought he wasn't really bothered.

'Can't see much at all in this light,' he said.

There was a bit of a scuffle at the door as Sally came in. She pushed her way through the blackout curtain and was silhouetted briefly against the light outside. The woman behind the table knew her and tried to offer her a badge but Sally ignored her. The DJ was watching the scene too, with the same detached amusement as when he'd been looking at the dancing.

'That's Sally Spence,' Rosie said, wanting his attention again. 'She's my mum's best mate. We're staying at her hotel tonight.'

'Oh, I know Sal very well. When you see her say Chris sends his love.'

The track he was playing came to an end. He murmured a few words into the microphone. No one seemed to be listening. Hannah was deep in conversation with a tall man, dressed in black. He had more style than the rest of them and Rosie might have fancied him if he'd been twenty years younger. Suddenly Sally broke in on the couple. She said a few words to Hannah then steered her away from him. From her position on the stage Rosie watched. Caught in a livid green spotlight, with Roxy Music in the background, she saw her mother's face crumple. The normally sharp features fell in on themselves. Sally led her out of the room and Rosie followed. At the door she stopped and looked up at the stage. Chris, the DJ, gave her a little wave and a knowing grin.

Outside it was still light, and at The Old Rectory four guests sat on the flagged terrace having drinks before a late dinner. Sally had driven them back from the reunion immediately. Rosie thought it was a fuss about nothing. Sally playing the drama queen. An old body dragged out of the lake. What could that have to do with her mother?

Roger insisted that they shouldn't decide anything until after dinner and Sally had deferred to him.

Hannah seemed to think she had no right to express an opinion. Rosie thought Roger had been transformed. That afternoon he'd been a crabby and grey old Latin teacher. Now, talking to his guests, dressed in a brocade waistcoat and floppy bow-tie, he was in his element. When they arrived he was taking a tray of drinks to a couple in the lounge and he sat beside them for a moment to chat. He flattered the woman without annoying her husband, camping it up a little to make himself harmless. Rosie, who was no mean actor herself, appreciated the show. She knew the effort which went into a performance.

Over dinner Sally and her mother talked in a series of elliptical comments which made little sense to her. At one point Sally said to Roger, 'But you must remember Michael Grey, even if you didn't teach him. Everyone knew Michael.'

Roger stared into his wine. 'Of course I remember him,' he said in a sad, solemn voice. Then he made an excuse to go into the kitchen and when he returned he was his old self, solicitous and funny.

At the end of the meal they were the only people left in the dining-room. The main lights were switched off. Their table was lit by a wall lamp with an engraved glass shade, which could have covered a gas lamp. The room had been designed to look like a Victorian parlour, with glossy-leafed pot plants, red plush, heavy furniture and silver. For Rosie it took on a nightmare quality. She prided herself on being able to hold her drink, but Roger had filled her glass every time it was empty and by the end of the meal her head was swimming. She listened to snatches of the women's conversation, and the image of the white corpse from the lake caught her attention immediately and stayed with her.

It was partly to shake off this feeling of melodrama, partly because she was so drunk that when the thought came into her head she couldn't stop it coming out, that she interrupted their conversation.

'Oh, by the way, Chris sends his love.'

'Chris?' Her mother seemed puzzled.

'The DJ.'

Hannah looked at Sally. 'That was Chris?'

'Didn't you recognize him?' Sally seemed pleased. 'He hasn't worn very well, has he?' Then she seemed to think Rosie deserved an explanation. 'Chris,' she said, 'is my unmissed ex-husband.'

Soon after, Rosie left them to it. Roger winked and wrapped a half-drunk bottle of wine in a napkin for her to take with her. Hannah would have objected if she'd noticed but she was too preoccupied to see what was going on.

In her room Rosie drew the curtains. The window was open and she heard young voices, smelled the grilling flesh of a barbecue. By the edge of the lake someone was having a party. She switched on the television and flicked through the channels, but nothing held her interest for long.

She poured wine into a beaker from the bathroom and wished she were outside. Leaving the set on, but with the sound turned right down, she dialled the Prom on her mobile. Frank answered.

'Hi,' she said. 'It's me.'

He recognized her voice. She wondered idly if he'd

know all his part-time staff by voice. 'Good God, girl,' he said. 'Can't you keep away from the place? I thought it was your night off.'

'Sad, isn't it?' She thought it really was sad.

'You're pissed,' he said. It was a statement of fact.

'Shit, Frank, you sound like my mum. Is anyone in?'

'Can't you hear them?' He must have held the receiver over the bar. The roar was deafening.

'Not *anyone*. Anyone I know.'

'Nah. They were in earlier. The whole crowd.'

'Except Mel and Joe.' She thought they'd be in Portugal by now, sitting by the pool under the orange trees.

'I've got some news about them.' He was like an old woman about gossip. He paused, tormenting her, knowing she'd be gagging for the information.

'What?'

'They're still here.'

'Why?'

'Mel refused to go, didn't she.'

'What do you mean?'

'She refused to go on holiday. They called in here on their way to the airport. Bags all packed. It was supposed to be just to say goodbye. Then all of a sudden she threw a wobbly. She said her parents wanted to get rid of her. The holiday was a trick to get her out of the country. They never intended to let her back.'

She kept her voice flat. 'Was Joe OK?'

'He didn't say much, but what was there to say? His girlfriend had practically accused him of kidnap. That girl needs help.'

She switched off her phone and dialled Joe's house. The answerphone clicked in straight away. She left a message for Joe saying she'd call him the next day. She thought then that she should phone Mel and check that she was all right but knew that should wait until she was sober. She'd only lose her temper. She seemed to lie awake for hours but she didn't hear her mother come in.

Chapter Ten

Sally was very eager that Hannah should go to the police station as soon as they returned from the school reunion.

'It'll be all over the papers tomorrow. They've got a picture. Someone will tell that detective you were Michael Grey's girlfriend. Better he hear it from you. Of course, I'll come with you if you like.'

Of course, Hannah thought. That was what Sally wanted. She was a journalist, even if not a very grand one. She saw a story she could sell.

'Let the poor woman eat,' Roger said.

Hannah was grateful. Perhaps it was the shock but she was ravenous.

In the end two detectives came out to the hotel. It was Sally's suggestion. She said the national press was already sniffing around in the town. On second thoughts this would be more discreet. And, thought Hannah, it would give Sally more control. Hannah didn't mind. She felt very tired. She didn't think she could face going out.

It was after ten when the detectives arrived, just dark, still very warm. Rosie didn't seem to have grasped the significance of the body in the lake. She went, a little unsteadily, to their room. The staff were clearing up in the dining-room and there were still guests in the lounge, so Sally let them use her private sitting-room. Roger brought in a tray of coffee. There was a bowl of roses on the table. Later Hannah would remember their fragrance, the scent of filter coffee and another smell which she realized was pipe tobacco. Although the older detective made no attempt to smoke on that occasion, it seemed that he was an addict and his pipe was always in his pocket. It must have been hard for him to sit there for so long without it.

She couldn't decide at first which was the senior officer. The older man was shorter, slight and dark, with an accent which suggested he came from the coast, from one of those villages where the pits used to be. He had the look of a collier about him. He wore a grey suit. The trousers were too big for him and held up by a thin belt. His shoes were as black and shiny as a prison officer's boots. The younger man was tall, prematurely balding. If she'd met him on a social occasion, Hannah would have guessed that he taught humanities at a college for further education. He could even have been a librarian. He wore odd socks and scuffed suede boots. The older one was called Stout, the younger Porteous. They must have given their ranks when they introduced themselves but Hannah had been in too much of a daze to take in the information.

They were very polite, but something about their manner put Hannah on her guard. She drank a cup of Roger's good, strong coffee and tried to clear her head. She had heard the prisoners talking and knew that the police weren't always to be trusted. What they wanted now was to clear up their case as quickly as possible.

There wouldn't be two detectives here, at this time of night, if they didn't think there was something in her story for them. For the first time she wondered what Sally had told them. There had been a muttered conversation at the door before she'd shown them in. She had been surprised when Sally had left them alone together without any fuss. But perhaps she was standing at the door now with a glass to her ear. Or perhaps there was a tape recorder hidden under one of the cushions on the sofa.

'I don't know what Sally has told you . . .' she said. She wanted to take the initiative, to appear purposeful, to let them know she couldn't be browbeaten.

Porteous, the younger, answered. He seemed diffident, almost apologetic. The voice was educated, but somewhere behind the polish there was a Midland whine.

'She said that you and Mr Grey were close at the time of his death.'

Stout interrupted briskly. 'We think it's possible, Mrs Morton, that you were the last person to see him alive. That, at least, is the information we've been given.'

Hannah stared at them. Trust Sally to stir things up. Trust her to turn this into the plot line of a soap opera. Hannah thought her judgement had been right all along. She should never have been persuaded to come back.

'I know it's a long time,' Porteous said. 'But if you could just take your mind back . . .'

'How did he die?' Hannah demanded. 'You must have done a post-mortem if you know he was murdered. You pulled him out days ago.'

They seemed shocked and the words sounded callous even in her own head, but Hannah needed to get the facts straight, neatly catalogued like books on a shelf. Stout looked at Porteous who nodded imperceptibly. She realized then that Porteous must be the superior and was glad to have another fact sorted.

'He was stabbed,' Stout said, 'with a sharp, wide-bladed knife.'

Hannah had an image of Jenny Graves at a school play rehearsal. It must have been a dress rehearsal because she was in costume. Her dress had been hired from the local amateur-dramatic society and was scarlet, laced at the front, daringly low cut. She had fake blood all over her hand. Mr Westcott had been so pleased with her performance that he had clapped. Hannah realized that the detectives were staring at her, waiting for her to speak.

'Have you told Michael's family?' she asked, not putting off answering but fishing again for information. She was still curious about Michael's family.

Again Stout and Porteous looked at each other. Again, it seemed Stout was given permission to answer.

'Ah,' he said. 'Well, we seem to have come up with a bit of a problem there. We're having some difficulty tracing them. He seems to have been a real mystery your young man, a real mystery. That was one of the reasons why we were so keen to talk to you.'

They looked at Hannah expectantly. At last she felt obliged to tell them at least something of what she knew.

'When we were at school together Michael Grey lived with foster parents. His mother had died and his father had worked abroad a lot. Or was ill. I'm not sure.' It had seemed to Hannah even in the beginning that Michael had made himself up as he went along. He changed his story to suit his audience. She had caught him out a few times and at first it had seemed to disconcert him. Later, when he realized how she felt about him, he had only grinned.

'What did the father do?' Stout asked. 'Work, I mean. The boy must have said.'

'I got the impression that he was employed by the Government. Some high-powered diplomat or civil servant. Something that took him away a lot.'

'He must have come back sometimes to see his son.'

'No. Never. Not that I remember. I never met him.'

'Didn't that strike you as odd?'

Hannah didn't answer. Michael's strangeness had been part of his attraction.

'What about the foster parents?' Porteous asked. His voice was gentle. Hannah thought he had set out to win her round. 'You must be able to tell us about them.'

She knew he would have got that much at least from the school records, but decided to play the game.

'Their names were Brice. Stephen and Sylvia. An elderly couple, more like grandparents than parents. They'd never had children of their own. Stephen was a retired vicar. They were devoted to each other, kind to everyone, into good causes. They lived in one of those terraced houses near the school.' She looked up at him sharply. 'You must know all this.'

'Part of it. I haven't been able to speak to anyone who knew them.'

'I didn't really know them,' she said quickly. 'I only met them once or twice.'

They had come to the performance of *Macbeth*. From her position as prompt, Hannah had seen them sitting proudly in the front row. At the end they had stood up and cheered, more like elderly eccentrics on the last night of the Proms than the audience of a school play. She could imagine them dressed up and waving a Union Jack. They had seemed to her then very old and even now, looking back from middle-age, she thought they must have been in their late sixties or seventies. They both had silver hair. Sylvia wore hers long, pinned back with a tortoiseshell comb. Their house was the quietest Hannah had ever been in. There was no television or radio. She remembered a ginger cat which purred and a clock which chimed the quarter-hour. She presumed this was not the sort of information which would be of interest to Porteous or Stout.

'They never reported him missing,' Stout said in a slightly aggrieved way, as if he took the Brices' failure to make a fuss personally. 'Nobody started looking for him until they died. Then the solicitor tried but couldn't trace him.'

Hannah wondered what had happened to the small, tidy house. It seemed unfeeling to ask. She had gone there first for tea. Michael had asked her. Although the Brices hadn't been expecting her they were thrilled to see her. 'We're always telling Michael he should invite his friends in.'

His attitude to them was delightful. He was thoughtful and playful. He called them Sylvie and Steve. But as they sat in front of the fire in the tiny drawing-room, eating seed cake and crumpets, the thread of the conversation had led Hannah to think that they knew little more about his past than she did. It seemed that Stephen had been invited to a theological college in Idaho to give a lecture on the Psalms. They had been discussing flight plans, when Sylvia asked suddenly, 'Have you ever been abroad, Michael? I can't remember your saying.'

It was as if they had depended on what he told them for their knowledge of him. Hannah struggled to explain that to the detectives. 'I don't think they were relatives. They probably didn't think there was anything sinister in his disappearance. They'd be sorry he hadn't kept in touch, but they wouldn't see it as their affair to meddle.'

'What was he doing with them then?' Stout demanded. 'You wouldn't just invite a strange teenager into your house.'

'I think they were the sort of people who might.' She paused. 'They called him their gift from God.'

She'd always thought it was a strange thing to say. Michael had spoken of it in a slightly shamefaced way. 'Look, Steve, that's a big thing to live up to, you know?' But the detectives remained impassive and unsurprised. She continued talking, trying to give an explanation they would accept as reasonable. 'He arrived with them out of the blue, then disappeared in the same way. Perhaps that's why they never reported him missing. They felt they had no claim on him.'

'The Lord giveth and the Lord taketh away,' Stout said. 'That's all very well, but they must have met up with him somewhere. He wouldn't just have knocked on the door.'

'Perhaps it was arranged through a charity,' Porteous suggested. He looked at Hannah hopefully. 'Was anything like that mentioned, Mrs Morton? Can you remember the name of any organization which might have put Michael in touch with the Brices?'

She shook her head. 'He wouldn't have told me,' she said. 'He liked being a mystery.'

'All the same he must have said something. When you asked about his family, his previous school, he must have given some scrap of information.'

Despite her resistance, memories were already clicking into her brain, jerky images like an old home movie.

'He told me a lot of things,' she said. 'Not all of them were true.'

'But . . ?' Porteous prompted.

'But I really think his mother died when he was little. He was quite specific about that. She died of leukaemia and he could remember the funeral. Nobody had explained to him properly what was going on. He couldn't understand where his mother was. When a black car turned up at the house, he thought it was to take him to see her.' Hannah stopped, then continued hesitantly, 'It was early spring. There were crocuses on the lawn. I don't know if that's any help.' She thought: Unless that was one of his fictions too.

Porteous said, 'At present everything is helpful.'

'There is something else.' She paused. She didn't want to make a fool of herself and she had a sense too that she was betraying Michael. But it was a matter of self-preservation. She had to give the detectives something to get them off her back. 'He resat the lower sixth. He was a year older than the rest of us.' Again she saw she was telling the men something they already knew and wondered what other secrets they were keeping to themselves. 'He made up a tale about his having been ill, but it was quite similar to his story of his mother's illness. I was taken in by it at the time. Why wouldn't I be? But now I work as a prison librarian and it's occurred to me that there might be another explanation for his missing year. I wondered if he might have been in trouble. Youth custody. Borstal, I suppose it would have been then. That would be something he wouldn't want to admit to the Brices or to me. That wouldn't fit into the Michael Grey myth.'

She realized she sounded bitter and to hide her confusion poured herself another cup of coffee, though by now it was cold. Porteous jotted a few lines in his notebook but gave no other indication of what he thought of the theory.

'Was he the sort of lad who might have been away?' Stout asked.

'What do you mean?'

'You work in the nick, Mrs Morton. There aren't many well-read, nicely spoken blokes in there.'

'More than you'd realize.' She thought of Marty, whose consideration had led to her being there.

'But you know what I mean,' Stout persisted. 'Most of the men will have been brought up with some degree of physical and emotional deprivation.'

It seemed an odd thing for a policeman to say. She took his point more seriously.

'Michael was a brilliant actor. And he was quick and bright. He could be whatever anyone wanted him to be. Do I think he was brought up in the west end of Newcastle or on a council estate in Wallsend? Probably not, but I wouldn't be astonished if that turned out to be the case.'

'Where *was* he brought up then?'

'West Yorkshire. At least that's where he said he went to school.' Hannah waited for another question: And before that? But it never came. Besides, she had told them the truth. On Michael's first day a girl from the upper sixth had asked which school he'd come from and he'd answered, without pausing a moment, giving her a smile: 'A place in West Yorkshire. You won't have heard of it.'

When Hannah told Porteous that, he wrote it down and said seriously to Stout, 'It seems a strange thing to make up, that, off the cuff. Check out approved schools, borstals and detention centres for that period in Yorkshire. Or perhaps that's where his family lived. We might find his mother's records.'

I don't think you will, Hannah thought, and wondered why she didn't speak the words out loud. Porteous turned to her with his diffident smile, which wasn't very different from one of the expressions in Michael's repertoire. 'Is there anything else you remember from that first meeting, Mrs Morton?'

She didn't answer. She thought she'd given him enough.

'You don't know how much this is helping us. We're very fortunate to have found a reliable witness at this early stage. What about his voice? Could you believe that he came from Yorkshire?'

'It depended to whom he was talking.'

'Sorry?'

'It was a habit. I explained he was an actor but I don't think this was self-conscious. He didn't realize he was changing his voice to suit the occasion. But he was. When he was speaking to us he spoke as we did. With the Brices it was old-fashioned English. We had a biology teacher from Edinburgh. She thought he came from there too because when he spoke to her he had something of the accent. It wasn't imitation or that he was trying to impress. He was a sort of verbal chameleon.'

Hannah sipped cold coffee. She thought she had nothing left to tell them. Surely now they would let her go. But Porteous shifted uncomfortably in his very comfortable chair.

'Tell us about you relationship with Mr Grey,' he said gently. He was more like a counsellor than a police officer. 'In some detail if you wouldn't mind, Mrs Morton. If you could cast your mind back.'

'We were friends,' Hannah said.

'More than friends surely.'

'Not at first.'

The men waited for her to say more.

'What are these questions about?' She'd had enough. 'You know who he is. Sally told me you found the dental records. There must be more efficient ways of finding what you want than listening to my ramblings.'

Porteous gave another little apologetic smile. 'Unfortunately not. Apart from your ramblings we've very little. We know that the body in the lake was that of a young man known as Michael Grey. One day he had toothache and Mrs Brice took him to her dentist. We're lucky that the practice kept records, but it hasn't provided us with a conclusive identification. It hasn't helped us to trace the victim's family. Because no birth certificate was issued to Michael Grey on the date he gave as his date of birth. There are no medical records or child-benefit records for him. There is no record of his having existed before he started school with you.'

They looked at her. It had been a long time since anyone had given her their full attention. She found it flattering. No doubt it was a technique they often used. She was taken in by it. She dragged her memory back almost thirty years.

Chapter Eleven

Her father died the summer Michael arrived. He committed suicide. He rigged up a hose-pipe from the exhaust of their Austin and the fumes killed him. Hannah didn't find him. He had timed it so her mother would do that when she went into the garage to fetch potatoes to peel for their supper. Mr Meek had an allotment. He kept the potatoes in the garage in wooden trays in the dark to stop them sprouting.

Looking back, Hannah thought her father and mother had never got on. He was nervy, quick to snap. Any noise or disruption to his routine threw him. She thought perhaps she'd inherited her own intolerance of change from him. He was a chain smoker. Every evening he came home from work, threw down his briefcase and would sit for an hour, sucking on cigarette after cigarette, going through the imagined slights of the day. He felt he was much undervalued at the bank. No one appreciated the work he put in. The only time he was anything like content was in the allotment. Perhaps the physical activity helped him to relax. Perhaps in the mindless routine of digging and weeding he could forget his troubles.

Hannah's mother didn't like the idea of the allotment. She pretended it didn't exist. She had been pretty as a girl and could have had her pick of the lads in the town, the ones who came back after the war. She had chosen Edward Meek over the plumbers and bricklayers because he worked in the bank. He wouldn't have to get his hands dirty. It put her on a par with other professional wives. Perhaps she imagined dinner parties and coffee mornings, but in fact she was awkward in company and if the invitations had ever come they soon dried up. When Hannah was a child Audrey Meek seemed to have no friends at all. She confided in her daughter, shared her loneliness and her disappointment with her. She had spent her life being disappointed.

At first Hannah thought that this disappointment had been reason enough for her father's suicide. She supposed he felt responsible for her mother's unhappiness; he had never been able to live up to her expectations. Then Hannah learned it was much worse than that. By the time of his death he'd progressed to the post of assistant manager, and he'd been stealing. Perhaps he hoped to buy his wife's approval with little luxuries for the house, but Hannah thought it was more that he felt the bank owed him what he took. It was his way of fighting back. Of course, he wasn't very good at covering his tracks and he knew he would be caught. He couldn't face it. But Hannah and her mother *had* to face it. They had to face the questions from the bank and the police, the prying neighbours, the dreadful sympathy. And Hannah had to come to terms with the fact that her father hadn't loved her enough to stay alive. He had put her through this embarrassment to save himself the ordeal of it.

Then it was September and time to go back to

school. Hannah was dreading it. Her father's face had been plastered all over the local paper. Even if the teachers were too sensitive to mention the suicide she'd be aware of their curiosity, and some of the kids, at least, would be merciless. Hannah wasn't popular. She was known as a swat. Rock music was important then. Status was conferred by knowledge of obscure groups and Hannah couldn't join in those discussions. There wasn't even a record player in her house and anyway she wasn't really interested. Over the holidays she'd avoided most of the people from school. She'd seen Sally a couple of times, but only in her home. She'd kept away from the pub and the parties.

On the first day of term Michael Grey turned up. There weren't many new kids at the school and he was immediately the centre of attention. For Hannah his appearance was a relief. It took the heat off her. While the rest of them were gathered around him at registration she slid into the room, dumped her stuff in her locker and slipped away to her first class. There was such a crowd around him that she didn't even see his face. At the mid-morning break she wanted to hide again, but Sally dragged her to the common-room.

'Look,' Sally said. 'You'll have to face them sometime. Better now when they've got the beautiful Michael to distract them.'

He always was Michael. Never Mike or Mick.

The sixth-form common-room was a mobile class-room. It was square, flat roofed, freezing in the winter, but that September was hot, an Indian summer. Sixth formers didn't have to wear uniform and they'd all chosen their clothes on that first day with care. It was a season of peasant fashion. The boys wore wide trousers and cheesecloth shirts. The girls, even Hannah, were in smocks and long flowery skirts. Michael stood with his back to the window so the light was behind him. That could have been deliberate. He had what Mr Westcott called a theatrical eye. He wore a pair of denim jeans which looked new, a black T-shirt, and desert boots with black leather laces. His hair was blond, almost white. He had a suntan. Foreign travel was unusual those days and it was hard to get a tan in her northern town, so that made him stand out too. There was something about him that made the others listen. It wasn't just the novelty.

Sally nudged Hannah in the ribs. 'What do you think?'

'I think he's cocky,' Hannah said. 'He's good looking but he knows it.'

He can't have heard what she said. There was music playing and everyone talked at once. But he looked over the heads of the others towards her as if he knew what she was thinking. He gave a self-deprecating little shrug. I know, he seemed to be saying. This is all bullshit. But it's a game and I've got to go along with it.

Later Hannah saw her first meeting with Michael as a turning point. After that she was seen differently within the school. She could face them all without embarrassment. It was possible that her memory played tricks – that there were unpleasant comments about her father, days when she wanted to stay at home. It was possible that her re-creation of her friendship with Michael was as great a fiction as the story he told about himself. But his arrival did make a difference. Some incidents remained clear and vivid. These, she was convinced, were true.

There was the day he first invited her to the Brices, for example. Hannah remembered that as soon as she started talking to the detectives. Michael was placed in the same English group as her, and on the day of his arrival he chose the seat next to her, at one of the old-fashioned desks with the lift-up lids that you never see now. Despite her disdain, her sense that he was too cocky by half, there was a rush of excitement when she turned and saw him there. Through habit they kept the same seats all term. They were reading *Middlemarch*. The rest of the group hated it. They found it tedious and Hannah suspected that most of them didn't make it to the end. She loved it and so did Michael. There'd been this guy in the old place who'd been passionate about it, he said. Who'd done it as part of his Ph.D. and passed on his enthusiasm. Hannah presumed then that the 'guy' was a teacher, the 'old place' a school. Later she was to presume nothing. Michael said he had some notes at home. Perhaps she'd like to borrow them to help with an essay they'd been set? If she wasn't in a hurry she could go back with him, have a cup of tea. The old folks would be thrilled to bits.

Recreating the scene in her head, Hannah thought it had been the beginning of December. She could remember the cold. He must have been in the town for three months but still she had no idea that his family was different from anyone else's. They hadn't talked about it. She hadn't told him about the drama with her father, though it was possible that the others had been whispering behind her back. At that age families weren't as important as friends.

'Old folks?' she said. It seemed an odd way to talk about parents.

'Sylvie and Steve. You'll see.'

'You call your mum and dad by their first names?'

'No. They're not my parents. My mother's dead. My father . . .' He seemed thrown for a moment. 'Well, I don't get to see much of him.'

They walked slowly up the school drive to the house. It was almost dark by the time they arrived at the house, one of a small row, flat faced. As the light went the temperature plummeted. They stood for a moment on the pavement, looking in. There was a street lamp and they could see their breath as a white mist. The lights were on inside but the curtains had not been drawn. There was a fire in the grate and an elderly man sat on a leather armchair, with a cat on his knee, reading.

'That's Steve,' Michael said with enormous affection. He took out a Yale key and let himself in.

Inside there was a smell of fruit and spice. A small kitchen led straight from the hall and she'd seen Sylvie, red faced, turning a cake on to a wire tray. She looked slightly flustered. Her hair had come loose from her comb. Michael put his arm around her.

'This is Hannah,' he said. 'She's a George Eliot fan too. I've brought her home for tea. You don't mind?'

'Of course we don't mind.' She smiled at Hannah. 'We haven't met any of his friends before. I think he's ashamed of us.'

'How could I be?' he said.

Hannah didn't know what to make of the relationship between Michael and the Brices. Usually she was jealous of other people's home lives. Her own was so bleak. Her mother struggled on to keep the house as she wanted it. They hadn't been forced to sell, though at one time that had been a possibility. There was even less money than there had been before and Audrey hated the forced economies. She pretended not to mind the gossip and in fact seldom went out to hear it. Television had become her consolation. Hannah was grateful because it provided a safe topic of conversation. Without it they would have had little to say to each other. Later she thought that her mother had been depressed and had been brave to keep things as normal as she did. Then she longed to be a part of a different sort of family. That's why she spent so much time with Sally. Her dream family would have been quite like Sally's, but the parents would have been younger, interested perhaps in different things. There would be a brother as well as a sister and they would have shared meals together discussing ideas about books and plays. There would have been noise and laughter. At the time she didn't consider Michael's situation as ideal. It was too different from her dream. Everything was so quiet. There was discussion but it was calm and measured.

There was one room which served as living- and dining-room. They sat at a round mahogany table and drank tea from translucent china cups, ate crumpets which Michael squatted by the fire to toast, and the cake Sylvie had baked. They talked about Stephen's lecture on the Psalms. At one point Michael reached out and touched Sylvie's hand.

'Why don't you go too?' he said. 'You know you'd enjoy it and I'll be perfectly fine here on my own.'

'I'm sure you would be.' Her voice was serene. 'But Stephen and I have had a lifetime together and I'll have your company for such a short while. I'd prefer to stay and make the most of it.'

Then she asked him the question about his having been abroad.

Hannah had always been an observer. Even in her youth she could usually work out what was going on between people. But the situation in the Brices' home confused her. She couldn't make out at all where Michael fitted in.

After tea the Brices refused the offer of help with the washing-up and Michael took Hannah to his bedroom to find her his notes. She was tidier than most of her friends but his room was almost Spartan in its lack of clutter. She wondered if he had planned to invite her back and had cleared it specially, but she went there on subsequent occasions and it was always the same. It reminded her of a cell.

'Are they your grandparents?' she asked.

'No, we're no relation. They're just friends.'

'Friends of your father's?'

'Yes,' he said, seeming grateful for an explanation that worked. 'That's right.'

It was a small room but there was a big desk under the window, of the kind that you'd have found in offices everywhere. It had three drawers on each side of the knee-hole. It wasn't well made. The varnish was scratched and the top was chipped. Michael seemed flustered when he couldn't find the notes where he'd expected them to be, with others in the top drawer.

'Sorry, I thought I'd brought everything with me. But obviously not.'

'Couldn't they be somewhere else?' Hannah yanked open a bottom drawer which was wider than the others. When it came to school work she was competitive. She wanted the notes, a chance to shine in the essay. She hadn't come along just for the chance to know Michael better. She had expected to find more files in the drawer, neatly labelled, but it was empty apart from a shoebox, the sort she had collected when she was young for use in *Blue Peter* projects. He must have had the box for a long time. It was too small to hold shoes of the size he wore then.

Michael slammed the drawer shut with a ferocity which almost trapped her hand.

'There's nothing in there. I told you, I must have left them behind.'

'Sorry.' She looked at him, expecting an explanation. He said nothing.

The incident seemed to have thrown him. Hannah thought he was angry about the invasion of his privacy and apologized more profusely. It was something she could understand. He hardly seemed to hear what she was saying and when she said that her mother would be expecting her he seemed relieved to see her go. When Hannah saw him at school the next day he greeted her as if nothing had happened.

For several weeks she was haunted by the mystery of the small, blue shoebox. She imagined it contained answers to her questions about Michael.

Just before Christmas she was invited back to the Brices for mince pies and mulled wine. She made an excuse to go upstairs, slipped into Michael's room and opened the drawer. She hated herself for doing it. Her hands were sweating as she tried to turn the knob. She had kept the door open so she would hear if anyone was coming. But it was an anticlimax. The drawer was empty. When she returned to the others Michael looked at her as he had on his first morning in the common-room, as if he knew exactly what she'd been up to.

Chapter Twelve

Throughout the interview both Porteous and Stout went on about Michael having been Hannah's special friend, as if they had been lovers from the start. But they were never lovers, not in the sense the detectives meant, and they didn't even start going out with each other until after the lower-sixth exams. She tried to explain that to them. The detectives listened but she wasn't sure they understood.

The town itself had nothing to attract young people. The cinema had shut and the pubs were gloomy and unfriendly. In the summer at least, they were drawn to the lake. A couple of years before, the valley had been flooded to provide water for northern industrial towns and the biggest man-made lake in Europe was created. It was news at the time. Although it was surrounded by forestry plantations and was miles from everywhere, the novelty of the development and the scale and spectacle of it attracted tourists. An enterprising farmer opened a caravan site, then built a bar and a club, so it was more like a small holiday camp. It hardly provided a sophisticated night life but it was livelier than anything else the town had to offer and it drew the kids like a magnet.

The Saturday after the end-of-year exams they

gathered on the shore in the afternoon and collected dead wood to build a bonfire. Hannah had expected Michael to be there but he didn't turn up. You could never guarantee his presence on these occasions, and he never offered explanations. They ate chocolate and crisps as a makeshift picnic and later moved on to the caravan park, to the bar where Sally's boyfriend was DJ. It was only supposed to serve residents but no one asked questions when they all piled in. It was June, early in the season. No doubt the owners were glad of their money. The bar was a horrible place, furnished like a transport café with Formica tables and plastic chairs. Along one wall a row of one-armed bandits clacked and flashed. Hannah and her friends didn't mind. There were no awkward questions about under-age drinking, and they took it over and made it theirs. When they arrived there were two residents, an overweight Brummie and his wife, leaning against the bar. Soon they shrank away and the Cranford Grammar brigade had it all to themselves.

Hannah still found events like that evening daunting, but she began to enjoy herself. She thought she'd done well in the exams, better than she'd expected. And she'd arranged to spend the night with Sally, so for once she didn't have to worry about her mother. Since Edward's death, Audrey had become increasingly anxious, in an obsessive, unhealthy way. It seemed that anxiety was the only way she could express her concern or her love. When Hannah went out Audrey always waited up. She would be pacing up and down the dining-room, her face knotted with tension, although Hannah was always back before the agreed time. Later she was to understand something of what her mother had gone through – she could never sleep until Rosie was in – but then it had seemed an unnecessary intrusion.

The evening of the party it was a relief to know there would be no prying questions to answer and she felt she could let herself go. She started drinking her usual halves of cider but later Sally's boyfriend, Chris, bought all the girls vodka. He was always throwing his money about, trying to impress. They made him play the music very loud and they started to dance. At closing time, as she stumbled and giggled with the others down the sandy path to the shore, Hannah thought this must be what it was like to be drunk. She had led a very sheltered life.

The bonfire was already lit. They could see the flames from the path, reflected in the water beyond. Sparks from the burning wood shattered in the sky like fireworks. Michael had lit it and he was there, alone, tending it, throwing on more wood as soon as the flames subsided. While the others ran down the bank to join him, pretending to be angry because he'd started the fire without them, Hannah stood and watched him. He was absorbed in his watch over the flames and seemed not to notice the approaching crowd. Even when the others crowded round him, yelling and cheering, he didn't look away.

Of course, she fancied him like crazy. In the beginning she *had* thought him cocky, still did if it came to that, but that was part of the fascination. And perhaps he'd seen her resistance as a challenge, because he'd made an effort to win her over. No one else had bothered to do that. She wasn't seen as much of a catch – skinny with no figure to speak of, black oily hair and the hint even then of dark down on her upper lip. He said she looked Mediterranean. Perhaps he had heard about her father and felt sorry for her, though if his friendship was prompted by pity he hid it well. She could usually pick up a reaction like that. It turned her spiky and moody. Perhaps their unusual homes in this conventional town of happy families gave them something in common. She thought he was happy in her company and for a while that was enough.

After Hannah's first visit to his home the relationship continued to revolve around the books they were reading, the essays they had to prepare. When school finished for the day they went to the library together. Not to the school library where the few recommended books of criticism were fought over but to the dark building in the town centre, a Victorian heap, with enormous polished tables and rows of reference books smelling of damp. Hannah never wanted to go home immediately to face her mother. The Brices placed no restrictions on Michael's movements. That always surprised Hannah. She would have expected such elderly people to share her mother's anxieties. He would have stayed with her all evening if she'd wanted. As a friend, of course. Not a lover. But she had her pride and sent him home at five o'clock in time for the tea Sylvie would have prepared. She knew that the pretty girls with the short skirts who lusted after him never felt jealous of the time they spent together. They didn't consider Hannah as any sort of competition.

By the night of the bonfire he'd been at the school for nearly a year, but he'd never had a proper girl-friend. Some of them saw it as a challenge. He tantalized them with the possibility, snogging them at parties, but nothing came of it. He was indiscriminate in his physical contact in a way which was unusual at the time. He liked to put his arm round people, boys and girls. He often hugged Sylvie, making her blush with pleasure. He had never touched Hannah though, not even a hand on the shoulder, not even brushing against her by mistake. She longed for it.

She didn't make straight for Michael when she reached the shore. The booze had made her up for the games other people played. Let him come to her if he wanted to. That night there was a huge orange moon which lit the scene, so she would be able to see Michael even if he moved away from the fire.

She latched on to a tall lad from the upper sixth, who was a figure of fun, because his picture was once in the paper when he got a Queen's Scout award. Someone had torn it out and stuck it on the noticeboard at school. He had stood in the photo in the ridiculous uniform, blushing in a way which made his acne stand out. Since then he'd got rid of the acne, but the reputation of being what they now called a geek had stuck with him. He did science and maths, and was considered brilliant at both, which didn't help. He came along to parties like this, but always ended up on his own.

'Isn't this brilliant, Paul? I mean this enormous sky. The landscape seems so huge, doesn't it, tonight. It seems foreign. Like we're in a country with wider spaces.'

She leaned against him, knowing as she did it that it wasn't fair. It was the sort of trick that had been played on her. Tentatively he slid his arm around her shoulder. She felt his breath on her neck. On the other side of the fire Michael was watching. She saw him get up. He walked over the pebbles towards the caravan site and the road into town. Hannah waited for a second, then pulled away from Paul Lord and ran after him. She caught up with him by the jetty where the water-sport freaks launched their dinghies and canoes. She took him by the elbow and swung him round to face her, exhilarated by the first touch and her daring. She felt muscle and bone under the denim shirt.

'Where are you going?'

'Home.' He paused. 'To Steve and Sylvie's.' As if the two were not the same thing.

'Where *is* home, Michael, really?' She hadn't had the nerve to ask him about his personal life before. After the incident in his bedroom, she'd been scared of frightening him off. 'What is going on here?'

He shrugged and walked off like a sulky child, not bothering to turn on the charm. She realized he resented the attention she'd given to the other boy, even though it was Paul Lord, who was a figure of fun, almost a charity case. He wanted her to himself. She was flattered but felt a sense of injustice. It was all right for him to flirt and kiss and touch, but she had to be there for him whenever he wanted the company. On other occasions she would have been apologetic, grateful that he needed her. Tonight, because of the vodka, she had more confidence.

'Suit yourself,' she shouted and started back towards the party.

'No.' He called after her and she heard something like panic in his voice. She hesitated, determined not to give in too easily, then continued walking. The tactics paid off because he scrambled over the pebbles towards her. He put his arms around her and clung on to her as if she were the most important person in the world. Triumphant, she stroked his white hair and told him everything would be alright.

'Shall we go for a walk?' He took her agreement for granted. He knew she wouldn't let him go again. He took her hand and led her along the edge of the lake. Sheep-cropped grass fell away into sand so it was almost like being on a beach at the seaside. But there were no waves. The water was glassily still. If the others saw them she presumed they'd think she was just another of his party conquests.

'Poor Hannah,' they'd say. 'She's been hanging round him for months and now he's taking pity on her.'

At that point the road skirted the edge of the lake. There was the flash of headlights. For a moment she thought it might be the police, that there'd been a complaint about the fire, or even something more serious. She wondered sometimes what Sally was getting into. There'd already been rumours about Chris and drugs. But it was a blue 1100. It stopped and the driver got out, leaving the engine running. He was a small middle-aged man, rather nondescript. Hannah thought it must be a parent, come to collect errant offspring. He peered over towards the fire trying to make out individuals, trying, it seemed, to pluck up the courage to go over. He couldn't see Michael and Hannah. They were in the shadow. But they could see him quite clearly, caught in the headlights. She turned to Michael to make a comment about the man, to ask him to guess which of their friends he belonged too, but saw at once he already recognized him.

'Who is it?' she whispered.

'I'm not sure.'

'But you do know him?'

'Perhaps.'

The man gave up his search, got into the car and backed it erratically up the lane.

Michael put his arm around Hannah and they walked on.

'Why don't you ever talk to me?' she said.

'I do.'

'Not about the important stuff.' Or the not so important. Like a bloke in a Morris 1100 looking for his kids. 'Is it just that you like the mystery?'

'No. You don't understand.'

'Whatever it is I won't be shocked. You must have heard about my dad. So you know about my shady past.'

'That was him. Not you.'

'What do you think I'll do? Shop you? Dump you?'

He didn't answer at once. 'I'm frightened,' he said. 'Not just for me. For you.' She thought that was the old Michael again. The attention seeker. The boy who made up stories in his head and almost believed them himself. She didn't care.

He pulled her beside him on the grass. She thought he was kissing her to stop the awkward questions. By the fire someone had started playing the guitar. There was a smell of pine and wood smoke. She lay on her back and looked at the orange moon.

All that came back when she was talking to the detectives, but of course they weren't interested in the detail, only in the clues which might lead to information about their victim's past. The party by the lake had taken place a year before Michael's disappearance. What happened then could have no relevance to his death.

Chapter Thirteen

So they became a couple. Michael Grey and Hannah Meek. She always liked the way their names scanned. Now, listening to Porteous and Stout talking about the mystery of their victim's birth, she thought it would be a shame if that turned out not to be his name, if the rhythm were lost. Though now of course she was Hannah Morton and she had more important things to worry about, like convincing these policemen that she knew nothing at all about Michael's murder and that she had no reason for wanting him dead.

If their friends thought about it, they must have assumed that Michael and Hannah were lovers. Porteous and Stout, of course, had made the same assumption. After all, they went out with each other for nearly a year. Their intimacy was for everyone to see. They walked round the school hand in hand, despite a rule banning physical contact. It only got them into trouble once. They were walking across the yard towards the common-room for morning break. Michael had his arm around Hannah's waist and they were laughing at a joke, some piece of nonsense. There was a shout and they turned to see Mr Spence bearing down on them. Spooky Spence. Now husband of Sally.

'Mr Grey, Miss Meek. A little decorum, if you please.'

They looked puzzled. Like the ban on smoking in the common-room, the rule was never enforced. Spence must have taken their bewilderment, their failure to comply immediately with his instruction, as impertinence, a personal insult. Suddenly he lost his temper. He stood in the middle of the playground, gathering a small crowd of giggling onlookers, and he ranted about the younger generation in general and Hannah and Michael in particular, about their lack of morals, their failure to comport themselves with decency and modesty. As he yelled flecks of spit came out of his mouth. It took them a moment to realize what had provoked his anger. At last they got the message and pulled apart. Spence regained a shaky control and walked away. They didn't mention the incident to their friends. They were embarrassed by it. It wasn't the way adults were supposed to behave.

They never went to bed together. Spence and the gang they hung around with would have found it hard to accept, but they never even discussed it. Hannah thought that was because Michael was living with the Brices and felt he should conform to their standards. An exaggerated idea of good manners. She wouldn't have known how to raise the subject. Later she wished she had, that she'd lost her virginity to him and not to a plump mathematician after a drunken freshers' ball in her first week at university. Sally was certainly sleeping with her disc jockey. At weekends she told her parents she was staying at Hannah's house, but she'd spend the evening with Chris and the bed in the Meeks' spare room was never used. Her parents never checked up on her. Perhaps they didn't want to know what she was up to. Hannah was worried about her, concerned she'd get caught up in his shady deals. It wasn't only the drugs. There was an air of aggression about him.

'Are you sure you know what you're doing?' she asked once.

Sally had told her not to be stupid. She wanted Chris and he wanted her. That was all that mattered. Sally also wanted the things Chris could provide. He had two jobs, more cash than the rest of them could dream of. She liked the presents, the fact that she never had to buy her own drinks. On the evenings when Sally was supposed to be at the Meeks, she would go with him to work, to the disco at whichever village hall or hotel had hired him, or more often to the caravan site which was his regular gig and seemed to have become her second home. Then she would go with him to the scruffy flat he was renting over the betting shop in a back street behind the police station. She once took Hannah there when Chris was away for the weekend. He'd given her a key to feed his cat – an angry black tom. Inside the flat was surprisingly ordinary. There was the same utility dining suite as Hannah's mum had in their house, and a floral carpet. One of the bedrooms was locked and Sally didn't have a key to that. She said it was where Chris kept his sound system, but Hannah wondered what else was inside. Sally agonized about going on the pill as if it were a decision Hannah must be making too. 'Doesn't it make you put on weight? Chris would hate me fat. It's all right for you. You could do with a few extra pounds.'

Hannah was noncommittal and Sally was too wrapped up in her own affairs to notice. Michael and Hannah didn't spend all their time together. They were ambitious. It was the A-level year and they wanted to do well. Hannah for herself; Michael, she thought, for the Brices. Hannah went through the process of applying to university, filling out UCCA forms, going for interviews. Michael, however, refused to make any plans. None, at least, that he would talk about. It was as if he wanted to shroud his future as well as his past in mystery. He said he'd take a year out, travel perhaps. Hannah wondered if he had more specific ideas. He worked for his exams with a purpose which suggested he had a project in mind. He spoke once of a crusade. He had a responsibility, he said. There was something he had to put right. When she asked what exactly this mission was, in a teasing voice, because she refused to let him take himself too seriously, he clammed up. She didn't push it. Talking to the detectives she thought it was incredible that she should have taken any of his stories at face value. Why didn't she ask where his father was, why they never saw each other? Because she was perfectly content. She knew she would never be so happy again. She was determined to do nothing to spoil it.

The school play was planned for the end of the Easter term. When Michael went for the auditions, just after Christmas, she thought he was mad.

'You *are* joking. Our last full term before the exams. You'll never manage it all.'

'Sod the A levels,' he said, much as Rosie would do, then gave her a grin to show he didn't mean it. Perhaps managing it all was the challenge. Perhaps it was part of his game plan.

Hannah went with him to the audition, not to try for a part, but to offer her support. She thought he might be given a small role. When she saw that Spooky Spence was one of the auditioning panel, she thought he'd be lucky to get that. It never occurred to her that he would go for Macbeth. She perched on a window-sill at the back of the hall and waited for his turn. The teachers sat in judgement on a row of chairs at the front: Spooky Spence, Miss Davies who taught English and drama, and Mr Westcott, still slightly tipsy from his lunchtime in the pub. The actors stood on a block to read, but when it was Michael's turn he didn't stand. He sat with his legs crossed, quite relaxed, and when he spoke, despite the language, it was as if he were speaking just to her. She knew at once that he would be chosen to play the lead.

Hannah saw Jenny Graves audition that day too. She was in the lower sixth, a year younger than them, tall and willowy, rather nervy. Hannah thought it was typecasting. The panel had gone for the look. She wasn't sure she would have chosen Jenny over some of the others. She realized that Michael and Jenny would have lots of rehearsals together. It didn't bother her at the time, but nearer to the performance she thought she could afford to get involved and she volunteered to help with props and to prompt. She never admitted to herself that she wanted to keep an eye on him.

One Saturday, at about the time of the *Macbeth* auditions, Michael and Hannah took a trip to the coast. Occasionally they wanted to get away from home and homework and explore the surrounding district. Hannah liked to have Michael to herself. On this day they went to Millhaven, the seaside town where Hannah would end up living. Where Rosie would be born. Where her husband would fall in love with a PE teacher called Eve. They caught a bus into Newcastle, then another to the coast. It was the longest trip they had made and she wasn't sure how they came to decide on it. On the bus Michael said he liked seaside towns in winter.

When they arrived, however, she could tell that he had been there before. It was a freezing day. Flurries of snow blew in from the sea, gathered like piles of confetti against the lampposts and wrought-iron benches. They walked shoulder to shoulder, hands deep in coat pockets, heads bowed against the wind. But not in an aimless way. Michael knew where he was going, where he wanted to be. He found his way immediately to the sea front, knew which way to turn for the funfair, closed and deserted for the winter. He stood there for a moment, looking in over the pad-locked gate at the entrance to the ghost train and the helter skelter, at the still and tarnished horses under their gaudy awning. Hannah guessed he had been taken there as a child, though it didn't seem to hold any happy memories for him.

'A penny for them,' she said lightly.

'Sorry?' He turned to her, still preoccupied.

'What are you thinking about?' She had to yell above the wind and felt a bit ridiculous. They weren't ideal conditions for a deep and meaningful discussion.

'My mother,' he said. 'Actually.'

She sensed that he was ready to talk, took his arm and pulled him into a pub.

Talking to the detectives, she was aware on a number of occasions of coincidences, links between her life as an eighteen-year-old and her life as a mother. Often she caught herself thinking, What would Rosie have done if that had happened to her? Certainly she would have been more assertive. She wouldn't have waited for almost a year, content with a kiss and a fairly chaste grope. She would have wanted to know what was going on. The pub was the most obvious coincidence. When Rosie first started work in the Promenade, Hannah thought the name was familiar. She called in occasionally to collect her daughter from a late shift but the place stirred no memories. By the time Rosie worked there the Prom had become one big room with long windows painted white. One evening, when she wasn't quite ready for her lift home, Hannah looked at the old photographs on the walls. They hadn't been bought as a job lot by the brewery; they showed the place as it had been before it had been taken over. With a start she realized it was the pub where she and Michael had sat on that winter's day. Then, the Promenade had two small bars separated by a gloomy corridor. The walls were half panelled in wood covered in a sticky yellow varnish, wrinkled like custard skin. They had sat all lunchtime in the corner of the snug, with their half-pints in front of them, and nobody disturbed them.

That was the time he told her about his mother's funeral, the story Hannah passed on to the detectives, without giving them the context, without telling them where she sat to hear it. He talked in short phrases, not trying to call attention to himself this time, but trying to get it right. He described the big car whose purpose he could only guess at. The stern people in black clothes. The crocuses on the lawn.

But the funeral hadn't taken place in Yorkshire. Hannah was sure of that. It had taken place in the windswept town on the coast. Why hadn't she passed on *that* particular gem of information to Porteous and Stout? She had her reasons. Because they had irritated her with their insinuating questions. Because Michael wouldn't have wanted them to know.

In the pub it was cold, so cold that she found it hard at first to concentrate on what Michael was saying. At one point she put her hand on the radiator and pulled it away because it was freezing, almost literally, so she felt her skin might stick to the pipe. They sat, huddled in jackets with the hoods still pulled up, Michael talking in spluttering fits.

'I don't remember much of the time she was ill. A visit to the hospital with my father. He was holding flowers – orange lilies, I think – and when we got to the bed he pushed them into my hand. The smell. In hospital and at home. Disinfectant, I suppose. Her face. I think I remember her face, but I've struggled too much to hold that in my mind and I'm not sure how accurate it is. You lose something, don't you, if you try too hard?'

'You must have photographs,' Hannah said. Even after just a couple of years her memory of her father seemed to come from family snaps. There was one of him, taken at Christmas, with a paper hat on his head and a forced smile on his face, which she'd have been glad to forget.

But Michael shook his head. 'I don't know where they all went.'

'Doesn't your father have them?' He shook his head again. He was so upset that she didn't feel she could push it. Later she knew that to be a mistake.

'Did she take you to the fair?'

'I think she must have done. It's one of the pictures I have in my head. We went down the helter skelter together. I sat between her legs. She wore tan nylons. I remember the mat we sat on. I was wearing shorts and it was prickly like coconut fibre. The sun was shining.' He paused. 'I chose the wrong day, didn't I, to re-create the atmosphere?'

'We can come back in the summer.'

'She was buried here,' he said suddenly. 'In the cemetery by the lighthouse.'

'Shall we go to look for the grave?'

He shivered. 'No,' he said. 'I've had enough now. Let's go home.'

He placed an emphasis on the last word as if he'd come to a decision. Home was the Brices' house. It wasn't this place.

Chapter Fourteen

Rosie stood behind the bar of the Prom with her back to the punters and took a moment to catch her breath. It had been a crazy evening. Friday nights were always busy, but this had been wild. On Friday night the locals came out and trippers and people from the city. They dressed up and paraded along the sea front from one pub to another, ending up after closing in the clubs. On Friday nights every pub along the sea front had a bouncer outside. The clubs were heaving. Scantily dressed waiters and waitresses pranced between the tables with trays held high above the customers. The Prom wasn't really part of this circuit, but some people who did the Friday-night gig as a bit of a joke started off there, because the beer was cheaper, and to show that they weren't really taking it seriously.

Early on, a visiting rugby team had arrived and taken up residence in front of the widescreen television.

'Isn't rugby a winter thing?' Rosie had asked vaguely.

They had explained it was a special tournament but she had already lost interest. She had never seen so many similar-looking men before. They were like clones, she thought. They wore matching sweatshirts with a sponsor's logo on the back. All had square jaws and squat, square bodies. All drank the same brand of lager. As the evening wore on they grew more raucous. They bought two pints each to save queuing at the bar. They whistled and shouted at the female images on the television, but when Rosie went to clear the tables they seemed not to see her.

Tonight was even busier than usual because they were one person down. Lindsay, their most experienced barmaid, had called in sick. Frank was grumbling. Rosie, preparing to dive back into the fray to collect glasses, heard him muttering to himself. She grinned. It'll be his age, she thought. Poor old thing. He can't stand the pace.

Just before closing time the crowd suddenly thinned. The rugby team stumbled away to look for a curry or a late-night bar. The holiday makers returned to their B&Bs. In the distance she heard the wail of a police siren. Then Joe came in. Mel wasn't with him.

Rosie hadn't seen him since she'd come back from The Old Rectory with her mother. He hadn't returned her calls and she'd almost given him up. She'd tried to talk to Mel but hadn't got through to her either. Mrs Gillespie always answered the phone – even during the day, which was a sign that something was wrong. Mrs Gillespie was usually as much of a workaholic as her husband, certainly worked the same sort of hours. At first when Rosie phoned, Mel's mum had been evasive – Mel wasn't available and she wasn't sure when she'd be back. Later she'd come clean.

'Look, I'm sorry, Rosie. She's really not very well.'

'I could come round.'

'Not just at present. Maybe when she's a bit better.'

So when Joe turned up at the Prom on his own that night, Rosie wasn't surprised. She pulled him a pint.

'On me,' she said, because she knew he'd have no money, even if he hadn't been on holiday.

He sat on one of the high stools by the bar.

'How's Mel?' she asked, though if she was honest by now she really didn't care. He cared though, which is why she asked.

He shrugged. 'Her mother says she doesn't want to see me.' He looked over the glass. 'I don't know what to make of that woman. When Mel first introduced us I thought she was OK. Smart. Funny. Mel always made out she was some kind of monster but I didn't get it. Now I don't know . . . I've spent the last few days at home waiting for Mel to phone. I'm not even sure if her mother passed on the messages. I had to get out. I need some air. Or space. Whatever . . .'

'Why wouldn't she go to Portugal with you?'

'I don't know. She was excited at first. We were all set to go. It must have been something I did.' He went on in a rush. 'I do everything wrong. I always say the wrong thing. Perhaps it would be better if we finished. What do you think?'

Yes, she cried silently. But he didn't want an answer. Not that one at least.

'She's so delicate.' He spoke slowly, struggling for the words, looking to Rosie to help him. 'So fragile. And I'm clumsy. Perhaps she'd be better off without me.'

Then, for the first time in such stark terms, Rosie saw what she was up against. She understood the competition. She was a size fourteen. Healthy. As strong as an ox. She laughed too loudly and could drink Joe under the table. He didn't want that. He was a romantic. Mel was frail and needed looking after. Consumption would have been better, but now that was no longer feasible, anorexia came a close second.

'Well?' he demanded.

She shook her head. What was the point of speaking?

He drank the beer without thanking her. To be fair that wasn't like him and she couldn't use it as an excuse to be mean. She felt like howling but she couldn't freeze him out. No point throwing a wobbly like Mel. Really she'd always known the score.

'My mum's a suspect in a murder inquiry.'

She thought that would grab his attention. It might not have the romantic appeal of anorexia but she thought it deserved some sympathy, some interest. It should take his mind for a moment off Mel's skinny body, her huge and haunting eyes. And he did look up, suitably curious.

She told him about the corpse in the lake. 'He was the love of Hannah's life.' Keeping her voice cynical, though she had been moved by the tale of first love, at least the bits of it which Hannah had told during the drive home.

Frank was getting rid of the last of the drinkers. As she talked to Joe she was washing glasses, holding them over the machine, then standing them on the draining board to dry.

A taxi stopped outside for three of the other barmaids. Frank asked, 'Do you want to go in that?'

'I'll walk home with you,' Joe said, so she shook her head.

She undid her tie and her apron, rolled them into a ball and stuffed them in her bag. Frank waited at the door for the women who were catching the taxi. The driver was getting impatient and hit the horn. They scurried out swearing and laughing. He watched for a moment until the car drove off then he shut the door and switched off the main lights. Even with the door shut they could hear the noise outside. The street was full of people moving from one club to another.

'Fancy a nightcap, you two?' Frank had never suggested anything like that before. Rosie was glad Joe was there. She thought her boss must be lonely. Word in the pub was that his ex-wife was getting funny about access and he was missing the kids. Rosie didn't particularly want a drink. It wasn't that her mum would kick up if she were late. She was always late on a Friday. Sometimes it took over an hour to clear up. Sometimes she went on to a club with her mates. But she was knackered. And she wasn't too proud to want a bit of time with Joe to herself. Joe seemed to take the invitation as an honour though and brightened up.

'Yeah. Great.'

Frank didn't ask what they wanted. He stood by the optic and poured three whiskies. He'd taken off his jacket and as he stood with his hand above his head they could see the flab spill out over his trousers. When he turned round with their drinks he was sweating slightly. He set one of the whiskies in front of Joe.

'Did that bloke ever catch up with your lass?'

'Which bloke?'

'There was a bloke in here a couple of nights back asking after your Melanie.'

Frank kept his voice casual but Rosie could tell he

was desperate to know what had been going on. That was probably why he'd invited them to stay. She thought it was really sad, this need he had to know all their business.

'What sort of bloke?'

'Middle-aged, respectable. A mate of her dad's maybe. I didn't like to say where she lived. He didn't seem that bothered so I expect he had some other way of catching up with her.'

'Perhaps she's into older men.' Rosie had meant it as a joke, but when she saw Joe's face she wished she'd kept quiet.

'Didn't he leave his name?' Joe said.

'No,' Frank had drunk his whisky and was getting another. 'I asked but he seemed in a rush. He didn't even stop for a drink.'

Out on the street Joe took her arm as he often did and steered her through the crowd on the pavement. A middle-aged woman in a see-through leopard-print shirt was throwing up in the gutter. A teenage girl was sobbing on her friend's shoulder. Joe held Rosie's hand and pulled her at a run across the road and on to the sea front. She had learned to take no notice of these gestures of affection but she still enjoyed them.

'Where are we going?'

'The scenic route.' He paused. 'You don't mind going the long way?'

'No.'

There was enough light from the street to see the white line of foam fall on to the beach. They walked in silence. She was thinking of her mother, of the body in the lake. If Joe disappeared into thin air, Rosie thought she'd make some effort to find him. She'd hassle his family, contact the rest of his friends. If they couldn't help she'd go to the police. Yet from what she could gather her mother had done none of these things. Michael Grey had disappeared and she had accepted it without a fuss. That was a very Hannah-like way to behave, but even so it just didn't make sense. She hadn't even been to see the couple Michael had been living with. She hadn't gone to the police. She'd sat her exams as if nothing had happened and then she'd left the area without trying to trace him to say goodbye. And she'd never gone back.

Rosie stopped. Without the noise of their footsteps they could hear the tide dragging back the shingle.

'That stuff I told you about my mother being a suspect in a murder inquiry. It was a joke, right?'

'Of course it was a joke.' He sounded amused. That was all she was to him. One big joke.

'It's just she's had enough to put up with. Everyone talking about my dad . . .'

'I know.' He squeezed her hand.

Of course her mother hadn't killed anyone. She was the least violent person in the world. When Jonathan walked out on her, she hadn't even raised her voice in anger. But it was odd all the same. Her mother couldn't have told the full story. Something had happened.

They had come to the lighthouse, which had been converted years before into an art gallery. It still had a whitewashed wall around it. There was no need for the light now. The rocks in the bay were marked by navigation buoys on the water. Looking back towards the town, they saw the flashing neon which marked the entrance to the funfair, the strings of street lamps, the inevitable blinking blue light of a police car.

From the lighthouse a footpath led inland, skirting the cemetery and arriving at last at the housing estate where Rosie lived. The free drink and the walk seemed to have cheered Joe up. He didn't mention Mel again, or the stranger who had been looking for her. As they sauntered past the cemetery he started making howling, ghostly noises. There were houses banking on to the footpath and Rosie had to tell him to shut up.

Outside her house Joe lingered. If she'd invited him in for coffee, he'd have accepted like a shot. She could tell he was too wired up to go home. But Rosie couldn't bear any more confidences. Not tonight. She might end up confiding in him. A small wind had got up. Down the street a Coke can rattled against the kerb and startled them. The trees threw strange shadows.

'You'd better go,' she said. Then she imagined him turning up at the Gillespie house, making a scene. 'You're not going to try to see Mel?'

'God no.'

He kissed her on the cheek as if she were a favourite aunt. She gave him a quick hug. Then he loped off. Inside her mother was still up, watching a late film on Channel Four, half dozing.

'Sorry I'm late.' Since the drama after the school reunion Rosie had been sporadically worried about her mother. She wasn't getting much support. When Rosie had told her father about the police investigation he'd had difficulty in stopping himself laughing. 'Hannah! Mixed up with the police. God, she'll hate it.'

Yet if the murder had happened recently, everyone would have considered it horrifying. Rosie could tell that the past had become very real to her mother. She seemed to have become lost in it. Hannah said nothing, but Rosie could tell that in the long silences she was reliving it. Now, half asleep in front of the television, she was probably dreaming it too. To bring her back to the present Rosie offered her a piece of information. Usually she never told her mother anything about herself unless she could help it.

'Joe walked me home.'

Hannah stirred at this but wasn't, Rosie thought, sufficiently distracted. Not as distracted as she normally would have been. Usually she took an unhealthy interest in Rosie's relationships with men.

'The police phoned,' she said. 'They want to come here to talk to me. More questions. After work on Monday.'

'I'm sorry. It must be shitty.'

Hannah was usually prudish about language and Rosie expected her to object to the word. Instead she repeated it. 'Shitty. Yes, it is, rather.'

'It can't be important if it can wait until Monday.'

'I suppose not.'

At the top of the stairs there was a landing window which looked over the street. She stopped and looked out, not expecting to see anyone because Joe walked very quickly and would have been long gone. But someone was there, half hidden by a windblown sycamore on the pavement opposite. Her mother called downstairs to ask if the front door was locked. Rosie turned away to answer her. When she looked again, the figure had gone.

Chapter Fifteen

That Monday the weather broke and Hannah went back to work. She woke too early, unrested, to bright sunlight, but by the time she went out to the car the sky was hidden by thin cloud like smoke. She ran back to the house to fetch an umbrella just in case. The prison was five miles to the north. She drove along the coast road towards mountains of cloud. The first rain started just as the barrier lifted to let her into the staff car park. The drought which had brought Michael's body to the surface of Cranford Water was over.

Apart from the weather it was just like any other morning. She queued at the gatehouse with the officers. Some spoke, others didn't. No one realized she'd been away. After she'd collected her keys she bumped into Arthur, who was sheltering from the downpour, blocking the doorway so the officers had to squeeze past. She thought he'd enjoy being an irritation.

'I thought it might blow over. It was fine when I left home. I'm not really prepared.' Grinning at himself, liking looking such a mess.

He was wearing a short-sleeved shirt, jeans and open sandals. Everything was dripping. His dress was another excuse for the education department's disapproval. The principal thought it set the wrong tone. Hannah had heard comments from the inmates too. They didn't know what to make of him. The officers were openly hostile. Despite his lack of hair there were muttered comments in the mess about ageing hippies.

She opened her umbrella and they ran together towards the education block. The rain was a deluge which had already formed a lake over the hard-packed ground. Inside, she walked with him as far as his room.

'Did you have a good break?'

She paused. 'It's a long story.'

'I'm not doing anything for an hour. I can make you a coffee.'

'My orderly will be waiting. Perhaps I could meet you at lunchtime.' She thought she sounded like a teen-ager suggesting a date, regretted the words as soon as they were spoken.

'Sure,' he said easily. He unlocked his door and went inside, his sandals squelching on the tiled floor.

Marty was waiting outside, his face pressed to the glass door to see if anyone was in the room. There was no porch and by the time Hannah had opened the door he was soaked. He was wearing a thin, prison-issue shirt which clung to him.

'Oh God.' She pulled the hand towel from her cupboard-sized cloakroom and threw it to him. 'I'm so sorry. I went in the other way and I was talking.'

He rubbed his hair and looked like a five-year-old just out of the bath.

'I'll make some tea,' she said, realizing she was staring. 'Warm you up.'

'It's OK, really.' He folded up the towel and handed

it to her, pulled his sodden sleeves away from his wrists.

'Everything been all right?'

'I'm glad you're back. The guy they sent didn't know the ropes. And he didn't want to be told.'

'No bother then?'

He shook his head.

'The lad that kicked off before I went on leave wasn't in?'

'Don't worry. He'll not be back.'

'You've not done anything stupid?' She was thinking threats if not actual violence.

'Nah. Too much to lose. He's out soon. Doing his pre-release course now. He's lucky you didn't say anything and that Dave's a good sleeper.'

Hannah made the tea, handed a mug to Marty.

'I could get used to this,' he said.

'Don't tell anyone. You don't want to spoil my reputation.' Which was, she knew, as a tough bitch, a bad-tempered cow who was OK at sorting out books, would move heaven and earth to track down a requested title, but who wouldn't listen to excuses about lost or damaged copies, would have you up on report for a bit of chewing-gum stuck to a page.

He smiled. The rain hammered on the flat roof, streamed down the windows so it was impossible to see outside. The perimeter wall had vanished. They could have been in a rain-soaked library anywhere.

'Do you mind if I ask what you're in for?' she asked. Suddenly she felt she had the right to know. Perhaps it was that being the subject of a police investigation gave her some fellow feeling. It made her position in the prison more ambiguous.

'Don't you know?'

'I suppose it was in your file. If I ever did know I've forgotten. Look, it doesn't matter. It's none of my business.'

'Manslaughter.'

She thought that was all he was going to say. She didn't blame him for not wanting to go into any detail. She shouldn't have asked. He'd been kind to her and she'd been rude. But he continued.

'It was a fight in a pub. Stupid. I was pissed and I can hardly remember now what started it off. The court accepted it was self-defence. To be honest I think I was bloody lucky. I had a good brief.' He drank the tea. Hannah didn't know what to say. 'The lad I killed had a wife and a baby. Sometimes I think, well he shouldn't have been in the pub then should he? Getting tanked up and gobby, spoiling for a fight. He had responsibilities. He should have been at home. But that's bollocks, isn't it? I can't blame him. You can't blame the victim.'

Hannah thought of Michael Grey. 'No, I suppose not.'

'Listen to me,' he said. 'I sound as if I've been on one of those courses. Victim awareness.'

'And have you?'

'Not here. But I've been through it all. I can talk the jargon standing on my head.'

'Where then?'

He didn't answer directly. 'I've done supervision, care, probation, community service. Spent more time in prison than I've been out. Long enough to know the right thing to say when you're after parole.'

But he'd meant it, she thought. That thing about not blaming the victim. He'd meant that.

'Have you got a release date?'

He shook his head. 'First board comes up next month.'

'Then what?'

'Then I'm going to stay out of trouble. Of course.' He gave a twisted grin. 'That's what all the cons say, isn't it? I bet you've heard it before. "I'm serious, miss. You won't see me in here again." Then a couple of months later, there they are at your reception talk.'

'And you?' she asked. 'Will you be back?'

'No. Not this time.'

'What's different this time?'

'I've grown up, I suppose. About time.'

'And?'

He smiled. 'You're in the wrong business. You should be a cop. You've got a better interview technique than most of them. *And* there's a girl.' He corrected himself. 'A woman. She's an actress. Younger than me but not that much. Dunno what she sees in me. Crazy.' He shook his head in wonder. 'She said she'd wait. This time. No second chances. We got together when I was on bail. My solicitor wangled me a hostel place. She was running a literacy course. A volunteer.'

'Does she visit?'

'Yeah. Regular as clockwork. With a list of books I should be reading.'

'So. A happy ending.'

'For me, yeah. One last chance. Up to me not to blow it. Not so lucky for the guy in the pub.'

Or for Michael Grey, she thought.

'You said you'd been in trouble when you were a kid . . .'

'Oh yes.' Now he'd started talking about himself it seemed he couldn't stop. 'We were the classic dysfunctional family.' She could hear the quotation marks in the self-mockery. 'My dad beat up my mum. My mum left him and took me with her. She couldn't cope so I was in and out of care. Where I met real little thugs. I was brighter than them so I didn't get caught so often. But often enough to go right through the system. I never did drugs but I drank too much, even when I was a kid. It clouds your judgement. If I hadn't been a boozer I'd probably have been a brilliant criminal. But I needed the drink.'

'Did you ever do youth custody in West Yorkshire?' This is ridiculous, she thought. A waste of time. Leave it to the police. But she held her breath while she waited for an answer.

'Why?'

'I'm just after some information.' She wasn't quite daft enough to trust him with the truth. He might keep it to himself, but if it got round the prison that she was involved in a murder inquiry her position would be impossible. 'A long shot. Something came up at the school reunion. Someone we're trying to trace. There's a place at Holmedale isn't there?'

'Yeah. I was there for a few months. It was all right. There was a farm. Pigs. Some of the instructors were OK.'

'When would that have been?'

'Early seventies.' He was older than he looked. 'I'd have been fourteen.'

'The timing would be about right. Like I say, it's a

long shot but do you remember a lad called Michael Grey? Very blond hair. He'd be a few years older than you.'

He paused and she thought for a minute he'd remembered the name from the news reports. But he must have sorted the daily papers without reading them. Certainly he hadn't seemed to have made the connection.

He shook his head. 'It's a long time ago. And I knocked around with so many lads over the years.'

'He might have been using a different name. You'd have noticed him. Posh voice, well educated, bright.'

He used almost the same phrase Stout had done. 'You didn't get many like that in borstal. Nice boys in trouble got probation or were sent off to see a shrink. I think I'd have remembered a lad like that.'

She could tell there was no point pushing it. 'Thanks anyway.'

There was a jangling of keys. Dave the prison officer came in, snug in his uniform waterproof. He raised an eyebrow at them drinking tea and the papers not sorted. Hannah could tell he would have liked a cup himself but was too idle to make it. He took off the coat, shook the water all over the floor and went into the office for his kip.

When Hannah went to find Arthur at lunchtime he was still running a class. He'd got them to pull the tables together and they sat round as if they were at a board meeting. The prisoner who'd pushed over the library shelf was standing at the front, writing on a flip chart with a fat felt-tip pen. This must be the pre-release course. Hannah knew it was feeble but she didn't want to meet him again so she waited in Arthur's office until they all streamed out. There was a list of the men attending the course on his desk, with their dates of birth and release dates. By a process of elimination she identified her troublemaker as Hunter. The next day he'd be gone.

Despite the rain Arthur took her out of the prison for lunch. It was her choice. The food in the officers' mess was cheap but she hated the noise in there, the banter, the unspoken implication that anyone not in uniform was an outsider. They went to a pub in the nearest village. Often that was full of prison staff too, but today it was empty. They sat in the bay window but low cloud hid the view. Arthur went to the bar for drinks and to order food. As soon as he returned he said, 'I'm sitting comfortably. Let's hear the story.'

She didn't know where to start. She would have liked to go back to the beginning, to her first meeting with Michael and the bonfire on the beach. She would have liked Arthur's opinion. He was an expert. But the friendship hadn't developed to the stage of discussing ex-lovers. And besides, they only had three quarters of an hour for lunch.

'Did you meet up with your friends?'

'Yes, and I'll go back. It's broken the ice.'

'But something happened?'

'Yes.' She sounded abrupt and ungrateful – Rosie on a bad day. She'd found it easier to talk to Marty. Arthur was a professional. The reassuring voice, the laid-back manner, these were techniques he'd perfected. He listened to people's confidences for a living. She felt resentful. She didn't want to be one of his clients. Anyway, wouldn't he resent her spilling out all her fears in his lunch break? It was like asking a mechanic

164

to check your brakes in his dinner hour. Still, she couldn't stop now and she stumbled on. 'Did you hear on the news that a body was found in the lake?'

'Exposed after the drought. Yes.'

'I knew him. When I was at school he was my boyfriend.'

There was a minute of silence. It was obviously the last thing he'd been expecting. 'I'm so sorry.' The response seemed genuine. But so, she supposed, would his Monday-to-Friday compassion with the inmates.

'The police think he was murdered.'

'Can they tell after all this time?'

'There's evidence of a knife wound. Apparently.'

'You went to the hills to escape all the crime and punishment thing here, then you ended up with that.'

'I know.' She forced out a laugh. 'As Rosie says, it's shitty.'

'How is Rosie? Is she giving you grief?'

'No. She's being a sweetie.'

There was a slightly awkward pause. 'She seems a nice kid. Protective.'

'She is. Usually. I'm sorry she was so prickly when you met the other night.'

He shrugged. 'Understandable, isn't it?'

A middle-aged waitress approached with the food. She had flat feet and they could hear her as soon as she left the bar. Arthur waited for her to put down the plates and retreat.

'Just because it happened thirty years ago doesn't mean you won't go through the normal stages of bereavement. You're bound to feel anger, guilt, all the usual junk.'

Of course he was right. Hannah supposed she

should be grateful. No one else had given her the right to mourn. But it wasn't what she wanted to hear. It wasn't any of his business. She didn't need a psychologist.

'It was all a long time ago,' she said briskly.

'But you'll have memories. Intense at that age.'

'No danger of forgetting,' she said. 'The police are coming tonight to interview me.'

'Whatever for?'

She was about to make a flippant remark. Something like – Perhaps they think I killed him. But that was too close to the truth. That was what really frightened her. She didn't want to tempt fate by saying it, even as a joke.

'After all this time they can't find out much about him. They haven't even traced his family. They think I can help.'

'Ah.' That satisfied him. He hesitated. 'Would you like me to be there with you? Not to interfere. Just for support.'

It was tempting. If she hadn't dismissed his earlier kindness she would probably have accepted. But she'd decided the body in the lake was none of his business. She couldn't have it both ways.

'No,' she said. 'Really. It's just a few questions.'

She looked at her watch. It was time to go back inside.

Chapter Sixteen

When Hannah got in from work Rosie was in the kitchen and there was a smell of cooking. A wooden spoon hung over the edge of the bench and dripped tomato sauce on to the floor. Pans were piled on the draining board. Hannah moved the spoon. 'This is a surprise.' A nice surprise. Since the end of exams, Rosie had seldom been there to share a meal with her.

'I'm supposed to be at work at seven but if you want me to stay while the police are here I can phone in sick.'

'Don't be silly. You can't do that.'

Usually they ate in the kitchen but Rosie had laid the table in the dining-room with the white linen cloth Hannah saved for Christmas and special events. It was a monster to iron but she didn't suggest changing it. Rosie proudly carried dishes from the kitchen – a tomato and aubergine casserole with a yoghurt topping, a green salad. She'd bought a bottle of wine.

'You should cook more often,' Hannah said.

Rosie smiled.

Afterwards there was the usual scrabble for uniform and she ran off to work. Hannah watched her through the window. Rosie wore a thin hooded jacket which hardly kept out the rain and every so often she looked at her watch and put on a spurt of speed. She ran like a toddler, legs flailing out from the knees. Then she disappeared round a corner and the house seemed very quiet. Hannah was finishing the washing-up when the doorbell rang. There was wine left in her glass and she drank it guiltily before going to the door. Porteous and Stout stood outside. They wore almost identical waterproof jackets. The sight of them – one tall and lanky, one short and squat – reminded her of a music-hall double act.

'Come in.' She had made sure the living-room was tidy before starting on the dishes. The gloom outside had made it seem almost dark and she turned on a table lamp.

'On your own?' asked Stout. He took off his jacket and waited for Hannah to take it.

'There's only my daughter and I. She's at work.' Usually she hated that explanation, but tonight it made her rather proud.

She offered them tea and was surprised when they accepted. She thought it wasn't a good sign. They expected to be here for a long time. On the way to the kitchen she hung the coats in the cupboard under the stairs. Stout's smelled of tobacco and reminded her of the night in The Old Rectory when she'd learned that Michael had been stabbed.

When she returned from the kitchen with a tray the men were perched side by side on the sofa. They sat with their cups and saucers on their knees, looking all prim. Hannah thought they could have been a committee of volunteers, perhaps organizing a charity jumble sale. She had sat on many such committees. It would have been more appropriate for them to interview her in the prison. That was the natural home for what Arthur had called the 'crime and punishment thing'.

'I'm afraid we're no further forward,' Stout said. 'We checked out your idea that Michael might have been in trouble when he was young. I know you thought he might have done time in Yorkshire. But no joy. There is a youth-custody institution near Leeds . . .'

'Holmedale,' she said.

'Holmedale, yes. It was a borstal in those days. But no one called Michael Grey was there in the years in question.'

'I thought you said he must have changed his name.'

'We've tracked down a couple of staff. There's an officer who's since retired and a senior probation officer who was a young welfare officer there at the time. No one recognizes the lad you describe.'

'It was a long time ago and they'd have worked with a lot of boys.' She wondered what made her push it. Marty hadn't known Michael either. Why was she so sure he'd been inside?

'Not many posh ones,' Stout said. 'Not many who go on to take A levels.'

'We've been looking at boarding schools in Yorkshire too.' Porteous gave a polite little smile as if to say – You see, we did listen to you, we did take your ideas seriously. 'Just in case Michael was telling the truth when he said he'd gone to school there. We started with boarding schools. If his father were a diplomat as you thought, that would be his most likely education. Don't you agree? We've been asking for a list of boys with the same date of birth as Michael gave to the dentist. We've tracked down every individual. They're all accounted for. No one's gone missing. Of course, it's an incomplete picture. Places close, records are destroyed. The team is working through the state schools now.'

'I see.' She didn't know what to say. Did he want a pat on the back for his thoroughness?

'We haven't found the mother's grave yet,' Stout said. 'But that's hardly surprising when we don't have a name, a date or a place.'

That would have been the time to tell them about the cemetery by the lighthouse. It would be possible to explain it away as a stray memory which had returned. But the tone of Stout's voice frightened her. He made it clear he hadn't believed her, that the story of the funeral was a fantasy she'd made up for her own ends. How would he accept she'd forgotten a detail of such significance, something which might finally pin an identity on Michael Grey? The moment passed without her speaking.

'So we thought we'd look at things in a different way,' Porteous said. 'From the other end, as it were. Not looking into Michael's origins but into where he was going. Or where you thought he was going. Because you didn't report him missing either, Mrs Morton, and that does seem rather odd. You had been his girlfriend for a year. We've been speaking to your friends, to teachers at the school, and everyone says you were very close.' He gave a sympathetic smile. 'Deeply, madly in love, someone said. I don't think you'd simply accept his disappearance. So he must have given you an explanation. Perhaps he told you the same story as he'd told the Brices.'

Hannah wondered which friends had been talking to him. The prose style sounded like Sally's.

'No,' she said. 'No story.'

'Oh but there was.' He sounded apologetic, as if he didn't like to contradict her. 'At least there was a story for the Brices. Unless they made it up.'

'They wouldn't have done that.'

'So it was a story they believed, even if it wasn't told to them by Michael himself. Let me explain. You were all sitting A levels. Michael's first exam was art. We know because we've spoken to the school. It hasn't been easy but we've chased up some of his subject teachers. The art teacher is retired but still living in the area. Michael didn't turn up for the exam. He was one of the few pupils in the class predicted to get a top grade. It was a subject he enjoyed, so it wasn't a case of last-minute nerves. The teacher was frantic – perhaps Michael had made a mistake about dates. He phoned the number on the school record and got through to Stephen Brice, who was perfectly calm, who seemed bewildered by all the fuss. "Didn't Michael tell you?" he said to the art teacher. "He's gone back to his father."

'If there was any other information given during the conversation the teacher can't remember it. He assumed it was a case of family illness or bereavement. It must have been something serious, he said, because Michael had been working hard for the exam and was determined to do well.'

Oh yes, thought Hannah, remembering lunchtimes in the art room, watching Michael, smudged with paint, working on his display. He was certainly determined.

Porteous set his teacup carefully on the coffee table. 'You never heard that story?'

She shook her head. 'I didn't see anyone much at that time. I went in for the exams and straight home. As soon as the A levels were finished I left the area. I'd found a summer job in a hotel in Devon. I didn't even come back for the results. They were posted on to me.'

'You must have noticed that Michael wasn't around?'

'Yes. I realized he'd gone. Back to his family, I thought. Dramatically. The way that he'd come.'

'But you didn't go to see the Brices, to ask what had happened, to get a forwarding address?' Porteous was faintly incredulous.

'No.' She hesitated, unsure how much to say. 'It was a bit embarrassing. We'd stopped going out with each other actually. I suppose I didn't want them to think I was chasing him. Pride, you know.'

'A row, was there?' Stout asked. 'Lovers' tiff?'

He said it casually enough, but then they both looked at her in a way that made her realize the answer was important to them. She sensed the danger just in time. Sally hadn't just told them how much in love she'd been.

Hannah matched her voice to his. Kept it light. Implying, You know what dizzy things teenage girls are. 'I suppose so, but I'm blessed if I can remember what it was all about. Not wanting to face the details, even after all this time.'

'Serious though, at that age.'

'Not as serious as passing the exams. That was our priority at the time. That was probably why we fell out.'

'You were jealous of the time he spent studying?'

'I think it was more likely the other way round.'

They looked at her. They were still sitting side by side on the sofa. It was leather. One of Jonathan's affectations. It didn't go in the room at all. Hannah thought of Michael's audition for *Macbeth* – Jack Westcott and Spooky Spence sitting in judgement on the red plastic chairs at the front of the hall. Porteous and Stout were sitting in judgement too. They thought she was lying but they were trying to decide if it was because Michael had dumped her and she didn't want to admit it, or because she had killed him. It was impossible to tell if they'd reached a conclusion.

'Why don't you take us through the last couple of days of his life?' Porteous said.

'Is that possible? Do you know when he died? Exactly?'

'Perhaps not,' he admitted. 'But we know when he disappeared. If we can believe the Brices.'

She was starting to panic. Incoherent thoughts pitched one after another into her brain. She forced out a reasonable voice. 'It's a long time ago. I'm not sure how much I'll remember.'

'We can help you.' Porteous leaned forwards so his elbows were on his knees. He clasped his hands. More like a priest than a cop. Or a counsellor. Not very different in tone from Arthur. 'There was a school play. *Macbeth*. I've seen an old programme. Mr Westcott has kept them all over the years. There was a photograph of Michael – we'll call him Michael for now, shall we? It's different from the one which was in the paper. It's rather faded and grainy, but it gives an impression. He was a striking boy.' He stopped, miming a man who's had a sudden thought. 'I don't suppose you kept a photograph, did you?'

She shook her head. She'd always regretted not having one.

'No? Pity. Still . . .' He seemed lost in a thought of his own, then ditched all the make-believe vagueness. 'The final performance of *Macbeth* was on the Friday night. You were prompting and looking after the props?'

She nodded, remembered like a slow-motion replay the Brices rising in their seats to cheer.

'Did you talk to him that evening? In the interval perhaps, or afterwards?'

'I'm not sure. Probably.'

'So you were still going out with him on the Friday then. So far as you're aware. The disagreement between you must have happened on the Saturday or the Sunday.'

'The Saturday,' she said. She felt she was being boxed in, tricked. She should have claimed not to remember. How could she be expected to have perfect recall of that sort of detail after so many years? But she did remember. She had played the scene over and over in her head ever since.

'You're absolutely certain about that?'

She nodded. She wished suddenly that Arthur were there. So much for pride. They wouldn't push so hard if another person were present. They'd be more circumspect. She wondered if she should refuse to answer their questions, demand to have a solicitor there. But she'd never been much good at demanding. Besides, then they'd assume that she was guilty, that she had something to hide.

Porteous straightened his back and looked satisfied as if it were just as he had supposed. He was taking the lead in the questions. Stout had taken out a soft, thick pencil and was making notes on a shorthand pad. As Porteous had waited for her answer Hannah had heard the lead move over the paper.

'We'll come back to Saturday later,' Porteous continued. 'If you could cast your mind back to the Friday.' He paused, gave her a look of reluctant admiration. 'You do have a most remarkable memory, Mrs Morton. It was the same during our previous conversation. So tell us what happened in the interval. Did all the actors remain backstage?'

'Yes.' An easy question. 'Mr Spence, the producer, was strict about that. There was to be no running around the hall. The PTA organized refreshments for the audience and took juice and biscuits for the actors and crew.'

'But *you* were prompting, I understand, from the front of the audience. It wasn't a traditional stage with wings.'

'That's right.' Good God, she thought. He's a magician. How can he know all this?

He closed his eyes as if he were picturing the scene. 'Did you go backstage in the interval or stay where you were?'

'I stayed in my seat. Mr and Mrs Brice came to speak to me.' That had been a relief. Her mother had been in the audience too, a gesture of support which she should have welcomed. Hannah wouldn't have known what to say to her and the Brices kept her away. Hannah had seen Audrey from the corner of her eye, circling at a distance.

'Did they mention that Michael might be leaving the area?'

'Definitely not. They talked about the play.'

'Of course. So either they didn't know about his plans at that stage – if indeed there were any plans – or Michael had asked them to keep a secret. Otherwise they would have discussed his leaving with you.'

'Yes, I'm sure they would.'

'What did you do after the performance?'

'We walked into town together and bought fish and chips.' Again to avoid her mother. So she wouldn't have to talk to Audrey on the way home. She saw he was astonished that she had remembered a detail like that and added, 'At least I think that's what we did. It could have been another time.'

'What about the props?' he asked. 'Did you clear them up that night?'

She thought, He knows about the knife. Felt the last of her control slipping. Held it together.

'Some of them. While I was waiting for the others to change and take off their make up. A team of us came in on the Saturday afternoon to do the rest.'

'What did you do with all the stuff?'

'Packed it into boxes. I don't know what happened to it then.'

'Did any of the cast keep anything? A souvenir perhaps. Something to remind them of the play?'

She shook her head. She couldn't trust herself to speak.

'Was Michael there that afternoon?'

'No,' she said sharply. 'He was the star. Too grand to muck about with props and costumes.'

Porteous smiled. 'Well that takes us nicely to Saturday evening.'

'There was a party,' she said. 'For the cast and the crew and a few of the teachers who were involved in the production.'

'Mr Spence?'

'I'm not sure. Yes, perhaps he was there.'

'Mr Westcott?'

'I don't think so. It was mostly the younger staff. I believe there was someone from the art department . . .'

'Don't worry. We can check the names if we need to.'

'We weren't allowed the party in school. Not the sort of party at least that we would have wanted. We hired a room on the caravan park. The DJ ran the disco for nothing.' She paused. 'Chris Johnson. He's still around in the town. He's got a record. You probably know him.' She was going to add that he'd been married to Sally but decided that would be petty. They'd find out anyway if they asked around. She watched Stout scribble furiously on his notepad.

'And you and Michael had a row?'

'Not a row.' She'd had enough. She could hear her voice raise a pitch. 'We just decided it would be best if we didn't see each other until after the exams.'

She expected him to probe with more questions but he nodded understandingly.

'Did you see Michael on the Sunday?'

'No. I had an exam next day. I didn't go out at all. I was working.' It wasn't a lie.

'And on the Monday the Brices told the art teacher that Michael had gone back to his father . . .'

He sat for a moment as if he was musing the significance of the detail for the first time, but it was all show. He must have gone over that information dozens of times before visiting her. He stood up suddenly, seeming to take Stout by surprise. Hannah fetched their coats and showed them to the door. Stout was still stuffing his notebook and pencil into his pocket as he left. It had stopped raining so Stout was able to light his pipe on the way to the car, curling his hand around the match to nurture the flame.

Chapter Seventeen

Frank sent Rosie home early. Perhaps that's what she'd been hoping for when she told him about the police and her mum. He was a good boss. It had been quiet in the pub anyway and she knew she'd been ratty. Raging PMT. Sometimes it got her so she wanted to roar with frustration. Like a huge lioness. She'd made a real effort with her mum earlier so she'd taken it out on Frank and the others at work. No wonder he'd wanted shot of her.

When she got in Hannah was sitting in the living-room. She must have heard the door, but she didn't get up or turn around. There wasn't the usual inquisition about what had happened to Rosie at work. No television. The only light came from a small table lamp. Hannah was sitting in shadow. She'd opened another bottle of wine and nearly finished it. She hadn't got drunk even on the night Jonathan had walked out, but tonight she was ratted. Rosie sat on the arm of the chair and put her arm around her. She took the glass from her hand.

'You'd better let me have that. You're not used to it and you've got work in the morning.'

'I was used to it once. When I was your age.'

Is that how I'll get? Rosie thought. Pissed after a couple of glasses of wine.

'I take it the police came,' she said. 'Was it dreadful?'

'They were all right. Polite. Just doing their job.' Hannah turned to her and Rosie saw lines on her face she'd never noticed before: on her neck and framing the bottom of her jaw. 'But they think I killed him,' Hannah said in the same flat voice. 'They think we had a row and he dumped me and I stabbed him.'

The next day Hannah must have got up in time to go to work but Rosie didn't hear her. She never woke up much before lunchtime unless she was on an eleven o'clock shift. Today she had a day off. She hadn't made any plans.

She was jerked awake by the phone, which didn't stop, even after the seven rings when the answerphone usually clicked in. Her mother must have forgotten to switch on the machine before leaving for work. Rosie got out of bed, saw it was only nine thirty, swore and took the call in Hannah's bedroom. The bed was made, the few clothes left out were neatly folded on the chair. Even with a hangover her mother couldn't bear to leave the house without tidying. Talk about anal.

'Rosie? That *is* Rosie Morton?' The caller had waited so long that he seemed surprised to get a response. She didn't recognize the voice. It was a middle-aged male. Somewhere in the background a woman was talking very quickly.

'This is Richard Gillespie.' She was still fuddled with sleep and didn't answer so he added with a trace of impatience, 'Mel's father.'

'Oh yes. Hi!' She'd never met Mel's father. She'd seen him on the telly, but whenever she was at the house he was working. 'How's Mel?'

There was a pause. 'We've a bit of a problem here. I wonder if you'd mind coming round.'

'Is Mel OK?' Rosie wondered if it was Mel's voice she could hear in the background. If so, she was almost hysterical.

'I don't really care to discuss it on the telephone. Look, if you like I'll come and pick you up.'

'I can walk thanks.'

'As soon as possible then.'

He hung up. She wished she'd put up more of a fight. She thought she knew what it was about. He wanted her to persuade Mel to go into hospital. Mel hated hospital, always had. She'd hinted darkly about past experiences. Rosie imagined scenes from *One Flew Over the Cuckoo's Nest* and wasn't going to force her into something she didn't want. Then she thought there must be something seriously wrong with Mel to keep Richard Gillespie away from his microchip empire. She dialled Joe's number. He might know what was going on. The line was engaged. Was Mr Gillespie enlisting him to do his dirty work too?

Outside, the rain had cleared the air. The sun was shining again but the day didn't feel so humid or sticky. She paused in front of Joe's house, considered calling in to find out if he had any news of Mel. But there was a car in the drive. Joe's mum only worked part-time. Once she'd seen Rosie very drunk and ever since Rosie had sensed the disapproval. She couldn't face it today. Besides, Richard Gillespie had made it clear he expected her immediately and even over the phone she'd found him intimidating.

She loved Mel's house. It was three storeys, set back from a quiet road. An old brick herring-bone wall separated it from its neighbours. At the back there were apple trees and blackcurrant bushes. There was nothing flash or showy about it. The Gillespies had money but didn't feel the need to flaunt it. Even the Volvo parked in the drive was a couple of years old. She thought that showed real style. Jonathan insisted on a new car every year.

Despite all that, Rosie wasn't sure she'd want Richard and Eleanor Gillespie as parents. Perhaps it was because style mattered to them too much. Image at least. Eleanor had made a career out of it. She was head of marketing for the big brewery which owned the Prom. According to Mel she'd been responsible for the huge posters which had recently appeared all over the city, featuring an elephant and a beer bottle and a slogan about gigantic thirst.

Image mattered to Richard too. Rosie had seen him on television talking about his family. The picture he presented was of a close and supportive group. 'Really, I couldn't cope without them.'

How did a nervy anorexic fit in with that? Mel said he had ambitions to go into politics. 'Power. That's what really turns him on.' It must have bugged him that he couldn't turn her into the daughter he wanted.

Richard opened the door to her. She recognized him from the newspaper articles and television reports. He looked younger than Eleanor, hardly old enough to be Mel's dad. She wondered if he dyed his hair.

'Hello. You must be Rosie.' A firm handshake and a smile. Charm on tap. A habit.

He showed her through to the kitchen. It looked over the garden and she thought, as she always did, that you could fit the whole of her house inside it. The style here was farmhouse chic. There was an Aga, a rack of stainless-steel pans hanging from the ceiling, a huge dresser with shelves of glass jars full of beans and pulses. Rosie had never seen either of the parents cook but she imagined them having dinner parties here at the weekends. Of course, the guests would sit at the scrubbed pine kitchen table. Richard would probably do the cooking – Thai perhaps or Mexican. She could imagine him in an apron. Melanie wouldn't be invited. She couldn't be trusted around food.

Mel's mother was sitting in a wicker chair by the Aga. She was wearing leggings and a big sweatshirt – aerobics-class clothes. Rosie knew she belonged to a gym but had never seen her dressed casually before. Without the suit and the make-up she looked like a different woman. She sat with her feet on the edge of the chair, her knees near her chin, her arms clasped around her legs in a sort of foetal coma.

'Where's Mel?' Rosie demanded, thinking from Eleanor's desolation that an ambulance had already come to cart her away.

Eleanor came to life, shifted position, put her feet on the floor. The wicker creaked. 'She didn't come home last night.'

'I thought she might be at your house,' Richard said. 'But obviously not.'

'Have you tried Joe's?' Rosie wasn't quite sure why they were so worried. Not after one night. They weren't usually like Hannah, who panicked if Rosie was half an hour late.

'She's not with him either. But I've asked him to come round. Between us we should be able to work out where she is.'

Rosie sat on one of the reclaimed pine chairs. 'Is there any chance of a coffee? I came straight out.' Usually she wouldn't have had the cheek to ask, but they needed her help, didn't they?

'Of course.' Richard filled the filter machine.

'Where did she go when she left you last night?' Eleanor demanded.

'I didn't see Mel last night. I haven't seen her for days. You said she was too ill.'

'Last night she insisted on going out. She said she was going to the Promenade. It was only down the road, so we thought . . .' her voice tailed off. 'Anyway, we couldn't stop her.'

That explained some of their anxiety. Mel had left in a strop after a fight. They'd be feeling guilty too.

'What time did she leave home?'

'Late,' Richard said. 'She told us she'd just go in for last orders. She knew you'd be working. We thought she'd be all right with you.'

Christ, Rosie thought. As if it's my fault.

He went on. 'It was probably about quarter-past ten. We went to bed soon after, assumed she'd go back to your house or Joe's and let herself in late. It was only this morning when Eleanor got back from the gym that she realized Mel's bed hadn't been slept in.' And had an attack of anxiety and guilt and summoned Richard back from work.

'I'd already left the pub at ten,' Rosie said. 'Frank let me go early.'

'Were any of her other friends in the pub?'

Rosie thought, shook her head. Monday was usually quiet; people spent all their money at the weekend. 'Have you spoken to Frank?'

'Frank?'

'The manager. To check that she arrived there.'

'Not yet. We didn't want to make a lot of fuss until we were sure it was justified.'

'Do you want me to phone him? He needn't know she's missing.'

'Yes,' Richard said. 'That'd be helpful.' Another flash of the smile.

Rosie would have preferred not to have an audience, but they obviously expected her to use the phone in the kitchen. She looked at her watch. Ten o'clock. Frank should be up by now. He answered quickly. 'The Promenade. Frank speaking. How may I help you?' Very brisk and efficient. He must have been expecting a call from his boss at headquarters.

'Hi. It's me. Rosie.'

'Hey, lass. I hope you're in a better mood than you were last night.'

'Did Mel come in after I left?'

'Aye but only to poke her head round the door to ask where you were. I'd have bought her a drink if she'd hung around. She looked like she could do with one.'

'Do you know where she went after?'

'No idea, pet.'

Rosie replaced the receiver. 'Sorry,' she said. Both

Gillespies were staring at her. 'She *was* there but only for a couple of minutes.'

Eleanor gave a little whimper. Rosie felt sorry for her though she'd never much taken to her before. She'd been friendly enough, but in a desperate way. She tried too hard to be one of the girls.

There was a knock on the door. Richard touched Eleanor's hand, extinguishing the hope before it was lit. 'That'll be Joe.'

Joe looked shattered. He was still wearing his uniform from the supermarket. It had been one of his nights for work. Any other time Rosie would have teased him about the shiny grey trousers, the blazer with the company logo on the breast pocket.

Now she just said, 'You must have had time to change.' His night shift finished at seven thirty.

'It's been a nightmare. I borrowed my mum's car. It broke down on the bypass on my way home. It took the AA an hour and a half to get there and then they couldn't fix it. By the time they'd got it to the garage . . .' He stopped, shrugged, turned to the Gillespies. 'Anyway, I got your message.'

Richard seemed to have forgotten about the coffee. Rosie tipped some into a mug, waved the jug towards the others.

'Yeah,' Joe said. 'Thanks.' She poured one for him and replaced the jug on the hotplate.

'Mel's gone missing,' Rosie said. 'She came to see me at the Prom but I wasn't there. She didn't come to your house? It would have been between ten thirty and eleven.' She felt the need to take charge. Even Richard seemed to have given in to lethargy. He was staring out of the window.

'It was one of my regular work nights,' Joe said. 'She might have forgotten and gone to the house but no one would have been there. Mum and Dad were at the theatre and Grace spent the night with a mate.' Grace was his thirteen-year-old sister.

They sat round the table looking at each other. Eleanor had moved away from the Aga to join them. Richard was at the head. He dragged his attention away from the garden. The chairman of the board, Rosie thought, trying to hold his team together.

'She has other friends,' he said. 'She'll have wanted to teach us a lesson. That's what this is all about. It would be best if the kids phoned around.' He looked at Rosie and Joe. 'You know the names and the numbers and they'd be more likely to tell you the truth.'

They started with a pretence of enthusiasm, but soon it was obvious to them both that Mel wasn't with any of the usual gang. Eleanor would have had them phoning all day. It was Joe, hollow-eyed and fraught, who said, 'Look, I think you should go to the police.'

Eleanor and Richard shot a look at each other which Rosie couldn't interpret.

'This evening,' Richard said. 'I promise. If she's not back this evening . . .'

Soon after, they left – Rosie to town to check on some places Mel might be and Joe to sleep. They were standing, talking together on the corner of the street before going their separate ways, when the Volvo pulled out of the drive and accelerated away. Richard Gillespie off to do some other deal. Rosie imagined Eleanor Gillespie curled up again in the wicker chair waiting for the phone to ring or the door to open.

Chapter Eighteen

Hannah's father had been cremated. Her mother had wanted the whole business over quickly, without any fuss. Hannah remembered the undertaker coming to the house to discuss arrangements. He was young, with impeccable clothes and a nervous cough. Perhaps Edward had been his first suicide.

'No fuss,' Audrey said immediately, before he had a chance to sit down. 'No show.'

'Nothing in the papers then?'

'Certainly not.'

'Flowers?'

'No!' She spoke very fiercely and he asked no more questions.

Hannah and her mother stood alone in the crematorium and watched the flimsy coffin slide behind the curtains. Afterwards they went home for tea and Battenberg, a cake Edward had always particularly disliked.

Michael's mother, however, had been buried. There had been mourners dressed in smart clothes, a black limousine which had taken Michael from wherever he had been living as a child to a church and then to the cemetery by the lighthouse. Had he mentioned a church? Hannah thought he had. The crocuses on the lawn, a church filled with weeping people, then another ride in the car to the cemetery.

Hannah had felt lousy all day. The encounter with the detectives had left her with a thick head and a jumpiness verging on paranoia. She was frightened that they'd turn up at any time to ask more of their questions. In the prison Marty saw at once that she wasn't well and had the kettle on before she asked him. She was tempted to seek out Arthur at lunchtime but something stopped her. More pride. She didn't want to admit to a hangover at her age. She didn't want him analysing her problems, coming to conclusions about her weakness and loneliness. She'd always been a person to give support, never to need it.

When Hannah got home, the house was empty. There was a cryptic note on the table from Rosie saying something urgent had come up and she'd be back by eleven. Hannah'd had nothing to eat all day but she couldn't face supper. She couldn't settle. So she went for a walk to the cemetery to look for Michael's mother.

Michael hadn't started school when his mother died. She was sure of that. It was the way he'd spoken of the wrench of her going into hospital. She must always have been around before. So, Hannah thought, when his mother died Michael would have been five at the oldest, three at the youngest. His memories had a clarity and sophistication which would have been unlikely in a toddler. The death would have occurred between forty to forty-two years previously. Even then it would have been unusual for a woman to die so young. Perhaps on the headstone there would be mention of a child. At the very least, Hannah thought, she should be able to provide Porteous and Stout with a short list of possible names. Information for the team to check, to get them off her back.

She walked along the sea front towards the lighthouse. The salty breeze and the smell of seaweed cleared her head for the first time that day. The car ferry from Bergen slid past on its way to the dock further up the river. Hannah remembered a family holiday in Norway. Rosie had been six. She'd been sick on the boat. Jonathan had sulked all week because the food in the farmhouse hadn't lived up to his expectations and he hadn't been able to get hold of a decent bottle of wine. Even before the arrival of Eve the temptress it hadn't been much of a marriage. 'You'll be better off without him,' her friends said. Until now it had been too much like admitting failure to agree.

The cemetery was almost empty. In the distance a workman was mowing the grass paths but the sound of the machine hardly reached her. At first she wandered aimlessly, her attention caught and held by unusual names, ornate carvings, simple messages of bereavement. Then, as the shadows lengthened she brought more order into the search. The modern graves – those dug within the last twenty years – were at the far end, the furthest inland. Those could be ignored. The remaining plots were in a more random jumble. There seemed to be no chronological order. The space was divided occasionally by a high cypress hedge or a stone arch. Rooks were gathering in the trees which separated the graveyard from the road. She walked up and down the lines of headstones to the jarring sound of the rooks, moving on quickly if the deceased were a man or too old, only stopping for a woman and if the date was right.

Most of the women had been elderly when they died. Most, it seemed, had been widows. The Elsies, the Mays and the Maggies had all joined dear departed husbands. She had almost given up hope when she came across one which fitted her dates. The grave had been planted with ivy and she pulled the plant away from the headstone to read the letters. Frances Lumley, aged thirty, daughter of Elizabeth and Miles. Hannah crouched on her heels to clean the rest of the text, convinced that her search was over. But Frances Lumley had been drowned at sea and there was no mention of a husband or child. And she had died in September, not a season for crocuses.

Michael's mother was buried in the grave next to Frances Lumley's and, despite her care, Hannah nearly missed it. In comparison to Frances's headstone the white marble was clean; the engraving looked as if it had been chiselled the day before. And there were fresh flowers in a brass pot which gleamed in the last of the sunlight. At first she thought this was a new grave, slotted in amongst the others to fill a space. It was only when she read the date that she saw the occupant had been buried the year after Frances. She had died on 19 February.

So there were relatives who lived near enough to tend the grave. She hadn't expected that. She still thought of Michael as he had been then. Quite alone. With only her and the Brices to care for him.

She read aloud. 'Maria Jane Randle née Grey. Daughter of Anthony and Hester. Beloved wife of Crispin and mother of Theo.' The facts were as bold as the carving. There was no comforting verse or religious text.

She knew her search was over. If she had opened the shoebox in Michael's bedroom on that day after school she would have found a birth certificate, and probably a passport too, in the name of Theo Randle. She couldn't guess where Michael – because that was how she would continue to think of him – had filched his first name. The family name he'd taken from his mother's parents. All the same she continued her walk past the last two lines of graves. She had to be sure and she hated a job half done. There were no other women of the right age buried in the place. She returned to Maria's grave and though she could remember them by heart she jotted down the details of her death and her birth, copying the engraving word for word. The sun had almost gone and she was starting to feel cold.

Hannah hadn't managed to eat anything after her interview with the detectives the night before, and after her walk along the sea front she was starving. In the town she queued up with the trippers to buy fish and chips and sat on a bench looking over the sea to eat them. She finished everything, even the thick pieces of batter she usually left behind, and licked her fingers. She had to pass the Prom on her way home and looked through the open door, thinking that Rosie's urgent appointment might involve a drink with her friends. But there was no sign of her or of anyone else Hannah recognized.

She had intended phoning Porteous as soon as she got home, had been gearing herself up to it all the way home. But when she got in the answerphone was blinking and there was a message from Arthur. 'Hi, I was hoping to see you today. How did you get on last night?' The taped voice had a stronger Liverpudlian accent than she remembered, was even more mellow and laid back. He'd left his home number and she dialled it quickly before she thought too much about it. He answered after a couple of rings. 'Hi,' again, as one of the kids would. Her mother, who'd been very strong on telephone etiquette, would have had a fit.

'Arthur. It's me. Hannah. Are you doing anything?'

'Nah, a couple of reports. Nothing interesting. Nothing urgent. And have you seen what's on the telly?'

'Would you come over? I could do with your advice.' She felt breathless. She thought he must be able to tell from her voice how nervous she was.

'Do you want to go for a drink?'

'Not a drink, no.' The idea of alcohol turned her stomach. Even the fish and chips seemed a mistake. 'Would you mind coming to the house?'

She gave him directions then sat and waited, thinking she'd made a fool of herself. Melodrama wasn't her style. It didn't suit her. He'd think, as Jonathan had done, that she was menopausal and hysterical. Or he'd get the wrong idea entirely and see her as one of those pathetic women, recently dumped, who'd do anything for the company of a man.

He arrived sooner than she'd expected. It hadn't given her time to work out what to say so she opened the door and stood awkward and tongue-tied in the hall.

'Are you OK?' He'd come out so quickly that he was still wearing carpet slippers – battered suede moccasins. Jonathan would never wear slippers. He said they were old men's garments, like pyjamas.

193

She began an explanation for calling him, but stumbled over the words. He put his arm around her.

'Hey. What is it?'

She pushed him away gently. 'Look, I'm really sorry to have dragged you out.'

'Just tell me what's going on here.'

So she sat him on the sofa where the night before Porteous and Stout had played their double act and she told him about it – about Michael Grey whose real name was Theo Randle, about the detectives who thought she was a murderer, about her discovery of Maria Randle's grave in the cemetery. He listened. He didn't move or give any of the usual verbal encouragements to prove he was listening, but she could tell she had his full attention.

'Can you be sure,' he asked, 'that Theo's the same person as Michael?'

'There's no other explanation. Maria's the only person buried in the cemetery who could be his mother. His memory of the funeral was so clear and precise that I'm sure he was telling the truth. And it can't be a coincidence that he chose Maria's maiden name as his surname.'

'Of course, you'll have to tell the police.'

'I know. But what will they think? I could have told them at the first interview that Michael's mother was buried there.'

'They'll think you were in shock, intimidated. I don't suppose they're stupid. They know how law-abiding people can react to police questioning.' He stretched his legs. He was wearing paint-stained sweat pants. He'd bought a cottage near the prison and seemed to have been decorating for months. 'Do you

194

want to phone now, while I'm here? Then I can stay if they want to come to talk to you.'

'Yes.' Again she knew she was being pathetic but she couldn't help it. 'Are you sure that's all right?'

The phone was answered by a young woman who said that Porteous was no longer in the office. She was polite but distant. Any secretary talking about any middle manager. Was it urgent? She could find someone else to speak to Hannah. Otherwise, if Hannah wanted to leave a message she could be put through to his voicemail.

'Yes.' It was some sort of reprieve. 'I'll do that.'

She listened for the beep. 'Hello. This is Hannah Morton. I've remembered something which might be useful for you. Perhaps you could get in touch.' She replaced the receiver. Arthur pulled a face of mock disappointment.

'Bugger. So I miss out.'

'What do you mean?'

'I was hoping for the chance to play detective.'

'You can't be serious?'

He put out his hands, palms up, a gesture of being caught in the act. 'OK I admit it. I love crime fiction. I'm a sucker for all those crappy cop shows on TV.'

'This is hardly the same!'

'I know.' He paused, continued slowly, a dream confided. 'I've always thought I'd make a good psychological profiler. At least in my work I meet real criminals and I'm not sure how many academics could say the same.'

'You're welcome to be here when the police talk to me.'

'Right.' He paused. 'What about making a few enquiries on our own? While we're waiting for the police to get in touch?'

'This isn't a game, Arthur. Not for me.'

'I know.'

But she couldn't bear to disappoint him. It was like when Rosie *really* wanted something. She always gave in. She thought, Being a mother is like trying to please the world.

'What did you have in mind?'

'We might find something which would divert attention away from you . . .'

'That's an excuse.'

'What about having a shot at tracing the boy's father? I don't mean camping out on his doorstep. Just finding out where he is.'

'How would you go about that?'

'Through the records office, the archives of the local paper. There may have been a death notice when Maria died, an address. If the Brices said Michael was going to meet his father just before he died I'd say Crispin Randle makes an adequate suspect. If we hand him to Porteous on a plate it'll give him someone else to harass.'

'Why would he kill his own son?'

'Why would he desert him? We'll have to find out.' He was like an overenthusiastic boy. Michael was a stranger to him. A puzzle to be untangled. He must have sensed her reservation, her distaste. 'God,' he said. 'What an insensitive git. Look, I'll clear out and leave it to the police.'

'No,' she said. He must have known she would give in eventually. 'You play detective. If it makes you happy.'

Chapter Nineteen

Rosie spent the day looking for Mel in some of the places she could be lying low. There were days when Mel couldn't face the Prom. Then she'd turn her back on her friends and Frank's teasing and she'd go walkabout. Usually she wanted to be on her own but sometimes on the trawls around town she'd take Rosie with her. She didn't speak much. She just waited for Rosie to follow her round the arcades, the sleazy snack bars, the tiny back-street pubs where a couple of pensioners sat all evening in silence. Everywhere people seemed to know her. Rosie stuck with her because in that mood Mel frightened her.

Rosie went first to the snack bar next to the bus station. A Formica shelf ran shoulder-high around the room and there were tall stools bolted to the floor. A water heater steamed behind a counter. The windows ran with condensation. There was a smell of frying bacon, which made her want to throw up.

A pimply youth was wiping tables with a grey cloth.

'Hey, Robbie. Seen Mel?'

Robbie was one of Mel's admirers. She had them everywhere, picked them up. Robbie was from Edinburgh, had run away from a loutish stepfather and lived now in a hostel run by a children's charity. Rosie had never talked to him about any of this but Mel had told her. Robbie was passionately in love with Mel. You could tell by the way that he blushed whenever she spoke to him. Mel encouraged him. He was into Idlewild and they'd talk about album tracks, Mel strumming an imaginary guitar, the boy banging out a rhythm on a tabletop until the manager came out from the back to shout at him.

'No.' He squirted cleaner from a spray, turned his back to her. He could be lying. If Mel had asked him to, he'd lie.

'Her parents are worried about her. They're talking about getting in the police.'

He faced her. 'Really. I haven't seen her for ages.' He seemed scared, but perhaps that was the talk of the police.

'If you see her, tell her to get in touch. With me or Joe if she's not up to going home.'

He nodded. His face was blank. Years of practice at not letting on what was going on in his head.

The amusement arcade was next to the funfair, old fashioned in the same sort of way. It was decorated in red and gilt and a cashier sat in a booth in the entrance. Mel said the booth reminded her of one of the windows in Amsterdam where a prostitute would sit. Carol, the cashier, wasn't one of Mel's admirers and the hostility was mutual. Mel went to the arcade to play the machines, not to chat. Carol was a middle-aged, once-upon-a-time blonde, a single mum. She was outraged by the money Mel lost; enough, she'd say, to feed her kids for a week. Mel didn't taken kindly to the lectures. She played the machines as if nothing else mattered, completely focused on the patterns which spun before her. The money was irrelevant. Sometimes she left her winnings in the tray and had to be reminded to go back for them.

On rainy days the arcade was packed. Today there was a middle-aged couple playing on the penny scoop and a few teenage lads bunking off school. Carol waved to Rosie. She got bored out of her mind imprisoned in her booth and she wanted the company. She'd keep you talking all day given the chance.

'Mad Mel not with you then?'

'No. I was wondering if she'd been in.'

'I've not seen her since she went away on holiday. Portugal, was it? Did she have a good time?'

'She didn't go in the end.' Rosie inched her way towards the door. She couldn't face explanations.

Carol seemed to realize she'd not get much more from the conversation and picked up a copy of *Hello*! magazine from a shelf under her desk. She began to flick over the pages. Her nails were sugar pink. She looked up once more to flutter the nails in Rosie's direction to wave goodbye.

It was early afternoon. Joe would still be sleeping. Rosie tried a couple of pubs without much hope. There was one in a back street, near the health centre, run by an ex-jockey, a little wizened old man with no teeth. Another of Mel's fans. The bar was full of men studying form in the racing pages. Rosie had never been able to understand why Mel went in the place. She had become a sort of mascot. She sat at the bar on a wooden stool and the punters asked her advice, though she admitted she knew nothing about horses or racing. Today her stool was empty.

'She needs looking after,' said the landlord

sentimentally when Rosie explained that Mel had gone missing. 'Proper loving care.'

Rosie thought secretly that Mel had been loved too much, spoilt rotten at least. But she kept that opinion to herself.

She walked down the steep hill from the health centre towards the sea front. Terraces of pastel-painted guest-houses ran away from the road. In the windows were signs saying 'Vacancies' and 'Contractors welcome'. On the corner was the hostel where Robbie lived. A young woman was hanging sheets out on the washing line. Rosie thought Mel could hide herself away in this town for months if she wanted to. The Gillespies would make sure there was money in her bank account. Eleanor obviously wanted her found, but Rosie thought Richard wouldn't pry too much as long as he knew she was safe and she didn't cause a fuss which could be picked up by the press. At the sea front Rosie crossed the road and went down to the level of the beach. The traffic became a distant hum above her.

The Rainbow's End was a café, two arches cut out of the bank of the promenade. It was run by middle-aged drop-outs selling organic food and herbal teas and it was one of Melanie's favourite haunts. She said it was like a cave. She would sit near the counter, as far away as possible from the natural light, her back turned to the sea. She'd drink decaffeinated coffee and smoke roll-up after roll-up although there was a big sign saying NO SMOKING. Maura, who ran the place, turned a blind eye. Another example of one rule for Mel and another for the rest of the world. In the Rainbow's End, Mel was drawn to the food. Sometimes she'd buy a slab of carrot cake. She'd sit and look at it, a paper napkin folded on her lap, but she'd never eat. In the end she'd push the plate across the table towards Rosie.

'I don't feel hungry. You have it.'

Rosie was always hungry but she didn't know what to do for the best so the cake would sit there, the cream-cheese topping slowly melting, until they left.

Maura was a big woman, an earth mother in an Indian-print caftan and beads woven into her hair. She looked out for Mel. If the café was quiet – which it usually was – she'd sit with her and talk earnestly about the things which would 'get her head straight'. Things like plant remedies, hypnosis, acupuncture. Mel would listen with a bored expression on her face. So far as Rosie knew she never followed up any of the suggestions.

Today two young women sat near the window. The tide was in, right up to the concrete walkway, and it felt like being in a boat. The women had children with them – a toddler apiece in pushchairs and a baby in a sling. Maura was going gooey-eyed over the baby, talking about the benefits of terry nappies and breast milk. The women agreed about the breast milk at least. They all seemed very smug.

Perhaps that was Mel's problem, Rosie thought facetiously. She probably wasn't breastfed.

She interrupted the baby talk and ordered a sandwich – mozzarella, tomatoes and basil on ciabatta.

'Has Mel been in?'

Maura shook her head. 'Not today.'

'Yesterday?' In the evenings the place had a licence. It sold veggie meals and organic wine in candlelight.

So you couldn't see what you were getting. Often there was live music.

'Yes. Last night. First time in ages. She stopped for one beer and then she left.'

The Rainbow's End only had a table licence but that had never bothered Mel.

'Was anyone with her?'

Maura shook her head again. The beads and the braids swung and clacked. 'I felt a bit mean actually.' She had a surprisingly classy voice, very deep and well modulated. 'She wanted to talk. But we were busy. We'd hired a student band and they'd brought all their friends. You know what it's like.'

Rosie didn't really. She didn't go there in the evening. She thought the people and the music a bit pretentious. She liked something you could dance to.

'How did she seem?'

'Not brilliant. A bit jumpy. Sort of desperate actually. I let her have the drink and told her to wait. Adam was on his break. I thought when he came back I'd take her out for a walk, calm her down a bit. But when I looked again she'd gone. She didn't even bother to say goodbye.'

When Rosie had finished the sandwich there didn't seem much point in staying and she couldn't think of anywhere else to look. She went home and snoozed on the sofa in front of a black and white movie. She didn't want to talk to her mother – she couldn't face the fuss of explanation – so she wrote her a note and at five o'clock she went round to Joe's. Joe's sister Grace let her in. She was a gawky thirteen-year-old with pointed elbows like the legs of a tree frog and a mouth full of metal brace. Grace yelled up the stairs. There was no answer. She shrugged.

'He's in. You'd better go up.'

Joe's room was in the attic. It had a sloping roof with a big velux window and even more crap on the floor than Rosie's. Divine Comedy was rolling away in the background.

'I was just going out,' he said, guilty because he'd been sleeping all day while Mel was missing.

'I've been everywhere I can think of.' She sat on the bed.

'Anything?'

'She went to the Rainbow's End after the Prom. Maura said she was a bit jumpy, but nothing new there . . . It was a student gig. Maybe she met someone . . .'

There was a pause.

'The police think she might have been kidnapped.' He couldn't keep a shiver of excitement from his voice. He was still worried but kidnapping was something out of the movies, glamorous even.

Rosie frowned. 'The Gillespies went to the police?'

'Eleanor did. I think she cracked. Richard didn't sound very happy. I phoned just now and I could hear him in the background. He says everyone's overreacting.'

So do I, Rosie thought. I think she picked up a bloke at the Rainbow's End out of boredom or desperation or devilment. She's hiding out in a hall of residence or a grotty bedsit, waiting for the maximum fuss before making her appearance. Rosie wouldn't have told Joe but it wouldn't be the first time Mel had gone home with someone she'd met on one of her walkabouts.

'Why do they think she was kidnapped?'

'Apparently it's not much more than a theory. Eleanor and Richard are high-profile parents. And there was a case a couple of months ago. The kidnappers got away with a half a million. Since then there has been a spate of copycat attempts. Mostly amateurs, the police say. Mostly easy to deal with.' He paused and sat beside her on the bed. His feet were bare. She could see every bone and joint under the skin. 'Do you remember Frank saying someone was in the Prom looking for her? An older bloke.'

'Yes. Do the police think he might have been the kidnapper?'

'I told Eleanor anyway. It's up to them. She thought they might want to talk to us sometime.'

'Me too?'

'Why not? You know her as well as anyone. You're best mates.'

Suddenly she felt sick with guilt. She remembered the good times. The girlie sleepovers with bottles of wine and soppy videos, the gossip about lads, mega shopping sessions in the city. She imagined Mel being held somewhere and what they might be doing to her. And she'd been thinking it was all some attention-seeking stunt.

'Let's go and look,' she said. 'Just in case. I can't sit here doing nothing.'

They spent the evening in the city, tramping through all the pubs, even those Mel had never set foot in so far as they knew. They asked in the arcade and the pizza places and the roller-skating rink. No one had seen her. They ended up with Maura in the Rainbow's End, shouting their questions over a flamenco guitar. Had there been an older guy in the night before? Anyone taking a special interest in Mel? Maura tried to answer their questions but in the end she got fed up with them and sent them home.

Joe walked Rosie all the way to her door. On the step he held on to her in a desperate bear hug. She pushed him away in the end, feeling confused and guilty. As guilty as if she'd played some part in Mel's disappearance.

Chapter Twenty

Hannah had been expecting Arthur to be waiting for her at the prison but she went through the gate to the library without seeing him. It was halfway through the morning when he bounced in.

'Can you spare a minute?'

She turned to Marty. 'Are you OK on your own? Dave's in the office.'

Marty rolled his eyes towards the ceiling. 'Is that supposed to be reassuring?'

'Well . . .'

'Go on. I'll be fine.'

They sat in Arthur's office drinking coffee. He was a different man: the super-cool Scouser had gone; he was bubbling, the words falling over themselves. She regretted her impulse of the night before to involve him. She could tell there would be no stopping him now.

'I've been to the Central Library, tracked down the back copies of the local rag. It's great that they've still got them.'

'Aren't they all on microfilm?' She wanted to slow him down, rein back some of the enthusiasm. Stop, she wanted to say. You don't know what you're getting into.

'Mm?' The interruption only checked him for a moment. 'It's amazing what you can find in the births, marriages and deaths columns.'

'You haven't wasted any time.'

'I started with Maria's death. The notice said she died after "a brave struggle with illness". Cancer isn't mentioned but that's the implication.'

'That would fit in with Michael's memories.'

'Then I went back a few years and found the report of her marriage. A front-page spread. Obviously a big do. The wedding of the season. Crispin Randle seems to have been a member of the local gentry. He owned land not far from here. He was an MP. Tory of course. Master of the Hunt. You know the sort of bloke. He married Maria Grey in 1952. Two years later Theo's birth was announced. He was named Theo Michael, so I don't think there's any doubt we're on the right track.'

She nodded, felt irrationally pleased that she could continue to think of her ghost as Michael.

'I almost gave up the search then. I mean, I'd got enough for the police to be going on with. But I thought Randle was still a young man. What if he'd re-married . . .'

'And had he?' Just to show she was still listening.

'Yeah. Three years later. That wedding was a much quieter event. The bride was Stella Midwood, who'd been working as his secretary. A year later they had a daughter, Emily.'

The names and dates washed over her. She thought she'd have to write it all down like a family tree to make sense of it.

'Why didn't they have Michael to live with them?' she asked. 'Why board him out with the Brices?'

'Wait. There's more drama to come. In 1964 when Theo Michael was ten, there was a fire in the family home. It was big news. The place was burned to a shell and Emily, the little girl, Michael's stepsister, was killed. Crispin Randle sold the estate and some months later he resigned his seat in the Commons. Michael isn't mentioned in the account of the fire or the resignation.'

'Is that significant?'

'Dunno. Perhaps it was too painful for Crispin to have him around. Perhaps Michael reminded him of the death of his first wife and his daughter. Perhaps Crispin had some sort of breakdown and couldn't cope.'

'Michael was only ten!'

'Old enough to be shipped off to boarding school.'

'Why did he come to Cranford then? And why the change of identity?'

Arthur shrugged. 'Teenage rebellion? It's possible he didn't get on with his stepmother. Perhaps he resented the way his father dumped him.'

'Perhaps.' It's all guesswork, she thought. Really, despite Arthur's excitement we're not much further forward. 'Do we know where Stella and Crispin are living now?'

'There's no record. But the police will find out easily enough. We've done all the hard work for them.' He hesitated. 'Don't you have an early finish today?'

'Why?' She knew he wanted something from her. Living with Rosie had given her a sixth sense about people bumming favours.

'What about going to Cranford? This afternoon. We

can give all this information to Porteous in person. That'll stop him hassling you.'

Who are you kidding? she thought. That's not what this is about. This is about you showing off to the police. You want the glory. You want to sit there and gloat.

'We could stay the night. I could meet your friends. We could be back in time for work tomorrow.'

'Go on then.' She couldn't think of an argument against it and, as Rosie knew, she'd always been an easy touch.

She phoned Porteous from the library. Dave had sloped off and Marty pretended not to listen.

'Mrs Morton,' Porteous said. 'I was hoping to speak to you. More questions I'm afraid. Something's come up.'

'I can't talk now. I'm at work.' She couldn't face an interview over the phone. She wanted Arthur there.

He said he was tied up all day and that he'd come to The Old Rectory in the evening. She sensed he was preoccupied and wondered if there'd been a development in the case. Perhaps he'd discovered Michael's background without Arthur's help.

Later she phoned Sally and asked if she could put the two of them up for the night as paying guests.

'A double room?' Sally asked mischievously. 'The honeymoon suite?'

'Of course not!' Hannah thought her humour hadn't developed since they were children. She'd always been a tease about sex.

Arthur hadn't quite finished his class when she arrived at his room at lunchtime. Some form of role-play was going on. Hannah walked back down the corridor so she wouldn't be tempted to watch. She found that sort of exercise embarrassing enough without spectators, though she'd come to realize that Arthur liked play-acting and games.

He admitted as much in the car. He'd been asking about the people who'd been around at the time of Michael's death. She described Roger Spence, Sally and her disc-jockey boyfriend, Stephen and Sylvia Brice. By the time they arrived at The Old Rectory she had the feeling that he knew them as well as she did and probably understood them better.

'What's all this about, Arthur?' It was her librarian, who's-been-turning-down-the-page-corners voice. 'I really think we should leave it to the police.'

'Come on, girl. Don't spoil my fun.' She was about to say tartly that it wasn't fun for her when he added, 'I might leave it to them if I could be certain they'd get it right.' He paused. 'You must have met men inside who don't deserve to be there.'

'I've met men who *say* they don't.'

'Well, I don't want any cock-ups in this case.' He smiled but she wasn't reassured. He worked for the Home Office. He should have had more faith in the system.

It was just after two when they arrived. Hannah had expected Sally to be at work but she was there to meet them. Curiosity about Arthur, Hannah thought, and a nose for a story. Sally hustled them into the dining-room and organized a late lunch. Later, over coffee, Roger joined them too.

They talked about Michael Grey. It was Arthur's

doing, but perhaps the Spences were eager to talk about him anyway. Sally had her own agenda.

'I had the impression he'd come from the private system,' Roger said, 'but his Latin wasn't up to much. Hardly prep-school standard. Not what you'd expect.'

'Was he doing Latin A level?' Arthur gave the impression he was just being polite. Hannah knew better.

'No, but I dragooned him in to help with one of my first-year groups. In the end I let him go. He wasn't any use at all.'

'Perhaps he just wanted his free period back.'

'Perhaps. I don't think so. It's quite hard to fake genuine ignorance, isn't it?'

'How did you get to know him if you didn't teach him?'

'Through the school play. I coached him. Individual rehearsals.'

'Were you surprised when he disappeared?'

'Not very surprised. Not at first. He liked mysteries. I remember one session when I talked about him bringing his own experience into his acting. He said he was already doing that but he refused to discuss his past with me. I was more surprised when he never returned. I kept expecting him to turn up out of the blue to astound and amaze us.'

Arthur turned lazily to Sally. 'How well did you know him?'

'Only as Hannah's boyfriend. And I'm sorry, pet, but I didn't really take to him. He was a bit arty-farty for me. There was too much pretence.'

'Whereas you . . .' Roger interrupted, 'you had your own bit of rough.'

She laughed, not offended in the slightest. 'Quite right,' she said. 'And very nice it was too. You'll be able to meet him tonight, Arthur. Chris. My ex-bit-of-rough.'

She narrowed her eyes. Hannah thought Sally knew what he was up to. Perhaps journalists and psychologists had similar techniques when it came to ferreting out a story.

Sally continued, 'There's a wedding party in the annexe and Chris is doing the disco. He's still playing the same sort of gigs. I think it's a bit sad that he's never moved on.'

In the afternoon they left the car at the hotel and walked to the lake. There was a footpath through an old deciduous wood and then a strip of forestry-commission plantation. The footpath was overgrown and looked as if it must have been there in Hannah's time, but she couldn't remember having used it, and at the lakeside everything was so different that she found it hard to get her bearings. A group of teenagers in orange life-jackets stood where once Chris had bought her vodka. A woman was spelling out the rules of safety on the water, shouting to get their attention. Hannah thought that if they capsized they'd be able to walk back to the shore. The water level was even lower than she'd expected. The beach, which she'd remembered as a narrow strip of sand, had widened to an unsightly expanse of mud, rock and shingle. The trainee sailors had to push their dinghies to the water on trolleys, lifting them occasionally over the larger rocks. A new island had been formed at the north end of the lake.

She didn't know what Arthur hoped to gain by the walk. A sense of place perhaps. She'd told him about her first romantic encounter with Michael by the bonfire on the beach. But this scene, on a sunny afternoon, with the giggles and squawks of the school party coming to them over the water, had nothing in common with the night after the exams. She felt it was an anticlimax. She'd waited so long to come back and now it meant nothing. Arthur seemed dissatisfied by it too, because he sat for a moment in the sun then suggested that they return to The Old Rectory by the lane. On the walk back she started to fret about what Porteous would want from her and how she would explain her failure to pass on the information about Maria's grave. She said nothing to Arthur. How could she tell him she felt like a schoolgirl, waiting for one of Spooky Spence's beastly tests?

Outside the hotel a battered white transit was parked. One headlight seemed to be held on by gaffer tape. Chris was standing by the sliding door, shuffling a loudspeaker towards him so he could get his arms around it. Hannah didn't want to face him yet and touched Arthur's arm to stop him from approaching. Chris shifted the balance of the speaker so he was taking all the weight and walked slowly with it round the side of the building. His hair was a lot shorter and he was a bit thicker round the waist but he hadn't changed much. It could have been the same black T-shirt as the one he'd worn to the party after *Macbeth*.

'I don't suppose you recognize him,' Hannah said.

'No. Why should I?'

'He's been done for dealing. He might have ended

213

up in our place. If he did he never used the library. I wondered if you'd come across him.'

'No. Look, why don't we talk to him now? Once all the wedding guests turn up it'll be impossible.'

'I wouldn't know what to say.' Again she regretted starting all this. But Arthur was unstoppable.

'Just introduce us. Leave the rest to me.'

The party would take place in a room Hannah hadn't seen before, a large one-storey annexe built on to the back of the house in stone. It had a polished wood floor for dancing, a bar at one end and a scattering of small tables around the walls. It was quite different from the rest of the hotel – more up-market working men's club than country house – but she supposed that in the winter the dos held here would make up most of the Spences' income. Chris was setting up his equipment on a low stage. He was bending over so his T-shirt had ridden up his back. He heard their footsteps and turned round.

'Hannah Meek,' he said. 'Well, well, well. The police haven't locked you up yet then?'

She blushed. She'd always known Chris was hostile. He'd thought her stuck up and prudish. But she hadn't expected such an obvious display of rudeness.

'Why should they lock her up?' Arthur sounded interested, a bit amused.

'Who are you?'

'Arthur Lee. I work with Hannah.'

'Oh? Where's that then?' He pretended to stick wires into sockets but his heart wasn't in it.

'I'm a librarian. I work in Stavely Prison.' She threw that out as a kind of challenge but he didn't seem bothered.

'I never got there. Not a long enough sentence.'

'Perhaps another time.'

He laughed. 'Nah. I'm too old for that now. Didn't Sal tell you? I'm settled. Content. I've got a lady. She's expecting our kid.'

The kitchen door must have been open. Hannah could hear the clattering of pans. There were cooking smells.

'What were you like then?' Arthur asked.

'What do you mean?'

'When Michael Grey was murdered. You weren't so settled then.'

He accepted that as a compliment. 'We were all a bit wild I suppose.' He paused. 'Except Hannah. You never did wild, did you, H?'

'What about Michael? Was he wild too?'

'I never knew him that well.'

'You didn't know anything about him before he came to live here? You'd never met him before?'

'How would I? He went to some sort of posh school.'

'Did he tell you that?'

'Him or someone else. How should I know? Anyway, what's it to do with you?'

Arthur ignored that, continued with the questions, sharp and impersonal.

'What was he like? You were older than the others, more experienced. What did you make of him?'

'He wasn't the angel they all thought.' It came out grudgingly.

'One of your customers, was he?'

'No,' Hannah said. She glared at Arthur. 'He wouldn't.'

'Come on, Hannah,' Chris was fighting back. 'You

know as well as anyone that Michael Grey was hardly the perfect gentleman. Don't you?'

She didn't answer. She wanted to drag Arthur away, to drive immediately back to the coast, but knew there was no way he'd give up now. She'd have to stick it out.

'Have the police been to see you yet?' Arthur asked.

'Of course they've been to see me. Anyone farts in this town, they knock on my door.'

'What did they want?'

'They wanted me to tell them about the party at the caravan site. The last time any of us saw Michael Grey alive. The party after the play. You remember the one, Hannah.'

'Did you tell them?' she asked.

'Of course I told them. I'm a law-abiding citizen now. What else could I do?'

He smiled. His teeth were brown and uneven. Then he turned back to the large, black speaker.

Chapter Twenty-One

Macbeth had gone well. Everyone involved in the production felt the buzz, lapped up the success. Even Hannah, who was on the edge of it. It was a manic time. Exams were only days away. People were up all night revising. You'd have thought it was the worst possible day for a party, but everyone had so much nervous energy and they felt like celebrating.

Hannah never knew whose idea it was to hire a room at the caravan site. Perhaps one of the cast was related to the manager. She thought it was something like that. She spent the afternoon at home getting ready. On her own. She'd asked Sal to come round. Sal was better than she was at clothes and make-up. But Sal hadn't had much to do with the play and anyway seemed to spend all her free time with Chris. Years later Hannah would be able to remember the clothes she was wearing that night. She wanted it to be special. After the exams everyone would move away. It would probably be the last time they'd be together.

She soaked for an hour in the bath, got dressed and looked at herself in the long mirror on the landing. She was wearing a long skirt with tiny green flowers printed on to a cream background. It had a drop waist and she'd made it herself. There was nowhere in

Cranford to buy clothes. It was the first time she'd worn it. A cream top with a gathered neck. A shawl which Sylvia Brice had crocheted for her birthday. Jesus sandals. And masses of black eye make-up. The last throes of flower power, which anyway had come late to the town.

Then, just as she was about to leave, her mother threw a wobbly. Hannah should have seen it coming. It had been building for days – resentful comments every time she went out, tearful self-pity when she returned.

Now Audrey blocked the front door, stood in front of it with her arms outstretched.

'Don't go.'

Hannah was panicking. 'I must. They're expecting me. It's to do with the play.'

She didn't say it was a party because Audrey would have played the guilt card – I never go out, you see your friends every day. That sort of thing. And Hannah had to go. During rehearsals she'd hardly seen Michael. He'd seemed to be slipping away from her.

Audrey crumpled. Her knees buckled and her back slid down the door until she was sitting on the floor. She began to sob. The tears gouged drains in her face powder. Hannah could see the tops of her tights and her knickers. Words came in muffled, snotty bursts.

'I'm so sorry. You mustn't mind me. I only want you to be happy.'

Hannah couldn't leave her like that, though more than anything she wanted to ignore the tears, step over the body and force her way out of the door. She took Audrey's arm and coaxed her to her feet, settled her on the sofa and made her tea. She switched on the television. Immediately Audrey became absorbed in one of her favourite programmes.

'I'll go now, Mum, shall I?'

Audrey turned, waved briefly and returned her attention to the set.

They'd hired a minibus to take party-goers to the lake. Courtesy again of some anxious parents. A disabled lad had gone missing a couple of years before and for a while there'd been a fuss about youngsters out on their own. Hannah was too late to catch it. She began to walk, sticking out her thumb for a lift every time a car went past. She'd never hitched on her own before but now she was too desperate to think of all the adult warnings. It was still light and the road was busier than she'd expected – mostly families on their way back to the site. They didn't seem to see her. Each time a car sailed past she stared after it with loathing. Her sandals were new and a strip of leather cut into her toes.

Then, when she was thinking she'd have to walk the whole way, someone stopped. A young bloke in a rusting estate car. He was chatty and in the few minutes it took to drive the rest of the way she found out he was visiting his girlfriend. She worked on reception in the site office and had been given a free caravan for the season. He was obviously smitten.

She heard the music as soon as she got out of the car.

'Some party, that,' he said, before driving off through the maze of caravans to find his love.

The party wasn't in the bar, but in a room next to it, which sometimes held bingo for the older visitors and talent competitions for the kids. In natural light it would be gloomy, but Chris had rigged up some coloured spots and someone had decorated it with balloons and streamers. It was full. The dancers jostled for space. The first person she saw was Mr Spence, who was dancing with the fifth former who'd played Hecate. Some of the cast had dressed up in their costumes and hers was black, floaty and long. Ribbons of frayed black cloth trailed from her cuffs. Mr Spence danced with his eyes half shut, his body twisting and swaying to the music. Hannah saw at once that Michael wasn't there.

She didn't ask any of her friends if Michael had been with them on the minibus. The music was so loud that her ears were already singing and the room was full of people she didn't know well. Boyfriends and girlfriends and stray hangers-on had gatecrashed. Sally was there, though her only contribution to the play had been to hand out programmes at one of the performances. She was beside Chris, dancing on her own. She already seemed drunk. Hannah didn't want to ask her about Michael. Chris would have made some sarcastic comment. He always did.

She went outside, walked down towards the lake where the noise of the music wasn't quite so loud. She told herself that Michael might have gone for a walk on the shore, that he might be waiting for her there. The sky was a crazy mix of colours. Violet streaked in the west with gold and grey. Soon it would be completely dark but now it was light enough for birds still to be singing and she could make out the paler strip of sand and the reflection of the last light on the water.

They were lying on the spiky grass between the road and the lake. Jenny Graves, otherwise known as

Lady Macbeth, was sprawled naked on the grass with Michael Grey, otherwise known as Theo Randle. The picture had the quality of a photographic negative. The background was grey, their bodies milky. Michael's hair was startling white, her black braid lost in the shadow. It wasn't a shock. She'd looked out for Jenny in the dancing crowd too and registered that she wasn't there. Hadn't even expected her to be. Throughout the rehearsals she'd watched Michael and Jenny, his charm, her flirting. But Hannah hadn't felt able to demand an explanation, because then he'd have told her, not using the exact words of course, that he wanted her as a friend and an audience, not a lover. That is was Jenny Graves he'd write his poems for. Hannah stood for a moment staring, fascinated despite herself by the entwined limbs, the panting, the moans, thinking in a dispassionate way – So that's what happens, that's what it's all about.

Then she turned and ran. They must have heard her footsteps on the shingle but she didn't care. She hoped Michael did hear, that the encounter would be spoiled for him. It serves him right, she thought. Over and over again, spiteful and childish, a schoolyard chant. She stumbled back towards the music, not because she could face going back to the party, but because it was the only way home. A figure was standing outside the building. He leaned against the wall rolling what she realized later was probably a joint. It was Chris. There was an outside light fixed to the bar and she was caught in the glare of it. He saw her tears. He gave a mocking smile and beckoned her towards him. She turned away and hurried down the lane. She didn't try to get a lift. By then it was pitch black and she had more sense. And she didn't want anyone to see her crying.

She was home earlier than her mother had expected. Audrey was still watching television, though she'd moved from the sofa to her usual upright chair and there was a plate with some crumbs on the coffee table. The earlier panic was forgotten. She was touchingly pleased to see Hannah, who sat on the floor beside her to watch the end of the programme. She found herself making allowances for her mother's behaviour now, as she would with someone who was very old or very sick. Audrey seemed not to notice that Hannah was upset until they went upstairs together, then she asked suddenly, 'Are you all right, my dear?'

'Of course.' Audrey would be the last person she'd talk to about her troubles. What could parents know?

'You should leave this place,' Audrey said sharply. 'As soon as your exams are over. I stayed far too long.'

'Oh yes,' Hannah said. 'I will.' She spoke as if it had been her plan all along but it had never crossed her mind before that evening.

'Good.' She shut the bedroom door firmly behind her, but Hannah still heard her repeat the word to herself. 'Good.'

The next morning Michael phoned. It was Sunday and her mother was still in bed. Hannah hadn't been able to sleep. She knew it would be him before she picked up the receiver but she couldn't let it go unanswered.

'Hannah, I have to see you.'

'No.'

'You don't understand. I'm scared.' He did sound

terrified, as if he'd just woken from a nightmare. But she told herself he was a good actor. 'No one else will believe me.'

She didn't say anything.

'There are things you should know. We should talk.'

'Talk to Jenny.' She knew it was petty but she couldn't help it.

'This isn't anything to do with Jenny.'

'And it isn't anything to do with me.'

If Chris hadn't seen her running away from the beach she'd probably have agreed to meet Michael. She wanted to see him. But Chris had seen her and she could tell from the way he'd grinned that he knew about Michael and Jenny. He'd have told Sally. Hannah was proud. She couldn't bear to be seen scuttling back to Michael after she'd been so publicly betrayed. She wanted to help him but knew it was impossible.

'I'm sorry,' she said, as firmly as her mother had said the word 'good' the night before.

She was replacing the receiver when she heard him say goodbye.

That was the story she told Arthur as they sat on the terrace waiting for Porteous to arrive at The Old Rectory. It was quiet. The newly-weds and their friends hadn't yet arrived. It was the story they agreed she would have to tell the detectives.

Porteous was late and when he did arrive he was looking crumpled and breathless. She was thrown because he was on his own. She felt she should ask after Stout. It was as if a husband had turned up at a dinner party without his wife.

'Oh,' Porteous said. 'We're very busy . . .' She had the impression that he'd been rushing around all day.

'You don't mind if my friend joins us. He's responsible for most of the information.'

'No,' Porteous said. 'Of course.' Though he seemed surprised. Perhaps he thought she wasn't the sort to have friends.

They sat in the lounge where he had interviewed her on the evening of the school reunion.

'I remembered something. Michael once mentioned the cemetery on the coast . . .'

Porteous's head shot up. He'd been taking notes. It seemed an overreaction.

'Which cemetery, Mrs Morton?' The voice as bland and polite as always.

'Near the lighthouse. Do you know it?'

'I've heard of it certainly.'

'I looked at the graves, narrowed down the possibilities. I think I've found Michael's mother. She was called Maria Randle. If we're right, Michael's first name was Theo.'

Arthur took him through the dates and the family history. Eagerly. A magician pulling each new bit of information from his hat. 'Theo's father, Crispin, remarried his secretary Stella. They had a daughter. She died in a fire in the family home. Since then there's been no mention of the boy.'

Porteous wrote meticulous notes, but Arthur seemed upset by his lack of reaction. He must have been expecting gratitude, to be welcomed with open arms into the investigation.

'You don't seem surprised,' he said. 'Had you worked all that out for yourself then?'

'No, Mr Lee, you've been very helpful.' Still polite but dismissive. Porteous turned his attention back to Hannah. 'When did you say you were at the cemetery?'

'Yesterday evening.' She added in a rush, 'I did try to phone you then.'

'Did you?'

'There's something else. I've remembered the party after the school play.'

'Ah,' Porteous said. 'Michael and the young Lady Macbeth. Yes. Mr Johnson told us about that.'

'Yes. And the next morning Michael phoned me. He sounded anxious, scared even.'

'Tell me, Mrs Morton, why are you telling me this now? It's not something you'd have forgotten. Seeing your boyfriend with another girl. Not when you remembered other details so clearly.'

She was saved from the need to answer because her mobile phone rang. It was Rosie.

'Mum. Something terrible's happened.'

She was almost screaming and Arthur and Porteous couldn't help overhearing. They both stared out of the window but Hannah could tell they were listening.

'What is it?' Her first thought was Jonathan. A car accident. He drove like a maniac.

Rosie was panting, trying to steady her voice so she could speak.

'It's Mel,' Rosie said. 'She's dead. Someone found her body today on one of the footpaths by the cemetery. She was stabbed.'

Hannah's first thought was, Thank God it's not

Rosie. Then she pictured her daughter frightened and alone in the house.

'We're coming,' she said. 'Leaving straight away.'

She clicked off the phone and stood up. Porteous was already on his feet, blocking the door. 'Do you know Melanie Gillespie, Mrs Morton?'

'Not well. She was my daughter's best friend.'

'Why?' Arthur asked.

Porteous looked down at him as if he were considering whether or not to answer. 'I'm running the investigation into her murder.'

'A bit far from your patch, isn't it?'

Hannah knew what Arthur was up to. Being deliberately provocative in the hope of prising more information from the detective.

Porteous hesitated then chose his words carefully. 'We have reason to believe that the deaths of Michael Grey and Melanie Gillespie are connected. Go back to your daughter, Mrs Morton. Of course she's upset. I'll be in touch shortly when I've checked the information you've given me.' He paused. 'You've nothing more to tell me now? About your visit to the cemetery?'

'No!' She understood for the first time how Audrey had felt, when she'd crumpled in a heap on the floor.

'There will be more questions. Of course you understand that.' He turned and let himself out.

PART THREE

Chapter Twenty-Two

Peter Porteous stood in front of them looking more than ever like a teacher at a second-rate college for further education. He'd set up a flip chart and there was an overhead projector to show slides of the victims and crime scenes.

'If Carver hadn't done the Gillespie post-mortem we'd probably never have made the link,' he said. 'But the Michael Grey inquiry was still fresh in his mind. He's convinced the same knife was used in both murders. If not the same, so similar that it's still significant. Not an ordinary kitchen knife. A dagger. Short bladed but wide. Very sharp.'

He flicked through half a dozen slides – grey flesh, Carver's hands holding steel instruments, wounds which looked now very tidy and clean – then he paused. It was hot again. He'd taken off his jacket, loosened his tie just a touch.

'So, let's look at the victims.' He turned a page of the flip chart. Stuck to the next page was the old photograph of Michael Grey playing Macbeth. Porteous stretched and wrote in felt-tip at the top: Theo Randle. He had no problem accepting the new name of the boy. He had more important things to worry about. He flipped the page again and scrawled a rudimentary family tree. The felt-tip squealed on rough paper.

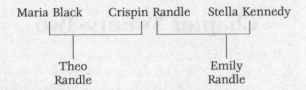

'Maria died when Theo was very young. Crispin remarried and had a second child, Emily. She was killed in a house fire when she was still a baby. Two tragedies. Perhaps that explains the family breakdown and the fostering.'

A young DC at the back stuck up a hand.

'Yes?'

'How did we get a positive ID on the boy in the end, sir?'

Porteous thought the man already knew the answer and intended to rub salt into the wounds. He was a cocky little sod. And it did come hard to admit that an enthusiastic amateur had got there before him. But he kept his voice friendly.

'With the help of a member of the public. A psychologist who works for the Home Office. He had information we didn't have access to, but I'll come to that later.

'Let's turn now to what we know about Theo Randle. Quite a lot, considering how much time has elapsed. He was bright, well educated, personable. He seems to have come from a wealthy family. Just before he died he had a row with his girlfriend because she caught him making love to someone else. He was a talented actor and was starring in a production of *Macbeth* in the week before he disappeared. One of his props was a dagger. According to witnesses it was very sharp. I'd like to trace it. The school is doing its best but I don't hold out much hope . . . He was lodging with a couple called Sylvia and Stephen Brice. Everyone says they were very fond of him. There was no question of ill treatment or abuse and I think we can rule them out. They're dead now, but perhaps we can trace friends who knew Theo, knew how he came to be living there. None of this might be relevant, but I want to know.'

He turned to the next page on the chart. This was covered with a montage of photographs of Melanie Gillespie. Before she'd dyed her hair red she'd been blonde. In the centre there was a picture of her, blown up. She was half turned, caught unexpectedly. She had a wide mouth, high cheekbones and she was super-model thin.

'Despite the gap in time these two have a lot in common. Not just their age. The Gillespies are wealthy. They're both prominent business people, often in the news. Theo's dad was an MP. Melanie was bright and articulate. Her teachers say she could be moody but she was often charming. She wasn't into art and acting like Theo, but she was a skilled musician. So they had similar backgrounds. Now, let's look at the differences. Most obvious, of course, is gender . . .'

The cocky DC raised a hand, languidly, as if it were hardly worth the effort. 'Is that important?'

Porteous wanted to yell: Don't be fatuous. *Everything's* important. Two young people have been killed.

231

'We don't know at this stage. There was no indication of sexual assault on Melanie Gillespie, according to Carver.'

He turned his back on the audience as he regained control, wrote DIFFERENCES on the flip chart, added GENDER, then AGE with a question mark. 'Theo was a year older than Melanie, though as they were both in their A-level year, that hardly seems important.'

'Could we be looking for a teacher?' Claire Wright asked.

'Possible, isn't it? I'd be very interested to know if anyone who taught Theo at Cranford Grammar went on to work at Melanie's school. Can you take responsibility for checking that out?'

She nodded.

'Then there are the temperaments,' he went on. 'Not so easy to pin down, but we seem to have a difference here. Theo is described as organized and conscientious but he doesn't seem to have been overstressed by exams. He still felt able to take part in the school play. One witness says he told stories, you couldn't believe what he said, but she was his girlfriend and he betrayed her. I'm not sure we can rely on her objectivity. There was no record of any emotional problems, nothing more than you'd expect in any adolescent. On the other hand Melanie was moody, given to bouts of anger and depression. For the past two years she'd been seeing a psychiatrist for an eating disorder.'

Porteous looked out at his team. Some were scribbling notes. He thought that soon they'd have no need for that. Soon they'd know these teenagers as well as they knew their own families.

'So,' he said. 'Two victims. The big question is – Are there any more? Would a killer keep a knife for nearly thirty years, resisting the temptation to use it, then murder again, out of the blue? We need to check the old files and make sure this isn't a part of a wider pattern. Pull up all the post-mortem reports for stabbings when the victim was a teenager. I don't want the search restricted to the local area – I'm sure we'd have picked that up. But the killer might have been working away.'

He stopped again, abruptly, and seemed lost in thought for a moment. A fan on one of the desks in a corner hummed. Someone coughed uncertainly. His audience didn't know him well enough to tell whether or not he'd finished the briefing. He let them sit in an awkward silence for a few minutes longer before continuing slowly.

'So that's one theory. We've got an undetected serial killer. We'll find other crimes that fit the pattern – teenage murders and that particular knife. At least it's something we can check. Carver's happy to work with us on it.' More than happy, Porteous thought. The pathologist had almost begged to be involved. He'd seen the chance for fame, mentions in influential journals and the opportunity to star as an expert witness in an important court case.

'The other theory is that the second murder came about as a result, somehow, of the discovery of Theo Randle's body, that there was a causal link between the incidents. If that's the case it won't be an obvious connection. Melanie hadn't been born at the time of Theo's death.'

'Couldn't we be talking a random nutter?' The

contribution came from Charlie Luke, who'd been sitting in the front row, his brow furrowed with concentration throughout the presentation. He had the build and squashed features of a boxer. Approaching middle-age he was still a constable and would remain one. No one was quite sure how he'd slipped through the assessment process to get into the service. Claire dismissed him as having the IQ of a gnat, but Porteous didn't care and rather liked him. He was dogged and did what he was told. He didn't let the job get under his skin. Beer and sport would always be more important.

'Nothing's ever completely random, is it, Luke? The killer must have met these young people somewhere. Their paths crossed even if he only came across them opportunistically, if he had no other motive than the thrill of killing. It should be possible to learn something about the pattern of his life from theirs.'

Luke seemed bewildered by the concept but he nodded enthusiastically.

'Of course,' Porteous went on, 'we've already discovered one connection between Theo Randle and Melanie Gillespie . . .' He turned towards Stout who was already rising to his feet. 'Eddie, perhaps you'd like to tell us that part of the story.'

'Hannah Morton,' Stout said. 'Maiden name Hannah Meek. She works as a librarian in Stavely nick. She's recently separated from Jonathan, who's deputy head of a high school on the coast, the high school where Melanie Gillespie was a student. There's one daughter, Rosalind, aged eighteen, still living at home and waiting to go to university. On the surface you couldn't find anyone more respectable than Mrs Morton. Anyone less likely to commit murder. But she did know both victims.

'We were already interested in Mrs Morton before the Gillespie murder. She was Theo's girlfriend, the love, she thought, of his life. She caught him . . .' Stout hesitated, seemed to be searching for an appropriate euphemism.

'Shagging?' Luke suggested helpfully.

'Quite.' Still Stout couldn't bring himself to say the word: ' . . . the young actress who played Lady Macbeth. *They* were together by Cranford Water after an end-of-performance party. That's the last record we have of the boy alive. Mrs Morton claims he phoned her the following day but after all this time it's impossible to check.'

Stout paused. 'She has a surprisingly clear recollection of all the details. That, in itself, raises suspicion. She didn't tell us about Theo two-timing her until she knew we'd find out anyway. She was stage manager for the school play so she'd have access to the dagger which could well have been the murder weapon. She had motive and opportunity. There's no one else in the frame.' He rocked back on his heels. 'But I don't see it. I don't see her as the sort of person who'd stab the boy she was in love with, tie an anchor round his body and hoy him in the lake. I certainly don't see her living with herself for thirty years afterwards—'

'Unless she'd repressed the memory,' Luke interrupted. He looked round as if he expected congratulation from his colleagues for the contribution. When none came he added defensively, 'Well, it happens. I saw this programme on the telly . . . And when the boy's body was dredged up from the lake

235

perhaps it all came back.' He looked at Porteous for help.

'You'd have to ask a psychiatrist,' Porteous said. 'Not my field.' Recognizing the irony of the words as he spoke.

'Unless she repressed the memory,' Stout said impatiently. 'But then why kill Melanie Gillespie? She had a motive for killing Randle, but none at all for murdering the girl. Melanie couldn't have been a witness to the first murder. She couldn't be any threat.'

'How did Mrs Morton know Melanie?' Claire Wright asked.

'Melanie and Rosalind Morton were best friends. They went to the same school. Hannah met Melanie when Rosalind had friends to the house.'

'Quite a tenuous connection then.'

Porteous, who'd been leaning against a table at the front of the room, stood up to answer.

'Quite tenuous,' he said. 'And as Eddie's said, Hannah Morton has no motive for the Gillespie murder. She does, however, have opportunity.'

He picked up the remote control and another slide was projected. It showed a narrow footpath with a stone wall on one side and a hawthorn hedge on the other. The footpath was crossed with blue and white tape. 'Melanie's body was found wrapped in black plastic at the bottom of the hedge.'

He clicked the remote and there was a shot of a lay-by on a main road, the entrance to the footpath. 'Melanie wasn't killed where she was found. The murderer must have parked here and carried the body the fifty yards or so to where it was dumped.

We've already said she was anorexic so she wasn't heavy. But not a pleasant job. It would have taken nerve.'

Another click and the footpath was seen from a different angle, so it was possible to see over the stone wall to a row of headstones.

'Hannah Morton admits to having been in the cemetery the evening before the girl's body was discovered. She claims to have remembered suddenly that Randle had told her where his mother was buried. She found the grave and that's the information Arthur Lee, the Home Office psychologist, used to dig out the boy's identity. If she's telling the truth, then it's some coincidence.'

The screen went blank. 'All the same,' Porteous said, 'I don't think we should become too fixed on the Morton connection. Not yet. Certainly there are other avenues to explore. I haven't spoken to the Gillespies today. The doctor said they needed time. But before Melanie's body was found they gave important information to the team looking into her disappearance. The case was taken seriously from the beginning because it was thought to be a kidnap. Melanie left home some time after ten, and went to a pub, the Promenade. When none of her friends were there she went to a café on the sea front called the Rainbow's End. We need to trace everyone who was in either establishment that night. It was the last time she was seen alive, though Carver thinks it more likely she was killed the next day.'

He paused for long enough for them to catch up with their notes. 'There's someone else we need to get hold of too. A middle-aged man went into the Promenade looking for Melanie the week before she disappeared. Who was he?'

He let the question hang. Luke's mobile rang. Embarrassed he fished in his pocket and switched it off.

Ignoring the interruption Porteous went on, 'This afternoon I'm going to see Stella Randle, Theo's stepmother, his only surviving relative. Perhaps something will come of that. Some other connection to make more sense of both cases.'

Eddie Stout listened and he thought that his boss had no soul. A fish on a slab had more emotion. Porteous spoke about connections and links as if he were forming a mathematical theory. Not as if a young girl had been stabbed to death. He thought of his Ruthie, excited and dressed up to go out, and said suddenly, trying to shock Porteous, 'Wouldn't there have been a lot of blood? A stabbing like that.'

'Certainly.'

'Not an easy thing to hide then. There'd have been stained clothes, marks on a floor, walls. Someone would have seen. Shouldn't we put out the usual plea through the press? Wives and girlfriends who noticed anything odd . . .'

'Of course, Eddie. It's already in hand.'

Porteous stayed behind when they all filed out, collecting his papers into an ordered file. On the way to the door he stopped and glanced behind him. Melanie Gillespie, half turned in the photo, her mouth wide in a grin of recognition, seemed to be looking at him. He had an image of her alone and in pain, heard the screaming. He turned his back on the photo, deliberately distancing himself from the smile. That way lay madness.

Chapter Twenty-Three

Crispin Randle, father of Theo, former Tory MP, had died. Porteous thought, with some satisfaction, that the fat psychologist hanging round with Hannah Morton had missed that bit of information. *He'd* dug it out from the registrar. Crispin had died five years before from liver failure. The doctors Porteous tracked down suggested that alcohol consumption had been a major contributing factor.

Stella Randle, the widow, was living in Millhaven, in a flat close to the sea front, not very far down the coast from the cemetery where Melanie Gillespie's body had been found. Porteous had made the appointment to visit by phone and she had been strangely uninterested, rather vague, so he turned up not even sure that she'd be in. The flat was in a crescent built around a communal garden. It had always been a poor Victorian imitation of Georgian grandeur but now it looked shabby and down at heel. A locked wrought-iron gate prevented him from parking right outside so he left his car on the promenade and walked. The grass in the garden was long, the borders overgrown.

Stella Randle opened the door to him herself. She had a faded charm, which matched the building. When he introduced himself she seemed not to recollect that they'd spoken earlier in the day and throughout the interview he was unsure whether her vagueness was genuine or an attempt to deceive. She was in her mid-fifties, dressed in what seemed to Porteous to be a parody of the character she was playing. She wore a pleated skirt, a little cashmere cardigan and even a string of pearls. In her youth she would have been pretty, a little foolish but aware of her limitations. Now she still tried to be girlish.

'Come in. An inspector. What fun! You will stop for tea?'

There was a wide hall, then a huge high-ceilinged room with a bay window looking out to sea. He had been expecting clutter, furniture from a big house crammed into a flat, but the room was surprisingly empty. There was one sofa – well made but modern – and a couple of coffee tables. On one lay a library book, a romantic novel, face down. The floor had been stripped and varnished and in front of the marble fireplace there was a Moroccan rug of a startling indigo blue.

She must have sensed his surprise.

'Crispin drank everything away,' she said. 'If he hadn't died when he did the flat would have gone too.' She looked round the room, saw it perhaps through his eyes. 'Why don't we go into the kitchen? We'll be more comfortable there.'

The kitchen was shabby too but less austere. There were herbs in pots on the window-sill, a bunch of flowers and a brightly coloured oilskin cloth on the table. A portable television stood on one of the counters. A plate and a cup were draining next to the sink.

'Tea then,' she said and set a kettle on the gas

ring. Still she hadn't asked Porteous what he was doing there.

'I'm afraid I may have some bad news,' he said.

'Oh?' She seemed untroubled. Perhaps years of living with an alcoholic had inured her to the possibility of bad news.

'It's your stepson Theo.'

'Theo?' It was as if she barely recognized the name. She seemed to trawl back through her memory before it made sense.

'Have you seen him recently?'

'No, no. Not for years.'

'Had your husband kept in touch with him?'

'My husband was very ill, Inspector. Long before he died.'

It was hardly an answer but he let it go.

The kettle gave a piercing whistle. She seemed grateful for the distraction. Her attention was taken up then with warming the pot and making the tea. Porteous set the photograph of Theo as Macbeth on the table. 'Is that him?'

'Oh goodness, after all this time, really I couldn't say.' She'd only glanced at the picture, was more intent on looking in the cupboard for matching cups among a jumble-sale assortment.

'Please look at the photo carefully, Mrs Randle.'

'I haven't seen him since he was a young boy.'

'All the same.'

He spoke firmly and her resistance went. She sat at the table, took a pair of reading glasses from the pocket of her skirt and studied the photograph.

'It could be him,' she said at last. 'That hair. Yes, I rather think it is.'

'Do you have any photos of him as a young boy?'

He could tell she was about to say no without thinking about it, then she caught his eye and changed her mind.

'There was one. He was pageboy at our wedding. Even Crispin didn't have the heart to get rid of those. Not that they were worth anything . . .' She jumped to her feet. He thought she was about to fetch the album, but she poured out the tea and arranged chocolate biscuits on a plate.

'If I could look at it . . .' he prompted.

'Yes.' The forced gaiety disappeared quite suddenly. 'I don't see why not.' She left the kitchen, shutting the door behind her. When she returned some time later her eyes were red. He wondered what had made her cry. He hadn't told her yet that Theo was dead. She hadn't asked.

She had certainly been happy when she married. She beamed from every shot. The photos were in a red leather album, separated by flimsy sheets of tissue paper. They had been taken in a garden. She hadn't worn a traditional wedding dress but a short white frock with a lacy white coat over the top. She must have been in her early twenties but had the enthusiastic grin of a school girl. She held a posy of garden flowers and there was a circlet of ox-eye daisies in her hair. Randle stood beside her, proud, rather paternal. His face looked a little flushed and Porteous thought he might have been drinking heavily even then.

'They were taken at Snowberry,' she said. 'That was Crispin's house. It had been in the family for years. It was foolish of course but I thought I'd grow old there. I imagined it full of grandchildren at Christmas. I was very young. Perhaps I fell in love with Snowberry as much as I did with Crispin.' She gave a sad little laugh. Her hands had stopped turning the pages of the album.

'You said there was a photo of Theo,' Porteous prompted gently.

'Theo. I did try very hard with Theo. I'd hoped he might dress up for the wedding. I can't remember now what plans I had . . .' She stopped, lost in thought. It seemed to be very important to her to remember what she had wanted the boy to wear. She looked up smiling triumphantly. 'A sailor suit,' she said. 'I think that was it. I'd seen a picture in a magazine . . . I didn't have bridesmaids. It wasn't a big affair. Crispin didn't want the fuss. He'd done all that the first time round. Anyway Theo wasn't having any of it. I don't think he resented my taking his mother's place. I don't think it was anything like that. Crispin said not at least, and we always seemed to be good pals. Perhaps it was his age. At the last minute anyway, he refused to wear the costume I'd chosen for him. Had an almighty tantrum.' She smiled and it seemed to Porteous that she remembered the boy with genuine fondness. 'Crispin was furious. I said it didn't matter. Why should it? So Theo came to the wedding in his school clothes. Short grey trousers and a cherry-red tie. Very festive and perfectly appropriate. He was very sweet actually. He came up to me later and said he was sorry for making a fuss. I said I supposed the sailor suit *was* a bit sissy and he gave me a kiss. First time ever.'

'Where was Theo at school?' Porteous asked.

'A place called Linden House. A little prep school. He went as a day boy. Crispin had been sent away as a boarder as a very young child and he didn't want that for Theo. Not then.' There was no hesitation. As she talked, the details of her life at Snowberry seemed to become sharper. She had more confidence in her memory.

'The photograph . . .' Porteous prompted her again.

She turned a page and there it was. A boy of about seven or eight standing on his own, looking into the camera, apparently enjoying the attention and the chance to show off. Instead of a traditional buttonhole he had a daisy pinned to the lapel of his blazer. There was a scab on one of his knees and his socks needed pulling up. He looked as if he'd been eating chocolate sauce.

'I did want a photo of him,' Stella said, 'but I knew he wouldn't stand being cleaned up first.'

Porteous was looking at the face, at the shock of white hair, the long straight nose. It would take an expert to check both pictures to confirm the identification but he was prepared to bet a year's salary that Theo Randle had turned into Michael Grey.

'I'm afraid,' he said, 'that Theo's dead.'

She had been staring at the photograph, apparently lost in memory, and he had to repeat the words to be sure she'd heard. Then she gave a little moan. 'Oh no,' she said. 'Not him too.'

'We believe he died a long time ago,' Porteous said. 'When he was only eighteen.'

'How?' Her eyes were bright, feverish. The question demanded an immediate and an honest answer.

'He was stabbed.'

She seemed almost relieved by the words. 'Quick then?'

'Oh yes. He wouldn't have felt any pain.'

'That's good.' She got up from the table and poured more hot water into the teapot. Then she stood at the sink with her hands over her eyes as if she wanted to pretend Porteous wasn't there.

'Mrs Randle,' he said gently.

She lowered her hands and asked fiercely, 'Did Crispin know about this?'

'I don't see how he could have done.' Unless, Porteous thought, he was responsible. 'The body was only discovered last week.'

'Crispin didn't tell me everything,' she said. 'He kept things from me. He didn't want me upset. He said it was for my own good. But I never knew what was going on. It's very confusing, Inspector, to be kept in the dark. Sometimes I thought I was going mad.'

'Would you like me to phone someone to be with you? A relative perhaps?'

She shook her head.

'I will have to ask questions,' Porteous said. 'About Theo and your husband. Would you like me to come back another time to do that? Perhaps now I should call your doctor. You've had a great shock.' He wasn't sure he should leave her on her own.

'No.' Her voice was sharp. 'No doctors.'

They sat for a moment in silence, looking at each other.

'Ask your questions, Inspector. It'll give me an excuse to talk about it. Talking helps. Isn't that what the doctors say? That's what they said after Emily died. It was a lie of course. Nothing helped. Except the pills. Crispin drank and I became a junkie. Not heroin. Nothing like that. Prescription medicine. All quite legal. Nothing for you to worry about. Professionally.'

'Are you still taking medication now?'

'No,' she said. 'I took myself off them when Crispin was very ill. I needed to feel angry. The pills stop you feeling very much at all.'

'That must have been hard.'

'The hardest thing ever. At least it stopped me blaming Crispin for his drinking. He'd been through more than me. First Maria. Then Emily. How could I expect him to give it up? When I knew what he was going through. It brought us together at the end.' She wiped her eyes with the back of her hand. 'I did love him, Inspector. People thought I was after him for the money and the house and there was some of that in it. How could you separate them? It was all a part of what he was. But I wasn't a gold-digger. I loved him. And Theo. I took them on as a package.' She looked at him across the table, gave him her young woman's smile. 'So, Inspector, why don't you ask your questions?'

'When did Theo stop living at home?'

'It was after the fire,' she said. 'After Emily died.'

'Would you mind telling me about that?'

She shook her head. 'I don't mind but it's very confused. You mustn't be cross if I get things wrong.'

'It's a long time ago.'

'No,' she said impatiently. 'It's not that. When Emily was born I was ill. Post-natal depression. I thought it would be easy. Like with Theo. I loved *him* without any bother. Why couldn't I do the same with my own child?'

'Not so easy building a relationship with a baby.' As if, Porteous thought, I'd know.

'But she was my own daughter. They wanted me

247

to go into hospital. I refused. I thought Snowberry was the only place I had any chance of getting well. You don't know what it's like, Inspector. Sometimes I'd wake up in the morning feeling better. For no great reason. The sun coming in through a gap in the curtains. The taste of toast for breakfast, though they brought me toast on a tray every morning. And I'd think – This is it. The start of the recovery. Sometimes the feeling would last for days. Crispin still had his seat in the House then and I'd send him off to London telling him I'd be fine and I didn't need him. Then the depression would return, as bad as ever. It was at the end of a really bad period of depression that we had the fire.'

'Was Crispin at home when it happened?'

'Yes. He came back that night. It was unusual to see him in the middle of the week. He'd been spending more and more time in London. He had a flat there of course. I think he probably had a mistress though I didn't ask. I couldn't blame him. I wasn't much of a wife.'

'Do you remember what happened on the night of the fire?'

'Not very well. As I said, it was all very confused.'

Porteous didn't push for details. There should be a fire investigator's report, a coroner's judgement. But Stella added quickly, 'I think it might have been my fault. I smoked then, heavily. We had a nanny for Emily. A nice girl. We hired her before the baby was born even. I thought we'd be friends. We were about the same age. I thought we'd be able to share Emily. In the end of course she looked after her pretty much single-handed. But that evening she asked for some time off. She bathed Emily and put her to bed and then she went out.'

'Do you remember the nanny's name?' Porteous asked.

'Lizzie. Lizzie Milburn. She came from Newcastle. Her parents were teachers and she was crazy about babies. Just as well.'

'You think your smoking might have started the fire?'

'No one said. I told you Crispin tried to protect me. But going back over the facts I think that's most likely. I went to look at Emily. Crispin came with me. There were no baby alarms in those days and I did feel responsible for her. Perhaps if I'd had the nerve to let Lizzie go, if I'd been forced to look after Emily myself things might have been different, but really I don't think so. I was very ill.' She paused. 'I'm sorry, I'm rambling. Crispin and I had dinner together. He'd come back from London in a foul mood. He'd always been ambitious and someone had said something to make him believe he didn't have a chance of promotion in the next reshuffle. He probably blamed me. I was hardly an ideal MP's wife. Certainly nothing like Maria, who was perfect apparently in every way. A saint is a hard act to follow. Crispin had a lot to drink over dinner. I had a couple of glasses with him. Not sensible considering the strength of the medication I was on. When we went up to the nursery we were both a bit unsteady. Crispin didn't stay long. He wanted to get back to the brandy. But I loved to watch her sleeping. That was the one time I could really believe I loved her . . .'

'You think you might have been careless with a cigarette?'

'I think it's possible. I'm sure Crispin blamed me. I wonder sometimes if he thought I did it on purpose. An act of madness. He thought I was crazy. Certainly he believed I was responsible for the fire one way or another. That's why he took Theo away. He said he couldn't trust me to look after him any more.'

Chapter Twenty-Four

'She says the boy never lived at home again after that,' Porteous said. 'I've seen the fire investigator and the coroner's reports. There was no real structural damage to the house. The fire started in the nursery and was contained there, but the girl was trapped in her cot and when the bedding and nightclothes caught, there was no hope for her.' There had been a photograph in the fire investigator's report of a small charred body pushed to one end of the cot as if she had been trying to escape the smoke and the heat, the arms raised in the pugilistic stance common in burn victims.

'I suppose it *was* an accident.' It was evening. Eddie Stout had come out to Porteous's home. It had never happened before. Porteous had reciprocated the Stouts' hospitality with a meal in a restaurant. He'd told them it was because he couldn't cook, but that wasn't true. He liked home and work kept apart.

He'd been home for an hour and had almost finished writing up the notes of his interview with Stella Randle, when his doorbell rang. He'd seen Stout's car from his window and had gone down, planning to keep him outside, thinking they could talk in the garden, even walk to the pub at the end of the lane if it was going to take a while. But Eddie had been so diffident and apologetic that a response like that was impossible. It called for something more friendly.

'Of course, you must come in. No, really, it's a pleasure. I was just going to have a beer. I'm sure you'll join me.'

And Porteous had found it helpful to describe again his conversation with Randle's widow. They were still standing, each with a glass, looking at the view down the valley. Stout continued without waiting for an answer to the original question.

'It couldn't have been an insurance scam turned tragic? Nothing like that?'

'No. The fire officer said it was consistent with a cigarette or match having been carelessly dropped, not an attempt at large-scale damage. It started in or near the nursery. If it had been deliberate they'd not have done that. I know the technology wasn't so precise then, but the officer was experienced and he was confident of his decision. When the fire really took hold the parents were at the other end of the house and hardly conscious – Crispin was drunk and Stella doped up to the eyeballs. Luckily the nanny came home earlier than expected or they might all have been killed.'

'Where did Randle take the boy?'

'Stella was very vague about that.' After her description of the fire and her daughter's death she'd hardly seemed to hear his questions. 'Perhaps to stay with relatives until Crispin could arrange a boarding place for him.'

'We've finally found out where he was at school then?'

'No. Crispin would never tell her where Theo was.

Not precisely. It was as if she'd relinquished all her rights over the boy. A way of punishing her for the death of his daughter. Theo came home occasionally for holidays, she said, but she was never allowed to be alone with him. As he got older he seems to have found better things to do. It can't have been much fun at Snowberry. Randle had resigned his seat in the Commons and was drinking. I presume Theo invited himself to friends' homes for the vacations. By all accounts he was a charmer. I don't suppose it was difficult. Or there may have been other relatives.'

'Where do the Brices fit in?'

'I don't know. Stella didn't recognize the name.'

'Not much further forward then.' Eddie didn't sound too disappointed by the lack of progress.

'Oh, I think so. We should be able to trace Theo's school with the information we've got now. Two schools probably if he was only ten when he went away. There must be someone who remembers him . . . I've been thinking that the reason for his leaving boarding school could have been financial. Crispin could have run through the family money very quickly. Perhaps he just couldn't afford the school fees.'

'Is this background relevant to the murder do you think?'

Is it? Porteous thought, and realized that he'd hardly considered the real business of the murder investigation all afternoon. He'd been wrapped up in the domestic tragedy. They'd all suffered – Crispin, Stella, Theo and Emily. When the wedding pictures were taken they must have seemed an ideal family. Porteous could imagine them posing for a similar photo to go with the constituency Christmas card. But the happiness had been shattered even before the fire.

'I can't imagine Stella Randle tracking down Theo and sticking a dagger through his ribs if that's what you mean. She wouldn't know where to start. And why would she?'

'Could she have blamed the boy for the little girl's death?'

'She might have been psychotic when she was very ill, and dreamed up something like that, but she didn't strike me as delusional today.'

'Perhaps it wasn't a delusion.'

'What do you mean?'

Eddie shrugged. 'Perhaps he did kill his sister. An unsupervised boy playing with matches could have the same result as a cigarette fire.'

'There was no mention of that at the time.'

'It would give another slant on Crispin keeping Theo away from his stepmother. Perhaps she was threatening to harm him even then. Much easier to blame the boy than take responsibility for her own negligence.'

'It's a possibility . . .'

'But you don't think it's likely.' Eddie finished his beer and grinned. 'It's OK. You don't have to humour me. I'm not a kid. I'm . . .' he paused. 'What's that technique they always use on the team-building courses? Brainstorming.'

'I'm not dismissing any ideas. It's just that Stella *did* take responsibility for Emily's death as soon as I asked her about it. And she'd almost forgotten about Theo. I don't think she'd have been able to do that if she'd killed him.'

'Did you ask her about the Gillespie girl?'

'Yes.'

On the way out. He'd stood on the doorstep looking across the garden to the wide sweep of the bay, with the lighthouse at one end and the mouth of the Tyne at the other, then turned back to her as if the question had just come to him: 'Does the name Melanie Gillespie mean anything to you?'

She'd stood with her arms clasped across her chest as if she were cold. A breeze was coming off the sea and her cardigan was thin, but Porteous still felt warm. Then she'd giggled. 'What's this, Inspector? A sort of quiz?' Then she'd gone into the flat shutting the door behind her without answering the question.

The sun was so low now that it shone up at them through the long window of the barn and they were dazzled. They turned away and sat down. Porteous offered Eddie another beer but he shook his head and for the first time Porteous saw how excited he was. It had been a struggle to contain himself in the conversation about Stella Randle.

'What is it, Eddie? What have you got for me?'

'I went to see Jack Westcott. You remember, he was the history teacher in the high school. Just retired.'

Porteous nodded.

'I turned up before opening time this morning. Caught him when he was completely sober. We went for a walk in the park. His wife's the house-proud sort. You could tell she was glad to have him out from under her feet. He was glad of the company, I think. He'll miss those kids.'

Porteous nodded again, thought Eddie would get to the point in his own time.

'I just wanted to get him talking. Claire Wright hasn't found any teacher who moved from Cranford to the school on the coast, but I thought there might be some informal connections – specialist music teachers, drama festival, sport. That sort of thing.'

'Anything?'

'Not that Theo was involved in. So I asked about the other kids in the school. It occurred to me that Melanie's mother and father would be about the same age as Theo if he'd lived. But Westcott couldn't remember a Richard Gillespie or an Eleanor of any description, so I could kiss goodbye to that theory.'

'Worth checking though. And it's possible that Richard Gillespie was at Theo's boarding school.'

'Aye. From what I've seen of him on TV he's got the air of a public-school boy about him . . . I'd pretty much given up hope of anything useful when Jack said he'd been digging around at home and he'd found some more photos of the *Macbeth* production. Would I like to see them? Most likely an excuse so he wouldn't have to face that dragon of a wife on his own, but I thought he might have a sharper photo of the boy we could give to the press, so I went along with him.'

Porteous was finding it difficult to give the story his full attention. He didn't mind Eddie Stout being here as much as he'd expected, but the evening sun was making him drowsy.

Eddie continued. 'You'd have thought he was a schoolboy himself, the way he spoke to his wife. He took me upstairs to a sort of den where he hides away from her. There were cardboard boxes full of snaps. There must have been pictures in there of every school play in the past thirty years, but he'd sorted out the ones he thought were relevant.'

'Anything of Theo we could use for the media?'

'No. Jack must have had the shakes even then. None of them were brilliant. But amongst them I found this.' Carefully, holding the picture by the edges with his fingertips, Eddie handed it over. It was a black and white photo of the audience, taken probably from the side of the stage just before the show was about to start. Parents clutched hand-printed programmes on their knees and chatted to their neighbours. There was no indication that they'd been aware of the photographer. Eddie pointed to a couple in the front row.

'Those are the Brices.'

They looked ordinary, elderly. They could have been anyone's grandparents. Stephen wore a hand-knitted sweater over corduroy trousers. Sylvia had made more of an effort about dressing up and had a high-necked blouse over a long black skirt. There was a brooch at the neck. They were holding hands.

'Interesting,' Porteous said. He always found it helpful to put a face to names. But he couldn't quite understand Eddie's excitement. It was hardly worth a trek into the country at tea time.

Eddie took a deep breath. 'That,' he said, pointing to a pale, insignificant man sitting next to Sylvia, 'that is Alec Reeves.'

Then Porteous did understand the excitement. This was Alec Reeves who'd worked as assistant manager in the hardware store in Cranford high street. Alec Reeves, uncle to Carl Jackson, the lad with the learning disability who'd disappeared not long before Theo.

Alec Reeves, who, according to Eddie, liked young boys and had gone off to get a job in a children's home.

'I thought Sarah Jackson said he'd left Cranford by then.'

'She did. He must have come back.'

Porteous looked again at the photo. Although Sylvia was holding Stephen's hand she was talking to Reeves. Her head was turned to him and she was smiling. It was the relaxed conversation of friends. 'You said they knew him.'

'Aye,' Stout said bitterly. 'You'd have thought they'd have had better taste.'

'This changes things,' Porteous said. Slowly. Not wanting to wind Eddie up any further. But Eddie was buzzing already.

'Of course it does. Alec was there that night. It must have been the last performance, because Hannah Morton says that's when the Brices were in the audience. No reason why he couldn't have got hold of the knife. I bet when we check the records we'll find other lads in his care who've mysteriously disappeared.'

'Theo wasn't in his care,' Porteous said. 'Not as far as we know.' And Melanie Gillespie wasn't a lad, he thought.

'He could have been. Perhaps the Brices asked Alec to have a word with the boy. Perhaps Theo was depressed because of the mess he'd made of his love life and they asked Alec to help. He was always a sympathetic listener. I'll give him that. Maybe he offered to take Theo out for the day, offered a shoulder to cry on. He was nearer the boy's age than the Brices. More like a father.'

'How would he explain Theo's disappearance?'

'I've been thinking about that.' Eddie's words tumbled over each other. 'Someone told the Brices that Theo had decided to go back to his dad. It must have been Alec Reeves.'

'It's certainly a plausible theory,' Porteous said. Then gently, 'Where does Melanie Gillespie fit in?'

'Maybe she's the last of a string of teenagers who've disappeared. We don't take missing teenagers very seriously, do we? Not the restless, unsettled ones. We put them down as runaways and hope the Sally Army will do the business for us.'

'Melanie didn't disappear though, did she? Her body was found. No attempt was made to hide it.'

'Perhaps Reeves was disturbed. Or all the publicity about the body in the lake made him want to come out into the open. Could be he's been enjoying the glory.'

Porteous said nothing. He wished he knew more about the subject. Perhaps after all he would have to talk to Hannah's fat psychologist, ask his advice. He drank his beer absent-mindedly. He hadn't eaten and felt it go to his head, mixed with the medication he'd taken earlier in the day. Like Stella Randle, he thought, I should take more care.

'Sir?' Eddie was on his feet. He was obviously desperate to move the case forward.

'Peter. Call me Peter here, please.' He set the glass on the table, stood up too, tried to sound decisive when all he had were questions. 'I want to know where Reeves is. Don't go to Sarah Jackson. I don't want him frightened off. Put a watch on her bungalow. But be discreet. When you find Reeves, don't pull him in. Tail him but leave him where he is. We'll need more evidence, any evidence, before we question him. At present he doesn't know there's anything to connect him to Theo Randle and that's how I want it. Show this photograph to the barman in the Promenade who said someone was looking for Melanie. Reeves will have changed since then, but it's better than nothing. Tomorrow we'll talk to her parents. See if the name means anything to them.' He paused. 'Go easy on this, Eddie. Bet will be expecting you back for a meal. Most of this you can do from home.'

But as Eddie bounded down the stairs Porteous knew he was wasting his breath. Eddie was a man with a mission and was losing the power of rational thought.

Chapter Twenty-Five

When Porteous arrived at the police station the next morning – early for him though he'd still walked, still kept to the same routine – Stout was already there. He looked as if he'd spent all night at his desk. He'd shaved but he was wearing the same clothes and he spoke too quickly, feverish through lack of sleep.

No use to man nor beast in that state, Porteous thought. Then recognized that as the pious sentiment of the newly converted and he listened to the steps Stout had already taken to track down Alec Reeves.

'There's an empty bungalow over the road from Sarah Jackson's. The council were going to do it up before the next tenant anyway. I talked to a chap in building services who goes to our church. He pushed the work to the top of the list. They're going to start this morning.' He looked at his watch. 'Should be there already. I've sent Charlie Luke along as part of the team.'

'Won't the council workers talk?'

'No, they think he's a management trainee. They have to do work experience in every department.'

Porteous smiled at the thought that Luke could pass as management material, but Stout was continuing. 'He'll have a key and can let our people in at night. If the neighbours get used to workmen being in the place it shouldn't cause so much gossip.'

'Good.' Porteous thought the plan unnecessarily elaborate. They had no evidence that Reeves would try to contact his sister. But he knew Stout wasn't in the mood to take criticism. Counselling had taught him the futility of knocking his head against a brick wall.

'I got an address for Reeves from the DVLA. He lives in a small town in the Yorkshire Dales.'

'Back to Yorkshire,' Porteous said. 'Hannah Morton thought Theo had been at school there but we didn't get anywhere when we checked earlier. Could Alec have introduced Theo to the Brices, I wonder? I suppose it's more likely to be coincidence. Theo would have been in a boarding school and Alec a care assistant in a Social Services assessment centre so it's hard to see where they'd have met. Not that I've traced either establishment yet. But it shouldn't be difficult now.'

'I've found out where Reeves worked.' Stout was jubilant. Porteous tried to be gracious in his moment of glory. 'It was a place called Redwood. It wasn't run by Social Services. Not officially. They bought in places there for difficult kids they couldn't persuade anyone else to take. It was operated by a charitable trust. It closed about a year ago when the person in charge retired. A woman by the name of Alice Cornish. Apparently she's famous.'

'Oh yes,' Porteous said. 'She's very famous.'

He was surprised Stout had never heard of her. Alice Cornish had been committed to providing quality care for children before the improvement of residential services became a fashionable cause. She'd worked in local-authority children's homes in the late sixties and resigned, very publicly, exposing a series of scandals. The press hadn't known what to make of her and in some quarters she'd been portrayed as an idealistic but rather hysterical trouble maker. She'd gone on to qualify as a doctor and then to set up an establishment of her own – Redwood – in a farmhouse in the country. Her peers found it hard to understand why she was bothering with grubby and disruptive children when she could be earning a comfortable living within the health service, but her qualifications made them take her seriously. She welcomed research teams into Redwood and they had to admit that her methods worked. She had gone on to be hugely respected in the field of social welfare. She had been made a Dame and chaired committees of inquiry into widespread abuse. Yet still she maintained her personal contact with Redwood and the children who'd lived there spoke of her with great affection. It seemed inconceivable that she would have employed anyone suspected of abuse. Porteous said as much, tactfully, to Stout.

'She wouldn't have known, would she? He was never convicted. Never even charged.'

'I just don't see how he would have got away with it at a place like that. Dr Cornish's whole philosophy was about listening to children. The kids wouldn't have been frightened to talk if Reeves had tried anything on.'

'He's clever,' Stout said stubbornly. 'Cunning. You don't know.'

Again Porteous saw no point in arguing. 'Is Reeves at home now?'

'I got in touch with the local nick. They sent a

community policeman round there yesterday evening. If Alec had answered he'd have got a pep talk about the neighbourhood watch, but nobody was in. According to the neighbours he's a model citizen, keeps his lawn cut, does his stint driving meals on wheels round the village and – get this – he helps organize the Duke of Edinburgh award scheme at the local high school.'

'Perhaps that's how he met Theo Randle,' Porteous said, almost to himself.

'Perhaps that's still how he gets to meet young lads.'

'Had the local bobbies heard that anything like that's going on?'

'They didn't say.' Stout sounded disappointed. 'But he's known as a loner. Well thought of in the village, but no real friends, no wife, no ladyfriend.'

You could say the same about me, Porteous thought.

'Did the neighbours have any idea where Reeves had gone?' he asked.

'Away for a week to visit an old colleague. They think he'll be back today or tomorrow.'

'I don't suppose they mentioned where the old colleague lives?'

'No. The old lady who lives next door asked but he wouldn't say. It wasn't like him. Usually he was happy to have a cup of tea with her and a chat.'

'Suspicious . . .' Porteous said, but only to please Stout. He didn't want Reeves to be uncovered as a child-abuser and serial killer. His employment at Redwood would be seized upon by the press. Alice Cornish would lose her credibility. And it would mean that Stout had been right all along. He hated to admit it but an element of competition had crept into the inquiry. Stout had found an address for Reeves, but still Porteous hadn't discovered where Crispin Randle had taken Theo to be educated after the fire. He didn't want Stout to be proved right about this.

'I've made an appointment to visit Mr and Mrs Gillespie,' he said. It would be the first formal interview with Melanie's parents. According to Richard Gillespie the doctor had said Eleanor wasn't up to it before. Gillespie still wasn't keen but Porteous had persisted and he'd reluctantly given way. He must have realized it would have to happen eventually. 'One o'clock. Is that all right with you?'

'You want me to come?'

'I don't want to miss anything. And while we're at the coast I thought we'd see Melanie's friends. Rosalind Morton and the boyfriend. You're good at teenagers.' He'd thought Stout would be pleased to be asked. 'Don't worry. They'll let us know if there's any news on Reeves.'

When Stout left the office Porteous made his decaffeinated coffee and spent most of the next hour on the phone. His first call was to an official in the Department for Education. He needed to find out where a child had been at school thirty years ago. It was urgent. A murder inquiry. Was there any way of finding out? There was a moment of silence and Porteous sensed the usual shock and excitement.

'State sector or private?'

'Private.'

Another silence. Then: 'Did he take any public examinations?'

'O levels. He must have taken O levels because he went on to the sixth form.'

'You could try the exam boards then.' The official hesitated then offered tentatively: 'If you don't mind giving me the details I can phone round for you. Call you back later.'

Porteous didn't mind. He gave both Theo Randle's names and his date of birth. 'We think he was in school somewhere in Yorkshire.'

He replaced the receiver and felt he was easing back into contention in the race with Eddie Stout. Then he remembered two kids had died and wondered how he could have been so petty.

The next phone call was to Hannah Morton's house. It was answered sulkily by a girl who sounded as if she'd just woken up. If anything when he identified himself she was even ruder. 'Don't come to the house,' she said. 'I'll be working. The Promenade. A big white pub on the front. You'll need to talk to Frank anyway and I'll make sure Joe's there. Make it mid-afternoon when we're not so busy.' She replaced the receiver before he had a chance to object.

He was wondering whether to break his routine and have another cup of coffee when the DFEE officer phoned him back.

'I think I've traced your lad.'

'Go on.'

'He took O levels in the name of Michael Grey. Passed seven well. A grades in Art and English. Failed Latin.'

That's all it took, Porteous thought. One phone call. Why didn't I think about the exam boards before?

'Have you got the name of the school?'

'Marwood Grange. It doesn't exist any more. I checked.'

'Where was it, when it did exist?'

'Out in the sticks. Yorkshire.' He paused. He was good at dramatic pauses. 'I tracked down one of the teachers. He works in the state system now. You can phone him if you like. Name of Hillier. This is his number.' Porteous was just about to replace the receiver, when he added, 'By the way. There's no record of A levels.'

'No,' Porteous said. 'There wouldn't be.'

Hillier must have been waiting for his call because he answered immediately. 'Marwood Grange,' he said. 'What a nightmare. It put me off private education for life.'

'Do you remember Michael Grey?'

'No. I was only there for a couple of terms before the place closed down and that was a bit of a blur. Like I said. A nightmare.'

'Why did it close?'

'Well, the fire was the final straw, but I don't think it would have survived long anyway. A couple of parents had complained and several more had taken their kids away.'

'Tell me about the fire.'

'It started late one night. I was junior house-master. It started in a classroom they think, but it spread to the dormitories. We got all the boys out but only because a kid got up for a pee. There were no fire doors. No extinguishers. There should have been a court case. It was gross negligence. I'd have been a witness . . . The guy in charge must have had friends in high places because it never came to that. He cut his losses, claimed the insurance and agreed not to run a school again.'

'You're sure you don't remember a boy called Michael Grey?'

'Certainly. I really only remember the boys in my house.'

Porteous saw Stout hovering outside his office door, ready for his trip to the coast, and waved him in. Another fire, he thought. Can that be a coincidence?

Chapter Twenty-Six

The Gillespie house had the dense quiet of an old church. It struck Porteous so strongly because he could tell that usually it wouldn't have been like that. As they approached the front door he saw through the living-room window an electric guitar and a practice amp, a battered upright piano with music on the stand and scribbled manuscript in a pile on the floor. In the hall the telephone had been unplugged.

Richard Gillespie let them in and took them to a room on the first floor which he called his office. It had a desk and a computer but it was big enough for a leather sofa and a couple of armchairs. He left them there while he went to fetch coffee. The room was at the back of the house and looked over the garden to public tennis courts. Two women were playing a scrappy if energetic game and occasionally shouts of triumph and cries of 'well done' floated through the open window, emphasizing the quiet inside.

When Gillespie returned with a tray he was still alone.

'Mrs Gillespie will be joining us?' Porteous asked.

'If you insist that it's necessary. She's resting.'

'It is, I'm afraid.' Porteous was glad Eddie Stout was with him, solid and unimpressed. He found Gillespie intimidating without being able to work out exactly why. Perhaps it was an impression of anger, only held in check with great self-control. Without Eddie as minder he wasn't sure he'd be able to stand his ground.

'While we're on our own I want to know what's going on,' Gillespie said. 'No one's told us anything. I've a right to know.'

'Of course. We're linking your daughter's murder to that of a boy called Theo Randle, nearly thirty years ago. Does the name mean anything to you?'

'Any relation to Crispin Randle?'

'His son.'

'Crispin never told me his son had been killed.'

'He didn't know. We retrieved the body from Cranford Water a couple of weeks ago.'

'*That* body?'

Porteous nodded. 'Did you know Crispin well?'

'Through business really. We had a couple of boozy nights together, but everyone who worked with Crispin ended up drinking with him.'

'Was Mr Randle involved in the computer business?' It was hard to picture.

'Hardly. No. And I was never a computer scientist or engineer. Still don't really understand the technology. I trained as a lawyer and worked my way up through the company's legal department before becoming MD. When I first qualified I worked briefly for a firm of solicitors in town. We sold some property for Crispin.'

'Snowberry?'

'No, he'd already sold that. This was a house in Gosforth. We got a good price for it considering it was nearly falling down round his ears.'

'Tell me about your daughter,' Porteous said.

Gillespie shifted in his seat. For the first time the suppressed anger gave way to uneasiness.

'It must seem like prying but we'll need all the information you can give us.'

Eddie sat with his pencil poised over his notebook, waiting.

'She wasn't my daughter.'

'I'm sorry?'

'I mean, not biologically. Legally of course. I adopted her when I married Eleanor.'

Porteous wondered if that explained the anger. His position was compromised, ambiguous. Eleanor's grief would be more straightforward. Had she made him feel he couldn't possibly understand what she was going through?

'Does Melanie's natural father know that she's dead?'

'I shouldn't think so. We've no way of tracing him. He's a musician. That, at least, is what he calls himself. I think there was a card at Christmas. From North Africa, Marrakesh, somewhere like that. He travels a lot. I don't know how he supports himself. Not now.'

'What do you mean? "Not now"?'

There was a pause. Eventually Gillespie said, 'I gave him money. Enough to last for a while.'

'Why did you do that, Mr Gillespie?' Eddie Stout spoke for the first time, shocking them both. Both, too, sensed the disapproval in his voice. Not now, Eddie, Porteous thought. Now's not the time for a moral crusade.

But though the question seemed to make Gillespie defensive, he wanted to explain. 'It was when Eleanor and I married. I didn't want Ray around, dropping in every afternoon with his unsuitable friends, confusing Mel. I wanted to be her dad.'

'So you paid him to go away?'

'And to agree to the adoption, yes.'

'How old was Melanie then?'

'Five. Six by the time we went through the whole process.'

'And he just disappeared from her life?'

'Yes. Look, I thought it was the best thing at the time, all right? Ray Scully was mixed up in all sorts. He'd been convicted of fraud. He'd even been to prison. What could someone like him give Melanie?'

'Did Mrs Gillespie know about the financial arrangement?'

'Look, it was no big deal. A one-off payment. I wasn't stopping him keeping in touch for ever. Like I said, he wrote to her, sent her cards.'

'So Mrs Gillespie knew?'

'No. She just thought it was Ray being irresponsible again. He'd been disappearing on and off since Mel was born.' He stood up and stared blankly out of the window. The tennis game was over. 'I shouldn't have told you.'

'No,' Porteous said. 'I'm very pleased that you did.'

'You won't tell Eleanor?'

'I really don't think that's any of my business. Though we'll want to trace the father. Is there any possibility that he's been in touch with Melanie recently?'

'She didn't say anything. But I don't suppose she would have done. Communication had pretty well broken down here.'

'You know a middle-aged man went into the Promenade looking for her. It didn't occur to you that it might have been her father?'

'No. He knows where we live. He could have come to the house.'

'That wasn't part of the deal, was it? You'd paid him to stay away.'

Gillespie shrugged. The fight seemed to have gone out of him. 'Eleanor thought that was the start of all Mel's problems. Ray going away.'

'What problems?'

'She was never an easy child. Bright of course, but attention seeking, hyperactive. Then in the last few years there's been the anorexia.'

'Was she being treated for that?'

'Oh, she's been treated for everything.' He must have realized that sounded callous. 'We wanted her to be happy. I don't think she ever has been, really. When we moved here and she started making friends I thought things were looking up. But in the couple of weeks before she died she was more disturbed than I remember.'

'Who was her psychiatrist?'

'Dr Collier at the General. He seemed a decent enough bloke, but I don't know how effective he was.'

Oh, he's effective, Porteous thought. Trust me. I know.

'He wanted to treat Mel as an inpatient. She hated the idea. He was talking about sectioning her. Not on the food issue. She was eating enough, just, to keep her alive. But because she seemed to be depressed.'

'How did that manifest itself?' Porteous thought he sounded a bit like a doctor himself.

'Listlessness, insomnia, withdrawal.' He paused. 'Sometimes I thought she'd lost all touch with reality.'

'In what way?'

'She seemed to hate her mother and me. She couldn't believe we were trying to help her. There was some fantasy about us trying to control her.'

Just because you're paranoid, it doesn't mean they're not out to get you, Porteous thought and stopped the facetious words slipping out just in time. It was true. In hospital he'd met a man who was convinced he was about to be blown up by the IRA. The staff thought he was psychotic. A week after leaving the place he'd been killed by a car bomb. He dragged his attention back to the present, was aware of Eddie staring at him. He nodded at Eddie to take over the questions.

'Had Melanie complained of any unwanted attention? Unusual phone calls, perhaps, strangers trying to engage her in conversation.'

'I told you. In the last few days before she was killed she didn't go out.'

'She hadn't had a problem with her boyfriend?'

'What do you mean?'

'They hadn't had a row, for example?'

Clever Eddie, Porteous thought. On the look out for another connection. But Gillespie shook his head.

'I don't know how Joe put up with her but he was always remarkably patient. Eleanor and I like him a lot. He's respectable, despite the hair and the clothes. Comes from a good family. He was devoted to Mel. It was a relief when they started going out together. It was someone else to keep an eye on her. You know?'

Porteous nodded. 'Would it be possible to speak to

Mrs Gillespie now? We could talk in her room if that would be easier.'

'No. She won't want that. But you'll have to wait while she gets ready.'

'Perhaps in the meantime we could look in Melanie's room. Is it as she left it?'

'Yes. The police said not to touch anything. I'll show you.'

The room was on the next floor, long and narrow, with two bay windows, each with a padded seat. The furniture was expensive, much of it custom built to fit the space, but the posters and cards on the walls, the candles and joss-sticks, the piles of clothes and papers turned it into any other student pit. On the desk there was a CD player and a rack of tapes. A door in the opposite wall led to a small bathroom.

'You'll have to excuse the mess,' Gillespie said. 'She wouldn't let our cleaning lady in. Something else to fight over.'

'You can leave it to us, sir. We'll come down when we've finished.'

Gillespie turned. They waited in silence until they heard his footsteps retreating down the polished wood stairs.

'Well?' Porteous asked. 'What do you think of him?'

'He's told us some of it.' Eddie had already started on the dressing table. He pulled the top drawer right out and began feeling carefully through an octopus of tights. 'Thrown us a few crumbs – like the fact that he'd paid the dad to go away. But he's not told us everything. Not by a long chalk. Perhaps it's not relevant. If he's having an affair with his secretary, for instance. I don't suppose that would have anything to do with the murder. But he's keeping secrets and I don't like it.'

'I'm not sure.' It was unlike Eddie to get so heated. Lack of sleep, Porteous thought. He felt more sympathy for Gillespie. 'Perhaps he just feels guilty because he sent the father away and screwed up the kid.'

'No,' Eddie snorted. 'His sort don't do guilt.'

They sorted through the mess but they didn't find a hiding place. No cache of love letters. No diary, which Porteous had been hoping for. He'd thought an introspective young woman like that would have kept a written record of her thoughts and feelings. No photo of her father, which he'd been looking for too. He'd have liked something to show the manager of the pub.

In the bathroom there was still a dirty towel on the floor. There was a small wall cupboard empty except for a bottle of anti-depressants on a shelf inside. It was dated a month before but it was still full. Had she stopped taking her medication because she thought she could manage without? Or was she saving the pills for a grand suicidal gesture?

Eddie was replacing the final drawer. 'Nothing. Still, if Gillespie knew there was anything incriminating he'd have had plenty of time to get rid of it. There's this . . . for what it's worth . . .'

It was the National Record of Achievement from her school. The academic reports were glowing. There was a number of unaccounted absences, but allowance had obviously been made. The teachers had written sympathetic comments about Mel's courage in the face of her medical difficulties. Eddie snorted again.

'You don't think she had serious health problems?' Porteous asked.

'Well, it's not like cancer, is it? Self-induced and self-indulgent. If you ask me she could have done with a bit of healthy neglect.' He opened the door of one of the wardrobes. Porteous had already been through the clothes checking the pockets. 'Look at all that stuff. She didn't get that in C&A or New Look. My Ruthie would give her eye-teeth for one of those frocks.'

'Not a justification for murder though, is it?' Porteous said quietly. 'Being spoiled by your parents.'

Stout stopped, horrified, his arm still flung out in a gesture of righteous indignation.

'You're right. That was crass. I don't know what came over me. It was that man. I let him get to me. One of the first rules, isn't it? Don't blame the victim.'

'Have we finished?' Porteous asked, a bit embarrassed to have had such a dramatic effect.

'Just a minute.'

Stout straightened the cover on the crumpled bed. It was dark blue with gold stars and moons, too young for the sophisticated young woman they'd come to know, perhaps a relic from childhood. He felt under the pillow and came out with a photograph in a small silver frame.

'The boyfriend?' Porteous asked. Then more interested. 'Or the father?'

'Neither.'

It was of a small girl, perhaps eighteen months old, with blond curls tied with a ribbon. She had a plump face and dimples.

'There's no younger sister, is there?'

Porteous shook his head. He slipped the photograph from the frame. On the back of the print was written 'Em'. 'Another coincidence,' he said. 'The Randle child who was killed in the fire was called Emily.'

'The photo's much more recent than that,' Stout said. 'Unless they had Teletubbies thirty years ago. Look at that top she's wearing.'

'Perhaps the Gillespies will know.'

'Aye,' Stout said. 'And perhaps they'll tell. Which is another thing altogether.'

Eleanor Gillespie had joined her husband in his office. Porteous thought perhaps they didn't want their personal space contaminated by the police. Eleanor wore jeans and a big sweater. She seemed very small inside it. She hardly looked up when they came in. Porteous apologized for the intrusion but couldn't tell if she was listening.

'It won't take long.'

She shrugged. 'We've got all the time in the world.'

'We need to trace your husband, Mrs Gillespie. Do you have any idea where he is?'

She shook her head.

'Is there anyone who might know?'

'His mother, if she's still alive.' She gave an address.

Porteous handed the photograph of the baby to her. 'Could you tell us who this is, please?'

Eleanor looked down listlessly, then seemed to jerk awake. She shot a look at her husband.

'It's Emma,' she said. 'Emma Leese. Just a little girl Mel used to babysit for. Before she got tied up with exams. I didn't realize she'd kept a photo.' She gave a sob. 'It's so unfair. If Mel had gone away on holiday when she'd planned she wouldn't have been here. She'd have been on some beach in Portugal soaking up the sun.'

'What made her change her mind?'

'I don't know. Perhaps Joe wasn't keen. He never seemed very happy about the idea. Perhaps Mel was so low that she just couldn't face it.'

She turned again to her husband. 'We should all have gone. As a family.' An accusation. He turned away and didn't respond.

Porteous stood to go.

'Does the name Alec Reeves mean anything to either of you?'

She seemed about to answer but Gillespie stood too and spoke for both of them. 'No,' he said firmly. 'I've never heard of him. Have you, Ellie?'

She said nothing and stared dumbly after the men as her husband led them down the stairs.

Chapter Twenty-Seven

Eddie said he was starving so they queued at a baker's for a sandwich and sat on a bench on the sea front like trippers to eat.

'I wouldn't give that marriage long.' Eddie cupped his hand to catch the oozing tuna mayonnaise before it splashed on to his lap.

'No?' It wasn't the first time Porteous had been surprised by Eddie's cynicism. 'I thought they were well matched. He seemed supportive. Protective even.'

'Nah. She blames him already for the lassie's death. I'd give it six months. She doesn't trust him. We should get her on her own.'

'What have you got against him? Besides his money?'

'That'll do for the time being. And the fact that he was lying.'

After the glare of the afternoon sun the pub was inviting. Rosie had been right. At this time of day the place was quiet. She was on her own behind the bar, chatting to a thin lad with a pony tail. She realized who they were as soon as they came through the door, and went to the back to call a plump, balding man, before greeting them.

'Do you want a drink?' It was an offhand snarl.

Porteous thought if she was as ungracious as that to all the customers she was lucky still to have a job.

'Orange juice.' He raised his eyebrows to Stout, who nodded. 'Two.'

She poured the drinks then turned to her boss. 'Can I have my break now, Frank?'

'Aye. Take as long as you like. We're hardly rushed off our feet.'

She helped herself to a Coke and led them to a table in the corner. The skinny boy followed after.

'This is Joe,' she said. 'Mel's boyfriend.'

'It was good of you to come.'

'What do you want?'

'To talk about Mel, that's all. To try to get a clearer idea what she was like. Her parents are upset.'

'We're upset too.'

Porteous wished Eddie would help him out. He hadn't expected the girl's hostility. Didn't Eddie know about teenagers? But Eddie drank his orange juice and seemed content to let his boss struggle on.

'It's not just that. She'll have told things to you that she'd never let on to her parents. Wouldn't she?'

'Yeah. I suppose.'

'So just talk to us. Describe her. Joe?'

'She wasn't like anyone else I'd ever met.'

That hardly helps, Porteous thought.

'She was delicate, fragile. It wasn't just the anorexia. I mean, I could never get to the bottom of what that was about. It didn't seem to be about food. Not image even. I mean, it didn't seem to be about the super-model thing. She didn't want starvation chic. She had more about her than that. It was as if she didn't feel she deserved to eat. Which was crazy when you knew her, because *everyone* thought she was brilliant. Not just the teachers but her mates. People liked being around her. I couldn't believe it when we started going out. I was on a high for months.'

Hadn't that been how Hannah Meek had described her relationship with Michael Grey? Porteous thought. But perhaps it could be a description of any teenage infatuation.

'Did she talk to you about her dad?'

'You know about that?' Joe seemed surprised. 'My God, you'd have thought *he* was a murderer the way Richard Gillespie made her keep it secret. I think that made her dream about him even more. She had this romantic notion that Ray Scully, the great musician, was going to turn up and take her away from all that respectability.'

'Richard wasn't Mel's real dad?' Porteous could tell Rosie was hurt.

'No.'

'You never said. Even when she went missing.'

'I couldn't,' Joe said. 'She'd made me promise . . .' Like a six-year-old in the playground.

'Had she heard from her dad recently?' Porteous asked.

'No, I'm sure she would have said.'

'How were things between you before she died?'

'I hadn't seen her for a few days. Her parents said she was too ill.'

'You'd spoken on the phone though?'

'They'd said she wasn't up to it. I don't know. Maybe she didn't want to talk to me.'

'Why wouldn't she? Had you had a row?'

'No!'

'But?'

'But something had happened to freak her out. I don't know what it was. Maybe it was something I'd done or she'd thought I'd done, but she wouldn't say.' He paused, drank his beer. Porteous thought that despite his grief part of him was enjoying this – the attention, the drama. At university it would make an unusual chat-up story. The murder of the love of his life would demand sympathy. Women would go for it in droves. 'We were going on holiday. It was her parents' idea. They thought she should get away. The stress of waiting for exam results was getting to her. They knew someone with a villa on the Algarve.'

'Eleanor said you weren't very keen on the idea.'

Joe seemed shocked by the interruption. Porteous thought he'd already conjured a fantasy in which there'd been no disagreements in their relationship.

'I just wasn't sure I wanted the responsibility.'

'She could be disturbed?'

'Not mad!' Joe said. 'Troubled, depressed maybe. I'm not saying she was insane.'

'So you were all set for a holiday to the Algarve. What happened?'

'We were in here. All packed. Our suitcases with us. It was an evening flight and we'd arranged for the taxi to pick us up outside at six. We were having a few drinks, saying goodbye to our friends. Not Rosie. She'd gone away with her mum.'

Porteous turned slowly to Rosie. 'That was the day of the school reunion?'

She nodded.

'Was the television on in here?'

'Yes.' Joe had finished the beer. He put the empty glass on the table. 'Why?'

'An idea. Humour me.'

'Mel started watching it. Suddenly she shouted for everyone to keep quiet. She was ratty. I mean really ratty. The moment before, she'd been laughing, then suddenly she was screaming at people because she couldn't hear.'

'What was on the television?'

'I'm not sure. Local news, I think.'

That was the day they'd issued the press release naming the boy in the lake as Michael Grey and shown the photograph. Porteous felt a hit of adrenalin, breathed slowly to keep his voice calm.

'Did she say what had interested her?'

'Not really. Nothing that made sense. She got up and switched off the telly. Not angry any more, but serious. I asked her what was so important. "Nothing," she said. "I think I've just seen a ghost. That's all." Then she said the holiday was off. "You go," she said. "Take someone else. Take Rosie if you like." But she didn't mean it. And anyway I couldn't just fly off and leave her like that. The taxi turned up then and we got it to take us home. The driver was moaning because he'd been expecting the full fare out to the airport and he'd turned down other work. I said we'd pay him anyway. I sat in the back next to her and she was shaking. She wasn't causing a scene. She was really upset. She wouldn't let me go into the house with her. "You've paid all that money. You might as well get him to drop you at your doorstep." That was the last time I saw her.'

'Rosie, did you ever see her after that, after you came back from Cranford?'

She shook her head.

'Does the name Alec Reeves mean anything to either of you?'

'Is he the suspect?' Joe asked, almost with relish. Again Porteous thought the boy would survive this experience without too many scars. He wasn't so sure about Rosie.

'Just someone we're trying to trace.'

'Never heard of him.'

'Rosie?'

Again she shook her head.

'What about Emma Leese?'

'Wasn't she the little girl Mel used to babysit?'

'Do you know her?'

'No. It was before Mel moved round here. But she used to talk about her. About how cute she was.'

'When did Mel move to the coast?'

'A couple of years ago. At the beginning of the sixth form.' Rosie gave Joe a brave grin. 'That's why all the lads fancied her. Because she was new, exciting. Him and me started infant school together. No secrets at all.'

Another connection with Theo, Porteous thought, almost automatically. But his mind was moving on in wider speculation. Wasn't the relationship between Mel and the baby girl more intense than that between a young babysitter and her charge? Could Mel be the child's mother, the photograph her only souvenir of a baby handed over for fostering or adoption? It would explain Richard Gillespie's hostility and his reluctance to answer questions. Even after her death he wouldn't want details of a teenage pregnancy made public. It might explain too why the family had moved just before she started her A-level course, why Mel was so mixed up.

'Did Mel ever talk about having children?' he asked.

Rosie picked up on what he was on about at once. 'You *must* be joking.'

'Where did she go to school before she started with you?'

'Don't know. Some private place inland, I think. Did she ever tell you, Joe?'

Or a special unit, Porteous thought, for pregnant schoolgirls. With very wealthy parents. Then immediately – I wonder if Redwood would take a kid like that. But wouldn't Carver have picked up the fact that she'd had a child at the post-mortem? Perhaps it was in the final report which still hadn't arrived.

'Don't you want to know,' Joe demanded, 'about the guy that came in here looking for her?'

'Of course.'

'I'll get back behind the bar,' Rosie said. 'Then Frank can come and talk to you.' She walked away from them. Joe watched her wistfully, unsure whether or not he should follow.

Porteus could tell immediately that Frank wouldn't be any help. There'd been a brief discussion with Rosie behind the bar. He'd been reluctant to let her take over. Now he did approach them his face was greasy with sweat.

'Look.' He held out his hands, palms outward, a gesture to distance himself from the policemen and their questions. 'I can't remember anything. Honest. I wish I could. It was really busy. A guy came in asking about Mel. I didn't tell him anything and he left. That's all.'

'Middle-aged, you said. Respectable.'

'Aye.'

'Not elderly then? Not an old man?'

'Compared to these kids they all look old, don't they?'

Stout had got hold of a recent photograph of Alec Reeves. He'd been in the paper in his home town handing over Duke of Edinburgh awards to a bunch of school children. He looked younger than his years. It must have been all that walking in the hills. He stood, fit and tanned, in the centre of the frame smiling shyly. It was hard to think of him as a monster.

'Could that be him?'

'Do you know how many faces I see in here?'

Porteus could feel Eddie beside him, winding himself up for a row.

'Please concentrate,' he said quietly.

'All right. Aye. It could have been him. But I wouldn't swear to it. Certainly not in court.'

Chapter Twenty-Eight

At the police station in Cranford, Claire Wright was waiting for them. 'I've traced Elizabeth Milburn, the woman who was Emily Randle's nanny. She's head teacher now of a nursery school in the city but she lives out this way. She'll be in this evening after eight if you want to get in touch.'

'Any news on Reeves?' Eddie demanded.

'Nothing. He's not visited his sister and he's not gone home.' She was sitting at her desk and didn't look up from her computer screen. Eddie walked away. He knocked an empty Coke can off the desk and didn't bother picking it up. 'What's wrong with him?'

'Reeves,' Porteus said. 'Eddie's convinced he killed a disabled lad before Theo Randle, and he likes him for these two. If there are only two.'

'Looks that way at the moment. We've pulled up all the serious-crime reports that might be relevant. I can't see anything which fits into a pattern with Randle and Gillespie. Not yet.'

'Anything else?'

'Members of the public have been ringing in all day, claiming they saw Melanie on the evening she died. It's taken time to sort through. We're following up anything that looks promising this evening. OK?'

'Sure.'

He went to his office to start tracking down Ray Scully. Scully's mother still lived at the address given to him by Eleanor Gillespie and she answered the phone on the first ring, shouting a little so he realized she was hard of hearing.

'Yes? Who is it?'

He explained, repeating the questions louder when she didn't seem to understand.

'Ray isn't here.'

'I know that Mrs Scully. Where is he? We want to talk to him.'

'What about?'

It was obvious that she didn't read the newspapers and the Gillespies hadn't bothered telling her. He didn't want to break the news of her granddaughter's death over the phone.

'He's not in any trouble, Mrs Scully.'

'Are you sure?' The deafness made her sound truculent.

'Absolutely.' Crossing his fingers, wondering if this was true.

There was a long pause.

'Mrs Scully?'

She made up her mind suddenly. 'He's in Cromer. Norfolk. Summer season in the theatre at the end of the pier. Playing in the band for the musical turns.'

'Has he got a telephone there?'

Suspicion returned. 'No. He phones me. Once a week. Regular as clockwork.'

'Can you ask him to contact me? Tell him it's about Mel.'

He repeated the question to check that she'd

understood, but she'd already gone. He left a similar message with the theatre manager.

It was six o'clock. Too early to visit Lizzie Milburn, so he could make a start on finding out everything there was to know about Frank Garrity, the manager of the Prom. A treat to himself after a dispiriting day. There was nothing he liked better than a dig through the files and records. He found what he was after quickly, made himself a celebratory mug of coffee and went to look for Eddie. He was at his desk, engaged in an earnest discussion with Charlie Luke, who was holed up in the bungalow opposite Sarah Jackson's.

'Nobody's been there all day except a bloke selling dodgy dusters.'

'I know why Frank was so reluctant to talk to us,' Porteous said.

'Why?'

'He was charged with rape twenty years ago. It never came to court. The girl changed her story. But he was held on remand for a few days. It must have made an impression.'

'Could he have killed Melanie? No one else saw the bloke who asked for her. He could have made it up to muddy the waters.'

'He could. But he'd have still been in primary school when Theo Randle was killed.'

'Could Carver be wrong about the links between the deaths?'

Could he? Porteous thought about it. It wouldn't be the first time a team had wasted weeks following up connections which didn't really exist.

'I don't think so. I don't like the man, but he's a good pathologist. And he's put his reputation on the line.' Another thought occurred to him. 'Has his completed report been sent over yet?'

'I've not seen it.' As if he didn't really care. As if all he cared about was nailing Reeves.

'I want you to talk to the Spences and Chris Johnson tomorrow,' Peter said.

'Why?' As truculent as Mrs Scully.

'Back to basics, I suppose. They were at the party where Theo was last seen alive. Ask them about Reeves. Did they know him at the time? Show them a photo. Both photos. Did anyone see Reeves and Theo together? Has he been knocking around recently?'

'Yes,' Eddie said slowly. 'I could do that.'

Then he was on the phone again, asking for an update from Charlie Luke.

Lizzie Milburn was in her fifties, but rather glamorous in an efficient, power-dressed sort of way. Certainly more glamorous than he'd expected someone who spent her days with three- and four-year-olds to be. But it seemed she ran the Early Years Centre on a big council estate on the edge of the city and spent little time these days with paint and sand. Porteous arrived at her home before her. She had a flat in what had once been a large country house. When there was no reply he was about to walk back to his car to wait, but she drove up, very quickly, and pulled to a stop beside him, scattering gravel. She was in a convertible Golf and the roof was down. She slid one slim leg out and stood up to greet him. She smelled expensive. Her skirt was short. Her shoes were dusty.

'You wouldn't believe the mess on the estate,' she said. 'It's like a dust bowl. They're knocking down most of the flats and putting up houses. A good thing. No one wanted to live in those high rises. But they seem to be taking for ever. And it's worse in the winter. You need wellingtons to get from your car.' She didn't expect any response and went on, 'Sorry I'm late. Parents evening. In a place like ours it's hard to get the parents there and we don't feel we can chase them away.'

At the door she slipped off her shoes. 'I'm sorry, Inspector, but I really must have a very large G and T. I don't suppose you . . . ?'

'Just a tonic,' he said.

She'd been married, it seemed, but it hadn't worked out. He had the impression that she'd got rid of a husband who hadn't lived up to her expectations, re-assumed her maiden name, and carried on as if he'd never existed. There had never been any children but she'd done well financially out of the divorce. All this he gathered in the first few minutes. They sat, without ceremony at the kitchen table and he was reminded of his conversation with Stella Randle. Another kitchen. Two women of a certain age, but remarkably different.

'What's all this about, Inspector?' Her hair was rinsed auburn and cut short. Her make-up was still intact. Despite the difference in their ages, despite the fact that she wasn't at all the sort of woman he usually went for, he found himself attracted to her.

'Theo Randle.'

'Oh? Usually when the police come to see me it's because one of the fathers has been suspected of abuse. Or the mums have been shifting stolen property on our premises. Or some little vandal has set fire to the place again.'

'It is about a fire I want to talk to you.'

'Is it true that the body you found in Cranford Water was Theo?'

'Yes. He'd changed his name before he died but it was Theo.'

'Poor boy.' She went to the freezer to fetch ice for their drinks. 'You'd have thought he started out with every advantage. Compared with the children I work with now. But he didn't. He didn't stand a chance of a normal life.'

'Why?'

'Before I arrived at Snowberry he'd been left almost to his own devices. Crispin went to pieces after Maria died. Kept up a show for the constituents but he was hitting the bottle even then. Theo was minded by a series of women whose main job was to keep the house clean. He got whatever he wanted so long as he left them in peace. And it was much the same when Crispin was there. I suppose things were better when he started school but it was a snotty little prep place and I think it must have been pretty bleak. Theo must have been well screwed up even before Crispin married Stella.'

'Did he resent his stepmother?'

'No. Quite the opposite. He worshipped her. She took time to listen to him, read him stories, played with him. She wasn't much more than a girl herself – a bit giggly and silly – but she made a real effort to get on with him. I met her first when she was pregnant. We were about the same age but she made me feel about a hundred and one. She treated the whole thing as a game. As if having a baby was all about parties and presents. She'd been totally sheltered. Mummy and Daddy were friends of Crispin's. She'd done boarding school, a year's finishing in Switzerland. The job as Crispin's secretary was to give her something to do with her time before marriage and of course she didn't have to look very far for a husband. It was hardly surprising that she went to pieces when Emily was born. Her depression was a nightmare for everyone at Snowberry but especially Theo. He thought he'd found someone who cared about him. Then suddenly she didn't care about anyone. She couldn't. The doctors Crispin got in didn't help. They just pumped her full of drugs. I tried to spend as much time as I could with Theo, but I couldn't replace her and I was pretty busy with Emily.'

'Did you keep in touch with him when he went away to school?'

'I didn't keep in touch with any of them. Crispin made it quite clear my role in the family was over when Emily died. The day after the fire he gave me a month's wages in lieu of notice and he sent me away.'

'Tell me about the fire.'

She swirled the remaining gin in her glass. 'I'd been out. It didn't happen often. Snowberry was miles from anywhere. The only entertainment was the pub and those days a woman didn't go out drinking on her own. One of the lads on the estate asked me to go to the pictures in town. He had a car. That was the only reason I went and I made sure I wasn't late back. The nursery was at the back of the house and I couldn't see the fire from the front. The first thing I did was check on Emily but I couldn't get near her room. You wouldn't believe the heat and the smoke. Sometimes I wake up at night and I can still taste it. Theo was asleep but I managed to get him out. Crispin and Stella were still up. They'd both been drinking and they hadn't noticed a thing.'

'Was anyone else there?'

'Not in the house itself. There was a couple who looked after the place, but they lived in a cottage at the end of the drive. They didn't know anything until the fire engines woke them up.'

'Are you sure it was an accident?'

'You think the fire's related to Theo's murder?'

He shrugged. 'I hope I've got an open mind.'

'Stella wouldn't hurt a fly, even in her maddest moments. Crispin had a fearsome temper. I can imagine him lashing out at Stella, but he loved the baby. And even if the fire was his fault, why kill Theo after all that time?'

And what, Porteus thought, could any of this have to do with Melanie Gillespie?

Chapter Twenty-Nine

Porteous had made an appointment to see Melanie's psychiatrist. Walking from the car park to the day hospital, all glass and concrete like the superstore next door, he tried to walk in her footsteps, see it through her eyes. On the step by the entrance, a young couple stared blankly into space, smoking cheap smuggled cigarettes. In the waiting-room a middle-aged man with wild hair paced backwards and forwards talking to himself about God. Sitting on one of the orange plastic chairs in the corridor a plump woman in a neat, grey raincoat sobbed discreetly into a handkerchief. What would Melanie have made of them? Would she have considered herself different and sat apart? Would she have visited the place alone, her parents too busy to be there? He found it hard to imagine Melanie here at all. He thought Richard Gillespie would have arranged somewhere private, an exclusive clinic where discretion would be guaranteed, the sort of health farm where customers were force fed instead of starved.

The receptionist on the main desk gave him a brief smile of recognition, but when he showed her his warrant card she shook her head. A sort of apology for mistaking him for one of the patients. The waiting-room was unusually busy. The hospital tried to see patients on time. If they were kept hanging around some lost their nerve and walked out. Others turned nasty. Porteous had a sudden qualm of conscience about taking up the doctor's time.

'Mr Porteous, the doctor will see you now.'

They watched him, aware he was jumping the queue, but too apathetic or too cowed to comment. The nurse started walking with him.

'It's all right,' he said. 'I know the way.'

He followed the corridor with its jolly posters promoting healthy eating and adverts for self-help groups, until he came to the door. He stopped outside, feeling for a moment the old anxiety, the breaker of rules outside the head teacher's study, then he knocked lightly and went in.

Collier was a red-headed Scot with freckles and blue eyes. He ran marathons and looked horribly fit.

'Peter. You're looking very well.'

Despite himself he felt pleased. Collier had always been honest. If he looked lousy he'd have said so. This meant he must be doing OK.

'I'm not here for me. Didn't they say?'

'Yeah. There's a note somewhere.' He scrabbled through a pile of scrap paper. Porteous would have loved the opportunity to go through the desk, to reduce it to a series of neat piles. 'And I had a phone call,' the psychiatrist continued. 'From Mr Gillespie.' He lay back in his chair. 'What you might call a warning shot across my bows.'

'Oh?'

'Oh aye. I'm to respect Melanie's confidentiality although she's dead. The cheek of the man. You'd think he was paying me.'

'Isn't that odd? I mean Melanie being treated on the NHS. He must have private health insurance.'

'I'm the best,' Collier said, quite seriously. 'If he'd asked around he'd have been told that. And I don't do private.'

'I do know. That you're the best.'

Collier grinned. 'And they might have gone private before they came here. They said not, but I wouldn't have been surprised if they'd tried something else. Herbal remedies. Acupuncture. Hypnosis. Any damn thing to avoid having to face what was going on. You'd be surprised by the number of patients who've been fooled by some quack but who're too embarrassed to admit it.'

'So,' Porteous said cautiously. 'There's nothing you're prepared to tell me. You've been warned off.'

'I can't tell you about the lassie's illness.'

'When did you last see her?'

Collier opened a desk diary. The pages were covered in scribbled notes and crossing out. The lack of order made Porteous wince.

'A week ago. It was a house call.' He paused, frowned. 'Oh bugger Gillespie! But just be discreet. He says he'll sue. He couldn't, of course, but he could make things awkward. Eleanor, the mother, phoned up in a state. She said Melanie was delusional, in the middle of some sort of crisis. She needed to be in hospital. I offered to send in a community nurse but that wouldn't do. By the time I could get there Gillespie had turned up. He said the same as his wife but more forcefully. I had to treat the girl as an inpatient.'

'But you didn't admit her?'

'No. I wasn't going to be bullied. I'd have liked to

talk to Melanie alone but the parents weren't having any of it and I didn't think I could insist. It was an awkward situation. I was on my own. Sod's law. I'd been trailing a female student around with me the rest of the week.'

'How was Melanie?'

'Angry. She'd had some sort of tantrum, throwing furniture around, smashing plates. It was over by the time I got there but I presume that was why Eleanor phoned.'

'The anger was directed at her parents?'

'That was the impression I had.'

'Was it about the anorexia?'

'Melanie used food as a weapon in every situation. But as to what triggered the scene . . .' He shrugged.

'Could it have had anything to do with her natural father?'

Collier looked up at him sharply then shrugged again.

'I don't know. By the time I arrived Melanie was very controlled and she wasn't giving anything away. She insisted she didn't want to be in hospital and I don't have the beds to admit every young person who causes their parents grief. She was perfectly rational and I didn't think she was suicidal. No grounds for sectioning. I made her an outpatient appointment.'

'When for?'

'I would have liked to have seen her immediately. Get her here, away from home territory. I felt there'd been some sort of breakthrough, that, you know, she trusted me for standing up to her father. But I couldn't make it for a couple of days. I was speaking at a conference in Edinburgh. I gave her a chance to see a colleague but she wasn't happy about that.'

'When was the appointment?'

'The morning her body was found in the cemetery.'

There was a pause. Porteous was aware of the patients in the waiting-room, their nerves twisting to breaking point as the minutes ticked on. He knew Collier was thinking of them too.

'Had she ever been in Redwood?'

'The assessment centre? Alice Cornish's place? Not so far as I know. Why?'

'One of our suspects was a social worker there. It would be a link. And that's privileged information too, even if I can't sue.'

'They never said. I mean, I took a history. Schools. You know the sort of thing. But I didn't check. Why should I?' He paused, tilted back in his chair. 'Redwood was an amazing place. I did a residential placement there. One of my options. There's no reason why the Gillespies wouldn't have admitted to her having gone there. It was harder to get into than Eton. Something for them to brag about.' His eyes flicked to the clock on the wall and Porteous realized his time was up.

Outside the sun splashed off the big glass windows of the hospital and the superstore. His car, trapped between the buildings, was sweltering. He opened all the windows but didn't start driving. He couldn't face Cranford and Eddie's obsession, the rest of the team expecting answers and leadership.

When he did start it was to go up the coast towards Stavely Prison, knowing he was running away. In the low fields on the coastal plain the combine harvesters moved relentlessly over the crop, followed by swarms of herring-gulls, as if the machines were trawlers. By the time he'd arrived he'd persuaded himself that the trip was vital. Hannah was still the best link they had between the killings.

Because he hadn't told the prison in advance that he intended to visit, he had to wait at the gatehouse while they found someone to take him to the library. There was a tiny room which he shared with a nervous young solicitor, who farted loudly then blushed. The walls were posted with mission statements about racism and bullying. They weren't as colourful as those in the hospital but they had the same improving tone.

He'd led the officer on the gate to believe that Hannah was expecting him. 'No. Don't disturb her. Just get an escort to take me over.'

The escort was a stocky young woman who seemed new to the job. They walked past a group of inmates who were weeding a huge circular bed, planted with geraniums in the shape of an anchor. The inmates whistled and shouted and the officer turned scarlet. Porteous didn't think she'd stick it long.

The library was closed and the officer had to unlock it. Inside, an orderly sat at a desk, covering books with transparent plastic.

'Mrs Morton about?'

'In the office. Hannah, there's someone to see you.'

She came out carrying a pile of new books. She seemed so shocked to see him that he thought she might drop them, but she recovered her composure well. She ignored him and spoke to the officer. 'That's all right, Karen. You can leave us to it. I'll see Mr Porteous back to the gate.'

The officer went reluctantly, obviously curious about what he was doing there.

'Do you want to go out for a smoke, Marty? Just give us a few minutes.'

When they were on their own she turned on him with a ferocity which surprised him.

'What the hell do you think you're doing here?'

'I had another appointment on the coast and I thought I'd call in, see if you could spare a few minutes.' I'm playing hookey. Hiding from my team.

'You don't get it, do you? In a prison a visit from the police means arrest, guilt, trouble. It'll be around the place in minutes that you've been to see me. There'll be rumours, stories. It's hard enough to work here as it is.'

'I'm sorry.'

'What do you want?'

'Really just a few questions. Would you like Mr Lee with you?' He would quite have liked to talk to the psychologist, get some informal advice about what might be going on with the Gillespies.

'Arthur can't be here. He's taking a class. If you'd phoned in advance we could have arranged it.'

'Really, it's no big deal.'

'Yes, Inspector. It is a big deal. Two murders nearly thirty years apart are linked by the same weapon. I knew both victims. I'm not stupid. I know how it looks.'

'I talked to your daughter yesterday.'

'She told me.'

'They're nice kids. Her and Joseph.'

'What is this about, Inspector? Marty and I have work to do. The library opens in twenty minutes.'

'Did Theo mention anyone called Alec Reeves?'

There was moment before she reacted. He saw that she still wasn't used to the boy's new name. Then she shook her head. He was disappointed. If she had met him, he thought, she'd have remembered. She remembered everything else. But he persisted.

'He was a friend of the Brices. You might have met him at their home.'

'I didn't meet anyone else there. They were content with their own company.'

'He was sitting with the Brices for the final production of *Macbeth*. In the front row. You told me you chatted to the Brices in the interval. You would have seen him then.'

She sat with her eyes shut and he knew she was trying to re-create the scene. He had heard of photographic memory but he'd never before met anyone with such vivid recall.

'A little man,' she said. 'Nondescript. Grey.'

'Yes.' He tried to keep the voice measured but she picked up his excitement.

'Did he kill Michael?'

'We want to talk to him.'

'So you're looking at someone else? Not just me.'

He smiled. 'No,' he said. 'Not just you.'

'You're right. He was staying with the Brices. He *had* been a member of the church but he'd been working away. There was a special service on the Sunday – a confirmation, I think. He'd come back for that and they'd persuaded him to stay the whole weekend.'

'What did Theo think of him?'

'He said he was boring. Boring but worthy.'

'He wasn't frightened of him? You said Theo phoned you on the Sunday to say he was scared and he needed to talk to you. Could he have been frightened of Alec Reeves?'

'I don't know. If he was, he didn't say.'

'Mr Reeves worked at a place called Redwood. Did Theo ever mention that to you?'

'Wasn't that the name of his school in Yorkshire?'

'No,' Porteous said gently. He didn't want to do anything to stifle her memory. 'I don't think it was.'

'Yes. I'm almost certain. Isn't it strange? I'd been trying so hard to remember if he ever told me the name and couldn't come up with a thing. Then you mentioned Redwood and the conversation's come back to me almost word for word.'

'Could you tell me? It is important.'

'It was the George Eliot essay.' She looked at him. She'd told him so many details of her time with Michael that she thought he knew it all. 'He was a George Eliot fan. As was I. There was a teacher who inspired him. When I reran the conversation in my head first he talked about "someone in the old place". But that wasn't what he said. Not at first. He corrected himself straight away but what he first said was "someone in Redwood".'

She beamed at him, delighted to have got it right. He could see why the fat psychologist fancied her.

So, Porteous thought, after the fire and Emily's death, Theo was sent to Redwood. He'd attended Marwood Grange as a day boy. That's why Hillier the housemaster hadn't remembered him. He must have lived at Redwood for years, until he moved to live with the Brices. Why? Because it was a place of safety and Randle had thought he was in danger from his step-mother? Or because he was so traumatized by the death of his sister, that he needed long-term help? If they could establish that Melanie had been there too, they'd have their link between both teenagers and Alec Reeves.

Hannah walked with him back to the gate. Marty was sitting outside on the grass. As they walked past him the orderly gave her a look which was almost protective.

Chapter Thirty

When he returned to the station Stout wasn't there. Claire Wright had sent him home to get a bite to eat.

'He was bushed,' she said. 'He was here most of the night again and then he went over to the old folks' bungalow to talk to Charlie Luke. And spent the rest of the morning mooching around town.'

'Looking out for Reeves?'

'What do you think?'

Porteous thought Stout was driven, losing it, but he didn't answer.

'Ray Scully's been on the phone.'

'And?'

'He's here. At the coast. He came up last night to stay at his mum's.'

'Can you go to see him? Check out his alibi of course, but let him talk. Anything Melanie might have told him. Did she write? Has he kept the letters? Find out if there's any possible connection between him and the Randles. Any gossip on the Gillespies would be useful too.'

'Sure.'

From his office Porteous phoned Carver. The pathologist was out and nobody else seemed willing to tell him if the report on Melanie Gillespie had been sent.

He sat at his desk for a moment then felt the old restlessness creeping up on him and went out.

He found Eddie Stout asleep in his garden. Bet opened the door to him. She'd been washing up and had on big yellow gloves like motorcycle gauntlets.

'Look at him.' She pointed through the open kitchen window to a neat patio, sheltered with a trellis covered by clematis and honeysuckle. Eddie sat in the shade in a green garden chair. His head was tilted back and his mouth was slightly open. He was snoring. 'I came in to make him a sandwich and when I went out he was off. He's still not eaten.'

'Leave him.' Porteous could smell the honeysuckle. 'He's been doing too much. It's not urgent.'

'No. He'd never forgive me if he knew you'd been and I'd not told him.'

Eddie woke with a start like a small boy startled from a dream. Bet left them. In the kitchen they heard her singing along to Classic FM, the sound of water running into a kettle. Eddie moved stiffly, easing the stiffness from his body.

'It looks as if you're right,' Porteous said. 'About Alec Reeves.' But even as he spoke he was trying to make sense of it. What had the Brices been playing at? They must have heard the rumours about Reeves but they'd invited him into a house where a young kid was staying. Then he thought – No, it was the other way round. Theo knew Reeves before he came to live with the Brices. Reeves must have introduced them.

'It looks as if Theo Randle was at Redwood,' Peter went on. 'Hannah Morton remembered his mentioning it. I haven't checked but I bet Melanie was there too, just before it closed.'

307

Stout shut his eyes, a silent prayer of thanks.

'Have they found him yet?'

Porteous shook his head.

'You'll be going public then? Tell the press we want to talk to him?'

'Tomorrow. I promise. I'm still worried about lack of evidence. Coincidence. It could be no more than that. If we come to trial I want nobody saying there can't be a fair hearing because of the ranting of the press. You can be sure all the old rumours will come out. Publicity works both ways. I've arranged to see Alice Cornish and she might have more information on Reeves. In the meantime you could ask again around the town. Discreetly. If he's come back here someone will know about it.'

'When are you seeing her?'

'I'm going straight from here. She still lives in Yorkshire.'

Eddie nodded with approval. 'I'm seeing the Spences as you suggested. And Chris Johnson.'

'Any problems?'

'Not with the Spences. She's a reporter, isn't she? All over me like a rash. Johnson wasn't so happy but he knew better than to object.'

'Look,' Porteus said. 'Take a couple of hours off. The rest of the day if you need it. Those interviews can wait until tomorrow.'

Stout didn't even bother to answer that. 'I think Reeves has done a runner. He's not gone home. He's not visited his sister. He's guessed that we're on to him.'

You're obsessed, Porteous thought, recognizing the signs. You're thinking of nothing else. Reeves is haunting your dreams. 'Alice Cornish might know where he's hiding out,' he said mildly.

'Please do me a favour.' Eddie leaned forward, put his hand on the arm of Porteous's chair, almost touching him. Fervent as he'd be preaching in the chapel on Sunday. 'Give me a ring when you get in. Let me know what she's said. Even if there's no news.'

'It could be late. You'll need some sleep.'

'I'll not be asleep. You phone me.'

Alice Cornish's house was less grand than Porteous had expected. She was a celebrity of a kind, a Dame, the author of a handful of books and dozens of reports. When he'd spoken to her that morning she hadn't exactly welcomed his visit. 'I don't understand, Inspector, why this conversation couldn't be conducted by telephone. I value my privacy.'

But he'd wanted to meet her. Not only because he thought he'd get more out of her face to face. He'd admired her work. And still he was itching with the need to run away. When he'd persisted in his request for a meeting she'd given in gracefully and instructed him precisely on his route from the motorway. It was an area he didn't know, too close to industrial centres to be of interest to second homers and holiday makers. As he left the main road there were views of the Pennines to the east and Emley Moor to the west. He drove down a steep hill into a valley bottom, turned at a disused mill and then he was there. A small stone cottage with a meadow beyond it and a garden in front so tangled with perennials that when he walked up the brick path he scattered pollen with his legs. A ginger cat was sleeping on a window-sill.

'Inspector.' She had the door open before he knocked, while he was still stroking the cat, and he was caught off guard and felt slightly frivolous to be petting the animal. But she must have liked cats because her mood was softer than it had been on the phone. 'Shall we talk in the garden?'

There was a small patch of lawn at the side of the house, the edges ragged with long grass where it hadn't been properly trimmed. They sat side by side on a wrought-iron bench.

'What is all this about? You said on the phone it was about Redwood. But I've retired. The centre is closed.'

'You employed a man called Reeves?'

'Alec, yes. One of our longest-serving employees. By the end he was part of the architecture of the place. He wasn't a demonstrative man. He never drew attention to himself. But it was impossible to imagine Redwood without him. His retirement and my decision to give up control coincided. I felt that was appropriate.'

'You liked him?'

'He didn't let anyone else get close enough to him for that. Not adults at least. He was very different with the children. But I respected him.'

'Were you aware when you appointed him that there were rumours he'd been involved in child abuse?'

'No!' She turned her face sharply so she was facing him. She wore her grey hair in a severe bob which must have been fashionable when she was a small child in the thirties. 'I don't believe it.'

'You had no suspicion when he was working for

you that he had an undesirable relationship with any of the children in his care?'

'None.'

'You didn't think it was odd that he'd never married?'

'Are you married, Inspector? Because I'm not.'

He could sense her hostility and sat for a moment in silence searching for words which might appease her, but she came at him again.

'Do you suspect Alec of child abuse, Inspector? A recent case?'

'Not exactly.'

'I'm sorry!' The sarcasm could have come from a ferocious headmistress. 'I'm not sure that I understand you. What do you mean "not exactly"?'

'We want to question Alec Reeves about two murders. We've been trying to trace him for a number of days. We hoped you might help us find him.'

She sat quite still with her hands folded in her lap, staring ahead of her.

'You've come from the north-east, Inspector?'

He nodded confirmation.

'Then one of the murders you're investigating is that of Michael Grey?'

'His real name was Theo Randle, but yes, I'm the senior investigating officer in that case.'

'I recognized the name when it appeared in the papers. When you phoned I thought you had questions about Michael . . . It never occurred to me that Alec was implicated.'

'We've no proof against Alec Reeves. But he was staying in Michael's home the weekend he was murdered. He had an unsavoury reputation in the town and was linked to the disappearance of another boy, a child with a learning disability of about the same age. You can understand why we want to talk to him. His disappearance is a cause for concern.'

'Yes,' she said slowly, 'I can see that it would be.' She turned towards him again. 'But I don't believe it, Inspector. I'll cooperate with you because I think that's what Alec would wish. But you're wrong about him. It's not unusual for him to disappear for a week or two in the summer. He's a hillwalker and he likes wild places and he avoids other people. He'll appear suddenly from the Highlands or the Peak District and make himself known to you.'

I hope he does, Porteous thought. But I'll not hold my breath.

'Can you tell me about the boy you knew as Michael Grey?' he said. 'You never knew his other name?'

'Not so far as I remember.'

'Perhaps you could check with your files?'

'There are no files. Not that we kept. It was part of the Redwood philosophy. The files remained the property of the children. They had open access to them while they stayed at the centre and they took all the records with them when they left.'

'Didn't that cause problems if you needed to liaise with other agencies?'

'No. It meant that we all had to involve the young people about their futures from the beginning.'

'There must be some records. A list, at least, of the children you cared for.'

'I have an autograph book. The children all signed their names when they left, added any comments they wanted. Towards the end of my time at Redwood there were names that I hardly recognized. I was so busy – lectures, reports, committees. Much of the day-to-day administration was left to my staff. That was when I knew it was time to leave.' She paused. 'At the beginning it was very different. We had so little money and we had to do everything ourselves. If it hadn't been for a generous benefactor the place would have closed only months after we started. It was a round of fund-raising, the school run, keeping the house from falling down and most of all finding time for some very disturbed children.'

'Was Michael Grey very disturbed?'

'Not as disturbed as some.'

'How was he referred? Social Services?'

'It was a long time ago, Inspector.'

'But you do remember?' He was sure that she did. Since hearing the news of Michael's murder, she would have gone over the details of his stay at Redwood. It was natural, what anyone would do.

'Michael was a private referral. It did happen occasionally. We were registered through Social Services and most of the children came through them, but sometimes we were approached by desperate parents who'd seen stories about us in the papers. Of course, they kept legal custody. Michael was unusual because he stayed with us for such a long time.'

'His father brought him to you?'

'I believe he did.'

'Don't you remember?'

'I wasn't here. I was in Geneva. Receiving some award.' She waved her hand as if it were of no importance. 'I wasn't keen but the staff thought I should go to raise the profile of the house. We'd not long opened. We were a democratic organization. I went. When I returned there was a new little boy. Michael. White hair, beautiful manners. Very distant. Very withdrawn. He didn't speak for months. I was told his mother had severe depression and his father a drink problem. A sister had been killed in a fire. The family didn't want Social Services involved but they thought we could help. I thought we could too. We were a good team . . .'

'Why the change of name?'

'I don't know. To me he was always Michael. Perhaps the family were in the public eye and afraid of publicity.'

'Perhaps.' Porteous thought it an extreme move. Once interest had died down after the fire, would anyone care what happened to a small boy?

'Did the family visit?'

'The father. Occasionally. Usually he was drunk when he turned up. When Michael was ready to leave we tried to arrange meetings with family members to discuss his future. But the appointments were never kept.'

'Michael attended a private school as a day boy?'

'It was what his father wanted. He made the arrangements. If Michael had been allowed to choose I think he'd have gone to the local grammar.'

'There was a fire at the school.'

'Yes.'

'Was Michael implicated?'

'Not in any way. The police came here first of course. We housed "problem" children. But he had an alibi. A member of staff was with him all evening.'

'Alec Reeves?'

'No. Not Alec Reeves.'

'How did he end up with the Brices?'

'Was that the name of the couple who took him in?'

He nodded.

'When Michael was sixteen we had a problem. Frankly he was taking a bed which could be better used by another child. He'd turned into a bright and well-adjusted young man. He'd enjoyed being at Redwood and he hadn't wanted to move, and we didn't want to throw him out. Of course we waited until he'd completed his O levels before thinking about it seriously at all. There was no interest from the family – we'd even had to subsidize his school fees because they'd stopped paying. So what to do with him? The fire in the middle of his lower-sixth year brought matters to a head.'

'Alec Reeves came up with a solution?'

'Yes. He'd not long started working with us. There was a retired clergyman and his wife, he said, in his home town. Childless, but full of love. We all met. Michael liked them. It seemed a wonderful solution.'

'Until he died less than two years later . . .'

'I never knew about that. Not until the press reports of his death.'

'Tell me about Melanie Gillespie.' If he hoped to shock her into some admission or indiscretion he was unsuccessful. She seemed lost in thought. The ginger cat had moved on to the grass beside her feet and she stopped absent-mindedly to tickle its ear.

'I'm sorry, Inspector. I don't recognize the name.'

'Melanie Gillespie was one of the children in your care. Much more recently. Within the last three or four years.' At least, he thought, I hope she was. Otherwise I've nothing to work on at all.

'I don't think so.'

'She had an eating disorder. Probably another private referral.'

'I've explained that in recent years my contact with the centre has been minimal.' She seemed tired now, rather than hostile. 'But we can check. Come inside and I'll show you my book. My record of achievement you might call it. More precious to me at least, than all the awards put together.'

She took him into a dusty and cluttered study. The book was gigantic, leather bound. It wouldn't have looked out of place in a cathedral. In it successive children had signed their names, written scraps of verse, drawn pictures.

'When do you think she left us?'

'Two years ago. Three perhaps.'

She turned the pages slowly.

'You see, Inspector. No Melanie Gillespie.'

'May I look?' Theo Randle had changed his name. Perhaps Melanie had too.

He found it immediately. *Mel Scully* written in spiky italics. Beside it a cartoon. A stick figure with cropped hair holding an electric guitar, with a balloon coming out of her mouth. Inside the balloon the words: *What now?*

'Scully was her father's name,' he said.

'I do remember her! Very bright. Very articulate. Self-destructive with her eating. A lot of aggression directed at her parents. Not nearly as confident as she wanted everyone to think her.'

'Had there been a child, do you know?'

'You think she'd been pregnant? Certainly not while she was here. Before?' She shrugged. 'She was someone we never quite got through to. She never felt able to trust us.' Porteous remembered Collier saying something similar. She closed the book suddenly. The air displaced by the heavy covers stirred the dust. 'What's happened to her?'

'She's dead too.'

Chapter Thirty-One

Despite his sleep in the garden Eddie Stout was tired. As he drove to The Old Rectory he found his concentration slipping, the car bouncing suddenly on the Cat's-eyes in the middle of the road. The Spences had agreed to see him at four. That was their quiet time, they said, between lunch and dinner. Sally would leave the paper early especially.

And they were waiting for him. A young woman in a black dress met him at the front door and led him to the lounge where the Spences sat, expectant and curious. Between them a small table was set for tea. There was a silver pot and china cups, tiny sandwiches, a double-tiered plate with scones and cakes.

'Just in time, Sergeant. I was about to pour.' Roger Spence wore a white shirt and a red bow-tie. He handed a cup and a plate to Stout, who juggled with them awkwardly, in the end balancing the plate on the arm of his chair. He noticed that Spence's fingers were very long, the nails beautifully manicured. Spence set down the teapot and rubbed his hands together. 'Now, how can we help?'

They both turned towards Eddie and smiled in a predatory way. Sally was dressed in a grey silk tunic over trousers. She filled the armchair, a huge grey walrus. He wondered how she would manage to prise herself to her feet. Jack Sprat and his wife, he thought. Throughout the conversation images and words came into his head unbidden as in a dream. Perhaps he should have followed Porteous's advice and waited until he was less tired. He felt he was no match for these two, especially now.

'I've been hearing rumours,' Sally said when he didn't answer immediately. Her tone was confidential, slightly flirtatious. She leaned forward and he could see the top of her bra. 'People are saying that you've linked Michael's murder – I still think of him as Michael – with that girl on the coast.'

'We're ruling out nothing at present.' The standard line. If she were any sort of a journalist she'd know anyway. And he thought she probably was very good at her job. She had the necessary ruthless streak

'We didn't know her,' Sally went on. 'The girl on the coast. We'd never met her.' She seemed very keen to make that point.

Eddie struggled to stamp his authority on the interview. 'It's the first murder I'd like to talk about.'

'Oh?' She smiled again, took a chocolate éclair from the plate and bit it in half.

Eddie turned to include them both in his question. 'You were at the final performance of *Macbeth*? The Friday before Michael disappeared.'

'That's right, Sergeant. I was selling programmes and Roger was helping to direct.'

Eddie watched the second half of the éclair disappear into her mouth. He unclipped his briefcase and took out the photograph given to him by Jack Westcott.

'Do you recognize the gentleman sitting next to Mr and Mrs Brice?'

Roger flicked his eyes towards the picture and immediately away again.

'I don't think I do,' he said casually. 'Why?'

'We're trying to trace as many people as possible who were there that evening. If you could try to remember, Mr Spence.'

'I know who it is!' Eddie almost expected her to clap her hands like a little girl who's just come top in a spelling test. 'It's Mr Reeves, isn't it? You must remember Roger. Alec Reeves, the scout master. There was talk . . .'

'Was there?' Roger licked his fingers with a long, darting tongue and patted his chin with a napkin.

'Probably all rumour,' she added quickly. 'You know what this place is like.'

'What exactly did the rumours say?' Stout asked, as if the information was new to him.

'Oh, you know. That he liked the company of young boys too much. I'd never met him. Not really. He ran the hardware store next to where my father worked, and I went into the shop sometimes on errands. My dad thought he was all right but then my dad said that about everyone. I didn't think there was anything particularly creepy about him, but then I was only a kid. But I'm sure Mr Reeves had already left the town when Michael disappeared. There was a new bloke in the shop when I was in the sixth form. Younger. Good looking in a dark, moody sort of way . . .'

'But Reeves came back for the performance of *Macbeth*,' Eddie said.

'He must have done, I suppose, if the photo was

taken that night. But I don't remember him. I was back-stage, helping with the costume changes. Roger was a real dictator. He wouldn't let us out during the interval.'

She grinned at her husband but he didn't respond.

'Do you remember seeing that man, Mr Spence?'

Spence took the photograph, holding it with exaggerated care by the edge of the print.

'No, I'm afraid not. Quite impossible after all these years.'

'Of course, he looks a lot older now,' Sally said.

They both stared at her.

'You've seen him recently?'

'About ten days ago. Don't you remember, Roger? He came in here with Paul Lord and his wife. I knew there was something familiar about him. I'm surprised that they stayed friends. Poor Paul, he was tainted by his association with Reeves when he was young. I mean, he was never going to be the most popular boy in the school. Not with that acne. Though I remember one night Hannah coming pretty close to snogging him . . . And he was a boy scout, wasn't he? His picture was in the paper when he won some award and he never lived it down. That awful uniform. But then it came out that he was big buddies with Alec Reeves, and when all those rumours started he was teased dreadfully.'

She continued talking but Eddie had stopped listening. Paul Lord was the lad who'd given Alec Reeves an alibi after Carl Jackson had disappeared. Eddie had interviewed the boy himself. He remembered a stuffy sitting-room, a mother, flustered and embarrassed, and Paul, hidden as Sally had said behind a layer of acne, stubbornly refusing to change his story. At last Eddie had given up and soon after Reeves had left the town.

'Is Mr Lord a regular customer?'

Roger answered. 'Yes. Mostly at lunchtimes. He's a businessman. He brings his clients here.'

'What is his business?'

'He's some sort of computer consultant. He and his wife are partners. They work from home. They turned the outhouses of the farmhouse where they live into an office.'

'The address please?'

But he knew it already. Porteous had phoned there when they were trying to identify the body in the lake. Balk Farm. Home to Balk Farm Computing. Once home to Carl Jackson, the lad with learning disability, and his parents.

In the car Eddie tried to phone Porteous, but his boss's mobile was turned off. Eddie saw that as an opportunity and didn't leave a message. He thought he'd be late for his interview with Chris Johnson, but that didn't seem important. Now he had to speak to Paul Lord, who'd been with Alec Reeves ten days ago, who must know where he was hiding out.

He drove too fast, still in the daze he'd been in since his sleep in the garden, his thoughts woolly, his eyes prickling with exhaustion. He came over the brow of the hill and had a flashback of himself, young and fit, standing in a line with other men and women, searching for Carl, prodding into the heather and bracken with a long pole. They'd improved the entrance to the farm, widened it and he sailed past, seeing out of the corner of his eye a big sign advertising the computer consultancy. It was only as he pulled into a lay-by to turn back that he thought what a fool he was being. Alec Reeves might be hiding out at Balk Farm but what could Eddie do about it, single-handed and without a warrant? Only warn him and drive him away. He drove slowly back to the town, his heart racing with panic at the damage he'd almost done.

He arrived at Chris Johnson's house without remembering how he'd got there. He was late and the conversation started badly. Johnson had recently moved into a small terraced house on a modern private estate. A woman, very young and very pregnant, opened the door. She wore a sleeveless dress which clung around her stomach and heavy breasts. Her frame looked as if it would snap under the weight.

'You're late,' she said. 'He's gone.'

'But his van's still here.' Stout nodded towards a transit pulled on to the pavement.

'He's not got time to talk to you. The soundcheck's in half an hour.'

Stout was too tired to argue. 'Just let me in. It'll not take long.' He pushed past her, not roughly, hardly touching her, but usually he would have been polite, and he was surprised at the change in himself. He walked straight into the living-room. Chris Johnson was watching television. In the corner was a flat-pack cot, still in its box, and a white fur rabbit. Eddie picked up the remote from the floor and zapped off the television. The woman followed him in and levered herself carefully into an armchair. There was nowhere else to sit so he leaned against the door.

'I want to know where you were one evening last

week.' He gave the date Melanie had been taken, but all the time his thoughts were racing about Alec Reeves. His hands were shaking at the thought of how close he had come to wrecking the whole investigation, and then he imagined Reeves driving down the track to the road by the reservoir before he'd had a chance to have it watched. He should have sorted out surveillance before coming here. He was losing it. 'Now!' he snapped. 'I've not got time to mess about.'

'I was working.'

'Where?'

'An eighteenth birthday party. Some village hall out in the sticks. Why?'

'Can you prove it?'

'You can check. Some of the kids got a bit wild. The police were called. It was that sort of place. No fun after nine thirty or the neighbours have a seizure. The cops came in and told me to turn down the sound.'

'What time did you get home?'

'About midnight.'

'Can you confirm that?' To the woman. Going through the motions. Though no way would Johnson have been able to pick up Melanie from the Rainbow's End and be back here at midnight.

'Of course.' There was a mischievous look in her eye which said – But how can you trust me? I would say that, wouldn't I? Eddie ignored it. Duty done.

'Does the name Alec Reeves mean anything to you?' The question was directed at Johnson. The woman wouldn't have been born when Alec was running the hardware shop in the high street.

Johnson shook his head. Stout got out the photographs. Reeves as he'd been at the performance of

Macbeth. Reeves more recently handing out Duke of Edinburgh award certificates. 'You don't recognize him?'

Johnson stood up quickly. 'I've told you no. I've got to get to work.' He pulled a leather jacket from the back of his chair, felt in the pocket for car keys.

Running away, Stout thought. What scared him?

'You weren't one of Alec's little boys were you, Chris?'

'Jesus, are you crazy?'

The blasphemy hit Stout, as it always did, like a slap.

'Nothing to be ashamed of if you were. Not your fault.'

'I told you. I didn't know the man.'

Chris went up to the woman, bent to kiss her on the forehead, stroked her belly, then he stood in front of Stout, challenging him not to let him out. Eddie opened the door for him. He watched for a moment as Johnson slid open the door of the transit, climbed in and drove off. The woman didn't move or speak. She looked at him from her chair, waiting for him to go.

Chapter Thirty-Two

They decided to go into Balk Farm early the next morning. Not mob handed. Porteous and Stout would knock on the door, very polite, very civilized. There'd be a car at the end of the track and someone on the hill behind the house with binoculars in case Alec tried to get out on foot. Because, as Eddie said, Reeves knew every inch of that hill.

The team had all crowded into Porteous's office to make the final arrangements, and Eddie stayed, even after the rest of them went. So wired up that Porteous knew he wouldn't sleep. Porteous wanted to get home and felt the nerviness was contagious. He tried to wind up the discussion.

'Then a team to search the house,' he said. 'Like we decided. Good people. Tidy and careful. It's all sorted, Eddie. Nothing left to do.' Still Stout didn't take the hint, so he added, 'Let's go home. We'll have an early start.'

But Stout wouldn't move until he'd gone through it all again.

Peter woke before the alarm went off. It was just light, a grey mist in the valley, the first blackbird screaming.

No walk to work today. A break from routine. He'd arranged to pick up Eddie from home and knew he'd be awake too, probably already dressed, pacing the floor. Porteous understood his sergeant. He'd been there. Like a reformed smoker he wanted to preach. He wanted to yell: It does you no good. All that stress and adrenalin. It'll make you crack up. Except it probably wouldn't make Eddie Stout crack up. *He* was tough, with a wife who was there when he came in at night, to help him relax and to stroke away the tension.

Peter showered, made tea, toasted a piece of wholemeal bread, forced himself to eat it. He was scared. Not of Alec Reeves, who was probably pathetic, not half the monster Eddie had described. But of cocking this up. If he made a mess of it he didn't think he'd be able to work with Eddie Stout again.

He was early but Eddie must have been looking out because he was halfway down the drive before Porteous had switched off the engine. He was carrying a foil-wrapped packet, which he threw on to the back seat.

'Bet insisted on making sandwiches. I told her it would all be over before dinner.'

They met up at the police station and drove in convoy round the reservoir, held up at one point by an ancient tractor. The only other traffic was a post van. They pulled into the lay-by where Stout had turned his car the day before while the team got into place. Stout didn't mention that. He didn't mention how close he'd been to going it alone.

At seven thirty exactly they drove up the track. That was the time they'd decided on. Not too early to cause offence if it did all turn out to be a mistake and Reeves wasn't there at all. Stout dismissed the possibility, but went along with the theory. These were business people, keen surely. They'd be checking their emails, planning their day. But it was still early enough to catch them on the hop, to emphasize that they were here on serious business.

'This has changed a bit. I don't think I'd have recognized it.' Stout was driving. He pulled into a marked parking bay in what had once been the farmyard. A brass sign by the door of a converted barn said 'Reception' but they ignored that and went towards the house. Everything was smart, spruce, clean. The garden was landscaped. A conservatory had been added. Porteous took a breath and rang the doorbell.

The door was opened by a child, a boy of about twelve, half dressed for school, his shirt hanging out, his buttons undone. Porteous hadn't expected that. There'd been no mention of children.

'Could I talk to your father please?'

The boy grunted. He still seemed half asleep. He led them through the house to a large kitchen, all new oak and terracotta tiles. There was a smell of coffee and faintly of cinnamon. At a table by a big window sat a couple, the woman in a silk kimono, the man, his hair wet from the shower in a short towelling dressing gown. The table was laid for three but it seemed the third place was for the boy because there was no sign of Reeves. Either the couple hadn't heard the doorbell or they thought the boy had dealt with it because they didn't look up. They were discussing work, planning a meeting for later in the day. If Reeves was there, Porteous thought they weren't aware of what he'd done. They had no sense of danger.

The boy stood dreamily. His bare feet had made no sound on the floor. Eventually he seemed to remember what he was doing.

'Dad.' Then they did look round and he nodded over his shoulder in the direction of the visitors before wandering off.

Paul Lord must have taken them for potential clients. If he was surprised or annoyed that they'd turned up at such an inconvenient time, he didn't show it. Perhaps it wasn't unusual. He stood up, held out his hands, a gesture of welcome, but also of apology for the dressing gown, the half-eaten breakfast. He was confident, rather good looking. There was no sign of the spotty schoolboy. His makeover had been as dramatic as that of the farm.

'Can I help you?' Then he turned to Stout. 'Don't I know you? I remember, you were a policeman. That dreadful case when I was a boy. Do you know, you've hardly changed.'

'Still am a policeman, sir. Here to ask you a few questions.'

And still Lord remained courteous and composed. Too courteous? Porteous wondered. Wouldn't most people be irritated, hostile, if they were interrupted in the middle of breakfast. But perhaps it had become a habit to be pleasant. Perhaps that was why he was so successful. He treated them now with a puzzled good humour.

He asked to be allowed to dress first and they let both of them go, because even if Reeves was hiding out somewhere in this big house and tried to do a runner the team outside would get him. That might be better even. Save them having to search and it would look better in court if he had been trying to escape.

'Does Phillippa have to be involved in this, Inspector?'

Phillippa, the wife, had remained silent throughout.

'We do have questions for both of you.'

And he accepted even that without a fuss.

While they were waiting in the kitchen the boy came in for breakfast. He shovelled in cereal, then, well trained, stacked the bowl in the dishwasher and returned the milk to the fridge. He showed no curiosity about who they were.

'Do you need a lift to school, lad?' Stout asked.

'No thank you.' Very polite, very well brought up. 'I get the bus from the end of the track.'

Like Carl Jackson, thirty years before. Doesn't that haunt Paul Lord? Porteous thought. He was involved in the case even if it was only as a witness. How can he send his son up that lane every morning without a worry?

They carried out the interview in the conservatory, drinking the best coffee Porteous had tasted for years from chunky, hand-thrown mugs. Stout took the lead. That was what they had decided.

'A bit of a coincidence you living here,' he said. 'After you were involved in the Carl Jackson case.'

'Not really involved,' Lord protested mildly. 'I gave Alec an alibi. That was all. And not really a coincidence. I'd kept in touch with Alec. When Sarah's husband died he knew she was wanting to sell. I was looking for bigger premises and he knew that too . . .

He put us together. She saved on agents' fees. We got the place for a good price.' He shrugged.

'It's Mr Reeves we're here about.'

'Why?'

'We'd like to talk to him. He seems to have disappeared.'

'I mean, why do you want to talk to him?'

Stout paused. 'It's in connection with a murder inquiry.'

'The body in the lake? Michael Grey? You've got things all wrong. Again. Alec had left town before Michael disappeared. Before he arrived even.' He kept his voice amused. Still he wasn't rattled.

'He came back,' Porteous said quietly. 'To watch a production of *Macbeth*. It was special because Michael was the star and Alec knew him very well. We'll call him Michael shall we, though that wasn't his real name. Michael had been staying at Redwood, where Mr Reeves was working as a care worker. Were you aware of the connection at the time?'

'No.'

'Don't you find that strange? You were the same age as Michael. Wouldn't Mr Reeves have introduced you? So you could help the boy settle into his new school.'

'He might have done I suppose, but he didn't. It wasn't necessary. Michael was confident, immediately popular. Alec would have recognized that he didn't need any help from me. Besides, after the business with Carl, all the gossip at the time, my parents didn't want me to have anything more to do with Alec. I expect he was trying to save me embarrassment.'

There was a pause, then Stout turned to Phillippa,

changing his tone. 'Are you a local woman, Mrs Lord? Had you heard about all this?'

'Only what Paul's told me. We met at university.' When she'd gone off to dress she'd put on make-up. Her lips were glossy, her complexion flawless. She was dressed in a neat little skirt and a sleeveless top. A jacket was hung carefully on the back of a chair.

'When did you first meet Mr Reeves?' Stout asked.

She gave a frown, not because the question worried her but because she wanted them to see how irrelevant all this was. It was eating into the important business of her day. 'He came to our wedding.'

'Did he?' Stout raised his eyebrows, a pantomime of surprise.

'Paul doesn't have many relatives. His side of the church would have been rather thin.'

'And Alec is an old friend,' Lord broke in. 'He was very good to me.'

'You've kept in touch ever since?'

'Yes. Phone calls. Christmas cards. If he visits his sister he calls.'

'Did he talk to you about his work?'

'A little. Not in detail. He wouldn't consider that ethical. Confidentiality must be very important in social work.'

'Quite.' Stout deliberately set down his mug. 'You can tell us now, Mr Lord. After all these years. You were under pressure at the time, we all know that. A boy. But now there's a chance to put things right . . . Where was Mr Reeves on the afternoon Carl Jackson disappeared?'

'With me. Just as I said.'

Phillippa looked again at her watch. 'Look, I've got a meeting. I really should go.'

'A few more minutes, Mrs Lord.' Stout didn't even look at her. He continued to hold Lord's stare. 'When did you last see Mr Reeves?' he asked suddenly.

'I can't remember the date. He phoned the day after the school reunion. He said he was going to be in the area, he'd like to take us out for a meal. We arranged to meet at The Old Rectory the following evening.'

'What did he want?'

'Want? Nothing. Our company perhaps. He's a kind, elderly man. Occasionally he must get lonely.'

'Did he talk about Michael Grey?'

'I think we must have discussed the identity of the body in the lake. It was a matter of interest. Everyone in Cranford was talking about it.'

'Did you introduce the subject, or did he?'

'I did. I remember Michael going away in the middle of exams. We all thought he'd gone back to his father.'

'At the meal at The Old Rectory, did Alec tell you that he knew Michael, that he'd worked with him at Redwood?'

'No.'

'Odd that, isn't it? You were gossiping about the body in the lake. Enjoying the drama even. Nothing wrong with that. But Alec didn't tell you it was through him that the boy had come to town?'

'I've told you. Alec was scrupulous about confidentiality.'

'So you did. Did he stay here the night after the meal?'

'No. We offered to put him up, but he'd made other arrangements.'

'What were those?'

'I don't know. I presumed he'd be staying with his sister.'

'How did he seem that night?'

For the first time Lord hesitated before answering. 'He seemed suddenly very old. We wondered if he might be ill. He said not, but it occurred to me that he'd arranged to meet us . . . almost as a way of saying goodbye.' He looked up, gave a little smile. 'Probably just my imagination. All that talk of death.'

There was a pause. Porteous could sense Phillippa's impatience but still Stout held the stage and she didn't dare move. When Stout spoke at last he was cheerful, a jolly surrogate uncle who should have been invited to the wedding too.

'You said you got a good price for Balk Farm. You've made a lovely place here, a real family home. Why was the price so low? A payment was it, for backing up Alec's story all that time ago?'

Lord stood up. At first Porteous thought Stout had succeeded in provoking him into losing control, but he held it together. All the taunting and bullying as a child had held him in good stead.

'I think you'd better take your sergeant away, Inspector, before he says something else you'll both regret. You're welcome to search the house if you don't believe me about Alec. Phillippa and I will be working in the office. We've wasted enough time already.'

The team searched the house but Porteous left them to it. He could tell it would be futile. He had to get Stout back to the police station, find some way to deal with his disappointment. In the car the sergeant sat mute, shaking his head. He didn't speak until they were in Porteous's office.

'I played it all wrong. But I don't know what else I could have done.'

'Perhaps he was telling the truth.'

Before Stout could answer the phone rang. Porteous listened, said little, replaced the receiver.

'You'll need those sandwiches of Bet's after all,' he said. 'Reeves's neighbour contacted the Yorkshire lads. She thinks he came home last night.'

Chapter Thirty-Three

Reeves lived in a tidy bungalow at the end of a cul-de-sac of similar houses. Porteous parked at the end of the street and they walked down, but still he was aware that they were being watched. Not from Reeves's place. The curtains there were still closed. But in the other bungalows neighbours were twitching behind the Venetian blinds and the bleached fancy nets.

'The old lady next door said it was very late when he got in. One thirty at least. Though according to the local lad who spoke to her she's as deaf as a post and he didn't think a car would wake her.'

The car, a red Metro, was parked on the drive, pulled right up to the garage door.

'She says it must have been late when he got here or he'd have put the car away. He always kept it in the garage. Security conscious. Head of the neighbourhood watch.'

'A model citizen,' Stout said sneering.

They knew there was no way out from the back of the bungalow. A thick leylandii hedge separated the garden from a railway embankment. Occasionally high-speed trains roared past, making conversation impossible. Porteous rang the doorbell. They stood back and waited. Nothing happened. He rang the bell again, then tried the door. It opened.

They stepped into a wide hall with a door on either side, and a corridor ahead which led, Porteous presumed, to bedrooms and bathroom. There was a pale grey carpet on the floor, a small table with a telephone.

'Mr Reeves?'

There was no answer. He opened the right-hand door into a kitchen. A yellow roller blind covered the window, but let in enough light to show empty workbenches, a spotless tiled floor. There were no plates or cups draining by the sink and the dishcloth folded over the mixer tap was dry and hard. Porteous looked in the fridge. It had recently been defrosted and was empty.

'He must have gone straight to bed,' Stout said. He couldn't stand still. He was fidgeting like a kid. 'Let's wake the bastard up.'

But Porteous shook his head. He went back into the hall and opened the opposite door into the living-room. The bay windows were covered by thick velvet curtains and it took his eyes a moment to adjust to the gloom. Stout came up behind him impatiently and switched on the light. The room was lit by two lamps on the walls. They had bulbs like imitation candles and heavy fringed shades. The central light was operated by another switch and didn't come on, but it was a chandelier with similar fittings. It must have been more substantial than it looked, because it supported the weight of Alec Reeves, who hung by a noose of blue nylon rope, twisted around the chain which fixed the chandelier to the ceiling. A kitchen stool, overturned, lay on the floor beneath him.

Stout was about to go into the room but Porteous pulled him back.

'There's nothing we can do. It might be a crime scene.' He wondered why he wasn't more surprised. Had he been expecting this as soon as he realized the door was open?

'What are you talking about? He knew we were on to him and he topped himself.' Stout was almost weeping with frustration. This wasn't the way it should have ended. He still had things he wanted to say to Mr Alec Reeves.

'Perhaps.'

'What do you mean, "perhaps"? He came in last night and killed himself.'

'Why didn't he lock the door?'

'What!' It came out as a scream.

'Suicide. It's a private thing. You wouldn't want to be disturbed.' Peter thought he was an expert. At the depth of his depression, he'd contemplated suicide in all its forms. Walking into the sea. Taking pills. Hanging. Jumping off a bridge like his dad. One of the things that had stopped him in the end was the possibility of an audience. The terrible embarrassment of being caught in the act.

Eddie was looking at him as if he were mad. 'Maybe he just forgot.'

'He wasn't that sort of man. He was careful. He had a routine. And the key was in the lock on the inside of the door. He used it to get into the house, took it out and put it in on the inside. A deliberate act. Why didn't he turn it then?'

'Maybe he didn't care.'

'Oh, I think he cared.'

'What are you saying?'

'That I think he was murdered.' He spoke quietly, apologetically. For thirty years Eddie had thought of this man as a monster, the human form of the devil he talked about in pulpits on Sundays. It was like expecting him to accept he'd got all the other Sunday stuff wrong too.

'Why?'

'I don't think he killed Theo and Melanie. I don't know about Carl. Perhaps not even him. I think we got it wrong.'

'Not "we"!' Eddie bellowed. A child having a tantrum. Wanting to be important, even if it meant taking the blame. 'If anyone got it wrong it was me.'

'We need the scene-of-crime team.'

'Why was he murdered if he wasn't involved?'

'To make us think he was. If the house had a Yale lock we'd have been taken in by it. The murderer would have been able to pull the door to behind him and we'd never have known any different. The pathologist should throw some light.' He paused, turned to Stout. 'Look, I might be wrong. I'm just saying how I see it.'

'No,' Stout said. 'I don't think you're wrong.' Then, muttering, just loud enough for Peter to hear. 'I don't think you're ever wrong.'

Porteous left him waiting for the local team and went to see the old lady who'd reported Reeves's return. She took a while to answer the door. She used a Zimmer frame and she was a big woman. Walking was an effort. But she'd moved as quickly as she could, frightened that he'd go without giving her the low down.

'Anything up?' she said, moving awkwardly aside to let him in.

'I'm afraid Mr Reeves is dead.' She'd see the trolley soon enough.

'I knew something were wrong!'

'Why?'

'Like I told that lad on the phone, he hadn't put his car away. I know it were late when he got in, but he always did.' She had a heavy Yorkshire accent. He saw the hearing aid, remembered what they'd said about her being deaf.

'Did you hear his car?'

'Saw the lights. I was awake and got up to get a cup of tea. You don't sleep so well when you get older. I was in the kitchen waiting for the kettle to boil.'

'Did you see him get out of the car?'

'No. I took my tea back to bed. The bedroom's at the back.'

'What time was it?' Just checking.

'Quarter to two.'

'It *was* just the one car?'

'What do you mean?'

'He didn't have a visitor? Someone who parked at the top of the road perhaps?'

'Not that I saw. Anyway he wasn't one for visitors at any time. Certainly not in the middle of the night.'

He was halfway down the path when she shouted after him. 'What was it that killed him then?'

He pretended he was deaf too and didn't turn round.

Eddie was waiting in the kitchen of Reeves's house, subdued. 'I had another look,' he said. 'Just from the door. You're right. It's the way that stool's lying. If he'd kicked it away it would be further from him.'

'The old lady didn't see anything.'

'The local lads are on their way,' Eddie said. 'We've made their day. It's two years since they had a murder.'

'Do you mind waiting for them?'

'Nah. Where are you off to?'

'I want to talk to Alice Cornish. I don't think we got it all wrong. Redwood's still the place that links the killings together.'

'You think she knows something?'

'I want to talk to her.' He thought, I don't want to be waiting here when they cut down Alec Reeves. I don't want to see Eddie realize it's partly his fault. He hounded Alec out of Cranford because he was lonely man who only felt comfortable in the company of kids. I want this over, with no more drama.

It was the last thought that stuck with him on the drive to Alice Cornish's cottage. It made him take the bends too quickly and hit his horn at a slow, elderly driver hogging the middle of the road. He felt the pressure and when he saw a café by the side of the road just before the turn-off into Alice's lane, he forced himself to stop. It was an ordinary living-room with two tables covered with gingham cloths; a jolly middle-aged woman brought him Earl Grey and a home-made scone with jam which she said she'd bought at the WI market. He ate it and told her how good it was, but he couldn't face waiting for her to bring him change, so he stuck a five-pound note under the plate when she was out of the room and he left.

He hadn't phoned Alice Cornish in advance. Partly superstition. If he phoned she wouldn't be there.

Partly because he needed to get out of Reeves's immaculate bungalow even if it were on a wild-goose chase.

She *was* there. The cottage door was open. Her briefcase and an overnight bag stood just inside. When she came to greet him she was dressed for a meeting – a smart trouser suit with a loose silk jacket. Her grey fringe was ruler straight. She was wearing lipstick.

'Inspector, I haven't time to talk to you now. I'm expecting a taxi to the station.'

'Alec Reeves is dead.'

'What happened?' The colour had drained from her face but her voice was even.

'I think he was murdered. It could have been suicide.'

'No. Alec wouldn't have killed himself. He'd have seen it as an act of cowardice.'

'Is there anything you have to tell me?'

She looked directly at him. 'Nothing.'

'I need to look at your book again. The book with the children's names inside.'

She hesitated. Down the track came a red Mondeo. It sounded as though the exhaust had a hole in it. He was aware that he'd been listening to it approaching for some time.

'My taxi. I'm appearing before a select committee. Not something I can put off.'

'Please.'

She paused again. 'All right. But you'll have to see to yourself. Just shut the door behind you when you leave. It's a Yale lock.'

She picked up her bags and went out to meet the

taxi. He stood, watching her. She turned back before getting into the car.

'Inspector?'

'Yes.'

'There's some coffee in the kitchen. It should still be hot.'

He smiled and waved his thanks.

He poured himself a mug of lukewarm coffee and took it to the study. He opened the big book with its scribbled signatures, its jokes and its drawings, turning the pages slowly, looking for anything he'd missed the first time round. Anyone else would have given up, but this was the only thing he was good at, this persistence, this love of the detail. When he found nothing the first time, he worked through it all again. And this time he saw it, wondered how he could have been so blind not to have picked it up earlier.

He shut the cottage door carefully and sat in his car to call Eddie and then the office. It was late afternoon. The car window was open and he could hear woodpigeons calling beyond the meadow. The ginger cat was back in its favourite spot on the window-sill. In the office he spoke to Charlie Luke.

'The pathologist's report has finally come through,' Luke said. 'Melanie Gillespie's never been pregnant. And we traced that kiddie you were interested in. Emma Leese. It all seems like the Gillespies said. Melanie used to babysit for her. But the baby died. Cot death. No wonder she was upset.'

That was it then, Porteous thought. The final piece of information. The tag line to the joke. The final connection.

PART FOUR

Chapter Thirty-Four

The afternoon the police came to talk to Rosie and Joe in the Prom, it was hotter than ever. Rosie thought that was why the conversation seemed so unreal. The heat seemed to shimmer, even inside the building, stopping her from thinking clearly.

When they walked in she was behind the bar. It had been one of those quiet afternoons she spent daydreaming. She'd look at the big clock in its heavy wooden frame and see that an hour had gone by and she knew she must have served half a dozen customers but she couldn't remember any of them. Then Joe had bounced in, excited somehow despite his grief, shaking her out of her reverie, and soon after that, the policemen. She'd never met them but she guessed at once who they were. Hannah had described them as a double act and Rosie knew what she meant. It was hard to imagine them working apart. But she couldn't work out why her mother had been so scared of them. They looked like two ordinary, middle-aged men. Out of place in here. They were dressed for the office, not the seaside in a heatwave. Doughy faces covered with a sheen of sweat.

They stood for a moment just inside the door and then the younger man came to the bar. He introduced himself and ordered orange juice. He was pleasant enough, but she couldn't forget he'd upset her mother and found it hard to be polite. Joe took a beer off him then they sat round one of the tables in the corner, staring at each other, not sure how to start.

'This isn't official,' the inspector said. 'Nothing formal. We just want to talk about Mel.'

Somehow that started them off, so he didn't have to ask any questions. It was like a real conversation, friends chatting. Frank wasn't there – he was minding the bar – but the rest of them did what Porteous wanted. They just talked about Mel.

But right from the beginning Rosie couldn't recognize who they were going on about. Slow down, she wanted to say. I mean, what *is* going on here? It was as if the person who'd been her best friend throughout the sixth form had disappeared to be replaced in their collective memories by a total stranger. Joe was worse than any of them. Really she wished he wasn't there. She felt constrained. While he was going on about how delicate Mel had been, how fragile, she wanted to yell at him: No, she was more than that, stronger than that. You know what she was like. She could be a manipulative cow. Ruthless. She had to get her own way. She wasn't the victim you're all making out.

But she couldn't do it to him. Not yet. Someone would have to put him straight, but it couldn't be her. She had too much to lose. What if he never forgave her? So she sat quiet while they warbled on, pussy-footing around the subject.

'What about you, Rosie?' Porteous said at last, leaning across the table, giving her a seriously deep and meaningful look, as if he expected *her* to give them the truth. 'What have you got to tell us about Mel?'

'Nothing new. Nothing that's not already been said.'

She could tell he was disappointed. They went on to talk about Mel's music, how talented she was and how she'd already got a confirmed university place at Edinburgh, the same old gushing stuff.

'They were so impressed,' Joe said, 'that they'd have taken her even if she'd failed all her A levels.'

Then Porteous tried again. He wanted to know if Mel had ever been pregnant. Not now, but at some time in the past. The question was so delicately put together that not even Joe was offended.

'No,' Joe said. 'Of course not. She'd have told me.'

'Would she?'

Joe didn't answer that because there were lots of things Mel hadn't liked to talk about.

Rosie though was certain. 'It's not possible. Mel would never get pregnant. She was paranoid about it, wasn't she, Joe?'

Joe nodded sadly in agreement and Rosie continued.

'She had to be in control of her body. Completely. That was what the food thing was all about. And if there was some accident, some mistake, she'd get rid of it immediately.'

'Was there ever any accident?'

'No,' Joe said. 'Not while she was with me.'

'Are you sure?' When there was no reply, he added. 'No matter. The pathologist will be able to tell us.'

Rosie was daydreaming again. She and Mel had talked about children on one of their girlie nights together. She'd slept on the sofa bed in Mel's room and they'd got through a bottle of wine each when they'd got back from the pub. Mel had got a bit soppy about the kid she used to babysit, but she'd made it clear a family wasn't part of her future. 'Your life's not your own if you're a mother,' she'd said, shuddering. Though what could she know?

'Eleanor seems to manage OK.'

'That's different. I'm old enough to look after myself. I don't bother her any more. She wasn't so keen when I was little.' She'd paused. 'I want to be someone. You can't concentrate on what you want to do if you're surrounded by screaming kids.'

And then, lying on top of her bed, propped up on one elbow, Mel had squinted across at Rosie. 'What about you? I can see you as an earth mother. Married. A cottage in the country. Four or five kids, a goat and some hens scratching about in the garden.' Rosie had laughed then, but something about the image still appealed.

She was brought back to the pub by a sudden blast from the jukebox, a couple of bikers laughing. Porteous gave her another pleading look but she ignored it. She told him she had nothing else to say and offered to look after the bar so they could talk to Frank.

Frank must have realized that Porteous would want to talk to him about the bloke who'd been in the Prom asking after Mel, but he didn't seem very pleased about it.

'Look, I don't think I can be much help . . .'

'Don't be daft, Frank. No one else can remember him.'

And she gave him a playful little push, sending him out into the room. He looked shaky, panicky, walking towards the policeman as if he were already about to go into the witness box. From the bar she couldn't hear exactly what the group in the corner were saying, but Frank was facing her and she saw him staring blankly, occasionally shaking his head. His eyes were unfocused, wandering. It was as if he wasn't really thinking about the questions and the answers. He was just trying to survive the interview, waiting for it to be over.

The next day she tackled him about it. She'd been thinking about it all night. Frank had liked Mel, in the way that he seemed to like all the young people who came into the Prom. He'd joked with her, acted sometimes as father-confessor, standing at the bar for ages listening to all her troubles. So why had he been so reluctant to discuss her with the police?

She waited until about five o'clock when they had their meal break together and she could get him on his own. They sat in the little staff-room which led off the kitchen. They propped the outside door wide open and sat beside it on old bar stools, their plates on their knees, looking out at the pavement. Families were already trailing back from the beach, the children fractious and covered in sand, the parents loaded with towels and toys. There was the hot smell of drying seaweed and frying onions from the burger stall at the fair.

'What was going on yesterday, Frank?'

'What do you mean?' He was defensive. He had the same unfocused look in his eyes as when he'd been talking to Porteous. She thought: But he can't be scared of me. Frank had always been the boss. He knew everything there was to know about running a bar. She'd been the dippy teenager who couldn't pour a decent pint, who couldn't get up in the mornings, who turned into work with seconds to spare. He teased her and poked fun in a slightly flirty way which kept her wary. Something new was going on here which she didn't quite understand. The power in the relationship had shifted.

'Well, it didn't look as if you were being particularly cooperative,' she said, carefully keeping her voice neutral.

He wiped his forehead with the back of his hand.

'Don't you want to catch the bloke who killed Mel?'

'I don't think the chap that came in that night did kill her.'

'How did you know that, Frank?'

He shook his head, a refusal to answer.

'If you knew anything you should have told the police.'

An open-top bus rattled past. A party of kids on the top deck all held helium-filled balloons. Rosie imagined the bus rising slowly in the air, carried slowly out to sea. Frank took a mouthful of sandwich, muttered something which she couldn't make out.

'What was that?' Sharply. Sounding like her mother trying to teach him table manners.

'I said I've had dealings with the police. I know what they're like. They'd set *me* up given half a chance. Best policy's not to say anything.'

'Nobody's saying you'd ever harm Mel. Why would you?'

He turned to her. Grateful, sad puppy eyes were focused properly on hers for the first time. 'I've got a record. That'd be enough for them.'

She hadn't known about the record. Again she looked at him in a new light. She wondered what he'd been done for and if he'd ever been inside. She imagined him in Stavely asking her mother to find him books, then thought she couldn't see him as the reading type.

'But they'll know you couldn't have done it. You were working the night she disappeared.'

'Only until closing time. I could have done anything after that. I live upstairs on my own, don't I? Lisa won't let the kids come to stay any more.'

Lisa was his ex. It was an old complaint. Rosie was irritated by the self-pity but she tried not to show it.

'Did you go out?' Rosie asked. She wanted to shake him. It was like speaking to a surly child.

He shook his head. 'But if they make out I'm tied up in this case I'll lose any chance I ever had of access.'

'That's ridiculous. The kids have nothing to do with this.'

Then she wondered if she'd been too hard on him. Frank doted on his children. Before Lisa started being awkward they'd come to stay at weekends. Rosie tried to understand what it must be like for him, how lonely he must feel. Perhaps that was why he was good at his job. He made an effort with the staff and the customers because without them he'd have no one to speak to. He ever talked about friends or other family.

'Why did you say that about the bloke that came in here looking for Mel? I mean, how did you know he didn't do it?'

'He wasn't the type.'

'Come on, Frank. What is the type? You must listen to the news. Anyone can commit murder. Teachers, doctors, anyone. And if they find him, you'll get the police off your back, won't you? There won't be anything to get in the way of the access application then.'

He put his empty plate on the floor. 'You're a good lass, Rosie. I'll miss you when you go to college.'

Oh God, she thought. A revelation. He wants to get inside my knickers.

'I've got a lot to lose,' he said.

'What are you talking about?'

'This place. It's all I've got.'

'So?'

'So people could make things awkward. With the brewery or the authorities.'

'Has someone been threatening you?'

He looked at her with those eyes again.

'For Christ's sake, Frank. Go to the police. Get it sorted.'

'Leave it,' he said. 'They always catch murderers, don't they? No need for us to get involved.'

'Yes, Frank, there is.'

But he hardly seemed to be listening. By now she knew exactly what was going on. Joe might not go for her heavy-bosomed, hippy look, but it appealed to middle-aged men. She fended off the flattery and the clumsy approaches every day at work. She'd always suspected that Frank fancied her. Now she was certain. She pulled her chair closer to his.

'Tell me,' she said. 'You don't have to see the police again. I can talk to them. I'll say one of the customers remembered seeing the guy that night. Give me a description, a name even. I'll pass it on. That way we can find Mel's killer and keep you out of it.'

He didn't answer immediately, but she knew she

had him hooked. It crossed her mind that it wouldn't be much fun working with him after this. Then she thought, Sod it. She'd just leave. She could do with a holiday anyway before she went to university. Her dad could pay up some guilt money.

She reached out and touched his arm and lowered her voice. She knew what a tart she was being, but found she was enjoying the role. The power thing again.

'Please, Frank. I'd be really grateful.'

Chapter Thirty-Five

Rosie's shift ended at seven. She tried to phone Hannah then. She was standing on the pavement outside the Prom, her hand cupped round her mobile, blocking out the sound of the traffic. She'd wanted to talk to her mother ever since Frank had spilled out his story. In the end he hadn't treated her as any sort of object of desire. There'd been no groping, none of the usual crap about how lovely she was. She'd felt like his mother, for God's sake, as he stumbled through his confession. She'd put her arm around him and told him she'd make everything all right. And she believed that she could.

Rosie hadn't liked to phone her mother while she was still at work. She didn't want everyone listening in and she didn't want Frank to know how important she considered his information. Not that he'd been around much after their talk. She supposed he was embarrassed. At one point he'd gone to the flat upstairs as if the exchange between them had exhausted him and he needed to rest. He looked as if he hadn't slept properly for weeks.

She let the phone ring until the answerphone was triggered, then she remembered Hannah had said she'd be working late at the prison. She tried the work number but no one answered in the library. A gate officer came on.

'Sorry, pet. You've just missed her.'

She switched off the phone. Before starting the walk home she glanced back at the pub. Both double doors were wide open and she had a clear view. Frank was staring out at her. She'd left without saying goodbye to him and she thought about going back in. It would have been pleasant to sit on one of the high stools on the right side of the bar, drinking a long glass of white wine and soda, plenty of ice. But perhaps she shouldn't lead him on. Anyway, he turned to serve a middle-aged couple, a big woman and a thin man, who had their backs to her. Something about them was familiar. She hoped they were regulars, customers who were as near as Frank got to friends. As she crossed the road to walk past the infant school, she had the sense that everyone in the pub was staring at her. Of course when she glanced back over her shoulder they weren't even looking.

He must have been watching for her outside the Prom but there was always a line of parked vehicles along the road and she wasn't aware of him until she reached the middle of the street where Joe lived. It was still warm. The tar oozed black where a patch in the road had been mended. Somewhere in the neighbourhood there was a barbecue. The street was quiet. She could hear children playing in one of the back gardens, the splash of water from a paddling pool, the occasional snatch of television through an open window, but no one was about. And until she got to Joe's house she took no notice of her surroundings. She was running scenes in her head. Rosie as heroine, giving the police vital information which would lead to the capture of Melanie's killer. Rosie talking to reporters outside court. Perhaps with Joe at her side.

That was when she arrived at Joe's house. The attic window was open and she could hear the thump of his music. She thought his parents must be out or they would have made him turn it down, then she remembered his saying he was looking after Grace that evening. At first Rosie didn't think of going in. She couldn't face listening to more delusions about Melanie and she wanted to talk to Hannah. But she liked Grace. She'd always wished she'd had a kid brother or sister. Even now she was almost grown up Grace was passionate about animals. Rosie enjoyed being shown the latest additions to the menagerie she kept in the garden – the motherless kittens, the baby hedgehog, the house sparrow with one wing. She stopped walking and looked towards the house, tempted.

A small grey van came up the street behind her. It was moving very slowly as if the driver were looking at the house numbers. It had a wing mirror held on with black electrician's tape and a loose bumper which rattled as the van went over the speed bumps in the road. When it pulled up at the kerb Rosie turned to face it, expecting the driver to ask for directions. But instead of winding down the window – it was a very old van and certainly wouldn't have had electric windows – the driver got out. He was a young man, about the same age as Rosie. She didn't recognize him and he didn't look as if he belonged in this street of wealthy professionals, even as someone's black sheep. He was thin with cropped hair and a tattoo running all the way down one arm. Still she paused, curious to see if it was someone who'd come to visit Joe. Joe had copied Mel's habit of gathering up strangers and oddballs and it wouldn't have surprised her.

But he went to the back of the van and opened the door. She decided he was making a delivery and lost interest. She turned and carried on walking down the street.

'Hey!' He didn't shout but his voice was urgent. She stopped. 'Are you Rosie?'

'Rosie Morton. Yes.'

He stood looking for a moment, squinting against the low, evening sun.

'Morton . . .' he repeated. 'Your mam must be librarian at Stavely nick.' As if this was a surprise, a new piece of information which needed consideration.

She didn't like being rude but she didn't want to encourage him. She continued walking. He covered the distance between them quickly. She didn't hear him running, but suddenly she could smell him, a strangely clean, chemical smell. He was behind her, so close that they almost touched, his bony chest against her shoulder blades. From a distance it would look as if he had his arms around her. She turned back to Joe's house but the sunlight was reflected on the windows and she couldn't tell if anyone was watching. Still she thought he might be some weird friend of Joe's, and any moment Joe would come out and rescue her, save her from having to make a scene.

'Get in.'

'What?'

'In the van. Now.'

Then he did have his arm around her. One hand

stroked her neck, in the other, clenched as a fist, was
a Stanley knife, only the blade showing.

'Not a sound.' The voice was almost caressing.

His head moved, turning quickly, his eyes darting
up and down the street. In the distance an elderly
woman in bowling whites stepped out into the road at
the zebra crossing. He waited until she walked away
in the opposite direction. Joe's music changed tempo,
became more melodic. As if they were dancing, the
boy moved Rosie to the back of the van.

'Get in,' he said again. Inside there was an old quilt
with a faded paisley design. It was shedding feathers.
She climbed in. He shut the door. The back of the
van was a sealed unit, separate from the front seats.
Everything was black, except for a thin crack of brilliant light where the door didn't quite fit. He started the
engine and the rattle of the broken bumper vibrated
through her legs and her back. She opened her mouth
to yell, but it was like a nightmare, when you scream
and scream and no sound comes out.

Later she spoke to Hannah. She sat on the floor of a
flat which was empty except for a sleeping bag and
a portable television. As far as she could tell. She'd
only seen one room and the toilet. Her hands were
tied behind her back, but the young man held her
mobile so she could speak. The flat was on the second
floor of a block on an estate she didn't recognize. It
hadn't taken them long to get here. Twenty minutes
perhaps. He'd parked at the bottom of the tower block
by a couple of skips, pulling her out of the van as if
he didn't care if anyone saw. She'd had a few minutes

to look around. There was a low building, some sort of school or community centre perhaps, and next to it a children's playground, which seemed surprisingly new and in good repair, though no children were playing there. There were giant hardboard pandas and chickens on huge black springs, with black seats and handles, swings made from tyres, a wooden fort.

In contrast most of the flat windows were boarded up and beyond the tower blocks there was a building site, where a crane and a couple of diggers were marooned on the hard-packed earth. A woman came out of the school. She had a bunch of keys like the ones Rosie's mum used at the prison, and she locked up the building, pulling at the doors to check they were secure. She looked smart and efficient and walked briskly round the corner out of sight. Her car must have been parked there because they heard the engine. She hadn't seen them standing in the shadows. Even if she had, she'd have taken them for a couple of lovers, mucking about. They hadn't passed anyone else on their way up the stairs to the flat.

'Hi, Mum.'

'Yes?'

'I'm not coming home tonight. Don't worry about me.'

'Where are you staying?'

She almost said Mel's because it came automatically. Perhaps she should have done. Perhaps her mother would have picked up the mistake and somehow understood. But the boy wasn't stupid.

'Laura's,' she said. 'She's having a party.'

'When will you be home?'

'I'll go straight to work tomorrow.'

He switched off the phone. 'Good,' he said. 'Very good.' But he seemed unsettled. He paced up and down the floor. She watched him, not terrified any more, her emotions somehow slipped out of gear, but her brain working like fury. Very sharp, very clear, as if this was the most important exam of her life.

'Can I ask you something?'

'What?' He stopped pacing, crouched beside her, so she could smell him again.

'Did you kill Melanie Gillespie?'

Chapter Thirty-Six

Hannah replaced the phone with satisfaction. She was proud of herself. At one time she'd have demanded details. Who was Laura? She'd never heard the name before. Where did she live? Was there a contact number? Today she just accepted Rosie's explanation and let it go. Treating Rosie as an adult. Besides, she had other things to think about.

For example, Porteous's visit to the prison earlier in the day. She could have died when he just turned up, unannounced, though he'd actually behaved with more discretion than she'd have expected. She wasn't sure Marty had been taken in by the detective's casual reference to needing witness statements, but Marty wouldn't talk. It wouldn't be all around the prison that she was a suspect in a murder inquiry. She could tell, though, that the orderly had been unsettled by Porteous. For the rest of the shift he'd been moody, demanding that the radio be turned down, snapping at prisoners who jostled to have their books stamped. Occasionally she caught him looking at her and she wondered if he'd say something when the place was quiet. But they were never alone. He asked to leave early, saying he had something important to see to. It wasn't like him. He always preferred to be in the library than on the wing, would have worked twelve-hour shifts given half the chance.

The other preoccupation was that Arthur was coming to supper the following evening. She'd invited him on impulse and immediately regretted it. She hadn't seen him all day, then met him in the car park on her way home. He must have been working late too. He'd seen her leaving the gate and was standing by his car waiting for her. His appearance had almost made her laugh out loud. He was wearing shorts which almost reached his knees and a shirt with horizontal stripes which made him look like an upended deck-chair. Dear God, she'd thought, with a jolt of affection which surprised her. Whatever is he like. No wonder the officers want rid of him.

'Are you OK?' He must have heard on the grapevine that Porteous had been there. And he'd be curious, of course, about what had happened. Since tracing Michael Grey's identity he thought he had a stake in the case.

'Of course.'

'I don't suppose you fancy a drink?'

She hadn't. At least not in public. What she'd fancied had been a long, hot soak to take away the smell of prisoners, a good book, a glass of very cold, very dry wine. But he'd looked so tentative, so sure of rejection, that she hadn't wanted to hurt him.

'I'm sorry. Not tonight.'

He'd given her a sad smile. 'Better things to do?'

'Just shattered. Why don't you come round for a meal tomorrow evening? Rosie will probably be working, but I'll get rid of her if she's not.'

'Haven't you got enough on your plate?'

'I'll enjoy it.'

But now she wasn't sure that she would. She hadn't entertained anyone in the house since Jonathan had left, and when he'd been around dinner parties had been daunting affairs, taking days of planning, sleepless nights of anxiety. She'd always admired friends who could throw together a bowl of pasta for half a dozen people, drink out of jumble-sale glasses, eat from ill-matched crockery. She'd never had that sort of confidence.

Now she worried about what she should cook for Arthur and whether she really wanted him in her house. He'd insist on going over the inquiry, picking at the threads of it. Would he be a rampant carnivore like Jonathan, who bragged that he never ate anything that hadn't breathed? She supposed there would have to be a pudding. And would he read more into the invitation than she'd intended? What would be expected of her?

She was about to set off to the all-night supermarket where Rosie's friend worked, in search of inspiration, when the phone rang again. It was Sally Spence, eager for a gossip. She had information to give, but throughout the conversation Hannah thought she was fishing too. She had a reason for calling which was never made clear.

'We had one of those detectives here again this afternoon. The ugly little one.'

'Oh?' Perhaps Stout had told Sally that Porteous had been to the prison. Perhaps she was phoning to see if Hannah had been arrested.

There was a pause, lengthened by Sally for dramatic tension.

'You'll never guess who's mixed up in this business.'

No, Hannah thought. Probably not. It was hard to remember that once Sally had been her very best friend, that she'd confided everything to her.

'Who?' she asked.

'Paul Lord. You remember him?'

'The spotty boy scout.' Hannah smiled despite herself. She remembered sitting next to him by the bonfire at Cranford Water the evening she'd first kissed Michael.

'Not spotty any more,' Sally said. 'Quite a hunk these days. You met him at the reunion, the night they identified Michael . . .'

'Of course.' Hannah replayed it all in her head – the curse of a memory which would let nothing go. She heard the conversation with Paul, his description of his computer business and the conversion of the farmhouse, the music in the background, Chris Johnson's muttered introduction to the next record. 'Why do the police think he's involved?'

'He's a friend of a man called Alec Reeves. Apparently this guy's disappeared from the face of the earth. They want to trace him because he knew both dead kids.' She paused again before adding grandly, 'At least that's what my sources tell me.'

'So Paul's not really implicated. Only by association.'

'Don't be silly, H. You can't see Paul Lord *killing* anyone, can you? He was always such a nerd.' As if she might admire him more if he did turn out to be a murderer.

Hannah thought the conversation was finished

then. She even began to say goodbye. But Sally seemed eager to prolong it.

'How's that lovely daughter of yours?'

'Fine. Out partying. As usual.'

'Oh.' Sally sounded shocked. 'I thought Melanie Gillespie was one of her best friends.'

'She was.' Hannah could have kicked herself. She didn't want to make out that Rosie was an insensitive little cow. Especially to a reporter. What right did Sally, who was obviously enjoying every minute of the investigation, have to disapprove? 'She's been really upset. I thought she needed some time out with her friends.'

'Right,' Sally said. 'Of course. Right.'

Hannah wondered if Sally had been hoping to talk to Rosie, to turn her memories of Mel into an article. Just as well she wasn't at home. There was a muffled conversation at the other end of the line.

'Roger sends his love.'

But I don't want it, Hannah thought. Really, I don't. I don't care if I never see either of you again.

She decided on a casserole for Arthur, something she could cook that night and heat up the next day. Chicken with tarragon, she thought. Then she could use some of the wine she had chilling in the fridge and she wouldn't end up drinking the whole bottle. The supermarket was quiet. There were a couple of single men in suits carrying wire baskets of ready-cooked meals and designer lager, sad disorganized women like her who had nothing better to do at nine o'clock at night than shop. She looked out for Joe. She would never do it because Rosie would be mortified, but she wanted to say, 'Look at my daughter. I mean really look at her. She's a beauty and she fancies you like crazy. What are you doing, letting her go?' She expected to bump into him at the checkout or filling shelves but he wasn't there. She hoped it was his night off and he was at Laura's party too.

The next day, Marty wasn't waiting outside the library for her to unlock the door and he still hadn't showed when the papers arrived. She tried to rouse Dave, the prison officer, but he was stretched out in the chair in the office and the rhythm of his snoring didn't alter a beat even when she shook him. She phoned the wing.

'Haven't they told you?'

If they had, I'd not be ringing, she thought. She didn't say it because she knew the wing officer and liked him. She didn't have so many friends in the place that she could afford to offend him. But she came closer than she ever would have done when she was living with Jonathan. Perhaps living on her own with Rosie was making her assertive.

'Where is he?' She thought Marty might have been shipped out to an open prison before release. Sometimes it happened without warning.

'He's in hospital.' The officer was from North Wales and spoke with a sibilant hiss which was mimicked by the inmates and other staff.

'The sick bay?' She was still thinking of it only as an administrative inconvenience. She ran through the library rota in her head, wondering if she could draft in another orderly, trying to think of a suitable candidate.'

'No. The General.'

That brought her up short. 'Serious then?'

'Yeah.'

'What's wrong with him? He seemed fine yesterday.'

'There was a fight. Nastier than most. We didn't get to it in time.' He paused. 'Marty started it. They all say that. Some new lad was winding him up. He can kiss goodbye to his parole, if he lives that long.'

'It's that serious?' What's happening to the people I know? She thought. He can't die. Not him too.

'I've not heard how he is this morning. The Governor will know, I suppose, but you know what he's like. He tells us nothing. It looked bad last night.'

'It's crazy,' she cried. 'Marty had so much to lose. I always guessed he had a temper, but he told me he'd learned to control it.'

'Did anything happen yesterday to upset him?'

She thought immediately of Porteous, but what did that have to do with Marty? 'I don't think so.'

'You two didn't have a row?'

'No. Why?'

'He seemed wound up anyway. I had a bit of a run-in with him earlier in the evening. I mean, sometimes you could tell that he was getting tense, but he'd take a deep breath and walk away from it. But yesterday, before lights-out, he had a go at me.' There was a silence at the end of the phone and she thought he'd finished, but he continued in a rush. 'I'm afraid it was about you. He wanted me to give him your home phone number. He said it was urgent, vital that he talked to you. I told him if it was that urgent to give me a message and I'd pass it on. And anyway he'd see you today. He calmed down in the end, but like you said, usually he managed to hold it together, and last night he was way over the top. I couldn't do it, Hannah. I couldn't give an inmate your home number. Not even Marty.'

'No,' she said, meaning it. 'Of course you couldn't.'

During the day Hannah tried to find out more about Marty. He hadn't had any close friends in the prison. He'd always worked on his own. But she thought someone might know what was behind the fight.

'Who was the lad he went for?'

'Don't know, miss. He was new. Just out of reception.'

'What did he do to wind Marty up?'

'I didn't see. Honest, miss. It all happened so fast.'

Apparently no one had seen. Or they weren't telling. She thought they were scared, but perhaps she was deluding herself. Perhaps she didn't want to believe Marty could have been such a fool.

At lunchtime she phoned the General Hospital, but the sister on ICU wasn't giving much away either. She said Marty was 'serious but stable'. And no, he wasn't fit to receive visitors. She sounded disapproving. Perhaps the prison officer who would be sitting on the end of Marty's bed was making a nuisance of himself. It wasn't always the most house-trained member of staff they chose for escort duty.

Hannah wished she had the name and number of Marty's girlfriend. Perhaps it would be possible to trace it through the bail hostel where she'd worked as a volunteer. But Hannah didn't feel she had any emotional claim on Marty and she didn't want to look as if she were interfering. In the end she shut the library early and went home. When Dave roused himself to complain she said it was a gesture of respect.

Chapter Thirty-Seven

The incident with Marty had stopped her worrying about dinner. She was glad now that she'd invited Arthur. He might know what had happened. Despite his outsider status he always seemed to understand what was going on in the prison. She took pleasure now in the preparations, set the table carefully, polished glasses, opened wine. She was coming out of the shower when the phone rang. Usually she'd have let the answerphone take it, but she thought it might be about Marty. She'd asked his wing officer to let her know if there was any news.

'Mrs Morton?'

'Yes?'

'Can I speak to Rosie?'

Because she was thinking about the prison it took her a moment to place the voice: Rosie's friend Joe.

'She's not here,' Hannah said. 'She's at work. Sorry.'

There was an awkward pause.

'No,' Joe said. 'I've just been to the Prom. Frank said she'd called in sick.'

Hannah's first response was irritation. It wasn't the first time Rosie had phoned in sick if she felt like a day's shopping or an expedition up the coast with her mates. Then she thought that Rosie would have told her what she was up to. Not just to cover in case Frank got in touch, but because she knew Hannah would be worried after what had happened to Mel.

'Did you see her last night?' she demanded.

'No. I met her the day before with the policemen, but not yesterday. My parents were out. I had to look after my sister.'

'You weren't at Laura's party then?'

'Sorry?'

'She was at a party last night and she stayed over. She phoned to tell me. Laura's party.'

'I'm sorry,' he said again. 'I don't know anyone called Laura.'

'She's not one of your friends from school?'

'No.'

Then she lost control of her body. She still had the towel wrapped round her but she started to shiver.

As if from a distance she heard Joe on the other end of the phone. 'Don't worry,' he said. 'I don't know everyone she does. She phoned you last night and Frank at lunchtime. She must be OK. I'll call round and ring you back.'

She replaced the receiver and dressed quickly. The shivering didn't stop. Feeling foolish for not having thought of it sooner, she dialled the number of Rosie's mobile. She heard her daughter's voice, delightfully normal, saying she couldn't come to the phone right now, but she'd return the call as soon as she could. The doorbell rang.

It was Arthur. He was clutching a huge bunch of flowers in one hand and a bottle of red in the other. Of course, she thought, he would be a red-wine drinker. She burst into tears. He didn't say anything then. He took her in, sat her on the sofa, poured her a glass of wine from the fridge and dumped the flowers in the sink.

'What is it?' he said. She saw he'd opened the red, poured a big glass for himself. 'News from the hospital?'

'Nothing like that.'

'Rosie?'

She explained about Joe.

'He's right,' he said. 'Rosie must be OK if she phoned you and the pub. Perhaps she's feeling the pressure and wants to go off on her own for a bit.'

'No. She wouldn't. Not without telling me.'

He sat beside her, put his arm around her shoulder. 'Could she be at her father's? She might feel awkward about letting you know she was there.'

'He's away. The Dordogne.' With Eve, the temptress. 'He gets back tomorrow. Rosie doesn't have a key to their house. It's something she complains about.'

'Do you think you should phone the police . . .'

She sensed he was thinking of Mel and that he was going to add 'in the circumstances'. She didn't want to hear it and cut him off.

'We'll wait ten minutes. See what Joe has to say.'

As if on cue the telephone rang. She answered it in the living-room so Arthur could hear what she was saying.

'Mrs Morton.' The same two words but it wasn't Joe. 'Mrs Morton, I've got a message from your daughter.'

'Where is she?'

'Not far away.'

'But she's safe?'

'She is at the minute. You could say I'm looking after her. You should be grateful.'

'Can I speak to her?'

He seemed to think about that. 'I don't think so. Not just yet.'

'When is she coming home?'

There was another pause. 'That depends on you.'

'What do you mean? She knows she can come home. Anytime.'

'I need something from you, Mrs Morton, before I can let her come back.'

'Money?' It was almost a relief. Something she could catch hold of. 'A ransom. How much?'

'I'm not greedy. Twenty thousand. You can manage that.'

'Not immediately,' she said. Her mind was racing. 'There are savings, bonds. Some things need my husband's signature.'

He lost his temper suddenly, shocking her. 'Listen lady, she should be dead already. Tomorrow. Eleven. I'll phone back then. And if you go to the police I'll know. And I'll kill her.'

She heard herself screaming as if it was somebody else. 'Of course I won't go to the police. I won't tell anyone. I want her safe.'

The line had gone dead and she wasn't sure he'd heard her.

Arthur took the receiver from her and dialled 1471 then held it to her ear so she could hear the number repeated.

'Rosie's mobile,' she said. 'He must have her.' She jabbed her finger on 3 and waited for the number to connect, only to hear Rosie's answering service say she couldn't come to the phone right now. 'He's switched it off.'

They sat together on the sofa, each clasping an undrunk glass of wine, double handed, like brides-maids each holding a posy of flowers, one white, one red.

'I know who it is,' Hannah said. 'That boy.'

She hadn't recognized the voice until he lost his temper, then the memory which was a curse, but which also served its purpose, replayed the scene in the prison library which had initially sent her back to Cranford.

'You know him too. Thin, cropped hair, young. He's got a tattoo of a snake running from his shoulder to his wrist. He can't have been out for long. You took his pre-release course.' She screwed up her eyes, saw the list of names on Arthur's desk. 'He's called Hunter.'

'Yes,' Arthur said. 'I remember. Are you sure it's him?' He kept his voice flat, but she could tell it wasn't good news.

'Certain.' She set her glass on the table. 'What was he in for?'

Arthur hesitated. 'Assault, I think.' He added quickly, 'Not rape. Nothing like that. He was a small-time dealer. Someone tried to muscle in on his patch.' He paused again. 'You know you must tell the police. They'll have an address.'

'What happened to the man he assaulted?'

'I don't know.'

'Don't lie to me, Arthur.' The anger was wonderfully liberating. 'You know all about these kids. That's what you do. You tackle their offending behaviour.' She was sneering as she used the jargon, just as the officers did when they talked about his courses.

'Hunter stabbed him, then slashed his face. He's got a scar.'

'But the victim lived?'

'Hunter isn't a murderer, Hannah,' Arthur said gently. 'He didn't kill Melanie.'

'He was out of prison in time.'

'What motive would he have? And he wasn't even born when the lad in the lake died.' He turned to her. 'You must tell Porteous about this.'

Again she ignored the point he was making. 'Why is he doing it? Why me? Personal revenge, perhaps. I upset him that day in the prison. Or is it Rosie? Has she done something to disturb him?'

'I don't know,' he said. 'You must tell the police. This is their area of expertise. They'll be able to trace him.'

'No!' The anger returned. 'What do the police know about why people do things? They haven't got very far in finding Melanie's murderer. And I can't risk it. What if he was telling the truth? What if he knows someone who works with Porteous?'

'He's a kid, a smack-head. He's not in league with the police. That's paranoia.'

She seemed about to give in, to agree to his phoning Porteous. Certainly she presented as the old Hannah, diffident and unassuming. She straightened her skirt over her knees and clasped her hands on her lap.

'You always wanted to play at detectives.'

'What are you talking about?'

'Well, now's your chance.'

'Hannah, what do you want me to do?'

'Bring Rosie back.' As if it were the most simple thing in the world. 'You must still have access to Hunter's file at Stavely. They won't have cleared it yet. You can find an address for him. You worked with him. You know what he's like. You're a psychologist, for Christ's sake. You'll know what to say to him. He won't be expecting anything to happen until eleven tomorrow. We can catch him off guard.'

'I don't know.'

She looked at her watch and was surprised that it still wasn't eight o'clock. 'If you go now to look at the file you won't even cause a stir on the gate. They're used to your working late.'

Still he paused.

'I'm sorry,' she said. 'I shouldn't have asked you. It could be dangerous. Just get the address and I'll go myself.'

'No.' It came out as a wounded bellow. 'It's not that.' He turned to her. 'Sod it,' he said. 'Sod the Prison Service and the Home Office. I'll do it. I bloody want to do it.'

Chapter Thirty-Eight

In the flat the boy was becoming more jumpy. Rosie thought of him only as 'the boy'. She hadn't asked his name. She didn't care. The television was on. He'd switched it on as soon as it got light, but he kept the sound low and the flashing images couldn't hold his attention. In the distance there was the scream of a police siren. He jumped to his feet and stared out of the window. Rosie saw his knuckles clenched white around the handle of his knife. He only started to relax when the noise disappeared into the distance. She couldn't see her watch because her hands were tied behind her back, but it was starting to get dark, the second night. He wouldn't put on a light. He didn't want anyone to know he was using the flat.

She'd stopped being scared. Now she was only hungry and uncomfortable. The water to the flat was still connected. The toilet flushed and when she'd complained of being thirsty he'd brought her a drink in a blue plastic mug with a moulded handle. They'd had an identical set to take on picnics when she was a kid. He'd given her a biscuit too because she'd said she was starving. It was soft and stale.

'Is this all there is?' she'd demanded.

At that, he'd been flustered and said she'd soon be

out of there. It wouldn't hurt her to go without for a couple of days.

Yeah, she'd thought. She could live off her bum for a week. If she came out of this thinner perhaps the adventure would be worth it. That had led to a picture of a skeletal Mel. She had pushed the image from her head. Remembering Mel, dead in the cemetery, had made her panic. She needed to think straight.

It was clear to her that there'd been no forward planning in the boy's decision to bring her to the flat. If he'd thought about it in advance, he'd have got food in. Even if he didn't mind starving her, he'd have wanted to eat and as far as she could tell he didn't have a stash hidden away. With the arrogance of someone who usually thrived on the challenge of exams, who found learning easy, she'd put him down as a bit dim. She'd worked out the sort of lad he was; there'd been someone like him in every class since she'd been an infant. The name for them in her school was 'charvie', meaning scally, loser, someone you wouldn't be seen dead with socially. Charvies were the kids who started school without being able to tie their laces. They wet their pants and came last in spelling tests. Teachers hated them. In primary school they started fights in the playground and failed their SATs, and in high school they got involved in petty crime, dealing in single cigarettes, then blow or smack. When they were at school, which wasn't often.

When Hannah heard Rosie talking like that, out would come the lecture. 'How on earth can you be so judgmental? You don't know anything about those kids. You don't know where they come from or what their families are like. Of course people can change if you give them a chance.' She thought she could change her prisoners by giving them books. What planet was she on? Rosie knew this boy was a charvie, always had been, and so he was no match for her.

She sat now with her hands behind her wriggling her fingers so she wouldn't lose the feeling in them, and she tried to work out the best thing to do. She couldn't rely on Hannah to go to the police. Hannah would do just as the boy said. She wouldn't take any risks. But Rosie wasn't going to see the boy walk away with all that money – money which could see her through university, buy her a holiday somewhere seriously hot, a little car and driving lessons. Then she wondered if Mel had died because her parents had refused to pay up.

When they'd come into the flat the boy had opened the door with a key, but he hadn't locked it behind him. It was a Yale lock with a snick, so if she got to it she'd be able to get out. Although he was thin and wiry she didn't think he was as fit as she was. He'd been smoking since they'd got there, tiny roll-ups. He crouched over a shiny tin to make them, so no stray strands of tobacco were lost and he used both hands. So while he was making his cigarettes he couldn't hold his knife. She wondered what he'd do when the tobacco ran out.

He hadn't made any sexual advance towards her. Even when he'd had his arms around her pulling her to the car, when his finger was stroking her neck, she hadn't thought he was interested. He had other obsessions. Her body wasn't something she could bargain with. She could tell.

It was possible that he didn't think she'd try to

escape. He'd probably grown up with the same sorts of prejudice about her as she'd had about him. He'd see her as a lardy wimp who couldn't look after herself. He even left her while he went to the toilet. It was off the hall right next to the entrance to the flat, and he left the bathroom door open, but if he'd thought she'd make a run for it, he'd have tied her legs. He just didn't think.

All the time she kept her eyes on the blade. She knew he could move quickly over short distances. He'd done that in the street outside Joe's. But she thought that once she got out of the flat she'd be able to outpace him down the stairs and into the road. Usually the knife was in his hand. Otherwise it was on the floor just beside him. He was as connected to it as some of her mates were to their mobiles. You couldn't imagine him without it. He'd said, as he let her out of the car when they'd first got here, 'I've used it before, you know.' Boasting. As if he were just waiting for an excuse to use it again.

As it grew dark, she let her head drop forward so her chin was on her chest, pretending to drowse. She'd slept a couple of hours the night before. Hannah always said it was a gift being able to sleep anywhere. But she wasn't sure the boy had. He must be exhausted. Despite his nervousness and his restless energy, he wouldn't be able to stay awake for ever.

There were no curtains at the window. She couldn't see from where she was sitting but on the way in she'd glimpsed the river, cranes, and the skeleton of an oil platform, half constructed. Light came in from the glow of the city on the horizon. It reflected on the blade on the floor beside the boy. He still had his palm flat on the handle, but his breathing was regular now. Rosie was leaning back against the wall, her knees bent. She stretched one leg, tensing and relaxing the calf muscles. The boy didn't stir. She repeated the movement with the other leg. Still his breathing didn't change.

It crossed her mind that it might be a trick. Perhaps he wanted her to try to run. Then he'd have an excuse to chase her and hold her down and threaten her. Perhaps that was what excited him. But she didn't think so. Charvies could be devious, but he hadn't tried on anything like that before. He saw her as a means of making money. That was all.

She bent her knees again and bent down, so her back slid slowly up the wall until she was standing. She shook the stiffness out of her legs. Still the boy slept. She walked quickly into the narrow hall towards the front door.

She had already realized there was no way she could free her hands. She'd spent hours the night before trying. She'd seen films where magically ropes had loosened sufficiently to allow one hand to slide out. That wasn't going to happen here. When she moved, the nylon twine cut into her wrists. They were still firmly fixed behind her back. She stood at the front door and turned her back to it, leaning forward so she could raise her straightened arms high enough to reach the Yale snick. The joints in her shoulders seemed to tear with the strain. Even when her fingers touched the catch, it was more difficult than she'd expected to open it blind. At last the knob turned. She gave a gentle tug and the door opened. The boy, caught in the orange glow from the window, muttered in his sleep. She froze but he didn't wake and she moved out on to the landing.

She'd reached the first floor when she heard him come after her, bellowing and stumbling as if he'd wakened suddenly and was still half asleep. She thought then that all the flats must be empty, because there was no response to the noise. She'd have to get out. There was just enough light to see where she was going, some dim, emergency lamp high on the wall. She carried on down, pumping her legs, one step after another, keeping the movements small and tight, saving her energy for when she reached the bottom. Her shadow danced ahead of her.

At the bottom the steel-plated double door was open. She supposed it had been left like that the day before when they'd come in. Outside it was warm and dusty and she thought she could smell the dry mud of the river. She paused for a moment. She didn't think the boy was gaining on her but in the distance there was muffled, amplified rock music – some sort of festival or outdoor show – and she wasn't sure she would have heard his footsteps anyway. She needed a main road, lots of people. The music was too far away. There was a general hum of traffic and she got her bearings. She saw the lights of speeding cars in the distance beyond the building site. She started to run towards them, moving awkwardly because her tied hands threw her off balance. In the distance there was a bang and the splatter of fireworks from the festival. No sign of the boy.

The scene was lit suddenly by car headlights. They shone on the animals in the children's playground behind its wire-mesh fence, a nightmare zoo.

He's fetched his van to head me off, she thought. Then: I underestimated him. Not such a charvie after all.

She heard the engine revving and sensed it coming towards her, but blinded by the lights after the gloom of the flats she was paralysed. She couldn't decide which way to run. At the last minute she twisted and started to move, but knew it was too late.

Then there was a shout. She felt the soft thud of another body, pain as she was thrown to the ground, winded and battered. Then came the movement of the vehicle past them, air on her face, and an enormous crash as it swung, out of control, into a wall.

Chapter Thirty-Nine

Hannah sat by the living-room window, counting the cars go past, telling herself, When I've counted ten more, Arthur will arrive with Rosie. But Arthur didn't arrive, so she counted twenty, then thirty, then fifty. She'd wanted to go with him to the estate by the river, Hunter's last known address, but he'd said she'd be better there, next to the phone, and he'd suddenly seemed to inspire confidence so she'd done what she was told. When the car did stop she thought it was a mirage, her imagination playing tricks. But the first person she saw, the only one that mattered then, was Rosie, who got out of the back seat. And she looked dishevelled and shocked, her white work shirt stained. Too solid to be a dream.

Hannah ran to the door and held her. She felt herself crying and wiped her eyes on her sleeve, because Rosie always said she was soppy, that she cried at the drop of a hat. When she looked up she saw Porteous and Stout coming up the path. No one else was with them.

'Where's Arthur?'

'They'll explain,' Rosie said. 'Is there anything to eat?'

'He's in hospital,' Porteous said.

'Shouldn't Rosie be too? For a check-up at least.'

'Nah.' Rosie shook her head and went to the kitchen to forage for food.

'Is Arthur badly hurt?'

'Serious but stable, they say.'

Like Marty, she thought.

Rosie wandered back in. She was drinking from the glass of wine Arthur had poured for himself earlier. In the other hand she held a slice of the cheesecake Hannah had finally decided on for pudding. Crumbs from the biscuit base were dribbling on to the floor. 'Any phone calls?' It was what she always asked. It was as if she'd only come back from a four-hour shift at the Prom.

She doesn't want a fuss, Hannah thought. 'Joe,' she said. 'Several times. He's been frantic.'

'I'd better phone him.' She drifted away upstairs.

Hannah watched her then turned to Porteous. She wondered what he was still doing there, hovering just inside the door like a Jehovah's Witness or a Kleeneze salesman. Shouldn't he be taking statements?

'Arthur is all right?' she asked. 'If it's serious, perhaps I should go to the hospital.'

Then Porteous and Stout walked in, flanking her on each side, so she thought for a crazy minute that they intended to arrest her after all. They sat beside her on the sofa.

'I don't think you should do that,' Porteous said. Hannah saw that both men looked exhausted, much worse than Rosie. He rubbed his eyes. 'Arthur Lee's under arrest. He's been charged with the murders of Theo Randle, Melanie Gillespie and Alec Reeves. And the attempted murder of Rosie.'

'No.' Again Hannah thought she was going mad. 'Rosie was abducted by a youth called Hunter. He phoned here for money. Arthur went to rescue her. I asked him to.'

'Mr Lee's just driven his car straight at her at fifty miles an hour,' Stout said crossly, grumpy as an over-tired boy. 'If the boss hadn't thrown your daughter out of the way she'd be dead.'

There was a silence. Porteous stood up. 'I think this should wait. You'll want to spend some time with your daughter.'

Hannah stood at the door and watched the policemen walk to their car. Through the ceiling she could hear Rosie's voice chatting, almost naturally, to Joe. There was a burst of laughter, tension relieved. Suddenly Hannah felt angry. How could her daughter be so arrogant, so foolish, not to be scared, not to recognize how close she'd been to danger? But later, when Hannah was in bed, pretending to sleep, Rosie crept in beside her and they spent the rest of the night cuddled together and occasionally Rosie cried out.

Porteous invited her to Cranford to explain Arthur's guilt. He was apologetic. He was so busy, he said, tying up loose ends. He didn't think he could make it to Millhaven. Would she mind coming to him?

It was the evening of the following day and still the sun was shining. They met at the picnic site at Cranford Water. The press was still at the police station, Porteous said. And anyway she wouldn't want to go there. They sat at one of the bench tables. A respectable, middle-aged couple taking the air. Porteous had brought an old-fashioned wicker shopping basket covered with a tea towel and fished out a bottle of wine and some smoked-salmon sandwiches. There were real glasses, linen napkins. Hannah wondered if this were another apology. I'm sorry I thought you were a murderer.

'How's Arthur?' she asked, wanting to start them off. Really rather hoping he was dead.

'Well enough to talk. Just. Did you know he'd worked as a psychologist at a centre for disturbed children called Redwood?'

She shook her head. 'He didn't talk much about the past. I knew he'd done research into families. The causes of delinquent behaviour. I don't think he ever said where he was based.'

'He was there for years. Almost since the place started. He went on to run training courses for other professionals, but he kept his links with the centre. He was a leader in his field. That's why the Home Office headhunted him for Stavely when Redwood closed down.' Porteous stretched back and closed his eyes against the sun. 'It started with Theo Randle, the boy you knew as Michael Grey. His mum died of cancer and his dad remarried. There was a little girl. Emily. You know all that. Arthur told you, didn't he? Once he knew we'd find out anyway. Theo's stepmother suffered from severe post-natal depression. His father started drinking heavily. The family was falling apart. A suitable case for Mr Lee's research. Theo hated Emily. She was only months old but he hated her. If she'd never been born he thought they might be happy.

It would have been like before his mother died. So he decided to do something about it. He started a fire in the nursery when the nanny had a night off. Emily was killed.

'Afterwards he was probably sorry. He went to his father and told him what he'd done. But his father didn't go to the police. He was a public figure. His wife was already suffering from depression. Imagine what the press would make of it. A boy that age charged with murder. Yet he couldn't face living with Theo either.

'Redwood hadn't long opened and was desperately short of money. There was a possibility that the place would shut before Alice Cornish had a chance to prove her ideas. Crispin Randle made a generous donation and Arthur accepted care of the boy. He probably saw it as a professional challenge. He promised he wouldn't tell the authorities that Theo had killed his sister and agreed to the change of name.'

'Was that wrong?' Hannah asked. 'Would Michael have been better off in a secure unit? A prison?'

'He would have been safe there,' Porteous said. 'And he wouldn't be a danger to other people.' He paused. 'There was another incident of arson. This time at Theo's school. He started the fire there too. Apparently he hated the place. Arson was his answer to difficult situations. His way of hitting out. Arthur provided an alibi for him. He didn't want people making awkward connections. Again Alice Cornish never knew. Soon after, the time came when Theo had to move on. He couldn't be protected in Redwood for ever and Arthur couldn't let on that he might still be a risk. Alec Reeves, a care worker at Redwood, knew the Brices. They agreed that he could live with them.'

Hannah didn't answer. She was thinking of Michael, sitting on the shore here at Cranford Water, so bewitched by a bonfire that he couldn't take his eyes off it.

'Then Arthur had a tricky moment,' Porteous said. 'Theo wanted to confess. Perhaps it was the Brices. Being surrounded by all that religion. Perhaps he kept getting flashbacks of Emily in her cot. He'd never been allowed to admit the truth of the memories. He phoned Arthur, telling him what he intended to do. Very self-righteous. Very dramatic.'

Oh yes, he'd have been that, Hannah thought.

'At first Alec was sent to sort him out. I don't think he was ever told the complete story but he knew the reputation of Redwood was at stake and he'd have done pretty well anything to protect that.'

'Did he have a blue car?'

'Why?'

'I saw him. He came looking for Michael here one night.'

'Poor Alec,' Porteous said. 'All those rumours about his nephew and he was just a lonely, middle-aged man who got on better with children than adults. He persuaded the boy to keep quiet, but in the end Theo couldn't let it go and Alec was sent back.'

'The weekend of *Macbeth*?'

'Yes. He realized immediately it wouldn't work and Arthur came up himself. He and Theo met on the Sunday evening after the performance of *Macbeth*, the day after the party, here on the shore. It was late at night. Theo must have had the dagger with him.

The prop from *Macbeth*. We'll never know if he intended any harm with it or if he'd kept it as a souvenir. He was a disturbed young man and he'd already tried to kill twice. There was an argument. Arthur says Theo got wild and angry and started to wave the dagger about. They had a scrap and Theo was killed. Hard to believe it was self-defence when the boy was stabbed in the back. And considering how cool and efficient Arthur was in dealing with the death. He weighed down Theo's body and threw it in the lake. Then he phoned the Brices and said that Theo was in the middle of some sort of crisis and had decided to go back to his father. Of course they believed him. Why wouldn't they? Theo had been their gift from God, only theirs on loan. Presumably Alec was given a similar story.

'And that's how it would have stayed if it hadn't been for global warming and a drought and a canoeist called Helen Blake, who found the body.'

'I don't understand where Melanie comes in.'

'Melanie was at Redwood too, briefly.'

'For her anorexia?'

'No,' Porteous said. 'It was history repeating itself. She killed a baby. A little girl called Emma. She was babysitting. The baby wouldn't stop crying, she got frustrated. She smothered it with a pillow. It was put down as a cot death. She confessed too. To Richard Gillespie. I couldn't accept the coincidence. Two babies dying. Richard was a public figure like Crispin Randle, but I don't think he was considering himself when he shipped Mel off to Redwood. He couldn't put her through a trial. There'd been all the publicity about the killers of the little boy in Liverpool. Even after her death he didn't want it to come out that she was a murderer. When he was young he'd worked as a solicitor for Randle. Apparently Randle got drunk one day and let slip about Theo and Redwood . . .'

' . . . so Melanie got shipped out there too.'

'Yes,' Porteous said. 'For a price. No wonder the girl was so screwed up.'

'Why did Arthur kill her?'

'Melanie was bright,' Porteous said. 'She knew what was happening to her. She was nearly fifteen when she killed Emma Leese, not a child like Theo. She was confused and mixed up and she wanted someone to blame. She knew Arthur was working locally. Rosie had talked about her mother's new friend at Stavely. She tracked him down, phoned him a couple of times at the prison. You can imagine the sort of thing. "You really screwed me up. How could you do that to me?" Wanting sympathy, someone to take her seriously. Arthur got jumpy and went to the Prom to try to talk to her. He knew Rosie worked there, thought it would be somewhere Mel would hang out.

'Mel might have let it go but she saw the photo of Theo on the local news in the pub on her way to the airport. She recognized him. Redwood was plastered with pictures of the kids who'd stayed there. The coincidence freaked her out. And she couldn't understand why Arthur didn't go to the police about the Redwood connection. Later that week the press reports were still talking about the mysterious boy with no past. She phoned him again and said that if he didn't tell the police Michael had been at Redwood, she would. He must have been frantic but he still thought he could reason with her. He couldn't get to her at home. She was so disturbed by then that her parents almost had her under house arrest. So he became more devious. He even followed Rosie and Joe home from the Prom one night, hoping they might lead him to Mel. At last he found her in the Rainbow's End. He persuaded her there was a reasonable explanation for keeping quiet about Theo. If she went back with him he'd tell her all about it. But whatever story he'd dreamed up she wouldn't accept it. She was hysterical . . .'

'And he killed her.'

'In his cottage.' Porteous hesitated, seemed to make up his mind to continue. 'The next night he took her body to the cemetery at Millhaven. He knew you'd been there. You were already a suspect and he wanted to implicate you.'

She sat in silence for a moment wondering how she could have been so foolish, so easily taken in. 'What about Rosie?' she asked. 'She can't have known anything about all that.'

'Rosie suspected him.'

'How could she?'

'Arthur got to know a nasty little boy inside, thought he might be useful.'

'Hunter.' Marty knew, she thought. Or guessed. It was impossible to keep secrets in prison. He'd wanted her to know too.

'Hunter went to see Frank at the pub and persuaded him it wouldn't be a good idea to remember the man who'd been looking for Mel. We thought Frank was uncooperative because he didn't like the police, but it was more than that. Rosie got an accurate description out of him.'

'Arthur.'

Porteous nodded. 'Later Frank had second thoughts and told Hunter what he'd done.'

'And Arthur told Hunter to kill her?'

Porteous didn't answer directly. 'Hunter recognized the name. Got greedy.'

'How did you work it all out?' *In time to save my daughter.*

'Dr Cornish had saved a book from Redwood. It was a record of all the kids she'd worked with, but Arthur's name was in the staff register at the back. I missed it first time. And his car was seen close to Alec Reeves's house on the night he was murdered. By then Arthur was panicking, desperate to throw suspicion elsewhere. Like Mel, Alec was starting to ask questions . . .'

There was a silence. 'Rosie's tough,' Porteous said. 'Brave. She'll be OK.'

Perhaps, Hannah thought. But will I? She looked out over the flat water to the hills on the opposite bank. In a few weeks her reckless daughter would be away to university. She'd live on her own and Hannah wouldn't know where she was or what she was doing. Hannah would retreat to the safety of the prison with its rules and its walls, but Rosie would dance and shimmy through the strange town in the south and there'd be nothing Hannah could do to protect her.

As Peter Porteous filled her glass his hand touched hers. 'Really,' he said. 'She'll be OK.'

Yes, Hannah thought. Of course we will. Both of us.

HIDDEN DEPTHS

Chapter One

Julie stumbled from the taxi and watched it drive away. At the front gate she paused to compose herself. Best not to go in looking pissed after all those lectures she'd given the kids. The stars wheeled and dipped in the sky and she almost threw up. But she didn't care. It had been a good night, the first with the girls for ages. Though it wasn't the girls that had made it so special, she thought, and realized there was a great soppy beam on her face. Just as well it was dark and there was no one to see.

At the door she stopped again and scrabbled through the eyeliner pencils and lippy-stained tissues and loose change in her bag for her key. Her fingers found the scrap of paper which had been torn from a corner of a menu in the bar. A phone number and a name. *Ring me soon.* Then a little heart. The first man she'd touched since Geoff had left. She could still feel the bones of his spine against her fingers when they'd danced. It was a shame he'd had to leave early.

She snapped the bag shut and listened. Nothing. It was so quiet that she could hear the buzz of the evening's music as a pressure on her ears. Was it possible that Luke was asleep? Laura could sleep for

England, but her son had never seemed to get the hang of it. Even now he'd left school and there was nothing to get up for, he was usually awake before her. She pushed open the door and listened again, slipping her feet out of the shoes that had been killing her since she'd got out of the metro hours before. God, she hadn't danced like that since she was twenty-five. There was silence. No music, no television, no beeping computer. Thank the Lord, she thought. Thank the fucking Lord. She wanted sleep and sexy dreams. Somewhere on the street outside an engine was started.

She switched on the light. The glare hurt her head and turned her stomach again. She let go of her bag and ran up the stairs to the bathroom, tripping halfway up. No way was she going to be sick on the new hall carpet. The bathroom door was shut and she saw a crack of light showing underneath it. From the airing cupboard there came the faint gurgle of water which meant the tank was refilling. And wasn't that typical? It took hours of persuasion to get Luke into the shower in the morning, then he decided to have a bath in the middle of the night. She knocked on the bathroom door but there was no urgency about it. The queasiness had passed again.

Luke didn't answer. He must be in one of his moods. Julie knew it wasn't his fault and she should be patient, but sometimes she wanted to strangle him when he went all weird on her. She crossed the landing to Laura's room. Looking down at her daughter, she came over suddenly sentimental, thought she should make the effort to spend more time with her. Fourteen was a difficult age for a girl and Julie had been so caught up with Luke lately that Laura almost seemed like a stranger. She'd grown up without Julie noticing. She lay on her back, her spiky hair very black against the pillow, snoring slightly, her mouth open. It was a bad time for hay fever. Julie saw that the window was open and, although it was so hot, she shut it to keep out the pollen. The moonlight splashed onto the field behind the house where they'd been cutting grass.

She returned to the bathroom and banged on the door with the flat of her palm. 'Hey, are you going to be in there all night?' With the third bang, the door opened. It hadn't been locked. There was a smell of bath oil, heavy and sweet, which Julie didn't recognize as hers. Luke's clothes were neatly folded on the toilet seat.

He had always been beautiful, even as a baby. Much lovelier than Laura, which had never seemed fair. It was the blond hair and the dark eyes, the long, dark eyelashes. Julie stared at him, submerged beneath the bath water, his hair rising, like fronds of seaweed, towards the surface. She couldn't see his body because of the flowers. They floated on the perfumed water. Only the flower heads, not the stems or the leaves. There were the big ox-eye daisies which had grown in the cornfields when she was a kid. Overblown poppies, the red petals translucent now. And enormous blue blossoms, which she had seen before in gardens in the village, but which she couldn't name.

Julie must have screamed. She heard the sound as if someone else had made it. But still Laura slept and Julie had to shake her to wake her. The girl's eyes opened suddenly, very wide. She looked terrified and Julie found herself muttering, knowing that she was lying, 'It's all right, pet. Everything's all right. But you have to get up.'

Laura swung her legs out of bed. She was trembling, but not really awake. Julie put her arm around her and supported her as they stumbled together down the stairs.

They stood like that, wrapped up in each other's arms, on the doorstep of the neighbour's house and the silhouette thrown on the wall by the street light made Julie think of people in a crazy three-legged race. One of those pub crawls that students went in for. She leaned against the bell until the lights upstairs went on and footsteps came and she had someone to share the nightmare with.

Chapter Two

It disturbed Felicity Calvert that she'd become so pre-occupied with sex. Once, in the doctor's waiting room, she'd read a magazine which claimed that adolescent boys thought about sex every six minutes. Then she'd found it hard to believe. How could these young men lead a normal life – go to college, watch a film, play football – when they were so frequently distracted? And what of her own son? Watching James playing on the floor with his Lego, it had been impossible to imagine that in a few years he would be similarly obsessed. But now she thought that an interval of six minutes between sexual daydreams could be a con-servative estimate. In her case at least. For a while now an awareness of her body and its responses had been with her whatever she was doing, an uneasy, occasionally pleasurable background to the stuff of everyday life. For someone of her age this seemed inappropriate. It was as if she'd attended a funeral wearing pink.

She was in the garden picking the first of the strawberries. She lifted the net carefully, sliding her hand underneath between the mesh and the straw bedding. They were still small but there should be enough for James's tea. She tasted one. It was warm from the sun and very sweet. Glancing at her watch she saw it was almost time for the school bus. Ten more minutes and she'd have to wash her hands and walk down the lane to meet him. She didn't always go. He claimed he was old enough to make his own way to the house and of course that was true. But today he'd have his violin and he'd be glad to see her because she could help him carry his stuff. She wondered briefly whether it would be the old bus driver or the young one with the muscular arms and the sleeveless T-shirt, then looked at her watch again. Only two minutes since she'd last considered sex. The thought returned that at her age it was quite ridiculous.

Felicity was forty-seven. She had a husband and four children. She had, for goodness' sake, a grandchild. In a few days Peter, her husband, would be sixty. The bubbles of lust surfaced at random, when she was least expecting them. She hadn't talked about this to Peter. Of course not. He certainly wasn't the object of her desire. These days they seldom made love.

She got up and walked across the grass to the kitchen. Fox Mill stood on the site of an old water mill. It was a big house, built in the thirties, a coastal retreat for a ship owner from the city. And it looked like a ship with its smooth, curved lines, the mill race flowing past it. A big, art deco ship, stranded quite out of place in the flat farmland, with its prow pointed to the North Sea and its stern facing the Northumberland hills on the horizon. A long veranda stretched along one side like a deck, impractical here where it was seldom warm enough to sit outside. She loved the house. They would never have afforded it on an academic's salary, but Peter's parents had died soon after he and Felicity had married and all their money had come to him.

She put the basket of strawberries on the table and checked her face in the mirror in the hall, running her fingers through her hair and adding a splash of lipstick. She was older than the mothers of James's friends and hated the idea of embarrassing him.

In the lane the elders were in flower. Their scent made her head swim and caught at the back of her throat. On either side of the lane the corn was ripening. The crop was too dense for flowers there, but in the field which they owned, close to the house, there were buttercups and clover and purple vetch. The pitted tarmac shimmered in the distance with heat haze. The sun had shone without a break for three days.

This weekend it was Peter's birthday and she was planning what they might do. On Friday night the boys would come. She thought of them as boys, though Samuel, at least, was as old as her. But if it stayed like this, on Saturday there could be a picnic on the beach, a trip to the Farnes to see puffins and guillemots. James would love that. She squinted at the sky, wondering if she could sense an approaching cold front, the faintest cloud on the horizon. There was nothing. It might even be warm enough to swim, she thought, and imagined the waves breaking on her body.

When she reached the end of the lane there was no sign of the bus. She hoisted herself onto the wooden platform where once the churns from the farm had stood to wait for the milk lorry. The wood was hot and smelled of pitch. She lay back and faced the sun.

In two years James would move on to secondary school. She dreaded it. Peter talked about him going to a private day school in the city, to the school which he'd attended. She'd seen the boys in their striped blazers on the metro. They'd seemed very confident and loud to her.

'But how would he get there?' she'd said. This wasn't her real objection. She didn't think it would be good for James to be pushed. He was a slow and dreamy boy. He'd do better working at his own pace. The comprehensive in the next village would suit him better. Even the high school in Morpeth, where their other children had been students, had seemed demanding to her.

'I'd take him and bring him back,' Peter had said. 'There'll be lots going on after school. He can hang on until I've finished work.'

That had made her even less favourably disposed to the plan. The time that she had with James when he arrived home from school was special. Without it, she thought, he would be lost to her.

She heard the bus growling up the bank and sat upright, squinting against the sun as it approached. The driver was Stan, the old man. She waved at him to hide her disappointment. Usually three of them got off at this stop – the twin girls from the farm and James. Today a stranger climbed out first, a young woman wearing strappy leather sandals and a red and gold sleeveless dress with a fitted bodice and full, swirling skirt. Felicity loved the dress, the way the skirt fell and the exuberance of the colours – the young today seemed to choose black or grey even in summer – and when she saw the woman help James off the bus with his bags and violin, she was immediately drawn to her. The twins crossed the road and ran up the track to the farmhouse, the bus drove off and the three of them were left, standing a little awkwardly, by the hedge.

'This is Miss Marsh,' James said. 'She's working at our school.'

The woman had a big straw bag strung by a leather strap over her shoulder. She held out a hand which was very brown and long and bony. The bag slipped down her arm and Felicity saw that it contained files and a library book.

'Lily.' Her voice was clear. 'I'm a student. This is my last teaching practice.' She smiled as if she expected Felicity to be pleased to meet her.

'I told her she could come and stay in our cottage,' James said and set off up the lane, unencumbered, not caring which of the adults carried his things.

Felicity was not quite sure what to say.

'He *did* mention I was looking for somewhere?' Lily asked.

Felicity shook her head.

'Oh dear, how embarrassing.' But she didn't seem very embarrassed. She seemed to be remarkably self-assured, to find the incident amusing. 'It's been such a nightmare travelling from Newcastle every day without a car. The head asked in assembly if anyone knew of accommodation. We were thinking of a B&B or someone wanting a paying guest. And yesterday James said you had a cottage to let. I tried to phone this afternoon but there was no answer. He said you'd

9

be in the garden and to come anyway. I presumed he'd discussed it with you. It was hard to say no . . .'

'Oh yes,' Felicity agreed. 'He can be very insistent.'

'Look, it's not a problem. It's a lovely afternoon. I'll walk into the village and there's a bus from there into town at six.'

'Let me think about it,' Felicity said. 'Come and have some tea.'

There had been tenants in the cottage before, but it had never quite worked out. In the early days they'd been glad of an extra source of income. Even with the money from Peter's parents the mortgage repayments had been a nightmare. Then, with three children under five, they had thought it might house a nanny or au pair. But there had been complaints about the cold and a dripping tap and the lack of modern convenience. And they hadn't been comfortable having a stranger living so close to the family. They'd felt the responsibility for the tenant as an extra stress. Although none of them had been particularly troublesome, it had always been a relief to see them go. 'Never again,' Peter had said when the last resident, a homesick Swedish au pair, had left. Felicity wasn't sure how he would feel about another young woman on the doorstep, even if it was only four weeks until the end of term.

As they sat at the table in the kitchen, with the breeze from the sea blowing the muslin curtain at the open window, Felicity Calvert thought she probably would let the young woman have the place if she wanted it. Peter wouldn't mind too much if it was for a short time.

James was sitting beside them at the table, surrounded by scissors, scraps of cut paper and glue. He was drinking orange juice and making a birthday card for his father. It was an elaborate affair with photos of Peter taken from old albums and stuck as a collage around a big 60 made out of ribbon and glitter. Lily admired it and asked about the early photographs. Felicity sensed James's pleasure in her interest and felt a stab of gratitude.

'If you live in Newcastle,' she said, 'I suppose you wouldn't want the cottage at weekends.' She thought that would be another point to make to Peter. *She'd only be here during the week. And you work such long hours you wouldn't notice she's around.*

The cottage stood beyond the meadow with the wild flowers in it. Besides the garden, this was the only land they owned. Viewed from the house the building looked so small and squat it was hard to believe that anyone could live there. A path had been trampled across the field and Felicity wondered who had been here since the grass had grown up. James probably. He used it as a den when he had friends to play, though they kept the building locked and she couldn't remember him asking for a key lately.

'Cottage makes it sound more grand than it is,' she said. 'It's only one up and one down with a bathroom built on the back. The gardener lived here when our house was first built. It was a pigsty before then, I think; some sort of outhouse anyway.'

The door was fastened by a padlock. She unlocked it then hesitated, feeling suddenly uneasy. She wished she'd had a chance to look around the building before inviting the stranger in. She should have left Lily in the kitchen while she checked the state of the place.

But although she was aware at once of the damp, it was tidy enough. The grate was empty, though she couldn't remember cleaning it after her youngest daughter and her husband had been here at Christmas. The pans were hanging in their place on the wall and the oilskin cloth on the table had been wiped down. It was pleasantly cool after the heat in the meadow. She pushed open the window.

'They're cutting grass at the farm,' she said. 'You can smell it from here.'

Lily had stepped inside. It was impossible to tell what she thought of the place. Felicity had expected her to fall in love with it and felt offended. It was as if an overture of friendship had been rejected. She led the woman through to the small bathroom. Pointing out that the shower was new and the tiles had recently been replaced, she felt like an estate agent desperate for a sale. Why am I behaving like this? she thought. I wasn't even sure I wanted her here.

At last Lily spoke. 'Can we look upstairs?' And she started up the tight wooden steps which led straight from the kitchen. Felicity felt the same uneasiness as when she'd paused at the door of the cottage. She would have liked to be there first.

But again, everything was more in order than she had expected. The bed was still made up, the quilt and extra blankets folded neatly at its foot. There was dust on the painted cupboard and dressing table, on the family photographs which stood there, but none of the rubbish and clutter which usually remained after her daughter's stay. A jug of white roses stood on the wide window sill. One of the petals had dropped and she picked it up absent-mindedly. Of course, Felicity thought. Mary has been in although I never asked her. What a sweetie she is! So unobtrusive and helpful! Mary Barnes came to clean twice a week.

Only when she was closing the padlock behind them, did Felicity think that the roses couldn't have been there for more than a few days, and Mary, an unimaginative woman, would never have thought of a touch like that without being prompted.

They stood for a moment outside the cottage. 'Well?' Felicity asked. 'What did you think?' She caught a falsely cheerful note in her voice.

Lily smiled. 'It's lovely,' she said. 'Really. But there's such a lot to think about. I'll be in touch, shall I, next week?'

Felicity had intended offering her a lift, at least as far as the bus stop in the village, but Lily turned away and walked off across the meadow. Felicity couldn't bring herself to shout or run after her, so she stood and watched until the red and gold figure was lost in the long grass.

Chapter Three

Julie couldn't stop talking. She knew she was making a tit of herself, but the words spilled out, and the fat woman wedged in the Delcor armchair that Sal had got from the sales last year just sat there and listened. Not taking notes, not asking questions. Just listening.

'He was an easy baby. Not like Laura. She was a real shock after Luke. A demanding little madam, either asleep or crying or with a bottle in her gob. Luke was . . .' Julie paused trying to find the right word. The fat detective didn't interrupt, just gave her the time to think. '. . . restful, peaceful. He'd lie awake all day, just watching the shadows on the ceiling. A bit slow talking, but by then I'd had Laura and the health visitor thought that was why. I mean, she was so bright and taking up all my time and sucking my energy, that Luke had got left out. Nothing to worry about, the health visitor said. He'd catch up as soon as he started nursery. Geoff was still living with us, but he was working away a lot. He's a plasterer. There's more money in the south and he went through one of those agencies, ended up working on Canary Wharf . . . It was a lot to cope with, two kids under three and no man around.'

Then the woman did respond, just nodding her head a touch to show that she understood.

'I started him at the nursery at the school in the village. He didn't want to go at first, they had to drag him off me, and when I went back an hour later he was still sobbing. It broke my heart, but I thought it was for the best. He needed the company. The health visitor said it was the right thing to do. And he did get used to it. He used to go in without screaming, at least. But all the time looking at me with those eyes. Not speaking but the eyes saying, "Don't make me go in there, Mam. Please don't make me go."' Julie was sitting on the floor, her knees pulled up to her chin, her arms clasped around them. She looked up at the detective, who was still watching and waiting. It came to her suddenly that this woman, large and solid like rock, might once have known tragedy herself. That was why she could sit there without making those stupid, sympathetic noises Sal and the doctor had made. This woman knew that nothing she could say would make it better. But Julie didn't care about the detective's sadness and the thought was fleeting. She went back to her story.

'It was about that time Geoff came home from London. He said the work had dried up, but I heard from his mate that there'd been some row with the foreman. He's a good worker, Geoff, and he won't be pissed about. It was a difficult time for him. He was never one for sitting around and he was used to making big money. He put in a new kitchen for me and did up the bathroom. You'd never believe what this place looked like when we first moved in. But then the cash ran out . . .'

Sal had made tea. In a pot, not with bags in the mugs as Julie always made it. Julie reached out to the tray and poured herself another cup. It wasn't that she wanted one, but it gave her time to sort out what she wanted to say.

'It wasn't a good time. Geoff wasn't used to the kids. When he was working in London, he had only one long weekend a month at home. Then it was a novelty for him being there. He'd make a fuss of them, bring presents. We were all on our best behaviour. And every night he was out at the club drinking with his mates. When he came back for good it couldn't be like that. You know what it's like. Baby clothes drying on the radiator and toys all over the floor. Mucky nappies . . . There were times when he lost patience, especially with Luke. Laura would giggle and play up to him. Luke seemed to be in a world of his own. Geoff never hit him. But he'd shout and Luke would get so scared you'd think he *had* been battered. I used to shout all the time but they knew I never meant it. They'd get their own way anyway. It was different with Geoff. Even I got scared.'

She was silent for a moment thinking of Geoff and his temper, the gloom which lingered over the house after one of his outbursts. But she couldn't keep quiet for long and the words started again.

'Luke was no bother in the infants' school. He even seemed to like going. Perhaps he was used to it, because the nursery was in the same building. He had a lovely teacher in the first class, Mrs Sullivan. She was like a grandma to them, sat them on her knee

16

when she was teaching them to read. She told me he had problems – nothing serious, she said – but it would be best to get him checked out. She wanted him to see a psychologist. But there was no money, or the waiting list was too long and it never happened. Geoff said the only thing wrong with Luke was that he was lazy. Then he left us. He said we got on his nerves. We were dragging him down. But I knew fine well that he'd been having a fling with a nurse from the RVI. They ended up living together. They're married now.'

She stopped again for a moment. Not because she'd run out of things to say, but because she needed to catch her breath. She thought Geoff had known all along that there was something wrong with Luke. You could tell by the suspicious way he'd stare at him when he was playing. He just didn't want to admit it.

It was eight-thirty in the morning. They were still sitting in her neighbour's house, in Sal's front room. Outside the postman walked past, staring at the cop standing by her front door. The kids further down the street were chasing and giggling on their way to school.

The fat woman detective leaned forward, not pushing Julie to continue, more showing her that she was content to wait, that she had all the time in the world. Julie sipped the tea. She didn't tell the woman about the way Geoff had looked at Luke. Instead she moved the story on a year.

'The tantrums started when he was about six. They came out of nowhere and you couldn't control him. Mam said it was my fault for spoiling him. He wasn't in Mrs Sullivan's class then, but she was the only one at that school I could really talk to, and she said it was frustration. He couldn't explain him-self properly and he was struggling with his reading and writing and suddenly it all got too much for him. Once he pushed out at this lad who was teasing him. The lad tripped and cracked his head on the playground. There was an ambulance and you can imagine what it was like waiting to pick up the bairns that afternoon – all the other mams pointing and whispering. Luke was dead sorry. He wanted to go and see the lad in the hospital, and when you think about it, it was the other lad who'd started it with his teasing. Aidan he was called. Aidan Noble. His mam was all right about it, but his dad came round to the house to have a go at us. Mouthing off on the doorstep so the whole street could hear.

'The head teacher called me in. Mr Warrender. He was a short plump man, with that thin sort of hair that doesn't quite cover the bald patch. I saw him in town the other day and I didn't recognize him at first – he's taken to wearing a toupee. He wasn't nasty. He made me a cup of tea and that. He said Luke had beha-vioural problems and they weren't sure they could cope with him in school. I showed myself up. Started crying. Then I told him what Mrs Sullivan had said about it being frustration and if they'd pushed for Luke to see a specialist earlier on then he might not have worked himself up into such a state. And Mr Warrender seemed to listen because Luke did see someone. They did tests, like, and said he had learn-ing difficulties, but he should be able to stay in school with some support. And that was what happened.'

Julie paused again. She wanted the fat woman to understand what it had felt like, the relief of knowing that the tantrums and the moodiness weren't her fault. Her mam had been wrong about that. Luke was special, different, had been from the beginning. Nothing she could have done would have altered the fact. And the woman seemed to know how important that had been because at last she allowed herself to speak.

'So you weren't on your own.'

'You don't know,' Julie said, 'how good that felt.'

The woman nodded in agreement. But how could she know, when she'd never had children? How could anyone know, if they hadn't had a child with a learning disability?

'I could put up with people talking about us and the whispering at the school gate about the special help he was getting, because it was out in the open and most people were dead kind. There was a class-room assistant who came in just to help him. And Luke did all right. I mean, he was never going to be a genius, but he tried hard and his reading and writing came on, and some things he was good at. Like, any-thing to do with computers he took to really quickly. They were good years. Laura had started school too and I had some time to myself. I got a part-time job in the care home in the village. My mates couldn't understand why I enjoyed it so much, but I did. It made me feel useful, I suppose. Geoff was never very interested in seeing the kids, but he was OK about money. I mean, nothing exciting ever happened, no holidays or wild nights out, but we managed.'

'It can't have been easy, though,' the detective said.

'Well, maybe not easy,' Julie conceded. 'But we

coped. Luke started getting into bother again when he moved to the high school. Other kids saw he was an easy touch and took advantage. Set him up to act out in class. He was always the one that was caught. He started getting a reputation. You must know how it happens. You must see it all the time. The police were called when he was caught thieving from a building site. Plastic drainpipes. What would he want with those? Someone had offered him a few quid to take them, but it wasn't that. He wanted people to like him. All his life he'd felt left out. He wanted friends.'

You could understand that, couldn't you? Julie thought. She didn't know how she'd have managed without her friends. The first trouble with Geoff and she'd be on the phone to them. Sharing her worries about Luke when he'd been ill. And they'd be straight round with a bottle of wine. Keen for the gossip of course, but there for her.

'He did have one special friend,' she went on. 'A lad called Thomas. They met up when Luke started at the high school. He was a bit of a scally. In and out of trouble with the police, but when you talked to him you could see why. His dad had been in prison for most of the time he was growing up and his mam never seemed to bother with him much.

'I'd never have chosen Thomas as a friend for Luke, but he wasn't a bad lad, not really. And he seemed to like spending time in our house. In the end he was almost living with us. He was no bother. They'd be up in Luke's room, watching videos or playing on the computer, and while they were there they weren't thieving, were they? Or taking smack like a lot of their mates. And they got on really well. Sometimes you'd hear them laughing at some daft joke and I was just pleased that Luke had a friend.

'Then Thomas was killed. Drowned. Some lads were messing about on the quayside at North Shields. He fell in and couldn't swim. Our Luke was there too. He jumped in and tried to save Thomas but it was too late.'

Julie paused. Outside a tractor and trailer with a load of bales went past. 'Luke wouldn't talk about it. He shut himself in his room for hours. I thought he just needed time, you know, to get over it. To grieve. He stopped going to school, but he was fifteen by then and he wasn't going to get any exams, so I thought I'd just let him be. I'd talked to the lady who runs the care home and she said she might be able to find some work for him there when he was sixteen, helping in the kitchen. He'd come to work with me a few times and the old folk really took to him. But I should have realized he needed help. It wasn't normal the way he carried on, but then our Luke never really was normal, was he? So how could I tell?

'He stopped washing and eating and he was awake all night. Sometimes I'd hear his voice, as if he was talking to someone in his head. That was when I got the doctor. He got him taken into St George's. You know, the mental hospital. They said he was very depressed. Post-traumatic stress. I hated visiting him in there, but it was a relief not to have him at home. I mean, I felt guilty thinking like that, but it was true.'

'When did he come home?' the fat woman asked. Her first question.

'Three weeks ago and he seemed better. Really. I mean, still sad about Thomas. Sometimes he'd burst into tears just thinking about him. And he was still seeing the doctor at the outpatient clinic. But not crazy. Not mad. This was the first night out I'd had in months. I really needed it, but I wouldn't have gone if I hadn't thought he'd be all right. I never thought he'd do something like that to himself.'

The woman leaned over and took Julie's hand, covered it in her great paw.

'This wasn't your fault,' she said. 'Luke didn't commit suicide.' She looked at Julie to make sure that she'd taken that in, that she really understood. 'He was dead before he was put into the bath. He was murdered.'

Chapter Four

They were sitting at the table in the kitchen eating breakfast and already it was sunny, the sunlight bouncing off the yellow crockery on the dresser, reflected onto the ceiling. Peter was buttering toast and talking, complaining about a record he'd sent to the British Birds Rarity Committee, which had been rejected. Felicity seemed sympathetic without giving the conversation her full attention. She'd had a lot of practice. When he was a young man Peter had been convinced that he was destined for greatness. He'd been described as the best young scientist of his generation. Now, close to retirement, he had come to realize that the natural history establishment did not recognize his abilities. He expressed his disappointment in a way Felicity considered churlish and ugly – there were snide comments about other staff in the department, their lack of rigour, and he dismissed other birdwatchers as chasers after rare birds, saying that they didn't appreciate the importance of covering a local patch. Felicity understood the background to his disillusion. She wished with all her heart that his talent would be recognized. How wonderful it would be if he found a spectacular rarity close to home. Or was given promotion within the university. But his complaining irritated her. Occasionally she found herself wondering if he really was the great man she had believed him to be when they married. Then she would look at him, at the anxiety and sadness in his face, and feel disloyal. She'd stroke his face with her finger or kiss him while he was still in the middle of a sentence, shocking him into a sudden grin which made him look twenty years younger.

'What time are the others arriving?' he asked, breaking into her thoughts. He sounded excited. The gloom seemed to have lifted. She thought he was more excited about seeing his friends than he was about her. She never had that effect on him any more.

Felicity had been wondering about Lily Marsh, the student teacher, about whether she would accept the offer of accommodation. Felicity realized that they hadn't discussed money. Perhaps that had been the problem, why Lily had run off in that way. Perhaps having seen the cottage, very picturesque, if a little primitive, Lily had thought the rent would be beyond her. She was only a student after all. Felicity wondered if she should send a note to school with James, something welcoming but very precise, mentioning a sum which wouldn't put the young woman off. She'd been composing the letter in her head when Peter spoke.

She turned her thoughts to the matter in hand. Peter's birthday meal. A ritual. The same three friends invited each year. 'I've told them dinner at eight, with a walk to the lighthouse beforehand.' The walk to the lighthouse was a ritual too.

She heard the postman's van down the lane and then the flop of envelopes onto the hall floor. She left

24

Peter to his toast and went to collect them. All the letters were for him. She recognized the children's writing on three of the cards. She set the letters on the table in front of him. He put them into his briefcase without opening them. He always did that, always saved them to open at work. She'd wondered once if he had something to hide, in a moment of fantasy imagined another wife, a secret family. But it had just become a habit. He did it without thinking.

As he shut the briefcase, he stood up. There was a flurry of activity; Peter had promised James a lift up the lane to the bus and stood at the bottom of the stairs shouting for him to hurry. There were bags to be picked up and the packed lunch was almost forgotten. Felicity realized the note to Lily Marsh had never been written. She almost shouted to James as he ambled towards the car. *Tell Miss Marsh to give me a ring about the cottage.* But Peter would want to know what it was about and she couldn't hold him up now. Besides, he might disapprove of the idea. She would need to sell the plan to him when things were less fraught. She put Lily Marsh out of her mind. At last the car drove off and the house was wonderfully silent.

She sat over another coffee and made a list for the farm shop. She had planned the weekend meals already in her head. There was a cake of course, already baked and iced. It was a pity the three older children lived too far away to share it. For dinner tonight she'd made a daube of beef, rich and dark, slippery with olives and red wine. It stood in the pantry and needed only to be reheated. Now she changed her mind. It was too hot for beef. If Neil at the farm had a couple of chickens, she'd do that Spanish dish with quartered lemons and rosemary and garlic. It would be much lighter, beautifully aromatic and Mediterranean. Samuel would like that. She could set a long table on the terrace under the veranda and they'd eat it with plain rice and a big green salad, and make believe that they were looking out over orange trees and olive groves.

Occasionally, when she talked to other mothers, who rushed in and out of her house to drop off their sons, or to pick up hers, she wondered if she was missing out by not having paid employment. They seemed astounded when they found out she was at home all day. But what could she have done? She hadn't had much of a life before her marriage. She had no qualifications, few practical skills. Besides, Peter depended on her being there, calm and rested, to look after him when he came back from the disappointments at work. Certainly he needed her to be no competition. Imagine if she had become a successful lawyer or businesswoman, if she had started to win awards in her own right! The idea made her smile.

The farm shop was cool, the door into the yard open, letting in the smell of cows and grass. She was the first customer. Neil was still filling the fridge. The huge wooden board, the cleaver, the long pointed knives were still clean. He weighed the chickens and packed them into her bag.

'They're not free-range.' He knew Felicity would be interested. 'But barn-reared, not battery. You'll taste the difference.'

'That was a wonderful piece of pork I had from you last week.'

'Ah,' he said. 'It's all in the cooking, Mrs Calvert. And in the growing. I only cut it up.'

Another ritual. Like Peter taking his letters to work every day and the same three friends being invited for his birthday. This exchange passed between them every week. He carried the veg box out to the car for her and winked as he had added a few extra links of sausage for free into her bag.

'I hear it's a special birthday for Dr Calvert.'

She wondered, as she always did, how the butcher could possibly know all her business.

When she unlocked the door the phone was ringing and she ran inside, leaving everything on the drive. It was Samuel Parr.

'I wondered if there was anything you'd like me to bring tonight. A pud?'

'No,' she said. 'Really. Nothing.'

She found herself smiling. Samuel always put her in a good humour. He, too, was always at the back of her mind.

Later, when the chicken was cooking and the house was full of the smell of lemon and olive oil and garlic, the phone rang again. Felicity was sitting outside with the paper and another cafetiere of coffee, enjoying the last hour of silence before she had to drive into Hepworth. James had chess club after school and she'd arranged to collect him. A heat haze covered the fields towards the sea and in the distance the lighthouse seemed to shimmer, insubstantial. When she heard the phone she hurried inside. Her feet were bare. The flagstones on the terrace were so hot that they almost burned and the tiles in the kitchen were cool. The contrasting physical sensations on her feet excited her, made her suddenly catch her breath.

She had been certain it would be one of the children calling, but when she answered the line went dead. She dialled 1471 and was told that the caller had withheld his number. That had happened several times recently. She wondered if she should mention it to Peter. There had been a couple of thefts in the area. Perhaps the phone calls were to check if the house was empty. But she knew she would not tell Peter. Her life's work was to protect him from unpleasantness and worry.

She finished her coffee, looking out towards the sea. A bath, she thought, using some of that expensive oil she'd bought in Fenwick's on her last trip to town, to relax her before the guests descended.

Chapter Five

'Do you fancy a bit of a walk?' the fat detective said. She stood up and Julie thought how strong the muscles in her legs must be to get all that weight off the seat in one go. Looking at her, you'd think it would take a crane to shift her, one of those huge cranes that towered over the river down at Wallsend. And it wasn't only her body that was like that, Julie thought. The detective was a strong woman. Once she was decided on something nothing would shift her. She found the idea somehow comforting.

'I thought you might like a bit of fresh air,' the woman said.

Julie must have looked at her bewildered, the way Luke would look at you sometimes, when he didn't quite get what you were talking about.

'They'll be coming to remove Luke's body in a bit,' said the detective gently. Her name was Vera. She'd told Julie that when they'd first started talking, but Julie hadn't remembered it until now. 'No doubt the neighbours will be gawping. I thought you might want to be out of the way. Or perhaps you'd rather see him off. It's up to you.'

Julie thought of the body submerged by water and felt sick. She didn't want to think of that.

'Where would we go?'

'Wherever you like. Nice day for a walk on the beach. You can bring Laura.'

'Luke used to like the beach,' Julie said. 'One summer he went fishing. My da gave him an old rod. He never caught anything, like. But it kept him out of mischief.'

'There you are, then.'

They'd put Laura to bed in Sal's spare room. The detective went upstairs with Julie to ask the girl if she'd like to come out with them. Julie thought Vera was nosy. She'd met people like her before. People who were greedy for other folks' business. Perhaps that's what it took to make a good detective. Now, she thought Vera wanted to find out about Laura. If they went out for a walk together, she'd make Laura talk about herself. She'd think the girl had been neglected, that Julie had given all her time to Luke.

Laura was still asleep. 'I don't want to wake her,' Julie said quickly. 'We'll leave her here with Sal.'

'Whatever you think's best, pet.' Vera's voice was comfortable, easy, but Julie could tell she was disappointed.

She didn't see anyone staring as she walked out of Sal's front door to Vera's car, but she knew fine well everyone was looking. Any drama like this in the street and Julie would have been just the same, in the front bedroom, her nose to the nets. Any drama that she wasn't playing a central role in.

Vera parked the car behind the dunes at Deepden. On one side of the track was a small nature reserve. A wooden hide looking over a pool and a couple of walkways built from planks. In the distance a bungalow, where birdwatchers stayed, the garden so overgrown you could hardly see the house. On the seaward side a stretch of grass, spattered with small yellow flowers, and then the range of dunes. They'd brought the kids here a few times when Geoff had been in the mood to play happy families, and they'd loved it. Julie had a picture in her mind of Luke, aged about eight, caught in mid-air just after leaping off one of the sand hills. Perhaps there was a photo and that was what she was remembering. She could see it quite clearly. The frayed cut-off denims, the red T-shirt, his mouth wide open, part fear, part delight.

Despite the sunshine there weren't many other cars parked there. Thursday morning and the kids still at school, it was only the active retired and their dogs who had the chance to enjoy the weather. Julie had a sudden thought.

'I'm supposed to be at work. The nursing home. Mary'll be expecting me.'

'Sal phoned her first thing. Mary got someone else to cover your shift. She said she sends her love.'

That made Julie stop in her tracks, caused a small landslide as the fine dry sand dribbled past her feet. Mary Lee, who owned the home, wasn't a sentimental woman. It wasn't like her to talk of love.

'Have you told my mam and da?'

'Last night as soon as I arrived. They wanted to come over. You said you'd rather be on your own for a bit.'

'Did I?' Julie tried to remember, but last night was all a blur. Like that time they'd gone on Bev's hen party and she'd ended up in casualty with alcohol

31

poisoning. That same nightmare sense of unreality, jagged images and flashing shadows.

She walked on and they reached the highest point of the dunes, began to slide down towards the beach. She'd taken off her trainers and had them tied by the laces and slung over her shoulder. Vera was wearing sandals and hadn't bothered to take them off. In the car she'd put on a huge white floppy hat and dark glasses. 'The sun doesn't agree with me,' she'd said. She looked a bit mad. If Julie had bumped into her in St George's on the way to visit Luke, she'd have put her down as one of the patients. No question.

They were at the southern end of a long sweep of beach, about four miles long. At the northern end it swung into a narrow promontory where the light-house stood, almost lost to view in the haze.

'It can't have been easy, living with Luke,' Vera said.

Julie stopped again. There was that salt breeze that you only ever get by the sea. Three tiny figures right in the distance: two old gadges and a dog running after a ball, just silhouettes because the light was so bright.

'You think I killed him,' she said.

'Did you?' Because of the hat and the glasses, it was impossible to tell what the detective was thinking.

'No.' Then the words, all those words that had been spilling out of her since she'd found the body, dried up. She couldn't explain that she would never ever have done anything to hurt Luke, that she'd spent the last sixteen years protecting him from the world.

She opened her mouth, felt as if she were choking on dry sand. 'No,' she said again.

'Of course you didn't,' Vera said. 'If there was any chance you'd done it, I'd be talking to you in the police station, tape recorder on and your lawyer sitting in. Otherwise the court wouldn't accept what you'd told me as evidence. But I had to ask. You could have killed him, you see. He'd not long died when you got home. Physically it was a possibility. And usually the murderer is a family member.' She paused and then repeated, 'I had to ask.'

'You believe me, then?'

'I've told you I do. You *could* have killed him. If he'd wound you up and you couldn't cope any more. But you'd have told us. Besides, you really believed he'd killed himself. When I arrived you thought he'd committed suicide and you were blaming yourself.'

They were walking on the hard sand that the tide had just left behind. Julie rolled up her jeans a couple of turns and let the water cover her feet. The detective couldn't follow her without getting her sandals wet. She looked out to sea so Vera couldn't tell she was crying.

'Someone killed him,' Vera said. Julie could hardly hear her. Although the sea was too calm for waves there was still the sucking sound when the tide pulled back. 'Somebody strangled him, then took all his clothes off. Someone ran the bath and lifted him inside and scattered those flowers on the water.'

Julie wasn't sure if she was supposed to answer, so she said nothing.

'Did you have the flowers in your house?' Vera asked.

Julie turned to face her. 'I never have flowers in the house. Laura has hay fever. They make her eyes stream.'

'What about the garden?'

'Are you joking? Nothing grows in our garden. My da comes and cuts the grass for us, but we don't bother with any plants. There's only room for the washing line out the back.'

'So the murderer brought the flowers with him. We'll say it's a *him* just for convenience. Most murderers are men. But we'll keep an open mind all the same. Why would he bring flowers? Does it mean anything to you?'

Julie shook her head, though something was picking away at her brain, some memory.

'They brought flowers to the place where Thomas was killed. They threw them onto the river. The people who lived on the estate where his mam stayed. I mean, even people who didn't know him or knew him and didn't like him. To say they were sorry, like. To say they understood what a waste it was. Him losing his life because of a few lads horsing about. Luke went too. I bought some daffs for him from Morrisons.'

'Flowers for remembrance and sorrow,' Vera said. 'Universal.'

Julie wasn't sure what she meant by that.

'Are you saying whoever murdered Luke was sorry for it?'

'Maybe.'

'But if you were sorry – sorry in advance, like, if that's what the flowers were for – why kill him? It's not like anyone forced him to break into my house and kill my son.'

'No one did break in,' Vera said.

'What?'

'There's no sign of a forced entry. No broken window. Nothing like that. It looks as if Luke let him in. Or Laura.'

'It will have been Luke,' Julie said sadly. 'He'd be taken in by anyone. He'd give to every lad begging on the street if he had the money. Anyone coming to the door with a story, he'd let them in. Laura has more sense.'

'Did Laura and Luke get on?'

'What are you saying?' She was angrier than she'd been when she thought the detective was accusing *her* of murder. 'Laura's a lassie, just fourteen.'

'There are questions that have to be asked,' Vera said. 'You're not daft. You understand that.' She paused for a moment. 'You realize I'll have to talk to her. She's not in a fit state yet, but when she's ready. It's better that I know how things were between them before I start. Is it possible, for example, that Luke confided in her? If he was worried about anything, would she know?'

'They weren't that close,' Julie said. 'It wasn't easy for her having a brother like that. He always got all the attention, didn't he? I tried to make her feel special too, but he was the one I worried about. It must have been embarrassing for her when she got to the high school. Everyone knew he got into bother. Everyone calling him names. That didn't mean she'd have wished him any harm.'

'No,' Vera said. 'Of course not.'

Two teenage lads ran down the dunes onto the beach. They were scallies, you could tell just by looking at them, kicking sand at each other and swearing. They were about the same age as Luke, probably bunking off school. Julie pressed her lips together hard to stop herself from wailing.

'Which taxi did you use from town last night?' The question came out of the blue. Julie knew Vera was trying to distract her and was grateful.

'Foxhunters, Whitley Bay. We booked it in advance. The driver dropped Lisa and Jan off first. I was last stop.' She paused. 'He'll confirm my story. I was only in the house minutes before I was banging on Sal's door. If he went to the end of the road to turn round, he might even have seen me on the doorstep.'

'I'm more interested in whether he saw someone else in the street. Did you see anyone?'

Julie shook her head.

'Take a bit of time,' Vera said. 'There might be something. See if you can rerun it in your head like a film. Talk me through it. From the taxi pulling up.'

So there on the wide and empty beach, with the gulls screaming over her head and the tide sucking at her feet, Julie shut her eyes and felt the dizziness that had hit her when she first stepped out of the taxi. 'I was drunk,' she said. 'Not fall-in-the-gutter drunk, but not really with it. Everything spinning. You know how it is?' Because she was sure that Vera had been drunk in her time. She'd be a good person to get drunk with.

'I know.' She gave Julie a minute. 'Did you hear anything unusual?'

'Nothing at all. I noticed how quiet it was. Usually there's traffic on the main road through the village.

It's always there so you don't hear it. Last night there was nothing. Not when I was opening the door.' She frowned.

'But later? When the door was open?'

'A car started up in the street.'

'Could it have been the taxi, turning round?'

'No. This was the ignition being switched on, the engine revving. It's a different sound, isn't it, from a car that's already running?'

'Quite different,' Vera said.

'It must have been parked down the street, near the junction with the road into town. That's the direction the sound came from.'

'So you'd have passed it in the taxi on your way in?'

'Must have done.'

'Don't suppose you noticed it? A strange car? Not belonging to one of the usual residents?' Her voice was so studied and casual that Julie knew it was important.

'Nah,' she said. 'I wouldn't have done.' But she shut her eyes again and concentrated. They'd come over the humped-back bridge and she'd leaned forward to tell the driver to slow down because they were nearly there. *There's a nasty right-hand turn just on the corner.* And at the same time she was pulling her purse out of her bag, so there wouldn't be that embarrassing last-minute fumble for payment. Lisa and Jan had already given her more than their share so she knew she had the cash. There'd been nothing coming in the opposite direction and the taxi driver had pulled into her street without having to stop. And there had been a car. Almost on the corner. Parked outside the bungalow where Mr Grey lived. She'd wondered about that because Mr Grey hadn't driven since he was diagnosed with Parkinson's and everyone knew his only son lived in Australia. She remembered because she'd wondered if the car might belong to the doctor, if there was some emergency. And she'd looked to see if there were any lights on, thinking of the gossip she could pass on to Sal. But the house had been dark. And anyway it had been a small car. Not the sort a doctor would drive.

All this she told Vera.

'I don't know what make it was.'

'Never mind, pet. It gives us something to work on. One of your neighbours might have seen it.'

The scally boys were throwing a football around, bouncing it hard in the wet sand, so muddy spray flew all over their clothes. Their mothers will kill them, Julie thought.

'Home,' Vera said. 'Are you ready?'

Julie almost said she never wanted to go home.

'Laura will be awake. She'll be needing you.' Vera stamped away towards the sand hills, leaving Julie no option but to follow.

Arriving back in the street, it was as if she was seeing it for the first time. Part of her was still on the beach with the sound of the gulls and all that space. Hard to think of this as home. A cul-de-sac ending in reclaimed farmland. Once there'd been the slag heap from the pit, but now there were fields all the way to the coast. Old folks' bungalows on one side of the street, each with a ramp to the pavement and a hand rail. A row of semis on the other, council once but all privately owned now. Julie thought: Would this still have happened if we lived somewhere else?

Vera asked her to point out the exact place where she'd seen the car the night before. She tried her best but her heart wasn't in it. All the time she was thinking of things she might have done to avoid the loss of her son. She could have moved, or not gone out with the girls, or had Luke put into a special school, a boarding school where he'd have been properly looked after.

Vera pulled up carefully right outside the house. There was still a policeman on the doorstep, but Julie knew that Luke had gone.

Chapter Six

When Vera arrived home that evening, there was a buzzard sailing over her house. The rounded wings were tilted to catch the thermals and the last of the sun caught it, so it shone like polished wood, carved in a totem. The buzzards were only just returning to this part of Northumberland. Common in the west of the county, the keepers here had shot them to buggery, stamped on eggs, put out poisoned bait. Vera knew there was a keeper on a neighbouring estate with murdering tendencies. Let him try, she thought. Just let him try.

Inside, the house was stuffy and untidy. She'd not been home for twenty-four hours. She opened windows, picked up mucky clothes from the bedroom floor and shoved them in the washer in the lean-to. Then she wondered if there might be anything in the freezer worth eating. Since the death of her father Vera had lived alone and knew she always would now. There was no point considering whether she could have survived a relationship. There had been someone once who'd kept her awake at nights dreaming, but nothing had come of it. It was too late now for regrets. Which didn't stop her, late at night, with a whisky in her hand.

She took a beer from the fridge, flipped off the top with an opener and drank it straight from the bottle. Even when she hadn't bothered to buy in food there was always booze in the old station master's house. She drank too much. Too regularly at least. Emotionally dependent, she told herself. Not addicted. She carried the beer with her back to the lean-to and ferreted in the chest freezer. Her father had stored the animals and birds for his taxidermy in there; she could do with a smaller freezer now. In the bottom she found a plastic tub of venison stew. The venison had been donated by the same keeper who hated raptors, but she'd accepted it without a qualm. Here in the hills you had to keep up a pretence of liking your neighbours. You never knew when you'd need a tow out of a ditch on a snowy day. She'd spent a wet Sunday afternoon cooking the venison, using lots of root vegetables to keep it moist, bay leaves from the garden and red wine. She'd thought it had all been eaten and finding a portion gave her a brief moment of joy, an uncomplicated pleasure of the kind you rarely experienced as an adult.

All the time she was stamping around the house, she had the Armstrong case at the back of her mind. Like an actor, she was feeling her way into the characters, living them. She already had a sense of Luke Armstrong. Julie's words had brought him alive for her, and anyway she'd met boys like him before. Mostly she'd bumped into them in police cells or Young Offender Institutions. The system had failed them, as it would have failed Luke without a mother like Julie to fight on his behalf. Luke had been a boy who had struggled. Everything had been difficult for him – school, relationships and the boring stuff of everyday life. He would have seen the world through a fog of misunderstanding. He hadn't ever quite made sense of it. He would have been an easy boy to manipulate. A few kind words, the prospect of a simple treat and he would have welcomed a stranger as a saviour. Vera could have understood if he had died in a pub brawl. She imagined him wound up and wound up and then lashing out with the frustration of a toddler. Even a street shooting would have made some sort of sense. He would betray without meaning to and a death like that could be a scrappy mistake or a message to others.

But this murder made no sense at all. The way Luke had been lovingly laid out in the bath, with perfumed oils and flowers, almost implied respect. It made Vera, who was more imaginative than her appearance suggested, think of sacrifice. A beautiful child. Ritual and reverence. And then there was surely a literary reference. O level English had been a long time ago, but the image was a striking one. Ophelia's suicide. And how many of Luke's scally friends and contacts had read *Hamlet*?

She had no idea yet what Laura was like. Her mother said she was bright and gobby. Was it credible that the girl had slept through the whole thing? The strangling, the bath being run. Had the murderer even known she was there?

Vera tried to imagine what might have happened. Someone was standing on the doorstep with a bunch of flowers. Did Luke let him in? Did he know him? Then what? The Crime Scene Investigators hadn't been prepared to commit themselves as to where the murder had taken place. At the bottom of the stairs? If that was the case, had Luke been carried up to the bathroom? Vera couldn't picture it. It didn't make sense. So perhaps the murderer had asked Luke to let him use the bathroom and Luke had shown him upstairs. Then the murder must have taken place in the room next to Laura's. Vera shivered slightly, imagining the girl still asleep while the boy was dying so close to her.

She ate her meal on a tray, sitting by an open window. Her immediate neighbours were ageing hippies in search of the good life. They had a smallholding, a couple of goats, one cow for milking, half a dozen hens, a small flock of rare-breed sheep. They had no use for pesticides, despised agri-business and their hay meadow was overgrown with weeds. Vera could smell the hay. There was a flock of twites feeding off the seed heads. She'd opened a bottle of Merlot and was a couple of glasses into it. She felt happier than she'd been for months.

Recently most of her work had been routine, boring. This was different and a challenge, something to pick over when she spent the evening on her own, something other than a gloomy play on Radio 4 to occupy her mind. God, she thought. I'm a sad old bat. She did feel some guilt in taking such a delight in a bonny lad's death. She liked Julie, thought she couldn't have done any better by the boy. But none of that stopped her relishing the case, the unusual details of the crime scene. She had few other pleasures in her life. She sat by the open window until it was dark and the wine bottle was almost empty.

*

The next day she brought her team together and she talked about Luke as if she'd known him.

'You'll have met the sort. A bit slow. You'd speak to him and you'd not be sure he'd understood. Say it again and you'd still wonder if he was any the wiser. Not a nasty lad, though. Soft-hearted. Generous. Good with the old folks in the home where his mother works. On the edge of trouble. Not bright enough to get into bother on his own account, but not bright enough either to stay away when his friends dragged him into it. And then only petty stuff . . .

'Luke witnessed a drowning. Joe has the details and will pass them round. It might be a coincidence of course, but it's the best lead we have at the moment.' She paused. 'The only lead.'

On cue Joe Ashworth played paper monitor, dishing out sheets of A4. Vera wondered suddenly if she treated him too much like teacher's pet. Did he resent it? Trouble was, he was one of the few members in the team she could trust absolutely to get things right. Perhaps that said more about her than about them.

She continued. 'The lad who drowned after the scrap on North Shields quayside was Thomas Sharp. One of *the* Sharps. Notorious family and we'll all have heard of them. Father is Davy Sharp, at present serving three years in HMP Acklington. There was no prosecution after the accident – it seems generally to be accepted as horseplay which got out of hand. It's possible of course that none of this is relevant, but ask around. Was Luke involved with people his mother knew nothing about? Is someone trying to send a scary message here?'

She paused again. She liked an audience, but preferred it if the listeners were responsive. No one answered. 'Well?' she demanded. 'Has anyone heard anything?'

They shook their heads. They seemed stupefied, too well fed, too hot. The room was airless, but she was surprised by their lack of excitement. Wasn't this what they'd joined up for? It didn't occur to her that she scared the pants off most of them, that even the ones who shouted their mouths off in the police canteen were too timid to commit themselves to an opinion which she might consider foolish.

'The crime scene,' she said. 'You'll have heard by now it was a tad unusual. The boy was strangled, then placed in a bath of water. Flowers had been scattered over his body. Luckily Julie didn't empty the bath when she saw Luke. The CSIs spent hours scooping out the water and saving it. There might be something. They're analysing the bath oil. We might even get a hair from the murderer if we're lucky. But we can't rely on that. We need to find where the flowers came from. Were they picked from fields and gardens in the village or did the murderer buy them? We need to know exactly what they were, then get someone to go round all the local florists checking that out. They didn't seem to me the sort you'd get in a standard bouquet. Mostly wild flowers, I'd say. So where were they picked? Is there a local botanist who can help? Joe, can you find out from the university?'

She didn't wait for him to answer. 'The more

important question is why. Why the gesture? It seems a risk, an unnecessary fuss. It's almost as if the killer wanted to draw attention to himself, make a grand spectacle. Julie was out for the night in Newcastle, but no one knew exactly what time she'd be back. She must almost have walked in on it. Laura, the sister, was in the house throughout. Fast asleep as it happens. Her mother says she could sleep through a bomb dropping. Is that significant?'

A hand rose tentatively. Vera liked a responsive audience but she could be as cruel to interrupters as a stand-up comedian to unwelcome hecklers. She was gracious to this one.

'Yes?'

'Does it mean the murderer knew the family? Knew that Laura was a heavy sleeper and that Julie was out for the night? She didn't often go out, did she?'

Vera nodded in approval. 'Maybe. Or that he'd been watching the place for a while, waiting for an opportunity.'

Another hand. 'Yes?'

'Could it have been the sister? A row that got out of hand?'

Vera considered for a moment. 'You could imagine them fighting,' she said. 'A lad like that. It must be a nightmare having him as a brother, especially the age she is. That age you want to be the same as everyone else, don't you? Last thing you need is a loony in the family. She could have drowned him too. If he was in the bath, it wouldn't take a lot of strength to push him under. But he was strangled and then put in the water. I can't see a fourteen-year-old girl doing that. She's a skinny little thing. Nervy. I don't think she's hiding anything, though. Where would she get the flowers from? The mother confirms there were none in the house. I think we can forget the girl unless anything else comes up. Everyone agree?'

There were a few half-hearted nods. Vera continued. 'The father, though, is a different matter. It sounds as if he always found it hard to cope with Luke. He and Julie separated years ago, but he's kept in touch with the family. Nothing formal. He calls in when he feels like it. The kids go to his house occasionally. If he killed the lad, it would explain why there was no sign of a break-in. Of course Luke would open the door to him. Julie says the boy always wound him up. You could think of a scenario when he was provoked to murder, to strangling.'

'You'd have the same problem explaining the flowers, though,' Ashworth said.

'Maybe. Unless he was clever enough to realize he'd be a suspect and knew that sort of elaborate staging would make us look elsewhere. All the more reason to get some details on the flowers. If they were available in the village, he could have picked them after the murder.'

Ashworth was sceptical. 'He'd have to be pretty cool. Dream up the theatricals, go out for the flowers, let himself back into the house. Surely someone would have seen him.'

'You'd have thought so, wouldn't you? Has there been any joy from the house-to-house? Was anyone seen in the street?'

She thought that later in the day she would go back to the village herself. Not that it was appropriate for her to be knocking on doors. Not according to her boss. Her last appraisal had mentioned an unwillingness to delegate. Her role, he said, was strategic, the management of information. But she liked to get a feel for what was going on in the neighbourhood. Not everyone was very good at that.

She looked at the blank faces, waiting for someone to reply. Is it any wonder, she thought, that I'm not keen on delegating?

At last Ashworth spoke. Teacher's pet again. Though she guessed they called him a lot worse than that when she wasn't around. 'No one saw anything unusual, according to the team who did the house-to-house.'

'What about the car Julie remembers seeing in the street on Wednesday night?'

He looked at his notes. 'It definitely wasn't there at nine o'clock apparently. A woman was bringing her daughter home from Guides. She says she would have remembered.'

No one else spoke. There was a moment of silence. Vera was sitting on the edge of a desk, as fat and round and impassive as a Buddha. She even closed her eyes for a moment, seemed lost in meditation. They could hear distant noise from the rest of the building – a phone ringing, a hoot of laughter. She opened her eyes again.

'If this wasn't the father playing silly buggers,' she said, 'we have to consider what was going on at that crime scene. It was like a work of theatre. Or one of those art installations. Dead sheep. Piles of elephant crap. The sort of art where the meaning's more important than what it looks like or the skill that's gone into making it. We need to know what this artist was *saying*. Does anyone have any ideas?'

They looked back at her, rather like dead sheep themselves. And this time she couldn't blame them. She didn't have any ideas either.

Chapter Seven

It was Friday afternoon and the traffic on the dual carriageway leading from Newcastle to the coast was heavy. People had left work early to enjoy the sun. Windows down, music loud, the weekend had already started. Luke Armstrong's father lived just off the coast road in one of the sprawling new housing estates on the outskirts of Wallsend. Vera knew it wasn't her job to talk to him. She should leave the legwork to the rest of the team. How would they learn otherwise? But this was what she was good at. She pictured Julie Armstrong holed up in Seaton with her daughter and her memories, and she thought she wasn't going to leave this to anyone else.

The house was a red-brick semi. It had a small patch of front garden, separated from the neighbour's with a lavender hedge, a block-paved drive, integral garage. The developers had squeezed every inch out of this land which had once held three collieries, but the estate was pleasant enough if you didn't mind communal living. It had been designed around lots of small cul-de-sacs so children could ride their bikes safely. Trees planted in the gardens were starting to mature. There were hanging baskets outside the houses, spotless cars on the drives. Nothing to sneer at, Vera told herself.

She hadn't been sure Geoff Armstrong would be in. When she'd phoned there'd been an answering machine, but she hadn't left a message. She'd just as soon catch him unprepared. She drove slowly down the street looking for the right house. It was three o'clock and the younger children were coming out of the primary school on the corner. Mothers waiting in the playground looked pink and dazed after an afternoon in the sun. Vera was standing on the step with her finger on the bell, when Armstrong walked into the drive. He was holding the hand of a little girl only just old enough to be at school. An ad-man's dream cute kid – blonde curls, freckles, huge brown eyes, dressed in a regulation red gingham frock.

'Yes?' he said. Only one word, but spoken with that undertone of aggression which had scared Julie.

Before she could explain, the front door opened. A slight woman was framed in the doorway. She was wearing a dressing gown, blinked out at the sunlight, but wasn't embarrassed to be caught like that. She knew she still looked good.

'Kath works nights,' Armstrong said angrily. 'I finish early on Fridays so I can fetch Rebecca. That way Kath gets an extra hour in bed.'

'Sorry, pet.' Vera spoke to the woman, not to him. 'No one said.' She held out her ID so they could both see. 'Can I come in?'

They sat in the small kitchen, leaving Rebecca in the lounge with juice, a biscuit and children's TV. Kath put the kettle on then excused herself to get dressed.

When Vera apologized again for waking her, she waved it away.

'It's impossible to sleep in when the weather's like this. Radios in the gardens and the kids playing out. Anyway, this is important. Poor Luke.' She stood for a moment in the doorway, then went upstairs. They heard her progress: footsteps, a cupboard being opened, the shower.

They sat on tall stools next to the breakfast bar. Vera thought they must look ridiculous. Two over-weight gnomes on toadstools. 'Did Luke spend a lot of time here?' she asked.

'Quite a lot, before he was ill. More than Laura. I thought she'd be excited when Kath had the baby. A little sister. But she seemed to resent her. Luke was better with Rebecca even when she was tiny.'

'He hadn't been here since he left hospital?'

'No. Kath wanted to have him over to stay last weekend, but I wasn't sure . . .'

'You were worried about your little girl?'

'Not that he'd hurt her, like. But that if he behaved strange, she wouldn't understand.' He paused. 'I never handled Luke well when I lived at home. Pride, Kath says. I wanted a boy who was strong, competitive, good at games. Like me only better. I suppose I was ashamed because he was different from other lads.'

Vera thought he'd changed since he left Julie. Kath must be a civilizing influence. Or maybe she'd just taught him how to talk a good game.

'You used to lose your temper with him.'

He looked up, shocked. He was a bereaved father. She wasn't supposed to talk to him like that.

'It was a bad time,' he said. 'I'd lost my job, no

money, Julie and me weren't getting on. Lately I'd been trying to understand him better. Then that lad he was knocking around with drowned and it freaked Luke out. No one could get through to him then.'

'Did you visit him in hospital?'

'Kath and I both went. I'm not sure I could have faced it on my own. First few times you could tell he was really doped up. I mean, I'm not sure he knew we were there. But even then he looked scared. He jumped whenever anyone came up behind him. When he got better we took him out for an afternoon. A pizza and a bit of a walk round Morpeth. He was more chatty then, but still very nervy. He kept saying it was his fault, that lad drowning. We got to the bridge, you know over the river by the church, and he really lost it. Shaking, crying. We'd only just got him calm when we arrived back at the hospital.'

'Did he say *why* he was scared? Did anyone blame him for the boy's death?'

'He was never able to explain himself very well even before the breakdown. We asked, but questions only made it worse.'

'You'd been to see him a couple of times after he came out of hospital?'

'Yes, and he seemed better. He didn't like to leave the house, Julie said. But he was more himself.'

'His sister will have been glad to have him home.'

Armstrong leaned forward across the breakfast bar. His hands were hard and callused, the nails very short. 'Aye, perhaps.' He paused, seemed to study his fingers. 'But it wasn't easy for her. She found it hard to get on with Luke at times. Maybe she's got too much of her father in her to make allowances. Maybe she was just fed up with him getting all their mother's attention.'

They heard a door shut upstairs, more footsteps and Kath appeared. She was wearing her uniform and had put up her hair.

'Is it OK? Or would you rather talk to Geoff on his own?'

'Come away in,' Vera said. 'I'm just about to get to the hard bit. Could do with a woman's common sense. Stop your man flying off the handle.'

'What do you mean?'

'I need to ask you both what you were doing when Luke was killed. That doesn't mean I think you had anything to do with his death. But I have to ask. You do understand?'

'Of course,' she said.

'Geoff?'

He nodded reluctantly.

'I was at work,' Kath said. 'The gynaecology ward at the RVI. There were three of us on. It was frantic. A couple of emergency admissions from A&E. I didn't even have time for a break. Geoff was here all night, babysitting Rebecca.'

'Do you always work nights?'

'I have done since I went back after Rebecca. It suits us. Geoff's self-employed. Most of his work comes from a builder in Shields, Barry Middleton. Geoff does all his plastering and joinery. Barry's well thought of and the work's regular, but Geoff can suit himself pretty well, fit it in round the family, school holidays. He has Rebecca ready for school in the morning when I get in and Fridays he picks her up. It's almost her bedtime when I leave for the hospital in the evening. Neither of us gets much of a social life, but it means Rebecca sees plenty of us.'

'Did your daughter wake up the night Luke was killed?'

The question was directed at Geoff, but it was Kath who answered again. 'She never wakes up! She's a miracle. She's slept through since she was six weeks. Once she's in her bed you don't hear from her till seven the next morning.'

There was an awkward silence. Almost as she spoke Kath realized the implication of her words. 'But he wouldn't leave her,' she cried. 'You've seen what he's like with her. He'd never go away and leave her on her own.'

'Geoff?'

'I didn't leave her,' he said. She knew he was controlling his temper, to prove to her and to Kath that he could, that he didn't lose it any more. 'I couldn't even go to the end of the road without imagining things. That the house was on fire. That she was sick. I wouldn't do it. Anyway, I could go to see Luke any time. Why wait till the middle of the night?'

'Right, then,' Vera said. 'Now that's out of the way, we can move on.' Though it wasn't out of the way. Not really. He could have got someone in to sit with Rebecca. Or if he was desperate enough he could have left her whatever he claimed in front of his wife. She'd get the team chatting to the neighbours tomorrow. Check if anyone was called in to babysit, or if anyone saw his car moved from the drive. She took a breath. 'Do you have any idea who might have wanted to kill Luke? Julie said he had no enemies, but a mam always thinks her bairn can do no wrong. I need something to work on here. Somewhere to start.'

From the living room they heard the little girl singing along to a rhyme on the television. Vera didn't know much about children but thought it must be unusual to get one this undemanding. It was a very different household from the one in Seaton where Luke had grown up. This was calm, ordered. The family lived by routine. Julie needed a bit of drama in her life to get through the day. Vera kept her eyes fixed on the adults, waiting for them to speak.

'Luke could wind you up,' Armstrong said. 'He didn't mean to. He just didn't understand what you were saying to him. You'd ask him to do something and he'd look at you like you were the daft one for expecting him to catch on. I can imagine that getting him into bother. Some of the people he mixed with, they were used to being treated with respect.'

'Like the Sharps?'

'Maybe.'

'Did the Sharps blame Luke for their son's death?'

It seemed Armstrong needed time to think about that. 'I don't mix with them,' he said at last. 'I wouldn't know. They're not famous for their patience, though, are they? And our Luke would have tried the patience of a saint. If one of them had asked him what happened that night Thomas died, Luke wouldn't have been able to answer. He'd get stressed, flustered. The words wouldn't come out and he'd just end up staring. Like I said, that would wind you up. Even if you didn't believe Luke was responsible, it would still make you mad.'

'Not mad enough to go round to his house and strangle him,' Kath said.

Armstrong shrugged. 'I can't think of anyone else who'd want to kill him.'

'Did Luke ever talk to you about the accident?'

'Not the accident itself,' Kath said. 'He came here soon after it happened. He talked about all the flowers that had been thrown into the river afterwards. How pretty they were. He'd gone with Julie and seemed really moved by it. There was a picture on the front page of the *Chronicle*. He brought it for me to see.'

Rebecca appeared at the kitchen door. She stood shyly, curious about the stranger.

'Do you mind starting on the tea, Geoff?' Kath said. 'I need to get ready for work.'

She followed Vera towards the front door. In the kitchen Geoff had switched on the radio and he and Rebecca were singing along to a pop song.

Vera had dozens of questions. She wanted to know how Kath and Geoff had met. What had she seen in him? How had she seen the potential doting father under the loutishness and the anger? But that was probably just prying and none of her business and she contented herself with a single comment. 'I was told your man had a bit of a temper,' she said. 'No sign of that now.'

Kath paused for a moment, reaching out towards the door handle. 'He's happy,' she said. 'There's no reason for him to get angry any more.'

Vera thought that sounded a bit glib. Too good to be true. But she didn't push it. She had an appointment, someone else to see.

Chapter Eight

Lying in the bath, the window open a crack, the water deep and very hot, Felicity found herself brooding on the past. She wasn't given much to introspection and wondered what might be the cause of it. Peter's six-tieth birthday perhaps. Anniversaries occasionally had that effect. Or a menopausal moodiness. Meeting Lily Marsh had unsettled her. She was jealous of the young woman's youth and vitality, the firm skin and flat stomach, and she had envied her independence.

Felicity had married too early. She'd met Peter at a party. She was an undergraduate, only six weeks into her degree. Her parents had tried to persuade her to apply to a university a bit further from home, but she'd been daunted enough at the prospect of a hall of residence. She needed the security of the vicarage only an hour away, an escape route. Her father was a priest, mild, relaxed about theology, but strict on kindness. In fact, she'd taken to university life, the friendships and the late nights and especially the men. She saw that she might be attractive to them. They quite liked her shyness, perhaps they even saw her demure demeanour as a challenge. But she wasn't sure how she should respond to them. She wandered around, bewildered and a little lost. Alice in an academic wonderland.

So, she was at this party in a student house in Heaton. There were bare floorboards and Indian cotton pinned on the walls, unfamiliar music and the heavy smell of dope which registered without her knowing what it was. It was very cold, she remembered, despite all the people crowded into the room. They'd had the first severe frost of the autumn and there was no form of heating. Outside, the soggy fallen leaves were frozen in heaps on the pavement.

Whatever had Peter been doing there? It really wasn't his thing at all and beneath his dignity anyway to fraternize with undergraduates. But he was there, dressed in corduroy trousers and a hand-knitted woollen jumper, completely anachronistic, as if he'd wandered out of a Kingsley Amis novel. He was drinking beer from a can and looking miserable. Although he'd been out of place in the student party, he had been a familiar figure to Felicity, a familiar type at least. There had been lonely men in the parish, attracted to the church because, surely, there they would not be rejected. The last curate had been terribly shy. Her mother had made fun of him behind his back, and the middle-aged spinsters in the village had taken to competing for his affection with lamb casseroles and spicy gingerbread.

But when she started talking to Peter, Felicity had discovered that he was nothing like the weedy young Christians she'd met at summer camp, or the amiable curate. He was abrupt and arrogant and quite sure of himself despite the bizarre clothes.

'I'd arranged to meet someone,' he said angrily. 'But they've not turned up. A complete waste of time.'

Felicity wasn't sure whether the person who'd failed to materialize was male or female.

'I've papers to mark.'

Then she realized that he wasn't a mature student. He hadn't looked thirteen years her senior. She was immensely dazzled by his status. She had always been attracted to men in authority, liking the idea of someone else taking control, of educating and informing her. She had so little experience of men and was convinced she would do everything wrong. Better let someone who knew what they were about lead the way.

She asked haltingly about his work and he began to talk about it with such energy and fire that she was enthralled, though she didn't understand a word. They moved into the hall where the music wasn't so loud, and sat on the stairs. They couldn't sit side by side because they had to leave room for the people stumbling up to the bathroom, so he sat above her and she took a place at his feet.

The conversation wasn't all one way. He asked about her and listened when she described her home and her parents. 'I'm an only child. I suppose I've been very sheltered.'

'This must all come as rather a shock,' he said. 'Student life, I mean.' She didn't like to say that actually she was enjoying the noise, the chaos and the freedom of university. He seemed taken with the idea that she was vulnerable and it seemed rude to contradict him. He was even tolerant of her religious faith, as if it was appropriate for someone at her stage of experience. As if she were a six-year-old who had confided a belief in the tooth fairy. 'Even I agree that not everything can be explained by science,' he said and that was when he first touched her, stroking her hair as if he wanted to reassure her that she wasn't making a fool of herself. Not really. And she was grateful for his understanding.

They left when the party was in full swing. He offered to walk her back to the hall of residence. They took the bus into town and then walked over the Town Moor. It was bitterly cold, everything white and silver, mist caught in the hollows and coming from their mouths. There was a swollen white moon. 'It looks too heavy,' she said. 'As if it should crash to earth.'

She expected then a brief sermon on gravity and the planets, but he stopped and turned towards her, taking her face in his gloved hands. 'You are delightful,' he said. 'I've never met anyone like you.'

Later she realized that was probably true. He had been to a boys' school, then straight to university and all his energies had been taken up with his academic work. Perhaps he had dreamed of women, perhaps they had haunted him, diving into his consciousness once every six minutes. Certainly he must have had sexual encounters. But he hadn't allowed himself to be distracted. Until now. When they walked on he put his arm around her shoulders.

Outside her hall he pulled her to him and kissed her, and he stroked her hair, not gently this time, but with a violent, rubbing motion which made her feel how frustrated he must be. This pressure on her hair and scalp was the only expression of desire he allowed himself. She felt the contained passion stinging and fizzing inside him like electricity.

'Can we meet for lunch?' he asked. 'Tomorrow?'

When she agreed she felt as if *she* was in control. She was the one with the power.

As he walked off, a friend wandered up. 'Who was that?'

'Peter Calvert.'

The friend was impressed. 'I've heard of him. Isn't he supposed to be brilliant? Almost a genius?'

He took her to Tynemouth for lunch, driving her there in his car. She had expected they'd go somewhere in town, somewhere close to the university. The car and the hotel restaurant full of businessmen again set him apart from her student friends. It took very little to impress her. Afterwards they climbed the bank to the priory and looked down over the river to South Shields. They walked along the bank of the Tyne and he pointed out a Mediterranean gull. He'd been wearing binoculars. She had thought that was odd because his subject was botany. She hadn't understood then the nature of his ruling passion.

'Do you have to be back?' he asked. 'A lecture?' He took her hand in his, drew on her palm with his finger. The sun was shining and today he had no need of gloves. 'I don't want to lead you astray.'

'Don't you?'

He smiled at her. 'Well, perhaps. Come and have tea with me.'

His flat wasn't far away, in North Shields, an attic overlooking Northumberland Park. Two elderly sisters lived in the rest of the house. One of them was in the small garden when they arrived, raking up leaves from the lawn. She waved in a friendly way, then went back to her work without taking undue interest in Felicity. The flat was very tidy and Felicity imagined that Peter had cleaned it specially. It was full of books. A large-scale Ordnance Survey map showing the area of his field study had been pinned to the wall and the way in was blocked by a telescope on a tripod. There was a living room with a cramped kitchen and a bathroom off and a door which she presumed must lead to the bedroom. The door into the bedroom seemed to hold a fascination for her and while Peter was making tea she found her eyes drawn to it. It was panelled and the grain of the wood showed through the white gloss paint. It had a round brass knob. She wondered if the bedroom was also tidy, if he had changed the sheets in expectation. She would have sneaked a look but he came in, carrying a tea tray. There were cups and saucers which didn't match and slices of fruit loaf, buttered.

Later that afternoon they went into the bedroom and made love. Her first time and nothing to write home about, of course. There was a lot of fumbling with a Durex, which he seemed as uncertain about how to use as she was, and they must have got the whole thing seriously wrong, or there had been an accident, because she found out soon after that she was pregnant. It must have been that first time. Later they became more proficient. The sex got better too. Even that first afternoon, though, she had a glimpse, an inkling of something wonderful, and that was more than she had expected.

She took Peter to meet her parents soon after, before she realized she was pregnant. It was a damp, raw day and, although it was only lunchtime, as they drove through the trees they could see the lights on in the living room, and a fire. 'It was always like this when I came home from school,' she said. 'Welcoming.' He never talked much about his parents. They were in business, rather driven. He made her feel as if her attitude to her family was sentimental and unreal.

Her mother had made a thick vegetable soup because it was Felicity's favourite and home-made bread. After lunch they took coffee and chocolate cake and sat by the fire. Peter had been very quiet at first. It was as if he felt out of place, much as she did in the university. He was feeling his way. Now, sitting by the fire, he seemed to relax. Felicity seemed unnaturally tired. She listened to the conversation as if she was half asleep. He was talking about his work and her father was asking questions – not out of politeness, Felicity could always tell when he was simply being polite – but because he was interested. That's good, Felicity thought. They get on. Then she must have fallen asleep because she woke with a start when a log fell and a spark cracked and spat onto the hearth rug. Her mother smiled indulgently and made a comment about wild parties. Felicity felt the same exhaustion in the first stage of all her pregnancies.

Marriage was Peter's idea. Her parents put no pressure on them. Indeed, they seemed unsure about the wisdom of such haste. 'You have been together for such a short time.' They would probably have supported her through an abortion if that had been her choice. Peter asked to speak to her parents alone. There was another trip to the vicarage and the three of them talked in the kitchen while she dozed once more over a book in the living room. She felt altogether that the matter was out of her hands. She lacked the energy to make a decision.

On the way back to Newcastle, she asked Peter what had been said. 'I told them I wanted to marry you the moment I set eyes on you.' She thought it was the most romantic thing she had ever heard and the wedding went ahead.

Felicity was so caught up in her memories that the sound of a door closing downstairs made her start with surprise. The bath water was tepid. She climbed out and wrapped a towel around her, went out onto the landing and shouted downstairs.

'Peter! I'm up here.'

There was no reply. She looked over the banister but there was no sign of him. She walked down the stairs, still wound in her towel, leaving a trail of damp footprints. The house was empty. She told herself she must have imagined the noise of the closing door, but a sense that the house had been invaded remained with her for the rest of the day.

Chapter Nine

Acklington Prison was up the coast and almost on Vera's way home. It hadn't been easy to arrange to visit Davy Sharp this late in the afternoon. Mornings were the time for official visits – solicitors, probation, police – and prison routine was rigid. It had taken called-in favours and tantrums on the phone before they'd agreed. She parked and walked to the gate. There was a heat haze over the flat fields towards the sea. Everywhere was quiet. Still the sun was shining and she felt the sweat greasy on her forehead and her nose just in the time it took to get to the building. The gate officer greeted her by name, though she didn't recognize him. He was friendly and chatted about the weather as she handed over her mobile phone and signed herself in.

'If it doesn't break soon, there'll be trouble,' he said. 'The heat gets to them. It's a nightmare in the workshops. Someone will kick off soon and we'll be lucky if there's not a riot.'

She waited in an interview room while they fetched Davy Sharp. All the heat of the day seemed trapped in the small square space and the sun still streamed through a high window. In winter, she knew, the prison was freezing, the wind blowing straight

66

from Scandinavia. She struggled to focus. She'd talked to Davy Sharp before. He could be sullen and uncommunicative, or charming. She thought of him as an actor or a chameleon. He could play whatever part he needed. It was always hard to know how to respond to him. Important to recognize that he was cleverer than he made out. And all the time her thoughts came back to beer, straight from the fridge, the condensation running down the outside of the glass. She'd had the picture in her head since leaving Geoff Armstrong's.

There was the sound of boots in the corridor outside, keys on a chain, and the door was opened. Davy wore a blue-and-white-striped shirt, blue jeans, trainers. He slid across the threshold without a sound. It had been the officer who'd made the noise. He stood, weighing the keys in his hand, then nodded in her direction, not really looking at her, not speaking. Vera could tell he was resentful about the disrupted routine, at being forced to unlock the prisoner, walk him here from the block, while all the other officers, his mates, were in the office, drinking tea, having a laugh. He moved outside, sat on an upright chair, stared into space. She shut the door, was aware of the smell of hot bodies, hoped it came from Davy and not from her. She took a packet of cigarettes from her bag, offered him one. He took it, lit it quickly, inhaled.

'You'll know why I'm here,' she said. They all had TVs in their pads now, he'd have seen the news, even if word of Luke's death hadn't got back to him in other ways.

'That lad who was a friend of our Thomas. Is that it?'

She didn't say anything, tried to banish the picture of the pint glass from her mind.

He leaned forward. Already the cigarette was half smoked. He knocked the ash into the foil ashtray. He was a thin, nondescript man. If you met him in the street you'd walk past without a second glance. It was an advantage. He'd grown up in a family where thieving came as second nature. Infamous. In Shields mothers said to kids who misbehaved, 'You carry on like that and you'll end up like the Sharps.' He specialized in credit-card fraud. It suited him that people couldn't remember his face. Vera never had any idea what he was thinking. Yet he couldn't be that good at what he did. He'd spent a third of his adult life in prison. Perhaps he was more comfortable inside.

He looked up at her, eyes narrowed. 'You don't think we had anything to do with that?'

'Luke blamed himself for your lad's death. I wondered if maybe you blamed him too.'

'It was an accident.' He stubbed out the cigarette. She saw his hand was trembling, wondered if that was part of his act too. She slid the packet across the table towards him, waited until he'd shaken the next one out.

'Did you ever meet Luke?'

'Not while Thomas was alive.' He gave a little smile. 'I haven't been home much recently. They let me out for my lad's funeral. I met the Armstrong boy there. Thomas had spoken about him, though, when he came here on visits. It sounded like they were real mates. Two of a kind maybe. Not the sharpest tools in the box. That was the impression I got from wor lass. We were pleased he'd taken up with the Armstrong boy. We didn't want Thomas following me into this game. He'd never be any good at it and he'd never survive a place like this.'

'Did you speak to Luke at the funeral?'

'Aye. Just a few words. They wouldn't let me stay on for the beer and sandwiches.'

'What did he say?'

'That he was sorry. That he'd tried his best to save Thomas. You could tell he meant it. He looked a real mess. He cried like a baby throughout the service, could hardly spit out the words when he was talking to me.'

'Was his mam there?'

'Big blonde lass? Aye. Thomas had talked about her too, said how good she was to him. I thanked her.'

'You were inside then, when Thomas died?'

'On remand.'

'But you must have tried to find out what happened.'

'I talked to a few people.'

'And?'

'For once your lot got it right. The lads had been drinking, horsing around. Thomas fell in. Like I said, an accident.' He paused. 'I wish there was someone to blame. But there isn't.'

'Did Thomas have any other friends?'

'Not really. There were kids he played with when he was younger, an older lad in the street who looked out for him, but Luke Armstrong was his only real mate just before he died.'

They sat for a moment in silence. Outside the officer must have shifted on the uncomfortable chair. They could hear the keys on his belt clinking.

'Is that it?' Sharp said at last.

'Have you any idea who might have wanted Luke Armstrong dead?'

He shook his head. 'No one I know would strangle a boy.' Vera knew that wasn't true but let it pass.

'He wasn't working for you? I mean, you weren't using the boys?' She was thinking something menial; maybe he'd given them a few quid to run messages.

'I told you, I'd never met Luke Armstrong until I saw him at my son's funeral and I didn't want Thomas caught up in my business. Besides, I wouldn't trust either of them. Not even to fetch me a bag of chips. Too unreliable.'

'Just seems a coincidence. Both of them dead. Couldn't be someone's trying to send you a message?'

'Coincidences happen,' he said grimly.

She looked at him sharply, tried to tell if there was anything behind the words, but his face was impassive.

'You could put the word out,' she said. 'Let people know you've got an interest.'

At first it was as if she'd not spoken. He continued to stare ahead of him. Then he gave an almost imperceptible nod. 'I'll do that.'

'And you'll let me know if you hear anything?'

He nodded again.

She felt she was missing something, that there was one question still to ask. They sat for a moment looking at each other. She wondered if she should mention the flowers scattered on the bath water where Luke had been found – might that have some meaning for him? But they'd managed to keep that out of the news and she didn't want it to become public knowledge. At last she pushed the packet of cigarettes across the table to him without a word. She waited until he'd slipped them into the pocket of his jeans, then opened the door and called to the officer.

'OK. We're finished here.'

While she was waiting at the gate to be signed out, she tried to picture Sharp's face, some expression she should have picked up, some message he might be trying to convey. But she couldn't do it. In her memory the features were a blur. She wasn't even sure if she'd select him out of an identity parade.

She'd switched off her mobile before handing it over to the gate officer. Walking back to the car, she turned it on. No messages. No missed calls. They were no further forward than the night Luke had died. She'd parked the car in the shade and the sun was lower now. She switched off the air conditioning and opened the windows. Away from the coast the roads were quiet and as she climbed into the hills she felt her spirits lift. At home there was a fridge full of beer and tomorrow she'd come to the investigation fresh and rested.

Her phone rang just as she'd parked outside the old station master's house. She didn't hear it at first, because the Edinburgh train was roaring north. Virgin not GNER. A flash of red. It rang again when the train had passed.

Chapter Ten

James loved chess. Clive, one of Peter's friends, had taught him, and perhaps because he considered it an adult pastime he'd been passionate about it ever since. It made him feel grown-up. Peter didn't often have the patience to play with him, but James always beat Felicity now. She waited outside the school, looking occasionally at her watch. She'd told him to make sure he came out on time, because she had the special meal to prepare, but still he was the last one to cross the playground. I should be pleased, she thought, that he's so laid back.

All the way home he talked about the game he'd been playing and she had to interrupt him to ask about the student who'd come to look at the cottage.

'Did Miss Marsh say if she wanted to live there?' she asked just as they turned into the lane which led to their house.

'No,' he said, so vaguely that she could tell he was still thinking of other things. 'I didn't see her today.'

She thought that was probably the end of the matter. It was a shame. It might have been fun to have the young woman as a neighbour just for a few weeks, until the end of term. Then she had to pull right into the hedge, because a Land Rover was turning out of the lane, and she forgot all about it.

Felicity had expected that Peter would arrive home early that night, but in fact he was later than usual. She had started to feel a niggle of concern; the road from town was a notorious accident black spot. But he arrived before that could develop into serious anxiety and relief made her affectionate. She took him into her arms and kissed his neck and his eyelids and followed him upstairs, sitting on the bed while he changed. Then they heard cars on the drive and she had to run down to greet their guests and the hall was suddenly full of male voices and laughter. She was pleased Peter had friends. There was nobody at the university he met socially. And she had always liked the boys, the courteous Samuel, the shy Clive, the lecherous Gary. She liked the taut bodies, fit from walking over the hills, and the way they admired her. She knew they thought Peter was lucky to have her. Clive especially adored her. She was flattered when he followed her around the room with his eyes. She liked to see him flush when she paid him attention. Yet when the four of them were together she couldn't help feeling excluded. The men had nothing in common except an interest in natural history, but that passion was all-consuming and she couldn't share it.

They were very polite to her. Samuel had brought her the script of his latest short story. 'I thought you'd be interested. You know I value your opinion.' She kissed them all in turn, enjoying the momentary touch of her hand on a muscular shoulder, a strong back. When Samuel's dry lips touched her cheek she had a shiver of excitement.

'Go through to the garden,' she said. 'I'll make you tea.'

But Peter, who was in an excitable mood, said they didn't want tea. They wanted beer, and they all followed her into the kitchen to fetch it, getting in her way when she wanted to prepare the meal. Peter was loving every minute of it. Felicity wasn't sure about Samuel – it was hard sometimes to tell what he was thinking – but the rest of them *were* true believers as far as Peter was concerned. They thought he was the cleverest man they knew, that he'd been overlooked at work because of politics. His records were only rejected by the Rarities Committee because of petty jealousies. This was their chance to show him how much he was appreciated by them. How devoted they were. And he blossomed under their attention, became charming and generous. He poured drinks for them and held court.

At that point she sent them on to the lighthouse ahead of her. She felt trapped by them, that she couldn't breathe. 'Go on,' she said. 'I'll just lay the table and I'll catch you up.' Usually she could cope with them en masse like this, enjoyed having them in the house, but today it was too much for her.

Samuel offered to help, but she refused him too and stood at the kitchen door to wave them off, a straggling, laughing line, her son bouncing around them like an untrained puppy. She watched until they'd climbed the stile and were out of sight and she was sure she had got rid of them.

She laid the table on the terrace, taking her time,

polishing the glasses with a tea towel when she took them from the tray, though they were straight from the dishwasher and there was no need. The sun was still warm, but the light was softer now. She poured a large glass of white wine from the bottle left in the cooler, chose one of the chairs at the long table and looked out over the garden.

At last she felt she should join them. She had promised. But she wouldn't follow them over the stile and along the edge of the cornfield. After collecting James from school, she'd changed into a simple linen dress. It was sleeveless and full length. Slit down one side, it allowed her to walk but not to climb with dignity over fences. She would take the path through the meadow, along the bank of the stream. It would take a little longer, but she knew they wouldn't return immediately from the lighthouse. James would want to poke around in the rock pools for crabs. The adults would humour him and then they would sit in the soft evening light and talk. By the time she reached them they would only just be ready to leave.

She set off towards the meadow then returned and checked that she had locked the house. Beyond the cottage the field dipped towards the burn. In winter, the land here was marshy and occasionally it flooded. A public footpath ran along the opposite bank and there was a simple plank bridge to join it. As she passed the cottage she checked the door. She still couldn't quite convince herself that she'd imagined the intruder in the house. It was locked. It occurred to her that this might have been another argument in her campaign to persuade Peter to let Lily live there; it would be a deterrent to thieves to have the place occupied. Close to the burn the grass was shorter in irregular patches. It looked as if someone had taken a scythe to it, but she couldn't imagine why anyone would. She stood for a moment in the middle of the bridge, looking down at the water. She'd heard that otters were back in the area and, though she had no idea what signs she should watch out for, she always stopped here, hoping to catch a glimpse.

Here, the burn was freshwater still, and very placid. There were cows in the field, released from evening milking. They'd softened the bank and she left the footpath briefly to avoid the mud. There was a small wrought-iron gate with a drop latch, and beyond that the character of the landscape changed. The grass was cropped by rabbits. There were scratchy bushes of buckthorn and bramble. The bed of the burn was sandy and it was shallow and wide and smelled of salt. The lighthouse was straight ahead of her. Although she couldn't see the others she fancied she heard them, a burst of laughter which could have been Gary, James shouting for attention. She looked at her watch. Already it was eight-thirty. Peter usually hated eating late, but he wouldn't mind so much tonight. She knew he would be enjoying himself.

She found them in the watch tower, which stood on the seaward side of the lighthouse. Once it had been a coastguard lookout. Now birdwatchers used it to watch for seabirds. They were sitting on the bench in a row, looking out over the bay. Although it was the wrong time of the year for seabirds, the watch tower pulled them in. Other men relaxed in the pub, but this was where they felt most at home. As she climbed the wooden steps she heard desultory conversation. She waited, silent, listening.

'What is it with sea watching?' Gary said. 'I mean can anything be more chilled? It's like Zen, or something.'

Felicity smiled to herself. What would Gary know about Zen? He knew about sound systems and rock music and acoustics. But Zen?

For a moment nobody answered. Clive leaned forward, his attention caught by something on the horizon. He had an old pair of binoculars which his mother had bought for him when he was about twelve, but his vision was legendary.

Then Peter spoke. Pedantic, as if he was in front of a class of students. Weighing every word.

'It's about possibility, isn't it? Possibility and chance. The random nature of the universe. We can sit here for four hours and see nothing but a few Manx shearwaters. Then the wind changes. A weather front shifts. And suddenly there are more birds than we can count.'

Clive moved in his seat. He lowered his binoculars. Felicity thought he was going to say something profound. Sometimes he did. But he just called two puffins going north and went back to staring out to sea.

Felicity climbed on into the tower. James jumped off the bench and came up to her, pulling a face. She could tell he was bored and restless.

'Can we go home now?'

'Go and have a look at the rock pools. As long as you don't go too far . . .'

Samuel stood up too. 'Why don't we all start back? It must be dinner time.'

She smiled at him. He could be such a kind man. 'It's a lovely evening. And Peter's birthday. Let's enjoy it for a while.'

When James started screaming her first thought was that the noise would make Peter irritated and he was in such a pleasant mood that that was the last thing she wanted. James did like drama. He'd probably found a live crab or a jellyfish stranded by the tide.

'Don't worry,' she said. 'I'll sort him out. And then perhaps we should start back.'

When the screaming continued she found herself panicking, imagining a dreadful accident, that he'd slipped and cut himself on a sharp rock, broken a limb. At first she couldn't see him. The noise was disembodied. It was as if her son had disappeared into thin air and that only added to her panic. She scrambled across the rocks, felt the seam of her dress rip as she slipped. Then she came upon him, found herself looking down on him. There was a deep gully with a shallow pool at the base and he was standing there, apparently unharmed.

Felicity saw the flowers first. They were scattered across the surface of the water close to the edge where her son stood, mouth open, rigid. There were poppies and buttercups, ox-eye daisies and pink clover. Someone must have waded in and placed them carefully on the surface. That, at least, was how it seemed to her. There was no breeze. She didn't think the blossoms could have drifted so far if they'd been thrown from the bank. They formed an irregular circle. Then she saw, in the middle of them, the blue cloth of the skirt and the corn-coloured hair. The pool was so shallow that the body lay just under the surface, and the water lifted the flimsy fabric and stirred the hair. But the gully was deep and the whole scene was in shadow. It was like looking at a painting a long way away.

'James,' she said. 'Climb back. Darling, come here to me.' She didn't think she'd be able to make it down and most of all she wanted to stop him screaming. Her voice seemed to wake him from a spell and he turned and clambered back towards her. She took him in her arms, looking over his head at the figure in the pool.

If Lily had been wearing the peasant dress of the previous day, Felicity might have recognized her, but she was convinced that this was a stranger. She stood, her arms clasped around her son, frozen. She knew there were things you should do. She'd seen the medical dramas on the television, doctors thumping on the chest and breathing into the mouth. But all that seemed beyond her. Small and ridiculous objections came into her head. *If I was wearing jeans I'd try. If I had on sensible shoes.*

Then the rest of them turned up. And they seemed no more able to act than she was. She had a horrible temptation to laugh at the four of them peering down into the bowl of rock. Then James pulled away from her and looked up into her face.

'Mum,' he said, his voice quite controlled now, just a little unsteady as if he was struggling for breath. 'What's Miss Marsh doing in the pond?'

And that was when she saw quite clearly that it was Lily.

Chapter Eleven

They were all sitting at a long table on the veranda at Fox Mill. It was dark and the scene was lit by fairy lights, which Felicity must have strung up along the outside of the house earlier in the day, and one fat candle, almost burned down now. Gary was feeling seriously weird. He thought this could be a stage set. Opera. The whole evening had that sense of melodrama. He could imagine some fat lass wandering in and belting out a tune, arms outstretched towards the dark garden. He sometimes did the sound for opera at the City Hall. Bits of it he quite enjoyed, but it was so over the top that you could never pretend it was real, could you?

He was drunk. He'd made an effort to cut down lately. It wasn't like the old days, just after Emily had left him. Then, the only time he was properly sober was when he was out birding. But tonight he had an excuse. Peter's birthday. And being involved in a murder. He pictured the body, spread out like a starfish just under the water, covered with flowers. It made him think of a collage, something you might see hanging on the wall in the Baltic Art Gallery in Gateshead. Bits of net and lace cut into pieces, seaweed and shells. Beautiful. If you liked that sort of thing. He reached out and topped up his glass from a bottle of red, pleased that his hand didn't shake and none of it spilled.

Felicity served the meal and it was amazing, just as it always was. A big pot of chicken smelling of lemon and herbs. He didn't know anyone else who could cook like her. Since he'd met up with Peter, he'd thought this was what he wanted – not just the food, of course, but the family, the wife. That was what he'd imagined when he'd proposed to Emily. Now he wondered if it was all too good to be true. It was as though they were part of a show. The Calvert family at home. I could do the sound, he thought, and imagined clipping the mic into the top of that simple black dress she was wearing. Her skin would still be warm. He'd be close enough to smell her perfume, the shampoo she used. He thought they'd all had dreams about Felicity, especially when she was younger. Even now they all fancied her. Sometimes he caught Clive staring at her, his mouth slightly open. He wondered if Clive had ever had a woman. Gary had offered to take him into town a couple of times, but Clive always refused. Perhaps he preferred fantasies of Felicity to the real thing.

It was late to be eating, even for him and he was used to meals at strange times. They'd had to wait for the police to arrive at the lighthouse, explain who they were, give their names and addresses. Then there'd been the walk home. Across the table from him, James, Felicity's son, was almost falling asleep over his food. The boy roused himself at one point to talk about the dead woman.

'What do you think happened to her?'

'I don't know,' Felicity said. 'Some dreadful accident.'

Gary knew that wasn't true. All the adults knew it was no accident. The flowers showed this death had been intended.

'If she'd come to live in the cottage,' James said sulkily, 'she'd have been able to help me with my homework.'

Gary didn't know what lay behind that comment and was too pissed to work it out. Felicity persuaded James to bed then. She put her arm around him, almost carried him into the house, and the men were left alone. Somewhere behind them a tawny owl screamed in the tall oaks up the lane. The dark shadows of bats flew in and out of the light. Other occasions, other birthdays, this was the time Gary loved best. The four of them sitting together after the meal, relaxed in a way he could be with no one else, sometimes quiet, sometimes following a conversation about old glories or making plans for the future – trips abroad, the definitive book about the county's birds. Tonight, though, there was an awkwardness. It was as if the dead young woman lay on the table between them, dripping seawater and demanding to be remembered.

'What did James mean?' Samuel asked. 'Was the dead woman going to come and live here?'

'No!' Peter said. 'It was just the boy being foolish.'

And they lapsed again into an uneasy silence.

Then Felicity came back and cleared the table. She brought out a plate of cheese and offered them coffee. Peter opened another bottle of wine. She took her place beside him. Samuel returned to the dead woman and how James had known her, but this time the question was directed at Felicity.

'Her name was Lily Marsh,' she said. 'She was a student teacher at James's school.' She was about to continue but was interrupted by a shout so loud that it made them all start. Gary could feel his pulse racing, wondered if he was old enough for a heart attack, thought again that he should drink less. He wasn't ready to die. Not now.

'Hello! Anyone at home?' The voice was deep and brusque. Gary wasn't sure if it came from a man or a woman. A figure appeared at the French window that gave on to the veranda. A woman. Tall and heavy, but wearing a skirt. She'd switched on the light in the room and she was silhouetted in front of it. 'You shouldn't leave your front door on the latch like that,' she continued in the grumbling tone of a teacher talking to idiots. 'Even when you're home, you never know who might walk in.'

They all stared at her, still shocked. She stepped down towards them until she'd reached the table. The candle shone upwards onto her face. She paused before she spoke again. Gary thought this was someone else who liked a drama.

'Inspector Vera Stanhope. Northumbria Police. Senior Investigating Officer in the case of that lass you found tonight.' She pulled out the chair where James had been sitting and lowered herself cautiously onto it. It was a director's chair with a wooden frame. The canvas creaked. Gary watched closely, expecting a ripping, tearing sound. Perhaps she was expecting it too. This was a woman who'd be able to carry off farce. But the canvas held and Vera continued cheerfully, turning to Felicity. 'I understand you knew her. The young woman who died, I mean. Weren't you just saying . . .'

Felicity answered, hesitating at first. She kept looking at Peter. Gary wasn't sure what that was about. She repeated the sentence she'd begun before Vera Stanhope's dramatic entrance.

'Her name was Lily Marsh. She was a student teacher at my son's school, the primary in Hepworth. She turned up here yesterday, on the bus with him. It seemed that James had said she could live in our cottage until the end of term. Without consulting us, of course.'

'You didn't tell me,' Peter said.

'There was nothing to tell. She looked at the cottage and left.'

'You'd said she could stay, then?' Vera Stanhope asked.

'I don't think either of us came to a decision. I couldn't even tell if she liked the place. She said she'd think about it.' Felicity turned to Peter. Gary could tell she was willing him not to make a scene, not to get all arrogant and pompous. Gary loved Peter to bits, but he could do pompous better than anyone he knew. 'Of course if the girl had decided she was interested, I'd have discussed it with you before deciding whether or not to rent. James really liked her.'

'Had any of the rest of you met this Lily Marsh?' The woman stared around the table at them. Gary thought she could make you feel guilty even if you'd done nothing wrong. 'Seems she was a bonny lass. You'd not forget her in a hurry.'

There was a murmured denial, shaken heads.

'Take me through finding the body. The boy found her first, then you went to look. Was there anyone else about?'

Clive raised his hand from the table. As if he was still a kid, Gary thought. A shy nervous kid. 'There was a family on the flat bit of grass by the burn. A father and two boys, I think. Playing football.'

'Any cars parked next to the lighthouse?'

Clive answered again. 'A people carrier. One of those big Renaults. Maroon. I don't remember the number, but registered last year.'

'Why would you remember something like that?'

'I notice things,' Clive said defensively. 'Detail. It's what I'm good at.'

'What were you doing in the watch tower anyway? It's hardly the right time of year for sea watching and the tide was right out.'

'What do you know about sea watching?' The words came out before Gary could stop them.

She looked at him, laughed. 'My dad was a bit of a birder. I suppose you pick it up. It seeps into the blood. He took me to the coast sometimes. Really, though, he was happier in the hills. He was a bit of a raptor freak.' She paused. 'Is that what brought you all together? The birding?'

'Aye.' Gary wondered if she really wanted to know and how he'd explain it. He'd always been interested in birds. Since seeing an old copy of *The Observer's Book of Birds* in the school library when he was ten, it had been a sort of obsession or compulsion. Music had done it for him too, but not in the same way. Music had been social, something to do with friends. At first the birding had been a secret passion. He'd started off collecting eggs in the park. Then at high school he'd met up with Clive Stringer. They had nothing else in common and now he couldn't remember the chance conversation that had brought them together. He must have made some remark which had given his interest away. Usually he was careful about what he said. He wouldn't have wanted what he did at weekends to be general knowledge in school. He had a reputation to keep up. It had been a revelation that someone felt the same way as he did about the natural world. He and Clive had started to go out birding together. Places they could get to on the bus. Seaton Pond. St Mary's Island. Whitley Bay Cemetery.

And one day, sitting in the hide at Seaton, waiting for a Temminck's stint to emerge into view, they'd met Peter Calvert. The famous Dr Calvert, who'd written papers for *British Birds* and had once been the chair of the Rarities Committee. He was dressed in black, a suit, a tie, a white shirt. Not the usual birding gear. Perhaps he'd seen them staring and thought it needed explaining. Perhaps that was why he started talking to them. He'd said he'd just been to a funeral. The wife of his best friend. Everyone else had gone back to the house for drinks, but he couldn't face it. Not yet.

Then he'd suggested that they might become trainee ringers. Casually. Not realizing that for them it was the most exciting suggestion in the world. There was another trainer, he'd said. Samuel Parr. He'd look after them. It was Sam's wife who'd just died and he'd need something else to focus on. Besides, they could do with some new blood in the Deepden team. After that Gary and Clive had spent most of their weekends up the coast at the Deepden Bird Observatory, sleeping on the bunk beds in the dorm at the cottage, waking at dawn to set nets and ring birds. They'd all become friends.

Gary realized the detective was still staring at him. 'Well?' she said. 'What were you doing in the watch tower if you weren't sea watching?'

'There's always a chance,' he said, 'that something good will fly past. But we'd gone for a walk. It's Peter's birthday. We do it every year.'

'A ritual?'

'Yeah. Kind of.' Gary wondered why someone else couldn't join in the conversation. Why had they left it to him?

Vera continued to look at him. She had her legs stuck out in front of her, big, rather grubby feet in sandals.

'What's your name, pet?'

'Gary Wright.'

She took a notebook out of a big, soft, leather handbag, flipped a page, looked at the squiggles written there. But Gary thought that was just for effect. She knew the facts already, had probably worked out who he was as soon as she'd sat down at the table.

'You live in Shields?'

He nodded.

'You're sure you didn't know the lass? Only it seems to me you're a bit of a party animal. You've got a history. A couple of cautions for drunk and disorderly, a conviction for possession.'

Gary looked up, suddenly sober. 'That was years ago. You've no right—'

'This is a murder investigation.' Her voice was

sharp. 'I've every right. Are you sure you never came across her?'

'I don't remember her. The town's full of students.'

'You didn't meet her while you were working?'

'I don't mix business and pleasure.' He couldn't understand why she was picking on him, felt an irrational panic. The mellowing effect of the wine had quite left him. 'I'm serious about my work.'

'Tell me about that.'

'I'm a sound engineer. Self-employed. It could be anything from an opera gig at the City Hall to the Great North Run. There are a couple of bands I do the sound for and I go on tour with them.'

'Glamorous.'

'Not really. Folk clubs, small arts centres. The same mediocre musicians singing the same boring songs. A night in a Travelodge before unloading the van somewhere equally forgettable.' Until he'd started talking he hadn't realized just how much he'd come to dislike it. He reached a decision he'd been hesitating over for a week. 'I'm giving it up. The freelance work. I've been doing quite a lot of work at the Sage Music Centre, Gateshead, and now they've offered me a permanent job. Regular wages, holiday pay, a pension. Suddenly it seems quite attractive.'

'So you're going to settle down? Why now?'

'Age,' he said. 'I suppose that's it. The late-night curries in small towns have lost their appeal.'

'Not a woman, then?'

He hesitated for a moment, then thought: What business is it of hers? 'No, Inspector,' he said. 'Not a woman. Certainly not Lily Marsh.'

He wondered if the use of the name was a mistake. Did that imply previous knowledge? But Vera Stanhope let it go and turned her attention to the others gathered at the table. Gary was relieved that he'd had to go first. He took a drink from his glass, surprised to find it still almost full. Now it was his turn to be the audience. Vera was about to speak when her phone rang. She got up, walked away from them to take the call and stood at the end of the veranda in complete shadow. They began to talk among themselves to prove that her conversation was of no interest to them, but when she returned they fell silent.

'Sorry, folks,' she said cheerfully. 'I'll have to go. Don't worry, though, I've got all your addresses. I'll catch up with the rest of you another time.'

But she stood there, not moving.

Felicity stood up. 'I'll just see you to the door.'

'Are you interested in how she died?' Vera asked, looking at them all.

'I thought suicide,' Felicity said, shocked. 'It was all so dramatic, so arranged.'

'She was strangled,' Vera said. 'Hard to manage that by yourself.'

They stared back at her, silent.

'One last question. Does the name Luke Armstrong mean anything to any of you?'

Nobody replied.

'I'll take that as a no, then, shall I?' she said irritably. 'Only he was strangled too. Not so far from here.' She looked at them, waiting for someone to answer. 'And the cases have certain things in common. I don't want you talking about this. Not to anyone and certainly not to the press. I hope you understand.'

Still there was no response and she followed Felicity into the house. Watching, Gary, who'd had one or two brushes with the law, thought he'd never come across police like her.

Chapter Twelve

Vera Stanhope drove back to the crime scene. It was a bugger to work, the Crime Scene Investigator said. They just didn't have the time to deal with it properly. The body had been found at low water. They had four hours before that stretch of the shore would be covered completely. And though it was mid-summer the light had started to go almost as soon as they arrived.

Vera parked by the lighthouse and saw that they'd almost finished. The body had been removed and the sea had slid up the gully and covered the pool. She wondered if they'd managed to retrieve all the flowers, imagined them floating out into the North Sea, tangled in the propeller of the DFDS ferry.

Billy Wainwright, the CSI, was still there, loading his bag into his boot. He was a pale, thin man and seemed not to have aged in the twenty years that she'd known him. She thought now that he had one of those faces which always look boyish. She got out of her car and wandered over to him. Even now, in the early hours, the air was heavy and mild. The beam of the lighthouse swept over their heads.

'Anything unusual?'

'A young woman. Strangled. Laid out in a public place in broad daylight. Flowers scattered over her body. Pretty unusual that, I'd have thought. What more do you want?'

'Would it have been broad daylight?'

'Must have been. Think of the tide. And anyway she can't have been there long. The place would have been crawling with people during the day, with the weather we've been having. I know it's a weekday and not school holidays, but all the same the sun always brings people out to the coast. My guess is she was put there not long before she was found.'

Not that public, Vera thought. You had to be right on the lip of the gully before you could see in. Getting her there, though. That would be quite a different matter. Someone must have seen that. And the killer must have wanted her seen before the tide washed all his elaborate stage set away. How would he have felt if James Calvert hadn't got bored and gone exploring?

'Do we know how long she'd been dead before she went in?'

'Sorry, you'll have to wait for the PM for that. John couldn't really do much at a scene like this. By the time he arrived we had to be thinking of moving her.'

'Are they doing it tonight?'

'I hope not. At least until I've had time for a pizza. I was just sitting down in front of a vindaloo when I got called out. I'm bloody starving.' Billy's appetite was a standing joke. He was as thin as a bean pole, but voracious. She pondered briefly on the injustice of genetics. 'We might leave it till the morning,' he went on. 'I'm waiting to hear from Wansbeck.'

On cue his phone buzzed. He walked away from her to talk. There were rumours he was having a fling with a new young pathology technician at Wansbeck

General and Vera, who was a great one for gossip and saw it as a tool of the trade, tidied away the information about the whispered conversation to pass on to Joe Ashworth. Her sergeant would pretend he didn't want to hear, but she knew he'd be interested. She wondered how Joe was getting on. They'd tracked down Lily Marsh's parents to a village just outside Hexham and Joe had volunteered to tell them that their daughter was dead. He'd said he didn't want just anyone doing it. He was a father himself. He couldn't come close to understanding what it must be like to lose a child, but thought he'd make a better fist of it than some in the team.

Wainwright finished his conversation and came back to her. Even in the dark she sensed a studied nonchalance which made her want to tell him not to be a muppet. He was a married man. Happy enough, she'd thought. The young technician was lonely, playing games with him. Then she told herself it was none of her business and she was hardly a candidate for relationship counsellor.

'John would like to do it soon,' he said. 'He's tied up later in the morning. Say an hour?'

'Fine. I'll be there.'

She stood, leaning against the bonnet of her car, listening to the waves breaking beneath the watch tower, until he'd driven away.

Her mind drifted back to the group sitting outside that strange white house which seemed so out of place in the Northumberland countryside. She'd gone to visit them because she'd had nothing better to do while the scene of crime team was working. They'd found the body, they'd all be together for the night and after that they'd disperse. The PC first at the scene had established that much. She thought she'd catch them while they were still in the area, check if they'd seen anything odd. She'd been hoping, she supposed, for the description of a car similar to the one Julie had seen in her road the night Luke was killed. But they'd caught her interest. It wasn't just that there was a connection to the dead young woman. Or that the men reminded her of her father, sitting in the kitchen at home with a bunch of cronies after an illicit raid on the raptors' nests in the hills. Something about the conversation had made her feel they'd need closer looking into. A smugness which irritated her and had something of a challenge in it. She tried to work out which of the individuals had so got under her skin, but couldn't pin down the source of her unease. In the end she got into her car and followed Wainwright down the track to the road.

John Keating, the pathologist, was an Ulsterman in his fifties, with a bluff, no-nonsense attitude which scared some of her younger officers. The only time she'd seen him show any emotion during a post-mortem was when he was investigating the death of a three-year-old child. And talking about a rugby match to a Welsh sergeant. He'd played when he was younger, still had a squashed nose. He made her coffee in his office before he changed for the autopsy.

'What were your first impressions?'

'She was strangled,' he said. 'But you'll have gathered that.'

'Similarities with the Armstrong lad?'

'I didn't have time to do a great examination in the field. Imagine your worst nightmare for a crime scene and this was it. A few hours later and the body would have been washed out to sea.'

'Then we'd never have seen the flowers, might not even have linked it to the Seaton case.' She came back to the point which had troubled her at the lighthouse. 'Is that what the murderer wanted? Was it a private ritual? Or did he gamble on the body being found earlier?'

'Hey! Don't ask me. I deal with dead bodies not live minds.'

She watched the post-mortem through the glass screen, not because she was squeamish but because she was conscious of her size and was always worried that she was in the way. There were so many people gathered around the stainless-steel table – the technicians, the photographer, Billy Wainwright.

They unwrapped the corpse from the polythene sheeting and to the flash of continual photography they began to undress Lily Marsh. They removed the blue cotton skirt and the embroidered white shirt. Vera saw she was wearing matching white bra and pants. But hardly virginal. The bra was deep cut, lacy, revealing. The pants had little red-silk bows at each side, a red-silk crotch. While Billy Wainwright bagged each garment, Keating gave a commentary, glancing at her occasionally to check that she'd noted the significance of what he was saying. 'There was little disturbance to the clothing. No apparent sign of sexual assault.'

Unless he dressed her afterwards, Vera thought. Let's wait for the results from the vaginal swabs before we come to a decision. But there'd been no evidence of sexual assault on Luke and she was already certain that the cases were linked.

Keating continued. 'No bruising. No lacerations. Can we have photographs of the eyes and lids, please. Note the petechiae.'

Vera had already noted them, had seen them at the crime scene – the pinpoint haemorrhages caused by obstruction of the veins in the neck. The classic sign of strangulation.

'Not manual strangulation,' Keating was saying. 'No finger marks. See the line around the neck. It hasn't broken the skin, so not wire, unless it was plastic-coated. Fine rope, perhaps.'

And that too was the same as in the Armstrong case.

She watched as he continued his external examination, saw Billy take all the samples – a trace of lipstick left even after her submersion in seawater, fingernail scrapings, a clip of pubic hair – but her mind was buzzing with theories and ideas. What could connect these two very different young people? Keating began his dissection and still her thoughts were racing.

When it was over, she sat with him again in his office. Outside, it was just getting light. Soon the hospital staff on early shift would be arriving. There was more coffee. Chocolate biscuits. She realized she was starving. She couldn't remember the last time she'd eaten.

'I don't think there's much else I can give you,' he said. 'There's nothing to suggest she was assaulted before she was strangled. She'd been sexually active, but not recently. No pregnancy and she'd never had children.' He paused. 'She had all that ahead of her. Such a shame.'

'She didn't struggle,' Vera said. 'Did she know the murderer?'

'Not necessarily. He could have surprised her.'

'It could have been a woman.'

'Oh yes,' he said. 'Physically a woman could have done it.'

But Vera could tell he didn't really believe in a woman as a killer. He was a chivalrous and old-fashioned man. Women who missed the opportunity of childbirth were to be pitied. I suppose, she thought, that he pities me.

Chapter Thirteen

The press hadn't yet tracked down Lily Marsh's parents, or if they had they were showing more than their usual restraint. The young police officer waiting with them said there'd been no phone calls, no visitors apart from the rector from the village church and Mrs Marsh's sister.

'I don't think it's sunk in yet,' he said. 'The way the mother talks, it's as if the girl's just gone away for a while and will turn up any time.'

The couple were more elderly than Vera had expected. Phyllis had been forty-four when Lily was born and her husband five years older. 'We'd given up, Inspector. It was like a miracle.'

Almost hope for me, then. But Vera knew she'd never have children. And the aching for them had almost passed anyway.

Lily's parents lived in a neat semi. They'd lived there since they were married. Phyllis explained this as she made them tea. 'It's all paid off. We thought it would be something to leave to our daughter. We've no other savings.' For the second time in a week Vera was listening to a bereaved mother talking too much, fending off thoughts and memories with words. When Vera and Joe arrived, the husband, Dennis, was in the small greenhouse in the back garden and they let him escape back there once they'd introduced themselves. Phyllis greeted Joe Ashworth like a friend, but Dennis was finding it harder than his wife to hold himself together. He had a blank, wild look on his face. 'I'll come out and chat to you in a bit,' Vera said, 'when I've had my tea.'

Through the window of the small living room they saw him perched on an upturned box, staring into space.

'He's always had trouble with his nerves,' Phyllis said. Vera thought she caught the hint of accusation in her words. Now, when she most needed support, her husband was falling apart, still making demands on her.

The three of them sat clutching cups and saucers. Phyllis apologized for forgetting the sugar, though none of them took it, and jumped up to fetch it from the kitchen. She was a small, energetic woman, in her late sixties. She wore her hair in a tight white perm. 'I was always worried that one of us would die before Lily was old enough to be independent,' she said. 'It never crossed my mind that she would go first.' She had to talk about Lily being dead, otherwise she wouldn't believe it.

Everywhere in the room there were reminders of her daughter. She kept getting up to point things out to them. The certificates for ballet and tap dancing, for piano. 'She got as far as grade five then she stopped taking lessons. Too much school work. But she was still a lovely little player. She was going to start it up again. She said it would be useful in teaching.' There were photos on the mantelpiece, the window sill, the upright piano. Lily at a birthday party, aged five or six, grinning out over a cake shaped like a hedgehog. The official school photos. By the time Lily was fourteen she was already so attractive she'd turn heads in the street. Even with a school sweatshirt and no make-up. That was something she had in common with Luke Armstrong. They were both physically beautiful. In all the chat, Vera was listening out for anything else which might provide a connection, but it seemed there was nothing. Then, in an enlarged, framed photo hung on the wall, there was Lily in her hired cap and gown on graduation day, head thrown back, a wide smile.

'It looks as though she was enjoying herself there,' Vera said. 'Did she like being a student?'

'She loved it,' Phyllis said. 'Every minute. I was so glad for her. Not that I wanted to let her go, of course. I missed her something terrible. But there was nothing much for her here. No brothers and sisters. Hardly any young people left in the village. And her father with his moods . . . He wanted her to live at home, travel in every day on the bus, but I knew that wouldn't do. I said to him, "Be grateful that she didn't end up in Kent or Exeter." They were universities on her list. "It's time she had some freedom." He saw sense in the end.'

'Did she work while she was at college?' Vera asked. 'Most students have to these days, don't they?'

'She worked in the holidays. Saturdays in term time. She got a flat in town with a couple of other lasses. In West Jesmond. A lovely flat. I wasn't sure how she could afford it, but apparently it belonged to one of the other girls' dad. He'd bought it, like, as an investment and rented it out to them. We helped her out as much as we could. Dennis got a bit of redundancy from the slate works when that closed so we had some savings.'

'Where did she work in the holidays?' Vera asked.

'In Robbins, that posh frock shop near the Monument.'

Vera nodded to show she knew the one Phyllis was talking about. She'd never been inside but she'd looked in the window. All tailored linen and crisp white blouses. Jackets £250 a shot.

'I'd hoped she might find somewhere in Hexham, one of the hotels maybe. Then she could have come home for the summer at least. But, like she said, she had to pay rent to keep her place and she'd never find wages as good as Robbins' out here. Besides, she always liked to dress well. She had style even when she was little. And she got discount on the clothes she bought from there. She brought me some lovely birthday presents . . .' Her hand started to shake, her cup rattled in its saucer. Ashworth stood up and took it from her. Phyllis pulled a tiny cotton handkerchief from her sleeve and began to weep. 'We thought she would come back now,' she said, still talking through the tears. 'She's a country girl, really, and there are lots of village schools crying out for teachers. I had this picture. Her married to a nice lad. Living local. Somewhere I could get to on the bus, at least. A grandchild before I get too old to enjoy it.' She took a deep breath. 'Take no notice of me. Nonsense.' She paused again, stifled a sob. 'Just you find out who killed her.'

Vera nodded imperceptibly to Ashworth to take over the questions. He had more tact in his little finger than she had in her whole body. She'd already put together her own picture of the family. An only child growing up with ageing parents, an overprotective mum, a moody dad. No wonder Lily hadn't come home in the holidays, had salved her conscience by buying cut-price clothes from Robbins for her mam's birthday. Who could blame her? But Vera needed details and Ashworth would get them out of Phyllis, without shattering her fantasy of Lily as doting daughter.

'When did you last see Lily?' he asked. 'It'll have been hard for her to get away from college much, I suppose. It's an intensive course, the PGCE. Demanding academically and then there's all the teaching practice.'

Just the right line to take, Vera thought. No implied criticism of Lily. Any of that and Phyllis would clam up.

'She was over for the Easter weekend,' the woman said.

'You had a good time?'

'Beautiful. It was just like old times. She came to church with me on the Sunday. It was one of those breezy, sunny days. All the daffs out.'

'You've not managed to see her since then?'

'She wanted to come over for the Whit half-term,' Phyllis said quickly. 'But she had an essay to write. She had to stay near to the library.'

'Of course.' Ashworth smiled. 'Her final term. She'd have been snowed under.' He paused. 'How did she seem at Easter?'

'Canny. She'd got the teaching practice she was hoping for. A little village school up the coast. You could tell that was the way her mind was working. She was looking for the right experience to get her back this way.'

And Vera saw this was where the dream had come from. The nice lad and the grandchild. The house just down the road. Lily had let slip some comment about her teaching practice and Phyllis had conjured up all the rest.

'I don't suppose she brought anyone home with her that time? A boyfriend?'

'No. I always said her friends would be welcome, but she was always on her own.'

'Did she mention a lad? A bonny lass like her, there must have been someone . . .'

'I didn't like to pry,' Phyllis said.

'Of course not.'

'They're very secretive at that age, aren't they? They'll tell you nothing.'

'You've been in touch since Easter, though? On the phone?'

'I phone every week. Sunday. It's cheap rate then. You couldn't expect her to phone us, the budget she's on.'

'Did you call her landline or mobile?'

'Mobile. That way she wouldn't have to stay in specially.'

'How did she seem?'

'Really well. Happy. Excited, even.'

'Do you know why she was feeling so good? Or was she always like that?'

'Not always, no. We all have our bad days, don't we? I thought afterwards about what might have made her so cheerful. I asked her if she'd sorted herself out a job for September. "There are things in the pipeline."

That's what she said. It sounds daft, but you could hear her smiling as she said it. I thought perhaps she'd applied for something locally. Near home, I mean. Maybe even got an interview. But she didn't want to say anything. Not to get our hopes up, like. In case we were disappointed.'

There was a moment of silence. In the greenhouse Dennis Marsh took a tin of tobacco from his jacket pocket and began rolling a cigarette. Phyllis frowned. She probably thought roll-ups common, something not to be done in front of guests. Not even when your daughter's just died.

Ashworth leaned forward, caught her attention again. 'Did Lily ever do a teaching practice in Whitley High?'

'No, she was a primary specialist. She didn't do high schools.'

'So she'd never have taught a lad called Luke Armstrong? Never mentioned him at all?'

'Why? Is he the one that killed her?' The words were spat out, so loud and so fierce that she shocked them both.

'No,' Ashworth said quietly. 'Nothing like that. He was murdered too. There are certain similarities.'

Vera left them then. Phyllis was making more tea, just about holding herself together with ritual chat, warming the pot, finding biscuits. She'd have liked Joe Ashworth as a son-in-law, Vera could tell. She might even have been thinking that as she prompted him to take another fig roll. There was a glass door from the kitchen into the garden and Vera went out through that, closing it behind her, shutting out the conversation, knowing she was a coward, but not able to bear it any more.

Dennis must have heard her approaching, but didn't look up until she appeared at the open greenhouse door. She pulled up a plastic garden chair and sat just outside, facing him. He had the drawn, defeated face of men she'd seen in the cells or sleeping rough. Phyllis would save him from that, at least. She'd make sure he washed and shaved, cut his fingernails, wore clean clothes.

'Tell me about Lily.' Vera planted her feet firmly on the grass.

'I should never have had a bairn,' he said.

She felt like saying she'd always believed children were pretty overrated herself, but thought that wasn't what he wanted to hear.

'I don't suppose anyone thinks they make a good job of it, bringing up kids.'

'I can't even look after myself.'

'Lily seemed to have turned out all right. University. Going into teaching.' Vera caught the cheerful tone of the social worker in her voice, hated herself for it.

'She was never happy, though,' he said. 'Not really. Not even when she was at school.'

'What was she like at school?'

'Bright,' he said. 'Oh yes, always top of the class in the little school. And when she started her A levels they put her down for Oxford.'

Vera was surprised Phyllis hadn't mentioned that, but understood why it hadn't come up when he continued speaking. 'Then she didn't do as well in her exams as they'd been expecting. There was this lad, I don't know, she was obsessed by him. Thought she was in love with him. Couldn't concentrate, it seemed. Got A levels, but not the grades she needed for Oxford.'

'It happens,' Vera said. 'Teenage girls . . .'

'It wasn't normal, though,' he said. 'Not a normal crush. She was fixated. Stopped sleeping. Stopped eating. I thought she was ill. She needed special help. Phyllis wouldn't see it.'

Vera said nothing.

'I knew,' he said. 'I recognized it. I've been in and out of mental hospital over the years. Not so much now that they've sorted out the drugs, but I had my first breakdown when I was Lily's age. Too much of a coincidence, isn't it? She must have got that from me. She got her mother's brains. My madness.'

'Do you remember the name of the lad she fell for when she was at school?'

He frowned. 'My memory's not so good. I blame the ECT but it's probably just age.'

She waited, hoping it would come to him. She didn't want to bring this up with Phyllis, cause her even more pain.

'Craven,' he said. 'Ben Craven. A nice enough lad. Not his fault.'

'What happened to him? Did he go on to university?'

Dennis shook his head. 'I don't think I ever knew.'

'You said you had a couple of spells in hospital, Mr Marsh. Where did you go?'

'St George's. That place in Morpeth.'

The first link between Luke Armstrong and Lily

Marsh, Vera thought. Tenuous, but something at least to work on.

'And Lily? Do you think she ever went there for treatment? Once she left home, maybe? Not as an inpatient. You'd have heard about that. But to one of the outpatient clinics?'

'I told her to go,' he said. 'I gave her a card with the name of my doctor on it. But I don't know if she took my advice.' He made a brave attempt at a smile. 'You know what it's like. Two women in the house. They weren't going to take any notice of me.'

Chapter Fourteen

'So what have we got here?' Joe Ashworth said. 'Some nutter who thinks it's OK to go round strangling nutters?'

They were in the car on the way to Newcastle. They'd arranged to see Lily Marsh's flat and to talk to the two students she'd shared with.

'Maybe.' Vera was thinking it was all too elaborate. Some game. Some clever bastard pulling their strings. 'But forget the window dressing. The flowers on the water. If we had two murders this close, same cause of death, what would you think?'

'I'd still think it was a nutter.'

'Serial killer?'

'Perhaps.' He was cautious, surprised she'd used the word even to him. *Serial killer* meant the press going wild, hysterical politicians, and that was the last thing she'd want. It wasn't something to speak of lightly.

'But if it wasn't random, if it wasn't some psychotic who'd taken against attractive young people?'

He took a moment to think. 'The second murder could be to cover up the first. I mean, we know that Lily Marsh was around in the area. She worked in Hepworth. What's that? Six miles from Seaton where

Julie Armstrong lives. If we can place her in Seaton at the time of Luke's murder, we'd have a reasonable explanation. She saw something, heard something. Or she was acquainted with the killer, guessed. Confronted him.'

'You're thinking a boyfriend?'

'Maybe. It's odd that the parents don't seem to know anything about him.'

'So what do we do now?' Vera shut her eyes as Ashworth drove too fast round a bend and had to brake sharply. A tractor was coming in the opposite direction. He didn't swear, it wasn't his style. She did, under her breath.

'Make the link,' he said, when he'd pulled into the hedge to let the tractor past. 'Find out where she was the evening of Luke Armstrong's murder. Talk to all her friends. Her tutors. The people she worked with.'

'Nothing difficult, then.' Vera stretched and yawned. 'A piece of piss.' Before he could answer she fell asleep.

She woke when they pulled up outside the house, lucky to find a parking place. It was Saturday morning; shoppers saved paying for city-centre parking by leaving their cars in West Jesmond and taking the metro into town. The flat was the ground floor of an Edwardian terrace; a bit grand, she thought, for a student place. There was blue-and-white tape around the door and Billy Wainwright was inside. She called to him through an open window.

'You're OK to come in,' he said. 'We're just about

finished. I'll soon be away to my bed. The search team
will be in any time.'

They all stood for a moment inside the front door.
Billy seemed tired but too wired-up to relax, fidgeting
with the clasp on his case.

'What can you tell me, Billy?'

'There's no sign she was killed here. No break-in.
No evidence of a struggle in her room. Apparently the
lasses she was sharing with were out for the evening.
They're at a friend's house up the road now, if you
want a chat.'

'You'll have had a look in the bathroom?'

'Of course. There were a few hairs in the drain, but
I'd bet a year's salary they belong to the tenants.
There's nothing to connect this place with the Luke
Armstrong scene.'

'Bath oils?'

'Plenty. We'll get them tested, but I couldn't recognize anything that smelled like the water when we
fished the Armstrong boy out.' He yawned. 'If you're
going to be here for ten minutes, I'm going. Like I
said, the search team is on its way. The victim's room
is the last on the left.'

When he'd gone Vera and Joe stood for a minute
in silence. The hall was cool. The floor was tiled, the
ceiling high.

'Not your usual student gaff,' Joe said. He pushed
open a door into the living room. They looked in at
the stripped wooden floor, cast-iron fireplace. There
was a sofa with a terracotta loose cover, an upright
piano. Everything very tidy, spotlessly clean. 'I
couldn't afford a place like this on my salary. How do

they manage it? And I thought students were supposed to be mucky.'

Vera had moved on to the kitchen, which looked like something out of the style magazines she dipped into at the dentist's. She opened the fridge. A box of eggs, a couple of bags of salad, some natural yoghurt. In the door two bottles of white wine. French.

There were three bedrooms, two at the front overlooking the small garden and the street, one, Lily's, at the back. Vera saved Lily's until last. The front bedrooms were in keeping with the rest of the house. So tasteful Vera had an urge to hang a Boots print on the wall or stick a cheap and nasty vase on the window sill. She'd always thought of the places she looked at in the magazines as fantasies, hadn't believed they actually existed. They weren't the sort of rooms she visited often through work.

Lily's room was different. It was the smallest in the house, smaller even than the bathroom. The furniture was less grand; perhaps it had been left behind by the previous owners when the flat was sold. There were net curtains at the window, which looked out onto a yard where the bins were kept. Inside, a single bed, a desk and computer, a post-war utility wardrobe like the one in which Vera still kept her clothes. One wall was covered with cheap, bare-wood shelving, holding paperback books. Vera pulled on latex gloves, but stood, looking around, not touching anything. The room was so small that Ashworth stayed in the doorway.

'A diary would be good,' Vera said. 'An address book.'

'Wouldn't she keep that on the computer?'

'More than likely. We'll wait for the experts to do

that for us.' The search team, specially trained. They'd not want her mauling through the evidence before they had a chance to do it properly. She opened the desk drawers. There were ring folders, envelope files, on the desk she saw a library card for the university and another for Northumberland Libraries. Exactly what you'd expect in a model student's room. But this was like no student's room Vera had seen. At least in the other two bedrooms there were personal touches. Family snaps, birthday cards, party invitations. Lily had lived in this room for nearly three years, but it contained nothing of her. No photos, no posters. It could have been a room in an anonymous, cheap B&B. She opened the wardrobe door and at last she caught a flavour of the dead woman.

The first impression was of colour. A rack held amber beads, a turquoise silk scarf with a silver thread running through it, long red satin gloves. She pulled out hangers holding a loose velvet jacket, blackberry-coloured, a dress in swirls of blues and greens, skirts in bright cotton prints. On shelves there were folded blouses, lacy underwear. Nothing cheap.

'So,' Vera said. 'She liked to dress up.' She looked at the labels at the necks of the jacket and the blouses. 'Some of it from Robbins,' she said. 'But not all of it. She wouldn't have got these at discount. She must have spent all her spare cash on clothes.'

And that, in the end, was all they learned about her. Nothing else in the room gave a clue to her life. They waited in the kitchen for the search team to arrive, not speaking, glad when they heard the van pull up in the street and they had an excuse to leave.

Chapter Fifteen

Lily's flatmates were staying with a friend who lived in the same road. Another big house, this time on the corner, with a garden at the back. It didn't seem to be split into flats. A student house, maybe. Vera rang the bell, hit it again when there was no response. She was about to ring it a third time when there were footsteps and the door opened. The young woman standing in the doorway was tiny, with chopped blonde hair, the build of a ten-year-old, eyes expertly made up to look enormous.

'I'm sorry,' she said. 'Annie's out.'

'I'm not looking for Annie.' Vera flashed her warrant card and walked in without waiting to be asked. 'It's Emma and Louise I'm after. Lily's friends.'

The woman seemed flustered. 'Of course. Sorry to keep you waiting. Annie's taken her daughter to ballet. Lou and I were having a late breakfast in the garden. After hearing about Lily, then camping out here, neither of us slept very well. Come on through. I'm Emma.' Not a local voice. Southern. Rich.

She was wearing leather flip-flops and tripped ahead of them, talking all the way. Not a student house after all. No beer cans or loud music, unsafe wiring or peeling wallpaper. A family lived here.

113

There was a small bicycle propped against the wall in the corridor, a child's paintings on the kitchen notice-board. But still wealthy. If Annie was a single mother she wasn't struggling financially.

'Is Annie a student too?' No reason for needing to know, but Vera had always been nosy.

'No. She's older than me. She lectures. On the course Lily was taking, actually. She's a sort of cousin of mine. Her husband works away a lot and when we were flat-hunting, we thought it would be nice if we could find somewhere close.'

'Very convenient,' Vera said, wondering what it was about this woman she disliked so much.

'Yes.' Emma turned briefly then led them out onto a flagged patio where four wooden chairs stood around a table. The garden was small, surrounded by a high wall. Blackbirds were calling somewhere in the ivy.

Emma continued talking. 'This is my flatmate, Louise. Lou, it's the police.'

Louise seemed still to be wearing pyjamas. Her feet were bare, her hair unbrushed. She nodded to them, played with the croissant flakes on her plate.

'I'll just put on some more coffee,' Emma said.

Vera sat down heavily. 'Not for us, pet. This isn't a social call. We've not much time. We just wanted to talk about Lily.'

'Of course.'

'How long have the three of you been living together?'

'Well, we met up in the first year. Same hall of residence, though we were all doing different stuff. Lily was into English, Louise did languages and I'm a medic. That's why the three of us are still here when most of our friends have left. Our courses last longer than the standard three years and Lily was doing a PGCE. We shared a kitchen then, got on OK, decided to move in together.'

'How could you afford to live in a road like this, like?' Emphasizing the accent, playing the dumb cop. It never hurt if they underestimated you.

'Well, it was down to my dad, actually. He thought he might as well buy somewhere. Thought it would be a decent investment. We'd pay enough rent to cover the mortgage. I mean, it's still not cheap, but when you look at some of the places other students live . . . My parents are great. They give me an allowance.'

'But Lily didn't come from that sort of background, did she? How did she keep up with the rent?'

Emma shrugged. 'She never said. I think her dad was made redundant at the end of her first year and gave her something to start her off. She didn't pay as much as us, because her room is a bit smaller. And she worked on Saturdays and in the holidays.'

'Tell me about her. Living together that long, you must have known her as well as anyone.'

For the first time Emma seemed lost for words. It was Louise who answered.

'Nobody knew her very well.'

'But three lasses together. You must have confided in each other.'

'Not really. Not Lily.'

'There'd have been nights out in town, a few drinks. She'd let down her hair then.'

'I don't think Lily ever let go in that way, Inspector. She was very controlled, very focused.

Ambitious, I suppose. Something to do with the background she came from. She worked much harder than the rest of us.'

'Was she ever ill?'

'Nothing serious. A cold, throat infection. Just like the rest of us.'

'You never worried that she might be depressed? Keeping herself so isolated.'

'No. I don't think she was that isolated. She just didn't include us in the rest of her life.'

'Where were you both last night?'

Louise answered. 'It was my birthday. We went out for a meal. A whole gang of us.'

'What about Lily?' Vera asked. 'Were you expecting her to be there too?'

'I asked her of course, but I wasn't surprised when she didn't turn up. It wasn't really her thing.'

Why not? Did you make her uncomfortable with your confident voices and your parents' money?

'Did she have a boyfriend?'

There was a silence. The women flashed a glance at each other. 'We think she must have done,' Emma said at last. 'There were nights when she didn't come home. But he never came to the flat. At least, not when we were in.'

'And she never talked about him?'

'Not to us.' Emma paused. 'Look, Inspector, in some ways Lily was a model tenant. Thoughtful, tidy. That's why I wanted her to come in with us in the first place. But we were never friends. Not really. I can't think of any reason why anyone would have wanted to kill her. But I wouldn't know. Her life was a mystery to us.'

*

It was lunchtime and Vera brought the team together, bought in sandwiches, proper coffee, doughnuts. Anything to keep up the energy levels. After the catnap in the car she felt on top of the world, but she knew the younger members didn't have her stamina. Still, they were a bit more alert now. A second body. A bright young woman. Somehow that made the case more exciting. They hadn't been able to get worked up about a lad with a learning disability, but a pretty student and suddenly they were buzzing. She told herself she was too cynical for her own good.

She filled them in on the visits to Lily's parents and the flat, walking backwards and forwards at the front of the room, in and out of the light streaming in from the windows.

'The lasses she shared with are camping out at a neighbour's house until the search team has finished. Of course we asked if Lily was at the flat on the night Luke Armstrong was killed. She wasn't there. It wasn't unusual for her to stay out. That's why they presumed she had a boyfriend.'

'Didn't they ask about him? They must have been curious.' This was from Holly Lawson. Eager, fresh-faced, looked like a sixth-former. 'I mean, you might say you respected someone's privacy, but really you'd want to know. Wouldn't you?' She looked around her.

'You're probably right. Go back and talk to the flat-mates,' Vera said. 'You might get more out of them. You're nearer their age.' She took a sip from the cardboard cup. The coffee had been OK at the beginning of the meeting, but it was already cold and she could feel the grounds on her tongue. She set the cup on the table, went up to the windows and pulled the blinds to keep the worst of the sun out of her eyes. The room seemed suddenly gloomy, the people in it blurred shadows.

'I think we'll have to bite the bullet and have a news conference,' she said. 'I don't want anything about the scene to get out. Not the flowers. Not the cause of death. The last thing we need is a copy-cat killer. I told the group who found the body that if they speak to the press they'll have me to answer to. But someone must have seen the corpse being carried from the car park to the rocks. There's that stretch of grass to cover and there's usually someone there. Dog walkers. Parents with young kids. We'll get the press liaison people to set it up.

'Now, what have you got for me?' Vera had landed on the desk at the front. Like a teacher. She wondered what sort of teacher Lily would have made.

'We've found someone at the university to look at the flowers,' Holly said. 'A Dr Calvert. Senior lecturer.'

'No.'

'Sorry?'

'Peter Calvert. He won't do. He found the second body. At least, his son did. He was on the scene immediately after. We can't use him.'

'Oh God, I should have realized. I tracked him down yesterday, before Lily Marsh was killed.' She blushed, stammered, waited for Vera to let fire the sarcasm. But Vera was feeling kind. She was thinking about Peter Calvert. It was probably a coincidence. It didn't take a botanist to scatter flowers on a dead body. But if they were looking for someone who liked to play games, it could be seen as a calling card, a signature.

'Get someone else,' she said. 'Not from Newcastle University. Try Northumbria or Sunderland. There must be another botanist somewhere in the north east. And check out what Dr Calvert was doing the night Luke was killed. Just to show we're tying up all the loose ends.' She remembered the scene on the veranda she'd walked into the night before. Four men sitting at the table. One woman. About the same age as her, but elegant, made-up. Desired. An interesting group, she thought again. 'On second thoughts, you can leave Dr Calvert to me.' It would be an excuse to go back. 'Can't trust you lot with the gentry.'

They smiled, not bothered. One less job for them and whoever heard of a university lecturer as a murderer?

She turned back to the group. 'Who's been checking out Geoff Armstrong's alibi?'

'Me.' Charlie Robson. Charlie was older than her. She thought he must be up for retirement soon. He didn't like working for a woman, but he'd had to get on with it.

'Well?'

'First I had a word with the guy he does most of his work for. Barry Middleton. Small builder. Does kitchens, bathrooms, loft extensions. He's known Geoff for years, even before he started passing work his way. He says Geoff always had a temper on him. One of those people who could take offence if you looked at him the wrong way. There were a couple of scraps on site. He lashed out at a foreman when he was working in London. That's why he turned up back here without a job. But apparently he changed completely when he remarried. Now he's a real family man, according to Barry. Devoted to Kath and the little girl. He'd even started to build bridges with Julie.'

'That's what he said to me.' But do I believe it? Vera thought. Do I believe people change that easily?

'I went onto the estate this morning,' Charlie went on. 'Geoff and the family were leaving just as I got there. Looked like a trip to the beach. They had towels, a picnic.'

'Very domestic,' Vera said.

'They didn't see me. I had a word with the neighbours. Everyone said the same. They're a lovely family. He's a bit quiet. Doesn't go to the pub or the club. Stays in to mind the bairn while the wife's at work. But nobody had a word to say against him.'

'What about Wednesday night? Did anyone see him leave the house?'

'No, and one couple is certain they would have done if he'd taken his car out. They were having a barbecue, had invited a few friends round. They'd even asked Geoff. They only live a couple of doors down the street and thought he could keep calling back to check the little girl was OK. He didn't go in the end, said he didn't like leaving Rebecca. But they were out in the garden all evening. It's on the corner and they'd have seen if he left. That's what they reckon.'

Vera was pleased they could count Geoff out of the investigation. She imagined the three of them on a beach somewhere. Tynemouth, maybe. Kath laid out on a towel catching up on some sleep, Geoff keeping the girl amused, holding her hand as she jumped the waves, building sandcastles, buying ice cream.

She must be going soft in her old age. She thought he deserved a second chance.

She realized the team was waiting for her to go on. 'Let's leave Geoff Armstrong, then. Unless anything else comes up. I want someone to talk to Luke's consultant. Find out if Lily Marsh was treated at St George's too. She probably wouldn't be an inpatient. Her flatmates would know about that. She might have gone to a clinic, though. We know her dad had a history of mental illness. It's an outside chance but worth following up. And I'd like you to check out Lily Marsh's finances. Bank account, credit cards. All that. The way it looks, she was living way beyond her means. Did she have some other income? A rich lover, maybe. And we need to trace the lad she had the crush on when she was at school. His name's Ben Craven. He could still be living locally.'

She thought there'd been enough talk. They all liked talk. Talk and coffee and buns saved them having to go out there and mix it with real people.

She stood up, made sure she had their attention. 'The first priority is to make some link between the victims. Something that places them together, a person they have in common.'

They sat, staring up at her.

'Well, go on, then,' she said, raising her voice, teacher again. 'You're not going to find it in here, are you?'

Chapter Sixteen

It was Saturday and the sun was still shining, but at Fox Mill there were no preparations for the picnic Felicity had been planning as an extra celebration for Peter's birthday. Everyone had stayed the night and they ate a late, subdued breakfast in the kitchen. The four men seemed preoccupied and washed out. Perhaps they were suffering from a collective hangover. Even James was unusually quiet and mooched back to his room to watch children's television.

She was glad when the guests left before lunch. Peter tried to persuade them to stay, but they must have realized she wanted them out of the house. Today even Samuel was no comfort. In the afternoon Peter locked himself in his office. He had a grand project. A book about the effect of weather on the movement of seabirds. One of the larger natural history publishers had expressed a vague, polite interest, but no firm offer had been made. They'd have to see the completed work, they said. Peter's theories had grown more complex as he analysed the material. There were days when she thought she would never see it finished.

Felicity went into the garden and began weeding the beds at the front of the house. She enjoyed the

methodical, mindless activity, the instant result.
There was the sound of a car in the lane. She ignored
it at first. Walkers sometimes parked on the verge
before setting off on the footpath to the coast. Then
she could tell it had turned into the drive and she
straightened, pulling off her gloves, tucking her shirt
back into her jeans, preparing to meet the visitor. She
had thought it might be Samuel. He would have realized she was upset. It would be like him to think the
matter over and come back to check that she had
recovered. She was already planning the words she
would use to him, the apology for being so crabby, so
inhospitable. The lie. *You know I didn't mind you being
here. It was the others. Just too much.*

But it wasn't Samuel. It was a car she didn't recognize. She felt a sudden disquiet, then saw the big
female detective from the night before struggle out
from the driver's seat. There was the moment of quiet
superiority she always felt when she saw a woman of
around her own age who had let herself go. The detective's face could even be attractive if she made more
effort. Her clothes were shapeless, her hair badly cut.
Did she really not care what she looked like? Felicity couldn't understand it. Somehow it made Vera
Stanhope invulnerable. *She*'d always enjoyed being
admired. She couldn't imagine not caring what other
people thought.

'Inspector.' She checked that her hand was clean
and held it out. The woman took it with a brief, sharp
grip, but her attention was on the garden.

'This is lovely,' she said. 'It'll take a lot of work.'

'Oh,' Felicity knew she was being flattered but was

still pleased. 'We have help, of course. An elderly man from the village.'

'Of course,' the detective said.

Felicity heard the sarcasm, wasn't sure how to respond.

'Can I help you?'

'Just a few more questions. You know how it is. Things come up.'

How can I know how it is? Felicity thought. I've never found a body before.

'Your friends have gone?'

'Yes, they had to get away. I think Gary is working tonight.' She felt awkward standing there, grubby and unprepared.

'What do they do? Gary told us, but what about the others?' Vera had moved into the shade of the house and Felicity followed.

'Samuel's a librarian. Also a rather fine writer. Short stories, mostly. Clive works as an assistant at the Hancock Museum. The natural history section.'

'Does he? I loved it in there when I was a kid. My dad used to take me. It had a smell all of its own. I haven't been there for years.' Vera seemed lost for a moment in the memory. 'Is your husband at home?'

'He's in the office,' Felicity said. 'Come through.'

'Is he working too?'

'On his research, yes.'

'I understand he's a botanist. That must be useful when it comes to gardening.' The voice was jolly, impressed. Felicity didn't know what to make of it. She decided not to explain about the seabird book. It might be considered a hobby, not work at all, and she wanted the detective to take Peter seriously.

'We often stop for tea at about this time. Perhaps you'll join us? I'll give Peter a shout.'

Felicity wouldn't have been surprised if the detective had insisted on disturbing Peter in his office, but it seemed she'd decided to be conciliatory.

'Why not? I'm gasping.'

'We could sit outside, make the most of the sunshine.'

'I'd rather not, pet. I have this allergy. Direct sunlight. Makes me come out in lumps and blotches.'

So they sat up to the kitchen table. Felicity had made to take the tea things through to the living room on a tray, but Vera had touched her arm to stop her. 'Eh, we don't want any fuss. I'm more the hired help than visiting gentry.'

Felicity knew the detective was playing with her and wasn't quite sure how to take it. She just nodded her agreement, sliced the scones she'd fetched out of the freezer the afternoon before and spooned homemade jam into a pot. When Peter came out from his office, Vera had her mouth full, and spattered crumbs over the table as she tried to speak. Felicity wanted to say to Peter: *Don't be taken in by this woman. She wants you to believe she's a clown. She's brighter than she looks.* But she could tell that Peter had already dismissed her as a fool. As she choked and coughed and swilled tea, he raised his eyes to the ceiling.

At last the pantomime was over and Vera began to speak.

'I got interrupted last night,' she said. 'There are a few questions. You'll understand. Formalities.'

'Of course.'

'You work at the university, Dr Calvert? Miss

Marsh was a student there. On the post-graduate education course. You're sure you didn't know her?'

'What did she take for her first degree?'

'English. She did that at Newcastle too.'

'However, I never met her, Inspector. My subject is botany. Our paths never crossed. I'm afraid it must be a coincidence. Her teaching our son, enquiring about accommodation and then our stumbling across her like that on the shore.'

A random occurrence, Felicity thought. Like sea watching. Like birds flying past just when you're there to see them. Except, of course, it wasn't chance which connected the birders and the birds, as Peter had described it in the watch tower the night before. They took steps to make sure they were there at the right time. They listened to the shipping forecast every night to hear which way the wind was blowing. They consulted tide tables.

'The girl was murdered,' Vera said suddenly. 'Strangled. But you know that already. I told you last night. Something that elaborate, staged, you'd think it'd be easy to find out who did it. They'd leave traces. A jilted lover, maybe.' She paused. '*Jilted.* That's an old-fashioned kind of word. And it seemed like an old-fashioned sort of crime, at first. Something from a gentler age. Looked peaceful, didn't she, lying there. The flowers. But there was nothing peaceful about her dying. I can't believe she wanted to go.'

Felicity felt tears in her eyes. As if, somehow, she was being held responsible. She was pleased that Peter seemed moved too, that he kept quiet.

The detective continued. 'And there are other complications. There was another victim. A lad was killed two days earlier. Name of Luke Armstrong.' She looked at them both. 'Are you *sure* you don't know the name?'

'You mentioned him before,' Felicity said. 'And I saw it on the local news. He came from Seaton.'

'What I didn't tell you was that he was put in a bath. Covered with flowers. Like I said last night, it could hinder our investigation if something like that became common knowledge. But you do see what I'm saying. It's not simple any more. A jilted lover isn't going to kill a sixteen-year-old boy as a sort of practice run. Why take the risk? Far too elaborate. I'm looking for links here. The mother's name is Julie. Julie Armstrong.'

'Wasn't that woman Gary was raving about called Julie?' As soon as the words were out of her mouth Felicity regretted them. It was such a stupid thing to say. Why point the inspector in the direction of Gary, who wouldn't hurt a fly? She could feel Peter glaring at her and tried to rescue the situation. 'I mean, it's a really common name. I'm sure it doesn't mean . . .'

'Why don't you tell me anyway, pet?'

'He met this woman, that's all. Some gig he was doing the sound for. A local band in a pub in North Shields. That place with the view over the river. Bumped into her in the bar after. They got talking and found out they'd been to school together. You know how it is.'

'I'm not sure I do. Why don't you explain?'

'He talks a big game, Gary. I mean, to hear him, you'd think he had women all over the country. But since his fiancée left him, I don't think he's had a real girlfriend. He loved Emily, really loved her. When she went off with someone else, he was devastated. I just got the impression that he clicked with this Julie. He hoped to meet her again.'

'Did he say any more about her? Like whether she had kids?'

'No, nothing like that.'

'What about you, Dr Calvert? Did he talk to you about this woman?'

'I'm sorry, Inspector. It's not really the sort of thing men talk about.'

'Isn't it?' As if she was genuinely surprised. 'Well, I can ask Gary about it, can't I? Get it straight from the horse's mouth.'

Felicity thought that the ordeal was over then. Vera Stanhope licked her finger, swept up the remaining pieces of scone from her plate, drained her teacup.

'What were you both doing on Wednesday night? Late. Between ten and midnight.'

Felicity looked at Peter, waiting for him to answer first.

'I was here,' he said. 'Working.' He looked at his wife. 'I was still in my office, wasn't I, when you got in?'

'And what were you up to, Mrs Calvert?'

'I was at the theatre,' she said. 'The Live, down on the quayside. It was the work of a young local playwright. I've seen some of his stuff before. It's very evocative. I think it's important to support new writing.' She stopped talking, realizing she was saying too much.

'Were you on your own?'

'No, I went with a friend. Peter doesn't enjoy the

theatre very much. Not that sort of play, at least. I was there with Samuel Parr. You met him here last night.'

'Of course,' Vera said. 'Samuel the librarian.' Felicity expected some sly comment, but none came. 'What time did you arrive home?'

'It probably was nearly midnight. We had supper after the show and it's quite a trek from town.'

'Thanks for that, then.' This time Vera did get to her feet. 'I'm sure you understand why I had to ask. I'll let you get back to your work, Dr Calvert.'

Felicity walked the detective back to her car. The sun was covered by a thin layer of mist, but it didn't look as if it would lead to rain. Gardening would be more pleasant now that it was a bit cooler. She didn't think she would go back to it, though. A bath, she thought. That would relax her. Then she remembered what the inspector had said about Luke Armstrong being found in the bath and the image of a body, strewn with flowers, flashed in front of her eyes.

Vera stood by her vehicle. Felicity started to walk back into the house.

'Just one thing, Mrs Calvert. Would you mind if I had a look at the cottage? The place you showed Lily Marsh the day before she died.'

Felicity had a moment of revulsion. She didn't want to be in the space where she'd been close to Lily Marsh, close enough to see the stitching on the hem of her skirt as she walked ahead of Felicity up the stairs. Then she told herself that was ridiculous. She'd have to go into the cottage sometime. Why not now? Better, surely, to humour the detective than antagonize her.

'Of course. I'll just get the key.'

They walked through the meadow to the cottage door. Inside, it was all as it had been since her last visit, except the roses in the bedroom were dead. Felicity took them from the jug to take to the compost heap, held them carefully because of the thorns. Vera followed her down the stairs, but then she seemed reluctant to leave.

'This was the last time anyone saw her alive,' she said. 'Last time anyone will admit to, at least. She didn't go into school on Friday. We talked to the head teacher this afternoon, finally tracked her down.' She looked sharply at Felicity. 'And that's not for public consumption either.' She looked out of the window. 'What a beautiful place. You'd have thought she'd have jumped at the chance to stay here.'

'I wondered if she thought she wouldn't have been able to afford it.'

'What rent were you going to charge?'

'I don't know. I hadn't really considered it.'

'Didn't she ask?'

'No,' Felicity said. 'She just said she'd think about it. Then she ran off.'

Chapter Seventeen

Julie was back in her own home. Her mother opened the door to Vera, pulled her close for a conspiratorial whisper.

'We've asked her to stay with us for a while, but she says she'd never face coming back. So I've moved in to keep an eye. Just for a week or two.'

Vera nodded, walked on into the house, kept her voice low too.

'What about Laura, Mrs Richardson? How's she?'

'Eh, I don't know. Not eating. Keeps to herself. I've asked if she wants her friends round but she says not.'

'Is she in now?'

'Aye, she's in her room.'

'I'll just go up for a quick word. I'll see Julie on my way out, if that's all right. Would you mind telling her I'm here?'

Laura was lying on her bed, curled on her side, a magazine beside her. It was open but she didn't seem to be reading. The window was shut and the room was hot. It was at the back of the house, looking out over a paddock, where a couple of tired ponies cropped the parched grass, and then a field of arable. Vera had knocked at the door and walked in without waiting for an answer.

The girl looked up. 'What do you want?' She was skinny, angular. Fourteen but no figure to speak of. Her hair was cut short and spiky. Eyes that glared at you. A rash of freckles across her nose which made her seem younger than she was. Soon, Vera thought, she might become an interesting beauty. Now she was sullen, miserable, lonely. There'd been a time when Vera had been desperate for children. The longing had come on her suddenly, when she was in her late thirties, shocking her with its intensity. It had been more potent than her dreams of men and sex. Just as well it never happened, she thought now. I could never have coped with someone like this.

'I'd just like a chat,' she said. 'Now you've had a chance to think about things.'

'I don't know anything about what happened that night. I was asleep.'

'I wanted to talk to you about that, pet. Are you sure you didn't hear anything? A knock on the door, voices, a scuffle. You might have heard, thought it was Luke and his mates larking about. Nothing to feel guilty about if you did.'

'I don't feel guilty.'

'Because I find it hard to believe you slept through all that.'

'I sleep like a stone,' Laura said. 'Ask Mam.'

She glared at Vera, who felt out of her depth. She would have pushed another witness, but this was a young girl who'd just lost her brother. 'Still,' Vera said. 'You might be able to help. I need to talk about Luke's mates, what he got up to, who he mixed with. You'll have a better idea about that than your mam.'

'No, I won't.' Aggressive. As if Vera was crazy even to consider it.

'He didn't talk to you, then?'

'No.' That tone again. The one teenagers did when they really wanted to wind you up. Sneering. The voice that made you want to slap them. 'I didn't want him to.'

'You didn't get on?'

Laura pulled herself up onto her elbow. 'I've had all the lectures, OK? From Mam and Nan and the teachers at school. I know it wasn't his fault, the learning disability. I know I'm a bitch. But I couldn't stand it. Everyone pointing at me, knowing I was his sister. Sniggering behind my back when he did something stupid. As if I could help it. We didn't *not* get on. I just wanted him out of my life.'

She realized the implication of what she'd said as soon as the words came out, but wasn't going to show she was sorry. She sank onto the bed and turned her back on Vera. Vera knew something of what she was going through. When she was a kid, people had sniggered about her too. She'd lived on her own with a mad father. No mother. No one to iron the school uniform or bake cakes for sports day. No one to take her to the hairdresser's or explain about periods. Just Hector, who spent his spare time prowling the hills looking for raptors' nests, who seemed to care more for his egg-collecting friends than his ugly daughter. But it wouldn't help if she talked about that to Laura. Young people saw the middle-aged as a different species. How could Vera's experience mean anything to the miserable girl lying on the bed?

She reached out and touched Laura's shoulder.

'Eh, pet, it's not your fault. And you might be able to help without realizing.'

The girl turned onto her back, stared at the ceiling.

'I didn't know any of his friends.'

'What about Thomas Sharp?'

'He's dead.'

Vera kept her voice even. The team back at Kimmerston would be astonished, she thought, that she could be this patient. 'But you must have met him when he came to the house.'

'Sometimes.'

'What did you make of him?'

There was a silence. Vera wondered if she'd pushed too hard.

'He was OK,' the girl said at last. 'Better than the others Luke had knocked around with. A laugh.'

She liked him, Vera thought. Fancied him, even. Had anything gone on between them? Furtive groping behind her mother's back? What had Luke made of that?

'It must have been a shock when he died.'

'It was dreadful.'

'Did you go to his funeral?'

She shook her head. 'Mam wouldn't let me take the day off school. She says I'm the only one with brains in the family and I have to use them.' She paused. 'I went with them to the river, though, when they took the flowers.'

'Did Luke ever tell you what happened when Thomas drowned?'

'He said he should have saved him.' The answer came back loud and angry.

'Do you think he could have saved him?'

'I don't know. Maybe. If he hadn't been such a daft sod. If he'd made more effort.' She started to cry, not for her brother, but for his friend.

'Do you know anyone called Lily Marsh?'

'I don't know any old ladies.'

'Why do you think she's an old lady?'

'It's an old lady's name, isn't it? Lily.'

It's the name of a flower, Vera thought suddenly and wondered why she hadn't realized before. Does that mean anything? Did Luke have any middle names? Something floral? Were there any male names connected to flowers?

Laura was getting restive, curious despite herself. 'Who is she anyway?'

'Not an old person,' Vera said. 'A student teacher. Did she ever work in your school?'

'Nah.' Laura picked up the magazine and pretended to read it.

Vera saw she'd get nothing more out of her today. 'I need to talk to your mam now,' she said. 'If you think of anything give me a ring. I'll leave my card here on the window sill.'

Julie was sitting in her front room, staring at the television screen. Saturday teatime. Daft celebrities getting families to do daft stunts. Despite the heat she was wearing jogging pants and a sweater. When she saw Vera she jumped up and switched off the television, embarrassed perhaps to be caught doing something so normal. The room was the same size as Sal's next door, but more cluttered. There'd be reminders of Luke everywhere – his clothes would still be in the plastic laundry basket next to the ironing board, his favourite video in the pile on the floor.

'Sorry about the mess,' Julie said. 'You know . . .'

Vera nodded, happy to accept the excuse, but she knew it would always be messy. Probably messier than it was now, because Mrs Richardson was here, keeping on top of things. Julie wouldn't be one for a tidy house. Not like Kath on the prim estate in Wallsend.

Mrs Richardson hovered just inside the door. 'Tea, Inspector?'

'Champion.' If I have more tea, I'll drown, Vera thought, but she didn't want the mother listening in to this. She sat on an armchair covered by a puce chenille throw, beckoned for Julie to sit down again too.

'It's about Gary,' she said. 'Gary Wright.'

Julie moved her head very slowly until she was looking at Vera. 'What about him?'

'You do know him?'

'Not really.'

'Tell me.'

'I was with him the night Luke was killed. I mean, not *with* him, not like that. We never left the club. But dancing together, having a laugh.' She snapped her mouth shut as if the thought of laughter was obscene.

'That wasn't the first time you met him?'

'No, a few weeks ago I was in the Harbour Bell with my mam and da. Sunday afternoon. Just before they let Luke out of hospital. Laura was spending the day with a friend. Da likes his music. If you let him, he'll bore you for hours about the old days. The Animals. The clubs in town where he used to go in the sixties. The Bell has live music on Sunday afternoons and there was a band he wanted to hear. I'd had my dinner at theirs and went just for the ride. I had a good time. Gary was doing the sound.' Julie's voice tailed off. She looked straight at Vera. 'You know, that could have been months ago. Years. It feels as if everything has changed. It's me I'm talking about but it's like I'm describing a different person.'

'I know,' Vera said.

'Gary made me laugh,' Julie went on. 'At first you could tell he was just showing off. Telling stories about his work. The musicians he'd done the sound for. You could tell he'd come out with the same stuff to anyone. Any woman, at least, aged between fifteen and fifty.'

Even me? Vera thought.

'Then we just clicked. We found out we'd been to the same primary school, started chatting about the people we could remember. Mam had to come and get me in the end. She was worried we'd miss visiting time at the hospital. She was coming with me to see Luke.'

'And you arranged to meet him in town?' Vera said.

'No. It wasn't a firm arrangement. Not really.' But Vera could tell it had been firm enough for Julie. Special. 'He just asked if I ever got into town, and I said, hardly ever. Then I remembered Jan's birthday and how the girls had asked me to go with them. So I said I'd be there. That night.'

Vera could imagine how that had been. The mother listening in. Julie keeping her voice casual, but making sure he'd made a note of the date, the places the girls always went. *Not the Bigg Market. We're a bit old for that.* She'd have been looking out for him all night. And he'd turned up. She'd have felt like a sixteen-year-old, giddy, triumphant. And she'd arrived home to find her son strangled, scattered with flowers.

Mrs Richardson appeared from the kitchen, a mug in each hand. Vera accepted hers, then tipped most of the contents into the compost of a sad umbrella plant when the woman went to get biscuits. Julie, staring at the blank television screen, didn't notice.

'A great cup of tea,' Vera said, slurping the dregs. 'Just what I needed.' Now the two women sat, looking at her. Perhaps they could tell she had something else to say. 'There's been another murder. A young woman. A student. She was called Lily Marsh. Does the name mean anything to you?'

They shook their heads. They didn't really care about the death of a strange woman. Luke was all that mattered to them. Vera found a space for the mug on the coffee table. 'I wanted you to know,' she said. 'It'll be in the press. And it might make it easier for us to find Luke's killer. It'll give us more to go on.' That was the theory, at least. She stood up. 'I'll be off now, Mrs Richardson. If there's any news, I'll be in touch.'

Julie got up from her chair too. 'Why did you want to know about Gary?'

'No reason, pet. Just routine.'

At the door Vera stopped. 'Did Luke have a middle name?'

'Geoffrey,' Julie said. 'Like his dad.'

Nothing floral, then. No connection there.

HIDDEN DEPTHS

As Vera walked into the street she could sense the eyes behind net curtains; the neighbours would wait until she'd driven off before getting on the phone to share the latest rumours.

Chapter Eighteen

One time, he wouldn't have admitted to living in North Shields, Gary thought. Certainly not if he was chatting up a woman, trying to impress. People from outside had a picture of it. All charity shops and boarded-up buildings, Wilkinson's and Poundstretchers the only stores doing business. Even now, if you waited at the metro, you'd share the platform with teenage mothers and gangs of lads who skipped off the trains whenever the ticket inspector arrived. But it was changing. Now if he said he lived in Shields people nodded, understanding. It was the sort of place where people in his business might live. Still not quite respectable, but interesting. There were new apartments, bars and restaurants on the Fish Quay. A couple of writers had taken up residence. House prices in Tynemouth were so high that people had crossed the boundary, blurring the edges. There was no shame to living in Shields these days. Sunday's Quiz Night at the Maggie Bank pub was full of lecturers and social workers. Gary had been a regular once, but only bothered going now to catch up with old friends. Even though he could score on the music round, he had no chance of winning.

He lived in a newish development on one of the

steep streets between the Fish Quay and the town, a four-storey block of flats, with a Gothic stone Methodist chapel on one side and a carpet warehouse on the other. He'd bought it soon after he split up from Emily; thinking back, he couldn't remember much about moving in. He'd been pissed when he signed the contract, swore at the estate agent about something that had irritated him. Clive had helped him carry the few bits of furniture they couldn't get into the lift up the stairs, organized Northern Electric to get the power on, even made the tea. That was the sort of friend he was. He never made a fuss but was there when he was needed. Gary hoped he'd act the same way if the circumstances were reversed, but he wasn't sure. Now the flat felt more like home than anywhere he'd lived since he was a kid. It would be a wrench to leave.

That morning, he'd given Clive a lift back from Fox Mill. In the car, they'd talked about the dead girl in the pool, tuned the radio to the local BBC station in case it had made the news. Gary had done most of the talking. Clive hadn't said much, but then he never did. Perhaps that's why they got on so well: Gary liked a ready-made audience. At school Clive had been a loner. He still didn't have any other friends. Only Gary, Samuel and Peter. The discovery of the body headed up the news, but there were no details. Nothing about the way she was found or the flowers. Not even her name.

Gary wandered out onto the balcony and looked over the town and down to the river. Upstream the ferry was sliding away from the South Shields jetty. He had his phone with him and leaned on the rail to dial. He was on the top floor and there wasn't too much noise from the street. He was about to press the buttons when the intercom buzzer sounded and he went inside to see who was waiting in the lobby. He wasn't sorry to have to put off his phone call. He still hadn't decided quite what to say.

'It's me, pet. Vera Stanhope.' The detective of the night before. He thought he'd answered all her questions and her presence threw him. At one time he'd have been able to take this in his stride. He'd had the confidence to talk himself into any event, out of any bother. Now, it wasn't so easy. But he couldn't leave her there, waiting.

'Come on up.' Keeping the voice light, to show he had nothing to hide.

He checked his appearance in the long mirror. Habit. Reassurance. Like spending a fortune on the right haircut, a decent pair of shoes. Then he opened the door of the flat and stood there, waiting for her to appear. He couldn't hear the lift and was wondering if she'd been called away on more urgent business, when she appeared at the top of the stairs, wheezing, heaving for breath.

'I don't like lifts.' The words came out in quick accusing pants, as if she was blaming him for living there. 'I'm never quite sure they'll carry my weight.' And he realized her appearance was something she was sensitive about. She'd have been bullied at school and the only way to deal with it would have been to get the jibe in first. Surprised that last night he'd been intimidated by her, he leaned back against the door and let her walk into the flat ahead of him.

Inside, he watched her checking out the flat, saw

it through her eyes. It would be tidier than she'd expect. He had lots of electronic equipment but it was all boxed and stacked on shelves along one wall. He didn't mind a bit of mess but he didn't like chaos. Against the same wall stood a long desk with a PC and printer, a pair of headphones, a pile of audio magazines. In the middle of the room a sofa and coffee table. In the corner a TV and DVD player. A couple of enlarged black and white photos on the wall. One of the river in the centre of town. Dusk. Looking through all the bridges to the Blinking Eye. But there was nothing really personal, he thought. Nothing to give himself away. He'd allowed himself to keep one photo of Emily, but it was on his desk, small, nothing flashy. The inspector wouldn't notice that.

'Sit down,' he said. 'Tea? Coffee?'

Her face was red with the effort of climbing the stairs. He didn't bother with the lift either unless he had heavy gear, but didn't even have to catch his breath when he got to the top. He told himself not to be such a smug bastard. She was an overweight, middle-aged woman. Hardly competition.

'I don't suppose you've got a beer, have you?' she said. 'I'm not fussy, pet. Whatever you've got in the fridge.'

He found himself smiling. Despite himself he couldn't help liking her. He brought out two cans of lager, a glass for her. She lowered herself carefully onto the sofa. He sat on the floor, legs stretched in front of him, felt her looking him over.

'Your file says you're thirty-five,' she said. 'You've not worn badly. If I was guessing, I'd say five years younger.'

'Thanks.' He was annoyed at himself for feeling flattered. It was an odd thing for her to say, an odd feeling to have her eyeing him up. It occurred to him briefly that women must feel like this all the time.

'This place must have set you back a few quid.' She looked out towards the window. 'A view like that.'

'Not really. I bought it from new six years ago. Everyone thought I was mad moving to Shields. I'd make a canny profit if I sold it now.'

'Live here on your own?'

'Yes.'

I'm not so sad, he wanted to say. Not really sad, like Clive. I was engaged once. To Emily. The love of my life. We were going to live together in a tidy flat in Jesmond. And since then there've been women. Not living in, maybe. Not real girlfriends. But I've never gone without for long. And now there's Julie.

She tugged at the ring pull on the can. He slipped a look at his watch. He still had that phone call to make.

'Expecting someone?' she asked.

'No,' he said quickly. 'Nothing like that. Is this about that student who died? I thought you'd finished with me last night.'

She made him wait until she'd taken a mouthful of beer, straight from the can, not bothering with the glass he'd set on the table in front of her. 'I'm going to ask you a question,' she said. 'You've heard it before. This time I want you to think about it.'

He was about to interrupt, to tell her she was wasting her time, that he knew nothing about the student's death. But she waved her can at him to stop him speaking and he did. She had a way of getting what she wanted. Again she waited until she was sure she had his full attention. 'Does the name Luke Armstrong mean anything to you?'

'No. I told you last night.'

'I said think about it.'

They looked at each other in silence. Gary shook his head.

'He has a mother by the name of Julie. A sister called Laura. Perhaps that jogs your memory.'

He froze, his beer almost to his mouth. 'Julie's son,' he said at last.

'Aye, Julie's son. The lad who's been ill.'

'I didn't mean to mislead you, Inspector.'

'You did, though.'

'I never met him. Julie talked about him. I know he'd been having a rough time. But the name didn't really register. I still think of her as Julie Richardson.' He looked up at her. 'He's dead?'

'Murdered,' she said. 'Didn't you see it in the press?'

'I don't read the papers much. I listened to the radio on the way back from Peter's this morning. It mentioned Lily Marsh, but not the boy.'

'We're not encouraging the media to make a connection.'

'And he was killed in the same way as Lily Marsh?'

'Not exactly. But there are similarities.'

'Oh God,' he said. 'Julie will be devastated. She said he wasn't an easy kid, but I could tell she was crazy about him. I mean, she said she loved both her children, but Luke was special. He needed her most. I don't know what to do. I was just about to phone her when you arrived. I was expecting her to phone me.

She said she would. I thought she'd changed her mind about wanting to see me again. Now I understand.' He paused. 'I don't suppose she'll want to hear from me now.'

'Typical man,' Vera said, speaking to herself. 'A woman's lost her son and all he can think about is getting his leg over.'

'No!' he said. 'I didn't mean it like that. I meant maybe she could use a friend. But probably not me. I mean, she'd be better off with someone who's known her longer, wouldn't she? I'd just be in the way. What do you think?'

'Eh, pet, I'm a detective, not a relationship counsellor.'

He looked straight at her. 'How is Julie?'

'Her son's just been murdered. How do you think?'

He stood up and walked towards the balcony. The door was still open. A couple of herring gulls screamed and squabbled outside. He knew it was pathetic, but he felt sorry for himself. He wasn't really thinking about Julie at all.

Vera heaved herself to her feet and followed him out. 'You do know he died that night you were out with her?' she said.

Gary turned, apparently horrified. 'Wednesday?'

'Aye, she got home from the night in town and found him.' She paused, narrowed her eyes. 'Some people might say it was a bit of a coincidence. You were chatting up the first victim's mother just before he was murdered and came upon the second soon after.'

'I'd never met either of them,' he said. 'Honestly.'

'Tell me how you got together with Julie,' she

said. 'I mean, were you set up? Some friend saw her, maybe, thought you were her type. Someone pulling your strings?'

'No, nothing like that. Why?'

'Probably no reason,' she said. 'I was just looking for a connection. It crossed my mind it would be a way of keeping tracks on her. Someone bringing you together would have inside information. But I've never been a great one for conspiracy theories.'

Gary found himself telling the inspector about the meeting anyway. He wanted to tell it. It was like one of those stories which become family legends, told to grandchildren. They stood together, leaning on the balcony rail and looking down into the street. 'It was a chance meeting. Pure chance. I saw her in the other bar. At least I heard her first, heard her laugh. She's got one of those laughs. You know, infectious. Then something about her was familiar. I'd not seen her since we left primary school, but I recognized her. Amazing, really, after all that time. And suddenly it hit me. That was what I wanted. To get together with someone like that. Someone who could laugh like that. I've always gone for younger women. Lookers, you know. But they've never stuck around. Thinking of settling down with someone, I suppose it was all part of getting old. Like taking the permanent job at the Sage after swearing I'd never stop being self-employed.'

She listened impassively. 'Aye,' she said. 'That's how Julie told it. But she kept to the facts. Left out the soppy bits.'

'She told you about me?'

Vera left the question unanswered. 'Did you tell anyone you were going to meet her that night?'

He couldn't stop himself grinning. 'All my close mates. I don't really do secrets.'

'All the people who were with you when you found Lily Marsh, they knew beforehand that you planned to meet up with Luke's mother on the Wednesday night?'

'Probably. I'd chatted to Felicity about Julie. Then there was a Bird Club meeting on Monday evening. All the lads were there. We went for a pint afterwards. I wanted their advice – how to play it. I probably bored them to death.'

'I didn't think men were supposed to talk about things like that.'

'Yeah, well. I never did the strong, silent thing.'

'And the others? Do they get touchy-feely too?'

'We're close.' Gary was suddenly serious. 'Nothing wrong with that.'

'I should go,' she said, but she didn't move. He could tell she was drawn to the view from the balcony.

'Did Julie tell you what triggered Luke's illness?' she asked.

'Some mate of his drowned . . .'

'Down there,' she said. 'Just off the Fish Quay. You didn't hear anything about it?'

He shook his head.

She wandered back into the room, stopped by the desk, nodded to the photo of Emily. 'Who's that, then?'

He felt himself blush, couldn't help it, thought she must be some sort of witch to go straight for the picture. 'An old friend.'

She stood for a moment looking at the picture.

'Strange-looking lass,' she said almost to herself. 'Pretty enough, if you like them anorexic.'

She was letting herself out of the door when he called her back. 'What do you think I should do about Julie? Should I phone her?'

She paused for only a second. 'Not my call, pet.'

Chapter Nineteen

Monday morning Gary woke up to the sound of his pager. He'd set it so it made a noise only when there was a mega alert, when an exceptionally rare bird had been seen somewhere in the country. It was six o'clock, but this time of year and this far north it had already been light for more than an hour. He slept with the pager on the floor next to his bed and scrabbled to reach it, pressed the buttons, screwed up his eyes to read what it said. He didn't travel all over the country to see rare birds any more, but there was still the rush of adrenaline.

It was a moment before he could take in the information. *Marmora's warbler. Deepden Nature Reserve. Northumberland.* His patch. The place where he and Clive started ringing with Peter and Samuel. The only place that had provided any retreat from thoughts of Emily. Then there was the intense stab of envy. *It should have been me. I should have been the person to find it. And if not me, then one of the others.* Really, it should have been Clive, he thought. It mattered to him more than any of us. Clive never really talked about his mother, but you'd been able to tell it was only the weekends at Deepden that had kept him sane. He supported the place long after the rest of them had moved on.

Those thoughts were at the back of his mind, but he was already out of bed with his mobile in his hand. He was the only one with a pager. The others pretended to despise the whole concept. They were into natural history, not ticking rare birds. He dialled Peter's number first. If they were any sort of gang, Peter Calvert was the leader and, though he pretended to be above keeping a list, he wouldn't want to miss out on this. He'd been part of the group which had founded Deepden in the sixties.

Peter listened to Gary's gabbling then swore under his breath. 'I've got a lecture at ten. Still, if it's showing well and I can get it straight away . . .' And Gary knew he would go for it, lecture or not. 'I'll phone Sam,' he went on. 'He should have time to go for it before work.' Gary thought Peter was the only one of them to get away with calling the writer Sam.

He ended the call then pressed the button again for Clive's number. There was no question that Clive would go. He'd throw a sickie if he had to, stay the night at the obs and look again the next morning. But he'd need a lift. By the time Clive answered, whispering, because of his dreadful mother asleep in the next room, Gary had his binoculars round his neck, his scope over his shoulder and he was already down the first flight of stairs.

Gary had heard the tale about the start of the Deepden Observatory hundreds of times. When he was a kid and they'd gone there every weekend, the older observatory members had explained it. Sitting in front of the fire after a day's ringing, drinking whisky or beer, they'd relived the triumph of raising the money to buy the cottage off the elderly woman who owned the place, the planting of the garden, the digging of the pond, the cutting of mist net rides through the undergrowth. The grand opening of the observatory which had attracted everyone of any importance in the field of natural history. Perhaps once all the work had been done, the excitement had passed, because even then they'd spent more time drinking tea in the cottage than going out into the field. Now a new generation of birders camped out in the two dormitories, staggered back late at night after a lock-in at the Fox and Hounds in Deepden village and found the rare birds.

The four of them had stopped going regularly a few years before. It had been a statement. A stand. Gary was already more attracted to sea watching and had been a sporadic visitor even then. He couldn't quite remember what the disagreement had been about. Some matter of politics within the Observatory Trust. Or Peter not feeling he'd been treated with the respect he deserved. Peter had resigned as chairman and the other three had supported him. The weekend ritual of staying in the cottage ended abruptly. It was harder on Clive than the others. He had no life at all. Unless he had an alternative existence which he kept quite secret, and Gary wouldn't have put that past him. They still visited of course, but it was strange to turn up as an outsider.

Clive was already waiting on the pavement outside his mother's bungalow. 'We should have gone there yesterday when we left Fox Mill.' His first words, before even saying hello, before getting into the van.

And all the way on the drive north he was tense, hunched up in the passenger seat, his shoulders rigid. Gary talked about Julie, about her lad being killed. They all talked to Clive because they knew he could keep secrets.

'It must be a nightmare,' he said. 'Imagine what it must be like, losing your son like that! And for her daughter. She was asleep in the next room when it all happened.'

Clive didn't say anything. He only moved when Gary's pager flashed its red light and then he read out the updated news on the warbler.

The observatory was a quarter of a mile inland, the first patch of cover for migrating birds once they hit the coast. The house was a low bungalow, built before the war as a holiday retreat, with an acre of garden which now formed the reserve. It had been the location that had made it so special. The bungalow itself wouldn't have been out of place in any seaside town – a squat, rather mean building of brick and white stucco, made a little more attractive now by the clematis which grew around the porch and which was just coming into flower.

They'd driven east from the A1, down a narrow lane, the rising sun in their eyes, through an ugly village and then down a dirt track. The observatory was at the end of the track and when they arrived there were already half a dozen cars pulled into the verge. Gary recognized Peter's Volvo and the sporty little Volkswagen which Samuel had recently bought. Clive was out of the van before Gary had the engine switched off and was heading through the wooden gate into the garden, leaving him to follow and shut it after them. The garden was an oasis in the flat, bare land which surrounded the house. Inland, there was a vast stretch of open-cast mining, a moonscape of rocky ridges and pits; already huge lorries with fat tyres crawled over it. Between the house and a line of dunes which marked the coast, cattle grazed in a long narrow field.

The garden had been designed to attract birds and insects. They'd dug up the lawn and replaced it with a pond. Now vegetation had grown up all around it and over it, so the water was hardly visible. There were the flat shiny leaves of water lilies, a patch of reeds. Where once there had been herbaceous borders, there were huge spikes of buddleia for the butterflies and bushes which in autumn would produce berries to pull in the thrushes.

The mist nets were unfurled, meaning a group of ringers was staying. They must have found the Marmora on their first round of the nets. Behind the house there was a small orchard which had been planted when the house was built and it was here that the group of birdwatchers stood.

The Marmora's warbler had been seen on the top of a hawthorn hedge which marked the boundary of the reserve. The birdwatchers stood in the dappled shadow thrown by the apple trees, binoculars raised, looking. From a distance it was impossible to tell if the bird was there or if people were searching for it. By the time Gary arrived Clive had his tripod set up and was staring through the scope.

'It disappeared into the bushes ten minutes ago,' he said. 'Nobody can tell me exactly where it went in.' He sounded murderous.

Gary thought they'd all have been talking when the warbler flew off. On the other side of the group he could see Peter and Samuel, smiling and chatting. Once you'd seen a bird there was a release of tension and you relaxed your concentration. He stared into the hedge, felt his guts as a hard knot of anxiety. He didn't enjoy this sort of birdwatching. It was too stressful waiting, knowing the bird had been there. Not knowing if it still was. Since Emily, he hadn't been able to handle stress. He preferred sea watching. That was the most relaxing experience he knew, sitting in the watch tower next to the lighthouse. There was nothing you could do to make the birds fly past, so no point getting anxious. Now, as he felt his heart beat faster, he tried to control his breathing and wondered if he'd been right to come.

'There it is.' Clive, still bent over the telescope, spoke so quietly that only Gary could hear. 'About four metres in from the fence, on the bare branch just below the top.' And then Gary was on to it and it was filling his scope. He could see the inside of the bill when it began to call and the colour of its eye. Mind-blowing. Only the sixth British record and it was here in Deepden. Worth falling out of bed at six in the morning and the tension of the drive.

Around him other people had picked up his excitement and they were looking at it too. Then the bird disappeared behind the hedge again and they were all standing around grinning. Some people started wandering off, talking about bacon sandwiches and work. Clive remained focused, though, and when the bird reappeared, further away on a dead tree by the lane, he was the person to find it.

Peter Calvert was full of it. You'd have thought he'd found the bird himself.

'Every year we get at least one *British Birds* rarity. A reserve this small. And when we started they all said we were wasting our time.' Gary thought with amusement that he was still claiming credit for something that had happened forty years before. It didn't bother him, but he could see why the man got up some people's noses.

'I've got to go,' Peter said. 'I'm giving a lecture this morning. Can't disappoint my students. Are you coming, Clive? I can give you a lift into town.'

And though you could tell Clive would have liked a bit longer with the bird, he twisted the legs on his tripod and followed Peter to the car. Peter was still his hero. Gary thought he'd have run into a burning house if Peter had given the order. Outside in the lane cars were still arriving. One of the observatory committee was standing at the gate with a bucket, demanding money before he'd let people in.

Samuel and Gary went into the house. They were still paid-up observatory members, so no one could stop them. Once inside the door, Gary was taken back to the time when they'd been regulars. It still smelled of wood smoke in there, though it must have been months since the fire had been lit. Wood smoke and the waterproofing you rubbed into Barbour jackets and leather boots. They made tea, stole a couple of soft biscuits each from the tin in the cupboard and sat outside on the rusty wrought-iron chairs by the pond.

'What did you make of that business on Friday night?' Samuel asked.

It took Gary a moment to realize he was talking

about the girl by the lighthouse. 'That business' seemed an odd way to describe the discovery of a body.

'I don't know. That detective turned up at my flat on Saturday. The big woman who was at Fox Mill. The lad who died in Seaton was Julie's son. She was with me in town on Wednesday night, then she went home and found him. It must seem a strange coincidence, but she appeared to believe me when I said I didn't know anything about the girl.'

Samuel took a moment to speak. Gary had read a couple of his stories. It always shocked him that Samuel, so good-humoured, so ordinary, could write stuff like that. Stuff that haunted you, so you'd wake up in the night with the pictures still in your head. It was impressive, but a bit scary.

'You didn't know Lily Marsh, did you?' Samuel said at last.

'No! I'd never seen her before.'

Samuel seemed pleased by the answer. 'Perhaps we should start coming back here,' he said. 'Show them how it's done.'

But Gary thought Deepden had too many memories for him, of how he'd nearly lost it when Emily had left him. He'd needed the place then and the three good friends who'd held him together. But now, he thought, it was time to move on. Although he didn't have to be in the Sage until the afternoon, he told Samuel he had to get off to work. He went back into the house to drop off his mug, then he went to his van. The lane was so jammed with cars that it took him nearly half an hour to turn it round.

Chapter Twenty

It was Monday morning. Vera woke up as she always seemed to these days with a faint hangover, a sense that she hadn't slept properly. Her window was open and her neighbours' cockerel was drowning out every other sound, seemed to be living somewhere just behind her eyes. She realized she was an object of curiosity to the couple who owned the smallholding. They'd moved from the city and had made an effort to get on with her, had this ridiculous notion that country people had a wisdom about nature, saw it as almost mystical. Then they found out Vera was police and she could tell they thought they should disapprove. They'd gone on marches, saw the police as the enemy. Vera didn't bother one way or the other. Except occasionally she dreamed about strangling the cockerel.

She shut the window and went to the kitchen to make tea, ignoring the pile of dirty plates in the sink. The first sip of tea and she was already engrossed in the case, her mind buzzing, the guilt about her drinking forgotten. The cockerel dismissed. This was what she was made for.

Today she was planning a trip to Newcastle, the big city. That was how she'd seen it when she was a girl and still thought of a visit to town as an adventure. She collected Joe Ashworth from home on her way through. She knew she wasn't fit to be let loose on the academic world on her own. She was too loud and brash and she'd end up offending someone. Joe lived in a small estate on the edge of Kimmerston. He too had grown up in the city and this was all he'd ever dreamed of: a new house, professional neighbours, a family. His wife was pregnant again, nine months and uncomfortable. When Vera turned up she'd just emerged from bed, huge belly and swollen tits wrapped in a cotton dressing gown, bleary-eyed. Joe was giving his daughter breakfast to the background noise of Radio 2. The little girl sat in the high chair beaming, while Joe spooned in Ready Brek on a plastic spoon. More happy families, Vera thought. There was all that talk of family breakdown, but wherever she went there were people making a go of it. Making her feel inadequate and depressed.

She'd phoned Peter Calvert at home on Sunday night and made an appointment to meet him at the university. She wanted to see him away from his ideal home and his ideal wife. She used the flowers as an excuse. 'It would be useful for us to know where they might have been collected. It will take time for the forensic people to release them. You saw them, at the second crime scene at least. It could give us a head start . . .'

And he'd been delighted to be asked. She could tell that. 'I understand you're an expert,' she said and had almost heard him purring.

They arrived at the university a little early and he was at the end of a lecture. They stood at the back of the theatre, listening. Vera didn't take in what he was saying, just watched him perform. She'd been sent on a course once. Body language. She tried to remember what the psychologist had said about it, but nothing of it came back to her. What she could tell now was that Peter Calvert liked the young women. There were a couple of pretty lasses sitting a couple of rows from the front. They wore frilled muslin skirts and lacy tops you could almost see through, and he seemed to be directing his words straight at them. When one of them asked a question he complimented her on making an intelligent point and gave a little frown, to show he was taking her seriously. But maybe all sixty-year-old men would be the same, Vera thought. No harm in looking, even if you did make a fool of yourself. She didn't mind looking at young men, though she tried to be discreet.

Calvert still seemed to be in a good mood when he took them into his office. He fiddled with a filter coffee machine which stood on the window sill.

'I can only offer you black, I'm afraid. I don't take milk myself. Though I could probably borrow some from a colleague. You wanted to ask about the flowers.'

'Informally,' Vera said quickly. 'Not as an expert witness. We'll deal with that later if we need to. But speed is important at this point in an enquiry.'

'Of course.'

'You did see the flowers when your son found the body?'

'Yes. I mean, my first priority was to move James away. He was upset enough as it was. Bad enough to come across something like that. Even worse when we found out he knew her. So I didn't have time to study the blooms in detail, but of course I noticed them.'

'What did you make of them?'

'There seemed to be a mixture,' he said. 'Some wild flowers, the sort you'd find in a hay meadow. Poppies, ox-eye daisies, buttercups. The rest garden flowers. Perennials. I didn't see anything exotic or unusual.'

'Not the sort of thing you buy in a florist, then?'

'Oh no. Nothing like that. Picked. And fairly recently. Or kept in fresh water. They hadn't wilted. At least I don't remember them looking dead or tired.'

'Were there any you'd have in your own garden? I was thinking you could show us. We can look them up in a book, but it wouldn't be the same. And it might trigger your memory.'

'I'm not sure,' he said easily. 'You'd think I'd know, but Felicity is the gardener. You're very welcome to come round and have a look. Any evening you like. We're usually both in.'

'And you're absolutely certain you can't tell us anything about Lily Marsh?'

'Positive, Inspector. As you can see, this is a big community. Our paths never crossed.'

There was a knock at the door. A young man stuck his head round. 'You said you wanted to talk to me sometime today, Dr Calvert. Is this a good time?'

'Ah yes, Tim. Just give me a minute. If you've finished, Inspector . . . This close to the end of term everything's pretty hectic. There are some students I have to see.'

Vera thought this was too convenient. She wouldn't have put it past Peter Calvert to arrange the meeting with the student so the interview with the police didn't drag on. That didn't mean he had anything to hide, of course. He could just be an arrogant bastard who thought his time was too precious to waste on catching a killer. She smiled sweetly and led Ashworth out of the room.

Along the corridor there was an open-plan office where three middle-aged women sat in front of PCs. There were plants on the shelves, photos of grandchildren. They seemed to be having an intense conversation which had little to do with the university. Vera thought these might be people who enjoyed gossip as much as she did. She tapped on the open door and walked in, leaving Ashworth lurking outside. The room fell silent, but she thought they were curious, not hostile.

'I wonder if you can help me. My name's Vera Stanhope. I'm heading up the investigation into the murder of one of your students.' That had them gripped, as she'd known it would. It would keep them talking through until the lunch break. 'Dr Calvert's been giving us some expert advice. He's with a student and I don't want to interrupt him. I was wondering if one of you looked after his diary. I need to check a couple of dates, see when he's next free.'

A plump, motherly woman with grey hair waved her hand, like an excited child at the back of the class with the answer to a difficult question. 'That's me, for my sins. Marjorie. Marjorie Beckwith.'

Vera beamed. 'He updates it on the PC, I presume.'

'He's supposed to,' Marjorie said indulgently, 'so the rest of the department knows what he's up to, but he's not one for following guidelines, I'm afraid.'

And she reached to a shelf behind her and handed a black, hard-back book to Vera. It was that easy. Vera took it to an empty table, sitting so she had her back to the room and flipped through the pages. The day of Luke's death, Peter Calvert had attended a meeting of the department in the morning. At five o'clock he'd planned a tutorial with two students. There were no names, only initials. The entry had been scored through with two lines and someone had neatly written *cancelled* in the middle of them. The following Friday – the day of Lily's murder – he had a lunch appointment. No name. Just *12.30–2.00 lunch out, unavailable.* Presumably that was for Marjorie's benefit. The rest of Friday was clear. Vera flipped back the pages. It seemed the lunch appointment was a regular feature.

'I was thinking of meeting up with him on Friday afternoon,' Vera said, turning the diary a week on, seeing the page was empty. 'There's nothing here. He doesn't have a regular commitment? A lecture?'

'Oh no,' Marjorie said. 'Dr Calvert never lectures on Fridays.' She looked up, eager to help. 'Shall I make you a provisional appointment?'

'No thanks, pet. I'll give him a ring later in the week if we need his assistance.' Vera put the book back on the shelf, gave a little wave to the three women and returned to where Joe was still keeping watch in the corridor.

'Well?'

'He was free both afternoons. The Wednesday before Luke's death and the Friday before Lily's. He cancelled a tutorial at five o'clock on the Wednesday.'

'So he had the opportunity,' Ashworth said. 'Along

with fifty per cent of the population of the north east. But there was no motive. No connection, even. So far as we know he hadn't ever met the victims.'

Vera was going to say she didn't care. She didn't like the man. But she couldn't face a lecture from Ashworth about detachment and objectivity so she let it go.

Outside, it was still hot. There were students lying on the grass or sauntering into town in the shade of the Gothic buildings. They had more than an hour to kill before the next appointment and Vera had a sense of time passing, time wasted. She got on the phone to Kimmerston but there was no news. Holly had arranged to meet Lily's flatmates later in the afternoon and Charlie was trying to prise information out of her bank. They had a news conference set up for the following day and local plods would be at the lighthouse in the afternoon to ask regular walkers if they'd seen anything. The press officer would take the news conference. Vera was pleased. Those occasions always made her feel like a performing bear. She switched off the phone.

'Coffee,' Ashworth said. 'And a bun. I didn't have time for breakfast.' He could sense her frustration, knew food might calm her for a while. Vera thought he treated her as he did his daughter; he was distracting her before she threw a tantrum.

He sat her in the shade of an umbrella, on one of the seats set out on the pavement, while he went inside. The cafe was close to the university and seemed full of idle students. A couple of young women approached her table and she glared at them, hoping to frighten them off. Then she recognized them. They were the lasses from the lecture theatre, the ones Peter Calvert had been performing for.

'Sorry,' she said. 'No problem. You're welcome to join us. Let me move my bag.'

They looked at her uncertainly. As if she were a dangerous dog, she thought. Were the young taught any manners these days? Didn't they know they should be polite to their elders? Then Ashworth turned up, all soft words and smiles, and she realized why she'd come to rely on him.

'Let me buy you a coffee,' he said. 'You're students, right? I remember what that's like. Especially at the end of term when the loan's run out.'

One of them laughed. 'My loan disappeared a week after we started.'

'I'll get them,' Vera said and she went inside to buy the extra drinks, leaving him to tell a story which would pull them in.

When she returned, carrying a tray, they were laughing, easy together. He could have been a student too, though she knew fine well that he'd never stepped foot inside a university.

They introduced themselves. Fancy southern names which she couldn't remember five minutes after they'd told her. Camilla? Amelia? Jemima? It didn't matter. Ashworth would have made a note of them.

'This is Vera,' Ashworth said. 'My aunty.'

They sipped their frothy coffee and looked at him with pity. A duty day out, they thought. A treat for her birthday. Or maybe he was taking her to an outpatient appointment at the RVI. Vera gritted her teeth and let him get on with it.

'So you do botany,' he said. 'A mate of mine did that a few years ago. What's the lecturer called, the famous one? Calvin?'

'Peter Calvert. He likes to think he's famous but it's years since he published anything.'

'You don't like him?'

'He's a creep. Like, he's *really* old, but he still comes on to you.'

'Yeah, and everyone knows he's got a wife and four kids. I mean, you'd think someone in his position would have a bit more dignity. The whole department knows what he's like. But some people play up to it. You know, flirt, in the hope of getting extra marks.'

'Just flirt?' Ashworth asked, keeping his voice light. Like he was cracking a joke.

'God, you'd have to be *really* desperate to go any further. Can you imagine him touching you? God, you'd just throw up.'

'There was that rumour,' the other said. 'You remember, at the beginning of the term. Someone saw him out in town with a much younger woman. It got round that he was having an affair with a student.'

'Oh?' Ashworth said. Not really interested. Just being polite. I've taught you well, Vera thought.

'It was probably just a story,' the student said. 'No one got any details. And we tried hard enough to find out what was going on. I mean, it could have been anyone. His daughter, even. It certainly wasn't one of us. Not a botanist.'

And they floated off to the sound of the bangles clinking on bare brown arms, soft twittering voices.

Chapter Twenty-One

Joe seemed happy to sit there in the sun, nursing his fancy coffee until it was time to meet Clive Stringer, but Vera was impatient and restless. 'I'm going to see if I can track down Annie Slater, the woman who put up Lily's flatmates the night she died. She was one of Lily's tutors. And they lived in the same street. I'll see you at the museum.'

And before he could argue or offer to come with her, she'd gone. She'd had enough of Joe Ashworth acting as her minder. She felt like a naughty kid bunking off school and wondered if her male colleagues ever had the same response. She found Annie in a staff common room, standing by the pigeonholes, reading a sheaf of mail. Lily's flatmates had talked about her children; Vera thought she'd left motherhood until the last minute. She was mid-forties, well preserved. Her hair was very black, cut in a severe bob and her lipstick was very red. She took Vera into a small office and frowned at her. 'I haven't got long. I've a meeting in ten minutes.'

'It shouldn't take long. Just a few questions about Lily Marsh.'

'Yes,' she said. 'Poor Lily. It was a shock. One hears about these things happening, but it's seldom to a person one knows.' Vera thought the shock seemed well hidden. Her attention was still caught by one of the papers in her hand.

'Would she have made a good teacher?'

Annie hesitated for a moment, focused for the first time on the conversation. 'I'd probably describe her as competent but uninspired. And that's more than I could say for most of the students in her group. She worked very hard, prepared the lessons, related OK to the kids, but I didn't think her heart was in it. I couldn't see her still being a classroom teacher in twenty years.'

'Did she ever seem depressed or anxious?'

'I didn't notice anything, but then I probably wouldn't. This is a short course and there's not much contact time. You'd be better talking to her friends about that.'

I would, pet. But I'm not sure she had any.

'How did she end up doing her teaching practice in Hepworth?'

'She requested it. She said she'd read the school's Ofsted report and thought she'd get a lot out of a placement there. I was pleased that she was showing some passion for teaching and tried to wangle it for her.'

'How was she doing?'

'Well. I had a chat with the head teacher a couple of weeks ago. She said Lily was making a real effort to build relationships with the kids. Before that, I'd felt her teaching had been a bit mechanistic. I was pleased.'

'Did you know anything about her private life?'

Annie Slater looked up then, apparently astonished by the idea.

'Of course not. We were never in any sense friends.'

'You lived in the same street, you socialized with her flatmates.'

'That's rather different. There's a family connection to Emma.'

You moved in different circles. Vera had been at the wrong end of snobbishness, could sense it a mile off. Perhaps that's what prompted her to persist. 'You'd not heard any rumours, then, about Lily having a relationship with one of the staff here?'

'I don't listen to university gossip, Inspector.' Which wasn't any sort of answer at all. She turned back to the letter and left Vera to find her own way out.

Vera met up with Joe outside the Hancock Museum. They had to wait until a crocodile of small school children had been shepherded inside by teachers and parents. There was a dinosaur exhibition – reconstructed skeletons, models which moved. The adverts had been all over the city; tyrannosaurus heads leered out from posters on buses, the metro and shop fronts. The children were unusually quiet, overawed by the building, the thought of enormous beasts, *Jurassic Park* come to Newcastle.

Vera and Ashworth followed them in and stood in the lobby, enjoying the coolness of the museum, when Clive Stringer arrived to collect them.

'Great, isn't it?' Ashworth said, watching the children disappear into the gallery. 'Hooking the kids while they're so young.' A couple of years, Vera thought, and he'd be bringing his own lass here.

'I don't know.' Clive blinked uncertainly behind thick round spectacles. 'I don't really deal with the public.'

His kingdom lay behind a wooden door, opened by a swipe card. There was a series of high-ceilinged rooms, rows of dusty cabinets. There seemed to be few other staff around. He led them into a workroom. It reminded Vera of the place in Wansbeck General where John Keating had performed the post-mortem on Lily Marsh. There was a long table in the middle, deep sinks at one end, the smell of chemicals and death. Though everything here was older, wood and enamel instead of stainless steel, and it didn't have the scrubbed, sterile feel. The windows were so dirty that the light seemed filtered through them.

On a board lay the corpse of a black and white bird. Beside it a scalpel, wads of cotton wool, small metal bowls. Another sort of dissection.

'Isn't that a little auk?'

'Yes. First winter. It was blown inland during those gales last November and found dead in a garden in Cramlington. The householder brought it in. I've had it in the freezer since then, but I want to do a cabinet skin.' He looked at Ashworth, saw he didn't understand the term. 'We preserve the skin for research, not display. It's kept here at the museum, a resource for students and scientists.'

Vera's father, Hector, had been an amateur taxidermist. He'd worked on the kitchen table in the old station master's house. He hadn't bothered with cabinet skins, though. He claimed his interest was about science, but Vera had known he was deluding himself even then. He'd prepared mounted birds, always moorland species. Usually the object of his attention was a bird of prey, a trophy for whichever game-keeper had killed it. That was art too in a way, she thought. At the end of his career the activity was illegal, but that had never bothered Hector. If any-thing, it had increased his pleasure and excitement. He'd been an egg collector too. When he died Vera had set fire to the whole collection. A huge bonfire in the garden. She'd drunk his favourite malt whisky and realized she wasn't grieving at all. She'd just felt relief that he'd gone.

'How long have you worked here?' Ashworth was asking Stringer.

'Since I left school.'

'You don't need a degree to do something like this?'

'I started as a trainee.' He paused. 'I was lucky. Peter knew the curator and put in a word for me.'

'That's Dr Calvert?'

'Yes.'

'You've known him for a long time?'

'Yes, he was my trainer when I started ringing. I was fifteen then.'

'Ringing?'

'The study of migration. Birds are caught in nets or traps and small metal rings are put on the legs. If they're caught again or found dead, we can tell where and when they were first ringed.'

'And Mr Parr and Mr Wright are ringers too? That's how you met?'

'We don't ring so much now. I'm the only regular

at the observatory up the coast at Deepden and I don't go so often. The rest have other lives. More exciting lives. But we're still friends. We still go birdwatching together.'

'Sea watching?' Vera asked, joining in the conversation for the first time.

Clive gave something approaching a smile. 'Gary's the passionate sea watcher. The right time of the year he'll spend hours in the watch tower. I say it's because he's so idle. He doesn't mind the waiting. He says it's a form of meditation.'

'It must have been a shock, coming upon the body on Friday night.'

'Of course.'

'But perhaps not so much for you as the others,' she said. 'You work with corpses every day.'

'The corpses of birds and animals. Not young women.'

'No. Not attractive young women.' She paused a beat. 'Do you have a girlfriend, Mr Stringer?'

When she'd first seen him at the mill, she'd thought he looked like an overgrown, prematurely balding schoolboy. Now he blushed, furiously, and the image came back to her. She felt almost sorry for him.

'No,' he said. 'I don't have a girlfriend.'

'Are you gay?'

'No.'

She looked at him, waiting for him to speak.

'I find it difficult to approach women,' he said at last. 'I suppose I'm shy. And I don't socialize much. I live with my mother. She was widowed when I was a baby and now she's not very well. I'm all she has.'

Vera wanted to tell him to get out and get a life while he still had a chance. But it wasn't her place.

'Does Dr Calvert have a girlfriend?'

Clive stared at her, horrified. 'What do you mean?'

'A mistress. A lover.'

'Of course not. He's married to Felicity.'

'This might come as a bit of a shock, pet. But some married men do commit adultery.'

'But not Peter. You've seen them together. They're happy.'

They put on a good show, Vera thought. That's not the same thing at all.

But she smiled at him. 'Aye,' she said. 'Maybe you're right.' She nodded towards Ashworth for him to take over the questions.

'Were you working last Wednesday?'

'Yes, until four-thirty. I start at eight and I'm supposed to finish at four, but it's usually half past before I leave.'

'What did you do then?'

'I went home. I called at the supermarket on the way. We had a meal together. Mother usually goes to bed early. Around nine. After that I stopped up and watched television. I'd videoed a documentary on the rain forest. Mother tends to talk through programmes which don't interest her.'

'You didn't go out?'

'No.'

'You seem to have a very clear memory of what you did that night,' Vera said.

'I do have a good memory. I told you on Friday night, I'm good at detail.'

'Do you drive?'

'I can drive. I mean, I passed my test and I hold a driving licence. But I don't enjoy it. I'm always aware of the potential danger. And I have a conscience about the environment. Greenhouse gases. I decided a couple of years ago to do without a car. Public transport's quite good into the city centre. And I have a bike.'

Vera could tell Clive was uncomfortable. Although the building was gloomy and cool, he'd started to sweat. He fidgeted with the scalpel on the board in front of him. She told herself not to read too much into it. This was probably the longest conversation he'd had with anyone other than his mother for years. When he was with his friends, he'd be a listener not a talker. Now, she kept her voice easy, gossipy. His mother would probably enjoy a good gossip.

'Did Gary tell you about his new woman?'

The change of tone in the question seemed to surprise him and he took a moment to answer. 'He told us all about it.' He paused. 'It wasn't unusual. There's always some new woman in his life. He's mad about all of them. For about a week. None of them stay.'

'He said this one's different,' Vera said.

Clive smiled again. Like smiling was something he did about once every six months. 'That's what he always says. Ever since Emily left he's been looking for someone to replace her.'

'Emily?'

'They were engaged. She dumped him.'

'Did you know Julie, the latest girlfriend?'

'No. He doesn't take me out on his dates.'

'Her son was the lad who was murdered,' Vera said. 'Strangled. Like Lily Marsh.'

'I'm sorry.'

'I don't suppose you know a family called the Sharps?' she said, not really expecting a response.

'Davy Sharp lives in our road. When he's not in prison.'

'You came across the boy, Thomas?'

'I saw him about. My mother looked after him sometimes when he was a baby. She took a shine to him. He was there sometimes when I got home from work. Not recently, of course. Not once he was old enough to fend for himself.'

'She must have been upset when he died.'

'Yes, we went down to the river. She'd seen the flowers on the water on the news and wanted to see. To pay her respects.' He paused. 'There wasn't much to look at when we got there. The tide was on its way out. It had carried the flowers out to sea.'

They sat in silence. Through the open window came the sound of a siren, shouted voices.

'Tell me about these mates of yours,' Vera said at last. 'Gary, Peter and Samuel. They are your mates? Only you don't seem to have much in common. Except the birding.'

'We're close. Like family.'

'With you and Gary as brothers and Samuel and Peter as mummy and daddy?'

'Don't be ridiculous!'

She knew she was pushing him, wanted to see if he ever lost that control. He was very flushed.

'OK, then,' she said. 'So they're not really like family. Tell me why you get on so well together, what it is that's kept you together over all these years.' She was really interested and it showed. She wasn't sure about friendship. She had colleagues, the people she'd grown up with, who lived close to her in the valley. But no one she felt any obligation to, no one she had to put herself out for. She thought it could be a two-edged sword, friendship. You'd end up giving more than you got.

'Partly it's the birding,' he said. 'People outside don't understand. They think you must be geeky, weird. But it's more than that. Although we're very different, we trust each other. I feel supported by them.'

She gave a chuckle. 'Eh, pet, you've lost me now. That sounds like something from a women's magazine.'

He shrugged. 'I wouldn't expect you to understand.'

'What about Friday?' Ashworth asked. He gave the impression that he too was irritated by Vera's comments and questions, that he didn't want to be here all day. 'What did you do before you went to Fox Mill for dinner?'

'I met Peter for lunch.'

'Another birthday celebration?'

'No, nothing like that. We meet most Fridays. Just a pint and a sandwich. When we were more active ringers that's when the weekend would start. I work flexi so I could take the time off, we'd have lunch then Peter would give me a lift up the coast to the observatory. The others would join us later. We don't go out so much now, but still have lunch when we can.'

Vera thought sadly that it was probably the highlight of his week. Lunch with an ageing, self-obsessed man who only wanted an admirer.

'How was Dr Calvert?'

'Fine. Like always. Looking forward to the week-end.'

'What did you talk about?'

'I'm not sure . . .'

'You must remember. You have a brilliant memory. Detail. It's what you do.'

'He's writing a book. We talked about that.'

'And after lunch?'

'I went home to spend a couple of hours with my mother.'

'What about Dr Calvert?' Ashworth said. 'Where did he go?'

'Back to the university. At least, I presume that's where he went. He didn't say, but he walked off in that direction.'

'How did you get to Fox Mill?'

'Gary gave me a lift.'

'He picked you up from home?'

'No, he was running late and coming straight from work at the Sage, so we arranged to meet in town. I got the metro.'

He picked up the scalpel again, turned over the dead bird on the board, ran his finger over the skull. 'Really, I should be getting on with this. I don't under-stand the need for all these questions. I was there when a body was found. That was all. I'd never met either of the victims.'

Vera looked over at Ashworth to see if he had any-thing else to say. He shook his head. 'We'll leave it at that, then,' she said. 'For the time being.'

'I'll show you out.' Clive dragged his attention away from the little auk, walked ahead of them down the corridors, through the dust caught in shafts of sunlight from the long windows. He opened the door which separated the staff territory from the public domain, hesitated as if reluctant to go further. Vera stopped too and faced him.

'Would you tell us if you suspected one of your friends of committing these murders?'

He answered immediately. 'Of course not. I trust them. I know that if they've done something as appalling as commit murder, they must have a good reason.'

He turned and walked away, leaving Vera and Joe staring after him.

Chapter Twenty-Two

Felicity wandered back from the garden. She was holding a colander of beans for supper, too many she realized. There would be only the two of them this evening; James had arranged to be out with a friend. In the kitchen she had a moment of unease as she imagined herself and Peter, sitting at opposite ends of the table, eating dinner. She wasn't sure what they'd say to each other. She imagined Lily Marsh there too. A beautiful ghost, coming between them.

It was ridiculous the effect the death of a stranger was having on her. She told herself not to be hysterical. But this life she'd spent years creating – the house, the garden, the contented family – suddenly seemed very fragile. She had a picture of Vera Stanhope shattering it with her loud, intrusive voice, her big feet, the heavy hands slammed against the table. With her questions, Vera would wreck it all.

She glanced at the clock on the kitchen wall. There were pictures of birds instead of numbers and their calls marked the hours. It was a joke present from Clive to Peter for one of his birthdays. She hated it but Peter had insisted on putting it up. It would soon be two o'clock. There were at least four hours before Peter would be home. She ran upstairs, changed

from trousers into a skirt, put on lipstick and a splash
of perfume. As the wren finished calling she snatched
up the car keys from the hall table and almost ran
outside.

She had never visited Samuel at work. She wasn't
even sure where he would be. Certainly, she thought,
he would disapprove of this unplanned meeting. He
kept his life in separate boxes. But she couldn't stay at
home fretting. She had never made demands before.
He would understand that the pressure was intolera-
ble.

She drove along the straight, narrow roads, impatient when she had to slow down for a tractor. It was
an old car, without air conditioning, and she had the
windows open. The sun shone hot on her arm and
shoulder. In the town she slid into a parking space
in the street next to the library. Now she sat for a
moment thinking again that this trip had been a terrible mistake. Samuel was a clever man. If he'd thought
it sensible for them to meet, to discuss strategies, he
would have suggested it. He would consider this a
rash, foolish gesture. In the end her desire to see him
made her give up on reason. She shut the windows
and got out of the car. She was a member of the library
after all. She had every right to be there.

Inside the building it was cooler. A couple of
students and an elderly man were hunched over
their public-access computers. Behind the desk was a
thin, rather untidy young woman in crumpled linen
trousers and a white cotton blouse. She caught Felicity's eye and smiled at her. She looked familiar.
Felicity thought vaguely that she might be the daughter of one of her book group friends.

The book group had brought her and Samuel together. She loved the company of the group, the excitement of trying a book new to her, and when she had been a member for a year, she had persuaded him along to give them a talk. A real published author. The group had read his most recent anthology beforehand and hadn't known quite what to make of it. The stories were so depressing, they said. Well constructed but twisted and rather horrible. One woman said they gave her nightmares. Generally they preferred happy endings. When he visited, though, they were more positive. They sat him in the big armchair in front of the fire. They were meeting for this session in the home of a large, capable woman who worked as a physiotherapist. Her husband was a surgeon and the room was quite grand. Green walls covered with paintings, large, old furniture. It was February, cold, and the curtains were drawn against the chill weather outside. The audience was wholly female. They drank white wine from tall glasses. Samuel had charmed them, speaking as if their opinions were important to him. He talked about the structure of the stories. These days people were obsessed about character, he said. Character was important, that was a given, but anyone could write faithfully about people like themselves, or people they knew. He was more interested in ideas. His themes were reflected in the construction of his plots. He wasn't so interested in portraying reality, but in creating a world where the most unlikely events were possible.

'It's the only way one has to play God,' he said.

One woman asked if that made him more like a poet than a novelist. He smiled, delighted, and said perhaps it did. Felicity had thought it all went way above her head. She worried about what she might say to him when they were alone.

'But wouldn't you make more money writing real, long books?' This came from a farmer, who read voraciously but understood nothing of literary snobbery. She never bothered with reviews or award lists. There was a moment of silence. The other women were afraid that he'd been offended. But it seemed that question had pleased him too.

'If I wrote a novel I'd get caught out,' he said. 'I'm not that good an author. I can't keep going for more than five thousand words.' He turned towards Felicity, giving her a look of complicity. The light from the fire caught his face. The women in the room laughed. She could tell that they all admired him.

Felicity had given him a lift to the book group and it had been arranged that she would take him home. In the car he suggested they go for a drink and she agreed. It was the least she could do. Her standing in the book group had changed because she'd introduced him to them. The pub was crowded and noisy, not the sort of place either of them would usually have chosen. Perhaps they landed there because it was so anonymous. They had a small table to themselves, crushed into a corner.

The announcement came out of the blue. He took her hands in both of his and said he thought he loved her. At first she couldn't believe he was serious. It was a joke. He was a great one for games. Nothing could come of it, he said. He was Peter's friend. Then she saw he was deadly serious and she was very flattered, moved. How noble and honourable he was! In the pub car park, which looked out over bare, open hillside, she reached up and kissed him. Droplets of mist clung to his hair and his jacket.

Later, back at his house, she asked, 'Aren't you going to invite me in for coffee?' She knew exactly what she was doing, had already considered which underwear she was wearing, remembered that she had shaved her legs that morning. He had hesitated for longer than she expected. Perhaps his friendship to Peter was so strong he would refuse. But at last he nodded, held open the door for her, took her hand once they were inside. That had been five years ago. They had been lovers ever since. Very discreet. There were no phone calls which couldn't have been overheard, no emails which might not have been read. They met every few weeks, usually in his neat little house in Morpeth. This was quite different from the public friendship – the trips to the theatre or the ballet. Nothing intimate ever took place on those outings.

Even after all this time, she didn't consider the relationship as an affair. There was nothing romantic about it – no flowers or presents or candlelit dinners. She knew Samuel felt a continual guilt. He never talked about love after that first meeting. And she had never once considered leaving Peter. He needed her. She saw the delight and excitement Samuel gave her as a wage, her dues for living such a boring and unadventurous married life, for keeping the Calvert show on the road. She knew it wasn't the way women usually looked at things, but couldn't see why they couldn't all maintain a civilized friendship. At least, she had thought that until Vera came blundering in with her questions.

Now Felicity wandered around the library shelves, as if she was having difficulty choosing a good read. She couldn't see Samuel, but that didn't mean he wasn't working here. He was a manager, would have an office somewhere behind the door which said STAFF ONLY. He would be there, or in a meeting with his staff, or out of the region altogether on a trip to one of the big library suppliers to select books. She encouraged him to talk about his work in the little house in Morpeth when they drank tea together before they separated. She was always fascinated by other people's working lives, and when she lay in her afternoon baths she imagined him sitting at his big desk, or chairing a meeting in his precise and authoritative way. It excited her that none of his staff could possibly guess what he did on his days off.

She was preparing to ask at the desk if he was in the building when he appeared through the STAFF ONLY door. He was carrying a briefcase and seemed to be on his way out. He was wearing an open-necked shirt and a pale linen jacket, a concession, she supposed, to the weather. Usually when they met up, if he'd come straight from work, he wore a tie. He dressed very well and cared what he looked like. At first he didn't see her. He was smiling at the young girl behind the counter. Felicity felt a stab of physical discomfort which she realized was jealousy. She wondered if he took other women to his house on his free afternoons.

Then he turned and saw her. He gave no indication that they knew each other. He said to the young woman, 'I'll be in Berwick for the rest of the afternoon. But if anyone phones, tell them to call back tomorrow. This is an important meeting. I don't want interruptions.'

Felicity caught up with him outside. He was walking down the pavement towards his car. If she hadn't hurried after him, perhaps he would have driven off without giving her the chance to talk to him.

'I'm sorry, Samuel. I had to speak to you.'

He must have heard her footsteps following, but he affected surprise.

'I really do have a meeting in Berwick.' He frowned, seemed more nervous than displeased.

'Just ten minutes.' Now that she was here, she wasn't sure what she wanted from him. Reassurance, she supposed, that everything would continue as normal.

He agreed to meet her in the Little Chef on the A1 and was already there when she arrived, apparently engrossed in the menu. Even walking towards him she sensed he was frightened, that he needed reassuring more than she did. The place was almost empty. The windows were all open and the traffic noise came in from outside. They ordered tea from a sweaty youth, stared at each other.

'You know something,' she said suddenly. 'Something about the girl. Lily. Had you met her?'

'No. Nothing like that.' But he was blustering, not at all his usual controlled self. This wasn't like one of his stories. He couldn't make the plot work out.

'The boy, then. Luke Armstrong. You'd heard about him?'

'I think Gary was going out with his mother. That woman he was talking about. She was called Armstrong. I'm sure she had a son. It's a link.'

'I told that detective Gary was seeing someone called Julie. He wouldn't kill anyone!'

'Of course not. But they don't believe in coincidences.'

It seemed a tenuous connection to her. A woman called Armstrong who had a son. How many Armstrongs were there in the phone book? Samuel must know more than he was letting on.

The waiter came back with their tea. As he lowered it to the table, liquid slopped onto the tray. He paused, expecting a reaction from them, anger, complaint, but they sat in silence until he left them again.

'I was worried that detective would find out about us,' Felicity said.

'How could she?' But she saw that the idea had occurred to him too. Perhaps that was why he seemed so uneasy, so unlike his usual urbane and confident self.

'I wondered if perhaps we should tell her, in confidence,' she said. 'That way she would know it could have no bearing on the girl's murder.'

'Of course it has no bearing!' His voice was impatient. She imagined he might speak in the same tone to a foolish library assistant. She felt tears come to her eyes.

'We know that.' She tried to sound reasonable. 'But Lily Marsh came to Fox Mill the day before she was murdered. You can imagine the police jumping to conclusions, building up a scenario. What if we were together that afternoon and she saw us? That might give us a motive for killing her.'

She waited, expecting another angry response, but he smiled. 'You should write fiction,' he said. 'A creative imagination like that. We weren't together, were we? Not in the afternoon. I was at work all day on Wednesday. Book selection, then Library Management Team. I'd be able to prove it. We only met up in the evening to go to the theatre. Besides, James was there with you when the girl was at your house.'

'Yes,' she said. 'He was.'

Samuel looked around the room. There were no other customers now. The staff were at the counter, engrossed in conversation. He reached across the table and took her hand. 'How can anyone know?' he said. 'We've been so careful. I'd hate it to come out. It would seem so squalid. How could people understand?' He pulled away from her and leaned back in his chair. His voice was still very low and she had a struggle to make out the words. 'I couldn't bear it if Peter found out. I'd die.'

Chapter Twenty-Three

When they'd finished with Clive Stringer, Vera took Joe home. She could tell he was fretting about his pregnant wife and his daughter. But she couldn't settle. She called into the police headquarters at Kimmerston and raged around the building, demanding action and answers. Holly was out, but Charlie was there, hunched over his desk, staring at the computer screen. His waste bin was overflowing – empty Coke cans, burger cartons, greasy chip paper. She remembered hearing that his wife had recently left him for a younger man. Like Vera, he probably didn't have much to go home to.

'Nothing unusual about Lily Marsh's bank account,' he said. 'She had a bit more money this year because they get a grant for doing the post-graduate teaching course, but she still spent pretty much up to her student overdraft limit. No mysterious payments to suggest a rich boyfriend. She was paid direct into her account by the dress shop, but it wasn't a fortune. Better than the minimum wage, but not by much.' He paused. 'Something a bit odd, though. I can't tell how she paid her rent. Not by cheque and it wasn't covered by standing order. No regular withdrawals of cash either.'

'Maybe she had a different account,' Vera said. 'Building society. Internet account. Perhaps there's a statement in that material we recovered from her flat. Get onto it, Charlie. She was living beyond her means. She should have been massively in debt. But she wasn't. Something doesn't add up.' And she stamped away without giving him the chance to complain.

She set off for home then, but she knew she'd only start drinking as soon as she got in. She was in that sort of mood. A large whisky before she scratched together a meal and downhill from there. Passing the Morpeth turn-off she decided to call on Samuel Parr. She'd have seen them all, then. The whole group. The four birdwatchers who claimed they had nothing to do with the murders except being present when the body was found, but who seemed tangled up with the case all the same. Gary, who had fallen for Luke Armstrong's mother. Clive, who, as a kid, had known Luke Armstrong's best friend. And Peter Calvert, who worked at the university where Lily Marsh had been a student. In the north east there were a lot of small communities, all interlinked. There were always going to be connections. Perhaps it was of no sig-nifi-cance, but she couldn't ignore it. And where did Samuel Parr fit in?

He looked as if he had not long arrived home. When she rang the bell of the small stone house, he answered immediately. He'd been standing in the hall. Perhaps he'd just shut the door behind him. There was a briefcase at the foot of the stairs. He wore a linen jacket, slightly crumpled.

'Is this convenient?' she asked. Samuel Parr was a minor local celebrity. She'd looked him up. His stories had been read on Radio 4. He'd got an OBE in the people's honours for service to libraries. She'd best treat him with a bit of respect. At first, at least.

'Yes, of course, Inspector. Come in. It'll be about that business on Friday night. Dreadful.' He took off his jacket and hung it on the banister. 'I'm late home. A meeting in Berwick. Awful traffic on the A1.' He was tall, bony and his hair was very short.

She remembered hearing one of his stories. She never bothered much with television, but the radio was on all the time at home. It had been a domestic tale. A man and a woman in a loveless marriage. A stranger in town who had become a lover. The ending had been horrific and quite unexpected. The couple had collaborated in killing the lover. They needed the stability and routine of their marriage more than the excitement of love or of loss. Vera tried to remember what they had done to the body. She knew it had been disturbing. Not explicit in the description of the violence, but so chilling, that it had haunted her for days. So chilling perhaps that she'd forced it out of her mind and the details wouldn't return. Now, looking at this quiet, middle-aged man, she found it hard to believe he had dreamed up the tale. She thought she should get the anthology out of the library. See how the story had ended.

'I always indulge in a glass of wine at this time of the evening. Can I tempt you?'

She thought he was playing up to the stereotype of the librarian. Surely he didn't talk like that while he was in the watch tower and the skuas were streaming past in a northerly gale. Then he'd shout and swear like the rest of them.

'Thank you,' she said.

'I only have red, I'm afraid. I live alone, so I just buy to suit myself.'

'You never married, Mr Parr?'

'I'm a widower.' There was a pause. 'Claire, my wife, committed suicide.'

'I'm sorry.' She'd always thought suicide the most selfish act.

'She'd suffered from depression since before I knew her. I didn't understand how desperate she was. Of course I'll always blame myself.'

He'd led her into a long narrow room, which covered the width of the house. He opened a window and let in the song of a blackbird, the smell of cut grass. He turned his back on her to stand at a Victorian sideboard and open the wine. She couldn't make out if he was as calm as he seemed. She wanted to ask how his wife had killed herself. Had she drowned? It wasn't a question to ask over a glass of Australian Shiraz, and anyway she'd be able to find out. There'd be a coroner's report. And where had she been treated for depression? On the wall, there was a photograph of a woman, her head thrown back, laughing. Claire? It seemed to be the only record of the woman in the room.

He turned now and held out a large glass of wine to her. She nodded at the picture. 'She was very pretty.' He didn't answer.

She took the wine, sat on a scarred leather Chesterfield, waited for him to speak. He told stories for a living. Let him go first.

'It was a terrible shock, finding the young woman's body,' he said. 'Hearing James scream, my

191

first response was irritation. I never felt any desire to have children, even when Claire was alive. I know we should encourage them into the library, but really my attempts are half-hearted. They're so noisy. Such a nuisance. Then when we saw that young woman, her hair floating to the surface, her dress . . . I was reminded of a Pre-Raphaelite painting. The muted colours in the shadow. Perhaps it was because we were looking down at her, seeing it at a distance.'

'It looked staged,' Vera said. 'Posed, like a model for an artist?'

'Yes.' He looked up, surprised that she'd understood him so easily. 'It wasn't just that someone wanted her dead, it was that a point was being made.'

'You didn't recognize her?'

'No.'

'And now, having had time to consider, you're sure you'd never met her?'

'She didn't look like a real woman,' he said. 'I can't be certain I'd know. But the name means nothing to me.'

'We found a Northumberland Libraries ticket in the belongings in her flat.'

'I don't know all our borrowers, Inspector.'

'Why would she join if she lived in Newcastle?'

'If she worked in Hepworth, she might find our branch there more convenient than the city library. It opens only a few hours a week, but it's very close to the school. Perhaps she just wanted to access her emails.'

'Would you be able to tell us what she borrowed recently?'

'Is it important?'

'Probably not,' Vera said. 'But I'd be interested to know. Curiosity . . .' She grinned at him. 'Probably something writers and detectives have in common.'

'I couldn't tell you now, even if I went into work. Our system will be shut down for the day. I could look tomorrow and let you know if there any books outstanding on her ticket. I can't do more than that.'

'Do you think you can tell what people are like from what they read?'

He laughed. 'Absolutely not. Many of our readers are gentle old ladies, who adore the most gruesome American thrillers.'

Vera found that she was enjoying herself. It was the wine, but he was good company. Easy. She'd been expecting someone restrained and dull, but now he seemed more relaxed too.

'What got you into birding?'

'A good teacher,' Samuel said. 'He took us on field trips. I grew up in a suburb of the city and it was a revelation to visit the hills. I suppose I have a romantic response to natural history rather than a scientific one. I enjoy beautiful things.'

'Dr Calvert takes the scientific approach?'

'Yes. We went to the same school. He's a few years older than me, but we met in the Natural History Society. Separated for university, but we've been friends ever since. He was into science; I loved reading.'

'Why did he do botany? Why not zoology?'

'He says he prefers to have birdwatching as a pleasure, not a chore.'

'Did you know that Gary had a new girlfriend?'

The sudden switch in conversation didn't seem

to throw him. 'I knew he'd fallen for someone.' He paused. 'It couldn't have been the murdered girl, you know. That was the sort of woman he'd usually have gone for. But his latest conquest was different, I think. Someone older, someone he'd gone to school with. We laughed at him, asked if he was growing up at last. He's in his thirties, but he's always played the part of wild adolescent in our group.'

'The new woman in his life is called Julie Armstrong. She's the mother of a lad who was strangled in Seaton the Wednesday before Lily Marsh died.' She looked up. 'Hadn't you heard? You're such close friends, I'd have thought one of them would have told you. The others know.'

'They might have tried to phone,' he said. 'I've been in meetings all day and I've only just got in.'

'If Gary is the wild adolescent, what part does Clive play?' She realized she'd finished her wine and put her glass on the table. She wondered if he'd offer her another, if she could accept it and still be under the limit.

Samuel thought for a moment. 'Clive's an obsessive,' he said. 'A brilliant birder. The best of us by far. He reads field guides like I read fiction, but he remembers every word. He's not wonderful company in the pub. He doesn't make us laugh. Not like Gary. Not like Peter even, if he's on form. But he finds the birds for us. He reminds us what brought us together in the first place.'

'Where were you on Friday before you arrived at Fox Mill for the birthday party?'

He looked at her over his glass. 'Am I a suspect,

Inspector?' He wasn't angry. He seemed to find the idea amusing.

'I need to rule out anyone involved with the victim, even peripherally.'

'I wasn't. Not while she was alive.' He set down the glass. 'I'm sorry, Inspector, I shouldn't take this lightly. You're entitled to ask your questions. I was working on Friday afternoon in the library in Morpeth. I took some time back and left early. At about four o'clock. Then I came home. I was re-drafting a story. I wanted it finished to take with me that evening.'

'A present for Dr Calvert? Something you'd written specially for his birthday?'

'Nothing like that. Peter never reads fiction. Felicity enjoys my work. And I value her opinion. I wanted her to look at it before I sent it off to my agent.'

Vera wanted to ask what the story was about, but could see that it probably wasn't relevant. Perhaps she just wanted to prolong the interview so she wouldn't have to return to an empty house.

'Can anyone confirm that you were here? Any phone calls or visitors?'

'I'm afraid not. And I never answer the phone when I'm writing.'

'Perhaps a neighbour saw you leave for the party?'

'You can check, Inspector, but I'd be surprised. This is a neighbourhood where people mind their own business.' He smiled. 'Some more wine, Inspector? Just half a glass as I know you're driving.'

She was tempted, but she shook her head and stood up. She wondered why he was being so pleasant to her. Men seldom bothered to make an effort with her and Samuel wasn't flirting exactly, but he wanted her to like him. Was that habit? He worked with eccentric middle-aged women. Perhaps he'd developed it as a management style. Or did he have some other reason for wanting her onside?

He walked with her to the door, shook her hand, and stood in the small front garden while she opened her car door. Driving away she felt she'd been in a small way seduced by him. He'd controlled the conversation. Things had gone just as he'd wanted.

Chapter Twenty-Four

Gary had been thinking all day about going to see Julie. The idea had got into his head and he couldn't get shot of it. It was a bit like those annoying bits of music that run in a loop in your brain. That Comic Relief song a few years ago, for instance. You try to replace it with something better, but the effort just makes it worse and the crap song gets louder and louder, so you can hardly think straight.

He'd been doing a technical rehearsal at the Sage, in the small space. He was working from the sound desk in the body of the hall. The artist was a poet, who spoke and sometimes sang with a band behind her. Usually when he was working, he couldn't consider anything but getting the sound spot on. The Sage was tremendous for large orchestras, but something small and intimate like this, it was tricky to get the balance right. The band was good, bluesy and moody, and he wanted to do them justice. Though poetry wasn't at all his thing he caught himself listening to the lyrics. Perhaps it was because the artist reminded him of Julie. She didn't look like Julie – she was black, for one thing, and younger – but there was a warmth about her and she was big and she laughed a lot. So all day he'd been wondering about Julie and how he could get in contact with her, and whether that would be a good idea or just gross.

He had a few hours free between the rehearsal and the performance. It would be a late-night gig, attracting people mellow from the bar and the arty crowd who didn't have to get up in the morning. He walked down the steps towards the river, the heat hitting him after the air-conditioned building. You'd never think Gateshead could get this hot, he thought. Gateshead should be a biting east wind and sleet. At the top of the bank the Ferris wheel turned slowly. Looking back, the Sage was lit up, so you could see the two halls inside the outer skin of glass. He thought they looked like two great ships. The large hall was like a liner, with rows of decking, number two like a snub-nosed tug. He'd been intending to wander across the footbridge and into town to get some food, but suddenly changed his mind.

He ran back up the steps to the car park and then he was in his van, the engine running, driving north. He wanted to see her house. It didn't mean he'd come to a decision about seeing *her*. He could drive down the road, turn round and come straight back. But that would be better than nothing.

Then he remembered them all in the pub after the Bird Club meeting, him talking about Julie and Peter mocking him. *My God, how romantic the young are these days. All moonlight and flowers*. And Gary, driving down the Heaton rat runs, avoiding the worst of the town traffic, knew that was what Julie had come back to on the night her son had died. Moonlight and flowers. That was what the inspector had meant when she said Luke's murder had been similar to Lily's. It had been posed in the same way.

He knew where Julie's house was. He'd looked up her address in the phone book. It was only a quarter of a mile from where she'd lived as a kid. He'd grown up in the village too, though the other end, on the new private estate, which wasn't new any more. It felt strange coming back. He'd come down the main road from Whitley every day on the bus when he was in high school. Memories came flooding into his head, at last pushing out his concern for what Julie would make of his turning up on the doorstep. Loud lads shouting on the top deck, throwing bags around. Him easing his arm round Lindsay Waugh's shoulders, nibbling her ear lobe, while she blushed bright scarlet and everyone cheered. And sitting next to Clive, on their way to a green-winged teal on the River Blyth, pretending not to know him, because he was such a nerd and a geek, and what would Lindsay and the others say if they'd known Gary was a birder too.

Without realizing it, he was in the village and turning into Julie's street. It was six o'clock and the kids were out playing. A couple of mothers sat on the doorsteps watching them. Since Luke's death he supposed this was how it would be. He was aware of their staring. A stranger in the street. If they hadn't been there he would probably have gone to the end of the road, sat in the car, lost his bottle, and driven away. But they made him defiant. And cautious. He was Julie's friend. What was wrong with paying his respects? Besides, one of them would probably have made a note of his registration number by now. If he drove straight off they'd be on to the police reporting a suspicious character, claiming they'd frightened him away.

So he parked up right outside the house, and without looking at the staring women he walked up the path and knocked on the door. Standing there, he thought he should have brought something with him. A gift. But what? Not flowers. How insensitive would that be! Wine, perhaps; but then that would imply that he was gatecrashing a party. He stood, his hands slid into the front pockets of his jeans, because he didn't know what else to do with them. Sometimes, after too much Stella and a vindaloo, he had this nightmare. He was standing on the stage at the City Hall in front of a full house, fiddling with a mic, the sound all wrong. Stark naked. That was how he felt now.

The door opened. It was a young girl in school uniform. Sort of uniform. White shirt, short black skirt. No tie. He wondered if he'd got the wrong house, then remembered that Julie had another child, a daughter. He scrabbled in his mind for a name. Laura. But before he had a chance to call her by it, a middle-aged woman scurried out from the back. She had a pair of oven gloves dangling from one hand and the air of an ineffective bouncer. 'Laura, pet, I told you to let *me* open the door.' The girl paused for a moment, staring at him, then she shrugged and disappeared upstairs.

The older woman turned to Gary, more aggressive now. 'Who are you? We're not talking to reporters. The police'll be back in a minute.'

'I'm not a reporter. I'm a friend of Julie's.'

The woman stared at him. She had very small eyes, fierce.

'Julie's not up to seeing anyone.'

He was about to give up, almost relieved. He could leave a message. That way at least Julie would know he was thinking about her. Then there was a voice, hardly recognizable. 'Mam. Let him in. I want to see him.'

The woman paused for a moment then stepped aside. Once he'd walked past her into the house, she shut the door loudly on the prying neighbours.

He went through into the living room, noticed in passing how untidy it was, wondered if it was always like that. Considered briefly if he'd be able to live in such mess. It was certainly nothing like Fox Mill, which had always been his ideal home. The windows were covered by thin white blinds which kept out the worst of the sun and the prying eyes. They made the room shadowy. It was hard to make out detail. Then he saw Julie, curled on the sofa. He sat beside her, took her hand. The woman stood in the doorway, anxious and protective.

'I was just getting dinner,' she said. She was almost growling, the words coming from the back of her throat.

'It's all right, Mam. He's a friend.'

'I'll be in the kitchen.' That was directed to Gary. A warning and a threat. She glowered at him and left the room.

'Sorry about Mam,' Julie said.

'Don't worry. I'd be just the same if I was here looking after you.'

She gave a brief smile. He stroked the back of her hand.

'I'm so pathetic,' she said. 'I can't do anything. I just sit here all day.'

'You couldn't be pathetic. Never.'

'I should be strong for Laura.'

He thought he could hear the echo of her mother's words in the phrase. He didn't know what to say. He wasn't sure what he thought of Laura, skinny and long legged. There was something about her which reminded him of Emily and he found that disconcerting. Behind the blinds the window was open. The bairns in the street were playing a skipping game, chanting. He hadn't heard anything like it recently. It was years since he'd seen girls skip. Perhaps one of the guardian mothers had taught it to them, dredging the rhyme out of her memory. It took him back to Seaton primary school, running round the playground with Julie Richardson, playing kiss chase on the green when nobody was looking. Perhaps she was having the same thoughts, because she joined in with the words.

'. . . *I never should, play with the gypsies in the wood.*'

She stopped suddenly. Outside, the rhyme continued without her.

If I did, she would say . . .

'I feel so stupid,' he said. 'Just sitting here. Nothing to say. Helpless.'

She squeezed his hand. 'No,' she said. 'You're helping. Honestly.'

'I wasn't sure whether I should come.'

Then she did something unexpected. She pulled him down to her and kissed him. A real deep kiss, pushing her tongue into his mouth, against his teeth, down his throat. He held her tight against him, felt her breasts soft against his chest, the beginnings of desire. Despite himself. Knowing that nothing could happen. Not with her daughter and mother in the house. Not while she was so screwed up. But singing inside, because in the end it would work out. All those dreams he'd had about her since meeting up with her again. Luke wouldn't get in the way of that.

He pushed her gently away from him, stroked her cheek, bent and kissed her hair at the parting, where he could see the darker roots. She was crying.

'Oh God,' she said. 'I'm sorry.'

He knew he shouldn't feel like this. He should be sad because she was sad. 'Nothing to be sorry about.' He kept his voice serious, low. Low voices were sexy, weren't they? 'Do you want to talk about Luke? I mean, I never met him, but if you want someone to talk to . . .' Behind her back he twisted his wrist so he could see his watch. He had to be back at the Sage for eight-thirty.

'No,' she said. 'I've done nothing but talk about Luke for days. To the police, Mam, my mates. I wanted to forget about him. Just for a minute. I wanted to see if I could.'

'Could you?'

'Not really.' She smiled. Not quite the old Julie smile. 'But I enjoyed trying.'

There was a noise at the door. He was expecting her mother again but it was Laura. She stood just inside the room, staring at them. Gary moved along the sofa so there was some distance between them.

'Laura went to school today,' Julie said, in a horrible, bright voice. 'I thought that was dead brave. How was it, pet?'

'All right. The teachers were nice. There was an assembly about it. About Luke and that. They said I didn't have to go.'

'Did you?'

'Nah. But I waited outside and I could hear what they were saying. It was all crap. I mean, it wasn't like they were talking about Luke at all. You wouldn't have known it was him they were talking about.'

'Nice, though, for them to remember him, to pay their respects.'

Laura looked as if she was about to say something rude and dismissive, but she kept her mouth shut.

'This is Gary,' Julie said. 'He's an old friend. We were in the primary together.'

It was as if Laura hadn't heard. 'Nan says tea's nearly ready.'

Gary stood up. 'I should get off.'

'Why don't you stay?' Julie said. 'Have something to eat with us?'

But he could tell she was back in coma mode. She was just going through the motions.

'I'm working tonight,' he said. 'A gig at the Sage.'

He started towards the door. He wondered if she'd rouse herself from the couch to see him out, but she seemed lost in thought again. It was Laura who opened the door to let him out. The kids stopped their game to stare and the women on the steps looked up from their magazines. He expected the girl to be intimidated by the attention. He found it difficult to handle himself. He wanted to shout at them: *What do you think you're looking at?* He thought Laura would shut the door on him immediately and hurry inside. But she didn't. She was still standing there while he got into the van and drove away.

Chapter Twenty-Five

Tuesday morning. Vera had called the team together for an early meeting. Charlie looked as if he'd slept at his desk; certainly he hadn't shaved. Joe had Ready Brek down the front of his shirt. Only Holly seemed awake and alive. Looking at her, so fit and bonny, Vera felt a horrible, destructive envy. Even when she was young, she'd never looked like that. When she arrived they were all sitting round a table. Joe was talking about Clive Stringer.

'What about him?' she said, coming in at the tail end of the conversation.

'If we're looking for a nutter, he's pretty weird.'

Is he? Vera thought. She'd grown up with several odd young men like that. Loners, obsessives. Acolytes of her father.

'I mean, he spends all day with his hand up a dead bird's bum, no friends apart from the group at Fox Mill, no girlfriend.'

Vera wondered if Joe would describe her as a nutter. She didn't have many friends either.

'What's his motive?' she asked.

'I don't know. Maybe he came on to Lily and she rejected him?'

'We'd need some proof that they met. And that doesn't explain Luke.'

'Envy, then? They were attractive and young. Perhaps that was enough for him.'

'There's no evidence,' she said. 'Nothing. And he doesn't have transport.'

'He has a driving licence. Nothing to stop him borrowing a car.'

'Who from?' Vera demanded. 'You said yourself he has no friends.'

'He could steal one, hire one.'

'Aye,' she conceded. 'He could. Check the car-hire places. They'd remember him.'

'We should talk to his mother too.'

'Of course,' she said, only just keeping her temper. 'But we'll keep an open mind.'

Joe shut up then and she had the sense that he was sulking. He thought she'd worked with him long enough to realize he'd not need telling that. Quite often he was the one who had to keep her on track.

'All right,' she said. 'What else have we got?' Implying, give me something useful. Not speculation or prejudice. She kept her voice calm. This wasn't a time for panic, though they should have a suspect by now. As they sat she was aware again of time passing, the possibility that these were random killings with no understandable motive, that they'd find another beautiful young person drowned and dressed in flowers.

Charlie shifted in his chair, cleared his throat in a way that reminded Vera of winos in doorways about to spit. It made her want to gag.

'I've found out where Lily's rent came from.'

'Where?'

'A building society account in her own name. The North of England. There was a passbook in the stuff the search team found in her room. She got a cheque made out from that once a month.'

'What went into it? Her wages from the dress shop?'

'Nah, I told you. They were paid direct into her current account.' He leaned back in his chair. Vera wanted to scream at him to get on with it. 'She paid in five hundred pounds every six weeks or so.' He paused again. 'Cash.'

'Where would she get that sort of money?'

He shrugged. 'Maybe she did a bit of high-class soliciting on the side. Some students do. So I understand.'

Another occasion there might have been sniggers. *How would you know about that, Charlie?* But they must have realized Vera wouldn't appreciate the humour.

Vera thought of the clothes in Lily's wardrobe, the expensive lingerie, the clothes that had the air of fancy dress. 'I suppose it's possible. Take a photo to some of the likely hotels in town. See if anyone recognizes her.'

Holly raised her forearm from the table. A polite student with a point to make.

'Yes?' Vera hoped her impatience didn't show.

'Or she could have a rich lover . . .'

'Any evidence of that?'

'I spoke to her flatmates.'

'They told me there *was* no one.' Vera could tell she sounded defensive, couldn't stop herself. 'At least, if there was, they knew nothing about him.'

'They were embarrassed to admit they listened in to one of Lily's phone calls. There's an extension in the kitchen. It only happened once. They were just desperate to know what was going on. I knew they would be; I mean, it's only natural, isn't it? I pushed them on it a bit. Lily was ringing out. They picked up the kitchen phone and listened in.'

'And?'

'No details,' Holly said. 'Nothing useful, like a name. Not even proof that she was having an affair with him. They think she must have suspected they were listening because she ended the call very quickly.'

'What *did* they get?'

'An older man. Educated, well spoken. An arrangement to meet for dinner.'

'That could have been anything. A relative. Colleague. Boss from the shop.'

'It doesn't sound like a relative,' Joe said. 'If there'd been anyone like that in the family you'd have thought Phyllis would have mentioned him. Bragged, like.'

'I don't suppose they did anything useful,' Vera said. 'Like follow her and see what he looked like.'

Holly grinned. 'Nah. They were tempted to book a table in the same restaurant, but they're well-brought-up lasses. Thought it wouldn't be right to spy on her.'

'I hate well-brought-up lasses,' Vera said.

'Luckily the women she worked with in the dress shop weren't so picky.'

Vera smiled slowly. She thought perhaps she could take to Holly after all. 'What did you get from them?'

'Nothing exciting,' Holly admitted. 'I mean, nothing really useful. But confirmation that the meetings with the older man weren't about a family connection or to do with work. She did talk a bit more freely with the girls in the shop. I think she felt more easy with them. She liked the idea of sharing the posh Jesmond flat with the classy southerners, but they didn't have much in common.'

'Tell me.'

Holly pulled out a small notebook, covered with her open schoolgirl writing. A swat wanting to impress.

'About six months ago she came into work wearing a new ring. Opal and silver. Antique. She said it was a present. He'd bought it when they were out for the day in York. It was the first time they'd spent the night together—'

Vera interrupted. 'Did they get the name of the hotel?'

'No. But one of them could remember what Lily had said about it. "That's the great thing about going out with someone a bit older. They know how to do things properly." They asked her how old he was, but she wouldn't say. "You wouldn't understand." One of them asked if he was old enough to be her father. She hadn't answered but she'd laughed so they guessed he probably was.'

'They never saw him?'

'No. Like I said, nothing really useful.'

'Oh believe me, pet. There's plenty useful here. Dig out the ring. Charlie, is it in the stuff the search team brought in?'

'I don't think so.'

'Check again. I don't remember seeing anything like that in the flat, but it must have been there. Then someone can have a fun day out in York, visiting the antique shops and the jewellers. Unless her mysterious lover paid for it by cash, we've a reasonable chance of tracking him down. And let's have someone on the phone to all the decent hotels.'

'Isn't it obvious?' Joe said.

'What do you mean?' Vera turned on him.

'We heard from Peter Calvert's students that he was having it off with a younger woman.'

'We heard there was a rumour going round,' she said. 'Nothing definite and no proof. And even if the rumour was true there are a fair few bonny young students in Newcastle for him to choose from. Doesn't mean it was Lily Marsh.'

Besides, she thought, Peter Calvert isn't the only older man floating around the edge of this case. There's Samuel Parr. Lily had a Northumberland Libraries ticket, could have bumped into him too. And if I had to choose between Peter Calvert and Samuel Parr, I know which one I'd go for every time. And the elaborate crime scenes were much more Parr's style. But she didn't say anything to the team. She kept her suspicion to herself. A private pleasure. A possibility to surprise them at the end of the case. If she turned out to be right.

She realized they were looking at her, waiting for

her to continue. 'Well?' she demanded. 'Anything else?'

Joe leaned across the table towards her. 'I've tracked down Ben Craven.'

She knew the name should mean something to her, but it didn't. He watched her. She could tell he was pleased with himself. *You're getting a bit smug for my liking.*

'The lad she was passionately in love with when she was in the sixth form. The one she got so obsessed about she messed up her A levels.'

'Of course,' she said as if she'd known all along. Fooling no one. 'What's he up to now?'

'He went away to university. Liverpool. Did a social work course. Moved back to the north east last summer. Guess what he's doing now?' He looked at them, savouring the moment, before answering his own question. 'He's a psychiatric social worker at St George's. The hospital where Luke Armstrong was treated.'

'Did he work with Luke?' Vera wasn't in the mood for games.

'I don't know. I haven't had a chance to talk to him.'

'Don't. Not until I've had a chat to Julie. We don't want to frighten him away.'

Why hadn't Joe told her this as soon as he'd found out? She felt like demanding an explanation. But this wasn't the place. Not in front of the others. He's getting complacent, she thought. Cocky. He thinks he can take me for granted.

Perhaps he sensed her anger, because he became

apologetic. 'I spoke to his mum only just now. Just before the meeting.'

I take him for granted too, she thought. Think of him as family, expect more of him than I should.

'Samuel Parr's wife committed suicide,' she said. 'I want the background, how she died. Charlie, can you look into that?'

He nodded and scribbled a note on a scrap of paper.

'Anything from the lighthouse? Anyone remember seeing a murderer with the body of a young woman under their arm?' She knew it wasn't funny, but it was getting to her. The nerve of the killer. The cheek of him.

'Nothing useful yet. Someone said Northumbria Water were working there for an hour. I'll check if their guys saw anything.'

'Well,' she said brightly. 'We've all got a lot to get on with . . .'

Charlie cleared his throat again. The ball of phlegm seemed constantly stuck in his gullet. 'There is something else. Probably nothing.'

'Spit it out, Charlie!' Thinking, as soon as the words came out: *But not literally, pet. No, not that.*

'I found this in the middle of all the papers we got from the search team,' he said. 'And I thought, with the flowers, like, it might be important.'

He held it in a clear plastic bag. A piece of cream card, A6 size, and, stuck to it, a pressed flower. Yellow, delicate. Some sort of vetch? Vera thought. There'd been a craze for pressing flowers when she was a kid. One of the teachers had started them off. You stuck the flower between blotting paper and weighed it down with heavy books – there'd been plenty of those in Vera's house – but she'd never much seen the point. Clearing out the house after Hector had died she'd come across one of her attempts among the pages of one of his field guides. A primrose, picked, pressed, then forgotten for more than thirty years. It had gone onto the bonfire with the rest of the crap.

'Anything written on the back?'

Charlie turned over the plastic bag. XXX in black ink. A row of kisses. It could have been a card made by a child for a mother. But this was something different, Vera thought. A love token?

'Was it in an envelope?'

'No, just like this.'

'No chance of DNA, then.'

'It suggests Peter Calvert, doesn't it?' Joe Ashworth said tentatively.

'Maybe.' She found it hard to imagine the arrogant lecturer taking the time and effort to make the card. Wouldn't it be just the sort of thing he'd sneer at? 'Perhaps Lily did it herself, but never got the time to send it. Or it could have been preparation for something she was planning to do with the kids in her class. Get it to forensics. They might give us something on the glue.'

She was still sitting at the table after the rest of them had gone. She poured the last of the coffee from the Thermos jug, took her time over drinking it. She couldn't get rid of the feeling that someone was playing with her. She was a piece in an elaborate board game. Real murders weren't like this. They were brutal and mucky. Unplanned usually, always ugly.

She tried to remember Julie Armstrong, staring at the telly in the front room at Seaton, Dennis Marsh hiding in his greenhouse; tried to persuade herself that she wasn't enjoying every minute.

Chapter Twenty-Six

The doctor had given Julie tablets to help her sleep. Every night she thought they weren't going to work, then sleep came in an instant. It was like being smashed over the head, a sudden unconsciousness. For the first time, that morning she remembered dreaming. She woke abruptly as she always did with the pills. It was early morning. She could tell by the noise of the birds and because there was no traffic in the street. The curtains were thin and the light came through them; it was sunny again.

Her first waking thought was of Luke, as it had been every morning since he'd died. The picture of him lying in the bath, the heavy scent, the condensation running down the mirror over the sink. But she was immediately aware too that he hadn't been the subject of her dream. It had been a sexy dream, the sort of daydream she'd conjured up after Geoff had left, when she'd thought she'd never have sex with a man again. In this dream, she and Gary were walking along a beach at night. There was a heavy moon just above the horizon, the sound of waves. The sort of thing you'd read in a cheesy magazine, one of those mags for old ladies which her mam took on coach trips. But then the dream shifted and they were in the dunes, making love. She remembered the weight of him on top of her, the sand rubbing against her back and her shoulders, his tongue in her mouth. Now it was like the memory of a real event, not a dream at all. Lying in bed she put her right hand on her left breast and believed it still felt tender, as if it had been pressed and squeezed. She started to move her hand down over her stomach and between her legs, then stopped herself. There was a shock of guilt. What was she doing? How could she even consider sex at a time like this? What sort of mother had she been? She should have sent Gary away the day before. What had possessed her to let him into the house?

She looked at the alarm clock by her bed. Nearly six o'clock. She zapped the remote and the portable TV on the chest of drawers came to life. She dozed, watching the moving pictures, not listening to the words, until her mother came in with a cup of tea and a pile of post. She could tell there were more cards. All her friends sending messages of support, telling her how sorry they were. She knew what they'd be like. Pictures of crosses and churches and lilies. She hadn't been in a church since they'd had Laura baptized, wondered what it was about dying that brought out the religion in everyone. She hadn't been able to face opening the mail and added the new envelopes to the mound of unopened post by the bed.

All morning she struggled to banish thoughts of Gary. Her mother seemed to sense she was more unsettled today and tried to distract her. Or perhaps she thought Julie had had enough moping around and it was time she pulled herself together. She wasn't given to sentiment and was easily irritated. She got

Julie up for breakfast, then set her to making a packed lunch for Laura to take to school. When the girl was out of the house and Julie was still sitting at the kitchen table, staring into space, she brought the bundle of letters and cards down from the bedroom.

'These need answering, Julie. You can't just ignore them. That'd be rude.'

Julie had been wondering where Gary was today. She had his number, hadn't she? She could phone him. She had this fantasy that he would come and collect her, take her to work with him. There'd be a dark room, flashing lights and a rock band. Really loud music which would blow away all the other thoughts from her head. The thumping of a bass which she'd feel vibrating through her body. Then the guilt hit her again and, as a sort of penance, she sat as her mother told her, a mug of milky coffee at her elbow, and began opening the cards.

When the doorbell rang, she felt her pulse racing. Gary had come back. Her mother was upstairs making the beds but she shouted down, 'Don't worry. I'll get it.' And Julie stayed where she was and made herself breathe slowly, telling herself over and over again that it was wrong to be thinking about a man at a time like this. Then she heard Vera Stanhope's voice, loud enough that you'd believe the whole street could hear, and she felt like bursting into tears.

Vera came into the kitchen and sat beside her. 'Sorry to interrupt again, pet. Just a few more questions.'

Then she noticed what Julie was doing, saw the one opened card on the table. 'That's bonny. Did it come today?'

And for the first time Julie looked at the image on the card. No church this time. It was one of those classy handmade things which cost a fortune. A pressed flower on thick cream card. She was going to pick it up to look at the message on the back, but Vera stopped her, physically stopped her by putting her great paw over Julie's hand.

'Humour me, pet. This might be important. Was it delivered today?'

'I'm not sure,' Julie said. 'I haven't been able to face opening them. They've been arriving since Friday.'

'Still got the envelope?'

'Aye, it's there on the table.'

She watched, dazed, while Vera took a pen from her pocket and flipped the envelope over so she could see the postmark and the address. She couldn't think what could be so important, didn't really care, stared out of the window at a tractor driving round and round a field in the distance.

'This isn't addressed to you,' she heard Vera say. 'It's addressed to Luke.'

Then she did look at the envelope, which was white, not cream, and didn't seem to belong to the card.

The writing was in black ink, in capitals. LUKE ARMSTRONG, 16 LAUREL WAY, SEATON, NORTH-UMBERLAND. No postcode.

She looked up at Vera. 'That's wrong,' she said. 'This isn't Laurel Way, it's Laurel Avenue. Laurel Way is round by the school.' Still she couldn't understand what the fuss was about.

'It was sent on Tuesday,' Vera said. 'First-class

stamp. If they'd got the address right it'd have got here on Wednesday.'

'If it'd arrived on Wednesday, Luke would have opened it. No way would I have opened a letter addressed to him. I might not have done it today, if I'd realized. I just assumed it was for me.' She watched Vera sitting there, frowning. 'It came with the others on Friday. Must have done. Is it important?'

'Probably not, pet. Let's just see what they had to say. Don't suppose you've got a pair of tweezers I could borrow?'

Julie went upstairs to fetch them, glad of the action. Her mother was in the bathroom. Julie could hear the sound of water, then the hiss of the spray cleaner. Every day her mother cleaned the bath, bent over it, rubbing away so you'd think the colour would come off on the cloth. It didn't make any difference. Julie still hadn't felt she could use it. But the bathroom door was shut so at least she didn't have to explain what was going on. Back in the kitchen, Vera held the card carefully with the tweezers and turned it over. The back was blank.

'Maybe some sort of joke,' Julie said.

'Aye. Maybe. But I'll take it away with me, if you don't mind. Get it checked out.'

Julie had a fleeting moment of curiosity, but it passed. Really, what did it matter what the inspector was up to? She flicked on the kettle to make Vera coffee. When she returned with a mug in her hand, the card and the envelope had disappeared.

'You said you had some questions?' She had no interest, just wanted to get this over as quickly as possible. Why? So she could return to her fantasy world of mindless heavy metal and a boy she'd first chased around the playground when she was six? She opened the biscuit tin and pushed it across the table. Vera took a chocolate digestive and dipped it in her coffee, bit it quickly just before it dropped.

'Did Luke have a social worker?'

'There was someone who came round when he first started having problems at school. Nosy cow.' Julie hadn't thought about her in years. She'd gone in for long cardigans and flat shoes, thick tights in strange colours. She'd had a mole on the side of her nose. In her head, Julie had called her *the witch*. 'I can't remember her name.'

'Anyone more recently?'

'I didn't need a social worker. I managed fine.' She looked at Vera suspiciously. 'And I don't need anyone sticking their oar in now. It's bad enough having my mother around the place.'

'I know you're managing,' Vera said, in a way that Julie knew she meant it. 'But we're looking for connections between Luke and the lass that was killed. It might help us find out what happened. Did you talk to one of the hospital social workers?'

'I don't think so. But it's possible. I mean, it's not like a real hospital where the nurses wear uniform and you can tell who everyone is. They all looked the same. Doctors, nurses, psychologists. All so young you'd think they were just out of school. They had name badges, but I never bothered looking at them. My head was so full of crap I knew I'd never remember. And every time I went, there was someone new.'

'This was a young man,' Vera said. 'Not long out of

university. Name of Ben Craven. Does that mean any-thing?'

Julie wanted to help. She wanted to make Vera smile, to please her, but when she thought about those visits to the hospital everything was a blur. All she could remember was the smell – stale cigarette smoke and old food – and Luke's huge haunted eyes. 'I'm sorry,' she said. 'He could have been there. I don't know.'

'But he never came to the house?'

'Oh no.' Julie was quite sure about that. 'He never came to the house. Not while I was here.'

'If someone came while you were at work, Luke would have mentioned it?'

Julie considered that. 'I'm not sure,' she said. 'He wouldn't keep thoughts for very long in his head. He couldn't pin them down. He wouldn't mean to keep it a secret, but it just might not occur to him.'

'Might Laura know?'

'Luke was less likely to talk to her than to me.'

There was a silence. She could tell the inspector wanted to get off, but after resenting Vera turning up, now she was reluctant to let her go. 'If you have any news,' she said, 'you will come and tell me? Straight away?'

Vera stood up and took her mug to the sink to rinse it.

'Of course,' she said. 'Straight away.' But she had her back to Julie while she was speaking and Julie wasn't sure she could believe her.

Chapter Twenty-Seven

Felicity saw James onto the school bus and walked slowly down the lane towards Fox Mill. Since Peter's birthday nothing concrete had changed. She still washed and shopped and cooked every night. She made sure James did his homework and over dinner she asked Peter if he'd had a good day at work. She lay beside him in bed.

She'd tried the night before to talk to him about the dead girl. Through the open window came the smell of the garden, but underneath cut grass and honeysuckle was an imagined hint of the sea. In her head she was taken back to the watch tower, to the clean salt air, the seaweed and the flowers floating on water.

'Do you think they know yet who killed her?' she asked.

She was lying on her back, staring up at the ceiling. She knew he was still awake, but he took so long to answer that she wondered if he was pretending to be asleep.

'No,' he said at last. 'I don't think they have a clue. They came to talk to me today. That woman inspector and a younger man.'

'What did they say?' She turned so she was facing

him, could just make out the shape of his face. At one time she would have reached out and stroked his forehead, his eyelids, his neck. His lips and inside his mouth. She'd loved the intimacy of his skin on her fingertips. Now, not even their feet were touching.

'They asked if I could identify the flowers. I'm not sure . . . That could have been an excuse.'

'They can't think that one of us had anything to do with it.'

'No,' he said easily. 'Of course not.' And he'd gathered her into his arms as he might have done when they were first married. A father comforting his child. She'd lain quite still, pretending to be comforted.

Walking down the lane, in and out of the shadow thrown by the elders, she thought that while on the surface everything seemed the same, in fact it never would be. Immediately after the idea came into her head she dismissed it as melodramatic nonsense. The trouble was that she had nobody to talk to about it. Of course she'd told her friends about finding the body, in fact over the last couple of days she'd described the incident so often – on the telephone, in different kitchens over mugs of coffee and glasses of wine – that she was no longer quite sure what was true. Had she embellished it slightly for effect? But what she couldn't share with her friends was the suspicion, right at the back of her mind, that someone she knew might be a murderer. Just as she had confided in none of her friends about her relationship with Samuel.

In the empty house, she thought what she needed was company. Peter's birthday had been ruined by the murder. She should organize a party, a barbecue, bring the boys back to do it properly. But she recognized an edge of desperation in the plans and knew that if she did go ahead with them the evening would be horrible, worse than the last time. A failure. Then she thought she would invite her daughters to stay, with their partners and families. They could have a grand family celebration. At least in her role as mother and grandmother she felt secure. She would talk to Peter that evening. It would be something to discuss. It would fill the deadly silence over dinner.

When Joanna, her youngest daughter, came to visit she and her husband always stayed in the cottage. It was a tradition which had started when Joanna first went to university. She'd come back one weekend with a group of friends and Felicity had thought they'd cause less fuss there. They could stay up all night drinking and listening to music without disturbing Peter or keeping James awake. Now Felicity decided she would prepare the place for their stay. She put cloths, a dustpan and brush, dusters and polish into a bucket and walked through the meadow to the cottage. Her mother, kneeling on cold stone to polish pews on which nobody would ever sit, had talked about the therapy of cleaning. She would put the theory into practice.

She hadn't been in there since the weekend, when Vera Stanhope had asked to see inside, and nobody had stayed since Christmas. Despite the weather it smelled damp and musty. She hadn't noticed it so strongly before. Perhaps that had put Lily Marsh off renting. Perhaps that was why she had rushed off without giving Felicity an answer. She propped the door ajar with a pebble and opened all the windows. With the door open the mill race seemed closer. As she worked she could hear the water outside.

She stripped the bed and put the sheets and pillow cases in a pile at the foot of the stairs, dusted the chest of drawers, polished it with beeswax. Then she stood on a chair to clean the bedroom window, lowering the sash so she could reach outside. Her mood was lifting already. She caught herself humming the snatch of a song which James had brought home from school. She fetched a broom from the cupboard in the kitchen and swept under the bed, pushing the dust ahead of her over the bare wooden boards into a pile. She gathered the pile into the dustpan, realized she hadn't brought bin bags with her and carried it carefully downstairs.

She washed the tiles in the bathroom, scrubbed the top of the oven and inside the kitchen cupboards, brushed more dust into a pile. Then she decided she needed coffee. There was a jar of instant in the cottage and some powdered milk, but she deserved better than that. She left the cottage open to air and went back to the house. The long grass was feathery against her bare legs as she walked across the field.

She put the kettle on and checked the phone. One message. It was Samuel. Bland and distant as he always was. *Perhaps you could phone me back if you have a minute. Nothing urgent.* But even that contact thrilled her. She thought he wanted to meet, imagined walking into the house in Morpeth, him greeting her. She dialled his direct line. No answer. She was disappointed, but pleased too. She'd try again later and it would be something to look forward to. Delayed gratification. She poured the coffee into a Thermos mug. She thought she would take it to the cottage, drink it sitting on the step looking out over the water. She recognized how childish the morning had been. Mary Barnes would have spring-cleaned the cottage a few months ago, would do it again if Felicity told her Jo was coming to visit. This morning she'd been behaving like a little girl playing house. At the last minute she remembered she'd need a bin bag and went back to fetch it.

Drinking the coffee she thought of Samuel, his long bony spine and his slender back. Behaving like a girl again, she thought. Really, it's time I grew up. But she smiled to herself. She went back into the cottage and closed the windows. She flushed the toilet to wash away the bleach. She scooped up the dust in the pan and tipped it into the bin bag. And saw something glittering. She set down the pan, stooped and picked the object out. A ring. Very attractive. Blue-green stones in an oval silver setting. An art deco design. Vaguely familiar. It must belong to one of the girls, she thought, pleased to have rescued it. Joanna probably. It was the sort of thing she'd love. How careless of her not even to realize it was missing.

It wasn't until she was back at the house, in their bedroom, on the wicker chair next to the phone, preparing to call Samuel again, that she remembered where she'd seen the ring. It had been on Lily Marsh's finger. Felicity had noticed it when Lily had reached out to help James with his violin after they'd got off the bus. She'd coveted it secretly even then. It must have been loose on the young woman's finger, slipped off sometime during the guided tour. Felicity set it on the bed. The quilt was of thick white cotton and the ring looked magnificent against it. She was tempted to keep it. She slipped it onto her own middle finger. It fitted perfectly. Who would know? Since her friendship with Samuel, all sorts of wickedness seemed more possible. She relished the idea of behaving against type, against the expectations of her family and friends who would have described her as a very *good* person. With the ring still on her finger, she dialled Samuel's number. He answered immediately.

'Parr.'

'It's Felicity. Returning your call.' She always identified herself though she knew he must recognize her voice. Even when there was nobody to overhear they maintained the pretence that there was nothing between them but friendship. Until they were alone together in his house.

'It was good of you to get back to me.' He paused. 'How are you?'

'Well,' she said. 'You know . . .'

'And James?'

'Oh he's fine too.'

'I wondered if you'd heard any more from the police.'

'They went to see Peter at work yesterday.'

'The inspector came to me too. At the house.' Felicity felt a moment of disgust. It was almost sacrilegious, that big, ugly woman sitting among Samuel's lovely things. He continued, 'I'm not entirely sure what she wanted.'

She didn't know what to say to that and found herself coming out with the inconsequential information which was still at the front of her mind. 'I've just found a piece of jewellery belonging to Lily Marsh. A ring. It was in the cottage. She must have dropped it while I was showing her around.'

'Have you told the police?' She was surprised by the urgency in his tone.

'No, not yet.' She kept her own voice light, playful. 'It is *very* pretty.'

'You can't think of keeping it!' He was shocked. 'You must tell them. Straight away. If you don't, they'll think you have something to hide.'

'It can't be that important. They know she was in the cottage.'

'All the same,' he said. 'They'll see it as evidence.'

'All right. I was only teasing.' She thought he could be very high-minded and preachy.

'And I was only thinking of you.' This was as intimate as he got on the phone and she was surprisingly moved. 'Please phone Inspector Stanhope. Now.'

'All right.'

'Promise?'

'Yes,' she said. 'I promise.' Then, 'Are you free this afternoon?'

'No, I've got a meeting.' She couldn't tell whether he was telling the truth or whether he was still nervous about them being together. Perhaps he imagined the inspector knocking at his door, demanding to be let in, while they were making love. How he would hate that, being caught when he wasn't entirely in control. She thought that her relationship with Samuel was something which had also been quite changed by the discovery of Lily Marsh's body.

'I must go,' he said. 'I'm wanted on the desk.' He ended the call without properly saying goodbye.

She sat for a moment, looking out of the window at the lighthouse shimmering in the heat haze, then picked up the telephone again to speak to the police.

Chapter Twenty-Eight

Vera arranged to meet Ben Craven in a day centre for psychiatric patients. He spent one day a week there meeting the clients who'd been discharged from hospital. It was on the edge of a coastal town which had once been famous for its docks. Now, it's only claim to fame was as the drugs capital of the north east.

On the way, she stopped at the library in the town centre, a Gothic red-brick building, with a clock tower and a huge painting in the lobby of a ship in full sail. She found a collection of Samuel Parr's short stories on a shelf marked LOCAL AUTHORS. She wasn't sure what he'd think about being displayed in that way. Was it an honour? Or did it mean he wasn't good enough to go on the shelves with the real writers? She stood browsing for a moment, but couldn't find the story she'd heard on the radio. In the end she decided to take it out anyway. When she handed over the book and her ticket the library assistant said, 'Such a lovely man. He came here to give a reading last year. He's one of our staff, of course.'

That made Vera think of her last conversation with Samuel Parr. He'd said he'd tell her what Lily had been reading. Still curious, but also interested what Parr's response to the request would be, she decided to follow it up. Sitting in the car she phoned Morpeth Library and asked to speak to him.

'Ah yes, Inspector. Let me just check the system. What was the name? Lily Marsh?'

What are you playing at? she thought. Of course you remember the girl's name. You found her body.

'There are no books outstanding on her ticket, Inspector. I'm afraid I can't help you.'

She switched off her phone, feeling unreasonably disappointed.

The psychiatric day centre had once been a nursery school and, walking in, Vera had the uncomfortable feeling that everyone here – even the staff – had regressed to early childhood. In one of the rooms an art class was taking place. The patients wore red aprons to protect their clothes, they used thick brushes and bright acrylic paint. In another, there was some sort of music lesson with tambourines, cymbals and a couple of glockenspiels. But everywhere was the smell of cigarette smoke. She'd never bothered much if other people wanted to kill themselves, but could feel this in her throat and lungs and she knew she'd have to change her clothes to get rid of the stink. She had to walk through the common room to find the social worker. The chairs were arranged in small groups, but nobody seemed to be talking to anyone else. Everyone was smoking. A thin woman was talking under her breath. Some long story about her rent and the council hounding her. The other people in the room ignored her.

Craven had a small office at the end of a corridor. His door was open and she saw him before he noticed her. He was sitting at a desk hitting computer keys with a speed she'd never master. Her first thought was that he looked good. He was the sort of young man you'd notice in the street, follow with your eyes just for the pleasure of seeing him move. Tall, blond, muscular. A tan to show off the eyes. He was squinting at the screen but she knew they'd be blue. He must feature in the fantasies of many of his female clients. No wonder Lily Marsh had fallen for him. What a couple they would have made.

He heard her approaching and looked up.

'Yes?' Just one word but that gentle, patronizing tone professionals use to mad people. A smile to make her feel at ease. He thought she was a patient. She wondered if she spoke to witnesses like that. Like they were children.

'Vera Stanhope,' she said. 'Inspector. We've got an appointment.' Brusque enough for him to feel awkward. A silly power game, which she'd usually despise.

He reached out and shut down the computer, stood up in the same movement, held out his hand.

'Inspector. Tea? Coffee?'

'No, thanks,' she said.

'Is it about one of my clients? Perhaps we should get my boss to sit in.'

She ignored that. 'Look,' she said. 'Is there anywhere else we can go to talk? Maybe get some lunch?'

'Do the mentally ill make you uncomfortable, Inspector?'

'Don't be daft, lad. I've worked with more loonies than you've had hot dinners. And I don't just mean the offenders.'

He smiled and she thought he might be human after all. 'I usually take a break around now.'

They walked out into the street. On the other side of the road was a narrow stretch of dune then the sea. In the distance a power station in the process of demolition. He led her down a terrace of double-fronted Edwardian houses, still stately despite their surroundings, and into a pub. The Mermaid. A carving like a ship's prow over the door. At night time they probably dealt drugs here, like everywhere else in the town, but now it was quiet, restful. A couple of old men with pitmen's wheezes playing dominoes in one corner. A middle-aged couple at a table eating steak pie and chips.

Craven ordered orange juice and a sandwich. She went for a half of Workie Ticket and a burger. Standing at the bar to pay, she looked at him, caught in the dusty sunlight, until she realized she was staring and turned away.

'Luke Armstrong,' she said, as soon as she sat down. 'Does the name mean anything to you?'

'Isn't that the lad who was killed in Seaton?'

'You knew him, then?'

'No, I never worked with him. But I heard other staff in the hospital talking. Gossiping. That's how I know he'd been an inpatient at St George's. I don't think he was ever referred to the social work department.'

'You didn't see him in hospital?'

'I might have done in passing while I was visiting someone else on the ward, but I certainly don't remember. Look, you really would be better talking to my boss. She'd know if there was any social work input with the family.'

'What about Lily Marsh?' Vera said. 'You *did* know her.'

He sat in complete silence. Still as a statue. Gilded by the sunshine. A bit of art she'd have in her house any day, she thought, only half as a joke.

'I haven't seen Lily since I was eighteen.'

'You heard she'd died too?'

'My mother phoned at the weekend,' he said. 'She told me there'd been some sort of accident. Lily was drowned. Up the coast somewhere.'

Vera wondered if that was the story Phyllis had spread round their village when she'd first been told of her daughter's death. Did she think it was shameful to be a murder victim? Not quite nice? It wasn't a fiction she'd be able to sustain for long.

'Lily was strangled. Just like Luke Armstrong.'

'You're saying the two deaths are connected?'

Bright too. Not just a pretty face.

'We don't get that many violent deaths in this part of Northumberland,' she said, not hiding the sarcasm. 'Not in one week anyway.' Then, watching him. 'You don't seem very shocked. It's a nasty business. You were very close to her at one time.'

'Of course I'm shocked.' He looked up at her. 'But not surprised. Not really. I don't believe in natural victims, but she wasn't an easy person to be close to. There were times when I felt like killing her. Not her fault. I saw that even then. I wanted to understand. Perhaps that's what pushed me into this line of work. But it didn't stop me feeling like strangling her.'

'Tell me.'

'I was in love with her,' he said. 'That mad, passionate obsession that you only get when you're a teenager. I wanted to write poems to her, spend every minute with her—'

'Fuck the pants off her,' Vera interrupted helpfully.

He laughed. 'Well, that too, I suppose. But in a very tasteful and romantic way. We'd been reading Lawrence. I imagined it in moonlight, on a pile of hay. Something like that. Young people are so pretentious, aren't they?'

Vera thought of Luke Armstrong and Thomas Sharp, stealing from building sites, mucking around on the quayside, standing up for each other when the bullying started. Not all young people, she thought. A plump, motherly woman walked up with their food. Vera waited until she'd returned to the bar before continuing.

'Did it live up to expectations?' she asked.

'At first.'

She wanted to ask if they'd done it outside, like his fantasy, but thought that was just prurient. She was like the sad middle-aged detectives who had their day made when they were asked to go through a mound of seized porn.

She was about to tell him to get on with it, but he continued without prompting. 'It was the autumn at the beginning of year twelve. I mean, that was when I plucked up courage to ask her out. There was a band I knew she liked at the City Hall. I managed to get tickets, asked if she'd like to go. I'd just passed my driving test and persuaded my mother to let me borrow the car for the night. There'd be no other way of getting home that late. I was so nervous before I asked if she wanted to go with me. I remember I was shaking. We were waiting at the bus stop on the way to school. We'd both got there early and I just took my chance. It was one of those lovely days you can get in October. Sunny with a hint of a frost. I stumbled over my words, felt about eight years old. She smiled. That was when I knew it would be all right. "I thought you'd never ask." That was all she said. Then some other kids turned up to catch the bus.'

'When did it start going wrong?'

'Just before Christmas the following year. We had coursework to get in for A levels. It was even more important for her than me. She'd got a conditional place at Oxford. But suddenly she didn't seem bothered about revising for exams. She expected to see me every night, even though we'd spent the day together at school. I was starting to feel suffocated.'

'So you finished with her?'

'Not at first. I suggested we should just go out at weekends. It would make the time we had together more special.'

'Did she go for that?'

He shook his head. 'I did still care for her, but she was starting to do my head in. She accused me of seeing other women behind her back.'

'And were you?'

'No! I was trying to get some decent A levels so I could get away to university.' He paused. 'We had this enormous row. We'd been to the pub in the village where she lived and I was walking her back home. She'd been drinking quite heavily. She suddenly lost it, started shouting and swearing at me. Said I'd never loved her, that I'd spent all evening eyeing up the lass behind the bar, that she couldn't bear it if things carried on like this. I'd had enough. "Fine," I said. "Let's call it a day." She was almost home, so I turned and started walking back. She chased after me, pleading with me to change my mind. "I'm sorry, Ben. I can't help it. I just love you so much." It was pissing with rain and I thought how crazy she looked standing there, sobbing, her make-up running down her face. I didn't know what to do. She was so upset. So I put my arm around her and went with her to her front door, waited until she'd got the key in the door and ran for it.'

'Quite the gentleman,' Vera said.

'It was too much for me to deal with. I should have spoken to her parents, explained why she was distressed, but I couldn't face them. They always seemed very old to me. Quite strait-laced. Anyway, things like that you didn't talk to your parents about.' He paused, played with the empty glass. 'That was a Friday. She wasn't in school the next week. Her parents sent in a message to say she had some sort of throat infection. I was relieved because I didn't have to face her. I thought that would be the end of it. She'd come back to school and everything would carry on as it had before we started going out. People were always breaking up. It wasn't a big deal.'

'But it was a big deal for Lily.'

'Apparently. Her mother phoned, asked me to go and see Lily. She wasn't sleeping, wasn't eating. I had enough sense to refuse. I knew if I gave her any encouragement, the whole thing would start over again. A couple of weeks later she came back to school. She looked dreadful, pale and ill. I wondered if there might be something physically wrong with her, had this nightmare that she had some incurable disease and I was making her worse. Really, I was sure her mother would have had her checked out. In a strange way I was flattered. To have that effect on someone I'd worshipped! Lily became very isolated and withdrawn. She'd never had real friends. I hadn't realized before we became close how alone she was. But still I thought it would be OK. She seemed to throw herself into her work. I thought she was starting to get over the separation. There were no big scenes. After a week or so she even looked a bit brighter. I mean, she started to take more notice of her appearance, she spoke to me when we met.'

'But it didn't work out?'

'I wish. Now, of course, I realize how depressed she must have been. She wasn't getting better at all. The new clothes, the chattiness, were all part of her delusion that I was about to take her back. There was a crisis over the Easter holidays. She turned up at my house all dressed up, all smiles. "Where are you going to take me?" She had it in her head that I'd arranged to take her out for the day. I didn't know what to do. In the end I took her home to her mother's. When she realized what was happening she started to sob. It was horrible. That was when the phone calls started. She'd ring dozens of times a day. I knew she was ill and I tried to be sympathetic but it wore me down. And it drove my parents crazy. We changed the number, went ex-directory. I don't know if she ever had treatment or if she just came out of it. Most of the next term was study leave before the exams. I didn't see much of her. Caught a glimpse occasionally in the distance on her way to a classroom and made sure I kept out of the way.'

'Have you seen her since then?'

'No. She wasn't even at school when we all went to get our exam results. I suppose she realized she'd not done brilliantly and couldn't face the rest of us celebrating.'

'Has she been a patient at St George's since then? Or an outpatient at the day centre?'

'I haven't seen her.'

'You must have been curious, though,' Vera said. 'You admitted she was partly why you took up this branch of social work. Didn't you check if she was in the system? I know I would have done.'

He didn't answer her question immediately. 'I still think about her,' he said. 'She was my first real girl-friend. Probably the most beautiful woman I've ever met.' Then he looked up at Vera. 'You'll have to check with the medical staff about whether or not she's been treated locally. But you're right. I was curious. And I couldn't find any trace of her.'

The landlady came to collect their plates and Ben stood up to go. Vera stayed where she was and he paused, looking down at her, realizing there was another question.

'Does the name Claire Parr mean anything to you? She was in her late thirties, depressed. She committed suicide.'

'No,' he said. She could tell he just wanted to get back to work.

'It doesn't matter.' Speaking almost to herself. 'I expect it was before your time.'

Chapter Twenty-Nine

Vera telephoned Clive Stringer's home number from her car. She'd parked behind the dunes and was looking out over the beach. An old man was walking along the shore, his head bent. Every now and then he stooped to pick up sea coal and stick it in an Aldi carrier bag. She thought he probably lived in a housing association flat now with central heating, but old habits would die hard.

She pressed the buttons on her phone. It went on ringing – there was no answer service at the other end – and she was about to give up, when a woman spoke. Her voice was faint, breathless. She gave the number.

'Mrs Stringer.'

'Yes?' She was suspicious, used to people selling things. Perhaps her son had told her just to hang up if a stranger called.

'My name's Vera Stanhope, Mrs Stringer. I work for the police. Perhaps Clive said I'd be in touch. It's about that lassie he found dead by the lighthouse.'

'I'm not sure . . .'

'Is Clive at home? Perhaps I could speak to him.' She crossed the fingers of both hands and her phone nearly slipped from her grasp. Early afternoon, surely he'd still be in the museum.

'He's at work. You'd best talk to him there.'

Again Vera thought the woman was about to hang up.

'Look, I'm going to be around your way in about half an hour. I'll call in then. We can have a chat.'

'Really, I'd rather you waited till Clive was here.' Vera thought she could hear panic in the voice. That meant nothing sinister. Plenty of old people were worried about strangers knocking at the door. They'd watched all the crime prevention ads.

'It's nothing to be anxious about.' Vera heard herself speak with Ben Craven's *You're mad and I know what's best for you* voice; she winced. 'I'll show my identification. You can phone the police station to make sure.' Then she pressed the button on her phone to end the conversation before Mrs Stringer started to protest again.

The Stringers lived in a low pre-war bungalow in North Shields. Once the street had been a main road, tree-lined, busy, with a shop at each end, but the surrounding area had been redeveloped and a new road system had left it stranded. Now Gunner's Lane ended abruptly in a breeze-block wall. Beyond that a glass and concrete sports centre threw a long shadow down the middle of the street. Vera knew the area. She'd been there a few times to visit Davy Sharp, had been surprised that he lived somewhere so unassuming and respectable. It was all part of his cover, his ability to fit in.

Mary Stringer must have been watching out for her. As soon as Vera knocked, the door opened immediately, just a crack. She was tiny, her features small,

241

her neck so thin it seemed impossible it could support her head.

'I phoned Clive. He said he didn't know anything about you coming to the house.' Even through the crack in the door, Vera could tell she was shaking.

Vera made no attempt to get in. She fished in her bag for her identity card. 'You must admit it's me,' she said. 'Look at that picture. There can't be more than one person in the north east with a face like that.'

'Clive said I didn't have to talk to you.'

'And he's quite right, but you don't want the whole street listening to your business, do you?'

There was no reply. Vera could tell she was weakening. 'H'away, hinny, and let me in. I called at the baker's on the corner and got a couple of custard slices. Let's get the kettle on and have a civilized chat.'

The custard slices seemed to swing it. The claw-like grip on the door loosened. Vera pushed it gently and went inside.

The interior of the house couldn't have changed much since Mary Stringer had moved in. It was clean enough and tidy, but the furniture was old, a little shabby. Vera stood just inside the front door, waiting for the old woman to take the lead. Having taken the decision to allow Vera in, now she seemed almost pleased to have company. She led Vera into a small, over-filled living room and bustled away to make tea. Above the mantelpiece there was her wedding photo. Mary in traditional white and a man, as skinny as she was, looking sharp and pleased with himself in an ill-fitting suit.

Mary came back with a tray and saw Vera looking. 'He died when our Clive was a month old. An accident at the shipyard. They were good, mind. I had a pension.'

'Hard for you, though,' Vera said. 'Bringing up the lad on your own. Did you have family to help out?'

'No one close by. The neighbours were smashing. I'm not sure how I'd have managed without them. It was a friendly street in those days. Still is, really.'

'Clive said you helped out with Thomas Sharp when he was a bairn.'

'Only as a favour,' Mary said quickly. 'I mean, they gave me a few pounds to mind him when they were stretched. You know what it was like – Davy in and out of prison. I wouldn't want the pension people to know. Or the social – I mean, I was never properly registered as a minder.'

'You were helping out a friend.' Vera wondered if that was all the anxiety was about. Mary had broken a few rules ten years before and still got into a panic about it. 'Nobody's going to worry about that now.'

And Mary did seem to relax then and to play the hostess. The tea was in proper cups with saucers. There were matching tea plates and Vera prised the sticky cakes from a paper bag, handed one to Mary then licked her finger.

'Did you ever meet Thomas's friend, Luke Armstrong?' An outside chance, but worth asking all the same.

'I hadn't seen much of Tom at all recently. Not to talk to. He'd wave when he went past to get the bus into town, but that was it. You can't blame him. What would he want with an old lady?'

'Clive would have known him quite well, then?'

'He was lovely with Thomas when he was a baby.

243

Even changed his nappy sometimes. You don't expect it of young men, do you? He took him out in his pushchair when he was a toddler.'

Vera thought it sounded as if Mary had done more than a bit of occasional child-minding for the Sharps, but said nothing. She bit into the custard slice; the icing was so sweet she could imagine her teeth crumbling at the roots. The vanilla custard spilled out, squashed between the hard, indigestible pastry. She scooped it up with her little finger and put it in her mouth.

Mary watched her fondly. 'My Clive likes his food,' she said, 'but he never puts on an ounce. He must burn it up.'

'A bit of a nervy lad, was he?' Vera asked.

'Maybe that was my fault. There was only him and me and I always hated being on my own. Perhaps I smothered him a bit. I couldn't have borne it if anything had happened to him.' She paused, gave a little complacent smile. 'He's a good lad. I had a stroke a while back. Not major, but some sons would take their opportunity to put their mam into a home. Not him. He took time off work, brought me home and looked after me here.'

'You're close, then?'

'Aye, very close.'

'You'd know if anything was bothering him.'

'Well, that's a different thing, isn't it? He's not one for wearing his heart on his sleeve, our Clive. I'm not sure I can ever tell what's going on in his head.'

'Has he been seeing a lass lately?'

'No!' She seemed to think the idea inconceivable. 'We're quite happy here, just the two of us.' Then she added, for form's sake, 'Not that it would worry me, mind. I mean, it would be lovely if he could find a good woman to settle down with. I'd love a grand-child.'

'Has Clive ever had any treatment for his nerves?'

'What do you mean?' She was suddenly suspicious. She'd been eating the pastry with small delicate bites, nibbling away at the edges, mouse-like. Now she frowned over the cake at Vera.

'I'm just asking, pet. Lots of people do.'

'He's not depressed, if that's what you're saying. We're very content here, him and me. We don't need anyone else prying into our business.'

Vera let it go, wondered if the woman was protesting too much.

'You don't mind when he stays away?' she asked.

'It doesn't happen much these days. One time, it was every weekend. Up the coast with those grand friends of his. I didn't complain, mind. He has his own life to live. But since I had the stroke he's been a bit more thoughtful. I said to him, "How would you feel if I had a turn and I was here by myself?"'

Vera was starting to think Mary was a poisonous old witch. She could have understood if Clive had wanted to do away with *her*. 'You knew he was going to be away last Friday?'

'Of course. He wouldn't have arranged it without asking me first.'

'He prepared you a meal?'

'Like I said, he's a good lad. He usually cooks if he's here. He didn't eat, mind.' She sniffed. 'He was going to get something fancy at the party.'

'What about the Wednesday?'

'He was a bit late home from work because he went shopping on his way home. I was waiting for him. When you're on your own all day, you look forward to the company.'

'He doesn't drive much now, he was telling me.'

'No.' She paused. 'I used to quite enjoy our jaunts out in the car, but he never much liked driving. When it failed its MOT a few years ago, he didn't bother having the car fixed and sold it for scrap. He says it's better for the planet to use public transport. It would be handy for me now, though. He'd be able to give me a lift to the outpatient clinic at the hospital.' She gave a quick look to the clock on the wall. 'Is there anything else? Only the quiz I like on television comes on soon and it makes my day.'

Vera decided she'd go before she said something she regretted. She'd checked out Clive's story. She couldn't see him as Joe Ashworth's madman, who killed young people just because he was jealous of the way they looked. He might be depressed, but who wouldn't be, saddled with the self-obsessed mother?

Mary had switched on the big TV. Vera had begun by being sorry for her. Now she thought the woman had her life organized very much the way she wanted it. Vera got up. 'I'll see my way out, shall I?'

The little woman nodded. 'If you don't mind. I'm not so good on my feet, since I was ill.'

Vera closed the living-room door behind her and stood in the hall. The signature tune from the television faded. The host made a joke. Mary chuckled. Vera pushed open one of the doors leading from the corridor. It had a thick white carpet on the floor. A double bed with a pink candlewick quilt. That old ladies' smell of worn nightclothes and talcum powder. The next door she tried was the bathroom. It was very small, a shower over the bath, the blue shower curtain with a pattern of beaming fish. The smell in here slightly more masculine. Shower gel? Aftershave? She looked at the bottles on the shelf. Had Clive always made an effort with his appearance, hopeful perhaps that one day he'd find a woman, an excuse to move away from his mother?

Then she was standing at the door of Clive's room. It was firmly shut but not locked and opened with a gentle click. The curtains were drawn and she had to switch on the light. She had been expecting something dusty, full of specimens like the workroom in the museum, but it was uncluttered, anonymous. A single bed and matching pine wardrobe and chest of drawers. A bookcase with standard field guides. In one corner a mist net packed into a canvas bag. So Clive must be into ringing birds too. A few fantasy novels, an upturned book on the bedside table. A computer desk with the ubiquitous PC. A chess set. No pictures on the wall. It was as if he knew his mother had access to his room and he wanted to give nothing away. There was just one photograph, propped on the bedside cabinet, where you might expect the picture of a girl-friend or lover. This was of the group of four friends – Clive looking shy and awkward, Gary laughing, and each side of them Peter Calvert and Samuel Parr. It had been taken at the lighthouse and they were all gazing out to sea.

Vera walked back into the corridor. There was a burst of laughter from the television studio audience.

She took advantage of the noise to shut the front door behind her and walk out into the street.

She stood for a moment then walked three doors down to where the Sharps lived. Now she was here, she might as well talk to Davy's wife.

Chapter Thirty

Vera could tell that Diane Sharp knew who she was as soon as the door was opened – not her name or where she came from but that she was a police officer. She must have developed some sort of sixth sense after years of practice. She was a plump woman in her forties, with very pretty features, hair which looked as if she had it done every week. She wore a pink blouse and a white linen skirt.

'You're wasting your time here,' she said. 'Davy's inside. Acklington.'

'I know. I spoke to him last week.' Vera was trying to remember if she'd met Davy's wife before, thought she probably hadn't.

'And our Brian doesn't live here any more. He's got his own place in town.'

'It's you I want to talk to,' Vera said.

The woman seemed surprised by that, so surprised that she stood aside and let Vera in.

'I don't get mixed up in their business.' As she spoke she led Vera through to the back of the bungalow. Everything was very neat, very respectable. She opened a door and suddenly light flooded into the space. There was a conservatory the width of the building, looking out onto a tiny patch of lawn. 'Davy had this done last time he was home,' she said. She settled herself into a wicker chair, nodded for Vera to join her.

'This isn't about what your men get up to,' Vera said. She paused. 'I was so sorry to hear about Thomas.'

The woman sat very still before replying. 'That was an accident,' she said at last. 'Nothing for you to trouble yourself about.'

'Are you sure about that, Mrs Sharp?'

'Aye, it'd have been easier if there was someone to blame, but it was just lads larking around.'

'You'll have seen in the paper that Luke Armstrong was killed?'

'Yes,' she said. 'He was a smashing lad. Tom spent a lot of time at his place.'

'Did he come here?'

'Not so often. Brian was still at home then. There were things going on. I didn't want Tom involved.'

'What sort of things?'

She hesitated, chose her words carefully. 'Brian mixes with a rough set,' she said. She could have been talking about a five-year-old mixing with bad company at school.

Vera knew one of the rough set had been convicted of attempted murder, a stabbing in a city-centre pub, but she let that go. 'Tell me about the memorial they did for Tom. The flowers on the river. Whose idea was it?'

'I'm not sure who started it.' Diane was looking through the glass at the trimmed lawn. 'Someone in the street probably. Everyone here was very fond of

Tom. I don't think it was organized. At first there was one bunch of flowers. Then everybody joined in.'

'Did anyone blame Luke Armstrong for Tom's death?'

The woman looked up. 'You're thinking of Brian? After revenge?'

'Your little brother drowns, you'd want someone to blame. Like you said, we all want that.'

She shook her head. 'It wasn't Brian. I'd have heard.'

Vera thought that was probably true. Besides, Brian Sharp would have kicked the Armstrong door down, battered Luke with fists and boots. He wouldn't have charmed his way in with flowers.

'Tell me about the Stringers,' she said. 'Your neighbours.'

Diane seemed surprised by the sudden change of subject. 'Why do you want to know about them?'

'Clive's a witness in another enquiry. I'm just curious.'

'Mary Stringer was like a mother to me when we moved here,' Diane said. 'Davy wasn't around much and I was pregnant with Tom. She was on her own apart from Clive. She lost her husband in an accident. Clive wasn't like either of my boys. He was very quiet. Always had his head in a book. No trouble. Not really. He was teased a bit as a kid, but Brian soon put a stop to that. We were almost like one family. Mary looked after Tom for me most days until he started nursery. I had my hands full with Brian and she was only on a widow's pension. She needed the money and I was happy enough to slip her a few pounds. Clive loved having Tom around. Most lads wouldn't have been interested, but for a few years they were like brothers.'

'Did Clive ever meet Luke Armstrong?'

'He might have done. Tom never said.'

Vera couldn't think of anything else to ask and stood to go. Diane shut the door firmly behind her. Outside, Clive Stringer was standing next to her car. He must have left work as soon as his mother phoned him about Vera's intended visit. He was wearing black jeans, a black polo shirt, black trainers. He had the sort of complexion which easily burns and his face was red, greasy with sweat. Vera could tell he'd stood there, fuming, getting hotter and crosser, waiting for her to return to her car.

'You had no right bothering my mother.'

'She didn't seem to mind, pet. We had a nice pot of tea.'

'Anything you want to ask, you can come straight to me.'

'You look as if you could do with a cup yourself. Is there anywhere round here we could get a drink? Save bothering your mam again. Stand here any longer and we'll start gathering a crowd.'

A gang of teenagers were slouching down the road on their way home from school and they'd already begun to stare. Clive shrugged. 'There's a caff on the corner.' He set off along the pavement leaving Vera to follow.

The cafe had set a garden table and chairs outside on the pavement. Any attempt to create a continental atmosphere was ruined by the smell of greasy burgers and stale cigarettes coming through the open door, but the pavement was in the shade now and they sat there anyway. Vera drank instant coffee, Clive a bottle of bright-orange fizzy pop. She thought again that he'd never grown up.

'It can't have been easy,' she said, 'growing up without a dad.' As soon as the words were out she thought that was a patronizing thing to say, but in the short walk Clive seemed to have become calmer.

'My mother's never been easy,' he said. He looked up with a sudden grin as if he'd made a joke.

'She depends on you?' Vera was feeling her way with him. One wrong word and she knew he'd clam up again.

'There's nobody else. No relatives. She's not very good with friends. She makes demands on them, but won't make any effort in return.'

'She made an effort with Diane Sharp.'

'Diane paid her. Besides Mam liked Tom when he was a baby. She could make believe he was hers. She didn't like him so much when he was old enough to answer back.'

'You never answered back?'

'No,' he said. 'I never got the hang of it.' She expected him to smile again, but he seemed quite serious.

'How did you get on with the Sharps?'

'At one point they were like family,' he said and Vera thought that Diane had said almost the same thing. 'It would have been easy to get sucked into all that. You know, the stuff they were into. But the bird-watching came along and that was a way out for me.'

'And another sort of family.'

'Aye,' he said, grateful that she seemed to understand.

'Do you have any idea what lies behind these murders? The flowers. The water.' Of all the people, she thought he might have. He had the sort of mind which could see the patterns in things. The question came out before she'd considered whether it would be sensible to ask.

He sat for a moment, his eyelids blinking wildly behind the thick lenses of his glasses.

'No,' he said. 'Of course not.'

Chapter Thirty-One

Felicity had assumed Vera Stanhope would collect Lily Marsh's ring and was a little confused to find a young man standing at the door. He introduced himself as Joe Ashworth and, when she still seemed unsure, he showed her his identity card and explained, 'DI Stanhope's my boss.' He could have been the junior partner in a small business. He was well mannered and engaging and she took to him at once. She realized then that she'd been foolish to expect an inspector to turn out on such a trivial matter.

Almost immediately afterwards, James arrived from the school bus. They were still on the doorstep and he ran past them into the house and into the kitchen, shirt untucked, trainers unlaced, ravenous as he always was when he got in from school. Even when they followed, he took no notice of the stranger and continued pulling biscuits out of the tin, talking with his mouth full about sports day. She wished he had given a better impression, been more polite. But Ashworth seemed to understand children and smiled at her over the boy's head. He sat and made small talk as if he had all the time in the world.

'Your husband says you're the gardener in the family.'

'I suppose I am. He's very busy. And though he's a botanist by profession, his real passion is birds. He'd much rather be out on the coast.'

'We live on a new estate,' Ashworth said. 'There's not much of a garden at all. My wife makes it pretty, though. She watches the makeover programmes on the telly.'

While he was chatting about his wife and daughter and the new baby on the way, Felicity thought what a *nice* young man he was and how she wished Joanna had married someone like that, instead of Oliver, who worked in television and hardly seemed to notice that he had a child at all.

'Recently wor lass has got into making home-made cards,' Ashworth was saying. 'They had someone to speak at the WI about pressing flowers. Sarah's started growing plants she can pick for pressing. She sells them round the village. She'll do a one-off if someone wants a card for a special occasion. There's not much profit in it, but she covers the costs and she loves doing it.'

'Goodness! I wish we could attract some younger women to the Institute here. The average age must be about seventy-five and I'm the youngest by miles.'

'Maybe you had the same woman as a speaker?'

'I don't think so. But all those talks on craft become a bit of a blur. I'm not really interested. Two left hands. Any spare time and I'd rather be in the garden. I'll show you round later, if you like.'

James ran outside to play with the girls from the farm, but Felicity and Ashworth stayed in the kitchen to talk. She set the ring on the table between them.

'Such a pretty thing.' She smiled, confessed, 'I was almost tempted to keep it.'

'You're sure it belonged to Lily Marsh?'

'Oh yes,' she said. 'As soon as I saw it I knew it was familiar. It was only when I got back to the house that I remembered where I'd seen it.'

'You didn't notice Lily drop it?'

'If I had,' she said primly, 'I'd have returned it to her.'

'Of course.' He paused. She thought he was more deliberate than Vera Stanhope, slower in his thought and speech. 'I'm not clear how she might have lost it. Did she use the bathroom there? Take it off, perhaps, to wash her hands?'

She played back in her head the young woman's appearance at Fox Mill. 'No,' she said. 'No, she went to the bathroom here in the house, before we went across to the cottage. Perhaps it had just come loose. If she'd lost weight since it was bought . . .'

'Yes.' He gave a doubtful little smile. 'Wouldn't you have heard it drop, then? Unless the cottage is carpeted?'

She was starting to lose patience. She wondered if she had been wrong about this young man. Had he taken her in with his stories of his wife and daughter? Was he trying to trick her? 'There's no carpet,' she said more sharply. 'Flags downstairs and wooden floorboards in the bedroom. Does it really matter? She must have dropped it. I'm handing it back.'

'It might matter. If she was still wearing the ring when she left, it would suggest that she returned. We still don't know where Miss Marsh was killed. You do see how important these details are now?'

Felicity felt suddenly sick. She couldn't quite get to grips with what the detective was saying. 'Do you mean she was killed in our cottage? That's ridiculous. Impossible.'

'I don't think it's impossible,' he said calmly. He could still be talking about pressing flowers and the WI. 'It's not that far from here to where her body was found. We know it was her ring. We know it meant a lot to her. It was a present from someone very close to her. If we can find evidence that it was still in her possession when she left you, that would be significant, wouldn't it? It would mean she came back. Probably on the day she was killed.'

There was a silence. Felicity realized she was staring at him, that she was expected to speak. 'I really can't remember if she was wearing the ring when she left me. But she was a stranger. Why would she come back? Do you think she'd changed her mind about renting the cottage?'

Ashworth ignored the last question. 'Are you sure your husband had never met her?'

'Of course. He told you.' But while she was saying the words she was wondering if that was true. Peter knew nothing of *her* affair with Samuel. It was perfectly reasonable that he might have a life which was hidden from her. The idea was horrifying. How hypocritical is that? she thought. What right do I have to be jealous or hurt? But Lily had been so young and pretty. Of course there could be no question of her having an affair with Peter, who must have seemed an old man to her. This anxiety was ridiculous. Then she realized the detective was speaking again and she tried to concentrate on his words.

'I'd like our crime scene investigators to look at the cottage,' he said. 'Just in case. You said you found the ring there this morning. Will anyone else have been in since you showed Lily round?'

'I took Inspector Stanhope in at the weekend.'

He gave a sudden broad grin. 'Her footprints'll be distinctive enough,' he said. 'Those sandals she wears. The size of elephants' feet. The CSI won't confuse them.'

'They won't find any footprints!' She didn't mean to be defiant, but realized that was how she sounded and she couldn't stop. 'That's what I was doing when I found the ring. I was cleaning. I brushed and mopped all the floors, scrubbed the work surfaces. It's not worth bringing in your experts.'

He stayed very calm and looked straight at her.

'What about bedding?' he said.

'I washed the sheets this morning. They're on the line. I told you, you're wasting your time. You won't find anything.'

'Oh you'd be surprised,' he said, 'just what we can find. You give us permission, I take it, for us to have a look?'

'Of course.' She knew it was too late to retrieve the situation. He must be convinced now that she'd cleaned the cottage to destroy any evidence that Lily had been killed there. 'We'll help in whatever way we can. We have nothing to hide.'

From the kitchen window she watched the drama unfold. He stood at the front of the house to make his phone call. He had his back to her and she had no idea what response he was getting. From his car he took a roll of blue-and-white tape. Had he been expecting this outcome? Had he brought it with him specially? He walked across the meadow and stretched it across the cottage door. She wanted to rebuild the rapport they'd had when he first arrived. Should she go out to him, offer him more tea? But she could tell he would consider it an intrusion. They might own the house, but this was his territory now.

He walked back to the drive, sat on the bank where the crocuses and snowdrops grew in spring and waited. He brushed the pollen and grass seed he'd picked up in the meadow from his trousers. His phone rang. She couldn't hear it from the house, but she could see him answer. A sudden grin. Triumphant. More scary than when he'd been so cool in conversation with her. She thought she should phone Peter at work, warn him what was going on, but when she dialled his direct number at the university there was no reply. The raucous call of a cuckoo came from the kitchen clock. It was six o'clock. He would already have left. She struggled to remember what she had planned for supper, but the thought slipped from her mind and she returned to look out of the window.

James wandered down the drive. The girls from the farm must have been called in for tea. He was wearing shorts and his knees were filthy. The detective raised his hand in greeting and James sat beside him on the grass. He was curious now about what the stranger was doing here. They talked for a few minutes. Felicity thought they were getting on well. They seemed to be sharing a joke. *Surely he must realize we wouldn't commit murder. We have a lovely son. Too much to lose. We're nice, respectable people. People just like him.*

James got to his feet and walked into the house.

He disappeared from her view for a minute, then appeared in the kitchen. She thought, knowing the image was a silly exaggeration: He's like a cold-war spy who's come across from the other side. He might have valuable information. But he opened the fridge and peered inside as if it was any other evening. 'I'm starving. When's tea?'

'Won't be long.' She tried to keep her voice even. 'What were you and Mr Ashworth talking about?'

'Is that his name?' He was drinking orange juice straight from the carton. She restrained the urge to snap at him to fetch a glass. 'He told me to call him Joe. He was asking me about Miss Marsh. What she was like as a teacher. How she got on with the kids in our class.' His voice grew more excited. 'They're bringing in crime scene investigators to look at the cottage. Like on the television. There might be some trace in there to help them find out who killed Miss Marsh. Wait till I tell Lee Fenwick.' Lee was his best friend and keenest rival. In winter they played chess together every evening.

She heard the faint sound of a vehicle turning in from the lane. She expected it to be Peter. *Please keep your temper. Please be polite. He's only doing his job.* But it was a white van. A man and a woman jumped out, greeted Joe Ashworth as if he was an old friend. They pulled on the paper suits she'd seen in films and started lifting equipment from the back of the van.

James had forgotten about food. 'Do you think I could go out and watch?'

'No,' she said sharply, then regretted her tone. Of course he was fascinated. So was she in a horrible, frightening way. 'Won't you get a better view from your bedroom?'

James ran off and she felt a sudden relief that she no longer had to pretend that everything was normal. When he'd opened the fridge she'd seen a bottle of white wine, started the night before, and realized she was desperate for a drink. She took it out, removed the vacuum stopper and poured herself a large glass. Her hand was shaking.

Back at the window she saw Peter's car coming down the drive. His normal parking place had been taken by the van. She saw him get out and prepare to demand it was moved. Then he realized what was happening. He saw the two figures dressed in white walking across the meadow. Their weight was tilted towards each other, because of the heavy metal box they carried between them. Like James, he had watched enough television to understand what they were doing. Felicity saw Joe Ashworth approaching him, hand outstretched, but Peter hadn't noticed. His focus was still on the cottage, the androgynous figures who had now reached the door. His face was very pale and still. My God, Felicity thought. He looks guilty. Guilty as hell. If I was Joe Ashworth I'd think he'd killed the girl.

She didn't dare ask herself if she thought the same thing. The thought hovered at the back of her mind and she pushed it away, concentrated on the fish she'd cook for supper and on whether she should make sandwiches for Ashworth and his friends in the cottage. Now Peter and Ashworth were deep in conversation. They walked together towards the house.

She prepared herself to be normal and welcoming, took a deep breath as the door opened.

Peter looked at her with the expression he put on when he'd received bad news, a paper rejected, a record dismissed. Aggrieved. She knew he wanted reassurance, but she didn't have the heart to give it. In the end it was Ashworth who spoke.

'Dr Calvert's agreed to come to the station in Kimmerston to have a chat with DI Stanhope. A few points we want to clear up. It shouldn't take long.'

She forced herself to smile. 'Of course,' she said. 'I told you, anything we can do to help . . .'

Chapter Thirty-Two

Vera thought Ashcroft had made a mistake bringing Calvert in. The botanist was hardly likely to leave the country. She believed they were showing their hand too soon. Perhaps *she'd* made a mistake in phoning Ashworth to tell him that Charlie had found the
a
bought. There was still no evidence that Calvert was the lover. An older man with an attractive young woman, the owner had said. Tall, fit for his age. That could describe a lot of people, including Samuel Parr. They'd found a photo of Calvert on the jacket of a textbook he'd written, but it had been published nearly twenty years before and his hair then had been l
nition. If Calvert had been the man in the shop.

The ring had been bought in January and paid for with cash. The owner had drawn his own conclusions about that. 'It's not unusual. He wouldn't want his wife finding it on his credit-card statements, would he?' And perhaps that did point to Calvert. Samuel Parr no longer had a wife to check up on him.

'Can you remember anything about the gentleman?' Charlie had asked. Vera could imagine him standing in the smart shop, looking scruffy and out of place. York wouldn't be Charlie's sort of place at all. Except for the races. He'd be quite at home there.

And then the owner had come out with the one useful bit of information they'd got from him. 'He was in town for some sort of conference. It was lunchtime and he said he had to go back for an afternoon session. The young lady didn't like that at all. She was trying to persuade him to miss it. There wasn't a row, not quite that. But a disagreement. That's why I remember. And because she was such a beauty.'

Vera would have liked some confirmation that Calvert was at a conference in York before sitting opposite him in an interview room. She'd phoned everyone she could think of, but this time in the evening there was no one around to ask. She'd set Holly onto the internet, university websites, botanical societies, but most of the sites had been updated. There was no record now of an event which had happened six months earlier.

She made sure he was treated with respect. She didn't want to waste time dealing with complaints and she wanted him to underestimate them. He'd give more away if he was feeling superior. At the last minute she asked Holly to join her in the interview room instead of Ashworth. Maybe Calvert would feel the need to show off in front of a pretty young woman. Among the rest of the team there was a bubbling excitement. They thought it was nearly all over.

She made coffee for Calvert – from her own supply, not the crap from the machine – and carried it through to the interview room.

'Sorry to ask you in before you've had time for supper,' she said. She took time to settle herself, let papers fall out of her bag when she put it on the floor, picked it up again to search for a pen. 'Still, this shouldn't take long. Just a few things to clear up. You don't mind if we tape the conversation? Standard procedure.' She looked at him for the first time. He seemed composed enough. Ashworth had said he'd almost fallen apart when he'd seen the CSIs walking towards the cottage and that was one of the reasons why he'd brought him in. She introduced Holly and Calvert nodded, gave an insinuating smile which was enough to make your flesh crawl.

'Did you attend an academic conference in York in January?'

He hadn't been expecting the question and it threw him. She saw his mind racing. He'd been so careful, paid for everything by cash. How could they possibly know? Ashworth had been right. He had been Lily's lover.

'Dr Calvert?' She kept her voice quiet, tentative. Then, when he still didn't answer, 'You do realize we'll be able to check.'

He pulled his thoughts together. 'I'm sorry, Inspector. Yes, I was there. I just can't see the relevance to your enquiries of my giving a paper at a conference.'

'You had a companion,' she said. 'Not at the conference, but in York.'

This time his response came more quickly. 'Ah,' he said. 'So my sins have found me out.' He gave the smile which was supposed to be charming. 'You must be able to understand why I lied about that, Inspector. I have a wonderful wife and family. So much to lose.

I hoped I'd get away with it, that they wouldn't have to be hurt.'

'You were having an affair with Lily Marsh?'

'Yes. At least, I'd had an affair. It was all over by the time of her death. But you can imagine the shock of seeing her body in the water. And of realizing that my son had known her.'

'You can't expect us to sympathize, Dr Calvert.'

'No,' he said quickly. 'No. But I'm trying to explain why I handled the situation so badly, why I wasn't entirely truthful.'

'You weren't truthful in any way. That has to end. I can't consider your sensibilities when I'm investigating a murder. Two murders.' She realized she sounded like a Sunday school teacher, but he seemed to respond.

'I really don't know anything about the first murder,' he said. 'Luke Armstrong. I'd never met him.'

'You had heard of him, though. Gary Wright had fallen for his mother. He was talking about it in the pub after the last Bird Club meeting.'

'Was he?' Calvert seemed genuinely confused. 'I'm sorry. I can't have been listening. Some things had been said at the meeting to which I took exception. A criticism of an article I'd written in last month's *Birding World*. I suppose it seems trivial now, but I was preoccupied.'

'Tell me about the affair with Lily. How did you meet her?'

'Quite by chance last summer. I went into the shop where she worked to buy a birthday present for Felicity. It's an awkward situation for a man. What do we know about women's clothes? She was very helpful. We talked briefly and she explained she was a student. Then I saw her at the university, bought her a coffee to thank her. At that point there was nothing more to it than that. I couldn't believe she'd be interested in someone like me. I suppose I was flattered, a foolish old man.'

'You gave her money?'

'Yes, something towards her rent. Her parents couldn't help out. My daughters had finished university. I suppose I wanted to make a gesture. Do something generous. I expect you think I was naive, that she was only going out with me for the money.'

Vera didn't answer that. It wasn't her job to reassure him. She didn't believe it was true, though. Lily had been an obsessive. Money hadn't been the object of her desire.

'So you started seeing her. Where did you meet?'

There was a slight hesitation. 'This does sound so squalid. Afternoons in cheap hotels. Occasionally in her flat when she knew her friends were away. At first I suppose the secrecy was part of the excitement. Later it all became rather unsatisfactory.'

'Did she ever come to your house?'

'Not to the house, no. That would have seemed quite wrong.'

She picked up the precise wording, the slight hesitation. 'Not to the house. But to the cottage?'

He hesitated again. 'Yes, we met in the cottage. A few times. When Felicity was at a concert or the theatre and James was staying with a friend. Lily loved it there. I found it a bit close to home. I could never quite relax.'

He was lost in thought and for the first time

Vera did feel a small moment of understanding. Was he remembering a specific evening? Winter, perhaps, frost on the grass in the meadow and a fire lit in the grate. But never really enjoying it, listening out for a car on the drive, the danger of interruption.

'Did she have a key to the cottage?'

'Yes,' he said. 'I had one cut for her. She never gave it back.'

'Who ended the relationship?' The question was peremptory. She couldn't allow herself sympathy here.

'Neither of us. Not really. We just agreed that it had to end. Before it became general knowledge.'

'That wouldn't matter to Lily, would it? She wasn't married after all. What would she have to lose?'

'She must have seen that the relationship wasn't going anywhere. I suppose she wanted all the things her friends had – a shared home, real companionship, a family eventually. She was very fond of children. I'd never have been able to give her that.'

It sounded very plausible. But Lily Marsh hadn't been like her friends.

'Why do you think she turned up to look at the cottage? If your relationship had ended amicably, it seems an odd thing to do.'

'Perhaps she was struck by the coincidence of having James in her class and came to look at the cottage for old times' sake. She might even have seen it as a weird kind of practical joke. She'd expect Felicity to tell me she'd been.'

'Was it coincidence, having James in her class?'

'Of course. What else would it have been?'

She arranged it, Vera thought. She was obsessed by

you in the same way as she was obsessed by Ben Craven. She found out where James went to school and she asked Annie Slater for a placement in Hepworth. She got to know the boy, orchestrated the visit to look at the cottage. Why? To put pressure on him? A form of blackmail? They sat for a moment in silence. Calvert seemed preoccupied, but not anxious. Was he so arrogant that he believed he could get away with murder? In the end he broke the silence.

'You are looking for the same person for both murders?'

'That's the theory we're working on just now.' She wasn't going to commit herself further than that. They'd kept the details of the Armstrong crime scene out of the press, but word got out. Friends and family talked. Police and CSIs were only human. A good story was for sharing. She couldn't rule out the possibility that Lily's death had been a copy-cat killing. Someone wanted her dead and had used the details of Luke's murder to muddy the water. The phrase stuck in her head. *Muddy the water*. She supposed it was apt.

'I couldn't have killed the boy. I was looking at the notes on my book. I made a phone call on Wednesday night. Ten-thirty. A detail I needed to check with a friend. There'll be a record, I presume, on my phone bill. It was a long call to a mobile.'

Vera didn't answer immediately and Holly spoke for the first time. 'That's very convenient, Dr Calvert. What a shame you didn't mention it before. We'll need to talk to your friend, of course. Otherwise the call could have been made by anyone in your house.'

The response irritated him. He struggled to keep his composure. He smiled again at Holly. He probably thought he was good with young women. 'I understand that I made a huge mistake not telling you about Lily. I'd expect you to check. But please believe me, I'm not keeping anything else back from you.'

'What will you tell your wife about the affair?' Holly again. She even gave him a grin. Cheeky, almost complicit. *What else do you get up to? What else have you got away with?*

'The truth. She deserves that. She knows me well enough to realize I'd never kill.'

'We found a card among her belongings,' Vera said. 'Made of pressed flowers. Did you send it to Lily?'

He paused. 'No,' he said. 'I don't go in for sentimental gestures, Inspector.'

'You're sure?'

'Of course I'm sure. It's not something I'd forget.'

So who did send it? And why was Lily's card marked with kisses while Luke's was blank?

'You were very close to Lily? I mean, you had a physical relationship, but you talked? You felt you knew her well?'

The question made him uncomfortable for the first time. He struggled to find appropriate words. At last he answered very simply. 'I was infatuated. I thought I loved her. For a while, at least. No, it wasn't just about the sex.'

'Did she tell you anything which might give a clue to her killer? Was she troubled, scared, anxious?'

'She didn't talk much about herself.'

She'll not have had the chance, Vera thought.

'Just before we separated, she said she'd met up with an old friend. Someone she'd known from the village where she'd grown up. It seemed to be a big thing for her. She was a loner. She didn't have many real friends.'

'Man or woman?' *Ben Craven?*

'A woman.' He paused. 'If you give me a moment I'll remember her name. Her first name, at least. She worked as a nurse at the RVI. Kath.'

It took Vera a moment to make the link. Kath Armstrong. Wife of Geoff. Stepmother to Luke.

Chapter Thirty-Three

Vera caught up with Kath Armstrong at the hospital. Her shift had just started and she was in a meeting with the day staff. Vera waited by the nurses' station and heard muttered voices coming from the sister's office, an occasional stifled laugh. Visiting was over and the ward was peaceful. The women in the side rooms were plugged into their televisions or reading. There was a little desultory chat. Further down the corridor the tea trolley was being wheeled away. On the window sill funereal bunches of flowers drooped in the heat. Vera had never been in hospital and knew she'd hate it. Not the illness or the pain. Not even the dreadful food and going without alcohol. But giving up control. Being at the mercy of people who knew more about her body than she did.

The meeting broke up and Kath came out. She was still chatting to a colleague, didn't notice Vera sitting in the orange chairs where patients waited to be discharged. 'I'd like a word,' Vera said. 'Sorry to bother you here, but something's come up.'

'Nothing's wrong, is it?' A moment of panic. Vera knew she was thinking about her little girl.

'No, nothing like that. Is there anywhere we can talk?'

Kath turned away to whisper to a motherly middle-aged woman in a sister's uniform. 'Maggie says we can use her office.'

They sat where the nurses had been huddled in their meeting. There was a photo on the desk of two small boys leaning against a farm gate next to a bearded man in specs. The ward sister's husband and kids. A child's drawing was pinned to the wall. More happy families.

'What's this about? Have you found out who killed Luke?'

Vera ignored the question. 'You didn't tell us you knew Lily Marsh.'

'You didn't ask.'

'She wasn't dead when I spoke to you, pet. You'll realize it's just a bit important. Two murders within a week and you knew both victims.'

'I didn't know her well. I mean, I just thought: What a weird coincidence. I couldn't contribute anything to your enquiry.'

She seemed genuinely puzzled. Vera wondered if she spent too much of her life investigating crimes, making connections which were insignificant, seeing motives which didn't exist. A sort of strange paranoia, which didn't allow for coincidence at all.

'How did you know her?'

'We grew up together. I mean, I'm quite a bit older than her, but we lived in the same village. My mam was good friends with Phyllis Marsh. You know how it is in a place like that. They'd been to school together, they met up at the church, the WI. Lily and I were both only children. I ended up looking after her when we were younger. We were close in a way. She loved coming to visit. You know what children are like with older kids. Especially girls. And maybe I've always had this maternal thing. We lost touch when I moved into town and started working here.'

'But you met up again more recently.'

'Yes.'

'How did you meet?'

'She came into the hospital as an outpatient. She thought she was pregnant. She'd missed a couple of periods, but her home pregnancy test had come up negative. She wanted to check. I bumped into her in the lift when she was on her way out.'

'Isn't that the sort of thing you'd see your GP for?'

'She'd have had to wait for an appointment. For some reason she was desperate to know.'

'She wasn't pregnant,' Vera said. It was a statement not a question. The post-mortem had been clear about that. She remembered the pathologist's sadness that Lily would never be a mother, would never carry a child.

'No. And I could tell she was upset. It was the end of my shift and I took her for a coffee. The mothering thing again. I should learn to leave well alone.'

'She wanted a baby?'

'Desperately. I said all the usual things. She was young. It would happen sometime. It would be better anyway when she'd completed the PGCE. I could tell that none of it was having any effect.'

'Did she tell you who would have been the father?'

'Not in any detail. She said he was an older man. That was all.'

'Was that the only time you saw her?'

'No. I was worried about her. I knew she'd had a

bit of a breakdown when she was in the sixth form. The stress of exams. Phyllis expected so much from her. Oxford, the glittering career. She didn't have much of a marriage and was living through Lily. Nobody would have been able to stand the strain. I asked Lily if she was seeing a doctor. She lost her temper, said she wasn't ill, everything was fine. I gave her my mobile number, told her to give me a ring if she wanted to talk.'

'And she did.'

'Oh yes.' Kath took a breath. 'To be honest she became a bit of a nuisance. She'd often be waiting in the car park when I finished work. After a night shift all you want is to get home, have a long bath and a few hours' sleep. And I didn't really think I could do any good. She needed psychiatric help. Then one day, a Saturday afternoon, she turned up at the house. We were having a day at home, one of those Saturday afternoons when you just want to chill. Rebecca was in the garden playing and Geoff was watching sport on the television. Luke was staying and he was glued to the box too. I was in the kitchen, keeping an eye on Rebecca through the window. And suddenly Lily was there, in the garden. She started chatting to Rebecca, then lifted her onto the swing and started to push. By the time I got out, she had Rebecca in her arms.' She paused. 'I'm not quite sure what would have happened if I hadn't been there.'

'You think she might have gone off with her?'

'I don't know. I'm probably overreacting. She was training to be a teacher, for goodness' sake. Why would she do something like that? But I made it clear that I didn't want her coming to the house. I said

Geoff wouldn't like it. Luke wandered out into the garden and was obviously a bit anxious when he saw I was upset. She went without a fuss, said she was sorry she'd turned up when it was obviously not convenient. The next time she waited for me outside work I made an excuse not to spend time with her. I felt mean, but she wasn't my responsibility. There was nothing I could do. I told her again she needed medical help, said I'd sort it out for her if she wanted. A veiled threat, I suppose. I never saw her again. When I heard she was dead, I suppose my first feeling was relief: Well, at least she won't come bothering us again. Isn't that dreadful?'

'Was she upset when you threatened to arrange a psychiatrist to see her?'

Kath paused. 'Not so much upset as angry,' she said. 'She didn't say anything but she glared at me, then turned away without a word. It was horrible. I felt she hated me. I was tempted to go after her, just to make things right between us, but I didn't. I couldn't face the idea of her turning up at the house again.'

'You never heard from her after that?'

'No.' Kath looked at her watch. 'Look, I should go. There's a patient coming up from casualty. I need to admit her.'

'She didn't say anything which made you worry for her safety? She didn't seem afraid of anyone? The man she'd been seeing?'

'Nothing like that. She said he loved her. I wondered if that was true. Perhaps he'd rejected her and that was why she seemed so upset. If I had any worry at all, it was that she might harm herself.'

'Suicide?'

'Perhaps.' Kath stood up and led the way out of the office. 'Look, I should probably have been kinder, made more effort to see she was OK. But my family came first.'

Vera drove home, pleased to be leaving the city and the investigation behind. Turning west into the hills she was almost blinded by the setting sun. When she arrived at the old station master's house, she sat for a moment in the car, too tired even to go in. Then she roused herself, got out of her car, unlocked the door. She stepped over the pile of mail on the floor, took a can of beer from the fridge and carried it outside. Even now, in the dusk, it was still warm. She sat on the white seat, where once passengers had waited for the small local train, and looked out over the valley. Everything was in shadow and drained of colour. Here, she thought, it should be possible to rest.

But her mind couldn't leave the investigation behind. She felt as feverish and obsessive as Lily had been, turning over details, chasing connections. If I could write it down, she thought, perhaps I could let it go. But she was too exhausted to get up to fetch paper and pen. And there was something creative in this concentration, in being forced to keep all the details clear in her mind at once. It came to her suddenly that this was what it must be like to be a writer of fiction. All the characters and stories and ideas spinning around her head. How could you bring some order to them? Make sense of them, give them shape.

If I was writing a novel, she thought, Lily would be the murderer. It would be one of those psychological thrillers, where part of the action is seen from the murderer's point of view, written in a different font or the present tense. Vera borrowed books like that from the library sometimes, enjoyed throwing them across the room when they got the details of police procedure wrong. So, Lily's the central character. She's been screwed up from childhood. A repressed mother and a depressed father. An illness that's been covered up by her mother, hidden away, never diagnosed. She's become a loner. A beautiful, obsessed loner. The reader will see her fall in love with an older man. Lily sees him as her salvation, even becomes happy for a while. Then he rejects her, because she's becoming too demanding, a nuisance, and she gets ill again. Imagines a pregnancy. And everywhere she goes there are happy families. Kath, Geoff and Rebecca. And Luke. Within the fiction she might kill the boy out of anger. A twisted revenge. Not realizing that he'd had a lot to put up with too.

Without being aware of it, Vera had wandered into the house, thrown the empty beer can into the box for recycling, opened the kitchen window to let in some air. She put the last two pieces of bread under the grill, sliced cheese to go on top, looked at the unopened bottle of white wine in the fridge and resisted the temptation. Took another can of beer instead.

All the time thinking, teasing out the different strands of the plot. Lily hadn't been a murderer, she'd been a victim. So how did that work out? How did that make sense?

She'd been a nuisance to Peter Calvert. He'd been happy to have a beautiful girlfriend, sex on tap, no strings attached. That would have done his ageing male ego no harm at all. Then she'd started to make demands, intruded into his respectable life of university big cheese and happy family man. No way was their separation mutual. Lily's conversation with Kath had made that clear. There couldn't be *another* older man in Lily's life.

Had Calvert killed her? Vera couldn't see it. He was too much of a coward, had too much to lose. His wife had indulged him in everything else in his life, why not in this too? Vera could imagine the conversation in the elegant living room at Fox Mill, the windows open to let in the breeze from the sea, the view to the lighthouse. *I'm so sorry, darling. I don't know what came over me. You will forgive me.* And of course she would because she had as much to lose as he had. Anyway, where did Luke Armstrong fit into that scenario?

If Lily had been killed first it might have worked. There was a motive for Lily's death. Luke could have been an involuntary witness. But this way round it made no sense at all.

Vera sat at the kitchen table and ate her cheese on toast. She switched on the light, so the clutter on the worktops, the stains on the floor near the bin, were all illuminated. Her thoughts turned to the four men who'd been there when Lily's body had been found. All different. But all screwed up when it came to women. Clive, so dominated by his mother that it made Vera want to weep. It was too close to home. She'd spent all her life in Hector's shadow, could get maudlin, if she let herself, about the missed opportunities when it came to men. Gary, who'd persuaded himself that Julie was the answer to all his prayers. But still pining for some slender lass with big eyes and no tits. Samuel, whose wife had committed suicide. And Peter, who pretended to have a perfect marriage, but had come under Lily Marsh's spell. It came to her suddenly that there was one logical suspect. But until she knew why Lily and Luke had been killed, that insight was no more than a guess. It couldn't influence the way she moved the enquiry on.

She drank more beer, knowing it was a mistake and she'd end up having to go to the bathroom in the middle of the night. Unsteadily she went upstairs to bed, still no nearer to any sort of conclusion. She took the collection of short stories by Samuel Parr from her bag and started to read.

Chapter Thirty-Four

Gary was having a quiet time at work. The band had
finished rehearsing and he'd got the sound as good
as it could be. Not that anyone else would notice the
difference. The musicians were Swedish. They played
experimental jazz, odd discordant noises which made
him wince. Now they were in the bar waiting for the
gig to start. There'd have been times when Gary
would be with them, matching them pint for pint.
He'd got into a real mess after Emily left him. It had
been such a shock. He still remembered in detail her
telling him there would be no marriage. He could
recreate the scene in his head – the jeans she had on,
the way her hair was tied back, the perfume she was
wearing.

They'd had everything planned. She'd bought the
dress, sent out the invitations. They'd found a flat to
buy in Jesmond. Emily worked for the Northern Rock
and got a cheap mortgage. It had scared the shit out of
him, the prospect of taking on a wife and a home all
at once, but he'd gone along with it because it was
what Em had wanted. He would have done anything
to please her. Her mother had never liked him, but
she *had* liked the idea of a fancy wedding. She had it

all arranged – the church, the cake, penguin suits. Nothing was too good for her Emily.

Then some lad Em had been at college with had turned up out of the blue, swearing undying love. He was a thin, weedy lad, not bad-looking if you liked them underweight and poetic. And it seemed Emily did, because she dumped Gary a fortnight before the big day. She was still with the bloke, who was a teacher now in some school in Ponteland. Gary'd seen him once in a bar in town and thumped him. The bloke hadn't made a fuss but Gary'd been done for breach of the peace. He'd been drinking a lot when that happened. He wouldn't react in the same way these days.

He'd idealized Emily and frightened her away. Who could live up to that? It wasn't the skinny lad's fault.

Now Gary never drank when he was working. *If you worked in an office, you wouldn't sit there with a bottle of wine on your desk.* That's what he told the other guys who sat in the cramped bit of corridor they called an office. Behind the scenes at the Sage was more like working in a submarine than a flash new music venue. All pipes and wiring and grey gloss paint.

He took his work seriously. It had always been the one thing he'd been good at, the one thing to hold him together. When his parents had bought their place in Spain, they'd said he should go with them too. There'd be plenty of work, they said. All those bars. Lots of them would have live music and they must need someone to do the sound. But he'd decided to stay in Shields. He had his flat there and his contacts. His birding friends. The chance to pick and choose the sort of gigs he wanted to do. He'd given up that flexibility now that he'd decided to take the job at the Sage, but he told himself he didn't regret it. Not really.

He walked up the steps of the small hall and swiped his pass at the door to get into the backstage area, then made his way down to the techie office. Neil, who was in charge, was leaning back in his chair thumping away on his computer.

'That offer of a permanent job,' Gary said.

'Yeah.' Neil didn't even bother to look up from the screen. He'd asked Gary loads of times before and the answer had always been 'no'.

'I've decided to take it.'

That got his attention. He swung his chair back to upright and his hands stopped moving. When he turned towards Gary his face was a picture. He jumped to his feet, took Gary's hand, slapped him on the back. Gary found himself grinning. But when he walked away, he was shaking. He wasn't quite sure what he'd done.

Now he had this picture of how things would be. Him and Julie living together in that house in Seaton. It would be a good place to live. Not too far from the coast when the wind turned east and the migrants came in. Not too far from the tower for sea watching. He couldn't rush her, of course. Not now that she was so upset about Luke. But he thought she'd come out of the tragedy whole. She was a strong woman. She wouldn't be changed by it. And he'd be there to support her and see her through.

He wasn't sure how he would have coped with a stepson. Would Julie have expected him to be like a dad? He didn't like to admit it, but he wasn't sorry Luke was dead, not really. It would have been a complication. Julie was always going to put the boy first. It was an awful way to look at things, but he couldn't help it. That led him to think of Laura. He pictured her as he'd last seen her, standing on the pavement outside the house in Seaton, watching him drive away. Weighing him up. That was how it seemed. He saw her in the short black skirt, the white shirt. He tried not to think of her in a sexy way. She'd be like a daughter to him if he got it together with Julie, and that was just vile. But something about her – her youth or her energy and defiance had got under his skin. Sometimes he thought he was haunted by Laura as much as he was by Julie. Perhaps it was safer not to consider moving into the house in Seaton until Laura had grown up.

There was still half an hour before he needed to start work and he went outside for air, walked to the front of the huge curved building and looked out over the Tyne. His parents had left for Spain because they couldn't stand the weather, but he couldn't imagine living anywhere else. He was proud of the city. He liked telling people he worked at the Sage. To his right and down by the river was the huge bulk of the Baltic Gallery. He remembered it as a decaying warehouse, kittiwakes nesting in the cracked stonework, its facade covered with bird muck. When it had first opened, he'd gone with Samuel Parr to see the Gormley exhibition. He wouldn't have wanted to go on his own. He was only comfortable backstage. But he'd loved the sculpture, all those figures of twisted metal, fine as spun sugar. Gary had found it odd to be there with Samuel, who was recognized by some of the staff. He was part of the Tyneside arts mafia, the set Gary despised as an alien race when they came into the Sage.

The river was at full tide, moving sluggishly, almost on the turn. On the north bank people were spilling out of the bars. He heard a line of melody, which faded before he could place it, the blast of a car horn. The low sun was reflecting from all the glass and turning the water red. Would Samuel or Clive or Peter Calvert find it strange to see Gary at *his* work, sat behind the deck, in control of the sounds coming out to the audience, making a difference, a real difference to the experience they had in the brilliant space? They knew him only as a demon sea watcher. They'd been friends for years, but really they knew very little about each other's lives. They knew he'd fallen for Julie, his childhood sweetheart, with her smile and her easy, comfortable body. They'd never guess he dreamed of the teenage Laura in her short black school skirt. They believed they were the closest of friends, but they all had secrets they would never share.

His mobile beeped to show he had a text message. It was from Julie and he felt a shock of guilt, physical. His face was hot as if he was blushing. *What are you doing tonight.* He pushed away his daydreams about Laura then and answered immediately. *Working. Wont be finished til midnight.* He had to wait so long for the reply that he'd almost given up. Perhaps she'd been offended, seen it as a rejection rather than a statement of fact. He should have taken more time to compose it. He fretted, putting together another message in his head. It was time for him to go in and do the final check. He always switched off his phone when he was working. Her reply came as he was walking back up the steps, with his back to the river. *Ill come and meet you. See you then.*

Chapter Thirty-Five

Julie felt that if she didn't get out of the house she'd scream. She'd stand at the top of the stairs and fill her lungs and open her mouth and the noise would be so loud that you'd hear it at the end of the road. Her mother was still there, cleaning. All day there was the hum of the Hoover, the background stink of bleach and polish, so it didn't even feel like Julie's house any more. And when she wasn't cleaning Mrs Richardson was talking, trying to prod Julie back to life with sharp words and guilt. As if there wasn't enough guilt around already. Julie had always found it easier to get on with her father. If he'd been there instead of her mother, they could have got pissed together. He'd have sat beside her on the sofa, watching the music channels on TV, telling his old stories about the musicians he'd known, holding her when she wanted to cry.

She couldn't tell her mother to leave. She thought she was being useful and it would hurt her. Then Julie would feel guilty all over again. So all day she tried to make up an excuse to get out. She concocted a story about being invited to Lisa's house. Lisa would cook her a meal and Julie would stay over in the spare room. Julie's mother approved of Lisa, who worked as a secretary for a big firm of solicitors in town. Then Julie went out into the garden and phoned Lisa on her mobile. On the other side of the horses' field they were cutting grass. She watched the tractor moving backwards and forwards, regular and mesmerizing. She could have watched it all day, but her mam would never have allowed it. She'd see it as idle and self-indulgent and would find Julie something useful to do.

'If my mother phones, I'm at your house, but I've fallen asleep and you don't want to wake me.'

Lisa was a good mate and didn't ask questions. She *would* have cooked Julie a meal and drunk wine with her and let her cry. But Lisa lived in a smart new flat on the front at Tynemouth and it had never been the sort of place where Julie had felt able to kick off her shoes and relax. Telling all these lies made Julie feel like a teenager again. By the end of the afternoon she was exhausted by it all. But she was a little bit excited too. She'd known all along that what she really wanted was to see Gary.

She had a shower before she went out, stood in the bath where Luke had been lying. Before, they'd had an old shower curtain, with pinkish spots of mould along the hem, but the police had taken that away. Her mam had been to Matalan to get another. Julie drew the curtain and shut her eyes to wash her hair. It was the first time since Luke had died. Until then she'd used Sal's place when she wanted a bath. She took her time getting ready, make-up, a splash of perfume. It wouldn't make her mother suspicious. She was of a generation when women didn't go visiting without making a bit of an effort.

Laura was in her room. She seemed to live there these days, only came out to eat and wee. Julie thought she'd been like that even before Luke had died. She knocked, poked her head round the door. Laura was lying on the bed. Not reading, not watching television, just staring at the ceiling.

'Are you all right, pet?' Julie sat on the bed.

Laura turned, managed a bit of a smile. Julie thought she should stay in. She was reminded of Luke when he'd started to get depressed. But she couldn't quite make the decision. If she didn't get out of the house she'd go mad herself.

'I was thinking of going out. Lisa's asked me to hers. Is that all right with you?'

Laura stared at her for a moment before shrugging. 'Sure.'

Julie thought she could never tell what Laura was thinking, never had been able to.

'I might stay over. Nan will be here.'

'I'll be fine. Really.'

Julie sat in the old Fiat she'd had since Geoff had left, which was held together now with filler and paint. Each year at MOT time there was a crisis and her friend Jan's mechanic son would work his magic and pull it through. This was another first. She hadn't driven since Luke had died. She imagined the neighbours looking through their nets, waiting for her to drive away. What would they think? That she was a heartless cow or that she was brave to start putting her life together. She wasn't sure herself which it was.

It was only eight o'clock but she went straight to the town. There was the usual panic when she hit the motorway at the old BT roundabout. She never knew which lane to take for the bridge. Then in Gateshead she missed the turn for the Sage and ended up in the car park for the Baltic. She couldn't face going back and stayed where she was. She sat for twenty minutes, her mind quite blank, before buying a ticket at the pay and display machine. Nine o'clock. The light was starting to go. She realized she was relishing the sensation of being alone.

She left the car and walked around the front of the Baltic Gallery. There was some sort of reception in the downstairs bar. Through the long glass windows she saw women in long dresses, men in dinner suits. They were drinking champagne from narrow glasses. A fat woman with very short hair was making a speech. Julie felt as if she'd travelled to a new country, as if these were exotic creatures quite different from her. On an impulse she walked across the new millennium footbridge from Gateshead to Newcastle. She'd never done that before either. She stood in the centre and looked upstream at the arcs and towers of the other bridges, the Tyne, the High Level, the Redheugh, familiar landmarks seen in a completely different light. On the Newcastle Quayside, she pushed her way through the crowd in a bar, just to use the toilet. She wasn't tempted to stop for a drink. She wanted to be clear-headed when she met up with Gary. She felt a bit mad as it was.

By the time she got back to the south bank of the Tyne it was quite dark. The river was draining towards the sea. The smart people were still in the bar at the Baltic, though the speeches were over. She sat on a bench outside, watching them. It was as if the big plate window was a giant film screen and though she couldn't hear what they were saying she got caught up in the drama. There was a pretty young woman who couldn't settle. She fluttered from group to group, talking and laughing, growing more and more unsteady. When she moved away, the groups turned in and talked about her. She seemed so lonely that Julie wanted to cry.

Her phone rang. She looked at the time as she answered it: 23.38. She'd been sitting here, watching, for more than an hour. And enjoying every minute of being alone.

It was Gary. 'Hi. I've finished earlier than I thought. Where are you?'

'I'm here already. At the front of the Baltic, by the river.' She was going to add that she'd just arrived. She didn't want him thinking that she'd been sitting here for hours waiting for him. But he was talking about the gig and how well it had gone, a joy. Despite the crap music and the small audience. How some nights were like that. Smooth and sweet. And then she saw him walking towards her, still talking on his phone. He'd walked down the steps from the entrance to the Sage. She stood up, so he could see her. The phone went dead and she stuffed it into her bag, so her hands were free. They stood for a minute just looking at each other, then almost stumbled together, awkward like kids. She expected him to kiss her, but he didn't. He held her for a moment, rubbing her back.

'Where would you like to go?'

'Can we go back to yours?' she said. 'I don't feel much like company.'

'Sure.'

'I'd better follow you,' she said. 'I don't know the way.' She hoped he'd suggest something different. *Why don't you leave your car here? I'll bring you back to get it in the morning.* But he didn't, so they were only together for a few brief minutes before they were separated again. He was giving her instructions about waiting for him in her car and what to do if she lost him. She felt like the girl weaving her way through the crowd in the Baltic bar. Lost and unconnected.

But she didn't want to make a fool of herself so she did as he told her. She waited at the car park entrance until the white van drove past and she followed it all the way back to Shields. If she lost him at lights he pulled in so she could catch up with him. She drew in behind him when he parked in a narrow street. Here there was another view of the river. Suddenly she was so nervous she wished she was back at home, sitting in her nightie in front of the telly, her mam wittering on.

In the flat it was easier. He opened a bottle of wine and she drank a large glass very quickly. Sod it, she thought. She'd never intended to drive home that night anyway. He put on some music she didn't know. They both sat on the sofa, leaning back against the cushions so they were almost lying down. He had his arm around her and he was talking about the music, what he loved about it, but in a whisper, so she could feel his breath on her cheek. He put his hand on her neck, stroked it just underneath her ear.

And suddenly she thought of Luke. How someone had put their hand on his neck, pulled a rope tight around it and squeezed until he was dead. She didn't scream. The last thing she wanted was to make a fuss.

But Gary must have felt her tense because he pulled gently away.

'Sorry,' she said.

'Nothing to be sorry for.'

She told him what she'd been thinking about. Luke in her bathroom and someone strangling him. 'Sorry,' she said again. 'I'm a bit of a liability.' But she'd drunk the wine too quickly and the word came out wrong. She giggled and he joined in.

'We can do whatever you like,' he said. 'Do you want me to take you home?'

She thought how lonely she'd feel in the double bed. Her mother would have made it, so the sheets would be stretched tight, tucked into the mattress. She never bothered making it herself, she preferred the sheets soft, slightly crumpled. 'No,' she said. 'Can I have more wine?'

He poured her another glass.

She woke with a hangover, lying on the sofa, fully clothed except for her shoes. There was a strange light, coming from a different direction, so she'd known at once it wasn't her own bed. The smell of proper coffee came from the kitchen. She hadn't thought he'd be into proper coffee. He must have been waiting for her to wake because he came in carrying a mug, a plate of toast.

'You could have had the bed,' he said. 'But I couldn't move you.'

'God, I feel dreadful. What time is it?' She did feel dreadful, but only the way she always did when she had a hangover, sick and heady, and that was reassuring, a sign of things getting back to normal. And she *had* slept, without the sleeping pills.

'Ten o'clock.'

'Oh my God. Laura will have already left for school. Mam will kill me.' She swung down her legs, so there was room on the sofa for him to sit beside her. 'Look,' she said. 'About last night . . .'

'It's all right, I had a great evening.'

'Really? I don't think so.'

'You're good company. Even when you're pissed. And we've got plenty of time.'

'Yes,' she said softly. 'I hope we have.'

She took the scenic route home along Whitley Bay seafront and past St Mary's Island, singing along to one of the compilation tapes her dad had put together for her. Motown. She was trying to put off the moment of going back into the house. Here, driving the Fiat so slowly that the guy in the Astra behind her hit his horn, yelling at the top of her voice, she could almost believe that the rest of it, all the nightmare stuff, had happened to someone else.

As soon as she opened the door, her mother appeared from the kitchen. She was like a figure in one of those mechanical clocks. Not a cuckoo, of course. A peasant woman in an apron, bobbing her head and wringing her hands.

'Thank God. Where have you been? I've been so worried.'

'I told you I'd be staying at Lisa's.' And that wasn't a lie, was it?

'I expected you to be back before Laura went to school.' The guilt again.

'Yeah, well, I had a bit much to drink. Did she get off OK?'

'She didn't have time for breakfast.'

'She never has time for breakfast.'

'I don't suppose you've had anything to eat either.' And immediately she popped back into the kitchen, to put on the kettle and start frying bacon. 'I got this from that decent butcher in Monkseaton. It's not all water and fat.' And though the smell of it almost made Julie want to throw up, she sat at the table and waited until the sandwich appeared, then forced herself to eat it. To make up for lying to her mother. To make up for having a few hours when she wasn't thinking about Luke.

It was only after the plate was clean that her mother brought in the mail for her to look at. Not such a big pile. On the top, a long white envelope.

'Look,' Julie said, trying to re-establish friendly relations. 'This is addressed to Laura.'

Her mam, already in her Marigolds at the sink, turned round. 'That's nice. Some of her friends from school, maybe.'

'Maybe.' But by now Julie had recognized the square capital letters, remembered Vera's response to the last card. 'All the same, I think I'll just give Inspector Stanhope a ring.'

Chapter Thirty-Six

When the call came from Julie, Vera was in her office, reading. The night before, she'd started a short story by Samuel Parr, one she'd never heard or read before. It was in the book she'd picked up from the library on her way to meet Ben Craven, a collection published by a small press based in Hexham. The title *Jokers and Lovers* had some sort of resonance, but she couldn't remember where it was from. It said on the jacket that the anthology had won a prize she'd never heard of. The story she'd been looking for, the one she'd heard on the radio, hadn't been in it, but she'd started reading anyway. Vera had fallen asleep after a couple of paragraphs but, perhaps because of the beer swilling round in her veins, the opening image had stayed with her all night. It had described the abduction of a teenager. The abduction had been described lovingly. A summer's morning. Sunshine. The flowers in the hedgerow named. It became a seduction, rather than an act of violence. The gender of the child was left deliberately ambiguous, but Vera imagined Luke. A great deal was made of the child's beauty. This was a form which would turn heads. And Luke could have been a girl with his long lashes and his slender body.

Half child, half man, he'd been an ambiguous figure too.

In the office, Vera held the morning briefing. Joe Ashworth had checked all the car-rental places in North Tyneside.

'Nobody of Clive Stringer's name or description hired a car on Wednesday night or Friday. I suppose that lets him off the hook.' He sounded disappointed.

Vera almost felt sorry for him. She described the interview with Peter Calvert. 'We know he was Lily's lover. We know he's a lying bastard, with an unhealthy interest in bonny lasses. We know she left her silver and opal ring in the Calverts' cottage. But we can't prove she didn't drop it when she looked round the day before. And we can't prove any connection between him and Luke Armstrong.' Then she'd gone on to describe the connection between Lily and Kath. 'Is it significant that the new Mrs Armstrong didn't tell us she knew the Marsh lass? God knows. It is to us, of course. But we're living and breathing the investigation. Maybe she just wanted to forget all about it and get on with her life.'

Then Vera had retreated to her office. She knew there were more important things to do, but she told herself that her team would already be doing them. She was pulled back to the story, the strange central character. Then the phone rang.

'Julie Armstrong on the line, ma'am. She won't speak to anyone but you.'

Vera listened in silence when Julie described the envelope, the writing. 'I didn't want to bother you, like. But last time you seemed to think it was important. We haven't touched it. Well, just my mam when she brought it in from the front door.'

'Has Laura got a mobile?'

'Oh aye, they've all got mobiles these days, haven't they?'

'Phone her and tell her to stay at school. She's not to go out with anyone, not even someone she knows until you pick her up. I'll send someone in a car and you can go and fetch her. I'll contact the school. Leave the card where it is. Don't open it.'

'She won't have her phone switched on,' Julie said. Vera could sense her confusion, the onset of panic. 'It's a rule. They're not allowed.'

'Don't worry, pet. Just send her a text and leave her a voicemail message. I'll see to the rest.'

She hung up and took a moment to compose herself. She'd picked up some of Julie's panic, could feel her brain start to scramble, the eczema start to itch. Then she phoned the high school in Whitley Bay, bullied her way past an officious secretary to the headmaster. He understood at once what was needed, motivated, Vera thought, as much by the possibility of tabloid headlines – *How did they let it happen? Young girl snatched from school gate* – as by concern for Laura's safety. Then she told herself she was a cynical old bag. He said he'd track Laura down and keep her in his office until Julie and the police car arrived. He'd phone Vera back and let her know when that had happened. Vera sat, waiting. Her eyes wandered back to the book on her desk, the atmospheric jacket in muted blues and greens. The phone rang.

'Yes?'

The headteacher didn't identify himself. She

heard the tremor in his voice when he spoke, thought he was starting to panic too. 'She didn't arrive at school. She was marked absent at registration.'

'Nobody followed it up?'

'We wouldn't. Not one day. And with what happened to her brother, we could understand she might want to take some time.' Justifying himself to her, and to the unforgiving press which would want someone to blame. Already making his excuses.

'Of course,' Vera said. 'Not your fault.'

But mine? Should I have seen it coming? 'Does she have a history of bunking off?'

'No. She's reliable. A worker. One of the bright ones.'

'Can you ask around, friends, people she might have come in with on the bus? I'll send someone to take statements.' She thought she'd send Ashworth. He'd be good with young lasses.

'Can you be discreet?' he said. 'I mean, no flashing lights and uniforms. I don't want to start a mass hysteria, parents coming to take their kids away. Luke was a pupil here too.'

She was distracted. 'You knew him? I mean, as more than a face, a name.'

'Yes, I like the kids like Luke. The ones who struggle. It's what I came into teaching for. Important not to forget that sometimes. I took an interest.'

'Can you think why someone would have wanted him dead?'

'No!' The answer was immediate and vehement. 'He was bit slow, but he was a nice kid. People enjoyed his company.' He struggled to explain. 'He was completely inoffensive.' He wouldn't be satisfied with that description, but she understood what he meant.

When Vera arrived at Julie's house, the door was open and she was waiting to go. Her mother was hovering in the background. Julie turned to say goodbye to the older woman, but by then Vera was out of the car and blocking the door.

'A change of plan,' she said comfortably. 'No rush now. Let's go in. Any chance of a brew, Mrs Richardson?'

She led Julie into the living room and sat her on the sofa. 'Laura's not at school, pet. Did she definitely get on the bus?'

'I don't know. I wasn't here. I stayed last night with a friend.' She looked up at Vera. 'I was at Gary's place. Don't tell my mam. But I needed to get away, have a few drinks.'

'What time did you wake up? A bit of a hangover, was it?'

'Aye, something like that. I was out of it till ten.'

'And was Gary with you all that time?'

'We didn't sleep together. I was on the sofa.'

'So he could have gone out without you knowing.' Vera was speaking almost to herself. She didn't expect an answer.

'Where's Laura?' It came out like a scream, brought her mother rushing from the kitchen.

'We don't know. We're all looking for her. The school. My team, and they're the best you'll find anywhere.'

'What time did Laura leave the house?' Julie turned to her mother. 'Did she get the bus?'

'She left at the normal time. In a rush, no time for

breakfast as usual. I'd made her a packed lunch but she wouldn't take it.'

'Did you have a go at her, before she went out?' Julie was red and angry. 'You always have to nag.'

The older woman was almost in tears. 'I didn't have a go at her. I said she was really brave for going and I hoped she'd have a good day.'

'Oh Mam, I'm sorry. It's my fault. I should have been here. I was so wrapped up in myself and she needed me. It's like Luke all over again.'

'We've really no time for this,' Vera said. 'You can save the tantrums for later, when we've got Laura back. I need information. The time of the bus. The names of the friends she travelled in with. Favourite teachers. Teachers she hated. Boyfriends past and present. You start making a list. I'm going to look at this card.' She tore a sheet of paper from a notebook and gave Julie's mother a pen. When she left them they were sitting side by side on the settee, both with tears drying unchecked on their cheeks, but working through the problem, coming up with names.

The envelope was lying in the centre of the kitchen table. From the moment she'd got Julie's call Vera had tried to tell herself this might all be a waste of time. The woman was probably overreacting. It was a card from a friend or a relative or a teacher. Nothing sinister. But when she saw it, she recognized the capital letters at once. This time there was the correct address. It even had the postcode. The envelope hadn't been sealed. The flap had been tucked into the paper at the back. No saliva. Nor on the stamp, which was of the ready-stick variety. Vera pulled tweezers and latex gloves from her bag, put on the gloves, lifted out the card. A pressed flower. Some-thing small and blue which she didn't recognize. The back was blank, just as the one which had been sent to Luke. No kisses.

She got on her phone to Holly at Kimmerston. 'It's definitely the same. I want it to the lab now and fast-tracked. And chase them up on the others.'

She phoned Ashworth, but heard immediately that he was surrounded by a gaggle of girls and couldn't speak. 'Call me,' she said. 'As soon as you have some-thing.' She knew he didn't need telling that but it made her feel better to be dishing out orders.

She put on her calm, slightly daft face before going into the living room. She wrote down the direct-line number for Holly and gave it to Beryl Richardson. 'She's a nice lass. Give her a ring and give her all the names you've come up with. Julie, I'd like you to come with me. Show me the way Laura would walk to the bus stop. I've got my mobile on me and they'll call as soon as there's any news. We could both do with some fresh air.'

She had Julie on her feet and out of the house before either of the women could complain. At the gate, instead of turning left towards the centre of the village and the main road, Julie turned right. 'Laura didn't like waiting with the crowd at the bus stop by the pub. Specially since Luke died. She always felt awkward with lots of people anyway, but since then it's been even worse. She walks along the cut here and gets on at the stop nearer town.' She stopped, turned to Vera. 'I should have given her a lift in. But I was such a mess myself. I couldn't face it.'

'This isn't your fault,' Vera said, slowly enunciating every word. 'None of it.'

Julie led her down a narrow alley with allotments on one side and the backs of houses on the other and arrived at a stile. Vera heaved herself onto it and waited, perched on the top, panting for breath, looking out at the landscape beyond. The footpath followed the side of the field which had been cut the day before, along the edge of a patch of woodland towards the main road. Laura would have been visible from the upstairs windows in Julie's street all the way. Vera thought she'd get a team to do a house-to-house. It was an outside possibility that the girl had been seen, but worth a shot. If Laura had been taken, this surely was where it had happened. Once on the bus, she'd be surrounded by other kids all the way to school. She lowered herself down the other side, pulled down her skirt so she was decent. Julie followed.

'Who else would have known Laura took this path to get the bus?' Vera stooped to pick a bit of straw from her sandal, tried not to make too much of the question.

'I don't know. The other kids, I suppose.'

'Geoff? Kath?'

'She might have mentioned it. I can't see it, though. She hasn't exactly been chatty lately.'

So it was planned, Vera thought. They knew that anyway because of the card, but this confirmed it. Someone had waited and watched, followed the family's movements. Not from the street. That would have been noticed. Perhaps from here on the edge of the wood, where you had a view of the village. A good pair of binoculars and you'd see inside the houses.

Then she thought that whatever the reason had been for the first murder, the killer was now enjoying himself. Or herself. It had become a game, an obsession. A piece of theatre. Not just in the staging of the body, but in the events leading up to that. She hoped the killer would want to make the pleasure last. She hoped it meant that Laura was still alive.

Chapter Thirty-Seven

The morning Laura Armstrong disappeared, Felicity Calvert walked back from dropping James at the school bus and tried to come to terms with the news that Peter had been Lily's lover. She supposed she should feel betrayed. Not by Peter – what right did she have to judge him? But by Samuel. She was convinced that Samuel must have known about Peter's affair with Lily Marsh. Probably all four of the men who were there when James found the body had known. Peter would have wanted to boast about the conquest. It was quite impossible that he would have kept something like that to himself and he confided in Samuel about everything. Perhaps that was why Samuel had seemed so weird lately, so wound up and tense.

Peter had told her about his relationship with Lily when he'd returned from the police station. He'd arrived back at the mill in a taxi, looking drained, rather vulnerable. By then James was in bed. The boy seemed to have accepted the story that the police needed to talk to his father as an expert witness and had gone to his room without a fuss. The house seemed remarkably quiet as she waited for Peter's return. Usually she had the radio on or listened to music, but tonight she could face neither. She had opened the windows and could hear the water of the mill race, very distant.

Felicity had watched Peter climb from the taxi and gone out to meet him. He'd taken her hand, as if they were teenagers, and led her inside. Without saying a word he'd lifted a bottle of wine from the fridge and opened it. This quiet was so unlike him that she was scared. He should have been raging against the indignity of his imprisonment, the impudence of the police in carrying him off. She almost believed that he was going to admit to murder. But he was free, wasn't he? It couldn't be that.

He poured two glasses of wine and sat at the kitchen table. The kitchen was her space and he seldom sat there in the evening. He preferred the comfort of the sitting room or the privacy of his office. To sit with her was an apology in itself.

'Are you hungry?' she said. 'Can I get you something?'

'Perhaps later.' He sipped his wine, met her eyes. There was another moment of silence, then he said, 'I was having an affair with Lily Marsh.'

She didn't say she'd worked that out. There was a more pressing question. 'Did you kill her?'

'No!' Horrified. He reached out and took her hands. She found herself excited, thrilled by the touch. In their everyday routine – the family, the house, even the sex – they seemed to slide away from a real encounter. This had the charge of being touched by a stranger.

'She was very beautiful,' she said. 'I can see how you might have been tempted.'

'I was flattered.' He paused, drank more wine. 'Do you want me to tell you about it?'

She thought about that. Did she want all the details? How they'd met? Where they'd made love? She worried she might find that exciting too. 'No,' she said. 'That's your business.'

'Would you like me to move out?'

'I don't know. No. It never even occurred to me.'

'Lots of women would.' He seemed puzzled that she was taking his revelation so calmly. Was he disappointed, even, in her lack of response? 'It would be their first reaction, at least.'

'Perhaps an affair doesn't seem so important with two people dead.'

'I didn't kill her.'

She stroked the top of his hand with her finger. 'I believe you.'

Now, walking back from the bus in the shade of the elder hedge, she thought that in this short, taut exchange there had been more communication than they'd had for years. Unbidden there came into her mind a possible headline for one of the women's magazines she only read at the doctor's and the hairdresser's: *My husband was suspected of murder – And it saved our marriage!*

Even the night before, sitting opposite him, she had found the exchange melodramatic and faintly ridiculous.

'It was over,' he said. 'Ages ago. I wasn't still seeing her.'

'Who finished the relationship?' More mag speak.

'I did. Lily was unbalanced. I should have realized no normal pretty young woman would fall for me.'

Perhaps there was a hint of a pause while he waited for contradiction. She kept quiet. At least his adultery meant she didn't feel obliged to play games with him. 'She'd become obsessed. She turned up at work. Phoned me.'

'I think she called here,' Felicity said. 'Several times when I picked up the phone, it went dead.' She remembered the roses in the cottage, the sound of footsteps in the hall. 'She might have been here too.'

'She seemed convinced that I'd leave you to marry her. I never promised her that. I didn't promise her anything.' He got out of his seat to fetch the wine from the fridge again, filled her glass then his own. 'I told the police that we'd parted amicably. I didn't want them to think I had a reason for killing her. But it wasn't true. It's been a nightmare. She was stalking me. I never knew where she'd turn up next. She must have arranged the placement in the school in Hepworth, so she could get to me through James. And then that charade, turning up here, pretending she needed to rent the cottage.'

'I don't think,' Felicity said, 'that you can expect me to sympathize.'

He was apologetic again. 'No, no, of course not.' And suddenly she felt ashamed and exhilarated at the same time, because her secret was still intact. Should she confess too? About her and Samuel? There was something addictive in the rawness of the conversation and she wanted that to continue. She felt as she had when she was a student, sitting late at night with her friends, the room lit by candles, something gloomy on the record player. Then, every discussion had the intensity of the confessional. But reason took over, a sly realization that while the balance of power had shifted between them she should make the most of it. Insist that James go to the local high school, for instance, rather than being shipped off to the institution in Newcastle which had screwed Peter up. In this penitent mood, he'd agree to anything. Besides, she told herself, this wasn't her decision to make. Samuel wouldn't bear it if their relationship became public knowledge. It would kill him.

Later that night they'd made love, with the windows open so she could still hear the water outside. Afterwards they stood together looking out towards the lighthouse. I'll finish it with Samuel, she thought. No one need ever know. It'll be as if it never happened.

The next morning they got up as usual, Peter left for work early while James was still having breakfast. The boy had been full of questions about the police and the CSIs. Peter had been patient, looked over James's head to give her a wry smile. He kissed her on the lips before he drove away. It would soon be James's summer holiday and she walked up the lane with him to meet the bus, making the most of their time together. Next year, she knew, James would insist on doing it on his own.

She reached the house and let herself in. She hadn't slept well and felt restless, edgy. The walk hadn't helped. If Samuel were asked to choose between me and Peter, she thought, Peter would always come first. That was why he didn't tell me about Lily, why he didn't warn me.

She made herself coffee and stood by the kitchen door to drink it. There was still blue-and-white tape across the cottage door, and while she was standing there a car appeared in the drive. It was one of the crime scene investigators from the previous day. He waved at her, before climbing into his paper suit and walking across the meadow.

In the cool of the house she phoned Samuel. It was quarter past eight and she thought he might be still at home. He lived only ten minutes from the library. Before dialling she didn't have any idea what she was going to say to him. When the answerphone clicked in, she was quite relieved. She thought she might have made a fool of herself by demanding an explanation. *Didn't it occur to you that I deserved to know my husband was having sex with a girl younger than our daughters?* But he could have retaliated. *You were having sex with your husband's best friend.* Besides, she'd never made any demands on Samuel. It was the basis of their relationship. She replaced the receiver without speaking.

On impulse she decided to go into Morpeth for the day. She wanted people around her, the feel of fabric between her fingers as she looked for something new to wear, coffee, a good lunch with a glass of wine. She didn't even bother to change or put on fresh make-up, just picked up her car keys and her bag and almost ran out of the house. As she locked the door behind her she heard the ring of the phone inside. She paused for a moment but she didn't go back in. She might call into the library to see Samuel later, but she needed time to plan what she was going to say to him.

Chapter Thirty-Eight

Vera had left a family liaison officer with Julie, with instructions that she should be taken away from the house – to a friend's, to her parents' home, anywhere as long as it wasn't in the village where soon a team would be doing a fingertip search of the length of the footpath leading from the allotments to the main road. Now Vera was back in the station. She'd called the team together, her three closest staff, shouted them into her office from her open door. Charlie was still on the phone to the officer who was coordinating the Seaton house-to-house enquiries. Joe Ashworth had just arrived from the high school, serious, rather flustered. She realized he was thinking of his own daughter. When Katie was fourteen, would he have the courage to let her get into school, into town, on her own?

'Laura definitely didn't get on the bus,' he said. 'The other kids didn't make anything of it. They thought she just hadn't been able to face school after what had happened to Luke.' He paused. 'I had the impression she didn't really have many close friends. They were shocked that she was missing, excited even. But none of them seemed terribly upset. The

312

teachers told me she kept herself apart from the other kids. One of them said she was a bit aloof.'

Of course she was aloof, Vera thought. Since she was young she'd had to put up with people teasing her about Luke. And for a moment Vera wondered if it was all much simpler than they'd been making it. Perhaps Laura *had* killed her brother. Revenge because he'd not saved Tom Sharp when he fell in the Tyne. Because he was always the centre of attention and he'd made her life a misery without even trying. And now she'd run away. Perhaps Lily's death was nothing but a horrible coincidence. Then she told herself that was ridiculous. The idea that there was no link between the two deaths was preposterous. And still at the back of her mind was the thought of the one obvious suspect.

Holly came in with a tray of coffee: four mugs of black liquid, a pile of plastic pots of milk on a chipped saucer. It was the first time ever Vera had seen her make drinks without being bullied into it.

Charlie finished the phone call and joined them. 'Nothing,' he said. 'Not yet. Some of the residents of the street are still out at work. I've told the team on the ground to get their phone numbers, call them at wherever they're working to see if they saw Laura this morning.'

In any other circumstances Vera would have been pleased that they were pulling their fingers out, working together, showing a bit of nous.

'I got the coroner's report on Parr's wife's death,' he went on. 'It was definitely suicide. She slit her wrists. The paper's on your desk.'

She nodded her thanks.

'This puts the focus back on the Armstrong family,' she said. 'Perhaps all the business with Peter Calvert was a distraction. Perhaps Lily Marsh was never an intended victim at all. She saw something, got in the way. Are we any closer to knowing what she was doing the night Luke Armstrong was killed?'

'The girls she shared the flat with were out that night. A trip to London to the ballet. Very classy. They stayed with friends in Richmond. They can't tell if Lily was there Wednesday night or not.' Holly had become an expert on Lily's flatmates.

'What would Lily Marsh have been doing in Seaton? An ex-pit village on the coast. I mean, it's just not her sort of place, those clothes she wore. She'd have stuck out like a sore thumb. Nobody saw her. I did the house-to-house myself.' Charlie had worked that patch as a PC and still had friends who were community police officers. 'There have been no strangers around at all.'

They sat, each of them trying to imagine Lily in her silk and her beads in the street where the kids played skipping games and the mothers sat on the steps watching them. All of them failing.

'Where do you think Laura's body is?' Charlie asked. The question they'd all had at the backs of their minds, none of them wanting to speak it.

'We don't know yet that the girl is dead.' Vera didn't shout, she kept her voice calm and reasonable. It wasn't the time for being showy. But she meant it. Or maybe she just wanted it to be true. For Julie and for herself. She wasn't used to failing and another death, the death of someone young, who'd never had the chance yet to be happy, would be the worst sort of failure.

'He didn't keep the other victims alive,' Joe said. 'Not that we can tell. Certainly not the boy.'

'This might be different.' Vera knew it was irrational, the idea she'd formed walking along the footpath with Julie, that the killer was enjoying himself, the game, the spectacle. That he might want to prolong the pleasure by keeping his victim alive.

Charlie knew better than to argue. 'If there is a body, where will it be?'

'In water,' Holly said.

'So where should we look? Every house in Tyne and Wear has a bath.'

'No,' Vera said. 'He won't use a bath again. Laura's a striking young woman. Not beautiful like Lily, but big eyes, cheekbones you'd die for.' She caught her breath at the phrase but nobody else seemed to notice and she continued, 'She looks odd, exotic. He'll want to turn her into a picture. It'll be somewhere dramatic.'

'Then he must be holding her,' Joe said. 'Either alive or dead. He won't risk posing the body in broad daylight. Not again. He got away with it with Lily, but he'd never try it a second time.'

'Did we ever hear back from Northumbria Water?' Vera demanded. 'Weren't they supposed to have blokes working at the outfall by the lighthouse the afternoon Lily was killed? Has anyone spoken to them?'

'That outfall hasn't been used for five years,' Joe said. 'Some European directive on sewage and clean beaches. The guy I spoke to reckoned a team must have just parked up there to have a break.'

'Well, talk to him again. Get the names of all the workers in the area that day. They're the closest we've got to witnesses.'

There was a moment of silence, then Vera jumped up, stood in front of them. 'I want ideas,' she said. 'Any ideas. Crazy as you like. Places to look. Places we can keep under surveillance.'

'The Tyne. That's where Tom Sharp died. That was flowers and water. The start of it.' Charlie again. More animated than she'd ever known him.

'Eh, man, that'll be some surveillance, the whole of the Tyne.' Joe looked around at them. Not being cruel, but demanding they be more specific. Joe was always the practical one.

'He's right, though,' Vera said. 'That's where it started.' She wondered if she could justify another trip to Acklington Prison to talk to Davy, wondered if by now he'd have something for her. She decided it would have to wait. She didn't want to be too far from Julie if the worst should happen.

'Where, then?' Charlie was sitting on the edge of her desk, hunched forward. This had become personal for him too. Vera wondered if he had a daughter, realized she'd never asked him about kids. She didn't like talking about other people's children. It gave her an empty, jealous sort of feeling. 'The Fish Quay at North Shields where Tom Sharp had the accident? There's that sheltered bit of the water where the boats tie up.'

'That's busy until the early hours. Bars, restaurants. People living in those smart apartments they've put up.'

'It would be some statement, though, if he could get away with it,' Vera said.

'Does it have to be a *he*?' It was Holly. She was the most detached of them all. She's still young enough to feel immortal, Vera thought, and to be self-absorbed, untouched by another person's tragedy.

'Physically a woman could have done the strangling. Carrying Lily across the rocks to put her in that pool, that's another question. Who were you thinking about?'

'Kath Armstrong is the one person who links all the victims,' Holly said. 'She's a nurse. They're trained to carry, aren't they?'

Not the one person. There's someone else too.

'What motive could she have?' In her head Vera was trying to find an answer to her own question. Perhaps it had something to do with perfect families. Lily, Luke and Laura had all intruded on the little family in the neat house in Wallsend. Were the crimes Kath's warped attempt to protect her own little girl?

She was imagining the Tyne at North Shields late at night. The shadows thrown by the buildings, the harbour master's office, the deserted fish market, the lights from the south bank. Within the dock the water was calm and oily. She pictured the dark shape of a girl, a silhouette against the reflected light on the water. But a body wouldn't float. Not at first. Perhaps the murderer would find something for her to rest on. A pallet? A fish tray? A small dinghy? And cover her with flowers. What a picture that would make. She tried to clear her head and leave her mind open to other scenes, other places.

'So, any other possible scenarios?'

'What about Seaton Pool?' Joe said. 'It's close to where the girl must have been abducted and isn't there a hide there? The birdwatchers would know about it.'

'The locals have looked there already,' Charlie said. 'It was one of the first places they tried because it was so near to her home, and they know some of the village kids hang out in the hide when they've bunked off school. They found a pile of empty lager cans and some graffiti. Otherwise nothing.'

But Vera thought it could very well provide the sort of setting that the killer would be looking for. Seaton Pool had been formed by the subsidence of mine workings, though there was no indication now of the industrial past. It lay between the footpath where Laura had walked to catch her bus and the sea.

When she was a girl, Vera had once sat in the Seaton Pool hide with Hector. There must have been some reason for him to have made a rare trip to the lowlands and it troubled her for a moment that she couldn't think what it was. Then she remembered. An American coot. They'd waited for more than an hour for it to appear out of the reed bed. It had been a cold sunny day and the pool had been ringed with ice. She'd been bored and Hector had been characteristically offensive to the other birdwatchers. The bird had occasionally been disturbed by people passing along the footpath which followed the west side of the pool. It was a favourite place for dog walkers. During the day, Vera thought, it would be a risky place to set out the body. But the murderer seemed not to mind risk. He seemed not to care whether or not he was caught. And later in the evening there would be no danger at all.

'Are they still searching along the footpath?'

'They'll be at it all day.'

'But not this evening. Not once the light goes.'

'No,' Charlie said. 'They'll call it off then.'

'I want someone watching all night,' she said. 'From the time the search team finishes up there and all the wooden tops go home. Hidden. Unobtrusive.' It crossed her mind briefly the effect that would have on the overtime budget but really she didn't care.

'Is there any chance he'd go back to the light-house?' Holly asked.

'Or there's the stream at Fox Mill,' Joe said. 'If the cottage is significant. If Lily came back, met someone there, lost the ring Calvert had given her, the place could have a special meaning for him. It'd be risky with people in the house . . .'

But he doesn't care, Vera thought again. The risk is all part of the game, part of the performance. He's come to realize that he likes an audience.

They were waiting for her to make a decision. There was a moment of quiet which sometimes occurs in busy buildings. Outside, a baby was crying in the street and a mother was trying to comfort him.

'Three teams,' she said. 'One at the Fish Quay. Talk to the harbour master. One at Seaton Pool, camped out in the birdwatching hide. And one in the house at Fox Mill. The least the Calverts can do is let you use the house, the runaround they've given us. I can't see him using the lighthouse again. The tide's such a variable there.

'But that's for tonight. Before that I want the detail checked. Go back to the beginning. By this evening it'll probably be too late. The girl will be dead.'

Chapter Thirty-Nine

When Felicity arrived back at the mill from town she saw that there was a car in the drive. A car different from the one belonging to the CSI. She presumed it was someone else to do with the murder enquiry and wondered when it was going to end, this invasion by strangers, the prying into their business. She supposed she should be grateful that the press hadn't got wind of their involvement and wondered even if the car belonged to some reporter. When she looked at the cottage she saw that the crime-scene tape had been removed.

She'd just had time to take off her shoes and put on the kettle when the doorbell went. From the kitchen window she saw the young detective sergeant who'd come to take Peter away the evening before. She went to answer the door in bare feet and she saw him looking down at her toenails, which were painted a very pale pink. She sensed his disapproval and wanted to say something to him. *Doesn't your model wife, who belongs to the Women's Institute, paint her toenails? Or don't you like it because I'm a grandmother?* But she said nothing. She stood, waiting for him to speak.

'We've been trying to phone you,' he said. There

was accusation in his voice and something else. Anxiety verging on panic.

'I've only just got in.'

'Where have you been?'

'Into Morpeth.'

'Were you with anyone?'

She didn't answer that. It was none of his business. 'Why, what's happened?' Because she could tell that there was something serious. 'Another murder?'

He didn't answer. 'It would be very helpful if you had some proof of your whereabouts this morning. Did someone see you?'

'No,' she said reluctantly. 'I was there on my own.'

'A till receipt, then. Something showing the date and time?'

Then she began to panic too. She imagined herself being carted off to the police station in Kimmerston, sitting in a cell, being questioned. Perhaps they thought she and Peter were involved together. What would happen to James then? 'I didn't buy anything. I intended to, but I ended up just window-shopping.'

Then she had an idea and went outside, still in her bare feet, the gravel on the drive stinging her soles, to look in her car. At last she found a parking ticket for the Safeway car park under the seat. The date and the time were clearly marked and Joe Ashworth's attitude changed slightly. He grew more polite and asked if he might come in.

'A young woman's gone missing,' he said. Back in the kitchen the kettle had already boiled and switched off automatically. She made coffee for him without asking if he wanted one. 'There's a possibility that it's linked to the two murders. I've been into the cottage.

I hope you don't mind. The CSIs have finished and you weren't here to ask. In the circumstances . . .'

'No,' she said. 'Of course. You must do everything you can.' But she was shocked he still considered the cottage as a potential crime scene. Did that mean the men in white paper suits had found something? Did it mean Peter was still implicated?

'Did your husband leave for work at his usual time?' Ashworth asked. His tone was polite and lacked urgency, but she wasn't taken in. She wasn't going to tell him that Peter had left early this morning.

'Yes,' she said. 'At about the usual time. And you'll be able to check when he arrived at the university. They sign in. Fire regulations.'

He smiled so she realized that had already happened. She wondered if Peter had actually been there when they'd checked or if they'd spoken to his secretary. She would have liked to ask, but had too much pride.

The kitchen clock squawked. Some bird call she didn't recognize. She saw it was already two o'clock.

'I haven't had any lunch,' she said. 'I'd planned to have something in Morpeth, but in the end I couldn't face it. I was going to make myself a sandwich. Can I get you anything?'

He smiled. 'I'm just going,' he said. 'But if you see anything unusual – a car you don't recognize, people hanging around the cottage – you will give us a ring?'

'Yes,' she said. 'Of course.'

She was walking to the door with him when the phone went. Her mobile, still in her bag in the kitchen. She knew it would be Samuel, and was preoccupied with the thought, so she didn't take in the implication of the detective's next words.

'Will you be in this evening? In case we have any more questions?' He seemed not to have noticed the trilling of the phone. Or perhaps he didn't care if she was inconvenienced.

'Yes,' she answered. 'Oh yes. We don't often go out.' She just wanted him to leave.

He smiled again as if that was the reply he'd wanted, as if that was why he'd come in the first place. 'Excellent. That's fine, then. I'll see myself out.'

By the time she returned to the kitchen the phone had stopped. There was no message. Call register brought up the number of Samuel's mobile. She tried to ring it but it had already been switched off. She left another message, but although she tried his home phone again, she couldn't get through to him. She kept trying until James came home from school, then she gave up.

Peter arrived home from the university a little earlier than usual. It was only half past five. From the kitchen window Felicity saw him get out of his car and stand for a moment looking over to the cottage.

He's thinking about the girl. He misses her. A lump of jealousy, solid, like food stuck in the throat, making her want to gag.

James must have seen him too from where he was playing in the garden. He ran round the house to greet him. She couldn't hear what he was saying, but he started talking as soon as he saw his father. Some news about school. Peter smiled and picked the boy up and swung him over his head.

Felicity watched, thought how fit he was despite

his age, how strong. Peter put his arm round his son's shoulder and they walked together towards the house. The land line rang. Felicity went into Peter's office to answer it, glad of a chance to compose herself before she greeted them.

It was Samuel.

'Hello,' she said. 'I've been trying to call you.' She had tried several times while she was in Morpeth that morning. There'd been no reply from his home phone or his mobile. She'd plucked up courage to go to the library, but the woman behind the desk had said he'd taken a day's leave. Then she'd gone to his house and knocked at the door. There'd been no reply.

'Why? What's happened?' His voice sounded strange, a little blurred. She wondered if he'd been drinking.

'I can't really discuss it now. Peter's just come home, if you'd like to talk to him.' She kept her voice light and easy as she always did when there was a possibility of being overheard.

'No. It's you I wanted.'

'Are you all right?' she asked. 'Where have you been all day?'

He didn't answer immediately. She heard Peter calling her from the kitchen, put her hand over the receiver and shouted back, 'I'm just on the phone. Won't be a minute. Stick the kettle on, will you?'

Still there was no response from Samuel.

'Where have you been?' she asked again.

'I thought you might have worked it out.' It was the sort of thing he might have said when they were alone together. Teasing. Implying a shared understanding. But now he just sounded bitter.

'Are you all right?' she said. 'Is something wrong?'

'I need to see you.'

'I don't think that'll be possible,' she said. 'Not this evening.' She'd forgotten all about her plans to accuse him of keeping the secret about Peter's affair with Lily Marsh. Forgotten the bubbles of lust which had sustained her since they'd got together, made her smile to herself when nobody was looking. Now she wanted to extricate herself from the relationship as soon as possible and with as much dignity as she could manage. With this phone call, she was starting to consider Samuel as a liability.

'It's the twentieth anniversary of Claire's death,' he said.

Of course, she thought, that had been mid-summer too. She remembered the funeral. A still, humid day. Swarms of insects under the trees as they waited outside the church. The awkwardness, because suicide was such an embarrassing form of bereavement. She'd felt almost that they should be commiserating with Samuel for being dumped. Later they'd brought him home with them and he'd described finding his wife. 'She looked more peaceful than I'd seen her for months. Her hair floating around her face.'

She had a sudden shock, as she realized he could be talking about the recent victims, then she pushed away the picture of Samuel as a murderer. Samuel was a gentle man. He wouldn't hurt a fly. 'I'm so sorry,' she said. 'I should have remembered.' She knew he was waiting for her to agree to meet him, and for a moment she hesitated. Perhaps she should go to him. Just as a concerned friend. James had switched on the television in the living room. She heard the signature tune of an early evening soap. Peter yelled from the kitchen that tea was ready. This was the important stuff, she thought. The everyday trivia of family life. This was worth fighting for. 'Look,' she said. 'I'm really sorry but I can't. Things are difficult here. The police took Peter in for questioning last night. Are you sure you don't want to talk to him?'

Samuel didn't answer.

'Everything's such a mess,' he said at last.

'Where are you?' she asked.

'Forget it.' More bitter than she'd ever heard him. He switched off his phone.

Peter had made her Earl Grey, with a splash of milk, just as she liked it. 'Who was that?'

She hesitated for only a moment. 'Samuel. He sounded a bit upset. It's the anniversary of Claire's death. I tried to get him to speak to you.'

'I'll talk to him later.'

'That young detective was here this afternoon. Another young woman has gone missing.'

Peter carefully set down his cup, but she could tell the news had upset him. Perhaps it reminded him of Lily.

'Do they think that has anything to do with the murders?'

'That was what Ashworth suggested. He wanted to know where I'd been this morning.'

'They've been trying to track me down all day.' Peter leaned back in his chair, stretched, implying that he'd been so busy that he was exhausted.

'Where were you?'

'A meeting. Extremely tedious and abysmally chaired, which is why it went on so long.'

'Really?'

'You can't think I had anything to do with this abduction?'

'No,' she said quickly. 'Of course not. Not that. I went into Morpeth this morning. I tried to phone you. But I couldn't get hold of you either.'

'You suspected I was with another woman?'

'I'm sorry. It did cross my mind.'

'Never again,' he said. 'I promise I'll never do that again.' He moved his head to take in the house, James in the next room, the view of the garden. 'This is all too important.' She realized he was echoing the thought she'd had earlier, when she was talking to Samuel.

After dinner, she and Peter watched television with James. Later, they went together to put the boy to bed, then they took their drinks onto the veranda and watched the huge orange sun floating low over the hills to the west. Peter seemed anxious, preoccupied. He returned several times to the subject of the abducted young woman. What else had Ashworth told her?

'Nothing,' she said. 'Really. But if they find her and catch the person who took her, you'll be in the clear, won't you? It'll all be over.'

But that thought seemed to give him no comfort. He couldn't settle. At one point he went into the house to make a phone call. She assumed it was to Samuel.

'How was he?' she asked when he returned.

'I don't know.' Peter was frowning. 'He wasn't answering.'

The police officers arrived just as it was getting

dark. She'd never met them before. She'd locked the front door and they walked round the side of the house, a man and a woman. They seemed impossibly young to her, gauche, inarticulate, though they made every effort to be polite.

'Sergeant Ashworth said we could watch the mill race from here. You told him it would be OK?'

'Did I?' She couldn't really remember what she'd agreed to.

'Perhaps there's a front room upstairs? We could watch from there.'

'Of course,' she said. 'Anything we can do to help.'

They were still in the spare bedroom when Peter and Felicity went to bed. She saw them sitting in the dark, peering out over the meadow towards the cottage. There was a moon now. It didn't give enough light to see detail, but would be enough to make out somebody moving as a shadow. But what will they do, if someone does turn up? Felicity wondered. They're hardly more than children.

She made them a flask of coffee and some sandwiches. They thanked her, keeping their eyes on the window.

She must have fallen asleep before Peter. She was aware of him lying next to her, very still, trying not to disturb her.

Chapter Forty

It was mid-afternoon when the search team found Laura's shoe. It was in a ditch by the side of the road, not very far from the bus stop. They'd started close to Julie's house in Seaton and followed the line of the footpath, spreading out across the field which was all stubble now. The residents of Laurel Avenue watched them from the upstairs windows, saw them as black figures against the bright sunlight and the gold of the cut field. The officers moved in sequence like dancers in a slow, elaborate ballet, their shadows shifting as the day wore on.

It must have occurred to some of the team, after being at it for so long, that they'd find nothing. Vera thought that in this situation she might find it hard to keep up her concentration; she'd start thinking of home and a shower, a cold beer. But when they hit the road the team didn't stop. They moved along the hawthorn hedge and down the ditch, which was almost dry now. They were still focused. They just stood up occasionally to stretch or rub an aching back. They worked almost in complete silence. Even after the discovery of the shoe they continued all the way along the verge to the big roundabout on the outskirts of Whitley Bay.

It was clear that the shoe had been dropped by accident. It was a mistake. Whoever had taken Laura hadn't realized she'd lost it. There was no sign that it had been placed in the ditch to hide it and it wasn't there to make a point. The water was so low that it was clearly visible sticking out of the mud. Vera was sure this had nothing to do with the placing of the bodies. There were no flowers. It was just a shoe. A flat, black shoe with no heel and no back, simple, the fashion of the summer. The kidnapper would know now that it had been left. Would it be preying on his mind? Would he think the forensic team would be able to work some magic with it, that they would deduce immediately who and where he was?

Julie recognized the shoe at once and began to cry. Until then it had been possible to convince herself that Laura had bunked off school. To pay her back for being such a crap mother. For not being there that morning when she set off for Whitley High. She looked at the shoe in its plastic evidence bag and she howled. Vera couldn't bear to see her in such a state. She persuaded Julie to take one of the tranquillizers prescribed for her by the doctor. This was more for her sake than for Julie's. The sound of the crying woman got under her skin and stopped her concentrating. Even when she'd gone outside to speak to the supervisor of the search team the noise remained with her.

Of course the shoe told them nothing. It could have told them about Laura. About how tall she was likely to be, about the way she threw her weight forward when she moved, about where she'd been walking. It didn't tell them anything about the man who'd taken her. But close to the spot where it had been found there were tyre tracks on the verge. The grass was very dry there. The tyres had only crushed the grass and left no real imprint. However, just where the grass sloped down to the tarmac was a small patch of reddish builder's sand. Perhaps it had been left during road repairs or spilled from a lorry. And there a perfectly formed tyre mark remained. Only a fragment, half the width of the tyre and about ten centimetres long, but enough to excite CSI Billy Wainwright, who crouched over it, like a toddler concentrating on making a perfect mud pie.

'Well?' Vera knew she shouldn't really be there. She should be back in her office, pulling in all the information, keeping on top of things. Only she didn't feel on top of things.

'I'm not sure we'll be able to identify the make of tyre from this.' Billy stood up. She thought he looked knackered and a bit stressed. He was too old to be playing away with his new young lover. Too decent to do it lightly. Again she wanted to tell him to be glad of what he had. A wife he could talk to at the end of the day. Not to throw it all away for some mid-life fantasy, however young and however bonny. 'But if you find me a suspect vehicle, I'll be able to tell you if there's a match. Look, there are very specific marks of wear, chips and nicks in the rubber.'

'So we're not looking for a new tyre?'

'No,' he said. 'The treads are very faint. This is hardly legal.'

It was a perfect late afternoon in mid-summer. Less humid than it had been earlier in the day, when everyone had been muttering about thunderstorms.

Vera stood for a moment watching the search team inch their way towards the horizon and the swallows swooping and dipping to pick up insects over the stubble field.

'If you can get an ID on that tyre, you'll get in touch?'

He nodded briefly and, looking at him, she thought he knew already how mad he was to take up with the pretty pathology assistant. He hated himself but he couldn't help it. He didn't want to admit he was making a fool of himself, or he was too old, or that the woman was using him. He'd persuaded himself that he loved her.

In Kimmerston, the incident room was unusually quiet. A strained expectant quiet, so every ringing phone or unexpected raised voice set nerves jangling. She'd just settled into her office when her phone did ring. Not an internal call. This had come through on her direct line. She gave her name and there was a pause. In the background the sound of echoes in an enclosed space, a metal gate slammed shut and locked, rowdy men's voices. Then a different, quieter voice. 'This is David Sharp.' Davy Sharp in Acklington Prison. It would be teatime. She pictured him on the wing. He'd have had to queue to get to the phone and there'd be a line of men behind him. All listening in.

'Yes, Davy. How can I help?' Keeping it easy. Her voice low too so only he could hear.

'More the other way round,' he said. 'More what I can do for you.'

'What can you tell me, Davy?'

'Nothing on the phone. You'll need to visit. And it could be nothing at all.'

'Run out of tabs, Davy?' She couldn't leave the investigation and rush off to Acklington just because he wanted a cigarette. Not without news of Laura. 'It's impossible today. Can I send someone else?'

'No,' he said, his voice still even. 'It's you or nobody.' There was a moment of silence and she thought the phone had been cut off before he continued. 'It's complicated. A bit odd. I don't understand it. But no rush. Tomorrow will do.'

'There's a girl missing, Davy,' she said. 'I need anything you have now.' But this time the phone was dead and she wasn't sure he'd heard what she'd told him. She replaced the receiver, angry with herself. She should have handled it differently.

Despite what she'd said to him, she was tempted to go. At least it would be action of a sort, the drive to Acklington, the banter with the prison officer on the gate. An escape from the waiting. But Sharp hadn't sounded urgent. There was no way she could justify it.

The collection of Parr's stories on her desk caught her eye and she was distracted by thoughts of the writer. She had a sudden picture of him, sitting with the rest of the group in the garden at Fox Mill, the night they'd found Lily's body. The four men and the one woman on the veranda. It occurred to her now that all those men were a little bit in love with Felicity Calvert. It wasn't the birding which glued them together. It was the woman. The ideal housewife with her flowery skirts and her perfect baking. The men were all lonely, screwed up, frustrated. Like me, she thought. Just like me. Then she was taken back to the story she'd been reading when Julie had phoned, the abduction of the young person at the height of the summer, the loving description of the capture.

Vera opened her door and yelled for Ashworth. He came immediately and she saw the people in the rest of the room look up from their desks to watch. She realized they were thinking there'd been a development. A body. It might even come as a relief for them, a break from the tension, if the girl was found dead. At least then they would know what they were working with.

'There's no news,' she said, speaking to the room in general. 'Soon as there is, I'll tell you.'

Ashworth shut the door behind him and leaned against it. She thought he looked tired, then remembered his wife, the baby due any day. Things got uncomfortable the last few weeks of pregnancy. Especially in this weather. So she'd heard. Perhaps neither of them was getting much sleep.

'Read this,' Vera said. She nodded to the book on the table. 'There's this story, written by Parr. It's not exactly like the abduction of the girl, but near enough.'

Joe looked at her as if she'd completely lost it, but he picked up the book and began to read.

'I started it last night,' Vera went on. 'Now I can't get it out of my head.'

Joe looked up from the book. 'You think it's a sort of fantasy. Parr's written about it and now he's playing it out.'

'Crazy, isn't it? Ignore me.' And really she couldn't believe it. It was too theatrical to be true.

'There's no evidence he ever met the Armstrongs,' Joe said slowly. 'Certainly no motive.'

'I told you,' Vera said. 'It's a stupid idea.'

'It's pretty weird stuff. And as you said, very close to the abduction and the murders. Not all the details perhaps, but . . .' he paused for a moment '. . . the atmosphere. How does the story end?'

She was pleased he was taking her seriously. Her earlier irritation at his lack of focus in the case was forgotten. For this she would have forgiven him anything. 'I haven't got that far. I don't know. And I'm too busy to sit here reading.'

His attention was pulled back to the pages. 'What do you need to do?'

'I want to pin down where they all are,' Vera said. 'The people who were there when Lily's body was found. What are they doing today?'

'Felicity Calvert's at home. I went to look in the cottage at the mill. Just in case the girl was being held there. This morning Felicity went into Morpeth. Shopping, only she never bought anything. And nobody saw her. The only proof she was there is a parking ticket from the car park in the town centre. I phoned Calvert at the university. He's there some-where. At least, his secretary said he signed in this morning and then went into some sort of conference which was going to last most of the day. She promised to track him down and get him to phone me back, but I've not heard anything yet. Clive Stringer's been at work. I spoke to him in the museum earlier.'

'Is he still there?'

'I presume so. It's not long since I spoke to him. Gary Wright's in North Shields. He's not working until tonight. One of the local men called on him earlier.'

'Did they look inside?'

'I don't know. Didn't ask.'

'I'm going to check Wright's flat,' Vera said. She knew it was probably a waste of time, but she was too restless to wait in her office for the phone to ring. She imagined Laura Armstrong locked in the room where she'd sat chatting to Wright, drinking beer. Even if the girl got out onto the balcony and started shouting, would anyone hear? 'And Parr? Where's he?'

'Nobody knows. He's taken a day's leave. Arranged it yesterday. He's not in the house in Morpeth.'

'I want to find him.'

Ashworth nodded. 'Look, do you want me to finish the story? I don't want to be too far away from home today anyway. Sarah had a few twinges in the night. Could be the baby.'

So that was what it was all about, she thought. He wasn't supporting her at all, just looking for an excuse to be in the office. She was about to make a sarky remark then thought it wasn't worth it. Office politics didn't matter so much with Laura missing.

'Stay in here,' she said. 'Give me a ring when you've finished the story. Earlier if anything occurs to you.' He nodded. She gathered up her bag and left the office. He was already engrossed.

Vera was in the car park when she realized she hadn't looked at the coroner's report into Claire Parr's death. She retraced her steps, ignored Ashworth who was comfortable in her chair, and dug through a mound of paper until she found what she was looking for.

'Oh Christ,' she said. 'Parr's wife. She *did* slit her wrists. But lying in the bath. Parr found her.'

Chapter Forty-One

Gary Wright opened the door to her with a sandwich in one hand and she realized that she should be starving. She wasn't, though. The thought of food made her feel sick.

'What's all this about?' He stood aside to let her in. 'One of your people turned up this morning, but they wouldn't say what was going on.' There was some music playing. Vera didn't really do music. Occasionally there was a song which stuck in her head, made her feel sentimental. Usually a tune she'd heard as a kid. Mostly she just considered it a distraction.

'Do you mind turning that off?'

He turned a knob and the music stopped. They were both still standing. 'Coffee?' he asked, then, seeming to remember her last visit, 'Beer?'

'You've not heard from Julie, then?'

'Not today.' He paused. 'She was here last night.'

'Aye, she said.' Vera sat down. 'You'll not have heard about her daughter?'

'Laura? What's happened?' He'd just finished the last of his sandwich and she had to wait for him to empty his mouth before he answered.

'Do you know her?'

'I met her once when I went to the house in Seaton.'

'What did you make of her?'

'Nothing. I don't know. We only exchanged a couple of words.'

'Interesting-looking girl.' She nodded to the photo of Emily. 'And you like them skinny.'

'For Christ's sake! She's fourteen!' But despite the bluster, Vera thought she caught something under the words. Guilt? Somehow the girl had got under his skin. 'I felt sorry for her. Being in the house while her brother was being strangled. I was saying to Clive the other day—'

Vera interrupted. 'She's gone missing. You don't mind if I have a quick look round.'

'What would she be doing here? She doesn't know where I live.'

'Humour me, eh, pet.'

She pulled herself to her feet, knowing all the time that she wouldn't find Laura. If Gary had taken her he'd be too clever to bring her back to his flat and she couldn't really see it. But now she was here she should go through the motions. She opened the door to his bedroom. The bed had been made and the room was tidy.

'What time did she go missing?' he asked.

'About eight-thirty. She never made it to the school bus.'

'I was here then, with Julie.'

'According to her she was sleeping off the effects of a bucketful of wine. Which you gave her.' Vera threw open the bathroom door. There was a row of shower gels and aftershaves on the window sill. More things to make you smell good than she'd ever possessed. No sign of Laura.

'She was determined to get pissed. I couldn't have stopped her even if I'd wanted to. And why would I? She wanted one evening when she wasn't thinking about Luke.'

Vera looked into the kitchen and through the glass door onto the balcony. Nothing. 'I know. I don't blame you.' She stood, quite still, in the middle of the room. 'You can imagine what sort of state she's in now. Are you quite sure there's nothing you can tell me? About Luke, or Lily Marsh? About any of this mess? Have you heard anything from Clive or Peter or Samuel?'

He hesitated for just a moment. Had he been tempted to confide in her about Peter Calvert's affair with Lily? Had he known about that? But in the end male solidarity took over. He shook his head.

'Sorry, Inspector. It was all just a horrible coincidence. I can't help you at all.'

At that, she lost patience with him and walked out. She'd only reached the top of the stairs when she heard the music again.

In her car she punched her own office number into her mobile, having to think for a moment what it was. Joe Ashworth answered immediately. 'Inspector Stanhope's phone.'

'Well?'

'No news on the girl. I'd have called.'

'What about the story?'

'I'm still only halfway through. I wanted to start at the beginning. It's fascinating, though, isn't it? The similarities.'

'I thought I was going mad,' she said. 'Obsession can do that to you. I'm going to see if I can track down Parr.' She switched off her phone before he could reply, slipped it onto the passenger seat. She'd never got round to fitting a hands-free set.

When she got to Morpeth, it was early evening. In the quiet street where Samuel Parr lived, his neighbour, a middle-aged woman, was dead-heading roses in the small front garden. Further away, children were splashing in a paddling pool, giggling and shrieking with delight. The woman tried not to watch as Vera got out of her car and knocked at the door. She would think it rude to stare, would hate to be seen as intruding. Vera thought Samuel Parr should be in. This was a time for preparing an evening meal, for the first glass of wine. But there was no reply.

Vera went up to the wall which separated the houses. The woman looked as if she wanted to escape inside.

'You don't know where Mr Parr's likely to be?'

'I'm sorry, I don't.' Tight-lipped, as if she begrudged the effort it took to form the words.

'It's all right, pet, I'm not selling.' Vera flashed her warrant card, grinned mirthlessly. 'I need to find Mr Parr. It's urgent.'

The woman looked up and down the street. 'You'd better come in.'

They sat overlooking an immaculate back garden. Away from public view the woman seemed to relax. 'I'm sorry, I really don't see how I can help. We've been neighbours for a long time, but never what you might call friends.'

'Did you know Mr Parr's wife?'

'Claire, yes. So sad. She always seemed happy enough. A little excitable, perhaps. We were all very shocked when it happened.'

'There was never any question that it was suicide?'

'Oh no, of course not. Samuel was heartbroken. I'm sure he blamed himself.'

'Why would he do that?'

'Well, it's a natural reaction in circumstances like that, isn't it?' the woman said. 'Guilt.'

'You don't think that he provoked the suicide? That he was having an affair, for example?'

'Of course not.' The woman seemed horrified. 'Samuel is a librarian!' As if his profession made the idea impossible.

They sat for a moment in silence, then she said, 'What are all these questions about?'

'I'm working on another enquiry,' Vera said. 'Mr Parr was a witness. His wife's suicide probably isn't relevant. I'm a little concerned for his safety.'

'Of course!' the woman said. 'It's the anniversary of Claire's death! My husband mentioned it this morning when he saw the date on the *Telegraph*.' She paused. 'You don't think Samuel's done anything stupid? That he can't face going on without her?'

'No,' Vera said. 'I don't think there's anything like that. But if you do see him when he comes in, ask him to give us a call.'

In the car, Vera realized she'd left her phone there when she'd gone in to speak to the woman. She'd had two missed calls, both from Joe Ashworth. She rang him.

'I've finished the story,' he said.

'And?'

'I think you'd better come in.'

Chapter Forty-Two

Back in her office, Joe was as excited as she could remember seeing him. 'Read the last few pages.' He moved away from her desk so she could sit down, hovered just inside the door.

Vera returned to the story. There was a description of a garden, where the kidnapped young woman was being held. It was an Eden gone to seed, a place of fleshy leaves, enormous flowers and overripe fruit. Vera found it oppressive, longed for a passage set in the hills, somewhere with lots of sky and a bit of a breeze, thought she'd been feeling like that since the beginning of the case. As the plot reached its conclusion, she grew more tense. She told herself it was fiction, wished she could throw the book aside and return to the reality of forensic tests and reason. But with Joe watching she had to continue reading. At last the inevitable ending occurred. The young woman was strangled. Parr had written the killing as if it was an embrace, a gesture of tenderness. The murderer was still anonymous; any relationship with the victim unexplored. In the final paragraph the body was placed in a pool, surrounded by water lilies.

'Well?' Ashworth demanded. 'What do you think? It must have been Parr.'

Vera didn't answer. 'I know where the story is set,' she said. 'I've been there.'

Vera's father had been part of the committee which had set up the Deepden Observatory. She wasn't sure who'd been foolish enough to ask him onto it. His brief flirtation with the birdwatching mainstream hadn't lasted for long. Hector had been too much of a loner to get on with the other committee members and his attention span had been too short for tedious meetings about fundraising events and the observatory constitution. Besides, he got his thrills from the illegal activities which surrounded his passion – the late-night forays into the hills for raptors' eggs, taxidermy carried out on the kitchen table. He wasn't really interested in the gentle and scientific study of bird migration. After about six months he sent an acerbic and libellous letter of resignation.

He had, however, been invited back to a party to celebrate the tenth anniversary of the opening of the observatory. Vera thought the invitation had probably been sent by mistake. He was on a list and nobody in authority had checked the names. The committee wouldn't have wanted him there. By that time, everyone in the Northumberland birding world had become aware of his illicit activities. He'd never been prosecuted, but it was a small world and there'd been rumours for years about his egg collection. When he was drunk he boasted about it. The best amateur collection of raptors' eggs in the country, he'd say. Probably the best in the world.

Hector, of course, had been delighted to receive the invitation and insisted on going to the party. She'd known better than to try to dissuade him. He'd always been a stubborn old sod and he delighted in making a nuisance of himself. By that point in his life he was drinking heavily and Vera had gone with him as a sort of minder, to stop him making a scene and to drive him home. It had been the same time of the year as now, another dry, still evening in mid-summer. Probably some of the people involved in the recent murders had been there.

What did stay with her was an image of the place. By the evening of the party the garden had grown up and everything was lush and green, an oasis in the parched flat land which surrounded it. There had been a conducted tour of the ringing hut, the mist net rides and through the orchard. Later, she'd stood by the pond, keeping a watchful eye out for Hector, ready to move him on quickly if he started to cause offence. But that evening he'd been on good form. A little loud, perhaps, but good-humoured, entertaining. As the night wore on she was able to relax. She even found herself enjoying the occasion.

She didn't tell Ashworth that story. 'I can't be certain, of course,' she said. 'But I think it's Deepden. Not far from the lighthouse where the girl was found and only just up the road from Seaton, where the Armstrongs live.'

'What are we waiting for, then? And if Parr's there with the girl, we'll need back-up, won't we? Do you want me to get on to it?' Now his anxiety about his wife was forgotten. He didn't want to miss out on the glory of an arrest.

'Let's keep it quiet for the moment. Low key. Any hint that we're on to him and he'll kill her. What's he got to lose?' But it was more a matter of pride for her than concern for the safety of the girl. Pride was her great failing. She didn't want a song and dance about this, in case they'd got the whole thing wrong. She hadn't got Samuel Parr down for the murders. She had in mind someone else entirely. And Laura could be dead. Vera imagined the gossip there'd be if she cocked this up publicly. *The boss got the idea out of a book. Talk about fairy tales. This time she's really lost it.* She would hardly be able to say then that it had all been Joe Ashworth's idea. She wasn't sufficiently sure of his theory to pull people away from the locations her team had come up with originally – Seaton Pond, the Tyne at North Shields, Fox Mill. Those places would still be watched.

'This'll be just you and me exploring an outside chance,' she said to Ashworth.

She could tell he believed the girl was at Deepden, he'd been seduced by the story, the flowers, the water.

She took a large-scale Ordnance Survey map from the shelf in her office and laid it across her desk. 'This is where we need to park,' she said, jabbing her fat finger onto the paper. 'If he's there, we don't want to be so close to the house that he can hear the engine.'

Before she left the station, she called into the incident room, sat on the edge of Charlie's desk, gave him her instructions. 'Then get off your backside. You could do with the fresh air and there's something I want you to check.'

As she drove towards Deepden she tried to recreate a plan of the place in her mind. The bungalow was side-on to the road, with the orchard behind it. The overgrown garden and the pond lay between the house and the flat fields running to the coast.

She didn't want anyone to know where they were, but Ashworth insisted on keeping his phone on until they got to the observatory. 'Sarah has to be able to get in touch.' She felt like screaming at him. *What will you do if your wife* does *go into labour? Leave me here on my own and drive off to play happy families? Or will you stay with me? Be in on the end of it and let your wife give birth without you?* She wasn't quite sure what he'd answer. Perhaps the same thought had occurred to him, because she could sense he was jumpy, sitting beside her, reading the map with his small Maglite torch, keeping his finger on the road.

'Nobody's booked into the observatory tonight,' he said. 'I checked with the secretary.' He'd told her that before. He couldn't cope with the silence. It wasn't like him; usually he was restful. Perhaps she should have left him in the incident room, so he could contact his wife every ten minutes. But Vera was used to having him with her at important times. She was glad she wasn't doing this alone. He cleared his throat. 'Apparently it was quite busy on Monday. There was some rare bird. But this time of year, people really only come for the weekends.'

She pulled into the verge, switched off the engine. There were no street lights and it was so quiet that they could hear the ticking of the car as it cooled. Outside it was almost dark, impossible to see colour or detail, but she could make out the shape of the hedge running alongside them.

'I'll walk up the lane,' she said. 'See if there are any lights on in the cottage, if there's a car there.'

Ashworth didn't answer.

The heat as she got out of the car made her think

of Spain. There should be cicadas, the smell of rosemary. Walking down the lane, keeping close into the hedge in case she heard a car turning off the main road, she was reminded again of her father. Until she was old enough to protest, he'd taken her out on his raids. She'd hidden in ditches and behind patches of scrub and drystone walls, keeping lookout for him in case the police or RSPB wardens should appear. She'd hated every moment. The panic. The fear of being arrested, locked up, of getting it wrong. What would she do if someone did turn up? But it had been exciting too. Perhaps that's why I became a cop, she thought. I got addicted to the adrenaline rush at an early age.

Her eyes were becoming adjusted to the dark and, before she came to it, she saw the five-bar gate which led into the observatory garden, and beyond that the matt black shape of the cottage. There was no car. Not on the lane, at least. It was possible that it had been pulled onto the drive and was hidden by trees and a bramble thicket. She wouldn't see it from here. She walked on down the lane in the hope of getting a better view of the front of the house, where there were windows. Would he take the risk of turning on lights? Was he there at all?

At first she saw nothing, then there was a flicker of light. The striking of a match or a torch being switched on and off. So brief that she could have imagined it. If she'd been the imaginative sort. Perhaps Joe was right after all. Perhaps Parr was here. She imagined how triumphant Joe would be when she told him there was someone in the bungalow. She allowed herself a daydream. She was in Julie's kitchen, her arm round Laura. *I've brought your girl home, pet.* Though she had no evidence that Laura was still alive she wanted that moment so much that it hurt.

She turned and walked back to the car, let herself in. She'd just shut the door when Ashworth's phone went, startling her so she felt her heart suddenly race.

He pushed the button after the first ring. 'Yes?' Even his whisper seemed very loud after the silence outside. Then she felt him relax and she could tell it wasn't his wife on the other end. She must still be tucked up at home with her cocoa. He wouldn't have to run back just yet to be present at the birth. 'It's Charlie,' he said. 'He wants to talk to you.'

She took the phone from Joe. 'Well, Charlie? What have you got for me?'

'I found Parr.'

'Where was he?'

'The first place you suggested. The cemetery. Next to his wife's grave. It's twenty years today since she killed herself. When I got there he was sitting on the grass. Looked as if he'd been crying.'

'You got someone to check his tyres against the mark on the road at Seaton?'

'Aye, and they're nothing like,' Charlie said. 'He drives a new car. Billy Wainwright said the tyre that left the mark was almost illegal. Besides, I don't think he's been in a fit state to snatch the girl. Sounded to me as if he'd been in the cemetery since early this morning. He puts on a good show, but I'd say finding that lass at the lighthouse brought it all back. When I got there he could hardly hold it together. I asked him about Laura Armstrong, if he knew what had happened to her, but he didn't have any idea what I was on about. Really, all he could talk about was how he'd let his wife down. I took him home, had a quick look round inside the house before I left him. There was no sign of the girl.'

'Thanks, Charlie.' She handed the phone back to Joe. 'They've found Samuel Parr. He had nothing to with abducting Laura.'

'So that's it, then. We can go back to Kimmerston.' She couldn't tell if he was pleased that his theory had come to nothing, or pleased that he could get back to his wife.

'Someone's in the cottage. I saw a light.'

'Are you sure?'

'Certain. I'm not given to visions.'

'One of the birdwatchers, perhaps. The members have keys. They're supposed to let the booking secretary know they'll be there, but they don't always.'

She saw him sneak a look at his watch, took no notice, shut her eyes to help her concentrate.

'Why don't we just go to the front door?' Ashworth said. 'Find out who's there and what's going on.'

She ignored him. It was important to think this through. Perhaps Samuel Parr's short story about the abduction of a child was irrelevant. A strange coincidence. She'd been so desperate to find Laura Armstrong that she'd allowed herself to be misled, swept along by Joe's enthusiasm. But the details were so similar, so consistent. She thought of the jacket of the anthology, the swirling greens and blues of the design, a stylized image of waves. The title in white, sharp against the patterned background. Parr's name at the bottom of the page. She'd borrowed the book in hardback from the library. Hundreds of people could have had access to it.

When she opened her eyes, she knew what had happened. She'd been right all along. It wasn't a surprise to her. She usually was.

Chapter Forty-Three

She was relieved when they found the door of the cottage was unlocked. Ashworth hadn't mentioned it again but she wasn't sure he believed her about the light. Not when they pushed open the five-bar gate, lifting it carefully on its hinges, and the place was dark. They walked across the grass to avoid the sound of their feet on the gravel drive. The grass was long and felt cool, slightly damp, through her sandals. Then a thin moon appeared and she even questioned her own judgement. Perhaps what she'd seen had been some sort of reflection. She'd wanted so much to find Laura here. She looked through the window, but could make out nothing inside.

But why would the cottage be open if the place was empty? She touched the door gently until it opened a crack, and listened. Joe Ashworth was making his way to the back of the house. She couldn't hear a thing, not even his moving. She stretched in her arm and ran her fingers over the inside wall, feeling for the light switch. Woodchip wallpaper, then the smooth plastic of the surround to the switch. She struggled again to remember the layout of the bungalow. She was sure there was no hall. This was the living room. Beyond it lay the kitchen and to the right two doors leading to the bedrooms which were used as dormitories. She gave Ashworth a few more minutes to take up position, switched on the light, pushed the door wide open.

The light came from a low-watt, energy-saving bulb which hung from the centre of the ceiling, but for a moment it blinded her.

'Police. Don't move.' She blinked as she shouted, heard a noise somewhere, a door being opened.

There was no one in the room. It was much as she remembered it. A table under the window. It might once have been a decent piece of furniture but now it was scratched and covered with rings from coffee cups and beer glasses. Two upright chairs pushed under it. A sagging sofa and two easy chairs facing the empty grate. On the walls photographs of birds and a number of paintings and drawings, mostly terrible. A few shelves with natural history books, maps and field guides. In the seconds it took to look around her, Ashworth appeared. The noise she'd heard had been him opening the door into the kitchen.

Without speaking she threw open the doors to the bedrooms. They were both surprisingly neat. Three sets of bunks in each. Grey blankets folded at the foot of each bed. A faint smell of mildew and socks.

She turned to follow Ashworth, who'd wandered back into the kitchen. It was the time to admit she'd been wrong. To get him to promise not to tell the world they'd cocked up and to let him go home to his enormous wife.

'Someone's been here very recently,' he said. 'The kettle's still hot. The light you saw could have been someone lighting the gas.'

So there was still a chance they'd find Laura before she was killed. She wanted to kiss him.

Ashworth seemed not to realize the effect of his words. 'He can't have gone anywhere. We'd have passed a vehicle in the lane. There's no car in the drive. He must have parked further down the track.'

'He knows we're here now,' Vera said. 'Switching on that light wasn't the brightest thing I've done in my career. You'll be able to see it for miles.' She ran out of the house and into the garden, stumbling on the last step from the front door. The pond was ahead of her. There was hardly any reflection from the water, only tiny patches of silver around the edges. In the centre a black shadow. She found herself praying in her head to a God she'd never believed in. *Please let her not be there. Not the girl. Not Laura.* She heard Ashworth close behind her, the sound of his breathing, the rustle of denim against denim as he walked. I hope you're praying, she thought. You're a believer. He might listen to you.

She crouched to get closer to the water. Began to make out the shape of a young woman's body, arms outstretched, when Ashworth switched on his torch. As the narrow beam swung over the surface, the image changed. She saw flat, waxy leaves, balls of tangled vegetation sucking in the light, but nothing human. Nothing dead. She realized she'd stopped breathing and took a lungful of air. She felt her head swimming.

The girl might already have been killed but she hadn't been posed. Not yet. She hadn't been used for effect, turned into a piece of art which had nothing to do with the real Laura. At least Julie had been spared that.

Vera straightened and tried to keep her thoughts clear, to remember the detail of what had happened during the Deepden party. Because she'd been determined to keep Hector on the straight and narrow, she'd been perfectly sober. The memories should be sharp. There'd been the guided tour: a walk through the orchard, sunlight sloping through the trees, a look into the cottage, which had been freshly painted for the occasion, a ringing exhibition.

The ringing exhibition. They'd stood in a semi-circle while a tall man in a blue smock reached out a bird for them to see. A yellowhammer, loosely held, the head caught between his second and third fingers. Through the door, they'd seen him weigh it. He'd slid it head first into a plastic cone which clipped onto a spring balance. He'd measured its wing with a metal rule. With his free hand he'd taken pliers from a shelf and a silver ring from a string hanging on the wall. He'd fitted the ring on the bird's leg, then squeezed it carefully into place. Then he'd stood at the door, the bird resting on the palm of his hand, until it had flown away.

It hadn't been the cottage door. She was sure of that. She dug in her memory for a picture of it. A flimsy wooden door held shut by a padlock which the ringer had unlocked when he'd returned from catching the birds. A door into a hut, the size of a big garden shed, made with stained wood panels. A corrugated iron roof. And surrounding the hut a thicket of bramble and buckthorn, so it was hidden from the garden and the house. They'd been surprised when the tour guide had led them there down a path cut through the undergrowth. The bushes had been cleared close to the front of the structure and that was where the group had stood, an audience waiting for the show to begin.

Now she tried to get her bearings. Standing next to Hector on the night of the party, while the ringer did his stuff, she'd felt her father start to get restless; he could only take not being the centre of attention for so long. She'd thought that he might escape, show his boredom by making an obvious run for it. It would have been easy enough for him to do that. The hut was right on the edge of observatory land, on the boundary with the field of rough grazing which led to the sea.

She began to move along the edge of the grass, looking for a gap in the vegetation. It seemed to her that the moon was brighter, or perhaps her eyes had adjusted to the dark. Then she found it, a narrow path leading through the bushes. She made herself walk slowly. She knew if she hurried, he'd hear them coming. If he was listening out for them he'd hear them anyway. Some noises she couldn't prevent – her laboured breathing, the snapping of dry undergrowth as it snagged on her clothing. The path was so narrow, she couldn't help that. But perhaps he wouldn't be listening out. Perhaps, locked in the hut, he hadn't seen the light from the cottage. Her fear was that if he knew they were there, he might be goaded into some grand gesture. It would upset him to be denied the water and the flowers, but he'd love a live audience.

He's forgotten why this started. He's become seduced by the glamour of it. He probably keeps a scrapbook of newspaper cuttings. Where will we find them?

The hut was just as she remembered it. Perhaps the paint had faded, the roof rusted, but in this light it was impossible to tell.

They stood on the edge of the clearing. Vera put her mouth so close to Ashworth's ear that she could feel his skin briefly against her lips.

'Wait. Until I call.'

She inched her way across the grass, aware of the weight she carried, the space she took up. As if, inside the hut, he'd sense the vibration of her feet on the ground, the displacement of the air.

At the door she stopped. There was no padlock. It had been pulled to from the inside, but she didn't think it had been bolted. She listened. No voices. Then she heard a rhythmic creaking, metal not wood, then a hissing. A white light appeared in the crack between the door and the frame.

Opening it, she tried to imagine she was visiting her neighbour. No fuss, quiet and easy. Wanting a favour. *I've run out of booze. Don't suppose you could spare a bottle of wine?*

Clive Stringer stood beside a narrow wooden table, his face lit by a tilley lamp. That had been the sound she'd heard, the creaking had been the pump as he'd primed it, the hissing the noise as it caught. Beside the lamp lay a bunch of flowers, mostly ox-eye daisies, their stems wrapped in damp newspaper. She tried not to look at them, or to peer into the shadow to look at the girl. Rolled up in bags in the corner, the mist nets used for catching migrant birds. And tucked inside, the thin nylon rope used as guys to anchor the poles. There'd been a mist net in Clive's room. She was sure now he'd used a guy rope to strangle his victims. She was glad of her size, blocking the doorway. He seemed very slight.

'It's all over now, pet,' she said. She kept her voice friendly. She didn't expect him to put up a fight, thought he might even be relieved to be caught. 'You'd just as well come with me.'

He stared at her without speaking.

She went on talking, keeping her voice even. 'You were the obvious suspect once I knew Lily was involved with Peter Calvert. You linked both families. But I couldn't work out why. You did it for them, didn't you? For Tom and Peter. Your friends.'

She thought he would answer, but he took the lamp by its wire handle and flung it against the wall. The glass smashed and the wood caught immediately; the paint bubbled and blistered and the flames licked along the line of the spilled paraffin. Stringer backed away from Vera into a corner. She ignored him, all her focus now on the girl, a still figure lying on the floor at her feet. Laura was wrapped in a blanket. Her face was covered. Vera picked her up, felt how thin and light she was. Ashworth was at the door, yelling for her to get out. Vera passed the bundle to him and turned to Stringer. He was almost surrounded by flame, though none of his clothing was burning. The red light was reflected in the lenses of his glasses. She wanted to get through to him.

'Come away out, man. Your friends wouldn't want this.'

He gave no indication that he'd heard her.

She was going to move towards him, but Ashworth took her by the arm and pulled her outside.

He'd laid the girl on the grass. Her face was filthy, her mouth covered by parcel tape, her hands and feet bound. Vera ripped the tape from her mouth, felt for a pulse. She didn't see the hut crumble in on itself, the heavy roof fall onto the man inside, trapping him so even if he'd wanted to escape he couldn't. If he screamed she didn't hear.

Chapter Forty-Four

Vera had dreamed of taking Laura back to Julie. From the moment she realized the girl was missing that picture in her head had kept her going. She'd seen herself in the kitchen, her arm around Laura's shoulders. *Look who's here, pet. I told you I'd get her back to you safe and sound.* And of course Julie had been grateful. In the dream.

It didn't happen like that. What happened was that Ashworth turned into the hero. When they stripped the tape from Laura's mouth she started choking and wheezing. The stress of the day finally bringing on an asthma attack. Or having her breathing restricted for that length of time. It was Ashworth who worked out what was going on, called for an ambulance, went with the girl to the hospital. He sat with her, holding her hand as the sirens wailed and they sped down the Spine Road to Wansbeck General. By the time they reached the hospital she was a lot calmer. They kept her in the hospital overnight, but by morning she was itching to be home. A little girl again, wanting her mam.

It was midnight when Holly brought Julie into the side ward where Laura was under observation. The woman was tense and frowning. Until she'd seen her daughter, she didn't dare to believe that Laura was safe. Ashworth was still sitting by the bedside when they arrived. He was the one to see Julie weeping and to receive her gratitude. And though Vera knew it was pathetic, she minded it. She'd wanted it to be her Julie thanked with tears in her eyes. But she'd been right about the killer. There was some consolation in that.

Instead of delivering the girl to her mother, she stood in the garden at Deepden waiting for the travelling circus which always followed a major incident. The fire engine arrived first. The fire fighters seemed disappointed that it was such a small fire, so easy to contain. She had the feeling that only the fact of a fatality made them think it was worth their being there. While she watched them she couldn't get rid of the image of Clive Stringer in the flame-red spectacles, standing quite still while the hut fell around him. He'd had his grand gesture after all. Later, when the scene of crime team searched through the wreckage, they found a couple of stems of daisies whole and undamaged.

Vera got to Fox Mill just as Peter Calvert was getting into his car. She saw Felicity watching them through the kitchen window, her face pinched with worry. The mood she was in, Vera couldn't feel much sympathy.

'I want a word,' she said.

Calvert began to bluster.

'You lied to me,' she said. 'I could charge you.' She wished she was a man. She wanted to hit him. 'We'll go and chat in the cottage, shall we? Back to the love nest. It might jog your memory. Don't worry, I've got a key. I rescued it from the CSI. We don't need to bother your wife with this. Not just yet.'

She started across the meadow, knowing that Calvert would follow. She had the door open and was sitting at the table when he came in.

'This is where Clive killed Lily Marsh,' she said. 'But then, you know that already. You suspected it, at least. Otherwise why lie about sending the card made of pressed flowers?'

He sat opposite her, gave a little smile. 'A small lie under pressure, Inspector. It means nothing.'

'You set Clive up. You were his hero. You knew he'd do anything you asked. You told him about Lily. How she was threatening to go public about the affair. When? At one of your cosy Friday lunches?'

'I needed someone to talk to, Inspector. It was a stressful time.'

'How did you put the idea into his head? "If only she were to have an accident . . ." You told him you'd sent the card. Were you worried she'd use it as evidence of the affair? "But at least I didn't sign it. No one will trace it back to me. We were very careful." But you didn't mention the kisses.

'Only Clive had a more elaborate plan than you'd anticipated. He was a chess player. He liked intricate patterns. And he had no real grasp on reality – my sergeant realized that after one meeting. It wasn't enough to kill Lily Marsh. He had to distract us from you. He had his own reason for wanting Luke Armstrong dead, so he killed him first. And to reinforce the connection to Lily, and to protect you, he sent the card. You must have known about that. Otherwise why lie when I asked if you'd sent a simi-

lar one to Lily?' She paused to catch her breath. 'When
was that, Dr Calvert? When did Clive admit he'd killed
Luke and Lily?'

The man didn't answer.

Vera thumped her fist on the table, so hard she
knew it would be bruised the next day.

'You're quite safe, man. I can't really charge you.
The CPS would throw out the case in minutes. You're
bright enough to know how these things work. But tell
me. Satisfy my curiosity.'

'There was a Marmora's warbler at Deepden a
few days ago. I gave Clive a lift back to town. He told
me then. As if I should be pleased with him. I was horrified.'

'Not sufficiently horrified to tell us what had happened, though.' Her voice was deceptively calm.
'There could have been another victim. But still you
kept your mouth shut. Why was that, Dr Calvert? A
warped sense of loyalty? Or were you scared Clive
would implicate you in the murders?'

'I don't have to listen to this, Inspector. As you
said, you can't charge me.'

He got up from his seat and walked out through
the open door. Vera watched him cross the meadow,
and stop to blow a reassuring kiss to his wife, who
must still have been looking from the window.

At ten that morning Ashworth's wife went into labour.
He phoned the office at teatime, to tell her they'd
had a boy. Jack Alexander. He'd been nearly ten
pounds, a real bruiser. Vera was just about to leave the
station for bed, but she agreed to meet up with him for

a drink. She found it hard to celebrate other people's babies but she'd rather have a few drinks with Joe than go back completely sober to an empty house. In the end, she suggested he come to the old station master's house on his way through. She knew she'd not be able to stick at a couple of halves and it'd save her having to drive. On the way home she stopped at the supermarket and got a bottle of champagne and a huge bunch of flowers for Sarah. She thought Ashworth would appreciate the gesture. Also in the trolley she put a ready-cook Indian meal and a bottle of Grouse. She'd need something to get her to sleep.

Ashworth arrived just five minutes after her. From her kitchen window she saw him leap out of the car, bleary-eyed and beaming. She'd already had a large Scotch. She rinsed out the glass and put it back on the tray, so he wouldn't know.

They sat outside. The house was even more untidy than usual and she didn't want him seeing it. She couldn't bear it if he started feeling sorry for her. She was light-headed through lack of sleep. Their conversation was punctuated by the sound of her neighbours' animals – sheep, goats, the inevitable cockerel.

'You were right, then,' she said. 'Stringer was a nutter.'

'You knew it was him, though, didn't you?'

'I thought it was a possibility.'

'You didn't let on.'

'No proof. And I met a few lads like Clive Stringer when I was growing up. Obsessives. Loners. They didn't all turn into serial killers.'

'Why did he?'

'He was a romantic,' she said. 'He believed in happy families.'

'That's no kind of motive.'

'It made sense to him,' she said. 'It had a weird sort of logic.' Looking into the distance, she thought the hills seemed very sharp and close this evening. She wouldn't be surprised if the weather didn't break soon.

'You'll have to spell it out.' Joe believed in happy families too, had done even before he got one of his own. But then he'd grown up in one. She caught him looking at her as if she was daft.

'Clive was a loner,' Vera said. 'No dad. No friends. Only that witch of a mother who tried to suck the life out of him. He had two surrogate families – the Sharps and Peter Calvert's birdwatchers. Both murders were committed to protect them. He was very close to Tom Sharp, looked out for him when he was a kid, blamed Luke for his death. The Calverts were his idea of a perfect couple. He idolized Peter and fancied himself in love with Felicity. He didn't want her hurt by news of her husband's affair.'

'We'll never really know what was going through his mind, will we?' Ashworth looked up from his glass. She could tell his head was full of the wonder of his new son, wrinkled and red and screaming. She'd had to hear all the details of the birth before he'd let her start talking about the murders. About how brave Sarah had been. 'All she had was a couple of puffs of gas and air.' He didn't care why Clive Stringer had murdered two people and kidnapped a third. Not tonight. *Nutter* was good enough for him.

But Vera cared. And she knew.

'Peter Calvert was his hero. Clive was doing what Peter wanted, saving his marriage, getting rid of Lily Marsh for good. Do you remember, we asked Clive in the museum if he'd keep quiet if he'd found out one of his friends had committed murder? He said of course he would. We should have asked him if he'd commit murder for his friend.'

She spoke almost to herself. The sun and the whisky and the lack of sleep had sent her into a sort of trance. 'If he'd kept it simple he might have got away with it.'

Joe looked up from his drink, his attention caught at last. 'What do you mean?'

'Lily Marsh was his first target. She was threatening to make life difficult for Calvert. We know she was starting to get awkward. That was why she turned up with James to look at the cottage. She assumed Felicity would tell her husband Lily had been there and he'd realize it was a threat. *Take me back or I'll tell your wife.* She was phoning Calvert at work. She'd even convinced herself she was pregnant. Calvert confided in Stringer. They met up for lunch every week. He knew he was Stringer's hero, has the sort of ego to allow him to believe a friend would commit murder on his behalf. We'll never be able to charge him with it, of course.'

She imagined Clive in the bungalow in North Shields, Calvert's words rattling around in his head, planning the murders while his mother watched television game shows in the other room. Obsessing about it, as he obsessed about birds and friendship. 'He played chess,' she said. 'He used to play with the

Calvert boy. He worked out the moves in this drama well in advance.'

'So why Luke Armstrong? And why was he killed first?'

'He had to be. Stringer didn't want Calvert implicated in any way with the murders. By making Luke Armstrong the first victim, he thought we'd concentrate on the boy in our search for a motive.'

'So the first victim could have been anyone? Stringer chose him at random to throw us off the scent?'

'No. It wasn't random. Stringer would never have worked himself up to commit murder unless he'd convinced himself that Calvert needed him, but I think he was glad of an excuse to kill Luke. He blamed him for Tom Sharp's death. Lots of people did. He looked on Tom as a brother. As I said the Sharps were his surrogate family. And he was there when Gary was talking about his plans to go out with Julie, so he knew she wouldn't be in the house that Wednesday night. Perhaps he saw it as a sign, decided it was time for him to make a move. He didn't know about Laura, though, didn't know she was there when Luke let him in. Gary told him later that Luke had a sister and she'd been in the house.'

'So that's why he abducted her?'

'Nah,' Vera said. 'He'd started to enjoy it. Being in control for the first time in his life.'

'And he got the idea for the flowers from Tom Sharp's memorial on the Tyne?'

'Maybe. He knew the best way to keep Calvert out of the frame was if the police considered the two murders as one case, the random killings of a madman.

They had to be linked. That was the reason for the flowers, the water. I don't see Stringer as naturally theatrical. The posed bodies and the dressing of the scene was part of the plan.'

'You wouldn't think he'd have that much imagination,' Joe said.

'Well, he didn't dream it all up himself, did he, pet?' Vera poured herself another drink, hoped Joe was too distracted with thoughts of the baby to notice. 'He got the idea from that bloody story. Parr's story. The one that almost had us convinced he was the murderer. In that the victim was strangled. How did Parr describe it? "Like an embrace"? And then the corpse was laid out in water. Clive had the book in his room when I visited the house. But it was in paperback. A different edition from the one I'd borrowed from the library. A different jacket. I didn't take it in at the time. He took his mother's bath oil to put in the water in the Armstrongs' house. When I looked round the Stringers' bungalow there were only male toiletries in the bathroom. I should have noticed.'

She reached out and finished her drink. Her third? Or her fourth? 'As I said, it was all planned. Very carefully. He knew Calvert had sent Lily a card with a pressed flower. So he sent one to Luke.'

In the distance her neighbour was calling her hens to be locked into the coop for the night, rattling a bowl of mash with a spoon to bring them in. The stupid woman had names for them all, cried when they had to wring their necks. Vera took the carcasses off her to casserole.

'He stole a car to get there. We checked car-hire firms, but not stolen vehicles. I was taken in by him, never had him down as a thief, but he'd knocked around with the Sharps for long enough to realize how it was done. He'd been good at it at one time, I heard today. Supplied cars for Davy on and off when he was still at school. Gave up when Calvert got him the job at the museum. After killing Luke, he dropped the vehicle back in Shields. If he'd stopped there we'd never have tracked him down. But that wasn't the object, of course. The object was killing Lily Marsh, saving Calvert's marriage, making himself indispensable.'

'Did he kill her in the cottage at Fox Mill?' Ashworth asked. Interested enough at least to put the question, drawn into the story despite himself.

'He must have done. How else would he get a woman like that alone? He wrote her a note, perhaps. Forged Calvert's writing or did it on his computer. We might never know. But I'm sure he was there. I phoned Felicity Calvert this afternoon. When I pressed her she remembered seeing a white Land Rover in the lane when she was bringing James home from school. Given long enough the CSIs would find a trace of him.'

'The white Land Rover,' Ashworth said. 'Stolen from Northumbria Water. That was how he got her body into the gully.'

'He took it from the depot,' she said angrily. 'Nobody missed it until I asked them to check. That was what Davy Sharp was phoning up for yesterday. He'd heard that Clive had been stealing again. Couldn't understand it when he had so much to lose. He'd heard that the girl had been abducted. With the Land Rover he could get all the way to the gully over the grass and rocks. That was why nobody saw him with Lily's body.'

Now, she was starting to feel properly tired, starting to relax. One more drink and she might sleep tonight. 'Clive must have gone back to Seaton, watched the house, maybe from the footpath by the pond. Seen Laura. He was a regular there. He'd been birdwatching in the area since he was a lad. If anyone saw him with binoculars it wouldn't register with them. The birders are a part of the scenery. The day of the abduction he'd have followed her almost to the bus stop, waited until the road was quiet. She was a skinny little thing, easy enough to overpower. He'd never had a girlfriend. Imagine the fantasies, as he lay awake at night reading that book. She'd have fascinated him. Especially as she was so similar to the figure in Parr's story. He'd have justified it to himself – that she might have seen him the night he was there with Luke, or he needed to throw our attentions back on the Armstrongs because we were getting so close to Calvert. But that wasn't why he went out early in the morning to take her while she was on her way to school. He kept her alive, because he liked the thought of having her there for him. He locked her in the boot of the car he'd stolen while he went into work and established his alibi. And all the time he was planning the murder, how it would look. How beautiful she would look when she was dead. He took flexi time and left early, took her up the coast to Deepden and locked her in the ringing hut.'

'But he intended to kill her?'

'Certainly. He had the flowers with him.'

Ashworth finished his drink, looked at his watch.

'I'll get back. Hospital visiting. And Sarah's mam's had Katie all afternoon. It'll be good to have everyone together at home tomorrow.'

Vera watched him walk to his car, the champagne in one hand, the flowers in the other. Thought that if she'd been married to someone like Joe Ashworth, she'd be so bored she'd commit murder herself.